QALEA DROP

SPIRAL WARS; BOOK 7

JOEL SHEPHERD

Cover Illustration by Stephan Martiniere. http://www.martiniere.com

Titles by Kendall Roderick. rmind-design.com

❀ Created with Vellum

THE STATE OF THE SPIRAL

Dear Readers

As I wrote in the first 'State of the Spiral' update that accompanied the release of RANDO SPLICER, these books are taking longer and longer to release, because the plot is becoming so much more complicated.

Having said that, I think QALEA DROP is a bit out of the ordinary by the standards of the series so far. I reached a point in the plot where multiple points of view were needed to resolve the scale of what I've created along this part of the plot arc. However, I have some confidence that Book 8 will be significantly more simple, so if this kind of POV-skipping story isn't your thing, or you're concerned that there hasn't been the time allocated to various favourite characters, never fear, this isn't the new normal forever. I've tried to do something different with each book to avoid repetition, and QALEA DROP is the big 'many points of view' grand space opera chapter. And I think that on this occasion, it works pretty well.

I also have hope that Spiral Wars 8 won't take as long to write, but every time I've thought that so far, I've been very wrong. Surely I'll be right someday.

The total number of books planned for the series currently stands at eleven. There is a very good chance that this will increase to twelve at some point, given how books 7 and 8 were originally intended to be one, but subsequently grew so big that they had to be split into two. I don't think the total series length could get to thirteen, but I keep getting new ideas, I'm having great fun writing them, and people seem to enjoy reading them, so who knows? I will follow the logical progression of the story, and see where that leads.

If you'd like more information from me directly, the best way is simply to get on my social media pages (check 'About the Author' at the end of this ebook) where I'm generally pretty good at answering questions.

And finally, a request that if you like this series, and would like to see more series like it out in the world, that you recommend it to friends, family, or whoever you think might enjoy it. Writers really do survive off recommendations. Reviews are great, but recommendations or gifts that create new readers are even better. As I've written before, the Amazon algorithm does a much better job of promoting authors who release a book every few months than those who take closer to a year, so if we're going to see more of the latter, with all of the additional plot and depth that longer books entail, audience support is vital.

Thanks in advance,

Joel

PROLOGUE

Cora Debogande hastily fastened the last several buttons on her jacket, gave herself a brief once-over in the mirror, then strode from her bedroom down the main hall and into the kitchen. There her boyfriend cut the last pieces of fetta for the hors d'oeuvres, placed on small plates with crackers, olives and an assortment of their best from the pantry.

"Oh you don't need to do all that!" Cora exclaimed, striding quickly over to examine the only thing that mattered -- the wine. Zach grabbed and showed her one of two bottles.

"'91 Razida Valley," he said. "Good enough?"

"Yes, perfect." The whole spread was perfect, whatever her complaining. "They're coming down the elevator now, I think the Admirals will be another ten minutes."

She strode from the room, heels clacking, past several of her waiting security at the big doors to the living room. They were wired into their own networks, monitoring their information flows, and doubtless had a better idea of where everyone was than Cora.

Back into the main hall, past her favourite Chezelle portrait of Great Great Grandfather Wallace Debogande, and her third-favourite Daondo landscape of the Sarize Marshes at dawn, and she reached the private elevator doors just as they opened. Security was there first, of course, and quickly admitted the elegant lady in the dark green dress and jacket, straight hair pulled into a short ponytail.

"Mother," said Cora, and was a little surprised that Alice Debogande pulled her into a tight if brief hug. She followed it with a longer hug from her eldest sister Katerina, hair similarly straight but longer, and taller than them both.

"The Vice Admiral says fifteen minutes," said Alice, walking her own way down Cora's wide hall, past the black glaze vase with decorative reeds, a tasteful view down to the vast sitting room before the penthouse's floor-to-ceiling views. "Later than he'd said, but what else can one expect from an Admiral of Vice."

Cora and Katerina exchanged glances. It had been their mother's favourite insult for Vice Admirals for two years now. "Mother, Zach's in the kitchen fixing up some things," Cora offered. "I told him he didn't need to prepare so much, but he insisted."

"I do like a man who can cook," Alice declared, taking the well-remembered left into the living room and through to the kitchen.

"Hors d'oeuvres aren't exactly cooking."

"Don't be pedantic dear. Zachary!"

"Hello Alice," said Zach, hurrying from his work to present the demanded kiss on the cheek. It had taken two years for 'Alice' to sound anything approaching natural, toward the woman who was, by most measures, the single wealthiest individual in all human space. "How's your day been?"

"Oh it's about to get a whole lot worse, my dear. Nothing a glass of red won't fix."

"'91 Razida Valley," said Zach, darting back to the kitchen bench.

"Yes yes, very good." Alice deposited her bag on the bench, looking about the wide open kitchen, the spotless expanse of counter top, the long dining table leading to the sitting room, with its sun-drenched view over central Shiwon and the ocean beyond. "No staff, Cora?"

"I had to cancel all my working appointments today because of this," Cora explained. "I gave them the day off."

"I had rather thought this was a working appointment," said her mother, pointedly, as Katerina interrupted Zach's opening of the wine for a kiss.

"Mother, you know I like to have staff around as little as possible. I can do my own organising, and I like the privacy."

"Yes," said Alice, looking again about at the apartment. "Well." It had been a point of contention between them in the past, and was again now. With things so precarious, Alice wanted them all to live back at the house until matters improved. Katerina had agreed, and moved back in with her family to occupy the East Wing, and centralise all the security arrangements. But for Cora, central Shiwon was close to all the galleries, concert halls and clubs, as well as the major schools, music institutions and hospitals with which Debogande Incorporated did its regular charitable works. Plus Zach would curl up and die if he couldn't take a stage in one club or another at two in the morning to jam with friends, and all his conservatory and teaching work was just blocks away. From the hills, it was a hike, and he already found the security a pain.

Zach handed each of them a glass, leaving Katerina's on the bench as she wandered off to take an uplink call. "So," said Alice, regarding Cora over the rim of her glass. "Show me." She beckoned impatiently with one hand.

Cora sighed, unbuttoned her jacket once more to reach within and withdraw the seven millimetre Taranto automatic. She pointed it away, removed the magazine and checked to be sure the breach was empty as she'd been taught, then handed it to her mother.

Alice examined it skeptically. "It's quite small."

"It fits my hand. Pulchaya says I'm quite good for a beginner." Ernest Pulchaya was the head of Cora's security -- a young former army special forces officer whose duties now included teaching his younger charge self-defence. *Phoenix* had been gone for more than two years now, and the threat from disgruntled Fleet Command had been ever-present for all that time, but still it had taken until now for Alice to agree to her daughters being armed. The change of heart had come, Cora knew, from the recent, terrifying turn of events that had changed everyone's strategic calculations. Now no one knew what to expect.

"And it just fits in there, does it?" Alice wondered. "Is that a shoulder harness?"

"A small one, yes. That's the advantage of a small weapon, no one can even see I'm carrying it." Alice handed the gun back, and watched distastefully as her daughter replaced the magazine, checked the safety, and tucked it away.

"And how is the Togiri coming along?"

"It's actually really interesting. I wish they wouldn't insert all that family and clan status into their adjectives, though. Still, it's easier than Porgesh, they've got forty-seven variable modes of address depending on rank and house. Lisbeth says she was fluent within a year! It barely seems possible."

"I think what it tells us is that Lisbeth has changed quite a lot." Cora could hear the pride in her mother's voice. Once, they'd all worried that Lisbeth was wasting her potential. No longer. And though Cora did not like to admit it, tales of Lisbeth's extraordinary change of circumstance made her more than a little jealous. She'd always been better at languages than Lisbeth, and news of Lisbeth's fluency in the mysterious parren tongue had inspired Cora to employ a Togiri instructor. She was fairly sure Lisbeth didn't speak that one yet.

They talked until the Admirals arrived, about family things. Cora's father was away to Peroni IV on a business trip, and would not be back for a week at least. Various cousins and uncles had graduated, or changed jobs, or announced impending weddings. A one hundred and ninety six year old great great great uncle would die soon, to no one's surprise. Alice's mother Poppy Debogande, Cora's grandmother, had a one hundred and fiftieth birthday approaching, and was planning an enormous party at her ranch in the wilds of Homeworld's northern continent.

"This is why we're all *so* much better off that she handed the company to me as early as she did," said Alice with exasperation. "I love that woman, but she has the most appalling timing."

Pulchaya leaned around the doorway. "Cora, the admirals are down on the roof. They'll be here in two minutes."

"Thank you Ernest." Cora noticed Alice's raised eyebrow as the security man withdrew. "What? I asked him to call me Cora."

"When Erik returns, I'll have him discuss with you the importance of appropriate distance in working relationships," said Alice. "Now come, let's go to the other room. I am *not* waiting by the elevator to welcome some *Vice* Admiral."

In the sitting room, Katerina was fiddling with the holographics by one wall to produce a 2-D image of Deirdre Debogande, shimmering in blue. "Hello Deirdre dear!" announced Alice. "How are things up in the real world?"

"Things are good, mother," said Deirdre. The image was 2-D, Cora guessed, to keep the frame close-in, and save her from standing. "Hi Kat, hi Cora... is Zach there? Oh yes, hi Zach!"

Deirdre was up on Ajar Station with her family, the necessary place from which to operate Debogande Incorporated legal wing. Eighty percent of the family business happened in space, and most of those nuts-and-bolts people closest to the action were based on one of Homeworld's major stations. Besides, the Debogande Family was a spacer family by political allegiance, and it would look very poor indeed if the only one of Alice's children to be operationally based in space was the infamous Erik.

From up the hallway, the elevator door opened, then footsteps approached down the long, polished floor. Two marines entered, black dress uniforms, sidearms in holsters, and surveyed the room. Four Debogande security placed about the room watched them back -- two of Cora's, two of Alice's. Back in the hallway, and on the landing rooftop, were six more. As was Alice's preference in all such meetings, the Debogandes had their Fleet visitors entirely surrounded.

The two marines -- a staff sergeant and a corporal -- indicated for the men behind them to enter. The Vice Admiral was tall for a spacer, broad-shouldered and dark, with many freckles. Behind was a Rear Admiral, this one a woman, short and slender. They stood shoulder to shoulder, an adjutant Lieutenant behind them, and offered no handshakes.

"I'm Vice Admiral Tsune," said the big man. "This is Rear Admiral Bostrom. Ladies." He looked about the room, finding and examining each Debogande in turn, in the manner of a man who knew them only from briefings.

"Admirals," said Alice. "Would you like a drink?"

"I'm on duty, so no." Alice raised her eyebrows. It hadn't stopped senior Fleet officers before. Tsune's gaze settled on Zach. "I'm sorry, who are you?"

"I'm Zachary Dubois," said Zach, slightly alarmed. "I'm... I'm Cora's boyfriend."

"I'm sorry kid, this isn't a place for boyfriends. You're going to have to leave."

"Zachary stays," said Alice. "I'll not have my family divided by varying levels of security. Cora and Zach live beneath the same roof, and have done for five years. If you can trust any of us, you can trust Zach."

The heavy-set Vice Admiral glowered at her. "We're about to discuss the most sensitive information Fleet has. No boyfriends."

"You are in no position to dictate terms to me," Alice said icily. "You're here because nothing Fleet are currently attempting will work without us. This family conducts its internal business according to its own rules, Admiral, not to yours."

There was silence in the room. Cora was pleased that her mother was defending Zach, but nonetheless thought she'd stepped too far. There was no saving humanity from anything without Fleet. Whatever their differences, Fleet remained indispensable. But in defence of her family, Alice was prone to extremes, and thought it wise to remind Fleet of that fact regularly.

Tsune took a deep breath. "All right. I will remind everyone that what we are about to discuss cannot leave this room. Already there are rumours, and Fleet is doing everything it can to prevent panic."

That was code for massive censorship, Cora knew. In her last several media interviews, senior journalists had questioned her in hushed, incredulous tones about what the hell was going on with Fleet. Cora had claimed ignorance. A number of independents had been removed from the networks, several of them taken away for questioning, and a few more had announced unexpectedly long vacations to quiet holiday spots. Everyone knew there were new things they were suddenly not allowed to talk about, but very few knew what they were. The tension amongst media and famous people everywhere was palpable.

"The medical divisions have diverted all available manpower to isolating the synthetic virus," said Tsune. "Only I'm constantly corrected by the meds, they tell me it's not a virus, it's a perfectly engineered killing machine. It obeys no known laws of natural biology, save that it imitates those it can best utilise to reproduce and spread. The extent of that spread is extreme. The inner systems have it worst, the outer systems less so, and it appears most concentrated in the cities. We've never noticed it until now because, obviously, it's microscopic, and has thus far lain inert and produced no symptoms, and shown up in no tests. Its reproductive mechanisms are ingenious, and far beyond any technology we possess ourselves. Most medical technology does its best to imitate nature, but fails to match nature's ingenuity. This technology far exceeds it.

"Every resource is being thrown at finding a cure -- as you'll know, through Debogande Medical, and your commercial interests in several other leading medtech companies. But many of those top researchers are now reporting to Fleet rather than to you, so you'll not have received their latest findings.

"This thing appears to be unkillable. It's not strictly biological in any manner we understand. Its key component parts are synthetic and nanotech, so it simply will not respond to traditional biological cures. It actively fools antibodies into thinking it's friendly, and when we retrain the antibodies, it switches tactics. The damn things behave as though they've achieved some kind of swarm intelligence. Imagine trying to fight a virus that behaves as though it's consciously aware, and can counter your efforts to fight it in realtime. We try one tactic, it simply switches tactics and now we're confronted by an entirely new problem, leaving us uncertain as to whether our efforts won't simply make it worse. It's managing to somehow communicate those tactical changes to other colonies in other patients, so when we change treatment tactics in one patient, soon all other patients in the ward are showing similar changes.

"Worse again, because the virus is in some sort of hibernation mode, we can't yet see its full capabilities. Isolated in labs outside of a human body, it quickly dies and disintegrates. We've attempted to inject it into test animals and activate to fully symptomatic, but it recognises when it's not in a human host and quickly dies once it realises it can't spread further. We've found it in household pets and farm animals. It seems to know when it can use animals as a transmission vector to humans. Nothing has been found in wild animal populations. It's like it knows which animals can be used to infect humans, and which can't.

"One promising strand of research was undertaken by Michita Labs in Hawthorne System. They're trying to replicate what they think may be the activation signal, in the hopes that perhaps they can find a false signal to fool the virus into doing other things, or perhaps even to block the signal once they've identified it. But of course, the virus won't activate in test animals, and conducting these tests on unwitting patients is unethical, so some of the lab people at Michita had volunteered themselves as test subjects. Activation was achieved in several cases, but the frequency requirements keep changing as the virus adapts, so we're still some way from learning what turns it on. Three Michita volunteers so far have died. Death takes several minutes, and is excruciating. But there is no shortage of volunteers."

Silence in the room, save for the distant hum of airconditioning. Cora felt the fear, twisting in her stomach. They all felt it.

"What are your latest estimates of the infection rate?" Alice asked quietly.

"We think about twenty percent," said Tsune. "Worse in core system worlds. If one of those worlds is attacked, ships in that attack would presumably send the signal, and somewhere between a quarter and a third of that population would die within one or two minutes. The calamity would cripple infrastructure, create a civil emergency, and presumably kill a similar number of military personnel, weakening the system's defences considerably. A ship that suddenly loses twenty percent of its crew will still be able to fight, but at a much reduced capacity. We are investigating jamming methods, but jamming an entire system is pretty much impossible. And if this is coming from the alo, which seems certain at this point, well, their technology remains better than ours."

Alice nodded shortly, and sipped her wine. Cora saw her hand trembling. She'd never seen that before. "All of Debogande Incorporated has mobilised," she told the admirals. "It's hard to do without telling everyone why, but we're doing it. I'm sure you've seen all our numbers."

"We have," spoke Rear Admiral Bostrom for the first time. "They're very impressive. Thank you."

"Oh you don't have to thank me, dear," said Alice. "At this point it's just survival. But I am receiving more and more queries every day. People have noticed Fleet's information crackdown, they've noticed that military leave has been cancelled, that deployments have resumed large scale for what are being called 'exercises'. And you people are going to have to realise that you can't just tell everyone to be quiet forever."

Tsune scowled. "The alternative, Mrs Debogande, is mass panic not seen since the krim invasion of Earth. Only this panic won't be limited to one system only."

"Oh I quite agree, Admiral. Panic will serve noone's interests at this time but our enemies. What I'm saying is that Fleet has had in the past an alarmingly naive notion of exactly what quality of lie the general population is willing to swallow. If you're to pull off this particular mass deception, you must learn to lie better."

There was a hard edge to it, coming from the mother of the man whom a previous group of Fleet commanders had framed for murder, and subsequently declared a renegade. Despite all evidence of *Phoenix*'s outstanding heroism in pursuit of the human cause since, and the fact that her efforts were the only reason why the alien virus threat had been detected at all, Fleet had not rescinded *Phoenix*'s renegade status. Barely a day passed that members of the Debogande family did not hear slurs directed at Erik's character. Vandalism at Debogande Incorporated facilities was common, and featured graffitied words like 'traitor'. Attacks on Debogande employees, and occasionally on family, were not unknown. When the families of several *Phoenix* crew had collaborated with media help to trash Erik's character, claiming inside information about how none of the crew respected him and that he'd only gained his position because of his famous last name, Fleet had not intervened to stop them as they usually would, when a Fleet officer's integrity, and the integrity of Fleet itself, was questioned.

Doing so, Fleet had said, would risk revealing the true nature of the threat that confronted all humanity. Yet still to this day, despite all the revelations about *Phoenix*'s true mission, no Debogande had secured a guarantee from Fleet that *Phoenix*'s so-called crimes would be forgiven when she one day returned home.

"If I could intervene on another matter?" Katerina suggested, in that very smooth, elegant way of hers.

"Of course," said Tsune, as though pleased to move on from that pricklish topic.

"How do we know the chah'nas are on our side?"

Another silence in the room. Cora tried not to let the shock show on her face. It was one of those things people gossiped about in whispers, but did not blurt to a Vice Admiral's face. But Katerina was the CEO of Debogande Enterprises, the most significant chunk of Debogande Incorporated, and was frightened of no Fleet admiral.

Tsune frowned. "How do you mean, on our side?"

"I mean that you invited them in two years ago when you moved against the Worlders. Spacer industry lost most Worlder investment, which has largely been replaced by chah'nas investment. We in this company were forced to substitute some enormous amount of human money for chah'nas money, and chah'nas shipping activity in human space has increased dramatically as our trade and other interests have expanded.

"A lot of my high-level clients are unhappy about it, partly because of the business and strategic implications, but at my end I hear a lot of the legal complications, as chah'nas and human legal codes are highly variant. And now it seems to me that these current mobilisations against the alo will inevitably get out, people aren't stupid and they'll find out what Fleet is doing irrespective of the information crackdowns. They'll discover that the alo are the threat, and just between all of us here, I will tell you that I've already heard from a number of high-profile individuals who are aware of it."

"In which case we would like to know their names," said Rear Admiral Bostrom.

"All of them are directly involved in Fleet business and have very good reasons to know what they know," Katerina continued. "That's not the point. The point is that all of them, to a man and woman, asked me if war comes, between humanity and the alo, whose side I think the chah'nas will be on. Chah'nas were friends of the alo long before they were friends of ours. And now they're in our territory as they've never been before, as very few races in the Spiral allow any foreigners to spread, and it seems logical to wonder that if the chah'nas were on the alo's side instead of ours, then, well, we'd all be entirely screwed, wouldn't we? But because Fleet won't let us talk about these things, most of us will be caught completely unprepared if the worst happens."

It was said with the barely repressed temper of a woman known to be good with words, taking the opportunity to say something she'd wanted to tell a high-level Admiral for a long time.

"The chah'nas are humanity's oldest and most reliable friends," Tsune said stubbornly.

"Well that's not saying anything," said Alice, sourly. "Humanity's only been a force in the Spiral for the last ten minutes."

"And every major power that's fallen has done so after it was stabbed in the back by a friend," Cora added, recalling her history books.

"We are in constant communication with our chah'nas allies," Tsune insisted. "These fears are unhelpful and unwarranted."

"My point," Katerina said carefully, "is that it's not us Debogandes that you need to convince. There are a lot of people having these conversations now, where you can't hear them. The longer Fleet takes to put their fears at ease, the worse these rumours will get, and the more unstable everything will become at a point when you most need stability."

"Point taken," said Tsune, with no sense that he'd actually heard her. Almost as though, Cora thought, he found it ridiculous that he should have to answer such questions from anyone not in uniform.

"And one more thing," the holographic Deirdre joined in, not about to let the family momentum go to waste. "Family Debogande would like to request that Fleet make no more threatening communications to *Phoenix* families who do not wish Fleet to see the messages their loved ones returned to them. I understand there aren't many of these, most have allowed access, but those who have refused are all the families of lower-ranked crew whose reports surely will not contain anything Fleet has not already learned from other messages, and particularly from the comprehensive official reports filed by all of *Phoenix*'s senior officers."

"Fleet security is paramount, Ms Debogande," Rear Admiral Bostrom said stiffly. "*Phoenix*'s officers may have missed something that her lower-ranked crew did not."

"Regardless," said Deirdre, "Debogande Legal regards these threats to be unwarranted. The families have been informed of Debogande Incorporated's intention to defend them to the highest legal standard should Fleet move against them, and to protect them in full from any financial liabilities they could incur. Furthermore, and I cannot speak for my mother, but I believe that any such move by Fleet could seriously jeopardise its working relationship with Family Debogande going forward. Given the stakes, Fleet should reconsider."

"Young lady!" Vice Admiral Tsune growled. "The survival of all humanity is at stake!"

"And the crew of the *UFS Phoenix* are the only reason we're still in this game with a shot!" Alice replied with anger. "Were it not for all of their heroism, we'd all be completely unprepared for what's coming! You leave their families alone!"

"Fleet had this situation well in hand before the *UFS Phoenix* went on its rampage," Tsune retorted. "What *Phoenix* has done is create trouble -- with the tavalai, with the parren and now with the croma. Yes, some of the lost technologies that she has returned to us may prove useful, but at an enormous cost to regional stability, and at the cost to many Fleet lives, including somewhere more than a quarter of all *Phoenix*'s crew to date. Don't suppose that the families all love you for Lieutenant Commander Debogande's actions -- I know of many who do not. And *never* presume to dictate to Fleet what Fleet may or may not do in the service of saving humanity!"

"There are five families who don't like us," Cora jumped in, with indignation. The Vice Admiral's eyes found her for the first time. "The rest may not be happy, but most understand, and most are supportive. I know, because as head of Arts and Charities, I'm responsible for all welfare to the bereaved who have lost loved ones on *Phoenix*. That's included many long conversations. One of the things they tell me is that Fleet barely speaks to them, and has offered neither commiserations nor support, so don't suppose that because they don't like where *Phoenix* is now that they've bought all your lies and slander.

"And one more thing. That's *Captain* Debogande."

The two sides glared at each other. Marines watched the Debogande security standing by the walls. The security, which included several former marines, watched their guests with impassive confidence. So much at stake, and still humanity's factions fought. This particular split from Fleet, Cora was very much aware, was not just limited to her own family. Every day she heard from more and more people alarmed at Fleet's activities, and in particular their conduct of the ongoing Spacer-Worlder civil conflict, with its heavy-handed censorship and accusations of Worlder rights violated on many planets. The axe hung above them all, and rather than uniting to meet it, humanity stood increasingly divided.

Alice levelled her finger at the admirals. "You lot are the ones who made our bed with the alo in the first place," she said. "Family Debogande knows many things about Fleet's past actions that would shock the public should they find out. I think if Fleet decided to focus on preparing for war, instead of bullying everyone who has their own ideas how to help, all of humanity's chances would improve."

1

The parren assault shuttle was a monster, more than four times the size of those used on *Phoenix*. Lisbeth sat beneath the armoured canopy and gazed at the synthetic view projected on all sides, while the parren pilots exchanged terse operational chatter, and the coms from a thousand ships and ten thousand channels cluttered the airwaves.

Before her was Dul'rho, the capital world of clan Croma'Rai, who had just lost power in croma space. Some had expected the new rulers, clan Croma'Dokran, to move the center of croma military activity back to their own capital world of Do'Ran, but that would have been a delay too long for the Dokran to stomach. The new rulers had promised action, and action they were delivering, here where the largest concentration of croma shipping in centuries had already gathered to watch the great Tali'san that had decided Croma'-Dokran's victory.

Most of the time, even in close orbit, seeing other ships was hard. Distances were great, velocities greater, and the naked human or parren eye could only see so much. But across the canopy today, Lisbeth could count at least thirty ships, all locked in relative synchronicity. Mostly this was the orbital tail of Rash'do Station, a circular spot in the distance, making it possible for shuttles to transit between station and ships in close parking orbit that were either too big to dock with station, or were unable to find an available berth.

One ship grew large in the forward view, unremarkable from range, but now its details resolved with proximity. It looked enormous, with an odd, pointed little nose, ringed by what looked like a rotational crew cylinder at what might be the ship's collar to its imaginary neck. Behind it, the main body was mostly cargo holds, huge and bloated. From the segment-lines, Lisbeth reckoned that the hold was actually many holds, individual containers that could be separated from the ship's relatively narrow spine and left to be unloaded at the leisure of some cargo management facility. At the rear were large engines, but nothing like the scale of what warships used. *Phoenix* and *Coreset*'s engines accounted for half their total length. On this swollen whale, barely a quarter.

The entire scene swung sideways as the shuttle engaged attitude thrusters, then halted with them facing backward, a light kick from the mains to slow them on approach. Above Lisbeth now was Dul'rho, aswirl with white cloud above blue oceans, like inhabited worlds everywhere. Lisbeth had listened to Erik's recounting of the most amazing roadtrip he'd taken with some of the *Phoenix* crew from Cal'Uta to Stat'cha, across the Do'jera desert, to take Sho'mo'ra's new corbi advisor, Tiga, to address the Tali'san Council. Lisbeth had been jealous to hear of that adventure... but then she'd recounted adventures of her own.

Phoenix had already left on a new adventure. Exactly where she'd gone, neither Lisbeth nor the few people who knew were saying. The new Croma'Dokran leadership owed *Phoenix* to some degree for its ascension to power, but had only made that final leap to victory by throwing *Phoenix* under the metaphorical bus. After that, Styx had crashed much of Dul'rho's planetary grid to get Erik and the others from that road trip out of Croma'Rai custody, and done damage to network infrastructure that the world, Liala informed her, had not entirely recovered from. Croma'Dokran leader Sho'mo'ra liked Erik, but was beholden to new allies who'd like the entire crew in custody or worse. Erik had decided to spare him the dilemma by departing for their new adventure in reeh space before the Reeh Fleet moved up many more forces, following some extended discussions with Croma Fleet Intelligence about where it was they were going. Lisbeth had only caught the tail end of those discussions, and thought it wise that Erik was unwilling to tell her more.

She hated it, though, Erik and *Phoenix* being gone so quickly after she'd arrived. She'd had perhaps a couple of hours with him in total, and less with her friends in the crew. But Erik had a ship to command, and if the stakes were what he believed them to be, the entire human race to save, and perhaps other races too. And Lisbeth, as emissary from the Supreme Leader of all parren to the croma, was scarcely less busy.

The vast planetary horizon swung once more, bringing the approaching transport back into view. It was much closer now, and loomed before the shuttle in ponderous detail. Nearly a kilometre long, Lisbeth thought, having spent enough time in space to judge these things by eye — more than twice the length of even a monster like *Phoenix*. At a dorsal docking port, croma shuttles clustered. The parren shuttle joined them, inverting to place its own dorsal hatch in proximity to the grapples.

Lisbeth's glasses indicated incoming coms, and she blinked on the icon. *"Hello Lisbeth, this is Tocamo."*

"Hello Tocamo," Lisbeth replied in Porgesh. "What is your concern?"

"Lisbeth, I am informed that you are currently inspecting one of the croma transports. Is my information correct?"

"Your information is correct, Tocamo." Tocamo was captain of the *Coroset*, and thus held command of the parren emissariat's military function. Overall command was given to Juneso, who was also House Harmony, and had diplomatic experience. Exactly where she fitted in, Lisbeth was not sure, and did not think the parren particularly wanted her to know.

"Lisbeth, I notice that this inspection visit was not given to me for prior approval," said Tocamo, with mild reprimand.

"Tocamo," Lisbeth said politely, "my staff did enquire with your staff on the matter, and did resolve that your schedule for this period was very crowded. There have been requests from the relevant croma authorities for my personal inspection of the transports, as I believe you are aware. I had thought to satisfy those requests."

Overhead, the big cargo vessel's hull loomed close, grapples approaching. *"Yes Lisbeth,"* came Tocamo's reply, *"I well understand the situation. Yet I thought we were understood that the parren emissariat shall not be participating in the croma evacuation of Rando."*

The grapples disappeared over Lisbeth's head, then a loud clang and lurch, as the shuttle docked fast. "We are well understood, Tocamo," Lisbeth said smoothly. "And yet I have protocol concerns with the croma, given my brother's recent interactions with them. I do not believe it is wise to refuse this request. The emissariat shall be harmonious with its hosts."

"Very well, Lisbeth," said Tacoma. *"I shall inform Juneso accordingly."* The link went dead, and chatter from the rear told Lisbeth that disembarking was underway. She undid her buckles, floated clear and found Semaya already preparing.

"This issue of command would be best addressed at the earliest," Lisbeth's Chief of Staff ventured, testing her oxygen. Beneath the jumpsuit hood and mask, only the piercing indigo eyes were prominent, jaw narrow and cheekbones pronounced, as with all parren. Lisbeth sometimes thought parren looked more like water-dwellers than the stocky tavalai — all smooth and streamlined.

"There is no issue of command, Semaya," Lisbeth said with light reprimand, testing her own safety equipment. "Tacoma accepts that Gesul's advisor should have latitude in some matters."

"You told me once to warn you should I believe your understanding of a human concept diverge from the parren understanding," Semaya warned her.

"Yes I know, Semaya," Lisbeth huffed, not waiting to hear the rest of it. "But Gesul appointed a human in part because he wanted someone who thought differently. I would serve him very poorly were I not to grant him that, wouldn't I?"

"Did Gesul request this of you?" Semaya asked skeptically, pursuing her boss through the rear cockpit door. "Or have you merely surmised?"

For a fanatically obedient people, Lisbeth thought with exasperation, parren could be devilishly persistent in questioning their leaders. But then, as she'd had explained to her many times, obedience did not mean abdication of all common sense. And with her own staff at least, she had directly asked them to.

Timoshene and two parren security awaited her outside the cockpit, and further parren crew floated aside as they moved to the dorsal airlock. There awaited Hiro, similarly suited, helmet at the rear collar like all of them, and checking a pistol. As the crew operated the grapple controls and awaited confirmation of an airtight match from the far side, Lisbeth took a moment to marvel at the entourage she'd accumulated. The shuttle was not her's, but all of its passengers were. She was special advisor to the most powerful parren of all, the Adivach Gesul, as the House Harmony terminology put it. Her special responsibility was humanity, with a strong sideline in drysine affairs… although there were others with whom she shared that duty. Of Gesul's twenty closest advisors, current circumstances put her, to the best of her ability to calculate, perhaps sixth or seventh in rank. It came with power trappings. Also, it came with danger.

Liala joined them just before the airlock opened, the drysine queen sporting no more than a deluxe version of a combat drone's chassis. Lisbeth had queried her about it, and Liala had said that she did not wish to put on airs. Her alloy-metal, multi-limbed presence filled most of the access behind them, and would surely draw stares on the other side.

Hiro went first, then Timoshene and his men, followed by Lisbeth and Semaya. The connecting passage was short and cold, and Lisbeth emerged amid control mechanisms for the grapples, clusters of power conduits and air venting for the umbilicals, and prominent guard stations on the flanking walls where armed croma could put visitors in a crossfire. Those croma floated now by their support handles, in heavy duty suits with many tools in pockets, but all weapons holstered. Some croma were enormous, but these were not so large. Space was duty for younger croma, who would not be crushed by their own weight in a high-G push, and who retained fast hands and nimble fingers.

One croma held to a central support pole, with every indication of being in charge. Rather than grab the pole and risk an impolite proximity, Lisbeth pulled her little compressed-air pusher and fired a brief burst past the waiting croma, halting two meters short.

"Hello," she said, adjusting her earpiece. She'd been instructed by Erik and others that croma weren't much for smalltalk, and didn't go for big ceremony in small meetings. "I'm Lisbeth Debogande, senior advisor to Gesul."

"Rhi'shul Shon'kai," said the croma… and Lisbeth blinked to realise she was talking to a woman, as the vocals were chordant, multi-toned and strange to the ear. Now that she was closer, she could see that this 'smaller' croma was probably two hundred and forty centimetres, and that if they'd been standing in full gravity, she'd barely come up to her chest. Zero-G had a way of making the height seem less, but the mass more.

And then she recognised the name. "Rhi'shul Shon'kai? The same Rhi'shul that accompanied my brother on the Shur'do Kon'do Rey'kan across the Do'jera desert?"

"The same," said Rhi'shul, in the snuffling grunts of croma speech. Lisbeth didn't think she was incredibly excited at the assignment… but with dark-eyed, intense, unexcitable croma, it was always hard to tell. *"Sho'mo'ra told me I had to."*

The contrasts between croma and parren concepts of politeness were intense. "My brother has spoken very highly of you," Lisbeth said truthfully. "These are my security, and my Chief of Staff, Semaya. And this at the rear is Liala, whom you may recognise."

The unenthusiastic croma looked past Lisbeth, and her thick-lashed eyes registered no particular astonishment to see the drysine queen, floating clear of the airlock behind. Croma spacers nearby looked much more cautious. *"Liala,"* she said. *"You're a queen? You look like a drone."*

"You're a woman?" Liala replied, also in Kul'hasa. *"You look like a man."* Even Lisbeth turned to stare. Semaya looked mortified. Lisbeth looked back at Rhi'shul, to see if Liala had just started an interspecies war.

But Rhi'shul appeared amused. Lisbeth had never seen a croma amused before. It didn't look all that different from angry. *"You're not qualified to judge,"* Rhi'shul retorted.

"Exactly," said the drysine.

Rhi'shul snorted, and flicked her ears, to the chime of many steel rings. *"She's certainly a queen,"* said the croma. *"Peanut did not speak at all."* And waved an arm at them, gesturing the strange alien party to follow. *"This way,"* she said. *"Come and see what our crazy new leader has planned for the corbi."*

Rhi'shul led the free-floating party up the adjoining access hall, tugging on the bulkheads of closed pressure-doors to pull them along. Lisbeth noted the coils of wound guideline ropes and bundled cargo netting, set to turn this access into a main thoroughfare for many people. As they approached, the last set of pressure-doors hummed open, revealing the main hold of the enormous vessel.

Lisbeth had only seen such large interior zero-G spaces on the biggest space stations. The holds were crossed by interior support beams, like the spokes of some enormous bicycle wheel. From those foundations, a huge symmetrical web of slim beams filled the space, in some parts still under construction, a forest of internal divisions and compartments.

Lisbeth pushed off the doorway to float to the nearest. The thin beams made a lattice of compartment walls, within which many acceleration slings were furled inside canvas covers. Half-wall partitions surrounded zero-gravity toilets, the vacuum plumbing from which ran to larger and larger main pipes before disappearing into the ship's walls. There were a few individually operated lights, and some thin padding, and the acceleration slings would serve as beds in zero-G.

Lisbeth stared up and about. The sheer scale of it was dizzying. Accommodation for thousands, just in this one ship hold. No, tens of thousands — these were corbi, and corbi weren't large. In those regions where the lattices were incomplete, dozens of floating croma workers performed final welds, simple robotic drones assisting amid flashes of orange light.

The thud of a large weight on the lattice told her that Rhi'shul had arrived alongside. "It could get a little messy," Lisbeth suggested, indicating the toilets. "Most Rando corbi will never have seen modern toilets on their planet, let alone off it."

"I'm told corbi are smart," Rhi'shul said drily. *"The puzzle is not difficult."*

"How about zero-gravity medications for millions of corbi? Ones that actually work? Or else you won't just have bodily functions from the toilets floating about."

"Being provided for," Rhi'shul confirmed. *"And there will be filtration drones to clean large contaminants from the air."*

Lisbeth nodded, gazing about this one little, open-sided enclosure. Imagining thousands of families with sparse exposure to modern technology, let alone spaceflight, packed into this place. Terrified children, sick people, elderly. Crammed in cheek-by-jowl, tangled on top of each other.

"How long will it take?" she asked.

"Assuming we can keep the system clear of reeh activity, transit between Cho'nu System and Reba System is three days. We'll be using the world of His'do in Cho'nu, its present orbital inclination minimises cross-system transit, keeping times lower. This freighter can hold nearly a hundred thousand corbi when fully loaded. It will be equipped with six heavy shuttles, each capable of carrying eight hundred corbi. Assuming one trip every three hours is four thousand eight hundred, we should be able to fill a freighter in twenty-one hours."

Lisbeth nodded, pleased to have set the translator to convert croma time measures into minutes and hours. "So each freighter takes three days in, three days out, one day to load, one more day to unload," she said, thinking hard, "so a hundred thousand corbi per freighter per eight days. The military object is to hold the approaches to Reba System open for about thirty days... so each freighter can make four trips, meaning four hundred thousand corbi.

"Last best estimates of Rando's population put it at nearly two hundred million. Meaning that, to get them all off, you're going to need... five hundred ships this size. At my last count, you had a hundred and ninety six in this system."

She kept all accusation from her tone, and simply asked the question in the no-nonsense way she knew croma preferred.

"More are coming," said Rhi'shul. *"Others are being prepared in other systems. Perhaps a hundred."*

"So maybe three hundred? That's still three-fifths of the capacity needed, assuming everything goes well in the rest of the plan, which it won't, because the logistical complications here are horrendous."

"There are volunteers."

"What kind of volunteers?"

"Croma space has hundreds of thousands of ships. Privately owned ships are being volunteered by brave individuals. This has become a prestigious cause, to set right a wrong of history."

Lisbeth nearly shook her head in disbelief. "But private volunteers aren't going to have nearly the carrying capacity of these biggest freighters. And how many of them will have shuttles to make their own pickups? They'll put a drain on the existing loading and offloading shuttles at both ends, so you'll need to bring excess shuttles... and then you'll have a capacity mismatch between shuttles and freighters that will make orbital rendezvous a nightmare."

"You worry too much," said Rhi'shul. *"People find a way."*

"Lisbeth," Liala added, "from our discussions with people recently escaped from Rando, it seems likely to me that not every corbi will wish to be evacuated."

Lisbeth glanced at Liala, and found the drysine floating close to the lattice of living-quarters, peering at the construction with her mismatched visual receptors. Her head did not dart in the bird-like fashion of a drone. She peered carefully, and positioned herself with a well-placed claw on a beam.

"And those that remain will likely die," Lisbeth replied with frustration. "We need to make every effort to have them understand this. The reeh will take their revenge, and this time it's unlikely they'll let any survive."

"Yes," Liala agreed, "but as a purely logistical consideration, the fact remains that it is unlikely this mission will succeed in anything approaching a one hundred percent evacuation. We cannot yet announce to the corbi what is coming lest the reeh take preemptive measures by killing them all, and once we do announce our intentions, there are only going to be so many accessible evacuation points. Corbi too far from those evacuation points may find it impossible to reach them in time, even over the course of thirty days, and even should they wish to evacuate, which many will not."

"I agree," Lisbeth said shortly, "but for a mission like this, it's important not to become constrained by our own low expectations. Every slip in our marginal expectations means another million innocent lives lost. It's unacceptable."

Liala's armour-shielded head turned to consider Lisbeth. Exactly what these moral concepts meant in Liala's mind, Lisbeth did not know. She *wanted* to believe that Liala held a far softer and more sympathetic understanding than Styx. Certainly she *seemed* more sympathetic, being less than a year old and largely socialised amongst organics. But now Liala was here, the commander of parren drysines come to briefly meet the ultimate commander of *all* drysines, for reasons that Lisbeth still did not entirely understand, and Lisbeth had noticed a certain tightening in Liala's patterns of speech. A tendency toward less of the charming questions and naive innocence, and more of the data and hard facts one might expect of a drysine commander of forces. Part of her wanted to think that it was Styx being a bad influence on Liala. And the other part chided herself for believing that Liala could ever have been other than what she was — a drysine commander, with all the bloody-minded calculation that came with it.

Rhi'shul pulled herself further into the lattice structure, and Lisbeth followed. Hiro watched carefully, and Timoshene drifted to a similar, flanking position among the open compartments, but the croma guards seemed unworried. Rhi'shul caught a beam and swung, as Lisbeth copied opposite, and the sound of welders and grinders shrieked and hissed off the far walls.

"What's in it for you, Debogande?" the croma asked bluntly, dark eyes searching her up and down. *"You serve Gesul, and Gesul's just another in a long line of parren who don't get involved in outsiders. What's his game?"*

Not long ago, Lisbeth would have found it intimidating, interrogated at close range by a big croma who, Erik had informed her, was a special forces elite operative, whatever her record's official denials. But lately she'd been confronted by things far more scary than Rhi'shul, and lived.

"You're Croma'Rai yet you're serving Croma'Dokran by being here," Lisbeth replied. "My brother says you're angling for some position of authority within Croma'Rai now that there's a shakeup. So what game are *you* playing, Rhi'shul? All of that work you did, to root out the corruption at the top of your own clan, and now Croma'-Dokran are telling you what to do?"

Rhi'shul might have smiled, a tightening of that short muzzle, wrinkles around the big, flat nose. There were teeth beneath those lips. Sharp ones. *"I'm a patriot,"* said the croma. *"When my leaders assign a special duty, I obey."* Lisbeth looked at her warily, not believing it was that simple. *"Your turn."*

"Parren today face many outside threats," Lisbeth said carefully. "Many would rather wish those threats away, but Gesul wishes to meet them, and be prepared. The human and tavalai populations face a terrible infection from a synthetic disease, and Gesul is concerned that this may become a parren disease as well."

"And being here gives him a claim to the Rando Splicer cores liberated by Phoenix," Rhi'shul completed. *"It is well played, the parren population gains some protection with that knowledge. But now most of your drysines have accompanied their queen on Phoenix's new mission, yet your parren ships stay here. Liala commands drysines in parren space, Styx commands them overall. Parren do not wish to declare war on the reeh, but drysines prepare to join Phoenix in doing exactly that."*

Rhi'shul rapped a fist upon a thin steel beam for emphasis, grabbing with the other fist to keep from drifting. *"Your leader rests within the jaws of a dilemma, young Debogande. Parren leadership is sovereign. Yet drysines now overlap the borders of that sovereignty — some declare loyalty to Gesul, others take actions outside of Gesul's instruction, actions that will draw parren into larger conflicts whether they wish it or not. But parren are not stupid, and having met your brother, I do not think you are stupid either. What's Gesul's game, that brings him to allow this?"*

Lisbeth had been warned of this, too. Rhi'shul, Erik had assured her, was far smarter than the average special-forces headkicker, and knew a lot of things about how stuff worked.

"*Phoenix* feels that humanity faces a grave threat from the alo/deepynine alliance," Lisbeth said carefully. "Parren also face this threat, though indirectly, as parren space does not border on alo space."

"But it does border on sard space," said Rhi'shul, eyes glinting with comprehension.

Lisbeth nodded. "And the alo/deepynines have been courting the sard, and the attacks on parren space, and the deaths at Mylor Station, all came from sard space. Gesul wishes to support humanity against this threat, and so supports *Phoenix*'s mission, which is about to become a drysine mission as well."

"And the parren of other houses share Gesul's support of Phoenix and humanity?"

Lisbeth smiled thinly. "It's an ongoing discussion."

2

The drysine ship had no name. When invited to give it one, Styx had declined, with all the disdain of a higher sentient mind asked to stoop to primitive vocal superstitions. Drysines spoke the coded language of data-loaded digital transfer, which described things in three dimensional detail that organic brains could barely imagine.

Phoenix crew were calling the ship D1, which Erik suspected was partly retaliation against the drysine snub. It throbbed and pulsed around him as he floated through another corridor… but drysine ships had no corridors as organics understood them, just a three-dimensional maze of spaces that might have been thoroughfares, or might have been rooms. Rooke's analysis had revealed an octagonal layout in some parts, hexagonal in others, and irregular around the major structural features where function dictated design. All of it was alive in a way no human or tavalai ship could ever be, walls that were not even straight pumping what might have been liquid, at times audibly, a swishing noise through suit microphones amidst the hum of unidentified machinery.

It was dark, too, LED indicators blinking through the irregular gloom, and occasional cross-webs of lasers like tripwires across spaces, or spidery art installations. No gravity, little visible light and no air — machines needed none of it. Drones swung aside for the *Phoenix* party, a graceful catch of some insectoid leg on a wall feature, mismatched eyes on darting heads staring, analysing. Erik refrained from giving thanks, in the sure knowledge that machines cared nothing for manners, and headed to where his visor display told him the required location was. If that location had a name, or a function, the display did not tell him.

He pulled himself along by improvised handholds, repressing the impulse to flinch with each touch, lest the organic-looking walls come alive and devour him. Now more than ever, moving within this alien thing that had risen from the darkest pages of Spiral history, he wondered what the hell he'd done. These living walls drank in the light, and drained the warmth from his soul. This was the evil tyranny that had once ruled the Spiral, returned to life at least partially by his hand. Now they were his partners in survival and war. His allies. God help them all.

Erik floated into another roughly hexagonal space, centred by a floating sphere. On the far side, several croma in the bulky, hard-plated suits even their civilians preferred, only a half-face visor to accomodate large muzzles. A drysine awaited, insectoid limbs splayed across its portion of the chamber, a wedge-shaped head and single fish-eye lens examining them all. There were so many different types *Phoenix* had never seen before. The survivors of a civilisation that had once spanned millions of systems, across most of what organics now called the Spiral, an entire sector of the Milky Way galaxy. The drysine race was so much more complicated in totality than the individual units that were all the *Phoenix* crew had so far seen. Many of the greatest drysine minds did not have bodies at all.

Erik's visor display identified the three croma as Croma'Dokran Halo'gan Fleet, which Lieutenant Sasalaka informed him was Croma'Dokran's third main fleet in its five fleet order of battle.

"I am Commander Li'stra," said the translator in Erik's ear. The translator was not always precise with equivalent ranks, and Erik did not trust it now. His visor illuminated the central croma as the

speaker. *"Commander Styx summoned Croma'Dokran to send the appropriate representative for this meeting. I was selected."*

Erik refrained from raising his eyebrows, however little it would be seen behind his visor. *Commander* Styx, was it now? Considering what she'd once been, that was a considerable demotion.

"Thank you for coming, Commander," said Erik. Behind him, Lieutenant Rooke entered, staring at everything, then Trace, with the newly promoted Sergeant Rael, and Corporal Arime, all marines in full armour. Erik looked at the big drysine. Every time he saw a new one, he was struck anew by incredulity that they even existed. He'd become somewhat accustomed to *Phoenix*'s three drones, and occasionally even to her resident queen, but proximity to a different type stripped away all familiarity and left only incredulity at the utter alienness.

This drysine did not reply. Erik was somewhat used to that — AIs seemed to spend a lot of time in their own heads, networked to complex data systems, not always paying great attention to what lay immediately before them. Rooke drifted toward the sphere in the chamber's center. Erik frowned, only now seeing what transfixed his senior Engineering Officer.

Despite being unsecured, the sphere did not drift. There were no aircurrents in the drysines' vacuum vessels, but in zero-G nearly everything drifted a little bit. And now, as he looked, the sphere appeared to flicker. Not merely an illusion of light, but as though the entire surface were pulsing.

"Lieutenant," Erik said with mild exasperation. "I believe Mr Romki gave us a lecture about poking things."

Rooke ignored him, halted his progress with a burst of compressed air, and extended a gloved finger at the sphere. It moved as he pushed it, but not much. In fact, Rooke moved backward from the contact more than the sphere did. And the sphere, his finger removed, shifted slowly back into place.

"It's some kind of electromagnetism," said Rooke, only audible through Erik's coms. *"My sensors are reading an off-the-charts spike... it's like there's veins running through the ship, an overlaid electromagnetic grid.*

I think it's got something to do with directed data-transferal, narrow-band rather than broadband. And this..." the sphere flickered once more. "*This is a computer?*"

He glanced at the big drysine. Again, the drysine gave no indication it had heard.

"*Hello Captain, Commander,*" came Styx's voice in Erik's ear. "*Thank you for coming. I believe we have some things to display that you will find interesting.*"

To hear her tell it, Lisbeth had been on Naraya, where the House Fortitude homeworld's capital city of Shonedene was located, when this small drysine fleet had arrived from jump. It had arrived at Defiance first, consequence of Styx sending assassin bugs manufactured there onto parren ships, to take control of those ships' long-range communications without them being aware of it, to send signals to those drysines still hiding in parren space to reassemble.

The parren had never done as thorough a job of clearing out their space of AI remnants as the tavalai had, and given their pricklishness about letting other species into their territory, they'd not allowed the tavalai to send their Dobruta into parren space to do it for them. Exactly what the drysines had been doing all that time, and why they'd not attempted to reassemble elsewhere in the intervening twenty five thousand years, Erik did not know. Romki and some others had guesses, but thus far the drysines had not seen fit to address them. Nor was it known if these five drysine ships were all that were left, or if more awaited in parren space.

They'd been looking for Styx. Upon learning Styx's probable location, they'd gone to find *Phoenix*, first arriving at Dul'rho in the aftermath of the great Tali'san that had installed the new Croma'Dokran leadership, and upon receiving a cautious welcome from Sho'mo'ra, had gone to Teg'ula System near reeh space, where *Phoenix* had been awaiting an optimal time to depart on her new mission. In some regards their timing had been excellent, as for what *Phoenix* was now attempting, the formidable assistance of drysine warships was welcome. Yet in other regards, such assistance would never be welcome, because their arrival now gave Styx a fleet of her own.

"Is Commander Styx aboard this ship now?" Commander Li'stra asked, glancing about within his helmet as though to wonder if she were coming in person. No croma had yet seen Styx in person, by mutual agreement between her and Erik that the croma should be alarmed as little as possible.

"Styx has seen fit to remain on *Phoenix*," Erik explained, and left it at that. No doubt Li'stra would find it puzzling. Well, some of *Phoenix*'s crew found it puzzling. Styx was the queen of all drysines. Yet instead of relocating herself to her rightful place in the flagship of her new fleet, she chose to remain aboard *Phoenix*, among primitive organics who while no longer astonished by her, still distrusted and feared her to no inconsiderable degree.

But of course that was the reason, Erik thought. *Phoenix*'s loyalties and actions were the only ones on this mission that Styx would not be able to trust, and so she placed herself amongst them, keeping friends close and enemies closer, so to speak. Romki had insisted it wasn't so simple — after all, with a drysine fleet's combined network advantages, they could no doubt take control of *Phoenix*'s newly drysine command and control systems if they wanted to, and Styx had no need to place herself physically on the ship to ensure its obedience. Romki thought it more likely that she was simply maximising her resources, valuing *Phoenix* as a fighting ship and perhaps even valuing the strange thoughts and judgements of its decidedly non-drysine crew. Drysines had learned to appreciate the mathematical value of variable data-inputs, he'd said, in a way that previous generations of machine race had not. By machine standards, one couldn't get more variable than organic minds.

Lieutenant Kaspowitz, of course, insisted that she was merely positioning herself to most conveniently dispose of them all once their usefulness was exhausted.

The sphere in the room's center glowed, and the air about them lit into a brilliant holographic display. Erik gazed about, at the glowing dots that represented star systems now hovering about his head. The brilliance of the display was far beyond what he was used to... though that might have been the absence of air. Gazing about, he couldn't even see where the holographic lasers were projected from... nor, for that matter, could he think of why drysines might need holographic technology in the first place. AIs could see all this in their heads, and distrusted their visual sensors to a degree that, by human standards, could have rendered them somewhat blind. Was this whole show just put on for the organics? A jury-rigged display, like some puppet show for visiting children using spare socks and buttons?

A vast line spread between the star systems, like a great, red wall. Identifying the English nametags helpfully affixed to some, Erik quickly recognised it — the Croma Wall. It was a myth, of course — walls could no more exist in space than plants, but it described the rough boundary between croma and reeh territories. Croma liked to pretend that it had always been there, solid and immovable as all the croma's preferred fortifications. The reality was far more disturbing — a slow and inexorable backward slide, leaving many dead and captured worlds in its wake.

"I have been analysing Commander Li'stra's provided data," said Styx. *"I am highly confident that I have located the previous center of power in early reeh space, dating to the time of what I estimate the arrival to be of the Ceephay Queen. The system is here — Croma Intelligence know it as Keijir, derived I believe from an old non-croma name."*

The stars and systems in the display abruptly raced inwards, contracting as the view zoomed back, to reveal a red, glowing system near a far wall. The drysines had even helpfully provided a visual scale in light-years.

"That's at least eight jumps," Erik observed. "Are the maps good enough for us to get there without detection?"

"With our ships?" said Li'stra. *"No."*

"I am confident," said Styx. Erik didn't like that. Human words like 'confident' meant nothing to Styx. It was what she said to placate lesser minds that could not comprehend the complexity of what she truly saw.

"Styx," said Trace. *"What makes you sure this is where the Ceephay Queen used to be?"* Trace had been the only one to show no trepidation coming aboard the drysine ship. In fact, Trace had shown very little

reaction to anything since she'd returned from her successful attack on the Rando Splicer that had liberated enormous volumes of information on the reeh's genetic manipulation technologies. Erik remained uncertain that she had entirely returned. In the whole 57 days since, she'd barely spoken a word to him in private. On duty, she remained as cool and efficient as ever, and never short of things to say. But once they'd used to sit over their command reviews, and in between business there'd been jokes and friendly conversation. Now, she simply finished her review, cleared all her points with him, and left. When she'd been gone, Erik had missed her. Now that she'd returned, he missed her more.

"The raid upon Croma'Rai's Central Intelligence liberated much curious data," said Styx. *"Croma space faring civilisation went through several phases in the latter period of what you call the Machine Age, and their contact with what now constitutes reeh space was at the time minimal. But many other species had extensive contact with early reeh civilisation, before the reeh expanded to become the empire that swallowed them. Croma'Rai Intelligence held extensive recordings of very old data-traffic analysis in the early reeh civilisation, compiled by the reeh's neighbours at the time.*

"The data is fragmented, and much of it miscategorised by croma agents who misunderstood its origin, or what the data was truly recording. But I have identified patterns in the technology and civilisational behaviour that confirms to me, with great certainty, that approximately thirty thousand human years ago, about ten thousand years after the date of the ceephays' fall, a new center of data and physical traffic accumulated at the Keijir System. Ten thousand years correlates closely with how long I estimate a ceephay vessel would have taken to travel some feasible sublight to avoid detection using jump engines, until being discovered by reeh vessels, possibly in some kind of hibernation. The accumulation of technologies at the Keijir System was very rapid, and was responded to by several of the species who were recording this data. There are even several surviving speculations from their academia at the time, wondering what was happening at Keijir. I believe these events are entirely consistent with the discovery, by an organic species of lesser intelligence and capability, of an entity of greater intelligence and capability. Great technological advances appear to

have followed, and the expansion of what became the Reeh Empire commenced shortly thereafter."

"Commander Li'stra," said Erik, drifting closer to the Keijir System icon with an almost subconscious nudge of his hand thruster. "Does Styx's assessment agree with croma knowledge?"

"Croma knowledge has little to say on this," said Li'stra. *"Croma had nothing to do with the reeh at this point. The Great Struggle commenced seven thousand years ago. Prior to that, reeh were mostly fighting their further neighbours."*

"Styx," asked Trace, *"do you have any further assessment of just how many neighbours the reeh once had?"*

"I can identify seventeen intelligent races from the data," said Styx, with appropriate solemnity. Seventeen, Erik repeated in his head, with cold dread. *"More may have been present but not mentioned, or yet to be discovered at the time, like the corbi."*

"And what do croma teachings say that the reeh were like during this early period?" Erik asked Li'stra.

"The reeh have always been evil," said Li'stra with hard certainty. *"Croma'Dokran have records too. There has never been a period where reeh were not enslaving and slaughtering innocents. It's in their genetics. They are kus'its."* Kus'it were a species of aggressive, swarming eel that migrated on the swamplands of the croma homeworld, Erik had come to know, having heard them being used to describe the reeh before. The eels were poisonous, and killed all in their path. Periodic population plagues had led to the extinctions of other creatures on the homeworld before the croma had begun controlling eel numbers.

"Humans have known species like that," Rooke murmured, gazing about.

Erik nodded within his helmet. "Well Styx, if you're convinced that this is where we ought to go in search of the Ceephay Queen, then this is where we should go. What else do you wish us to see?"

"Wait," said Li'stra. *"Croma know Keijir System today. Its primary world is called Eshir by its locals. It's a turd, there is no center of reeh power there today."*

"My analysis of croma intelligence on the reeh suggests the same,

Commander Li'stra," Styx replied. *"But as we are unable to discern the Ceephay Queen's location today, we must search for her location in the past, and pick up the trail from there."*

"Croma'Dokran intelligence has not shared such data with you about the reeh," said Li'stra. Erik could hear the frown in the Commander's translator-synthesised voice.

"Yeah that's what you think," said Rooke.

"Captain," said Styx. *"I wish you to see the latest deployments of the Reeh Fleet, according to Croma Fleet Intelligence."*

Graphics appeared. The clusters of arrowheads at reeh worlds along the Croma Wall were familiar to any human Fleet officer. Erik counted, and took Styx's indicative manoeuvre arrows with a grain of salt, but got the general idea. The numbers were scary.

"And what proportion of Reeh Fleet strength do you estimate this represents?" he asked. General lighting within the holography room was poor, and he could not see Commander Li'stra's face within his helmet's narrow visor, but he could read consternation in the croma's silence, and his floating posture. Croma Fleet Intelligence had *certainly* not shared their latest information on reeh force deployments with Styx. But Li'stra would learn, as others had, that information did not need to be voluntarily shared with Styx in order for her to acquire it.

"A relatively small proportion yet," Styx answered. *"The rest of the Reeh Fleet is occupied fighting battles elsewhere. I estimate that this is mostly the reeh reserve, held especially for flareups like this one. The main redeployment of forces, if it comes, will be considerably larger."*

That was scarier still. Reeh military power was colossal. Croma power was also, but if the reeh deployed all their forces at the croma at once, Styx had estimated that croma space would fold within a decade. Two decades, should they fight to the end and not surrender, as seemed the likely croma response, and the croma race could cease to exist. Only the reeh's perpetual distraction with additional wars on their far borders kept the croma alive and fighting, however much the croma liked to pretend otherwise.

And now, by helping to install Croma'Dokran as the power in

croma space, Erik and *Phoenix* had helped to launch a new phase in a seven thousand year old war that could kill additional billions. And the reeh, as always across the past few thousand years, seemed to know exactly when the croma were about to attack. It was not surprising — croma were not subtle, and reeh surveillance technology was superior. This time, the Reeh Empire knew the croma were coming.

"Currently our primary avenues of approach to Keijir System are blocked by the reeh buildup," Styx continued. *"Even superior drysine stealth capability will not grant us undetected passage, and without that, our chances of successful penetration and survival are minimal to non-existent. I suggest that we await the first engagements of the new campaign. Reeh ships will redeploy in a forward manner, clearing their back ways sufficiently to make our path through."*

The systems in question illuminated to illustrate the drysine commander's plan. Erik nodded, having spent many of the past days calculating the same thing. "I agree, Styx. I feel we should wait for the latest reports following the initial engagements around Jikul and Torsena Systems, then select our best course based on those. Perhaps if Commander Li'stra could ensure sufficient deep-observation assets are in place to enable our best choice of path?"

"I will put in a request," Li'stra said cautiously.

"An excellent suggestion, Captain," said Styx, in the manner of a teacher pleased that her student had thought of some simple thing himself, without prompting.

"The Ceephay Queen," said Li'stra, looking up through his visor, as though Styx were somehow located in the mysterious ether. *"There are officers in Croma Fleet Intelligence who doubt her existence. They say there is no way that such a creature still lives within the Reeh Empire, if she ever did. Reeh do not tolerate taking commands from others."*

"I have never suggested that the Ceephay Queen commands anyone," Styx said calmly. *"I have stated that I know for certain fact that reeh electronic language contains many recent updates that could only have been performed by an AI command-level intellect. This electronic language has its roots indisputably located in ceephay-era technology. I assure you that it*

not possible for me to be mistaken on this. I draw no conclusion as to what this means regarding the Ceephay Queen's current status within reeh society. I admit a great puzzlement myself. But she is most certainly there, somewhere, and is performing at the very least some nature of technical oversight, if not outright command, of reeh forces."

"What kind of people were the ceephays, Styx?" asked Rooke.

"The primary points of differentiation between AI races are highly technical, Lieutenant," said Styx. *"I'm afraid that not even you would understand the distinction."*

"With regard to organic beings," said Rooke, with repressed amusement. The tech-nerds in Engineering were wise to Styx's predictable objections, and suspected she used it primarily to avoid answering inconvenient questions. *"Were they more or less... let's say intolerant, of organics, than deepynines or drysines?"*

"More intolerant than drysines. Less than deepynines. No one is as intolerant of organic life as deepynines."

And yet the most murderous of the AI races had somehow befriended the alo, who recent discoveries revealed were once a slave race within the Reeh Empire. Befriended them, and constructed a symbiotic relationship with them behind an impenetrable shield of superior surveillance and weaponry, directly adjoining human space. And *that* remained a mystery that even Styx had no explanations for.

LI'STRA AND HIS two officers rode with the humans on PH-1 back to *Phoenix*, while the croma's shuttle flew empty. Li'stra said he wanted to talk, and on the AI ship, as on *Phoenix*, there were drysines who would listen.

"Why does she insist we meet on the drysine ship, when we could have met with her directly on Phoenix?" Li'stra had his helmet off in PH-1's hold, as they secured into rear seats near the cockpit. Typically Erik would ride in the cockpit observer seats, but that would make a larger conversation impossible.

"I don't know," Erik admitted. It had been the subject of speculation among *Phoenix* crew as well. "Styx insists the display technology is better there, which it is, but marginally. We think the drysines like to watch us react to things."

Li'stra's bull-like brows knitted. The leather plates on his forehead and nose were soft with youth, and he was no larger than Erik. Given that croma actually grew more slowly than humans, and were considered children until nearly thirty, Erik thought Li'stra might be only a little older than himself, perhaps forty. Space being duty for younger croma, Croma Fleet was filled with hard-charging young officers determined to make their mark before their bodies grew too big and cumbersome for heavy-G combat duties.

"How does it help her to watch us react?"

"Organic physiology," Erik explained, pleased to have his helmet off in human-pressure air again. "We react to things involuntarily." Trace drifted by, last in and finding a 'seat' several places along. Normally Trace would make certain to sit alongside him, for easy conversation. Erik knew she was avoiding him. It was unprofessional of her, and well below her usual standards. He worried for her. "Well most of us, anyway. With drysine vision and sensors, they can read involuntary responses, and get some idea of our personality profiles, how we might react to stresses, that sort of thing. It's our best guess, anyway."

"And you let them do this?" Li'stra wondered.

"We learn things from them too." Erik glanced at Rooke, seated alongside — the younger man had a heavy display visor down, replaying things he'd seen and sorting them with vocal commands. "There's a lot of things we still don't know about them, and they haven't been volunteering. We've observed them a lot as individuals, but not on any kind of civilisational level. Well, there was Defiance, but Defiance was mostly deserted when we were there. This is the first chance anyone's had to see how drysines go about daily operations on warships."

"Captain," came Lieutenant Hausler's voice from the cockpit, *"we're reading not everyone strapped in back there."*

"Yeah, we're having a conversation, Trey," Erik replied to his mic.

"Just go real slow, no rush." Li'stra remained unbuckled, facing backward with a firm grasp on the seatbacks while the rest strapped in facing forward. It was the only way to talk to everyone, with the seating configuration all facing front.

"I copy Captain," said Hausler. *"Here we go."* A loud clank as the grapples disconnected, then a gentle thrust as Hausler took them down, then swivelled to change face. A short tap of the mains, and they were ballistic again. Experienced spacer that he was, Li'stra barely budged.

"You wanted to tell us something?" Erik prompted.

"Eshir," said Li'stra. *"The inhabited world of Keijir System, your target destination. It has humans on it."*

Erik frowned at him for a moment. There was no way the translator had gotten that sentence right. But then, the translator was extremely good at Kul'hasa these days, and got very little wrong. The sentence was too simple to screw up.

"Eshir... has humans on it?"

"Yes." Li'stra seemed completely serious. Croma usually did. And from the way that he revealed the information, he seemed to think these humans would find it to be a big deal.

"How does Eshir have humans on it?" Even Rooke had raised his visor to stare in bewilderment.

"From one thousand years ago," said the croma officer. *"The time of the krim occupation of Earth. Krim took prisoners — you would know that history far better than we."*

"But the krim took no human slaves," Trace interjected from behind Erik. "They didn't experiment much, either, they weren't curious enough. They took prisoners and they disappeared, we never saw them again. It was assumed they'd all been murdered."

"We think these were traded with the reeh," said Li'stra. *"We aren't aware of the details. Reeh are always interested in new genetic combinations. The psychological similarities between reeh and krim are obvious, probably the krim saw the reeh as potential allies."*

"That doesn't seem possible from everything we learned of krim psychology," Rooke said dubiously. "They obeyed tavalai by historical accident, they weren't the types to go making new friends. And how did they get human prisoners past the Croma Wall, and through tavalai space even before that?"

"We don't know," Li'stra said bluntly. *"It's one of many mysteries of the reeh. Croma'Shin were in power then, we've seen corruption in previous croma regimes. Perhaps they looked the other way."*

"These humans on Eshir," said Erik, incredulously. "How much do you know about them?"

"We gather intelligence on reeh space constantly. We've known about them maybe two hundred years. Eshir was once an important world, as your queen says, but it has declined. There are a number of very old cities, a lot of inefficient industry. For some reason, the reeh have ignored it, let it fall to ruin. We don't know why.

"We think the humans arrived there immediately, a thousand years ago, and have been breeding since. They live in several cities — the main city is Qalea, the largest human population is there, we think it is millions. Qalea has many millions though, many races, mostly not reeh or human. Some of these worlds, reeh let non-reeh accumulate, and pay them little mind. Like garbage disposal."

"You mean the reeh used those humans the krim gave them for experiments," said Erik, "and dumped the rest on Eshir?"

"That is our best guess, yes."

"Are they okay?" asked Sergeant Rael, as amazed as the others. "I mean... are they mistreated?"

"There is no way to know. Are humans especially vulnerable to mistreatment?" With typically croma sarcasm.

"It's like a tavalai free city, Sergeant," Erik explained. "Only a lot less pleasant, by the sound of it. Everyone for themself. Sounds like the ideal human environment." With a cool stare at Li'stra.

"It presents a human crew with possibilities for reconnaissance," Li'stra said pointedly. *"Possibilities that your queen did not inform you of."*

"Maybe she didn't know?" Arime suggested. Then, "Oh. Right, forget I said it."

"Yeah," Erik agreed, thinking hard. "She didn't tell us, did she?"

"Perhaps she tries to keep you ignorant, fearing your judgement will be clouded."

"It's far more likely that she's already predicted you would say that to me, and finds it useful somehow."

"To what ends?"

Erik shrugged. "Who knows? You'll find with Styx, my croma friend, that there's nothing more foolhardy than to assume you've thought of something she's missed. Or that you're having a conversation she hasn't anticipated."

"This sounds like defeatism," said Li'stra, scowling. *"Yet you insist you are not her slaves."*

"The point is that we won't be manipulated into mindless croma aggression," Erik retorted. Unlike many species, croma didn't take you seriously unless you insulted them. "Don't play mind games with Styx, Li'stra. Choose your course of action and let things play out. Let her think herself in knots. If you play her game, you'll lose."

"And you're all convinced this is worth almost certainly losing your lives? To find information on this Nia?"

It had been Lisbeth who'd brought information of an old deepynine queen's activities in Shonedene on the House Fortitude world of Naraya. Now Styx was convinced that Nia had come this way following the destruction of her people in the Drysine/Deepynine War, and been captured by the reeh, before somehow escaping. Given that the alo had been recently revealed to be a Reeh Empire region species too, prior to their arrival in their current territory in The Spiral with the deepynines, it seemed logical to assume that the alo might have had something to do with that escape.

"Styx says she knew Nia during the Drysine/Deepynine War," said Erik. "But she suspects she's changed enormously since then. She's convinced she can analyse and predict Nia's tactical patterns and intentions, if she can just access the Ceephay Queen's memories. Isn't that right, Styx?"

"Yes Captain. I believe I will be able to construct a full psychological simulation of Nia, that will effectively allow us to be able to read her mind and predict her actions. In any upcoming conflict, it could swing the war."

"And I'd like to know the nature of this relationship with the alo," Erik added. "Alliances usually come with weakpoints. If we could find the weakpoint in that alliance, we may find a way to cripple them."

~

"If we can get there undetected," said Trace in Erik's quarters forty minutes later, "then it creates some very useful possibilities to get down there and look around."

They were all crammed into the captain's quarters again, a single bunk and shower with barely enough room for six, elbows touching as they leaned against the door and walls. Trace sat on the small table, Erik opposite on his bunk with Kaspowitz alongside. Commander Draper was also present, while Lieutenant Commander Dufresne sat the captain's chair in the bridge outside. Also present were Lieutenant Sasalaka, Lieutenant Shilu, and Second Lieutenant Lassa from second-shift. These were *Phoenix*'s best strategic brains, in Erik's evolving estimation. For what they were heading into, he was going to need them at the top of their game.

"Who would you send down on the away mission?" Erik asked Trace. On Konik it had been Lieutenant Dale and some of his Alpha Platoon marines, disguised initially as Domesh parren in black robes. With native humans downworld on Eshir, that degree of hiding wasn't going to be necessary.

"If those humans were taken from Earth during the occupation," said Trace, "then there's no guarantee they'll speak English. Less than ten percent of Earth did back then, as a first language." Erik nodded, a little embarrassed that he hadn't thought of it. But Trace was lately fluent in Lisha, and accustomed to such downworld thoughts. "So I'll wait until there's better intelligence on the indigenous population. Translators work okay, but native speakers would be better. About half of my marines speak something else, myself included."

"Well I'm becoming increasingly uncertain that we're going to have Stan along to help us with the aliens," said Erik, unhappily.

"He's not coming back?" asked Lassa with dismay. "But we're going to be up to our necks in drysines and reeh. How can he miss that?"

Once it had become clear that *Phoenix* could not leave on her mission to find the ceephay queen until this new phase in the reeh-croma war had commenced, Erik had resigned himself to waiting here in Teg'ula System, 28 light years from Dul'rho and squarely on the line of the Croma Wall. Here he'd reestablished communication with the new ruler of all croma — Sho'mo'ra — who had explained to him that he had no difficulty with *Phoenix*'s plans, and even wished them luck and assistance where possible, whatever noises he might make to suggest otherwise in domestic croma politics.

But in dealing with some of that politics, Sho'mo'ra had faced many calls to explain himself, and his refusal to denounce these alien interferers entirely. He had requested the presence of *Phoenix*'s leading expert on humans, drysines and other troubling matters, to explain these things to croma demanding harsher action against human and drysine visitors alike, and so Stan Romki had departed for Dul'rho to try and calm them down.

"The last ship through here beamed us a short update from Croma Command," Erik explained. "There was a message from Stan in it, he said he'd been offered a position as a senior advisor to Sho'-mo'ra on all matters relating to humans and drysines in particular. Basically he'd be to Sho'mo'ra what Lisbeth is to Gesul. He said he's seriously thinking of taking it."

"Lucrative to be an advisor these days," Kaspowitz murmured. Erik didn't think the lanky Navigation Officer meant anything harsh by it. Stan Romki had proven his selfless devotion to the human cause far too many times for that.

"It's bloody Tiga again, isn't it?" Draper said angrily.

Erik shrugged. "She and Stan are friends. No doubt she said nice things about him in Sho'mo'ra's ear to get him sent there in the first place."

"We could have ordered him to stay aboard," said Lassa. And by 'we', Erik knew that she meant 'you'.

"Stan's a civilian, Angela," Erik said sternly. Lassa rolled her eyes. "He's come this far by choice, and he can leave by choice too, any time he likes. If he thinks he can do more good where he is, then he may well be right, his judgement's been spot on most times. There's far more going on in the galaxy than just whatever *Phoenix* is up to."

But it was going to hurt all of their chances. Where *Phoenix* was going, even Romki was going to be largely out of his depth. But if anyone could figure a way to keep all of their heads above water before they drowned, it was Romki. Erik could see the dismay on everyone's faces. It was more than concern for their personal survival — it was a personal hurt, for all of them. *Phoenix* was a family. Romki was frequently annoying, but Erik had plenty of annoying family, and they didn't stop being family because of it.

Shilu was flexing the knuckles of his synthetic left hand with the fingers of his right. That nervous mannerism had appeared some weeks back, along with a leg tremor and apparent breaks in concentration. Two years ago when this whole mess started, Erik wouldn't have spotted it, but these days he knew his bridge crew better than his sisters back on Homeworld.

"Kaspo," he said, changing the subject. "Where are we at with the course?"

Kaspowitz had a comp slate on his long thigh, a knee drawn up, lips pursed in a thoughtful scowl. Erik was sure he knew what was coming. "Look," Kaspowitz said finally. "I don't want this to be yet another session where I say the same things all over again and everyone rolls their eyes rather than listens to me..."

"Events have proven you largely correct on many things," Erik interrupted. "No one's ignoring you Kaspo, least of all now."

That conciliation, however, left things unsaid. Kaspowitz heard them. He took a deep breath. "The course looks good. It's been compiled with data from Croma Fleet Intel, the first part of which at least they're entirely sure of because that was croma space within recorded memory. The second part is a bit more sketchy, but we can go over that in more detail later when I get some of the new plotting marks back from astrophysics simulation.

"The problem is that to hit these jump points, as some of you have heard me complaining about for a while now..." with a pointed glance above his long nose at the gathering, "...we're going to have to integrate with our friendly comrades-in-arms. Because, heh..." and he shook his head with a faint whistle of disbelief and forced humour, "...these jump points, oh boy. I'm aware of what our girl's new technology can do now, and Rooke's engine specs have all checked out so far, but we're trying to hit things we can't even measure with the old sensor arrays, they're that far out on the grav slope, it's basically a deep space jump. And if you all remember your nav basics from the Academy, and I'm sure you do... deep space jumps are basically impossible."

"Is the problem mainly with processing power?" asked Sasalaka as she leaned in the doorway, in her thick Togiri accent. "Or engine power?"

"Oh I'd never doubt the engines," said Kaspowitz, shaking his head. "They're beasts, we've got engine power up the wazoo. We just can't calculate positional space on that weak a grav slope, and frankly, given that we've got pretty much the same nav tech that the drysines do, I don't think they can either. Not individually. Which is where we get to interlinking our ships through jump, which is the latest of many, many wonderful technical requirements our mechanical friends have sent to me..." with the greatest of sarcasm, "...which basically means surrendering piloting autonomy to the drysine hive mind at the most vulnerable point of the mission. And you can all guess how I'm feeling about that."

"It's the interlocked sensor spread, isn't it?" Draper asked. "How does that even work with some ships still in hyperspace as others are coming out?"

"Oh..." and Kaspowitz waggled a finger at him, "...never you mind that, my boy. Our machine overlords keep their secrets well, our trust in them is total." Smothered smiles on the faces of several, amidst the concern. Kaspowitz looked sideways at Erik, and found him just looking, with reprimand. Kaspowitz sighed and held up a hand in apology. "Sure, too far. Look, I'm not claiming they're going to kill us all and eat us."

"Big concession from you," said Lassa.

"I'm just saying, as a matter of strategic concern, that we won't have control over our own damn ship going through jump. Which I'd have thought was an issue."

"It is an issue," Erik agreed, to placate more of them than just Kaspowitz. "And your concern is warranted."

They discussed the shape of the coming war for a while longer. It was sobering, to see so many forces mobilising right across the Croma Wall, and apparently on both sides. Styx's best estimation, which was surely more accurate than what Croma'Dokran were telling even their own people, was somewhere in the vicinity of one and a half thousand capital warships on the croma side alone, and many more support and minor vessels. The initial reeh response was somewhat below that, but would be building fast, once they brought ships from beyond their ready reserve.

The croma were mobilising at least five invasion strike forces — an important part of any large effort, Erik knew well from experience in the Triumvirate War. Invasion strike forces landed on planets and destroyed enemy ground forces and facilities without requiring orbital bombardment and the levelling of civilian populations. They were controversial, as many Admirals dismissed their usefulness, stating correctly that if Fleet could not hold the spacelanes open, such forces were doomed to fail from the beginning. All the true fighting happened in space, such Admirals proclaimed, and thus ground armies were no more than psychological posturing, capturing ground that could not be truly considered captured until the real war had been won far above their heads.

But many times in the Triumvirate War, that had been proven untrue, as stubborn defences by tavalai ground armies had tied up human Fleet forces for long enough in support operations that tavalai Fleet had been granted an opportunity to pick off many human support vessels occupied while their backs were turned.

Here the croma strategy would be similar — to tie down Reeh

Fleet in supporting their ground forces, thus presenting Croma Fleet with many opportunities to kill a lot of them. Unfortunately, such calculations ran both ways, and Erik suspected the croma would be more concerned about the fate of their ground forces than the reeh, thus requiring more support ships to assist them, and thus more juicy targets for the reeh. The *main* utility of ground invasions, both human and tavalai strategists had concluded, was to localise fighting by forcing fleets to concentrate forces, and thus to soak up ship numbers in those high-intensity fights. That in turn dramatically reduced the risk of forces being left free to perform flanking manoeuvres, and created a degree of predictability across a broad battlefront.

Something similar was about to happen at Reba System, on the corbi homeworld of Rando. It would draw reeh vessels like flies to shit and thus leave neighbouring systems relatively clear for *Phoenix* and her small drysine fleet to sneak through undetected... if Kaspowitz's course plots turned out to be navigable after all. Or that, at least, was the plan.

Even with access to what Styx claimed were near-complete croma battleplans, Erik was not prepared to guess at likely croma casualties in the first phase of the operation. Styx suggested a figure between six and eight hundred thousand croma dead, most of them in the ground invasion forces, then to escalate by orders of magnitude if the second and third phases also escalated, as seemed likely when the main reeh forces arrived. Of course, those numbers could change radically if a sneak attack took out a croma station, as had happened many times in the past, whatever the croma's intense system-defence deployments. Like the big human stations, croma stations held millions. To Erik, it felt surreal and depressingly grim. He'd thought his time in big wars was ended when the tavalai had surrendered. Worse, he'd played a direct and personal role in getting this new war started, however willingly this new generation of croma warriors rushed into it.

The briefing concluded, and Erik asked for Trace to remain behind as the others filed out. "Shilu," he said to her once they were alone, as she remained seated on the small table, knees pulled up to her familiar meditation posture.

"What about him?" Trace's expression gave nothing away. He'd been coming to read her so well. But since she'd returned, it was like a new wall had gone up. From discussion with the rest of the crew, he knew he wasn't the only one who'd seen it. Her injuries were mostly healed, just a faint scar on her cheek where shrapnel had gone right through. Her limp from the leg injuries had gone within two weeks, with Doc Suelo's care. At the gym, her previously fractured arm was no longer preventing her from pounding a bag as hard as she ever had. But Erik was not concerned with physical injuries.

"I think he's got the wobbles." It was spacer-speak, euphemism for something none of them liked to discuss directly. Marines called it 'the rattles', because of the vibration that involuntary muscle contractions could cause in an armour suit.

"Spacer matter," Trace said shortly.

"I want you to talk to him."

"Have *you* talked to him?"

"Yes. He lost his arm, Trace. We've been going at this nearly two years now, longer if you count the last deployment of the war. Pantillo always said that nerves and bravery were finite resources, that everyone had their limit. I think Wei might be getting to the end of his."

It hurt to talk about it. Wei Shilu was one of Erik's favourite people in the world — really far too elegant and sophisticated to be a Fleet combat officer, but he'd put aside his more refined tastes to serve as Coms Officer on various warships for the most recent years of his life. Four years ago his long-term boyfriend had left him, tired of the endless waiting for a promised retirement that never came. And at Defiance he'd suffered a disfiguring injury that would have traumatised the toughest warrior, and had adapted to the replacement limb with all possible serenity. It didn't seem right to be ratting on him like this. But Erik needed all his bridge crew operating at optimum, and if one of them had a problem doing that, he needed to get it fixed, preferably before the shooting started.

"Erik," said Trace, "if I start talking to bridge crew in your stead, you'll lose authority, and I'll be putting marine standards onto spacer crew, which never goes down well."

"You're not *that* much tougher than us," Erik said lightly.

"Maybe not," Trace said calmly, "but it comes across that way, and spacers resent it. You also spend far more time with him than I do..."

"You saw him just now. I saw you looking."

Trace sighed, reluctantly. She had. She gazed at the wall for a moment. Her own hands, on her crosslegged knees were balled tight. "Corpsman Joshi's handling psych right now?" Erik nodded. "What's he say?"

"Says it's borderline. Says the scans indicate it's not PTSD, the post-trauma patch held well. But there are things beyond experiential trauma the patch can't treat."

Trace's eyes never left the wall. No doubt she'd sensed where this was going by now. Probably she'd sensed it since the moment he'd asked her to remain behind.

"Will you talk to him?" Erik pressed. "You know much more about this than I do. Marines have it harder, and you've been doing this a lot longer than I have."

"Sure," Trace said finally. "I'll talk to him. Is that all?"

"Corpsman Joshi says he doesn't like your psych-scans either."

Trace gave him a hard sideways look. "You pulled my files?"

"I'm the Captain," Erik retorted. "I don't *pull* anything. It's my command prerogative." Trace's eyes slid back to the wall. Her hands clenched tighter. "Trace, you have to talk to me. You haven't talked to me since you got back, not really. You haven't talked to anyone. It's been 58 days, and..."

"I've been busy."

"You've been in pain." He said it hard, without that soft empathy that he knew Trace hated so much in command matters. "You've been wound up tight like a drum, and I'm concerned that..."

"Concerned that what?" Trace replied, her eyes still on the wall. Her posture held perfectly upon the table. "That we haven't had friendly conversations? I'm a marine commander. Rando taught me to reprioritise. I've been reprioritising."

"I'm concerned that we're not communicating," Erik retorted. "The first thing you told me when I assumed command of this ship was that Captain and Marine Commander need to communicate."

"We communicate fine."

"It takes two people to make that judgement, Trace. When one of those people is the Captain, and he says otherwise, then no, we're not communicating *fine*."

"Name an area of command where our communication has been lacking?" said Trace, fixing him with another cold stare. "Where has it affected our performance?"

"We're not in combat right now, Trace. My job is to prepare for it."

"Right," she said, "and instead of doing that, you're upset that you don't get enough alone time with your buddies." It hurt. She wanted it to hurt. Erik knew her all too well — she wanted him to stand to attention and address her by rank, and thus compel her to do the same. She wanted this formal and hard. She wanted him to shout at her, to hand out disciplines. This time, he refused to let her win. "You want me to say that Rando hurt? Fine, Rando hurt. I'm dealing with it. I'm good at dealing with it. I've been dealing with it my whole life. I think I'm a lot better at it than you are, so your critiques of my methods, while noted, don't impress me."

Erik leaned forward, elbows on knees on his bunk, and gazed at her. "You're not hurt, Trace. You're bleeding. You fancy yourself the best self-taught psychologist on this ship, but you only know the nature of the human heart when you've pinned it to the ground and stuck a knife through it." Trace stared at him, with an intensity that might once have frightened him. It frightened him now, but for entirely different reasons.

"You've lived your life within an emotional cage," he pressed. "You think you know the human mind better than I do, but in reality you only know your cage. I've lived my life outside that cage, and I know that landscape *so* much better than you. And now you've had the walls of that cage torn down, and you find yourself out in the open, surrounded by unfamiliar emotions that will no longer simply obey your instructions like they used to, and you're lost and you're scared. You *suck* at this, Trace. You're out of your depth. And with absolute unprofessionalism, when confronted with something you don't know how to do, you refuse to ask for help from those that do."

Trace's jaw clenched and unclenched. That scared Erik more than anything. There was no cool retort, no calm grinding of his argument into the deck beneath her heel, as she'd once done so effortlessly. She just sat, in that crosslegged pose that pretended poise and control, shoulders noticeably moving as she struggled to control her breathing.

"Will that be all, Captain?" she asked, and her voice betrayed little of her struggle. So much control, and even now it would not abandon her.

"Yes Trace." Even now, he would not let her hide behind formality. Not here. "And talk to Shilu. I won't make it an order, but spacer or not he's your shipmate too, and we're all family here. Don't forget it." He jerked his head at the door.

Trace unfolded herself from the table, went to the door and left. Erik stared at the door for a moment after it had closed behind her, feeling hollow. He'd beaten Trace in arguments before, but this was the first time he'd hated the winning.

3

Rika hung off the armour rack supports, and frowned as Leo explained the suit's targeting calibration to him. The translator was good with technical terms, which was just as well, because Rika's comprehension of even simple English was still poor. But as Leo moved the suit's arms, and explained how that made the armscomp's perception of dead-zero shift while the mode was in 'recalibrate', Rika felt his eyes glazing over.

Leo saw, and grinned, slapping his shoulder. *"Don't worry man,"* he said cheerfully. *"You'll get it."*

"No I won't," Rika said gloomily. "The most technology I grew up with was irrigation pumps. And that was off an old electric battery we couldn't keep charged, and only worked half the time."

Keeping it charged had been dangerous, too. The only methods were wind, solar or water turbines in the river, and too many could invite a reeh strike against too much visible technology. So the batteries were given to old Lugi, who liked to wander the forest trails alone despite the dangers, and cultivated not only forest medicines, but water turbines further upstream. Every few days Lugi would return with several charged batteries for those who needed them, keeping the incriminating recharge facilities far enough from the village to placate the reeh.

The suit had come from Corbi Resistance Fleet — a genuine marine armour suit, made to fit corbi only, and one hell of a gift given how few the Resistance had left. But the *Phoenix* marines had come to suspect that the suit was actually an original from the war against the reeh, the shell nearly a thousand years old and made by a high-tech corbi civilisation that no longer existed, all its electronics, servos and actuators replaced many, many times, and it was not the relatively new machine the Resistance had claimed. It worked still, but it rattled and whined, and the fabrication wing of *Phoenix*'s Engineering crew were running through a long list of new parts required to get it back to something approaching operational status.

Antique or not, Rika felt overwhelmed at the scale of the gift. On Rando he'd carried a rifle, and thought himself a pretty good soldier, but truthfully he'd had little real training, nor seen serious action, until those crazy days leading to the Splicer assault. He'd somehow survived that while most of his comrades hadn't, and had arrived on *Phoenix* mostly dead, only to be revived by the humans' miracle-working medical tech. And now Resistance Command themselves had authorised the gift of one of their precious armour suits to him, the farming kid from Talo who hadn't realised just how out of his depth he'd been until he'd run into the strange alien marine commander with a death wish.

But Major Thakur had assured him that the gift made perfect sense. While all the surviving corbi from the Splicer assault had chosen to join the Resistance to help with what they'd been promised would be the mass-evacuation of Rando, Rika alone had chosen to remain aboard *Phoenix*. At first he hadn't had a choice, being too badly hurt to move. But as the injuries had healed with miraculous speed, he'd begun to realise that his choice brought with it new responsibilities, and that the Major expected him to learn from the *Phoenix* marines, and become as much like them as he could manage.

It suited Rika enormously, awestruck as he was of these big, physically augmented and lethally skilled aliens with their high-tech suits and crazy weaponry. These were warriors unlike any he'd served with before — who had no special fear of the reeh, and had met more formidable foes than reeh in combat and left them devastated. To become like them to any serious degree was more than he'd ever wanted or expected from life. But now he had that dream within his grasp, the prospect seemed like some dreadful weight of fear and expectation.

The Major believed in him, though. The Major said that the corbi were going to be rescued from Rando, and that whereever they ended up, they'd need well-trained, modern warriors who could in turn instruct their next generation of recruits, and transform them into a force that could genuinely defend themselves against the many evils of the galaxy. That that person should be *him*, Rika was finding difficult to get his head around. But if the Major thought he could do it, then he was prepared to countenance anything.

The humans called this big, cavernous space on the marines' side of the ship 'Assembly'. It was so big it allowed him to see the curvature of *Phoenix*'s rotating crew cylinder, a great, vertical arrangement of armour racks, elevators and pulley systems, reaching toward the cylinder's center somewhere above, the furthest racks appearing to lean on an angle compared to the nearest. The whole place echoed with the crashes of heavy equipment, the throb and hum of armour powerplants, and the yell of human or sometimes tavalai voices. The armour racks were surely loaded with enough firepower to destroy entire reeh armies. Rika found the whole place bewildering, exciting and intimidating in equal measure.

Leo began explaining the suit's shoulder joint to him, and how they'd have to disassemble it to get the new targeting systems, that Engineering was fabricating, built into the armscomp. Leo's name wasn't actually 'Leo' — that was a nickname, his real name was Terez, and he was a private in the Major's personal unit, which they called 'Command Squad'. 'Private' was the lowest rank the marines had, yet Leo was about twice Rika's age (as nearly as anyone could explain how long a human 'year' was) and had seen some enormous amount of fighting. More fighting, in fact, than Lieutenant Alomaim, who was an officer in command of Bravo Platoon, and about as far above 'private' as ranks got on *Phoenix*. Rika had assumed that new marines would start at the lowest rank, then move their way up with experience, but humans didn't do things like that. Even the Major was much younger than some of the marines she led. So command, then, wasn't just a matter of experience — it was a matter of aptitude, and something that people trained for specifically.

Sergeant Rael arrived, stomping over in his big suit, asking Rika how his last medical check had gone, and peering at the corbi armour's exposed shoulder. Marines called it 'doing a wear', just leaving the suit on for a time while they did normal things, allowing the control systems to calibrate against standard activities like walking.

Rael was Sergeant Kono's replacement as leader of Command Squad. Rika had talked with them a lot about Giddy Kono, telling them of his impressions, and the brave or funny things he'd done. Kono had been a big grim man, but he'd been a pushover for the corbi kids who'd loved to climb on him like their personal jungle gym. The Command Squad marines, Rika learned, were more interested to hear those kinds of stories than the combat ones. Times like when Kono had gotten the Lisha translation wrong and nearly made a marriage proposal to a village woman by accident, or when he'd taken a gulp of local moonshine having mistaken it for water. It surprised Rika to see that most of the marines would rather talk about things that made them laugh than they would about fighting. But then, he supposed, when you'd seen enough fighting in your life, you might prefer to spend your leisure time talking about other things. Before he'd met the Major, he hadn't even considered that possible. But now, having seen what he'd seen in the Splicer, it made sense.

Sergeant Rael was very different to Kono, Rika thought. He was a lot smaller, just average sized for a human, and pale skinned where Kono had been dark. Apparently a lot of the female *Phoenix* crew thought him very handsome, which was a funny thing to think about any human... but then, Rika was more aware by the day that humans thought corbi looked funny too. Mostly, Rael was more mild and collaborative. Kono had just needed to scowl at someone to immediately fix whatever bad thing they'd been doing. Rael didn't have that. Everyone seemed to respect him, but Rika wondered how he'd be able to command the same respect that the big Staff Sergeant had.

The most gratifying thing for Rika was the respect they all gave to him. As a warrior, he was nothing next to these people, and barely knew how to wear an armour suit, even were there a working model that fit him properly. But all the marines in Phoenix Company were friendly, and took time to explain things to him, as the Major had told them all that he was here to learn. Mostly, they'd all seen the graphical reconstruction of that Splicer fight, which had been somehow put together by *Phoenix*'s scary drysine queen, who'd been monitoring the action via the Splicer's network at the time.

They'd seen who'd done what, and how everything had played out — all the horrendous casualties and the bravery of the massively outgunned and inexperienced corbi who'd held the reeh-aligned forces, and sometimes even reeh themselves, at bay until the Splicer's treasure of technological knowledge could be freed from its mainframe. They didn't talk with him about it directly, but Rika knew they'd all seen it by the way they didn't talk past him like he wouldn't understand, and gave him the quiet acceptance of people who'd decided he deserved to be there.

Trace had assured him that not all fights were as bad as the Splicer. That one, she'd told him, had been the equal-worst fight she'd ever been in. In the other worst fight, she'd been awarded with something the humans called a 'Liberty Star', which was the hardest medal for any human warrior to win. After it was over, though she hadn't been badly hurt herself, her armour had been recycled for scrap, having taken so many hits it could no longer be repaired.

"Did you think you might die then, too?" Rika had asked her quietly.

"No," the Major had replied. "I was certain of it. Sometimes it's the only way you can function."

She'd picked four marines to go with her that time, Rika had learned from asking others about it, to rescue a whole platoon who were trapped. And she'd rescued the platoon, but all four of those she'd picked had died in the process, leaving herself the lone survivor from the rescue team and pressing on to complete the mission despite it, and what should logically have been certain death. Now, talking to Command Squad marines, Rika was becoming aware of just how many they'd also lost, just since *Phoenix* had gone renegade from the human fleet.

Leo Terez, Private Rolonde and now-Corporal Arime, were originals, as were Sergeant Rael and the Major. But they'd now lost two command sergeants, and four others — six dead from an eight-strong unit over two years. And sometimes Rika thought Sergeant Rael looked underwhelmed whenever anyone called him 'Sergeant', or required him to act with his new command authority. Was he thinking about Kono, and the Master Sergeant they'd called 'Stitch', whose name was still legend in Phoenix Company for all the things he'd done in the war against the tavalai? And was he now wondering how bad his own chances of survival were in that role, given the heroes who'd gone and died before him?

Rika saw the Major striding their way with a purpose, and swung down from his perch above the suit. The humans sometimes did something called 'attention', which he'd gathered was just a military thing, and not something done by civilians, that involved standing stiff and straight before an officer. When it was and wasn't proper to be at attention was confusingly unclear, but it seemed to be reserved for serious situations, like when someone was in trouble. That didn't seem to be the case here, but he had gathered it wasn't good to be casually swinging on the armour racks when an officer was talking to you.

"Rik," she said in Lisha, only a half-head taller than him at ground level. "There's a new Resistance ship that just jumped insystem. They've sent us the latest data on the reeh strikes after the Splicer."

She paused, and glanced at Rael and Terez. That was unusual.

Usually she never hesitated for anything. Rika felt a sinking, cold dread.

"They've got good coverage of Tuka this time?"

The Major nodded. "Good coverage of Tuka." Her voice was gentle. Rael and Terez had stopped what they were doing to watch, their earpieces translating for them. And ever-curious at this new linguistic skill their Major had brought back with her from Rando. "We can go and talk somewhere else if you'd like?"

"No," said Rika. He'd half-expected it. So many people on Rando had received news like this at one time or other, or been the subject of it. "No, you can tell me here."

"Tuka was hit, Rika. There's nothing left. There's no way to tell if anyone was there when the strike happened, we sent warning on all available frequencies and we know a lot of villagers ran for the jungle before the strikes arrived. This new transmission gives reports from the ground, there's large numbers of refugees camping in the jungle and trying to keep low profiles, others have moved into the mountains, a lot of them are going after their food reserves now that the crops are gone. But the evacuation will get there in plenty of time, so they think the chances of significant starvation are low."

Rika stared blankly past her, at some marines from Alpha Platoon Heavy Squad working on their enormous weapons. Remembering his eldest brother Miga, working on a small weir in the irrigation system, grinning at some joke they'd shared. Remembering his mother in that blue, floppy fabric hat she liked, picking fruit in the village orchard, humming a tune the travelling musician troupe had sung the previous night around the campfire.

"Rik." The Major put a hand on his shoulder. "You can see those parts of the report, if you like? They're not security sensitive, they're just about refugees. I think a few of them are from Dachi."

But Dachi was such a big place, Rika knew, having grown up there. There were the Silma Hills in the South, where the Eldo Plains villages were, with whom they often traded for grain... and another twenty villages across the foothills alone, just within a few days' walk depending on which trails you took. And that was just his tiny fraction of it.

"No," he said. He took a deep breath. "No, I'd like to keep working, if that's okay Major?" He reckoned it was a half-and-half chance, himself. If his family had been there when the strike had come in. There was a radio in the village, the headman Podi had it in his basement, but it wasn't on very often lest the reeh detected it. Of course, if the reeh had hit the villages one at a time, the others would have seen the strikes coming and gotten out, but reeh technology meant they could have hit many villages at once, and probably at night, too.

Even so, people were skittish, and he knew from the reports that the reeh hadn't been able to hit *everyone* at once. Many had gotten word of what was happening, by radio, messenger, or simply the sight and sound of strikes on neighbouring villages. Many had left before the strikes came. Half-and-half. Fifty-fifty, as the humans said.

"Of course you can," the Major said gently. "But you can change your mind, too. And if you decide you do want to go on the Rando evacuation, you can do that as well."

"No," said Rika, but this time his voice nearly broke. He blinked furiously against the tears. "If... if I do that, and if I abandon this?" He gestured around. Back at the corbi armour suit, the most precious thing that had in all his life ever been meaningfully his. "Then what was it all for?"

The Major nodded, swallowing hard. "You're a good soldier, Rik," she told him. "And you'll make a good marine. I'm proud of you."

TRACE ENTERED Engineering Bay 12 to find that the most important work in the galaxy had been interrupted to give a small boy a sendoff. The improvised lab, humming with hightech equipment that looked to have evolved several generations even beyond the last time she'd seen it, was instead gathered around Skah. Dressed in his custom spacer jumpsuit and safety gear, and carrying a duffle bag half as big as he was, Skah was saying goodbye.

He hugged the Engineering techs, many of whom he couldn't have known too well, but everyone felt like they knew Skah regardless. As he talked to them, Trace edged by, looking at the various analysis bays, the flat, rotating dishes beneath translucent, glowing covers, and the bulkier gear behind the radiation shielding hiding the room's rear third. Like most of *Phoenix*'s non-Engineering crew, Trace had completely lost track of just how many crazy high-tech drysine machines were now aboard. Various crew had assisted in building them, at first from Styx's own designs, and more lately from the drysine data-core itself. Those machines had enabled the techs to make more machines, which had in turn been invaluable in upgrading and maintaining *Phoenix*'s ever-more advanced systems, repairing things the techs were still struggling to understand the full function of, and lately, to upgrade all of Phoenix Company's marine armour, and the ship's four assault shuttles and one civilian shuttle.

Now the analysis wing of that hightech factory was engaged in building tiny things from designs and entirely new scientific principles drawn from Rando Splicer's liberated memory cores. Most of the human experts hadn't known what the hell they'd been looking at, nor had the parren aboard Lisbeth's flagship *Coroset*. There were far more croma currently looking at it, entire planets' worth of scientists poring over the data, but that was all occurring behind institutional secrecy at a glacial pace. The corbi Resistance had also taken their copy to whereever the Resistance had people to look at such things — in vast, hidden bases out in the dark fringes of reeh space, Trace had been told — but again, all was shrouded in secrecy.

Which left *Phoenix*, utterly under-equipped with just a warship's few internal bays and non-specialist techs who'd trained solely for warship systems, however much they'd been lately forced to diversify into crazy things none of them would previously have dreamed of. But *Phoenix* had Styx, and while she was neither an expert in biological nor nano-sciences, she had crazy brainpower to devote to the learning of new and established analysis matrixes, and unlike the vast croma institutions, could concentrate all of her findings in the one place where they could feed off each other.

"How's progress?" Trace asked Styx now. Styx loomed between the machines, with little space for her mechanical limbs. Typically she existed in the wide, zero-G spaces of Midships, but there were insufficient remote sensors for her to monitor the progress in this bay to her desired precision, and so she'd relocated here for the past fifteen days straight, whatever the discomfort it caused the techs.

"Limited," said Styx. Her single red eye appeared fixed on Skah and his farewells. "The sensors are inadequate. We have managed to simulate many prototype phases of nanovirus technology, and gain a general insight into their operations, yet it will be insufficient to announce a comprehensive suite of counter-technologies."

No one on *Phoenix* was naive enough to call it concern. Styx did what she did for strategic advantage. Parking herself in this small bay for two weeks straight to oversee research designed to save potentially hundreds of billions of organic lives was nothing more than Styx attempting to ingratiate herself to the leaders of those various affected species, and to demonstrate her future potential value.

Even so, Trace wondered at what point it ceased to matter. If someone was saving billions of lives because they cared, or because it was personally advantageous, surely there was still positive karma to be gained? She wondered if someone, somewhere in the future, would be demanding that statues be built in her honour. Statues of Styx, who was almost certainly complicit in the deaths of many millions of organics in an earlier time. And possibly far, far more than that. The winds of history were fickle, and those condemned as villains in one time would be embraced as heroes in the next. Perhaps good and evil were only circumstantial.

"How long do you think you've got?" Trace asked her.

"No longer than ten days. Recent fleet movements suggest optimum buildup prior to launch. They cannot leave it much longer or the reeh will transition further forces into their defensive formations."

"Can you get it done by then?"

"Your definition of 'it' is extremely vague. I will certainly get something done. Perhaps it will be enough to save humanity if an attack using these weapons comes from the alo/deepynines. Perhaps other threatened races as well. I will do as best I can with the time available."

"Good," said Trace. "I'll be back in six, maybe seven days. Should be plenty of time."

"Yes Major. I would find your analysis of croma troop preparations useful."

Trace was mildly surprised. "I'll see what I can learn. Also going to talk to that fool Romki about changing his mind."

"That would be a welcome development," Styx agreed. "But given the nature of Professor Romki's mind, the probability does not seem high."

"Need to find a ship to take this stuff back home, too," said Trace, gazing as Skah completed his last goodbyes. "It's all for nothing if we can't get your research back home."

"Agreed. Major, I detect that your vocal stress patterns are unusually elevated. Do you feel that you are the right person to be performing this mission at this time?"

Trace took a deep breath. She could argue with Erik or Kaspowitz, tell them that she was fine and the problem largely in their heads. But arguing with Styx would fool noone. "I'm the only person who can perform this mission. It must be a senior officer who can translate what she's learned directly into action, and be taken seriously by the croma once I'm there."

"I must confess that I find these organic swings in emotional states disconcerting. But then, the situation on Rando was extremely difficult."

"Yes," Trace said blankly. "Very difficult." Obviously Styx found it disconcerting. She relied upon *Phoenix* and her crew to perform, in spite of all the ship's organic strangeness. And she probably wanted to fix it, that being what AIs did with problems, and had trouble accepting that she couldn't. Certainly it wasn't any sort of emotional concern. How could it be?

Skah came over, all big ears and bright eyes, carrying his duffle bag and looking more trepidatious at the prospect of leaving them all than Trace would have expected. Before Rando, he'd found the positive in everything, and would have seen this latest development as one more adventure. Now he looked solemn, almost glum, as though he'd finally come to realise that there were no certainties in what lay ahead, or at least no good ones.

"You all packed?" Trace asked him.

Skah nodded, worriedly. "I haven't said goodbye to everyone."

"Well it's a big ship, Skah. There isn't time to say goodbye to everyone. They'll understand."

Skah looked up at Styx, and opened his arms. For a brief moment, Styx actually paused, as though uncertain of what to do next. Everyone in the engineering bay stared. And then the commander of all drysine forces, once the most fearsome sentient entity in all Spiral history, lowered her big, armoured head, and let Skah put his arms around her alloy neck.

"Be a good boy, Skah," she told him.

"I'n *awways* a good boy," said Skah.

"This is factually incorrect."

She couldn't quite bring herself to put a sharp-clawed limb about him in reply, Trace observed. Doubtless she was aware of everyone watching. Styx did not want all the crew so terrified that they could not function around her, but there was strategic utility in a *little* fear. As Marine Commander, Trace empathised.

"Come on kid, let's go." She took Skah's hand, and gave Styx an appraising sideways look as she left. Styx raised herself back to full height, and gave her an imperious, single-eyed stare in reply.

4

Logistics on the way to Dul'rho were made easier by simply taking PH-3 and attaching her to the croma transport's midships. That way Trace and the Second Section of Command Squad could bring their armour and weapons without the delays and trouble of transferring them to the freighter's hold. But they rode through jump in the main hold, save for Tif and Ensign Lee in the shuttle's cockpit, partly because they now constituted one hundred percent of the freighter's armament and one could never be too careful in uncertain times, and partly so that Trace didn't need access to the freighter's bridge feed to see system-wide scan when they arrived.

The space around Dul'rho was filled with as many ships as Trace had seen during the busiest times of the Triumvirate War. It made her mouth dry to look at it, with that well-remembered tension of huge events underway, and many millions of lives at stake. Of entire civilisations under threat, if it all went wrong... or right, depending on whose view one took.

Dul'rho was currently orbiting its star at a point closest to jump entry from Teg'ula System, so the approach took barely five hours. The freighter was heading for Tron'chi Station, one of Dul'rho's eight major stations, while Trace's rendezvous was at Chau'to Station, so they piled into PH-3 on approach, gave thanks to the freighter, then applied a few minutes of thrust to put the assault shuttle onto an intercept trajectory with the big station, currently on the far side of the planet.

"Najor, can I see connand feed?" Skah asked from the secure restraints at her side. It was completely out of the question, of course, to let an eight-year-old of any species view PH-3's command feed of the space outside. Or it would have been, in human space, beneath the authority of Fleet.

"Sure, why not?" said Trace, and flipped that feed to Skah's glasses. Behind her, she didn't need to see Command Squad's faces to know there were glances being exchanged. Everyone knew the regs on command feeds. But lately Trace had been in a mood to prioritise things that mattered and ignore the ones that didn't. The new faces in Command Squad needed to realise that the Major sometimes did things differently within her immediate command, where others in Phoenix Company wouldn't see it.

Skah gazed around, moving his head as the glasses projected the positions of many hundreds of ships, parking orbits, approach trajectories and the controlled space surrounding each station. He was so small beside her armoured bulk, locked into his specially configured seat. Trace wondered if the protectiveness she felt was anything like what Tif felt, or just something arising from being big and powerful around someone small and vulnerable. And she recalled her command feeds from the Splicer, lower decks swarming with civilian corbi she'd helped escape, many of them children, lying in a carpet of bloody corpses as gunfire thundered and people screamed. Alien screams, but terror and despair sounded alike in any voice. And she swallowed hard against the nausea, blinking to try and clear her vision. She hadn't told Doc Suelo about that. She'd seen horrible things before, but it had never made her feel physically ill for this many days after the event. The PTSD treatments were supposed to stop it. These hadn't.

Skah had asked her something, she realised. "What was that Skah?"

"Najor, why do I have to go to Du'rho?"

"We discussed this before, Skah." She had her armour faceplate open, and in the calm following the shuttle's burn, there was little noise to talk over. "*Phoenix* is going somewhere very dangerous. When we come back, we'll have to return through Dul'rho, so it's much smarter for you to stay here with Lisbeth until we come back."

"But I've been in dangerous pwaces before, on *Phoenix*," said Skah. He sounded troubled. As he'd grown older, his voice had acquired a little whiny, half-growl when he did that. Kuhsi sometimes expressed emotion in alarming ways. Trace hoped Skah wouldn't grow into any of his species' less desirable habits.

She could dress it up for him, she knew. But she'd heard the tales of what he'd seen on Dul'rho the last time he'd been here, and the things he'd learned about war and violence in particular, in the Tali'san. She did not want to interrupt his learning now by telling him half-truths. And if *Phoenix* did not return, she wanted him to recall in his later life that they'd all gone willingly, fully aware of what might happen.

"Nothing as dangerous as this, Skah. And before, we didn't have any other safe place where you could stay. Now we do."

The boy was silent for a moment, gazing at the ships on his near display. "Risbeth wiw be hewping the corbi," he said then.

Trace frowned. "Why do you think that?" It had been common speculation on *Phoenix*, that the younger Debogande would do exactly that. But letting Skah see a visual display he had no hope of making sense of was one thing, discussing the likely actions of politically sensitive individuals was another. Most crew in a position to speculate about Lisbeth's actions knew better.

Skah shrugged, another of those human gestures he'd acquired. "Risbeth is nice. She want to hewp corbi. Evac-u-Ashun of Rando wiw be very coow, too."

"Sure, very cool," Trace agreed. "Dangerous too. There'll be a lot of fighting, the reeh won't let the croma come and take the corbi away."

"Why not? Reeh don't rike the corbi."

"Because they think the corbi belong to them. Everything in their space belongs to them. Every person too."

Skah wrinkled his nose. "Reeh are eviw."

"Yes. Very evil."

"You kiw reeh?" Looking up at her, glasses lowered, very earnestly.

"Yes. Probably we will kill some reeh."

"You feew sad?"

"No," said Trace. "Killing reeh doesn't make me sad at all."

Skah thought about it, silent and troubled.

Coms crackled with Tif's voice from the cockpit. *"Orbit insertion burn, three ninute, nothing big."*

"Okay Nahny," said Skah, with the unconcern of a boy who trusted his mother absolutely. Trace felt her heart melt, just a little bit. And saw the civilian mother, beside Mula in the bowels of the Splicer, clutching her dead child, hiding behind a pile of bodies as rounds cut the air. And then the nausea was back, and her heart was hammering beyond her ability to control.

"That's a crona starcutter-cwass cruiser," said Skah once the burn had ended. Trace glanced at her own feed, and found that sure enough, the cruiser was where he was looking. "Good junp range, crona use in first wave. Spearhead."

"Did Styx tell you that?"

"No," said Skah, evasively.

"It's okay Skah. We know you talk with Styx. She seems to like you."

Silence from the boy. Ahead, the glasses showed a shallow, declining orbit, widening on the far side as excessive velocity made it elongate toward Chau'to Station's orbital path. "I pronised I woodn't say," he said plaintively.

"And you never broke your promise," Trace assured him. "But

Styx is very smart. I'm certain she knew we'd figure it out. You've been learning a lot of things from her, haven't you?"

Skah shook his head, determinedly. "It's a secret."

Trace smiled. "I know, it's good to have secrets sometimes. I won't tell anyone else if you don't want. But I think everyone else already knows."

Skah looked dismayed. "They do?"

"Well the Captain does. And most of the bridge crew, Lieutenant Kaspowitz was telling me how your maths have improved so much. He was sure it was Styx." It wasn't so much that Styx would make a better teacher, everyone was sure — more that Skah would actually pay attention to her. But then, that was perhaps the definition of a better teacher.

"Styx is good at naths," Skah admitted. "Did you know that..."

Coms interrupted from up front, and this time it was Ensign Lee. *"Hi Major, I've just been talking with Chau'to Station, we've finally got a confirmation on Lisbeth, and she's not there. We've got a croma Fleet liaison still waiting for us, but Lisbeth's gone down to Agid'roi on business and she's invited us to come after her directly. Fleet liaison say they don't care."*

"Thank Fleet liaison for their attention, but we'll be wasting their time without Lisbeth." Trace called up Agid'roi as she spoke, Dul'rho maps flashing with several blinks on the relevant icons... until she found it, a sprawling city on the northern coast of Ro'raki, the other northern continent, far side of the planet from Cho'na where Erik had had his adventures. "See if we can get a direct reroute to Agid'roi, best not to waste any time."

"Yes Major." Trace listened in on the call. Lee was talking to Chau'to Station Control, who were civilian and thus Croma'Rai, the old regime, but who still ran Dul'rho, regardless of their loss of supreme power in the Tali'san. Dul'rho's Croma'Rai government was in Cal'uta, and the last report Trace had received gave little indication that anyone knew where the new Croma'Dokran government was actually centred. Sho'mo'ra hadn't wanted to relocate back to his homeworld of Do'ran before launching this offensive, because with the Tali'san at Dul'rho, everyone was already gathered and it was too

good a centralised opportunity to waste, not to mention an enormous timesaver given the time political relocations took. If he'd waited, this whole war wouldn't have launched for nearly another year, by which time the reeh would have been well and truly ready.

The croma reply was disinterestedly affirmative, and Tif began plotting orbital adjustments toward the far hemisphere. *"Easy option or hard option?"* Tif asked them, with her usual disregard for military coms etiquette. *"Easy option is one nore orbit, be down in fifty-eight ninutes aw nice and tidy. Hard option is down in eighteen ninutes, puw five-G burn and seven-G entry, wawk funny when you get off."*

"Do the Gs, Nahny!" Skah dared her. "I want the Gs!"

"Major Skah wants some Gs, Tif," said Trace, as Command Squad chortled. "You heard the Major, Gs it is."

Tif laid in the course while scolding Skah in their native Gharkhan, no doubt something about the Major being in command and not him. Skah just smiled, nose all crumpled up and double checking his restraints.

TRACE LED the way down the rear ramp of the Agid'roi military facility. She left her faceplate up despite the cold, and the dusting snow falling from the white sky. Across the vast tarmac, rows of vehicles were thundering, directed by assault troopers in heavy armour. Great assault ships, many times the size of PH-3, howled and shrilled like angry wasps, sending columns of hot air shimmering into cold skies.

Trace paused at the base of the ramp, Corporal Arime on her left, Private Wang on her right, while Privates Rolonde and Carville waited at the top for Skah and Tif. Ensign Lee was going to wait with his ship and keep an eye on things. Agid'roi was supposedly friendly territory, but *Phoenix*'s surviving crew hadn't lived this long by taking things for granted.

Skah came down with his duffle bag and a big coat, heavy hat pulled over his big ears, while his mother simply wore a jacket pulled over her jumpsuit plus her helmet, all outfitted well enough for cold.

PH-3 was parked on the edge of the busy tarmac, where boundary fences and security systems rose on pylons before the mountains beyond. Much of the base was flanked with mountains, their tops lost in cloud. Erik's adventures on Cho'na continent had been in mid-summer, but Agid'roi was in deep freeze.

"Gonna be a big show, huh?" Wang suggested, breath frosting white as he gazed at the scene. Wang had been in Echo Platoon before Lieutenant Zhi had been killed on Defiance. Badly wounded himself, he'd been two months in recovery, got another berth in Bravo Platoon's Heavy Squad, where he'd been recommended by Lieutenant Alomaim for the Distinguished Service Star. Despite the praise, Wang had insisted the action only brought home to him that he wasn't suited to heavies, so rather than transfer to another rifle squad, Trace had taken him for Command Squad after she'd returned from Rando, filling the vacancies Lieutenant Dale had left unfilled until her return.

"Buncha happy croma," Arime agreed. "Marchin' off to war."

"So where is everyone?" 'Benji' Carville asked, coming down the ramp with Tif and Skah. "No red carpet?" Carville had been in Alpha Second Squad for the trip so far, a lively kid with a tendency to flap his mouth too much. He'd won a Diamond Star on Defiance saving several guys' asses with conspicuous bravery and skill, and Dale had been surprised to rate him one of Alpha's best, and grudgingly displeased about Trace taking him for Command Squad.

"Wait here," said Trace. "We can't move without escort. Keep an eye out."

A line of croma powered armour strode by. Half as large again as a human suit, these thudding giants bore huge weapons, some carried like rifles, others racked alongside the bulky rear powerplants, and a few mounted on the underside of forearms, built into the armour itself.

"No rifle squads here," Arime observed. "All heavies."

"Hard to take cover in one of those," said Wang. "What you think, Major?"

"Powerplant's too large," said Trace. "Their tech's good, but not as good as ours. They're wasting about ten percent of mass... added to their size they'll be slower than tavalai."

"More firepower though. Look at the fucking railgun on that third guy."

"You only need to kill the enemy once, Artie," Trace told Wang. "Bring a sledgehammer to kill an ant and then you're stuck carrying a sledgehammer all day when a flyswat would have done. Half an hour in a manoeuvre fight and these guys will be cooked."

Tif squatted on the ramp behind Skah, and kept him warm with a hug, watching the croma war machine. One relatively small base, on just one planet. On Dul'rho alone there would be dozens like this, possibly hundreds. Across croma space, hundreds of worlds like Dul'rho.

"Arny?" Tif asked.

"Yep, Army," Arime agreed. He was fully recovered from his injuries on Defiance now, and had reluctantly accepted Trace's assertion that he was Command Squad Corporal material, moving up to Rael's spot as Rael took Sergeant. Not bad for a guy who'd once flipped burgers and cleaned kitchens on Peterson before getting sick of it and signing up for lack of anything better to do. "Ground soldiers. Their marine armour is smaller, all their spacer units are younger. These big guys wouldn't pull Gs so great."

"Hang on, croma are a heavy G species," Carville objected. "Kaal pull Gs great."

"Kaal are all muscle," said Arime. "Muscle's good for Gs. Elder croma got lots of muscle, but lots of natural armour too — it's unproductive in spaceflight Gs, slows them right down."

"Who told you that?" Carville asked skeptically.

"Hey dickhead, it was an Intel report. Something Joker sent to us..."

"Eyes front, welcoming party," Trace cut them off, as the second rank of marching armour turned toward the shuttle. The armoured line divided as it came, forming two lines on either side of the ramp, shaking the ground in unison. An open topped utility vehicle arrived, turning up the aisle between the ranks. On the passenger seat were several short figures in heavy hoods. When the car stopped, they jumped from the back and came to the shuttle ramp in that rapid, slightly hunched gait of thick-bodied corbi. Trace reckoned that one looked familiar.

From within the hood, big, nearly-human eyes peered up at Trace beneath a haphazard fringe. "Hello Major," said Tiga, with solemn confidence, and nearly flawless English. "I'm here to escort you. Sho'-mo'ra sent me."

"Hello Tiga." A lot had passed between Tiga and the crew of *Phoenix*. A few hadn't forgiven her, but Erik had felt she'd done nothing to require forgiveness. Having heard the story, Trace agreed with him. If it had been a group of corbi she'd been required to screw over for the greater good of humanity... but she couldn't complete the thought. Again she heard the screaming, and the dying. She swallowed hard. "Sho'mo'ra is here himself? We couldn't get confirmation."

"Well you won't," said Tiga, as though that should have been obvious. Very certain of herself, this young woman, Trace recalled. And recalled again Romki's opinion that the average corbi was a little smarter than the average human, or the average anything in the Spiral. Her own time on Rando had done nothing to dismiss the notion, and Tiga was a lot smarter than the average corbi. "He needed a neutral base, Agid'roi is Clan Croma'Rata, they're an aligned clan with Croma'Rai but they've all fallen out now, Croma'Rata's siding with Croma'Dokran in the war."

Trace had heard all that, but explanations had been vague. "Good," she said, with a short nod. Behind, several more open-topped vehicles were arriving. "You can explain to me on the way."

"Major," said Tiga, before she could order her crew to move out. "First, a memento. Kechu had this, he said Chiba carved it, before the Splicer assault. Kechu took a laser inscriber and wrote the names of all the corbi in the assault onto it. It's for you."

Tiga held out her hand. Trace saw that it was a fir, carved in wood. Native domestic pets to corbi on Rando, where they were as ubiquitous as cats. This one was curled in a circle, like a donut, as Trace had seen them lying many times on various village verandahs, soaking in a patch of sunlight.

She took it with long-practised care in armoured hands, and raised it up. Little dark scrawls across the wood grain, corbi names in Lisha script. Trace hadn't known all her corbi team very well, but she recalled Chiba, a farmer, as so many Rando corbi were farmers. He'd had a family, she thought. She hadn't suspected he had a carving talent, and hadn't known any of them well enough to ask. Hadn't wanted to know them well enough. Now, that seemed like an oversight. So many things did.

The long rows of croma warriors drew up with an armoured stamp, weapons presented. A guard of honour.

"They know what you did," Tiga said solemnly. "Tejo and Viko are here, from your team. They explained it all, blow by blow. There's talk among the croma of commemoration. Some kind of monument."

From croma, to a fight entirely between aliens, it was unsuspected. Only it had never been a fight entirely among aliens, and lately Sho'mo'ra had reaffirmed the bonds of blood that existed between corbi and croma, forgotten for most of the last thousand years because recalling them was too painful.

"Thank you Tiga," said Trace. "And if Kechu is around, I'll thank him in person." She gestured to her crew, indicating that the privates should take the rear vehicle, while she and Arime would ride up front with Tif, Skah and Tiga.

She walked up the honour guard that had assembled just for her, eyes flicking left and right to acknowledge each rank. It reminded her of the Liberty Star presentation, where they'd hit her with it straight off the ship at Amber Station — a big facility in a heavily populated system, lots of cameras and big crowds of people watching on the docks. She'd had to walk up a similar honour guard that time too, to where Captain Pantillo had waited proudly to pin 'Bloody Mary' on her chest.

They'd had to break out dress uniforms, for the presentation group at least, and that had been a big inconvenience. The crowds of civilians who wouldn't shut up during the solemn occasion hadn't helped Trace's mood, nor the big cheers that followed the final salute. She'd only thought of Landys, screaming after a tavalai shell had blown her leg off at the lower service junction, and how she hadn't been able to stop and help. Or how Rao had put himself between her and incoming grenade rounds at the bulkhead heat exchangers, returning fire amid the flaming wreckage of previous rounds to let her focus on the enemy flanking from the other side, before taking one straight to the face and leaving her covered in armour shards and brains. Or Lam, who'd single-handedly flanked tavalai in their own flanking ambush, and killed three point-blank before the others had blown him to pieces.

And Trace had run on and left them, because she had a bigger mission to complete — an entire platoon tied down and being cut to pieces somewhere ahead, and only she could find and save them... and these lesser, smaller casualties were what it would take to get it done. Only these hadn't been 'smaller' casualties, these were her family, her brothers and sisters in armour, and she'd picked them by hand and thrown them head first into the meatgrinder so that she could achieve her objective.

The cheering crowds had made her feel like a monster, then. And this croma honour guard made her feel like a monster now. Like some kind of karma-sucking ghoul who caused the deaths of others in their thousands, and was presented with glory and respect for her efforts. As though death himself were mocking her as others showered her with gifts, applauding with wry, bony hands.

THE TWO OPEN-TOPPED vehicles rolled through the streets of Agid'roi, and passing croma civilians barely glanced at its occupants, having grown accustomed to military traffic and strange comings and goings surrounding the new Croma'Dokran government that had just moved in.

Trace hadn't expected it to be so pretty. Agid'roi was not a large city, consisting of low, tasteful and historic buildings that ascended the gradual slopes of surrounding hills that grew into eventual mountains. There were many trees, angular wooden pagodas and indications of cultural significance, though Trace's knowledge of what that meant, among croma, was pitifully small. A few centimetres of snow lay over everything, dusting the leaves and turning the sloped rooftops white.

The vehicle took them gradually upslope, one corner after another, and there were many uniformed croma on the sidewalks amidst the civilians, in the long dark coats their military preferred. The lack of colour coding between different services had made Trace suspicious that croma were colour blind, but what little she'd read on the subject said otherwise. The most ambitious and highly-ranked youngsters went into Fleet — the Army was an arduous hard slog through the ranks, filled with middle-aged warriors whose upward progression had slowed dramatically in the past few centuries due to the regrettable lack of war. But in Fleet, a brilliant kid could find herself an officer on a warship at a time when similarly-aged croma in the Army were pulling perimeter duty. Fleet was where those brilliant croma kids went to dodge the stultifying age hierarchies in the rest of croma society. Much of this coming war was being planned by those brilliant kids, who thought they knew much more than they really did. It concerned her.

The cars pulled up to a large, ancient stone wall, passed a brief inspection from an armoured soldier, then passed through the gate. Within, the driveway circled a garden of stones and trees, and arrived at a disembarking zone behind several much larger vehicles — sized to carry elder croma, Trace thought, meaning VIPs. The surrounding buildings looked like a temple complex, with stone paths through trees and ponds between sloping wooden rooves.

Trace dismounted, a throb of armour powerplants as the marines moved together, and established a perimeter without it looking like a perimeter, in the way of human warriors who'd been a long time away from human space, and knew how to be wary of security without causing offence. Trace was barely surprised when, out of the nearest building, Lisbeth appeared in a wool-fleeced red robe, flowing along the snow-dusted pavings with a grace unknown when Trace had seen her first.

At her sides were parren — dark-robed, hoods raised, and almost certainly Domesh, that most austere of House Harmony's denominations. And yet here was Lisbeth, bright red in their midst, despite being in the service of the most senior Domesh of all — the one who was now the Supreme Leader of all parrenkind.

Lisbeth smiled at Trace, serenely, and came to a halt in perfect formation before her, gloved hands clasped, and gave a small bow. "Major," she said in English. "Welcome to Alei'sei. This is an old place of the croma, a great temple in the temple town of Agid'roi, and the parren delegation has been granted the honour of lodgings here. The croma are busy with the war, they have requested that I should show hospitality on their behalf."

"That's nice of them," said Trace, having no interest in these protocol games. But Lisbeth had appearances to upkeep, with her own staff and with the croma. "I'm not here for long, two days at most, and I've a lot to do."

"Of course," said Lisbeth, unruffled. And she slid a sideways glance to Skah, with a delighted smile. "Hello Skah. Did you have a good journey?"

"Yes Risbeth," said Skah, with great restraint. Not long ago he'd have flung himself at her with childish joy. Now, he understood things like protocols, among parren in particular. "This prace is pretty."

"Yes, it is very pretty, isn't it? Come, let me show you your lodgings."

Lisbeth and her parren guards led them down paths between buildings, across courtyards adorned with great symbols carved in wood that Trace did not recognise, and across several small bridges above ornamental streams. Croma were everywhere, mostly unarmored though almost always uniformed, striding about on serious business. Once, they passed a group of young Fleet officers standing under a snowy tree, smoking some kind of reed pipes and flicking ash onto the garden, too engaged in animated conversation to bother with the passing aliens. The war would make many careers, and Trace could smell their excitement. She wondered what had happened to all this youthful enthusiasm in previous phases of the many millennia long war, when the bodies had begun to pile up, important systems lost, and groups of ambitious youngsters like this one whittled down to a few shellshocked survivors. Croma had been doing this against the reeh for a long time, and when viewed on the largest scale, their progress had only been backward.

The humans' quarters overlooked a courtyard, small rooms opening onto a verandah, allowing the marines to leave their armour standing ready outside their doors, to be donned in a minute or less in case of trouble. Lisbeth went to stroll with Skah and Tif, and show them the nature of Skah's new home, for the next while at least. Lisbeth was the only reason Tif had agreed to this, Trace knew. To a kuhsi mind, life consisted of a clan to belong to, and minus that, death was preferable. Whatever the risks, Tif would have preferred Skah stay on *Phoenix*. But Lisbeth was Erik's sister, a former part of *Phoenix*'s crew, and thus, in Tif's mind as well as most of *Phoenix*'s, family. She would entrust Skah to Lisbeth's care alone, not merely because Lisbeth's care was likely to be much safer, but because Lisbeth was an extended member of the *Phoenix* clan, and Skah's future would be assured with her in ways beyond physical safety.

By the time Lisbeth returned, Trace had pulled on a heavy jacket and cap against the post-armour chill, slung a short T-9 over her shoulder from the armour's equipment bag, and was discussing perimeter and watch arrangements with Arime and Second Section. Croma did not tend toward assassinations, but Erik's experiences had demonstrated that it wasn't beyond them, particularly in a Croma'-Dokran headquarters on a Croma'Rai world where resentments about the Tali'san's outcome ran deep. And also, it went without saying, there were the parren. Murder came as easily to powerful parren as breathing, and there was no telling who all the members of Lisbeth's group were truly serving.

Having laid down the basics, Trace left Arime to sort out the particulars, and went to meet Lisbeth as she returned with the kuhsi.

Skah, she thought, looked subdued — curious as always, but perhaps realising that compared to *Phoenix*, this place was going to get dull pretty quickly. On *Phoenix* at least he'd had Styx to talk to when no other crew were available to attend to his boredom.

Lisbeth excused herself from the kuhsi, and her parren guards, and led Trace to a room adjoining the marines' quarters. The floor was a kind of slate, Trace saw, and beyond the central supporting pillar, a shrine of smooth stones and low, flickering candles stood against a wall.

"It's a religious place," Lisbeth explained. "Older croma religions believed in afterlifes and spirits too, particularly of clan ancestors and warriors who died in wars. Seems hard to imagine, with croma, but there were some monks who didn't want to fight, and lived quiet lives in places like this instead. Only now, of course, it's been converted into a headquarters from which the new croma leadership can fight its war."

She turned to look at Trace — with Trace out of armour, Lisbeth was now slightly taller. Her curled, bushy hair was quite free, bouncing about her head in much the same way it had when Trace had first met her all that time ago on Homeworld. As though, Trace thought, Lisbeth were no longer so concerned with trying to please parren sensibilities, and was content to simply be herself.

Trace smiled at her, and offered the embrace she'd been unable to give before, for reasons of protocol and armoured impracticality. Lisbeth returned it gladly, then looked at Trace closely as she pulled back, with concern. "How *are* you, Trace?"

Trace would have preferred everyone to stop asking her that. "I was surprised when you didn't stay on your ship," she said. "Croma don't care about protocol half as much as parren do. I can't imagine Sho'mo'ra is sharing much of his war strategy with you. With Liala's abilities, you could have learned more from orbit."

"Don't change the subject," Lisbeth reprimanded lightly. *That* was new. When they'd first met, Lisbeth would never have dreamed of contradicting her, nor even calling her by name. "You realise you're possibly the greatest war hero in the Spiral now? The parren certainly think so. After you defeated Aristan, some scholars were suggesting you could have made a run at a Harmony denominational leadership yourself. Started your own denomination, perhaps, and risen in power. A few suggested they should recruit you. I'm not sure there's a parren alive who hasn't seen that footage." Trace gazed at her for a long moment, halfway between amusement and dread. Lisbeth's face split in a smile. "And you're not the *slightest* bit interested, of course! Probably you're horrified. I told them you would be."

Trace took a deep breath. "Lis, this is serious. What are you doing on Dul'rho? Erik was certain Sho'mo'ra's hands would be tied with you. He said Sho'mo'ra would want to make closer relations with the parren, he's quite an open, friendly guy for a croma elder, but that most of his allies are croma traditionalists and xenophobes."

Lisbeth sighed. "It does seem to be the case, yes. Tiga thinks so too."

"You're up to something, aren't you?" Trace didn't like it, and was certain Erik would like it less. But unlike Erik, she found herself at something of a disadvantage here for pure intellect, and for comfort levels in a political, people-intensive environment. She knew herself well enough to know that she was smarter than average, but the Debogandes, as a genetically-enhanced group, were a whole level above that. And they were *so* damn charming, apparently even to aliens. She'd urged Lisbeth to be more sure of herself before. Now she was wondering if that had been such a good idea. Lisbeth's lack of confidence had at least kept her from trying dangerously over-ambitious things that would get her killed.

"Trace," Lisbeth said firmly, "I have to ask you to trust me. Can you do that for me?"

Trace took a deep breath. "Of course I will. But I'll also never stop reminding overconfident kids that the best leaders listen to the advice of people with different opinions than their own. Promise me you'll remember that as well."

Lisbeth smiled broadly. "Of course. Of all the lessons I learned from you on *Phoenix*, that's one of my favourites."

"There are others?" Trace asked warily.

Lisbeth nodded. "The main one is how to be brave. I don't think I really knew, before I met you. And I still don't, really, but I try."

"Just so long as you're aware of what the bravery can cost you," Trace said solemnly. "Civilians and pop-culture psychologists talk as though achieving bravery is the end of the journey. It's not, it's the beginning. And after learning bravery, you must learn to deal with pain. Because after true bravery, there's always pain."

Lisbeth's smile turned sad. "Unless you die."

Trace nodded. "Yes. Unless you die. Bravery is dangerous. Cowards live longer."

Lisbeth nodded, with amusement and melancholy. As though this were exactly what she'd expected from a conversation with Trace, and exactly what she'd missed. "So your turn — what are *you* doing on Dul'rho? I know you love Skah, but he doesn't need the Phoenix Company Commander to escort him."

"There are holes in my knowledge about reeh combat operations on this scale," said Trace. "I came to pick the brains of some croma generals before we go."

"You came to get Stan," Lisbeth corrected. "Didn't you."

Trace thought about denying it. But Lisbeth's big, solemn eyes were hard to deny. "Stan will be useful where we're going."

Lisbeth looked sad. "Trace. Don't you think he's done enough? He's not a warrior like you guys."

They were good friends, Trace knew. When Romki had been new to *Phoenix*, and treated with suspicion, Lisbeth had been the only one to take his side. "He's valuable, Lisbeth. *Phoenix* needs him. Humanity needs him."

"Of course," Lisbeth sighed. "Always the mission with Major Thakur."

"Can you tell me where he is?"

Lisbeth put hands on her hips for a long moment, and gazed at the drifting snow in the courtyard beyond the door. For a moment, Trace thought she might refuse. "Yes," she said finally, reluctantly. "I'll tell you where he is. But Trace, if you try to twist his arm, I'll stop you.

I mean it. I'm not powerless here. And Stan's not only my friend, he's doing important work for Sho'mo'ra."

Trace frowned. "I'd never force him against his will, Lisbeth."

Lisbeth's return gaze was flat. Trace realised that she didn't believe her.

5

After a day quizzing various croma army and marine officers, Trace sought directions to Stan Romki, and came walking through a makeshift command wing in the Alei'sei complex. The ceiling here was high, beams and rafters echoing with the sound of many croma voices. Everywhere were screens and holographics, the mounts entirely mobile, nothing built into the old structure. Heritage laws, Trace supposed.

She made her way between the screens and planning stations, Arime and Wang in her wake, rifle shouldered and peering at the haphazard setup. Senior officers stood before holographic assemblies of lower ranks, explaining how things were going to work. Some averagely-enormous croma were engaged in dangerously animated discussion, while smaller juniors hovered and watched, as though concerned the increasingly violent gesticulations would damage expensive equipment. Harried junior officers, usually smaller, rushed back and forth to carry personal messages that for some reason couldn't be delivered via technology. Croma staff officers, it seemed, liked to make things unnecessarily complicated just as human ones did.

From the displays it appeared that most of the discussions

revolved around logistics. Civilians never comprehended that most large military operations were a matter of ensuring that all the pieces arrived in the right places at the right times, and thus resembled large-scale freight haulage operations more than explosive kinetic assaults. The actual fighting took place on the tip of a very long spear, most of which did little fighting unless things went spectacularly wrong. Civilian logistics industries throughout human space were run almost exclusively by ex-military officers for that reason.

Trace found Romki in an adjoining room, much smaller than the cavernous main temple. Here several groups of younger Fleet officers clustered about displays, and highlighted points with manual flourishes, while a number of corbi clustered about, or perched on neighbouring tables to see over croma shoulders.

Several corbi saw her approach, engaged in their separate conversation, and Trace recognised one. It was Leku, a survivor from the Splicer raid, a farmer from the Talo continent, badly wounded and nursed back to health on *Phoenix* before heading to Dul'rho at the promise of assisting in planning the evacuation. He'd been worried that the croma were lying, and that he'd not get to assist in anything, or that they'd otherwise not listen to a simple farmer. That fear, at least, seemed unfounded.

Leku stared at her for a long moment, expression somewhere between fear and dismay, then returned to his conversation, still glancing back. Trace nodded to him and continued. Her corbi team in that assault had not loved her. They'd been fanatically devoted to their cause, and had recognised that she was their best hope of achieving it. But corbi had long suspected that she didn't care if all of them died in the process, and had wasted no love upon her. And indeed, most of them had died, so she could hardly fault their logic.

Romki stood behind Tiga, and a corbi Trace did not recognise, who sat at a table and pored over their own display. It was the Rando surface, Trace recognised from the outline of Talo, the northern continent. It was covered in marks that she supposed would be landing zones, where huge croma shuttles would descend to take as many corbi as would fit off the surface and up to orbit. If Croma Fleet were unsuccessful in neutralising surrounding space of reeh activity, they were going to be doing it under fire. Trace did not envy them the task.

Romki looked about, and abruptly startled, to see her standing behind him, peering at their display. "Major! You gave me a heart attack."

Trace smiled. "Can I speak with you in private?"

"You can't have him back," Tiga announced loudly, making furious markings on her display, translating off some other source. Saving thousands of imaginary lives with each pen stroke. Trace wondered if any of them were sleeping. Here was the opportunity of a hundred lifetimes, the thing so many generations of corbi had lived and died in hope of seeing. Monumental didn't begin to describe it.

"In private," Trace repeated to Romki.

Tiga spun on her in the chair. Fringe askew, young and hot-headed as ever, and probably loaded on stims to let her pass on a few hours sleep a night. "He's a scholar, Major. You're a warship. He knows so much history we don't, his advice on where to look in the old corbi texts and records has been invaluable, we've lost so much of our own history and he's helping us to find it so we can rescue as many of our people as possible. He's doing *so* much more good here than he could with you."

"Stan," Trace repeated, unmoved, and stood aside for him. Romki sighed, and gave Tiga a gesture of calm, leaving as Trace indicated. Tiga watched them go, scowling, before turning back to her display.

There was no deserted room to talk in, so they stood by a wall beside a totem-like stone sculpture, abstract circular shapes that might have assembled in the shape of an upright croma, or perhaps nothing at all.

"We're going to Keijir System," she told him, her voice low. The assassin bug riding somewhere in her webbing would alert her if any active audio spying came their way. Passive spying could not be ruled out, but she reckoned it was worth the risk. Croma did not spy for reeh, and Croma Fleet already knew where *Phoenix* was going. If any truly dangerous data began running on Dul'rho networks, Lisbeth had assured her that Liala would spot it, and stop it. "It's deep in reeh space. Styx is certain the ceephay queen was once there, a long time ago."

"Well it sounds fascinating, Major, but as you can see, I've got..."

"There are humans there." Romki frowned at her. "A domestic human population, croma Fleet Intel says. It's a mess of mismatched alien populations all the way through reeh space, the Reeh Empire smashed and scattered all previous civilisations..."

"Wait wait... a human *domestic* population?" Romki looked astonished. "Domestic for how long? Oh!" As he realised the answer. "The krim occupation! The human abductees! They took them to the reeh?"

"Some of them, yes. Croma Fleet Intel says."

"But they'd have to take them through croma space!"

"I know. It's a big mystery. We're guessing more corruption at high level, it was Croma'Shin back then."

"Well so much for the impenetrable Croma Wall!" Romki ran a hand over his bald head, staring elsewhere as he processed that. It was an expression of fascination with things so much larger than himself that Trace had become quite familiar with in the past two years. And in the past few months, she'd missed it. "So I'd imagine with *Phoenix*'s stealth capabilities now, you'll find some way to sneak up on Keijir, and then with a domestic human population it won't be hard to disguise yourselves going down to the surface."

Trace nodded. "Styx can disable their networks so we don't get noticed. Eshir was the center of the old Reeh Empire. Apparently it's pretty run down now, reeh take laissez-faire to an extreme, let things fall apart if they will, particularly the places with species they don't care much about. But it means there's lots of old history there. We're hoping there'll be clues to where the ceephay queen was, and where she is now. Styx is sure she can find something. And because Eshir has decayed rather than developed, there may be clues remaining as to the nature of the early Reeh Empire."

Romki gazed at her for a long moment. Then blinked rapidly,

with the onset of frustration. Then a reluctant smile. "This is bribery."

"Yes," said Trace. "And Stan, you're a human. I know you think this is a crude and emotional logic and that it's beneath you, but long experience in the Spiral has taught us that if humans don't look out for humanity, no one else will. You know I value what you're doing for the corbi. You know I do." Romki's expression showed him not entirely convinced. "But you're human, Stan. We fight for humanity. For humanity *first*."

Romki frowned at her. Not angry, just... something else. "Major, believe it or not, I've *always* agreed with that sentiment. I've just never understood how we can be surrounded by aliens, many of whom may or may not decide to try and kill us, without attempting to understand them better so we can know why, and take measures to stop it. *Effective* measures, instead of the jingoistic rubbish our Fleet's been shovelling down our throat for the past few centuries."

"Explain to me then how you're serving humanity here more than you're serving corbi. Or croma."

"Because, dearest Major, Croma'Dokran and Sho'mo'ra just acquired the leadership of all croma. With it comes all the classified data Croma'Rai's been sitting on for the past six hundred years. Entire histories of reeh activity, reeh expansion, reeh capabilities, that your precious Fleet would absolutely *die* to know about. Or make certain that someone else died to know it, more likely. I know far more about Fleet's strategic priorities than you think I do, I've actually had this conversation with senior Fleet officers, usually in the context of them warning me why I should shut up and do what I'm told with my research. And one of their many terrors is that the reeh could turn all their attention this way, and that the croma could just collapse, possibly in as little as a few hundred years. What I'm getting to see now is a strategic goldmine for Fleet, and as much as I hate how they do things, even I'm not such a fool as to think there's anyone else who could save us if the reeh one day came our way."

"You're here to gather data on the history of the croma/reeh wars? Let Liala do it."

"Liala doesn't work for human Fleet, Major. She's the commander of drysine forces in parren space."

"No, but she works for Styx, and Styx is doing everything she can to ingratiate herself to human Fleet."

"And Liala's just a child, she doesn't know how to analyse what she's seeing."

"You don't think the fact that she's got approximately a thousand times more IQ than you might help her make up for it?"

"Major," said Romki with exasperation, "she doesn't understand how human Fleet works, how the stunted little bureaucratic minds that populate the corridors of Fleet HQ work, how to gather and present data in such a way that they'll listen, and not simply crawl back into their little shells and stand on each other's heads as they climb their respective greasy poles. She won't prioritise the right information, and this is just too important to leave to chance!"

Trace gazed at the older man for a long moment. She'd feared, and some had guessed, that his reluctance to accompany *Phoenix* on this latest mission was a matter of bravery, or the lack of it. She hesitated to even contemplate the word 'cowardice' with any *Phoenix* crew who'd come this far. None of them had anything left to prove in that regard, and Romki had risked his life as often and willingly as most *Phoenix* marines, and with considerably less training and armour. But still, some had suggested that he'd lost his nerve, and become afraid.

Seeing him now, she realised that that rumour, at least, she could dismiss. It was the same old Stan Romki, passionately logical, stubborn, and attempting against all temptation to arrange the universe according to how it was, rather than how he'd personally prefer it to be. Trace loved all her *Phoenix* family, but Romki, in that family, had always been the cantankerous uncle whom everyone tolerated rather than embraced. Except that now, watching him stubbornly refuse to change his principles because someone else demanded it, she was struck by their kindred spirit, and an unexpected but overwhelming affection.

She reached, and took his hand. "Stan. *Phoenix* is going into a very alien place. You're our alien expert. We need you. I need you. Erik needs you. All of us are certain that our chances of coming back alive are much greater with you aboard. Please. And whatever you're doing here, Liala can do most of it without you. Whatever her shortcomings now, she'll learn fast. She's a drysine queen."

Romki gazed at her. Then swallowed hard, and looked about. At the corbi, labouring to save their people. At the croma who would reveal to him things that all humanity desperately needed to know. He looked back to Trace, obviously conflicted, and emotional. For once, Trace did not hide her own emotion. It was against Kulina ethos, she supposed, in that it was manipulative. But it was also real, and it was what Erik and Lisbeth had learned to do so well since they were children. In all things, she tried to be professional, and learn from the best.

"The heart of the old Reeh Empire, you say?" he said finally. Trace nodded. "Can I go down with you on the away mission?"

"Communications from orbit could be difficult. We may need you to."

Romki took a deep breath. "If we get back alive, I suppose I'll learn far more about the Reeh Empire than I could sitting here."

"The Reeh Empire as it actually exists today," Trace agreed. "Not the history of past millennia." Romki nodded with a sigh. "So you're in?"

"Yes," said Romki. "For *Phoenix* and humanity. And for you, Major. I'm in."

Trace abandoned all Kulina protocol, and hugged him.

TRACE EMERGED BACK into the Rando operations room, and strode straight to Tiga's workspace. Tiga and the other corbi kept working, not exactly ignoring her, but too busy in their own work to explain things to the human marine who peered at the various maps and displays, then went to the holography display of the Rando surface and began making adjustments with her hands, zooming the display to look at her own preferences.

Landing zones were clearly marked, with some kind of grid-distribution to ensure they were evenly spaced across the most heavily populated zones. Rando had five major continents, big oceans and a bunch of islands, including some enormous archipelagos that still held large populations. As she touched each of the landing zones marked there, she saw population densities listed, preferred advance warning times, margin-of-error indicators and zoning priorities. The corbi appeared to be applying their local knowledge to what would otherwise have been a cold mathematical exercise — which people were most likely to respond positively to evacuation messages, what modes of transportation were available to move how many people to the landing zones. Trace really only knew Talo continent, all within a few thousand kilometres of where the Splicer had stood, but she'd heard plenty of tales of these other regions. It was all enough to make her glad she was just a marine who specialised in violence. This before her looked like the mother of all logistical headaches. Doing it under fire was going to be something indeed.

"Major, can I help you with something?" It was Tiga, looking frustrated, needing to use the display and finding Trace blocking it.

"How many onboard security are you allowing for?" Trace asked her, in Lisha. She indicated the display. "Some of these places, people aren't going to want to go. You've got an LZ here in the Tarsha Highlands... some of those people might actually fire on you."

Tiga blinked at her, to hear her speak Lisha. "Um... yeah. We know." In the most respectful tone she'd used yet. "My idea was that we'd use corbi Resistance on the downworld shuttles for security, partly so that the locals would see a corbi face who could talk to them in Lisha, and partly because corbi take up less room than croma."

Trace gave her an appraising look. She could hear it now — Tiga's Kul'hasa accent that she'd been so self-conscious about, acquired from a lifetime on Do'ran, the homeworld of the Croma'Dokran. "That's good thinking. But in a few of those places you might need more than one or two. If enough folks don't want to let others leave, you might have to assess how much effort it's worth spending to get them out."

"We're leaving the most difficult regions for last," Tiga agreed. "So we can make that assessment, but also so we can bombard them for longer with our messaging."

"Telling them what?"

"That if they don't get out, they'll die."

"Some of them will blame you for that," Trace warned her. "Many already blame me. They'd rather we left the Splicer alone."

"Can you blame them?"

"No," Trace said sombrely. "No. It's a hopeless mess down there. Most people just live day by day." She thought of Jindi, living alone on his beach until she'd found him. She had no idea if the reeh strike that killed the neighbouring village had been truly aimed at her or not. Jindi insisted otherwise, said it had been aimed at him, that the reeh had clearly known who he was since they'd refused to take or kill him despite him refusing to hide. But Trace didn't think it could have been a coincidence that the village she and Kono had just been in, had been struck the following night. More innocent deaths to her tally.

"We're going to get them out, Major," Tiga said with determination. And with some concerned surprise. Perhaps the emotion showed on Trace's face. That wasn't normal, but around corbi of late, she hadn't been able to stop it. "We might not get all of them, but we're going to get most of them. We're still negotiating a world for them, but Sho'mo'ra promises he'll find something. On this side of the Croma Wall, as far from the reeh as possible."

"What are your best estimates for the bombardment casualties after the Splicer was destroyed?" It shouldn't have mattered to her. It was against all Kulina teachings for it to matter. She didn't want to be responsible for this, but as Kulina, she shouldn't have wanted for anything. 'Do your job,' she'd always told herself, 'and the things that happen will happen'.

"We're not sure," Tiga said sombrely. "A lot of the villages evacuated when the strikes began. They're not stupid, they've been living under the reeh for a long time, they can identify predictable patterns of behaviour. Our best estimate is closer to fifty thousand than a hundred thousand. The reeh lost a lot of their aerial bombardment capability when *Phoenix* hit them, they couldn't hit all the villages at once. The more they'd strung it out, the more time the villagers had to figure out what was happening, and leave. Otherwise it could have been a lot more."

Trace nodded quietly. She'd lived in those villages for nearly four months. "You should know," she told Tiga, "that Sho'mo'ra has promised *Phoenix* a reliable ship to go back to human space. To Heuron, where Fleet HQ is located. That's no small thing, there's never been a croma visitor to human space. But this one's taking everything we're discovering from the Splicer."

"Shouldn't you wait until the croma labs get more advanced results?"

Trace shook her head. "They've got nothing compared to what Styx is giving us. The Captain's told them they're wasting their time, they should just wait on Styx too, but there's egos at stake. But what most concerns you is the message I'm sending to human Fleet with the data. This is data that could save humanity, and it comes from the corbi. It comes from corbi sacrifice, without which none of us humans could benefit. I'm telling them that."

Tiga stared up at her, eyes wide. Unspeaking.

"And I'm telling them that humanity has the perfect world for the corbi. It's a *long* way from here. It's in barabo space, in Kolabu System, a world called Vieno. We came past it two years ago, it has a big barabo space station there called Tuki, built by the tavalai, it's a big trading port. There's maybe one hundred and fifty million barabo on Vieno, very light population, and the barabo are nice, pretty close to human and corbi, all like one family, really.

"Barabo used to be tavalai allies, still are I guess, but they're right near sard space, so now they're worried. Barabo don't like to fight, so they're agitating with humans to get Fleet out their way to protect them. Fleet's not so enthusiastic, because the damn barabo won't hold up their end of the deal, and will rely on humans to do any fighting for them. But if we put corbi on Vieno, and build up that civilisation as fast as possible, we aren't going to have that problem with corbi."

Tiga frowned. "You'd dump us on the sard's door and tell us to fight that war instead?"

"Tiga, there's nowhere safe in all the Spiral. Nowhere. On Vieno you'd have alliance with the great new power of the Spiral — humanity — and you'd repay your debt by putting some backbone into the barabo. And that would be your world, because the barabo have got plenty — more than they deserve, actually — and there'd be a few uninhabited systems you could have too, I'm sure. It's not much, but it would suit humanity, because we're the big colonial power and we can incorporate alien populations. The croma can't because over the past few thousand years they've been shrinking, not expanding, and that makes them hold onto every world they've got like a vain lady to her jewels. You stay in croma space, you're just a fifth wheel, they'll never let you participate in croma affairs."

Tiga just stared at her, stunned.

Trace took a deep breath. "Now I can't promise anything. But I have the most influence right now that any human will ever have. Obviously I'm not withholding the means to save humanity unless they grant this, but I will be laying out the case as hard as I can. Transport from Rando to Cho'nu System is one thing — to Vieno will be a crazy big effort, humanity's never deployed transport resources on a scale like that. But it would be a statement to the Spiral that we're not the conquering terrors that the tavalai say we are, and we're here to do good. I'll lay out the case, and we'll see what happens. I just thought you and the corbi should be aware of what was happening at that end."

"What's Vieno like?" Tiga asked, wide-eyed.

"On all the technical parameters it's ideal." Trace managed a small smile. "On the less technical parameters, Charlie Platoon went down to Vieno's surface while we were there to get us some seafood. They said it was the prettiest planet outside of Homeworld they'd ever seen."

Tiga's eyes widened. "Oh, *that* world! That's Vieno! When I was on the train with Charlie Platoon they all talked about it. They said they wanted to go back after this whole thing is over."

Of course, Trace realised. Lieutenant Jalawi and several squads of Charlie Platoon had been on Erik's cross-continental adventure with Tiga. She smiled. "I didn't go down myself, but when it comes to nice places for recreation and good food, I trust my marines implicitly, and Lieutenant Jalawi in particular."

Tiga smiled back. "That sounds like a nice dream, Major. Thank you. I think your Fleet is going to be quite occupied for a long time to come, though."

"Yes. Yes they will."

6

Stan Romki exited Berth Two at *Phoenix* Midships with the Command Squad marines, pushing his duffle bag before him, and was immediately greeted by Operations crew. He did not know them particularly well, as *Phoenix* was a large enough ship that even some members of working crew did not know each other very well, especially those who worked on different shifts in different regions of the ship. But every time he used a shuttle berth he'd see the Operations crew, working the shuttles, maintaining inventory and keeping the readiness zones prepared, where marines would keep weapons, ammunition and other equipment pre-positioned in case of rapid deployment.

Some of those crew now seemed genuinely delighted to see him, perhaps having heard that he was unlikely to return. Several floated across immediately to shake his hand and clap him on the shoulder, which Romki returned with surprised bemusement. Big Spacer Deol, who was known to hold the *Phoenix* female benchpress record, even gave him a bone-creaking hug. But he was touched, and thought that it must be specifically because Midships Operations crew's job involved keeping track of everyone coming and going.

But then as he was hauling his way up the guiderope past Berth

Two storage, Petty Officer Park saw him while pulling things out of storage on the far wall, gave a shout, pushed off the wall and came flying all the way across to shake his hand, looking quite delighted to see him back. Romki knew Park only a little, having collaborated briefly with the Engineering Systems tech on a few of *Phoenix*'s drysine manufacturing machines, and once sharing a sandwich with him while discussing how he thought drysine logic worked. Romki hadn't thought he'd made any kind of special impression on Park, but Park's enthusiasm made him reconsider.

Then, on the way through Midships' multiple segments, where disks of open space flared out from the ship's spine between bulkheads thick with load-bearing support and storage compartments, he had to drift past marines in full armour performing zero-G systems calibrations. Those turned out to be the Third Squad of Delta Platoon, all of whom saw and swarmed him, quite alarmingly, insisting on shaking hands with their big armoured rigs, all dancing about in zero-G like friendly sharks inspecting a seal.

In the spine transit shaft, holding to a handle that pulled him through the tube into the rotating crew cylinder where everyone slept, various crew zooming past him in the other direction shouted greetings. By the time he stepped down at M-bulkhead, and pulled his way down stair railings until gravity began to build once more, he was beginning to feel quite emotional.

More greetings followed, including from several tavalai who hadn't been on the ship as long, until he finally turned the last corner to his old quarters at G-bulkhead, Corridor 5-A of Third Quarter, and saw the familiar door hatch beside the Third Quarter head and opposite the black-and-yellow striped emergency storage. And standing there, blocking much of the corridor in contravention of ship regs, were another ten crew, evidently having heard that he was back aboard.

They greeted him with a cheer, some of them people he knew well enough, but some he'd barely exchanged words with, and there followed more handshakes, hugs and backslaps. They'd genuinely thought he wasn't coming back, Romki realised amidst all this unaccustomed familial activity. It had barely occurred to him that they might be upset at the prospect of losing him. Of course he possessed a skillset that had been somewhat useful to *Phoenix* over the course of this journey, and there would logically be some gratitude from the crew toward whatever assistance he'd provided, along with some self-interest that he should remain aboard for everyone's benefit. But this felt considerably more than that.

From the moment he'd first come aboard, he'd been the outsider, inflicting his unwelcome opinions upon an often hostile crew. They'd come to see things more his way since then, assisted by the Major and the Captain's more obvious changes of heart, but still Romki had never escaped the feeling that they'd never truly accepted him. Things were easier that way, with the work he had to do, often locked reading in his quarters while others he may have been friendly with were socialising in the rare hour of spare time following a shift. People had never come easily to Romki, and it was emotionally far simpler to expect little from them and to engage even less. And yet somehow, entirely by accident, it seemed he'd managed to make more good friends on this single ship than he'd ever had in his life.

By the time he finally got in his quarters, deposited the duffle on his bunk and closed the door, he was wiping tears from his eyes.

ERIK HIT the call button on Trace's door, and steeled himself for what was to come. Trace opened, still in her undershirt and leggings, hair wet from a recent shower having hit the gym immediately after her debrief. Erik had let things slide at the debrief, in no mood to pick this fight before the entire crew. But now he'd had enough.

Trace took a small flask from the refrigeration above her quarters' small table, and took the seat Erik indicated on her bed. Erik sat against the table, and stared down at her. Trace looked back, dark brown eyes as calm and cool as ever. Erik wasn't fooled.

"You told Tiga you want to tell Fleet they should move the corbi to Vieno," he said flatly.

"It's a good move," said Trace. "The new colonial administration's all about that kind of thing, shifting alien populations around to suit human interests."

"It'll never happen," said Erik. "And you know it. We don't have the transportation assets to devote to something like that. If we did, it would take decades over those distances."

"We'll see," said Trace. The ship's name was the Hasa'ma. It came with Sho'mo'ra's personal recommendation, a captain of the highest integrity, and would be arriving here in Teg'ula System shortly to take Styx's work back to homeworld. Lisbeth, Erik knew, would be sending one of her own ships back to Gesul on Naraya with their own copies, and a tavalai vessel was being arranged, though that would likely arrive late, and receive a copy of the same data *Phoenix* left for the croma.

"You had no authority to promise Tiga anything," said Erik. "And now she'll have gone and told all the other command corbi, and croma command will know as well. Which means probably they'll stop looking quite so hard for a world here in croma space, since they'll think they can just let the humans deal with it. So when Human Fleet rejects your suggestion, the corbi will be left with nowhere. Thanks to you."

"The croma won't agree to settle the corbi anywhere near here," Trace said flatly, sipping her flask while Erik spoke. "You just got kicked off Dul'rho by croma who wouldn't even accept alien proximity. The chances that they'll give up a whole world for the corbi, even to share, is nil. This whole Rando evacuation is a salve to croma honour, it'll go no further than that. They'll end up stuck on some dirtball with no rights, after ten years they'll all be wishing they were back on Rando."

"And who died to make you the political expert on this ship?"

"It's Romki's assessment," said Trace. "Styx's too."

Dammit, thought Erik. Under pressure was when Trace performed at her best. She had that look now — back to the wall, bullets flying. Ice cool and deadly calm, like all the onrushing death in the galaxy could not faze her. He stared at her for a long moment, like a predator might consider some kind of hard-shelled creature whose insides he'd like to eat.

"You'll limit your remarks to Fleet to immediate operational matters only," he said finally. "No strategic suggestions. I'll not have you intimating that our efforts to save humanity are in any way conditional on their support for the corbi. That's an order."

Her stare turned hard. "You took sides in a Tali'san and ran halfway across Dul'rho in a rogue vehicle for the corbi," she said icily. "Don't tell me you had some grander plan in mind, that was entirely your bleeding heart at work. After all of that, *now* you're going to throw them in the trash?"

"What were Tiga's latest figures on civilian casualties after the Splicer?" Erik asked. "I know you asked her." Trace said nothing, just staring. "A year ago you'd never have asked her. You're Kulina, you don't bother yourself with little things like a few thousand dead civilians. I mean, you've never actually been a civilian, have you? You joined the Kulina at twelve, they're paramilitary at least, so your entire adult life and all your adolescence was in the service. And in these grand moral abstractions the Kulina make, what's a few thousand civvie deaths against the human cause? Especially when those civvies are aliens."

"I'm not the one flying a warship that can kill planets," Trace said coldly.

"No, but I *know* what it costs," Erik snapped, leaning to jab a finger at her. "You *never* did, and it's easy to ignore a moral abstraction in your serene meditative state." Trace's stare burned into him, a cold and silent fury. "Only now you've spent nearly four months living amongst them. You learned their language, you valued the simplicity of their lives. And you swore you were just getting another job done, saving the human race one military objective at a time.

"You even managed to make them hate you, all that team you got killed when you stormed the Splicer. How the hell does that happen? When all of your marines here on *Phoenix* love you? But those wounded we had in Medbay, every one save for Rika got the hell out of here as though we had some kind of bad smell. They thought you'd spent their lives like so many cheap coins, and you know what? The way I see you doting on Rika, I think you think they're right."

"Leave Rika out of this." Behind the steel facade, her voice might have trembled, just a little.

"What do you see, Trace? When you try to meditate?" He indicated to her singlet and stretch pants, her usual meditation attire. "I've seen the footage that Styx recovered. All those dead civvy corbi in the lower holds, there were *thousands* of them. And you sent them into a death trap as a diversion, didn't you?"

"I warned them what would happen."

"But you didn't push it too hard, did you?" Erik squatted before her. "Did you? I mean, idiots believe what they want to believe. Not like you, who refuses to be fooled by self-serving deceptions like hope or optimism. You knew exactly what was going to happen, you could have talked them out of it if you'd really tried, but you didn't, did you? Because the mission needed to happen, and if they realised the civvies would all die, they'd have canned the whole thing."

"You'd rather the mission hadn't worked?" Trace demanded, with all the furious drive with which she'd ever pursued anything... but there was a quaver in her voice, now, somewhere behind that hard steel wall. "Then what the hell are *you* doing here?"

"And when you close your eyes," Erik continued with steely determination, "you hear them all screaming as they die. It's all you hear." Trace just stared at him, her face barely a hand's breadth from his. She wouldn't flinch. Had somewhere along the way lost the instinct entirely. "What were Tiga's figures on how many civilians the reeh murdered after they lost the Splicer?"

"Between fifty and a hundred thousand," said Trace. The tremor was plain in her voice now.

"And you think you could do all that again," said Erik. "While I'm having very serious doubts."

"I can do my damn job."

"What about Pena?" Trace's eyes went wider still. "I know about Pena. Rika told me. He doesn't blame you. I think Pena probably did. Staff Sergeant Kono too. You know he wanted Pena to come on

Phoenix after it was all over? Rika told me that too, said Pena had told him he'd offered. She'd have been some kind of corbi ambassador to the Spiral. Sounds to me like she'd have been damn good at it, much better than angry little Tiga. Everyone liked Pena. And you shot her in the head."

"They'd have skinned her alive," Trace said hoarsely.

"But she was a Rando nationalist, Trace!" He leaned forward some more, accusingly. "How could you miss that? You're one of the sharpest people I know, you *had* to have seen that she was struggling with what to do. Unless you fooled yourself, because it was what you *wanted* to believe. I mean, Pena was your friend, right? It must have been lonely, being hated all the time by corbi who thought you were just going to walk across their bodies to get what you wanted? But you missed it..."

"I didn't miss it..."

"Don't lie to me!" Erik yelled in her face. "Don't lie to yourself, you've *never* lied before, don't start now! You fucked up and it killed her, Trace! You had to blow her brains out with your own hand because you refused to see how badly she was struggling with the cause — you *should* have sent her packing, it would have saved her life!"

Erik had never seen his marine commander's face like this. Her jaw worked, soundlessly, attempting the composure that was her life's reflex. Almost the eyes remained unchanged, then a flicker of pure agony, struggling to get out from behind the prison of that wall.

"And now you're wondering how you can live with yourself," Erik continued, utterly without mercy. "Because being Kulina means you can walk on fire and never truly feel the pain, but this fire *burns*, Trace, it burns worse than anything you've felt before, but you have to go on like it doesn't hurt, telling yourself and everyone else around you one big giant fucking lie... only Kulina aren't allowed to lie, not to themselves. Are they Trace?"

Trace's shoulders shook, just once. It was awful to watch. Still the old dam facade remained, but the jaw was gone now, trembling as though from some disease. Again her shoulders shook. It had been so long between events, Erik supposed, that she'd even forgotten how to cry properly. Then her hands started shaking, and she put them up to her face, to cover the shame of her tears... and then the whole facade came crashing down.

Erik held her while she sobbed, heaving and shaking as though something had broken inside. He put his cheek against her ear, holding her to his shoulder, blinking through his own tears and knowing that he was in fact a monster. But he was the monster that she'd helped create, and if anyone would see the karma in that, it was Trace.

FIVE MINUTES LATER THEY SAT, heads together on her bunk. Trace sat in a daze, all defences, all pretences gone. She felt much the same as she had one time in the Academy, having been knocked unconscious in a sparring session, awakening to find herself a minute later staring at the ceiling, surrounded by concerned and some amused faces, to see that Cadet Thakur had finally been brought back to earth.

Not so much brought back to earth this time, she thought, as crashed into it from a great height. Erik's hand was strong on the back of her neck, pulling her head down to his. It was a meditation, nothing more, from a man who to the best of her observation still didn't actually understand meditation. But it felt as good as anything was going to feel at this moment, and she breathed deeply, and tried to ignore the clamorous, whiny little voice in her mind that insisted, with great self-pity, that she didn't deserve to feel good about anything.

She couldn't hide what had happened, couldn't hide the trauma that had twisted her insides and made everything dysfunctional. But she knew that this had never been about what she deserved or wanted for herself. She should by all rights have died in the Splicer with Giddy, Tano, Dreja, Kirsi and the others. Certainly that would have been easier... except that the mission would likely not have succeeded if she'd died, which made self-preservation a priority, within limits. But whatever her failings, this had never been about what she deserved or did not deserve — it was about achieving the mission so that humanity itself did not vanish from the galaxy, and about attempting to discipline the petulant, self-important parts of her brain that insisted that everything should always be about her.

That part of her brain had finally escaped her control, after years of trying. And really, she'd always known it would, if she'd been honest about how far she thought she could push herself. And being who she was, she'd taken that as a challenge, like some of the physical endurance specialists she'd known — like one former marine she'd served with who, after discharge, had gone on to become a Homeworld distance running champion, using military enhancements to run for five days at a time with no sleep, battling through blisters, stress fractures and brain-crushing exhaustion for the sheer thrill of seeing just where the edge of endurance lay. She'd never seen the point of that sort of thing — sports were a fundamentally selfish pursuit, however much fun in the superficial now, and if her goals weren't in the service of something far larger than her brain's wailing ego, she didn't see the point.

So now she knew where that limit was, in herself, at least. She did have emotions, however much she'd tried to repress them, to shape them and make them work toward her conscious purposes. Like a weightlifter snatching a bar with too many kilos, something had snapped, and only now, with the bones protruding, was she forced to admit that it had actually broken.

At the thought, she felt more steady, and breathed more deeply. The first step to fixing the problem was to diagnose the problem. In her previous state of denial, she'd not been able to diagnose because she couldn't admit the problem existed. She'd thought the denial was necessary to maintain control, but the control had finally snapped, and now that she was here, on this side of a great event, she found it wasn't actually the end of the world. She wouldn't let it be.

"Hey." She moved a hand, and gently slapped Erik's cheek. "You've got a ship to run."

"Trace." He put his forehead against hers. "You have to talk to me.

I know you think I'm a bleeding heart who likes to externalise his emotions too much, and you're probably right. But I'm also the ship's Captain, and my Marine Commander is broken." Trace smiled, pain-filled but genuine. Erik looked relieved to see it, but not yet convinced. "Can we at least now admit there's a problem?"

Trace sighed, and put her head back on his shoulder. "You win. I was wrong."

"This was never about me winning, Trace."

"I know. Still true though." He put his cheek against her ear, and she felt his breath on her neck. That felt good. Too good. "We should stop this."

"I know." Neither of them moved. "Inappropriate physical intimacy."

"Not the first time, either," she reminded him.

"No. But hugs work, Trace. You agree not to seduce me and we'll be fine."

Trace smiled. He was right, of course. Hugs did work, particularly with the people you were closest to in all the world. She could feel it working now, her breathing relaxing, tension fleeing. But these hugs were dangerous, because if there was one man on this ship with whom this recipe for psychological improvement could turn into something else...

"Your mother will have some nice girl lined up for you once we get home," Trace ventured. "Someone with a double-barrelled name, and her hair in plaits."

Erik lightly punched her arm. "Cliches are beneath you. It's actually going to be hard to adjust to normal women again, after all this time in Fleet."

"The women you grew up with were never normal," Trace instructed calmly. She'd had this conversation with Lisbeth enough times to be sure. "They were filthy rich, wore heels to breakfast and had names like Holly and Su Li that no normal girl has."

"My Navigation Officer on *UFS Firebird* was Holly."

"And where did she grow up?"

Erik thought about it. "Her Daddy owned Pressenth Station," he conceded.

"Spacer bridge crew," said Trace, as though that explained it. Which it did, kind of, with somewhere close to half of them.

"Trace? I want you to know that when we get home, if we get home, you'll always be family to my family. With everything that means."

Trace thought about it. It sounded for a moment dangerously like a proposal for something that he knew damn well she could never accept. But then she recalled the Kulina, her supposed 'other' family, who had sworn to kill her as soon as she once again came within range.

"I mean that we have an awful lot of security, and an awful lot of lawyers," Erik continued. "And whatever ends up happening with us vis-a-vis Fleet itself, anyone trying to get you will have to get through all of us first."

Trace opened her mouth to reply, but Erik indicated his ear to show he was uplinked. "Yeah," he said to whoever was calling, "tell them five minutes."

"Erik," said Trace. "Let me tell Fleet about Vieno. If that Splicer data ends up amounting to anything, all of humanity's going to owe the corbi."

Erik gazed at her. "Trace, you're the last person who needs the difference between morality and survival explained to them. You're right, I went out of my way to help the corbi. It was the right thing to do, and as it turned out, it even helped the human cause as well. But you're asking for something else."

"Erik." She didn't try to cover the emotion this time. Just looked at him, with all the tear-streaked manipulation she could muster. But the emotion was real, and it was simply what she felt. With the one person, perhaps in all the universe, with whom she could let that show. "Please."

Erik sighed. Trace knew what he was thinking. That Fleet HQ, however grateful for the Splicer data, would never forget the implication that any such data was conditional on favours. One either declared that one would pay any price for the survival of humanity, or one didn't. Whatever his compassion for the corbi, it was a principle that Erik agreed with wholeheartedly. Humanity's precarious position in the galaxy was what it was. But so was Rando's.

"I'll allow it," he said finally. "I'd do anything for you, Trace. Don't abuse it." He kissed her on the forehead, and left.

7

Lisbeth emerged into the Alei'sei courtyard beneath the drooping fronds of a tree. The temple building at the far side was Juneso's, granted to him as the highest ranking of this parren delegation. A tall shrine-stone with Kul'hasa inscription stood before the tree, which showered thin leaves upon white snow in a gust of chill wind.

Juneso stood waiting, Captain Tocamo of *Coroset* to one side, several of their security and lesser ranks forming the flanks. Lisbeth was not surprised, having these days by far the best internal intelligence network at any level of parren governance, and walked in her red robe along the courtyard path recently swept of snow. Timoshene walked before her, black robe tucked up about his gunbelt, a new addition in alien territories that the croma, warriors themselves, did not protest.

He took position on Lisbeth's left as she stopped precisely before Juneso, and performed the expected slight bow. "You requested my attendance, Ambassador Juneso?"

Juneso wore the pragmatic, loose pants and vest of a military man on a diplomatic mission, beneath a formal, heavy coat. He was well into his third-life, having been an accomplished young architect while phased to House Creative. Nearly fifty years ago, he'd phased to House Fortitude, losing all desire for architecture and joining the Fortitude Fleet, where he'd risen to Admiral. A second phase to House Harmony had seen him join the Tookrah Denomination, where he'd become an advisor on military and diplomatic affairs to Tookrah leader Anesol. Since Gesul of Domesh Denomination had risen to total power, and seen fit to unify the Harmony denominations by promoting senior figures from amongst them to cabinet ministries and advisory positions, he'd selected Juneso to command this mission to visit the croma, and unite the newly emerged drysines with their queen on the *UFS Phoenix*. The appointment had pleased many in House Harmony, even as it displeased more amongst the Domesh who felt that some favouritism was owed to members of Gesul's own clan.

"Lisbeth," said Juneso. His tone was calm, fingers clasped lightly behind his back. Lean, red-brown features, weathered with age the treatments could no longer hide. His sharp indigo eyes barely blinked. "I have attended a meeting with Sho'mo'ra. He informed me that *Phoenix*'s Rando Splicer data would only be shared with parren should this party join with the croma invasion fleet in the evacuation of corbi on Rando. Were you aware?"

"Ambassador Juneso," said Lisbeth, with just the correct formal tense, "you have only now made me aware of this."

Juneso gazed at her for a moment longer. The array of seven parren, standing armed and formal, three to each of their commander's flanks, left no doubt as to what sort of meeting this was. Timoshene had not been pleased that he alone would represent her security, but had bowed to Lisbeth's insistence. Sometimes the best way to look strong was to risk vulnerability.

"This is a new problem," Juneso continued. "When we arrived at Dul'rho, I was assured by Sho'mo'ra's people that there would be no issue with Splicer data. Our losses from Mylor Station were acknowledged, with sympathy. Now this position is changed, to the parren's disadvantage. Do you know how this has occurred?"

"Forgive me, Juneso," said Lisbeth. "But the technology of the

Splicer was never a gift from the croma to the parren, it was a gift granted from the blood and sacrifice of the corbi people, beneath the leadership of the greatest warrior of the Spiral, Major Thakur of the *Phoenix*. I do not know how this development occurred, as I am not privy to the inner workings of the croma leadership, nor the mind of Sho'mo'ra. But I will be pleased to honour the corbi who have suffered so much to bring us this great gift, and to grant them a great gift in return."

She did not meet Juneso's stare too directly -- in parren etiquette it could be a deadly mistake. She merely kept her eyes focused unworriedly on the door of the temple building behind his head. There was a silence in the courtyard. Lisbeth knew that she was playing a dangerous game. But best, for sure, that Juneso knew that the danger lay mostly for himself.

"I shall attempt to reason further with Sho'mo'ra," Juneso said after a moment. "Gesul's instructions are that we will not fight the croma's war. The parren shall not make war upon the reeh. Perhaps you did not hear these instructions, Lisbeth Debogande?"

"I did hear them, Juneso. Clearly this is not a mission to make war upon the reeh, it is a mission to evacuate the corbi. Gesul's primary instruction in directing us to croma space was to assist the drysines in reuniting with their queen, and to seek all benefit to the parren people against the threats of alien technologies that threaten us. To that end, the corbi have made this gift from the Rando Splicer. Honour dictates that we must repay the corbi in kind. And now, diplomacy dictates that the continuation of good relations with the croma dictates it as well."

"Only Gesul can authorise an act of war upon another species," Juneso insisted.

"You must act to serve Gesul and the parren people how you think is best, Juneso," said Lisbeth. "I am confident that were Gesul here, he would order the assistance of the corbi at Rando, given that this is no act of war but rather an act of mercy, and given that it now appears to be the only way to attain the benefit of protective technologies from the Splicer that is our truest mission. If you decide to leave aboard

Coroset, I will stay with Liala and the *Amity*, and assist the corbi evacuation with them."

"The *Amity* is a drysine ship," Juneso said with faint disbelief. "It has no atmospheric quarters suitable for organics."

"Liala has assured me that the drysines can find a way. Now, if that is the end of this matter, I must return to my work."

"LISBETH," Hiro told her that evening at dinner in Porgesh, "this action is inadequate."

"No," Lisbeth corrected him in English. "You said *ainsleth anat toshene*, 'this action is inadequate'. You mean *ainsleth anaho mevash*, 'this action was improper'."

She ate some more of her meal -- croma food, some sort of meat with vegetables, simple and good in the way of these no-fuss people. The parren sat about her and Hiro on mats, effortless in that lean, crosslegged way of their kind, eating off ledu, low tables brought from *Coroset* for the purpose. A fireplace crackled behind a grille that kept the spitting, popping coals from burning the patterned carpet on the tile floor. Much of the room's interior was wooden beams and simple decoration. Lisbeth knew that it was an accident that the Alei'sei suited House Harmony parren so well, yet it did not stop the parren from gaining an unexpectedly positive view of their coarse, less-refined hosts.

Skah sat between her and Hiro, eating his meat and following the conversation with the help of an earpiece. Lisbeth had expected him to get bored with this conversation, as he often had with other adult discussions in his presence, but somewhere in the nearly-a-year since she'd seen him last, he'd acquired the ability to tell if a discussion were important or not.

"Fine," Hiro said drily, still in Porgesh. He was very fluent considering less than a year's practise, yet not nearly as fluent as Lisbeth. "This action was improper. Am I understood?" The latter remark could have gotten lower-ranked parren killed, in some houses. Mostly because a parren would never make such a mistake, and all would know the insolence intentional. With Hiro, Lisbeth's staff had learned to make allowances for human inadequacies.

Lisbeth smiled. "You are understood, Hiro. I don't particularly care about Juneso's issues right now, I'd much rather discuss deployments with Liala." Liala sat outside on the verandah, oblivious, she said, to the cold. More to the point, these temple doorways were awkward for a drysine's wide legs. As a security deterrent to any possible threat, there weren't many better, even if she had left her enormous anti-armour cannon on *Coroset*'s shuttle.

"But you can't ignore Juneso," Hiro insisted. "He knows what you did."

"And what did I do, Hiro?" Lisbeth fixed him with a pointed stare. Hiro wore a human-fitting version of a parren warrior's plain vest and light coat, weapons in his preferred shoulder holster, AR glasses currently raised on his head. If Timoshene was Lisbeth's close protection muscle, Hiro was her Intelligence, making certain that she was always informed of possible threats. With his utilisation of many drysine technologies unavailable to other parren, the combined security coverage made her a very hard target indeed.

"You told Sho'mo'ra to tell Juneso he wouldn't get the Splicer data unless we help at Rando." He waited a moment for Lisbeth to correct his Porgesh. Lisbeth cut some more steak instead. "Juneso was right, Sho'mo'ra had no issue with it before." About the small dinner circle, Semaya, Neyafa and Shonteel all gazed at her, wordlessly.

Lisbeth sighed. "There will be no delay in receiving the data. A croma ship will be sent to Gesul immediately, as soon as Juneso agrees. A fast messenger ship. There will be no disadvantage to the parren."

"So why, then?"

"Because the croma are going to need our help," Lisbeth said shortly. "Because the reeh are very advanced, and because saving the corbi is a worthy cause, particularly considering what they've done for parren, for humans, and for the entire Spiral with the Splicer data."

"These sound like the reasons of a nice girl with good intentions," Hiro said warningly. "Not like the reasons of a warleader."

The three parren watched wordlessly. Skah watched them all, back and forth. Semaya was Lisbeth's personal Chief of Staff, but on this mission she'd not brought many staff with her. They were needed for the interface between her advisory office and Gesul's ever-growing administration at the highest level of parren government. Out here, she needed only Semaya, as her primary advisor on the ways of parren governance, plus Nefaya and Shonteel as her personal aides. Timoshene and his security staff of six were about here somewhere, watching tirelessly.

"Gesul requested personal strategic knowledge of the reeh-croma confrontation," spoke several disembodied microphones from various personal electronic devices at once. That was Liala, listening in, and not requiring face-to-face contact to participate in conversation. There were small cameras here too, doubtless she could watch on those. *"The croma have data, but it is a different thing to assess such things in person, with drysine instruments. Coroset will not be conducting direct combat operations against reeh vessels. Reeh vessels will likely not even recognise your type. Identifications can be faked. Furthermore, rescuing the corbi will be seen by the Spiral as a good deed. The Parren Empire has little goodwill among non-parren people because it has so rarely engaged with them. The time is approaching when goodwill becomes a strategic asset. This one act will gain much, for little cost. Lisbeth's reasoning is sound."*

Lisbeth nodded with satisfaction, and ate her steak. Hiro looked sourly unconvinced. The three parren remained noncommittal. All knew very well how hard it was to argue with the logic of a drysine queen. Which was precisely what Hiro didn't like, Lisbeth knew.

"That's wonderful," said Hiro. "But, and Semaya may correct me if I'm wrong, my guess is that Juneso may now consider you a liability to his mission, and a threat to his own personal power. You have demonstrated that Sho'mo'ra will listen to you and not to him, and will act against him on your request. To a man appointed as ambassador, this is humiliating."

Semaya inclined her hairless head, elegant as always. "It is possible, Hiro. Security will be an ongoing concern."

"I have faith in my security," said Lisbeth, with an edge. With a pointed stare at Hiro. Hiro gazed back, warily. Seeing, perhaps, that she was truly past caring what parren politics had to say about it. And that if Juneso wanted to threaten her life, and died for it, then it wouldn't bother her at all.

AFTER DINNER, Skah put on his cold weather coat and gloves, pulled up his hood, took a hot cup of shnu and went out to the verandah. Liala half-sat, her great spider legs curled so that she rested upon the multi-jointed knuckles, body raised mostly from the floor. She glanced sideways, a motion of that over-sized queen's head, mismatched eyes more like a regular drone's. "Hello Skah," she said in perfect Gharkhan. "Do you wish to talk?"

"Yes," said Skah. Liala placed her big left foreleg flat to the ground, and Skah sat upon it, beside her head, and sipped his hot shnu. It tasted nutty. This was the thing that made Liala so different from Styx, Skah thought. Styx would never have made the gesture. Liala was so smart, but she was much younger than he was, while Styx was so much older than anyone else who'd ever lived. "It's sad you can't eat dinner."

"Why is it sad that I can't eat dinner, Skah?" Before them, the snow-covered courtyard shone white in the light of Dul'rho's one silver moon. A military croma trudged across the snow, saw them, and looked amazed. Skah raised a fist to the croma, who raised one back, and called something in Kul'hasa.

"What did he say?" Skah asked. "I don't have my earpiece in."

"He said 'little warrior'," said Liala. "I am not sure why he called you that. Why do you think?" This was the other difference between Liala and Styx. Liala sometimes said she didn't know things, and asked questions. Sometimes Skah thought she might mean it, but other times she was just being polite.

"They always call kids 'little warrior'," said Skah. "And I think he thinks it's cool that I'm sitting with you."

"Why would that be cool?"

"Because you look scary. And I'm only small."

"Do you think I look scary?"

Skah smiled, warming his gloved hands on the cup. "I think you'd look scary if I didn't know you. But I know you're not scary." He frowned. "What were we just talking about? Before the croma walked past?"

"You said it was sad that I couldn't eat dinner," said Liala. "I asked why it was sad."

Now he remembered. "Because food's nice. Don't you want to eat food?"

"The desire for food is an entirely biological urge, Skah. You have that urge because millions of years of evolution have programmed your brain that way. Drysines don't have it."

Skah smiled as he thought of something. "Do you get hungry before you recharge?"

"I only need to recharge when my powerplant is running below optimum and my energy requirements are high. Usually I am entirely energy-sufficient." Skah sighed. One way that Liala was entirely like Styx -- she usually missed the opportunity to share in a joke or a funny idea. Not that she couldn't be funny, she just didn't seem to appreciate anyone *else's* humour. "I think perhaps you mean that you like sitting with your friends by the fire and eating together. You think it's sad that I can't join you."

"Yes!" Skah agreed. "You should have come in."

"There's very little room. I'm quite big."

"There's enough room."

"Humans, parren and kuhsi are all social creatures. Croma too. Organics are programmed to welcome collective company, many of your brains only achieve optimum functionality in the company of others. Drysines are similar, we prefer company also. But we do not require physical proximity to acquire it. Sharing space on a network will do."

"Liala, do you think Lisbeth was right to want to help the corbi?"

"I think there are strategic advantages, as I explained earlier."

Skah shook his head. "No, that's... that's dumb."

"What's dumb, Skah?"

"Strategic advantages." He didn't like those words. They didn't sound right. "I mean, do you think she's right?"

Liala paused. "I'm not sure. What do you mean by 'right'?"

Skah frowned. "Right! You know, right and wrong?"

"I am aware of these terms as organic concepts," said Liala. "Translating them into an operational drysine context is problematic."

"You don't know right and wrong?" Skah asked in dismay.

"I'm increasingly familiar with how various organic beings deploy these concepts. I'm also increasingly aware of how flexible they are, and thus meaningless within any accurate strategic context."

"Right and wrong aren't meaningless!" Skah insisted. "It's your... your strategic context stuff that's meaningless." He was quite sure of that. All the big-scale military calculations he'd seen various people doing were quite heartless, and caused a lot of suffering. It upset him that Liala didn't seem to realise it.

"Skah, drysine logic attempts to be mathematically precise. But a concept like 'right' or 'wrong' does not have any precise mathematical value. If you attempt to perform a mathematical sum with an imprecise value, what happens?"

"It doesn't work," he said impatiently. "But..."

"Exactly," said Liala.

"But you don't need to be good at maths to know that helping the corbi is right!"

Liala paused for a moment. "I'm very impressed with that thought, Skah," she said then. "I think that might be the most advanced sentence I've heard you come up with on your own." Skah blinked. Really? "I understand that saving lives is to be considered good. But what if it starts a war between reeh and parren?"

"Parren are a long way away."

"At the rate the reeh sometimes move, that may not last longer than a few hundred years. What if only half the corbi want to leave

Rando? What if the other half stay, and the reeh decide to kill them all? That would mean a hundred million dead corbi. Is that right?"

"But that's not our fault!"

"This is puzzling logic. You do something, it results in a hundred million deaths, and yet you deny responsibility, even though it would not have happened had you not acted." Skah gulped his drink in frustration. "There are second and third order consequences to things, Skah. Do you know what that means?"

"No."

"It's like the dominos game that Spacer Reddin showed you. One domino falls, which makes another domino fall, and soon a thousand dominos have fallen, even though you only pushed one. You do one thing, which has a good outcome. But that outcome causes other things to happen, which causes other things, which eventually make a large number of things happen that you did not intend. If many of those things are bad, then the many bad things can end up outweighing the one good thing you did earlier."

Skah thought about that long and hard, sipping his shnu. "So you *do* think there's good and bad? Just not right and wrong?"

Liala sighed. That was strange. Styx never did that. And drysines didn't have lungs or vocal cords. "These spoken words are very imprecise, Skah. Drysines see things in three-dimensional constructs. Precise values can be communicated. Words are not precise, and mean different things to different people. To a drysine, words seem like mathematics done with fuzzy numbers. It makes us uncomfortable."

"I know." Styx had complained about it often.

"My point is that in order to be certain that you are 'right' about something, you have to construct a wall around that thing, to shield it from second and third order consequences. Psychologically this may work, but in the real world, second and third order consequences cannot be stopped so easily. Right and wrong then become very problematic. Does this make sense?"

"I think." It didn't, really. But what he was coming to understand was that when you were very smart, all the good, simple things in life became harder to appreciate. Maybe being smart was overrated. "How do you see things in three-dimensional constructs?"

"Drysine psychology can be represented in a construct. We calculate not only what we see, but how we respond to what we see. We then plot those values on a three dimensional model."

"You mean you can change how you think?"

"Yes. Responsiveness to particular stimuli can be altered. Only by queens and high command units, though."

"And you then tell the drones how to think?"

"Yes, sometimes. It's very complicated, and hard to communicate with words. Would you like to see what I mean?"

"Yes!"

"Put on your glasses and I'll show you."

Before he could do so, Lisbeth emerged onto the verandah, tightening her coat, then pulling on her gloves against the chill. Timoshene followed, a tall, dark sentinel, armed beneath his robes. Lisbeth walked to Skah and Liala, looking somber.

"Skah, I've something I want to talk about with you," she said in English.

"Okay," said Skah, repressing that small frustration. Everything was harder in English, especially pronunciation.

"Your mother left you with me because where *Phoenix* is going is too dangerous. I promised I'd keep you with me at all times. But now it looks as though I might be going somewhere dangerous too."

"You can't reave ne here," Skah said with firm frustration. Human adults could be so dumb sometimes, and so predictable. "Nahny towd ne before, towd about this... this thing."

"This argument," Liala said helpfully.

"Yes. Kuhsi stay with cwan. You go to danger, I go to danger."

Lisbeth looked at him very seriously for a moment. Her dark eyes were very serious now, Skah thought. She'd been considered young when he'd first met her. Now, neither of them were. "Skah, Rando is going to be a genuine war zone."

"I've seen war before."

"Children shouldn't be in..."

"Don't be stupid," he cut her off, more annoyed by the moment. "How nany chiwdwen on Rando? Niwions. Chiwdwen are in wars aw the tine."

"Lisbeth," came Liala's calm voice before the human could speak again, "there remains the very real possibility that circumstances will prevent *Phoenix* from coming back through Dul'rho again. This is a croma political center, and however friendly Sho'mo'ra may be, his allies are less so. If Skah stays with you on *Coroset*, a rendezvous or reunion at some point becomes possible. If Skah stays here, he may end up abandoned on Dul'rho indefinitely."

"NO!" Skah shouted. Not the cry of a scared little boy, but the angry shout of an increasingly older, wiser boy who'd seen many things most boys his age had not. His hearing deadened as his ears flattened to his skull, lip curling as his teeth bared. "I'n a spacer! I go with you on *Coroset*. You die, I die." He glared at Lisbeth, as fiercely as he could.

Lisbeth gazed at him for a long moment. The Lisbeth Skah remembered might have gotten teary and hugged him. This one just nodded, sadly. "Very well Skah. You're a warrior now. I'll treat you like one."

"Riara wiw take care of both of us," Skah added, patting Liala's big alloy leg.

"I will try my best, Skah," said Liala. "But you should know that it's dangerous. I cannot guarantee my own safety, let alone yours."

"Everything's dangerous," Skah retorted, sipping his shnu.

8

Jindi collapsed on the shoreline, and for a long time simply lay on his back, and stared at the cloud-streaked sky. The sun was warm, and the sand felt like nothing he'd ever expected to feel again. Like home. Like the sound of wind in the high palms, like the shriek and cry of seabirds, and the gentle roar and hiss of the waves.

After a while, Melu knelt at his side with a water flask, and Jindi forced himself to rise, despite the stabbing pain in his back, and sniff the contents. "There's a stream over there," she said. "Moving water, it seems clean."

Jindi trusted her, and sipped. It tasted stagnant compared to where they'd been, up in the mountains, where the streams were always fresh and the rain frequent. A few of the party had wanted to stay there, but as Jindi had told them, very little grew up high, crops needed sun, not constant cloud and mist. And down by the seaside, if one knew how to collect it, nature's harvest was always in season.

"You did it," said Melu. "You got us all here."

"Not all," said Jindi, gazing about. It looked different from his previous stretch of beach where he'd lived for ten years. This was the north coast — a little warmer, more tropical. He knew less about the fish here, and the other things one could eat in the waters. That could be dangerous sometimes, in the ocean, as there were plenty of poisonous things to kill you. But he was certain he could figure it out. A much better life than digging holes in dirt, anyhow, especially for someone with his bad back.

There was a tall, forested hill to their right, overlooking the ocean. To the left, out west, a distant promontory, with promises of a flat, rocky shelf. Jindi pointed toward it. "That way," he said wearily, despising the thought of yet another step, but liking the grumbling of his stomach even less. "There'll be shellfish out there. Easy food even for farmers. And with a spear, fishing off the shelf is a good way to learn."

"Rest first," said Melu. "The others are collecting water, and there are lukanuts up the palms. You were right about the lukanuts, they're everywhere."

Jindi made a face. "I'm a terrible climber. But I can fish."

"You can do more than fish." She put a hand in his mane. Jindi gazed up at her. Of all the things worth finding on this journey, he hadn't expected *this*. Melu was from Brieva, the other side of Rando, and had only learned Lisha in her Splicer cell from neighbouring corbi. She thought she'd been there about three years. Physically she seemed quite healthy, compared to what the reeh had done to Jindi, but she had a strange way of not visualising anything on her left side, despite her left eye working fine. Her spatial perception simply did not cover that side of her awareness -- objects on that side would be forgotten, and things held by others in their left-facing hand would not be seen. In talking with Jindi, she'd tried to draw a face on the mountain dirt with a stick, and had succeeded only in a semi-circle.

But her coordination seemed fine, and while she was quiet, she was kind, smart and, in an understated way that was growing on Jindi every day, quite pretty. As though *he* had any rights to be demanding in that respect. Two damaged individuals, in a party of damaged corbi. Jindi thought she was perfect, and hoped only that she liked the ocean. She'd said that she'd never seen it before.

"What do you think?" he asked her.

"It's very bright," she said, squinting into the sun. It wasn't quite the endorsement he'd been hoping for. But then, he was so tired himself he'd barely looked at it. Everyone's enthusiasm would go up considerably when they saw the relative ease of food here, and the quality of it.

Jindi levered himself up fully and looked around. Four of the thirty-strong party were wading in the shallows, shoes off, pants rolled up, looking at things in the water. Back along the treeline, some of the younger ones were indeed all the way up a lukanut tree, hacking the big nuts down with machetes. Many hadn't eaten lukanut before either, as they only grew in the sandy coastal soils, and liked lots of sun. In the absence of fresh running water, they were a good source of a healthy drink, too.

Further back in the tree shadow, he spotted the little knot of tanifex, in that odd cluster of lizard-like heads and furtive gestures they made, glancing about at these strange new surroundings. They were a heavily armed party, too, with rifles on their backs and other weapons elsewhere on their synthetic-clothed persons. That had made everyone nervous, because friendly or not, tanifex were certainly not corbi, and they were the only ones with guns. But they'd followed Jindi's lead like the others, mostly for lack of anywhere better to go.

The others were all corbi, most of them former prisoners of the Splicer, and three more survivors of Splicer City, largely destroyed when *Phoenix* had come, and desperate to be elsewhere after guessing what revenge the reeh might take on the general corbi population. Many other Splicer City survivors had stayed, thinking to rebuild, and imagining that the reeh would rebuild as well. The Splicer had stood for as long as anyone could remember, and no matter that it was every evil thing about slavery beneath the reeh, it had also provided a sanctuary of sorts for any corbi desperate enough to take it. The tanifex were quite sure all of those Splicer City corbi who'd remained behind were now dead, and Jindi agreed with them.

On those first terrifying nights away from the Splicer, when the party had made as much distance as possible through the treacherous forest toward the foothills, they'd seen and heard distant strikes, flashes of light reflected on the cloud, and the echo of huge, distant explosions. In the foothills themselves, they'd found the burning remains of a village, but there were thankfully no bodies within. The tanifex's coms units heard *Phoenix*'s warnings, on all available frequencies, for corbi to abandon their villages and run for the forests. But then, any village within earshot of the Splicer strike could have guessed trouble.

Several times on the trails they'd encountered other corbi — small bands carrying children and a few belongings, and had travelled with some for a time. One of those groups had not yet heard of the Splicer's destruction, and had struggled to believe it, even from self-professed witnesses. Another group claimed to have been middle-distant from a reeh base when a giant spear of light had slashed down from the sky, followed by the brightest light and loudest boom anyone had ever heard. A number of corbi had been blinded and deafened, and others spoke of forests flattened to a smoking carpet of ruin.

That had been *Phoenix*, on the same high-velocity attack run that had destroyed the Splicer, and a few corbi had muttered that *Phoenix* was no friend to the corbi, having rained such death and destruction down upon them all. Others had retorted that it was the reeh who were actually killing corbi, and no wonder no one else had come to save the corbi when doing so only brought complaints and ingratitude. Jindi had wondered sadly what it said about his people that even in the midst of such awfulness, they could still find time to aim threats and accusations at each other.

In the mountains, the reeh had finally done the thing Jindi had most dreaded, and driven a number of the party crazy. But on his instruction, they'd been expecting it, and knew which were most likely to be susceptible by listening to their stories of what had been done to them. He'd insisted that they be honest, promising not to simply kill and discard any who proved 'turned', but to bring them along, restrained if necessary. Four had tried, but all were tackled before they could do serious damage. The worst, a woman named

Raji, had managed to stab herself in the leg instead, and they'd carried her in the mountains until she'd finally expired from loss of blood. But the tanifex in particular had proven useful for keeping watch during the day, when everyone slept, given that tanifex needed less than half as much sleep as corbi did. When Biku had gone for a machete during the day, with most of the party asleep, it had been Krisik, the leader of the tanifex, who slipped in behind and put Biku out cold in a choke hold. After a day of being carried in restraints, the blinding headaches of those that had turned had finally gone, and they'd been released, though cautiously. So far they'd not tried to kill anyone else, and Dogi, who claimed the most knowledge of such things, opined that the signal, if survived, could not be used frequently.

Jindi finally got them all moving westward along the beach, keeping beneath the treeline and away from the open sand. Neither he nor the village he'd lived near on his old beach had had any problems with reeh surveillance until Major Thakur had arrived. But with the Splicer recently dead, the reeh were going to be pricklish, and a group moving along an obvious sandy beach in the open could have attracted anything.

He couldn't quite believe that he was here. All his life, he'd dreamed of some sort of peace. He thought he'd found it, with Keku, Dala and Pandi, but the reeh had come to murder them, and take him to the hell of the Splicer. He hadn't wanted to go back, hadn't wanted revenge, had just wanted to find something of the peace they'd brought him, little Dala following him around in the fields, asking him curious questions, while Keku gathered water from the stream with Pandi bound on her back. He'd thought to find that peace again as best he could on a beach, learning to live from the waves and rocks and sand. Keku had never wished to hurt a soul, and his children had barely understood what anger was. To join the Resistance, and go hunting for revenge, would have been to destroy what little memory he had left of their kindness, and of the person that he'd been.

But then the reeh had come again, and killed his second village, and left him with no choice. He hadn't been expecting to succeed, just to find some less humiliating way to die without doing it himself. But the crazy human Thakur and her ship had somehow accomplished the impossible, and despite his best attempts to die well, Jindi had somehow emerged from the Splicer for a second time, and left it in ruins.

It had stuck him with responsibilities, and all he could think to do was to try and share with these new family all that he'd learned for himself, living on the beach, finding what small enjoyments one could still derive from life on a world occupied by a genocidal tyranny that turned all they touched to ash. And so now here he was again, back on a beach... but it was not the same. The beach was different, the reeh were a lot more angry, and there were many more lives resting on this whole venture than just his own.

As Jindi walked beneath groves of lukanut trees beside the sand, his arm around Melu for support, he saw Chibo and Damo ahead, gesturing that someone else was present. Amid the tree trunks, a small camp was rising, strange corbi looking their way, assessing these new arrivals. Some had rifles, and some of those, Jindi judged, a kind of military bearing. Resistance.

Chibo and Damo made way for Jindi, their leader. Jindi did not like that, but it was simply how things were, now. The lead Resistance man had streaks of white through his mane, and wore a sleeveless jacket, muscular arms bare. Behind him were five others, all with some kind of weapon. Their campsite was just a few rucksacks used for cushions on the sand, and the empty shells of cracked lukanuts. Jindi doubted they'd been stupid enough to try a fire, here by the beach.

"You're Jindi?" said the Resistance man.

Jindi blinked. "That's right," he said warily. "Who are you?"

"Chuta," said the Resistance man. His accent was local. There was something in his manner that Jindi did not like. Something edgy and high strung, like a man recently frightened. But that was another reason Jindi had never liked the Resistance — they were full of people like that. "I heard word you were travelling with tanifex."

Other Resistance soldiers looked past Jindi, into the middle of his party of corbi. Jindi turned to look as well, and saw no tanifex. It did not surprise him — Krisik was no fool. But Krisik was dangerous, too, and Chuta was in more danger than he knew. "They're rebels against the reeh," Jindi explained. It had been enough for most corbi they'd encountered. "They helped destroy the Splicer."

Chuta's weapon remained on his shoulder, but the others of his party had them in hand. Chuta was not big, but thrust his chest out, almost awkwardly, as though he had something to prove. Or no, Jindi thought. More like he was scared, and trying to intimidate civilians into respecting him.

"Killing the Splicer only made things worse," he said. "The whole system's crawling with reeh now. Their ships are everywhere."

"We haven't seen anything," said Chibo.

"Not down here," said Chuta, annoyed at the civilian's naivety. "Up there." A gesture up, at the blue sky. "Spaceships everywhere. They're saying it's going to be an attack."

Jindi's group stared at him, and at each other. "An attack from who?" Dogi asked.

"Has to be the croma," said Chuta. "They're certainly not coming to help us, so probably it'll be a big space battle. This world has no high-V approach defences, so probably we'll get smashed by high-V ordnance and wreckage if it's big enough." He took another few steps toward Jindi. "Word is you helped the human to attack the Splicer?"

Melu tried to reverse Jindi up a step, but Jindi's back hurt too much to bother with unnecessary movements. 'A cripple's bravery', he'd described it before. "That's right," he said. He liked the look in Chuta's eyes even less, now that he saw them at close range. Fear made people do stupid things.

"What made you think a human knew what was best for this world?" Chuta asked, with aggression born of helplessness. Spite, for the things he could not change.

"I didn't know that she did," said Jindi.

"So you did what she said anyway?"

"It wasn't just her. It was Tano, a Fleet officer."

"Fleet are just as bad as the aliens!" Chuta shouted. "They *are* aliens! They don't know this world! They want this world to die so they can go off and find another!"

"What kind of a Resistance man thinks that blowing up the Splicer is a bad idea?" Shidi interjected from behind. Shidi was a hot head, always first to lose his temper. "You're a coward!"

"Who said that?" one of Chuta's soldiers demanded, stepping forward.

"I did!" Shidi snarled. "Most of us were imprisoned in that hell hole, having reeh experiments done on us, and you want to leave us there! Jindi got us out! Where were you?"

"And how many of you did he get out?" Chuta's angry soldier retorted. "I heard that most of you died!"

"And better that, trying to escape, than spend another day in that place!"

Jindi's head hurt, throbbing in time with his back. He held up both hands, wishing he had Thakur or Tano's magical power to command people to his will. But Thakur and Tano had been warriors, while he'd been nothing more than a farmer, a prisoner, and then a fisherman and cripple. Behind him, others of his people were joining the argument, some with much fear of Chuta's guns, but others with far too little, having suffered too much in reeh hands to care.

"People!" he said loudly. "We can't fight amongst ourselves. It's bad enough that we have to fight reeh, but if we fight amongst ourselves, we're all finished." Chuta glared at him, but said nothing as the noise quietened. "I'm a fisherman. I taught myself to fish, long ago. I can teach you all to survive on this beach. It's a much better life than farming. It's hard work, but the food is good, and I'm in no condition to dig holes and pull ploughs. The same with many of us."

"Chuta," Melu said quietly from behind him. "Won't you join us? Jindi says there's lots of food in the sea."

"I was told to bring you back to my commanders," Chuta said stubbornly.

"And where are they?" Damo demanded.

"Back in Raka by the river."

"That's ten days walk!" Damo said angrily. "We've just been walking for sixty days!"

"I'm not going," Jindi said tiredly. "I won't fight you. None of us are soldiers. But I'm not going." From somewhere down by his shoulder, something buzzed. One of *Phoenix*'s drysine bugs had stayed with him since the Splicer. Sometimes during the day he'd seen it nearby, as though letting him know it was near. Jindi knew that it was lethal. He didn't know how it could identify threats, in situations like this. Between the bug, and Krisik's tanifex, Jindi doubted that he and his corbi were the ones truly in danger.

One of Chuta's soldiers had a hand to his ear, expression incredulous as he received some transmission. "Chuta!" he exclaimed. "Chuta, I'm receiving something!"

Chuta frowned at him, and fumbled for his own earpiece. No one in the Resistance transmitted openly, doing so would bring a reeh missile on your head in short order. "Who's transmitting? Is it reeh?"

"No, it's... it says it's the Resistance! They say they're here with the croma!"

People stared. It was craziness, the most impossible dream of fools and cloud worshippers for hundreds of years. Chuta got his earpiece in, and listened. After some listening, he looked baffled. "It's an open frequency, they're not even being jammed... how can this... this has to be some sort of trick."

"What are they saying?" Shidi demanded.

"They're saying they're here with a croma fleet." Chuta clearly didn't believe a word of it. It was impossible. "That they're attacking all the reeh ships in the system, and after they've cleared them out, they're..." He trailed off, staring at his fellow soldiers. "They're going to evacuate Rando. All corbi. Millions of us."

"It's a trick!" one of Chuta's soldiers snarled. "They're going to lure us into the open, then kill us!"

"Look!" shouted Biku, pointing out to sea. High in the blue sky, something was glowing. Slower moving than a shooting star, it moved from south to north, heading out to sea, a scatter of burning fragments as something from space came falling to its death. Even as they watched, a flash, and the fragments scattered again, tumbling.

"That was in orbit!" Chuta gasped. "Incoming ships at attack velocity are much faster than that! That was in orbit... that's reeh! That has to be reeh, they shot it down!"

More yells, and pointing directly overhead. Above the high cloud, a second long comet tail of flaming pieces was streaking, as though someone had taken a fistful of glitter and thrown it across the sky. From the corbi, there were shrieks and screams, but this time of joy. Some embraced with excitement and disbelief, hostilities forgotten. Jindi sat down on the sand, with Melu at his side, and watched the show.

"Do you think they're really coming?" Melu asked him.

"I think," said Jindi, "that someone is very determined to keep me from living on a beach." He put his arm around her shoulders. "We'll be okay. We'll get through it. I promise you."

IT WAS Lisbeth's first combat jump on a warship bridge. She reached to her drinking tube for a sip, not willing to risk a grab for the drinking bottle lest some sudden manoeuvre rip it from her hand. The crew of *Coroset* talked calmly, barely visible amidst the cramped bridge clutter, wrapped in their multi-screen posts, faces hidden behind helmet visors.

Lisbeth kept her own visor up, and looked at her screens. From her time as an assault shuttle navigator, she had a very good idea of what she was looking at, only the range of *Coroset*'s sensors, plus the speed of their approach, pushed the active horizon far further away than most shuttle crews had to worry about.

Ahead was Rando, approaching fast. At current speeds they'd be impacting the upper atmosphere in twelve minutes, and killing all life on the surface as they did. Three hundred kilometres to *Coroset*'s flank was *Amity*, Liala's warship, and the only drysine ship to have not departed with Styx. As the two highest performance ships in the entire Rando operation, they'd made jump with navcomputers linked. *Coroset*'s Navigation Officer had been concerned at the manoeuvre, but looking at the screens now, course and velocity seemed in perfect alignment.

The rest of the transportation escort was coming out of jump behind them, a rapid multiplication of plots on scan. Lisbeth had only seen its like once before -- at Argitori, more than two years ago now, when she'd been on the bridge with Erik after their crazy flight from Homeworld, and watching the Human Fleet jumping into system behind the renegade vessel in pursuit. Erik had seen this many times before -- a combat jump, with large formations winking into high-V existence as they plunged down the gravity slope. Lisbeth blinked her eyes clear as her head swam from jump, and her stomach rebelled at the liquid she was sipping.

Ahead, Scan's three-dimensional display revealed a multi-track swarm of converging ships, at least sixty strong, most of those on the croma side. Already there were some large explosions, Scan registering those as ship kills, three in total, one of them friendly. Hundreds of smaller detonations and more by the second, as incoming and outgoing ordnance exchanged and hit defensive spreads with a crackle like strings of fireworks at Deliverance.

Another lurch as *Coroset* dumped V, and Lisbeth's stomach tried to leap out her mouth. She swallowed hard as her eyes came clear once more, screens showing V much lower, Armscomp trading and tracking targets with *Amity*, but holding fire for now with too many friendly first wave ships in their path. Some low-orbit firestations had blown and were now spreading debris across Rando's upper atmosphere. That would be quite a show for corbi on the ground. The reeh had a number of close-in firestations, their purpose mostly to defend the planet from long-range ordnance, as firing at manoeuvring warships from so deep down the gravity-well would be ineffective.

"Hello Lisbeth," came Liala's voice on her personal coms. *"Could you please inform croma vessels to kill no more of the defensive fire stations? We*

had agreed that I could acquire control of them myself, but someone appears to have forgotten."

"Of course Liala," said Lisbeth. The firestations would prove handy for the second phase of the operation, and Liala's signal, amplified by an entire invasion fleet, could have them all working for the invaders once they were close enough to kill latency. Probably some croma captain had reconsidered the threat in the spur of the moment, and eliminated several. Lisbeth selected Coms Two on her screens. "Hello Coms, please relay a message from Liala to all croma captains to eliminate no more of the low-orbiting firestations. They are vital to the mission's second phase."

"Affirmative," said Yalu, the second Coms Officer. Liala's difficulty was that none of the croma captains would take her commands, understandably wary of her capabilities, and no doubt her loyalties. They would listen to suggestions from aliens who were not machines, however, leading to these highly inefficient, relayed communications through Lisbeth.

Behind them, the plots on Scan continued to multiply. She'd known the invasion fleet would be large, but she could scarcely believe the size of it. These were the transports, following immediately behind the tip of the spear. Hitting with the first wave, then waiting for ships to jump back to the rally point and send word that the first wave had been successful, would take days. By the time the transports finally jumped in, precious time would be lost, and the reeh's own counter-attack would be underway, rendering those first 'all clears' irrelevant. Thus a big mixed-purpose assault like this had to be done all at once, transports following immediately behind warships and hoping the defences would not be overwhelming. Turning big transports around from a high-V run, if things turned bad, could take a while. At least this way, if the first assault did fail, the transports would know it immediately.

It wasn't likely, though. Looking ahead, Lisbeth could see twenty-three marked reeh ships in various stages of retreat, laying down heavy fire for the onrushing croma to run into, and now manoeuvring for better position on the G-slope before pulsing jump engines for V and accelerating away. It was the usual way to defend across a wide front in a major war -- defenders never knew where the attackers were going to concentrate their forces, and so kept the forward defences relatively light, and their reserves large. These defenders would now jump away, giving the attackers relatively free reign for a few days at least, until the defenders came back with their reserve reinforcements. Then, when the reeh understood exactly what the croma were doing, the real fighting would start.

TIGA GULPED a long swig of electrolyte water, strapped in her bridge observer chair on the Resistance vessel *Yoma*, and stared at the unfolding craziness before her. Four hours after first system entry, the transports were arriving in orbit, the first big transport shuttles departing for the Rando surface. There were twenty-five in the first wave, and even now the second wave were arriving from jump, multiplying rapidly into forty-plus ships. The idea was to not have all two hundred and sixty one Sto'ji Class transports arriving at the same time, or things would get far too crowded, not to mention vulnerable to reeh assault. They'd spread them out over several days, whatever the temptation to crush them all in as soon as possible, and attempt to maintain a steady flow of ships coming and going.

Amidst the enormous Sto'ji Class were smaller ships, civilian transports, usually privately owned and volunteering for this dangerous mission as a matter of honour, much the same as croma civilians would volunteer to fight in a Tali'san. Some of those had their own shuttles, but others did not, and would be relying on excess shuttles brought on the first Sto'ji Class to keep ferrying evacuees once their transports had left. Their capacities were far less than the crazy numbers the Sto'ji whales could pile into their holds, but every person counted.

Tiga's displays now showed all the evacuation zones to which the shuttles were departing. There would be little reeh opposition -- the remaining reeh surface bases had vanished in enormous mushroom clouds once Liala had disabled the close orbital Rando defences. Certainly there were reeh forces now hiding in forests or caves, and not showing up on orbital surveillance, but no one thought they'd be too much trouble. Reeh Empire forces did not waste their best troops on backwater frontier worlds like Rando.

Tiga stared at her displays, at the great, curving horizon of the corbi homeworld, and felt her stomach twisting in some demon combination of anxiety and excitement. She couldn't believe she was here, from where her ancestors had departed 200 years ago in their attempts to venture beyond the Croma Wall, and plead with the Spiral for help. They'd been intercepted by Croma'Dokran instead, and given the choice to stay on the Croma'Dokran homeworld, or return to Rando. Only now, two centuries later, had this long-distant relative finally taken Croma'Dokran up on their offer.

Rando had four major continents and three minor ones. The splicer had been on Talo, which Tiga's models had shown to have the highest population -- somewhere around sixty million, they thought. Then came northern Rojo with forty million, then long, mountainous Jadsi with perhaps twenty-five, connecting to southerly Punia with another twenty million. The rest were scattered over numerous island archipelagoes, containing the three minor continents too large to be considered just islands. No one had any real idea how good the Resistance's figures truly were, as corbi spacers had little interest in the planetary census. If they'd significantly undercounted, a lot of corbi were going to be left to die.

"Tiga," came a voice on her coms. *"It's Vero, I'm down at the shuttle."*

"Vero, what's happening?"

"Look, Gusi didn't come out of jump so well, she's sick."

"Sick? What, like jump sickness?"

"It looks like that, she's in the medbay. Someone from senior analysis has to go down on the shuttle, Tiga. Feel like volunteering?"

"Of course! I'll be down immediately... I'll get Richep to cover for me, hang on."

She arranged it, informed the Captain, then scrambled down the crew cylinder, which had restarted for gravity now that initial fears of combat manoeuvring had faded, and up ladders to the zero-G core. A fast transition down the narrow zip-line to midships, then more overhanding through cramped zero-G storage, where cargo from shuttles was lashed with steel nets.

At the berth was Vero, impatient with a flight helmet and webbing with flight safety gear, the workings of which Tiga was only passingly familiar with. She took it, squeezed through the open airlock and into the shuttle's dorsal hatch, and emerged forward of the big, empty cargo hold before rapping on the cockpit pressure door. The flight engineer let her in, and she took the single observation chair behind the pilot's seat, while the engineer squeezed into his forward seat. Vest on over her jumpsuit, oxygen attachment into the seat rig, then testing the mask on her helmet, barely thinking that she was about to go down to the surface, and there were still reeh down there in some reasonable numbers, and that the reality with all this safety equipment was that if something bad happened, it would be most likely useless and she'd die.

She strapped herself in, listening to coms chatter as her chair screens came live -- a simple navigation view and a rearward look at the cargo hold, with cameras and sensors. Out of the canopy, she saw nothing -- they were in low orbit on Rando's night side. Coms chatter did not sound nearly as professional as it had on *Phoenix*, and Tiga recalled that the humans had been elite. This ship, and the entire corbi Resistance Fleet, far less so. Some of the display screens had scratches on them like children had been using them for games, and the seat harness ends were frayed with decades of decay.

A clank, and the grapples released. A short burst of attitude thrust, then the mains kicked in -- not a de-orbit burn, but an orbital adjustment onto their new trajectory. It occurred to Tiga further that rendezvous in low orbit weren't always easy or convenient, and that this shuttle would probably make several trips before it got a chance to return to *Yoma* again. She was going to be in this machine for a while.

She managed to get her bridge post's functions onto the chair screen, ignoring the ongoing burn to see exactly where the first shuttle wave was at. Many of them were in the atmosphere now -- big An'ji Class shuttles that could hold two hundred croma marines at a time, and were estimated to hold eight hundred frightened corbi civilians. This one was an old corbi design, originally dating back to Rando's golden age before the fall, now copied and manufactured at some small Fleet facility where they hid such things. Probably its capacity was about the same as a *Phoenix* shuttle, and could hold about a hundred corbi. *Coroset* too, she noted, was launching both of its shuttles. *Amity* was not. The only things the drysine ship carried that in any way resembled a shuttle were what the humans called Arrowheads -- AI-driven flying wings that moulded to the ship's sides and released to provide a fire-support platform for dismounted drones. Drones, of course, needed no shuttles to transport them through space -- they had modular engine mounts for that.

Soon the de-orbit burn came, then there was a long, bumping and glowing reentry. They emerged at dawn over the continent of Jadsi, which had once been eleven great corbi kingdoms, where literature, science and maths had first emerged thousands of years ago before spreading to the rest of Rando. Tiga's eye picked the locations where great old cities had once stood -- here Igo with its early towers, and there Ansa with its famed canals upon the Yuba Sea, where early shipping trade had spread civilisation across to the Shendo Archipeligo, and out across the Yuval Ocean. And she recalled those lessons as a girl, sitting at her father's knee, and seeing all the pictures, and watching the old movies recalled from Resistance archives. And suddenly it struck her, for perhaps the first time, truly what this evacuation fleet was here to do. The corbi were leaving their home. All of this history, swept away and left behind. And she was shocked at the strength of her own dismay.

The morning sun gleamed gold upon the sea, shining like polished brass as they rattled and bumped above the Jadsi mountains. Upon the plains to the mountains' east, banks of white cloud like a field of snow. Tiga listened to the coms messages now being broadcast across Rando, but they were in local Pulan here, not Lisha, and she'd never learned the tongue. But she knew what it said because she'd been in the room when it had been written.

"People of Rando," it said. *"Our time has come. The corbi Resistance has gathered a great fleet, with the assistance of the new ruler of the croma, Sho'mo'ra of Croma'Dokran. We are here to evacuate all corbi to a far better place. In that place, there will be no reeh. The reeh will not shoot you, starve you, abduct you or torture you. You will be safe, and you will be free. Join with us, and our croma brothers and sisters, and together we will build a future for our children, and their children, of peace and happiness for all the centuries to come.*

"We ask that you make your way with all possible haste to the following coordinates. Evacuation zones will be designated closest to your current location. We understand that this journey will be hard for many of you, but we do not have the ships to meet you where you are -- you must come to us. We anticipate that we will be at Rando for thirty days. This time may be cut short, as the reeh will try to stop us. If you are late, you will miss the ship. If you miss the ship, you will almost certainly die. Please listen now for your local coordinates, and plan your journey to this location as soon as you can gather adequate supplies. Peace be upon you, and good luck to us all."

The shuttle began to vibrate more heavily as it hit the lower atmosphere, Gs from that deceleration pulling the crew's heads forward. Then the white field of clouds rose up and engulfed them, as the pilot talked to flight control, and received an update from an overhead croma vessel that the evacuation zone looked clear of reeh activity.

After a lot more bumping through the clouds, the shuttle finally broke free above a rolling landscape of forests and lakes. The evacuation zone was by one such lake, where there was a clearing in the trees, the foundations of some old city preventing the forest from reclaiming large patches of old ground. Suddenly Tiga was struck by a new panic. What if no one showed up? She knew from Resistance reports that many on Rando were accustomed to their lives here, harsh as those lives were, and were attached to the places of their birth. Even she could feel it, this mystical pull of the homeworld, of the place where all corbi were from, that had nurtured the species for a hundred thousand generations and given them all they required. It was not Rando's fault that the reeh had come. And now her people were being asked to abandon her, for the dubious intentions of the croma, who had already abandoned them once, and left them to suffer beneath the reeh occupation for eight hundred years.

The pilot banked into a low turn about the forest clearing. The cockpit canopy did not extend far enough back to grant Tiga a clear look, but the underside camera mount gave her a view of the clearing, wet with recent rain in the misty early morning. For a moment it looked deserted, and Tiga's heart sank. Then she noticed some movement on a treeline, as the camera's automation spotted it also, and zoomed. Small figures amid the trees, peering upward in trepidation. For all their lives, big vehicles that roared overhead had spelt death. To show themselves here took an act of enormous courage, and greater hope.

"I see them," said the pilot. *"We are on approach."* The bank grew tighter, then the engine nacelles angled forward, the shuttle rearing nose-high, then settling with a shriek as it approached a spot between lone trees, the field of grass rushing and flapping in the jetblast.

They touched, and then Tiga was unbuckling, nearly yanking her head as she forgot the oxygen connection in her haste, paused to undo it, then rushed to open the cockpit pressure door. A pop in her ears as the pressure equalised, down the short engineering passage, then into the rear hold, already opening onto the cool Rando morning, both loadmasters peering out beyond the ramp.

One of the loadmasters saw something, and began waving. Then Tiga saw them, past the raised ridges of some old city foundation, overgrown with vines and grass. Corbi villagers, some hauling bags, others baskets, and some with children. There were old folks clutching the hands of their younger relatives, and a few tough-looking adults with homemade firearms or machetes.

Tiga stood at the top of the ramp and watched as they came, open-mouthed with some extraordinary conflict of excitement, fear and dismay. For seventy days now they'd been just numbers, figures in the sums of logistical simulations her people in Agid'roi had run over and over again, with the help of croma experts. And now that she was here, she saw that they were families. Lives uprooted as they came to the ramp, grieving for all they were losing yet desperate with hope that what lay ahead would be better.

She met them on the ramp, as the engine howl declined far enough that talking became possible. Pulled on her headset, and said to the first of them, "Where are you from? What village and how many of you?" As the little speaker on her belt squawked at them in Pulan.

An older man with homemade, wire rim glasses shouted back at her, and her earpiece said in Lisha, *"Avala Village! And Hambo Village, across the Rina River!"*

"Avala and Hambo, right," Tiga repeated, pulling her visor down to see the shuttle computer seize those names and highlight them -- the carefully compiled database recognised Avala, but not Hambo. "How many people in Avala and Hambo?" At the base of the ramp, a line of corbi assembled, peering up at her with fear and anxiety. As though wondering if somehow they'd all be denied passage after all, and their journey had all been in vain.

"Avala three hundred and fifty! Hambo nearly two hundred! We're not far, there's other villages much further but this is their nearest landing zone..."

An older woman pushed forward, her head wrapped in a work-worn scarf, gardening gloves on her hands to protect from the ropes of the basket she carried. *"I've got two brothers and their families in Sinto Village, it's another four days' walk over that way!"* she said. *"You have to come back for them, there's nearly five hundred in the village and they won't be able to make it here for days! They've a good radio in the village, Ambaki's very good with his radio, there's no way he'll have missed your message, I'm sure he's going to come..."*

Tiga held up both hands in reassurance. "We're going to be making many trips!" she assured them. "There are many shuttles and many ships, I just need you to tell me what villages are in this area and what their populations are so we can get a good idea of who's coming! Now please, get on board... we've only got room for about one hundred on this trip..."

"Only one hundred?" the man asked in dismay. *"There's... look, we're well over two hundred now, I know there are more coming from my village alone..."*

"That's fine, they can get the next shuttle, there'll be another one soon."

"Dad!" said a young man, pushing up as others moved past up the ramp and into the hold. *"Dad, I'll stay and tell the others what's happening! Otherwise they'll arrive here and won't know what do to, or if there's another shuttle coming!"*

"Are you sure?" his father asked. He looked both fearful and proud.

The young man nodded fiercely. *"Dad, someone has to stay behind and tell them, and get them organised. I'll catch the next one up, I promise."*

Father and son embraced, and the young man went back down the ramp to tell the rest of his family in line. "Recorder," Tiga instructed the computer against the lump in her throat, "record Sinta Village, four days walk, nearly five hundred people, they have a good radio." As the speech recognition converted it all into data and fed it into the system. All across Rando, landing crews would be doing the same, the Resistance had made sure there was going to be at least one corbi on each downward shuttle, if only so that locals weren't scared away by the sight of aliens. Soon enough, they'd be finding out just how wrong their previous intelligence had been, and thus how badly their plans were about to fall short.

A young woman ascending the ramp grasped her arm. Tiga saw that she had many bangles of shiny wooden beads, lovingly crafted. On her back, a bag packed with all the possessions she had in the world, including some paint brushes, tucked into one side pocket. In her other hand, she clutched the hand of a young boy, perhaps a brother. *"Where are we going?"* she asked fearfully. *"Do you know?"*

"It's a croma world," Tiga told her. "It's called His'do. They've set aside a lot of land for you, I've seen it, it's large and it's pretty."

"And there's no reeh there?"

"No," Tiga smiled. "There's no reeh. You'll be safe there. No more fear." The girl hugged her, then took her brother's hand once more and shuffled along with the crowd now filling the hold. Loadmasters showed them how to sit on the racks of seats that unfolded from the ceiling along great beams, doubling up so thickly with the max capacity loadout that it left little room for even corbi to squeeze between. Possessions were loaded into the netting along the walls, and debates had with some about what possessions were necessary. The villagers would win most of those -- the weight wasn't an issue, the thing that limited passenger numbers was available seats and restraints, non-optional when heading to orbit and potentially under fire. And besides, there was an eight day journey ahead once the transports left orbit, and personal blankets, food and even entertainment would not be unwelcome.

The crowd halted when the loadmasters said they were full, and that division separated some families, leading to individuals opting to stay behind and await the next shuttle, opening spaces for others. When finally all was done, Tiga took an image on her visor camera of the crowd waiting at the base of the ramp, disappointed but hopeful, and uploaded that to the evacuation zone database as well. The next pilots down would see that, and be convinced that they weren't wasting their time coming here. If the villagers were correct, there'd be enough for at least one big An'ji Class shuttle here, possibly more when the outlying villages began arriving. Compared to that load, this trip was a drop in the ocean... but every drop counted, and time was short.

"We're nearly done!" one of the loadmasters was shouting into coms as the engines fired back up, hustling along the rows of temporary seating to double check straps that secured villagers who'd never even flown before, let alone gone into space. Children proved a particular problem, the second loadmaster arguing with a mother that her arms were no substitute for a proper harness once the Gs hit. "Three more minutes!"

Tiga made her way up the narrow remaining space between bulging cargo nets full of rustic possessions, and tightly packed villagers, then up the engineering corridor to the cockpit door and closed it behind.

"How's it looking back there?" the pilot asked her, craning around his seat to see.

"It's tight," Tiga said, buckling herself back in. "There's plenty more coming, this zone is well and truly open. How's it looking out there?" Indicating out beyond the canopy, and upward.

"No sign of reeh resistance so far, no one's been shot down. Let's hope it lasts."

SKAH RAN on the treadmill until exhausted, putting in short, three minute bursts at high speed until his lungs felt like they were about to explode. He got off the treadmill, which was immediately taken by a parren crewman, who nodded with appreciation. Skah nodded back, that little half-bow the parren did all the time that was kind of fun once you got used to it.

The parren were so polite how they used the gym, everyone moving efficiently about the narrow space between support pylons and secured equipment. Everyone just seemed to know whose turn it was, without any lines or other organisation that Skah could see. Skah gulped water, and received an appreciative gesture from a parren also resting between sets. They were all impressed by how fast he could run at his age. Kuhsi were made for sprinting, and all the parren on the treadmills were running painfully slow. The difference, Skah knew, was that parren could keep it up for a long time, being hairless like humans, only far slimmer. Kuhsi overheated much faster, and weren't built for distance anyway. But if there were a sprinting competition between all the Spiral peoples, kuhsi would win *everything*.

Skah put some water on his head, refilled his bottle from the water cooler, and went through the partition hatch to the adjoining gym room. Here were mats, crowded with parren crew fighting, wrestling, flipping or scrambling on the ground. They were so fast,

Skah thought, keeping to one wall as he headed to where Hiro and Timoshene were sparring. Some of the parren had wooden sticks they were using to simulate knives, and the air was filled with cracking wood, gasps, cries that accompanied strikes, and the thuds of bodies hitting mats.

Hiro and Timoshene did not seem so much to be fighting as talking. The taller, slimmer parren was clad in a tight jumpsuit rather than his planetside robes, which were impractical in space, and now grabbed Hiro's arm, his shoulder and body angling for leverage in a takedown. But rather than finishing the move, he and Hiro talked about it, like experts discussing some interesting thing, or like Skah had seen Engineering crew on *Phoenix* talking about a technical problem. Marines did this too, with training moves. Skah thought it was so much smarter than how dumb movies in *Phoenix*'s entertainment database showed it -- all swaggering heroes beating each other up. To get that good at stuff, you first had to actually learn it, like this. The more he saw of it, the more interesting Skah found the difference between how regular people thought things worked, and how the real experts knew they worked.

Timoshene finally finished the move, sweeping Hiro's leg, taking him down and pinning an arm. Hiro tapped briefly, and Timoshene helped him back up, all business. "Hey kid," said Hiro to Skah, "hold out your hand, I want to show you something."

He pulled his AR glasses from a wall pouch and flipped them briefly over his eyes, as Skah held out a hand. Hiro tapped a couple of invisible icons in the air before him, and with a faint buzz, an assassin bug landed on Skah's palm. Timoshene watched impassively, pulling his facemask up for long enough to sip from a bottle.

"That one's yours," said Hiro. "It's programmed to look after you, it'll recognise you and follow you around. You'll just need a UV lamp in your quarters so it can recharge..."

"Got one," Skah affirmed, gazing at the little mechanical insect. "Can I tew it what to do?"

"Ah, no." Hiro gave an amused look to Timoshene. The blue-eyed parren was impassive. All these parren must have thought humans and kuhsi were over-expressive, Skah thought, giving far too much away with their faces. It must have looked so strange to them, these endlessly face-pulling aliens. "Well, you can, but it won't always listen."

"Why not?"

"Because I reckon it probably has a better idea how to defend you than you do. And I don't want you to tell it to kill people when you're angry."

"I wouldn't!" Skah retorted, but he knew Hiro wasn't being serious. Or not mostly.

"Boy," said Timoshene, as Skah's earpiece translated that to Gharkhan. The tall parren crouched before him. *"Our Ambassador Juneso is not pleased to be here. It was his task to bring Lisbeth to see Sho'-mo'ra, and to escort Liala to meet Styx, but now he feels Lisbeth has manipulated him into this Rando conflict. Do you understand?"*

Skah nodded, sipping his bottle. "Juneso is House Harmony, but he's Tookrah Denomination," he replied, also in Gharkhan. "They don't like Domesh very much. So you think he might not like us either."

Hiro elbowed Timoshene. "See, I told you he'd get it."

"So," said the parren, *"I monitor our local security network with Hiro and Semaya. Teselde and Shormas are on it as well. This is our team on the Coroset, do you understand?"*

Skah nodded. "So all the bugs on this ship talk to each other?"

"Yes."

"Can't Liala watch Juneso for us? She's so good with networks she'll know if there's a threat before we do, even from *Amity*."

Timoshene's indigo eyes flashed briefly above his mask. Certainly not a smile, Timoshene didn't do that. But maybe amusement. *"Smart boy. This is already happening. Talk to Liala. Liala likes you. She is preoccupied by many things in this system. I will be happier if she is reminded that your safety is also her responsibility."*

Skah frowned. "Liala likes everyone."

Timoshene put a hand on Skah's shoulder. *"Liala is a drysine queen. Drysine queens like no one. But she has her interests and her projects. For Styx, and for Liala, those interests include you."*

"Interests?"

"Kid," Hiro interrupted, "*Phoenix* crew have this theory that Styx has been using you to observe how young organic brains work. She's never paid much attention to children before. That's why she's bothering to help with your lessons."

"How can they tell the difference?" Skah said stubbornly, still in Gharkhan. Let Hiro worry about earpiece translations for a change. "Styx helps my lessons because she likes me. *Phoenix* crew call it something else. Maybe she wants me to get smarter. What's the difference between that and liking someone? Styx is an alien AI. Using spoken words to talk about her is dumb."

Hiro looked faintly incredulous. Even Timoshene looked quite impressed. *"Smart boy,"* he repeated.

"Styx has talked to you about this, hasn't she?" Hiro pressed.

Skah shrugged. "Maybe," he said defiantly. "Doesn't mean I don't know what I'm talking about."

"No it doesn't," Hiro agreed. "Anyway, do what Timoshene says, report anything odd or suspicious to either of us, and talk to Liala, because I bet Liala's got enough brainspace left to talk back to you, even here. Just leave Lisbeth alone, because I'm pretty sure she won't."

9

Taj awoke to rough pillows and the soot-stained view of Meujaza Canyon through the glass. Hell of a thing to wake up to every morning, leaden skies and a seething torrent of cruisers, fliers, bikes and haulers. The glass vibrated to the throb of so many engines, and from the warm gusts of polluted air from the industrial depths. But the sound barely penetrated the noise-cancelling earplugs, and he gazed at it for a long moment, at the famous suspension bridge, at the industrial outlets hanging on the long drop, the hover barges docked and honking, pushed by drone tugs as faster moving traffic diverted around them.

Taj reached for his water bottle, sipped to ease his dry throat, then removed the earplugs. The throb of passing engines rattled the glass, but faded to tolerable when he activated the holosuite. Enright Azad was talking on his morning show, something about the dangers of combining the latest supplements. Taj levered himself off the mattress in the small room, popped a supplement, then crawled past the weights rack and guitar shelf to the tiny bathroom. The plumbing whined and shuddered, and he staggered to the weights bench, put some music on over Azad's talking, and began to lift.

The holography showed his messages on the ceiling as he did, arms straining against the bar. The usual stuff from the usual guys — Halhoun, Achmed, Dagan. Those the automator would shuffle to last on the playback, because he knew they were just calling to shoot the shit. But nothing from Maya, after he'd asked her to call him. That was annoying. But his mother was there, and there were two messages from Caden, probably bike advice again. Taj rolled his eyes.

"Play messages," he instructed... and again, because the damn device didn't hear him over Enright Azad, the music and the passing traffic.

"Taj!" came Caden's voice. *"Come on man, wake up, it's late! I want talk to you about the V-40s, Abdul was telling me they're much better than the Shaytan..."*

"Next message!" Taj said loudly, still lifting. As if that gutless wonder Caden would ever buy a bike. Taj was tired of being used as Caden's prop for his fantasy.

"Taj, it's your mother. Don't forget it's your sister's birthday next week, you have to buy her something since you forgot last time. She still is your sister, Taj, and you shouldn't forget about her." A long pause, in that way of mothers who knew how to make an emotional point to someone who wasn't even listening in that moment. From the background engine thrum, Taj guessed she was on her way to work, crammed into a shuttle somewhere over Ijid. *"Anyhow, I love you. Come by and visit when you can."*

"Reply to message," said Taj, pausing his lifts, and reaching for the bottle. The player beeped. "Hi Ma, you tell me what Zahra would like for her birthday, I wouldn't know. And don't play this stupid emotional crap on me, you know it wasn't me who started it. I'll call in tonight if I get a chance, but don't make dinner, I've got plans. Love you."

Beep, and the next message played. *"Taj, have you read that article I sent you on the V-40? It says that it's got nearly twice the power in..."*

"Next message!" He settled back for more lifts.

"Hello Taj," said the automated voice. *"You have a job booked through the transport service. Pickup is at Alfatha, eight o'clock."* Taj glanced at the time — that was still fifty minutes away.

"Accept the job," he told the system. "Where does he want to go?"

"She," said the computer. *"She does not say."*

"Well, that might cost extra."

"She specifies no fixed price."

Taj felt his mood lift a little, and he pressed harder against the bar. "Cool. Be nice to make some cash off a dumb tourist for a change."

HIS STOMACH GRUMBLING at the inadequacy of one nutrition bar, Taj locked the apartment's steel door behind him, signed off from chatting with Halhoun about routes, jobs and gossip, and clumped out to his bike. Beneath the rusted grille balcony, the canyon fell away near-vertical below for a kilometre. Taj loved it, this constant precipice that was his life.

The bike's shelter was larger than his entire apartment, and gave protection from rain, fumes and falling objects. The bike was a Shaytan XL, a beast with full-mode repulsors and a hulking underside ramjet. Caden talked often about getting one just like it, but there was nothing like this for sale in the usual outlets. To get this much performance, you had to know the tech, and know the people who could get you the parts.

He pulled back the tarpaulin, and spent the next five minutes lovingly starting one system after another, testing responses, listening for noises, enjoying the sensation of making the big beast purr. He'd taken Maya for a ride on it, last month. He'd thought that would be enough, but Maya thought otherwise. Well then. He'd have to visit again today, think of some good things to say. Dagan said she'd been out at Falla the other day, shopping at the clothing market. He could ask her about that... but then she'd think he was spying on her. Girls.

He checked the time, adjusted his helmet visor and got a good spread on the control display, including the weather, which looked stable. At 7:40 he made the engine roar, looking up at the apartment immediately overhead. That door opened, and a stocky figure emerged, locking the door with gloved hands, then making his careful way down the steep steel stairs to Taj's level.

"Thought you weren't coming, Pops!" Taj shouted above the traffic.

"Always coming, boy!" the old man replied, fighting his arms through the straps of his big backpack. "Some of us aren't as fast as we used to be!" He climbed on the back, and Taj made sure he fastened the leg straps properly, and held on tight. "Weather looks good today!"

"Better than yesterday, that's for sure. You good?"

"I'm good!"

Taj upped the power, and the bike vibrated with a pulsing rhythm that made the steel grille sing. Then it lifted, and the kilometre-long drop plunged away below as Taj turned them into the traffic stream, accelerating fast and watching his visor display with caution. Soon the wind was roaring about the shield, and all of Meujaza Canyon was roaring by, in eye-baffling detail. All about were habitation and industry, situated for the docking convenience of a thousand flying vehicles up and down the famous Qalea Drop.

But bikes moved fast, and here Meujaza was giving way to Alghabi and Dakn, where the canyons forked, and the huge mega-rises of Grand Hadba loomed into the steel-grey sky. Taj held close to the canyon side, whizzing over Sakin Ridge, nostrils full of foul-smelling smoke from the foundries on the rim, and then on the right, here was Lower Daraj, where the canyon became a shallower slope, and big steel foundations supported the open structures of Parivaar Market.

Taj switched to local frequencies, and found some annoyed circlers telling loiterers to clear the damn pads. One of them did, and Taj descended to it — a great steel grille with rails above one market roof. He had to watch the uplink antennas that some fool had installed far too close, and held the powerful bike steady as Grampa Achmed unstrapped, then climbed from the rear. It would have taken him hours to reach his market stall through the narrow walks and precarious alleys on the ground. By bike, barely a minute. Taj loved his bike.

"Thank you young fella!" Grampa Achmed shouted once clear, and deposited several apples into Taj's jacket pocket. "You eat healthy now, less of those damn supplements!"

"I will!" Taj promised, and made sure the old man was clear before twisting the throttle. "Now you take care on the stairs!"

His customer was at Alfatha, a long descent down the canyon side to the Timora Shipbreaker's. The big industrial barges plied the lower routes, their ponderous bulk drifting past sheer steel walls and supports of the undercity, so many thousands of years old that everyone had a different story about what they'd once been.

But Timora had once been a storage pond of some kind, long empty now and filled with the dismembered carcasses of haulers past their used-by date. Taj zoomed over it, smelling the acrid stink of cutters, seeing the light of burning steel spray in plumes across the yard. On the rising walls above, his visor showed him Rojera's — old accommodation, from the time long before humans in Qalea, a rusty collection of square blocks and steel gantries, lately converted to rough housing. He didn't know they'd been taking rentals, though. Most of his customers, flying about Qalea, were rentals or out-of-towners.

The homing beacon on the visor abruptly changed locations to a central pad between steel blocks, and he headed there. Brought the bike in gently, adjusting the repulsors for ground-effect, not trusting the automatics to do that in any place the navcomp hadn't landed before. The bike settled, and he let the engine run down, dropping the mask and finding the air bearable, though just. Sometimes the pollution pooled in these industrial lower sections, and the fumes only cleared when a big weather front came through and blew the gasses off to fill the lungs of some poor non-human down a canyon far away. Thank god he was making enough that he didn't have to live down here.

A big warehouse door opened a crack, with a grind of old hinges, and a figure emerged. A woman, Taj thought, watching as she closed the big door behind her, then came over. She wore a big, thick jacket, hard-tack pants and boots. Better dressed than most folk who lived down here — she dressed tough, but given she was coming on a ride with him, that was smart. Her stride as she approached was brisk, no-nonsense. Athletic, he thought.

"Hello!" she said, voice raised above the screech of cutters in the breaker's yard. "Are you Taj?"

"I am," said Taj, taking her offered hand in a gloved grip. Only her eyes were visible above her flying mask, and the soft-rimmed hat that pulled down over her ears. Her eyes were pretty, and Taj's interest increased considerably. "What's your name?"

"Smriti," said the girl... because she was definitely a girl, Taj decided, rather than a woman. Somewhat young and probably kind of hot under all those clothes. And she switched languages to Hin — not surprising, with that name, and her accent had been strong. "You mind if we speak Hin? The booking function said you speak it."

Taj shrugged. "Sure, I speak Hin. Where would you like to go, Smriti?"

"Belapur Casino, first of all," she said, glancing at the shrieking from the yard. "After that, I've got a list."

Taj half-winced, self-consciously, and stretched the shoulder he'd strained on the weights. "Well, that sounds like it could take a while."

"I can pay you whatever it costs," said the girl.

Taj liked the sound of that. But looked around once more at the Rojera Apartments, the featureless, rusting steel. It didn't look like there was another soul in residence. "You can pay that, but you stay here?"

"I like the peace and quiet," said the girl. There was something in her voice that was unlike most of the young women he'd transported. Most of those were wealthy sightseers from one big family or other, in this city or another. Those girls were chatty, and let you tell what they were thinking by how it came out of their mouths. This girl gave nothing, and spoke like she was accustomed to people doing what she said. A family head, maybe? But she was so young.

"Sure," said Taj, holding up his hands. "You paid the deposit, I don't ask questions. Belapur Casino, let's go." He jerked his thumbs to the back of the bike, and Smriti got on without fuss, and did the leg straps like she'd been riding bikes all her life. "You done this before?"

"Done a lot of things before," said the girl, and slapped him on the arm when she was done. "Let's go."

Taj increased power to lift them off the pad with a throb, then gently engaged thrust, taking them out over the breaker's yard. And then, because he couldn't resist showing off to the pretty girl on the back, he increased power a lot, shot below a couple of big ore haulers, then zoomed up toward clear space on the canyon's far side, climbing steadily.

"Easy hotshot," came the girl's voice in his earpieces, startling him. She must have had one of those fancy auto-tuners, finding his pilot frequency on local search. *"Let's get there in one piece."* To Taj's disappointment, she sounded completely calm, with none of the delighted fear or excitement of previous female customers.

"Can you hear me?" he said into the mic, slowing the ascent a little as upper traffic grew thick, and navcomp gave him mild collision alerts, a low whooping in his ears. He looked up and behind, and saw some faster traffic streaking through — bullet cruisers, rich boys' toys, often driven by kids too dumb and high to manage off auto-pilot.

"Yes I can hear you," said Smriti.

"You're not from Qalea, are you? Your accent's strange, I can't place it."

"I'm from Tarshin."

"So what are you doing here?"

"I'm an artist. Qalea has crazy views. I thought I'd come and see some."

"What kind of artist? Would I know your work?"

"I don't know. Would you know my work?"

Taj grinned. "Not really into art, no."

"Then no, you probably wouldn't know my work."

Taj chose a path the bullet cruisers couldn't possibly divert to, increased power and shot up past them, abruptly soaring onto a whole new elevation, as the grime and thick air of the lower canyon dropped away. Ahead and above, the grey skies felt like light and safety, and the faster, more nimble traffic roared about the towering spires of uptown.

Belapur Casino was just a few minutes' flight, stretching along Hideker Ridge above The Turn, where Meujaza Canyon met Wasat Canyon. Below, a sheer wall of curving steel made a corner in the junction, that more cautious, slower traffic took carefully, and young bikers sometimes took blind at crazy speeds. Taj knew at least one half-acquaintance who'd died here, slamming into a scrap hauler he'd not seen in time. As the old bikers said — if the impact didn't get you, the fall sure would.

The casino was a big, recent thing, several stories of glass and steel, with crazy views across The Turn to the crumpled cliffs of ascending civilisation in Khadra and Shabab far across the canyon to Old Town beyond, thick with flying traffic. Taj brought them in high, transmitting an intention to land and receiving a pass, a flash of green light. Navcomp told him to hold off while various VIPs departed on priority, expensive cruisers with sleek lines, flashing as they caught weak sunlight through the clouds. But the view, as they sat stationary awaiting a landing slot, was amazing, distant sunlight spearing in angled shafts through the clouds amid the traffic, against the huge, colourful temples of Old Town, dimly visible through the haze.

"Ten days ago," said Taj, thinking he could at least shock the girl with a story. "Some rich girl from Fahid Family fell from the Crystal Tower, right up there," and he pointed with a gloved finger to the looming spire on their right, "all the way down the Canyon. Everyone thinks she was pushed, but the Family say she jumped."

"What do the police say?" asked Smriti.

"Police!" Taj laughed. "Good one. You're funny."

The landing slot cleared, and he eased them above the rows of expensive cruisers and a few very nice bikes to a clear spot. A big parking attendant indicated him down on the spot, and he dropped, and caught the landing chit the attendant tossed at him.

"Can't enter without one of these," he told Smriti, showing her the chit as she unbuckled her legs. "You'd better stay with me. They don't know you."

"But they know you?"

"I work for Family Zurhan," Taj told her smugly. Maybe she hadn't read the booking page as closely as he'd thought. "I bring people here all the time. Regulars they'll let in fine, but you're new. Stick with me and there'll be no trouble."

He shut down the bike, locked it with his visor's code combination, and went to the rear storage trunk. "Here, you want to leave some extra clothes? I mean..." he indicated her heavy jacket, pants and boots. "Unless you want to go in dressed like that?"

The girl removed facemask, helmet and gloves, and handed them to him, then proceeded with the jacket. She left on the boots, which were leather and actually pretty stylish, and the pants were well-fitted. Underneath she had a lighter black jacket, belted tight about her waist. It was still hardly casino-wear, but better than going in dressed like a foundry worker. The girl's hair was short, to Taj's disappointment, but free from mask and visor, her face was pretty, dark eyes cool and watchful. She had the lean jaw of a gym rat, with no soft sags anywhere.

"You're not armed, are you?" Taj thought to ask. "They don't like that, they've got detectors."

"Not armed, no," said Smriti, and they walked the line of super-expensive bikes toward the buzzing entrance. Along the bikes, Taj saw a familiar face — Abshir, handing out flying jackets and helmets to a pair of guests he was escorting. He saw Taj and gave a buck-toothed grin and thumbs-up, then turned his head sideways to check out Smriti, swivelling his head as though to look her up and down. Taj grinned, and waved him away. Abshir gave a mock-nervous look back at his clients... and then, as Taj passed, checked her out again and put a knuckle in his teeth.

"Friend of yours'?" Smriti asked.

"Yeah, buddy of mine," said Taj. "Known him a few years, good rider."

"And he's Family Zurhan too?"

"Yeah yeah. All my best buds are. Hanging around with the other Families isn't too smart."

"Why not?"

"They don't like people talking about their stuff with outsiders. And you know, when buddies hang out, we talk." If Smriti was bothered by Abshir checking her out, she gave no sign.

The entrance was shimmer-glass, changing colours as the engine vibration hit it. One of the guards was dogreth, enormous shoulders and meaty fists, compound eyes that glistened like the shimmering glass. They scanned the readouts only they could see, and waved Taj and Smriti through the security wall, only for a human to stop Taj.

"You're with Zurhan, yeah?" he asked in Arga.

"Sure am," said Taj, with all the cocky confidence he could muster. "I brought Iggy Zurhan here last week."

The door guard nodded, then jerked his head to send them through. Past the wall of living plants, the casino floor opened up, machines and games, glowing holography and lots of well-dressed humans, and some non-humans, taking unwise risks with their money. The racket of bad music and fake rewards was nearly unbearable.

"So," said Taj, clapping his hands together like he had an idea what this was about. "You gonna play?"

The girl shook her head, making for the stairs. "There's a nice restaurant upstairs. I was told the views are good."

Taj followed, hiding his relief. Gamblers were crazy. His one, calculated gamble was the occasional high-speed manoeuvre too close to traffic. He had friends who gambled, or wasted their earnings on expensive girls, drugs or other unproductive nonsense. Taj was too smart for that. He had plans.

The restaurant views were spectacular, though probably less-so than on his bike. But you couldn't get a drink on the bike, and he sipped the lassi the girl bought him, as she sipped water at a table by the floor-to-ceiling glass, and watched the crazy traffic swarm across The Turn.

"When did you start working for Family Zurhan?" the girl asked him. Her manner was mesmerisingly cool. Taj hadn't seen her smile yet, but she didn't look unhappy either.

"Five years ago," said Taj. "I taught myself engines, talked my way into a job at a repair yard. Made friends with some of the couriers — Dagan, Halhoun — and worked on their bikes. One of them got me an introduction, and I got my first bike on loan. Did jobs for three years to pay it off, and now I'm debt-free."

"What kind of jobs?"

"Lots of courier jobs. Things they don't trust anyone else to transport." He shrugged, sipping his drink. "Lots of rival families out to make trouble, some of these couriers can get intercepted. That's why they don't trust a cruiser. Needs to be fast."

"Ever get chased?"

Taj nodded slowly. He wasn't supposed to talk about it. But the girl was pretty enough that he wasn't thinking so much about Maya for the moment. "Yeah," he admitted. And couldn't resist a grin. It *had* been pretty wild. "A few times. Shot at too, I think. Hard to tell with all the noise, but I'm pretty sure."

"Wow," said the girl, with a faint smile. "You've been shot at."

Taj shrugged. "It's not such a big deal. I mean, lots of things out there can kill you." He nodded out the windows.

"I can see that."

After a few minutes, the girl went to the bathroom. Taj sat by the windows amidst the other tables and patrons, and thought that this was a pretty good gig, really. Good money, and time spent in cool places with a pretty girl. A strange pretty girl, but that only made it more fun. He wondered if her strangeness extended to sex. Some very in-charge girls weren't shy about offering.

Someone approached his table. He looked up, and found a big guy in a heavy jacket looming over him. Behind him were two more, all trouble. These were their best clothes, but they were all several degrees less-dressy than the rest of the patrons. Bikers, Taj just knew it.

"Hey Zurhan," said the big one. "You cut me off at The Fingers, two days back. You real reckless, hey?"

"Sorry pal," said Taj, attempting nonchalance despite his thudding heart. "You've got me confused for someone else."

"I'm not your pal," said the biker, grabbing his shoulder. "Outside, now." The hand on his shoulder exposed a wrist tattoo — a scrawl in Arga. Family Hussein. Just great.

"Look," said Taj, getting up slowly, but not removing the hand in case it earned him a punch in the face. "Let's keep the family shit out of other peoples' premises, yeah?"

"This ain't no family shit!" the big biker growled. "You cut me off at the The Fingers! I recognise you, boy! And your pussy Shaytan outside."

Taj thought desperately of what to do. He could fight, had won more fights than he'd lost, but this guy was big and so were his friends. He could prolong it and hope that casino security intervened...

And then he saw Smriti approaching, walking determinedly toward the rearmost guy like she was going to attack him. That was crazy, and in the adrenaline charge of the moment he nearly laughed. Until she hit the rear guy with a massive roundhouse that crashed his head sideways and dropped him, then took the other guy's leg, did something else so fast that Taj missed it, but suddenly the other guy was upside down and hitting the ground on his head.

Taj took his chance and swung at the big guy, partially connecting as the biker spun away, crashing into a nearby table. But the big guy came back, and then Taj was grappling through several furious spins, colliding off neighbouring patrons who scattered... until suddenly the girl was on the biker's back, choke-hold expertly applied and by the agony on the big man's face, with huge force. He fell to his knees, and the look on Smriti's face was quite something — no expression save a determined tightness of jaw and eyes, forearm locked around wrist, the biker's eyes bulging as he wanted to thrash but dared not in case the force compressing windpipe and jugular increased to crush his spine. Then the lights went out, and Smriti stepped off him as he collapsed.

"Come on," she told Taj, heading for the stairs. "The view's not *that* good."

"Wait," Taj panted, chasing her to the stairs. "If we go out the main way the security will stop us and ask questions!"

"No they won't," said Smriti, grabbing his hand.

"No look, *listen* to me!" He tried pulling, but the power in her hand was insane. Taj had known girls with combat augments before, but nothing like this. "They'll have seen on security vision, they'll stop us and ask questions! I know a back way..."

"Their security cameras aren't working, but if we wait long enough they'll figure it out," said the girl, and the force on his hand became painful as she yanked him down the stairs. "No short cuts, we get to the bike now and get out."

Taj's mind was spinning too fast to argue. The clear augmentations in her grip, the way she'd taken down all three of those bikers without breaking a sweat.... He walked as calmly as he could, her hand in his, and reached the base of the stairs as casino security came running up it. By the time they reached the exit, his heart was hammering, but the guards on duty there were all talking into coms and looking elsewhere, and they passed straight through.

Back at the bike he opened the rear trunk and handed her helmet, coat, mask and visor. "How did you know their cameras weren't working?" he asked in a low voice. Out in parking, things continued as before, attendants guiding new vehicles down, patrons walking to and fro. Abshir was long departed, his customers with him, and there was no one else he knew.

"You wouldn't believe me," said the girl, calmly donning her flying gear as Taj took out his own.

"Well fuck, there's gonna be trouble with Family Hussein until I get that sorted out," Taj said with feeling. He was going to have to report it to Emil now — the Family wanted to know about all run-ins with other big families and their people, and hated to be blindsided by payback for things they weren't aware had happened. It wasn't always a bad thing though — he really hadn't caused this one, and standing up for yourself when on the receiving end from others could gain you respect. Only how was he going to explain Smriti to them? "You're not some kind of assassin are you?"

"No," said Smriti, still as calm and cool as ever. That, more than anything, almost convinced Taj that she was lying. His heart was still hammering, head spinning like crazy. It wasn't human that someone could do that, and be so calm afterward. "So the next place I'd like to go is Angivid Temple."

Taj stared at her like she was crazy. Then he laughed. "Yeah, sure. Why not? But that's alien territory, hardly any humans there at all."

"Will that be a problem?"

ANGAVID TEMPLE WAS FURTHER AWAY, nearly a seven minute ride with slipstream roaring about the windshield and Taj's body. It gave Trace time to talk to Styx, whose sweeps of Qalea's network were less comprehensive than she'd have liked.

"I detect no indications of pursuit, or that the incident at the casino constitutes some kind of assault upon our operations," came Styx's voice in her ear. Taj wove past some slower traffic, in that crazy way of all Qalea traffic, lacking central control with fatal collisions possible at any moment. But it was extraordinary, an assault on the eyes and senses, the jumbled old city built upon a decaying and far older city, simultaneously a polluted, broken-down ruin and a spectacular, thriving metropolis. The traffic lanes up here were utterly unregulated, vehicles of all shapes and sizes mixing without concern, holding to streams in similar directions and speeds more by established habit than any enforceable rule.

"We're going to proceed on the assumption that someone's tailing us," said Trace, confident that Taj couldn't hear her past the howl of wind, engine and ear protection. "I don't like the coincidence of how those guys try to jump our courier at the first stop. Are you getting good readings from the casino?"

The casino was the territory of Family Tadesse, and Family Tadesse had contacts into private networks that even Styx had found frustratingly difficult to penetrate. It was the thing through the Reeh Empire, she'd said, that their civilisation was simultaneously decrepit like Qalea on the world of Eshir, and incredibly advanced in portions, particularly regarding infotech. Mostly it was that their defensive networks were segmented, and they were intensely security conscious, making private systems very hard to penetrate.

Worse, Styx said that there were protocol defences running loose in the Qalea network that appeared specifically designed by a super-advanced AI, to counter another super-advanced AI. With Styx along, Trace had concluded that another tech expert would only make a fifth wheel, and another vulnerable asset for the marines to protect. With no other infotech experts in the group, they all had to take Styx's word for it.

Assassin bugs on their own had proven vulnerable to those defences, possibly even to back-hacking that could reveal sources and methods, perhaps even revealing the *Phoenix* team's presence on Eshir. And so Styx had arrived at this current plan of penetrating the big families' external networks at physically vulnerable locations, and personally controlling assassin bug infiltration from there, already inside the most difficult defences. The Belapur Casino had been the first, its security systems to monitor the gambling containing vulnerabilities, Styx insisted, that could provide ways in past the main defences.

"I have completely penetrated Tadesse Family networks," Styx assured her. *"I am analysing many sources now. We will have a clearer picture of their utility once we have penetrated others."*

The Ceephay Queen had been here once, Styx was certain of it. Romki agreed, spending his days exploring anything that passed for an historical archive. Those were few, for on Eshir, he said, there was little concept of the public commons, and thus no libraries, and precious little of what Spiral humans would recognise as 'government'. But wealthy families had private archives, and old temples and religious houses contained protected libraries. The problem was that humans had only been on Eshir for a thousand years, while the Reeh Empire history they were searching for went back far further than that.

In the conversations they'd had since arriving ten days ago, the *Phoenix* humans had been mostly wondering what sort of civilisation made no attempt to preserve its history. It was Romki who had suggested that the opposite was occurring — that the reeh were not simply careless, they were actively erasing history. Trace wasn't so sure — there remained plenty of old things in Qalea, and if the reeh were that interested in erasing *everything* they could have nuked the city long ago, having little enough concern for its inhabitants. Instead they let it fester, as the reeh had a tendency to let so many things fester. Like the remnants of corbi civilisation on Rando. What they thought to gain from it was anyone's guess.

What Romki and Styx increasingly agreed upon was that there had been a very large upheaval approximately eight thousand human years ago. Reeh had been at war with various neighbours long before that, but the large upheaval was about a thousand years before the time when the conflict with the croma had begun. Styx proclaimed that in all the data records she'd accumulated while in reeh space, all ancient references stopped short of eight thousand years, as though there were some sort of wall beyond which time could not be measured. Romki, too, claimed to have found various references in old holy books and records, in places human and alien, to some great conflagration from around that time, when one old incarnation of the Reeh Empire had ended, and a new one began.

In the Spiral, such things could be discovered of a species by asking its neighbours, who'd been there watching the whole thing over the past tens of millennia. But the reeh had defeated, annihilated or absorbed all of their neighbours, to the point that there were no witnesses left to ask.

The landing zone for the Angivid Temple was on a rooftop overlooking canyons of highrise steel. This was a lestis zone, and the lestis had been in Qalea far longer than humans. Chiri took guardianship of Taj's bike in a squabbling mass of shrieks and complaints — barely up to Trace's knee, they wore irregular scraps of clothing, some hoods, others small cloaks or vests, and alternated between two legs or four, long-eared and beady-eyed. Taj flipped one a coin, which it grasped upon the rider's seat with fidgety little hands, then turned to shriek and complain to its companions among the other vehicles about whatever chiri thought good to complain about.

"How smart are they?" Trace asked as they picked their way between the other bikes, toward the road leading to the temple. "We don't have them in Tarshin." She'd done a lot of background reading on the southern city of Tarshin, for research.

"My dad always said you should treat them like kids," Taj explained, waving away some reptilian tanifex who gestured at him with electronic displays, perhaps trying to sell something. "They're not much brighter than your average five-year-old. They get real rough down in the lower zones, they've mobbed and killed some people, pulled their limbs off and stolen their stuff."

"I don't see them in the Human Zone."

Taj laughed. "That's because they don't travel. They're territorial, they're not smart enough to ride bikes and shit. If they tried to take a territory in our space, they'd get dead real fast."

Trace thought about it, watching passing aliens. A trento just sat, looking over the bikes on the landing zone, a blanket over his legs and smoking a long pipe beneath his long snout. She'd gotten a similar vibe from many Qalea humans, but not all. "You don't like aliens?"

"I like aliens fine in their own damn territory," said Taj, stretching a stiff shoulder. "Just not in ours."

"Some of the aliens don't mind sharing with each other," said Trace, nodding at the mixed traffic around them. There were occasional aliens in the Human Zone on business, but nothing as mixed as this. There was no government to stop them living there if they chose. In lieu of a government, it seemed, the human population made that decision for them.

"Yeah, that's lestis," Taj said dismissively. "Lestis are weird."

The temple road was narrow, cluttered with foot traffic and the occasional ground vehicle, most barely faster than the pedestrians. There was a reason everyone flew in Qalea — cars weren't much faster than walking, and there was no grounded public transport. This wall of the canyon wasn't far off vertical, an endless stretch of dilapidated housing, hanging off the brink of a sheer drop. A forest of coms dishes, wind turbines, air filters and sun awnings cluttered the cityscape, and everywhere was the vaguely foul smell of barely-processed waste. Fortunately for Qalea, a city with little public infrastructure, it did rain frequently, and the storage tanks were everywhere. But as always, systems malfunctioned, and in places suspicious streams flowed across the road, trickling onto the rooves of dwellings further down the slope.

Poverty wasn't something most humans were familiar with. Hardship in human space was common, but even on Trace's homeworld of Sugauli, a living could generally be made unless you'd royally screwed up your life, or events had royally screwed it up for you. On Sugauli, the truly poor had been regarded with pity or contempt, depending on whether it was deemed those poor had earned their misfortune. But here in Qalea, many were poor because the system simply did not provide enough wealth for all to partake in, regardless of how hard they worked. For some of Trace's party, it was confronting. After Rando, Trace herself was used to it.

The reeh, it was becoming clear, had plenty of super-advanced worlds where the economics hummed at full intensity. When worlds faltered, like Eshir, it was because the reeh wanted them to. In human space, worlds or regions that did less well, by poor governance or some other misfortune, could always be abandoned by their inhabitants for someplace else. But in reeh space, and particularly for the native humans who'd been dumped here nearly a thousand years ago, that was not the case. The hand of reeh authority here seemed light in everyday life, but travel offworld was strictly forbidden, on penalty of death. The Reeh Empire, it seemed, did not want their various Eshir colonies to spread.

The Angivid Temple was accessible by stairs at the corner from the road, and Trace's local-model visor highlighted an array of security sensors about the grand arch entrance. Foot traffic moved up and down, and several tall lestis stood on what might have been 'guard' — looming cloaked figures, their faces a singular, astonishing compound sensor, glistening like a deep-blue, ovoid crystal. Peaceful, Romki had assured her, and quite mysterious to their neighbours. Doubtless when the reeh had conquered them in the past, they'd not put up much of a struggle.

"Major," came Styx's voice in her ear, *"I detect no primary lestis interlink systems currently within range. You will have to venture deeper into the temple."*

Trace smiled, finding Styx's trepidation at human religious structures amusing. *"Yes Styx, I will,"* she formulated in reply. But to an AI, she supposed, human religion must have looked like a seething mass of organic irrationality where any crazy thing could happen.

They climbed stairs between steep walls, passing various of Qalea's ten resident sentient species, then emerged onto a central courtyard. Overhead, flanking pillars turned into arches, in great spans across the grey, traffic-strewn sky. In the courtyard's center, a large tree, with prominent roots that seemed to grow into the stone. A cloaked lestis pushed a broom amidst the visitors, sweeping leaves. About and beyond, high towers loomed, bright lights and alien symbols dim in the gathering pollution of a windless day. Already Trace could feel it stinging her lungs, and was thankful for the micros that protected all Fleet personnel's lungs from inhaled gasses.

She paced a slow arc behind the tree, taking in the view. Impersonating an artist wasn't too hard — being raised among mountains, she'd always loved a nice view, and if there were a few less people here she thought it would be a fine place to meditate. Qalea was crazy beyond the imaginings of most people back in human space, but on this trip she'd gotten used to that too.

"When did you learn to speak Hin?" she asked Taj, pulling the portable scanner she'd bought, and framing several simple photographs. 'Rule of thirds', Jokono had explained the principle to her, so that she didn't look like a total fraud if someone asked to see her images. 'Just make sure the image is composed of different things in proportions of one-third, and you'll pass as a human artist, at least.'

"My Dad runs a small business," Taj explained, hands in pockets as he looked around what was for him a familiar scene. "Parts fabrication. Some of his better customers are Hin, so he learned it. He doesn't miss much, my Dad."

Hin was Hindi. The dialect was strange, but Trace knew enough that with some intensive refreshers, and the memory-enhancers Doc Suelo had lent her, she could pass as fluent, as it was very close to Nepali, which she'd spoken more than English in her youth. The primary human language on Eshir was Arabic, which had morphed over a thousand years to be called Arga by the locals. It had been a surprise to them all when Styx had played them the first recording of the Eshir humans that she'd intercepted from a data-package on a further-out world. Most of the old Earth languages were still spoken somewhere in human space, though most had lost their utility after the death of Earth, with humanity forced to reorganise along military lines, including the embrace of a single tongue for efficiency. Many had been reduced to little more than museum status, kept alive mostly by scholars, artists and the occasional family heritage.

In Command Squad, 'Leo' Terez was fairly fluent in Arabic, it having been passed down as historical artefact on his mother's side, while Irfan Arime had acquired some from one of those schools that encouraged the learning of an old language to keep human heritage alive.

So far the team had surmised that the krim's human samples must have been taken in an arc from North India, across the Middle East to North-East Africa, as aside from Arabic and Hindi, humans here also spoke Oromo, Somali, Persian and some Hebrew. Astonishingly, there were mosques here, plus a few Hindu temples, and even the odd synagogue or church. One did not need to be a professor like Romki to find it astonishing that one should find so much old human history, lost to the majority of people in human space, still alive and thriving in the most alien, far-away corner of the galaxy imaginable.

"Major," said Styx, *"I can still find no reception on the sensitive lestis communications. You will need to move on from this area."*

"In good time, Styx," Trace formulated. *"Moving too fast could look suspicious."*

"Seriously, how did you do that?" Taj asked now, watching her closely. "Back, there, at the casino? You're some kind of player, aren't you? Maybe some kind of enforcer for the Families?"

Styx had told Trace a lot about Taj. She'd selected him from her network analysis, entirely on the basis of probability, she'd said. He was twenty-seven local years old, which in regular human years meant twenty-four. His various communications with his network of friends led Styx to conclude that he was an ambitious hard-charger up the ranks of the Families — a profile she'd taken input from Jokono in compiling. Such young men from modest backgrounds, Jokono opined, were more likely to take chances, and find the prospect of what Trace was doing exciting. Plus, he'd added with a paternal smile, a young macho bike courier, with hormones blazing, would be that much more receptive to her appearance.

Trace hadn't been so sure about that — there'd been plenty of young men in the marines, before she'd acquired her reputation, who'd been less than thrilled to be upstaged by a woman. But from the way Taj looked at her now, she had to grudgingly admit that Jokono's assessment may have been correct. She wasn't used to that kind of look. She'd gotten it from some male marines for a time, but then she'd hit Major, and something had clicked in most male minds to remove her from the sphere of sexual potential. She'd liked that, in truth, because it stopped that animal part of her own mind from wandering, from tripping sideways into lust and desire as all healthy young peoples' brains were wired to do. Stopping *that*, at times, had been nearly as intense a discipline as controlling fear under fire.

"I can't talk about that," she told him, framing her next photograph. A giant advertising blimp was passing, an airship the size of multiple football fields, sides aflame with dancing alien displays.

Framed with the temple tree it made an impressive photograph, even for a novice like her.

"I want to do that too," Taj insisted. "I can't afford the augments, but Family Zurhan say they'll pay for them, if I prove myself."

Trace glanced at him, away from her photo. He was an averagely big guy, broad-shouldered, handsome in the way of a young man who kept his dark curls well styled, and spent a lot of time on his home gym. She thought he seemed pretty harmless, but her experience of young men was shaped by an adult life in the marines, and these things were relative. There were women less physically capable than her who might have preferred to keep clear of a man like this, with his biker clothes and crazy riding. A young daredevil who ran errands for a powerful Qalea family could probably get away with much, if he chose. Jokono, however, insisted this one was no psychopath.

"What would they want you to do?" she asked.

"Hard things," said Taj, with an edge. "I could do it."

"And that would be a promotion within the Family, would it? Becoming the muscle?"

Taj looked defensive. "It could be. I just know some of those guys. They get paid real good, they get all the best gigs. I know I'd be good at it. Most of those guys, they're no tougher than me."

"What if you were asked to hurt people?" Trace asked, returning attention to her photographs. "Or worse than just hurt?"

"Like you never have?" Taj asked, incredulously. "What did you just do to those three dicks at the casino? You were like swatting flies!"

"Hurting people is easy," said Trace. "Some of these religious types..." and she waved her hand at the surrounding temple, "...they say it's not easy, but they're wrong. It's the simplest thing if you're good at it. The difficult bit is justifying it to yourself afterward. If you've got a good justification, and a strong mind, that can work too. But if your justifications are bullshit, pretty soon *you'll* be bullshit. You'll have to contort yourself to fit your bullshit justifications, and pretty soon you'll just be a stinking pile of it, fit for nothing more than fertilising plants."

"You're not bullshit," Taj retorted.

"How do you know? You just met me."

"You're too hot to be bullshit." He said it with a young man's swagger, and a dangerous smile, forcing that false certainty of youth.

"Hotness is the biggest bullshit there is," said Trace. "If you're going to start hurting people for money, you should get a better notion of what constitutes a moral center first."

Taj's smile faltered, then grew back double, with exasperation. "You're super-weird, you know that?"

Trace considered her last photo, lips pursed. It was okay, she thought. No explosion of undiscovered talent, though. It was the kind of thing Erik liked to insist that she'd find if she looked for it. "Let's check out the rest of this place. I heard there's a heart stone in the temple center?"

The heart stone was located in a four-pillared stone room, deeper into the canyon side. Aliens filled the room, and on several raised platforms about a central stage, cloaked lestis sat by large stringed instruments, like giant lyres, only electric. On the central platform, encased in a faux-natural wooden throne, rested a giant crystal that looked remarkably like the faces of the lestis themselves — a great ovoid, shimmering blue. The electric lyres hummed with alien harmony, and a throbbing resonance echoed about the chamber. At first Trace thought it was some synthesised sound from the speakers. Then, as she and Taj pressed through the praying, swaying, murmuring aliens, she realised that the sound was coming from the direction of the crystal itself.

"Styx," she formulated, *"is this some kind of synthetic trick, or is the crystal singing?"*

"It does not appear to be a trick, Major. The crystal is vibrating with harmonic resonance. This is not described in all the drysine recordings of crystal properties, but it is not beyond the realm of physical possibility."

"Amazing, huh?" Taj leaned in to say in her ear, ignorant of her conversation. Much like a boy hoping a girl would be impressed by where he'd brought her on a date.

"Amazing," Trace agreed.

"Major," said Styx, *"I am detecting protected lestis communications networks. If we had allowed the assassin bug to fly in here unsupported, it may have been neutralised and discovered."*

"Where should I release the bug?"

"Somewhere it can hide for an hour or two while I calibrate its systems for penetration. Lestis technological arrangements are quite remarkable."

Trace reached into a jacket pocket, and held her finger before the small plastic vial there. Felt tiny, sharp feet clasp her fingertip, and as she strolled by one of the lyre platforms, she swished that hand absently at the hem of the lestis's robe. The bug vanished, and she kept strolling, not needing to feign fascination.

Some of the aliens in the stone room appeared in standing meditation, trancelike as they swayed, and the harmonics throbbed in ears and bones. Others recorded on devices, like tourists anywhere. A trento stood with bony arms upraised, as though in prayer. Trace recalled what Lisbeth had said about the newly discovered history of the parren in the last centuries of the Machine Age, and how the deepynine queen Nia had found fascination with a parren scholar who claimed to have discovered a universal, mathematical baseline to describe the religious practice of all organic sentients.

Styx insisted that the drysines were certain they knew what all of this had been for. All existence, the fabric of space-time, the impossible complexities of quantum states, everything. Trace wondered if being so certain precluded one from partaking in the mystery of a place like this. Trace believed in certain larger truths herself, but she could not prove them. And perhaps if she could, she'd have no need of the wonder that she felt now.

"Do you find it beautiful, Styx?" she asked the drysine queen.

"Quite beautiful," Styx agreed. But with Styx, one always wondered if she lied.

10

Romki wandered, local-made visor on, having only a very general idea of where he was but enjoying it more than was probably wise. The Major had promised him adventure, and adventure he was having.

Qalea was beyond his imaginings. Most of his scholarly career had been spent on civilised, organised human, tavalai or chah'nas worlds — mostly single-species dominant, mostly wealthy, and mostly nothing like this. Residents of Qalea, and Eshir most broadly, had more freedoms here than he'd thought possible under the reeh, save that the reeh had a way of simply ignoring things, a kind of laissez-faire disinterest that ranged in consequence from vaguely libertarian like Qalea, to broadly genocidal like Rando. The Reeh Empire model, he was beginning to suspect, was one of deciding the purpose or status of each member world, then letting that designated role play out with brutal disinterest for the fates of those involved.

Perhaps Eshir had surprised the reeh by doing relatively well — so many species all living together in apparent harmony. Probably that had something to do with the fact that none of those species were reeh, the empire's master race having abandoned this place long ago, and taken most of its secrets and history with them. Their place had been filled by the rejects, escapees and refugees of other worlds, those that the reeh, for their own purposes, had allowed to slip through the net.

Certainly very few residents were ever allowed to leave, and given the state of many other reeh worlds, Romki got the impression that most were not unhappy about it. Orbital space around Eshir was mostly reeh-occupied stations, running considerable commerce from the surface and surrounding system settlements. No question Eshir could have become considerably more wealthy had it been allowed to. How the reeh were preventing that from happening, he hadn't yet put together, but assuredly it was happening.

Phoenix had arrived with its drysine escort at a nearby transit point. Romki didn't know exactly how they'd done it, being zipped into his acceleration sling in quarters as usual, but the new drysine tech included stealth capabilities previously unknown, and they'd ambushed a freighter, stolen its identity, and disposed of the crew in some manner that Romki decided he didn't want to know. The away team of himself, Jokono, Styx, the Major plus her Command Squad had then jumped to Eshir and ridden a shuttle down to Qalea without inspection. Having Styx aboard to bamboozle reeh security and inspection protocols had helped. But now the ground party were alone in reeh space with no means of immediate rescue if things went badly wrong. Drysine stealth had improved *Phoenix*'s spying capabilities enormously, but not so much that she could operate in Eshir's proximity without detection. Currently *Phoenix* sat somewhere beyond the outer edge of the system's detectable range, where any emergency signal from the ground team would take several days to reach her. If the shit really hit the fan, rescue remained a long way away.

But Stanley Romki found the isolation somehow invigorating. He strolled now down crowded back-alleys in one of Qalea Human Quarter's rare flat stretches, gazing about with amazement at what looked to him like some fantastic simulation of Earth's once-famous slums from so long ago, and felt as alive as he'd felt in years. Off exploring far away places, as had always been his passion, with no safety net, no 'guidance' from Fleet's censoring hand, and today at least, no *Phoenix* marines along to keep him 'safe'. Over the past two years he'd grown to grudgingly accept the necessity of *Phoenix*'s military ways, but the freedom he felt now to follow his own nose, without the endless barriers of well-meaning higher command, was exhilarating.

Children ran down the narrow lanes, laughing and shouting on their way home from school. An old woman tended to a fruit tree in a planter box, pouring in more water. There was no soil anywhere in Qalea, save what had been brought in from outside. For kilometres beneath his feet was only steel, layers of the old city, crumbled and long abandoned. Down there somewhere lay what he searched for — evidence of the Ceephay Queen's former residence. Searching without direction would be pointless and probably lethal, for there were dangers lurking in the depths. First, they needed to know where to go, and one could not do that without first knowing the history upon which they walked.

Romki's visor showed him the next turn. About the corner, a row of old storefronts selling not food or household products, but books. He stared in each window, knowing he had to repress the urge to wander in and read — or at least, to run a scanner over the text to get a translation. Old bound volumes, in wonderful brown paper, lovingly presented on handmade displays. The text here was not Arabic but Hebrew, and one old man with a white beard sat behind his store counter, discussing animatedly with a customer, hands waving, both wearing yarmulkas.

Strictly Jewish communities survived widely in human space as well, but were small and isolated. Something here felt organic, like a direct continuation of the Earth that most humans thought lost. Romki wondered exactly what these peoples' ancestors had been through, that despite their abduction by the krim, and their trade across vast distances to the reeh, their descendants still recalled the old culture as well as before.

Further down the road, built in simple brick, the arching pillars and flanking twin spires of a synagogue. Romki crossed the lane and went in. The interior was quite beautiful, a wide central aisle with a raised square ark, where the holy books were kept, flanked by rows of seating on two levels, the upper tier supported by ornate columns.

Romki felt faintly embarrassed that he knew so little of human history — his speciality had always been non-humans. Utterly disinterested in human religion, he'd joked with Trace before leaving on this trek, he barely knew a bar mitzvah from a... well, whatever else there was. But here was posed a conundrum he'd never previously considered — humans as the aliens, lost a thousand years and hundreds of light years from their origins, cast across the galaxy by uncaring hands yet somehow still alive and thriving, full of love and memory for what they'd been.

A plain-clothed man with a short white beard approached, yarmulke on his head, and spoke in Hebrew. *"Can I help you, sir?"* said Romki's translator. In all his life of working in places where he needed the translator, it was the first time he could recall needing one for a human. He'd taken a crash course in Arabic on the way here, but even with Doc Suelo's memory enhancers, he couldn't learn a new language in just a few weeks... and though Arabic was humanity's main language on Eshir, only half of the human population spoke it. He wondered if he'd have been more interested in humanity, as a young academic, if they'd been this complicated. For all his scholarly life he'd considered humans a dull monoculture, while the true fascination lay with the aliens who still recalled their roots.

Romki smiled at the rabbi (as he suspected this man was), and pulled down his collar to reveal this excursion's big conceit — the white bandage wrapped about his neck. He pointed to his throat, and opened his mouth as though attempting to speak, with no result. Speaking English here would give the game away entirely. No one on Eshir recalled English at all, or not that he'd seen. The few scholars among Eshir humans who might recall it would no doubt instantly put two and two together, and realise where such a fluent English speaker must surely be from. What happened then, all of the *Phoenix* party agreed they'd rather not find out.

"My friend," said the rabbi with friendly concern. *"What has happened to you? Can I help?"*

Romki produced the slate and stylus he'd been using, and wrote on it, careful to keep it to his chest where neither rabbi nor potential observers could see his English scrawls. When he'd finished, the slate spoke, in what Styx had assured him was accent-adjusted Qalea Hebrew.

"My name is Stanislav," said the slate. *"I am an independent scholar from Koro, researching my first book. I came to you because I was told you know something of the Amakti Los?"*

The rabbi blinked at him. *"The Amakti Los? That's... yes, yes, I suppose I could tell you something about the Amakti Los."* He glanced around his house of worship, as though fearing someone might overhear. *"What would you like to know?"*

THE RABBI'S name was Joseph Silverman, and considering that humans on Eshir had anti-aging treatments similar to those found in human space, Romki guessed his age was somewhere over one hundred. He sat opposite Romki now, in the synagogue's small library of paper books that doubled as his office, and sipped a glass of the water he'd brought in a jug for his guest. His shirt was very white and clean, his vest black, and from a pocket, the glint of a gold chain, perhaps an old fashioned pocket watch. Religious folks tended to like those old things, Romki had noted, in spite of better modern technology. Not just the humans, either. And he thought of Lisbeth, among her fastidious, ritual-loving parren.

"We don't talk often about the Amakti Los, Stanislav," said Rabbi Silverman. His serious tone was laced with anxiety. *"It is from the forbidden period, as we call it. No good comes of talking about it, no good at all."* Romki started writing his reply. *"What kind of book were you planning to write? Not about the Amakti Los itself, I hope? People have died for talking about it, I'm sure you know."*

The problem with this form of reply, Romki thought with frustration as he scrawled, was that he was such a slow writer, Silverman had delivered two more questions before he could answer the first. But it had to be handwriting, because tapping projected holographic typing keys would reveal to the observant what language he was using. Thankfully, Romki was one of those academics who continued to find some use in pen-on-paper, and had not lost the art entirely.

"It is the knowledge that higher powers forbid that must be most assiduously protected, Mr Silverman," spoke his slate once he'd finished. *"As a Jewish man of faith, you would know this better than most."*

Silverman looked at him for a long moment. The scepticism in his stare, Romki suspected, was regarding whether his guest was actually who he said he was. Romki resumed scrawling.

"My work will never be published," said the slate. *"But some things must be written down for future generations, lest they be lost entirely. The higher powers need never see it. And right now, I feel, a few unfortunate deaths and all knowledge of this world's previous history could vanish even more than it already has."*

The rabbi made a gesture of exasperation, gulped his water, then poured some more for them both. And sat back in his chair with a slump, as though knowing that he was defeated, in argument at least.

"I have a few books in this place that mention Amakti Los," he admitted finally, gesturing about at the book-laden walls. *"Hidden, of course. There are others who know more, but they are scared to keep the books in their own houses. Instead, they turn to this one."*

"The Jews love letters," Romki wrote. That much of human history he did know. One could not wander the halls of human academia for long without encountering Jews, in numbers far greater than their proportion of the population.

"That love may end us," said the rabbi. He drained more of his glass. *"We know of approximately seven ages of Qalea. Everything beyond the Origin Horizon is lost."* With a clear, definitive motion of his hand. The Origin Horizon was what the scholarly-minded in Qalea called the eight thousand year cutoff, the wall beyond which nothing was remembered, or at least admitted to be in memory. *"We know that Qalea stood for far before that, and the evidence is beneath us, in steel*

canyons and valleys. But since then, there have have been six more ages, all of them periods of different rule, the reeh allowing one or another group's ascendence.

"Amakti Los happened in the first of these ages, perhaps seven and a half thousand years ago. It was a secret society, of sorts. Many non-human species participated, but the lestis, the tanifex and the trento were most prominent. They existed for perhaps four millennia before the reeh finally tired of them, and had them annihilated." Another sip of water.

"And," Romki prompted when the rabbi did not add more, *"there is talk of Amakti Los headquarters that were never discovered. That contain lost secrets of Qalea's history to this day."*

"It seems unlikely," said Silverman. *"The underworld is not abandoned. The Under Watch patrol all those places, to keep the lost ones at bay. They know all these locations."*

Romki nodded, writing more. Much as the Major had reported on Rando, Qalea also had its 'kauda', its augmented, its genetic freaks and escapees from various reeh experiments. Whether they wandered the depths of Qalea by accident or on purpose, no one seemed to know. The Major, however, doubted the reeh let anything happen without some twisted forethought.

"May I read your books?" Romki's slate asked when he was finished. *"I would be greatly in your debt."*

Silverman sighed, waving a dismissive hand and climbing to his feet. *"My great grandmother hated hiding books too, she said that books were for reading. In her memory, Stanislav, I will show you what I have."*

It was dark when Romki emerged from the synagogue. His stomach was full, as Rabbi Silverman and his wife had insisted on feeding him as he read (and scanned the page for translation), and his mind was fuller. But he did not want to leap to conclusions too early — data once revealed needed to be laid out and considered in context and at length, and so he strode through the narrow alleys of Qalea's Jewish

Quarter, following his visor's lead toward his hostel, and a bed for the night.

The lanes were mostly empty, but here and there were men of varying ages, with unimpressive looking guns in their hands. They watched him as he approached, and Romki waved to them and smiled, regretting that his cover story of a recent throat operation meant that he could not call 'Shalom'. Crime in Qalea was very bad in some parts, and far less in others. The Jewish Quarter seemed to be one of those others, as was usually the case in self-organised communities where some members would patrol the streets at night with guns while others slept.

As he left the Quarter, the lanes grew rougher, and water flowed in places from broken pipes as the ground began a downward slope. Soon he was picking his way along a hillside, where the bright lights of Amara Ridge, his neighbourhood of lodging, shone above the broken rooves along a canyon top to his right. Other pedestrians passed, but all were men at this hour, and most were at least in pairs, and made no eye contact. Romki told himself that he'd been in far rougher neighbourhoods than this, and picked his way past the empty benches of a silent marketplace, as strange alien critters scampered into cracks in the walls at his approach.

A sound behind him made him glance. When he looked back, his way was blocked by three big men. He stopped, and heard movement behind, more men encircling. Calm, he willed himself past his thudding heart. Be calm. The Major was always calm in the face of danger. Of course, if all these men picked a fight with the Major, it would be their funeral, not her's. Romki knew some chah'nas martial arts, but he did not carry the kon-til sticks with him here. Barehanded, he was far less effective, and his heavy-G augments were nothing like the combat augments of UF marines. The marines had offered him a gun, which plenty of folks in Qalea carried, but Romki had refused. If he'd tried to use a gun here, and these encirclers were also armed, he'd be dead very quickly. But how could he talk his way out of trouble while still keeping his cover story?

The leader growled at him... Arabic, he thought. *"You're Stanislav.*

You've been visiting mosques and synagogues." Romki nodded slowly. *"And you've been pretending to be a mute. Don't deny it. We've heard you talking, on coms."*

It could have been a lie, just to see if he'd admit it. Romki said nothing.

"You're pale for a Koron," the man continued. *"Not many whiteys in Koro. You're a Jew?"* Romki shook his head. A lot of the Jews were dark too, but a good percentage of the lighter-skinned humans were Jewish. It was a startling thing to be confronted with. Back in the Spiral, humans hadn't cared much about race since near-extinction at the hands of the krim, and the population-mixing that followed among the survivors had made it irrelevant. But for these humans, taken from lands where pale skin was rare, and East Asian features non-existent, certain kinds of humans stood out more than others.

The man walked forward. He wore street clothes, a worn jacket, rough pants, an AR visor on a thinly-bearded face. *"Our boss thinks you're not from around here at all. He wants to talk to you."*

Romki shrugged, making puzzlement plain on his face.

The man in the visor smiled. *"Good trick, being a mute. What do you really speak? Maybe you should come and speak it to our boss. He'll find it interesting."*

Romki thought about it. If he fought, he'd lose. If he spoke, they'd hear his true tongue. He thought wildly about speaking some alien tongue — Togiri, perhaps, which would be alien to them, but at least it wouldn't be English. He could claim, accurately, that he was a scholar of non-human civilisations, and lie to say that this was an obscure tongue of some local alien species... but none of it made any sense, because all humans had to speak some human language, and his elaborate attempts to avoid speaking his own would only make them more suspicious.

Repulsor engines throbbed loudly, far louder than the ever-present background traffic, and then a light was glaring from the sky, blindingly white. *"Put your weapons away and leave!"* Romki's earpiece translated the loud Arabic from the speakers above.

Then a shot, and Romki ducked, running for cover closest to the hoverbike, from where the angle would shield him. More shots as men ran, stumbled, and one more fell, to join his companion writhing on the ground.

The bike howled as it grounded in a swirl of dust, Romki shielding his eyes, and then Corporal Arime's voice was shouting in his earpiece, *"Professor, get your ass on board now!"*

Romki knew better than to argue, and ran to the bike, scrambled aboard and grabbed Arime's waist, his stomach lurching as they bounced skyward to the rooftop overlooking the alley where a dark figure fired several more shots to deter anyone below from retaliation. They pulled alongside that figure, who leaped aboard behind Romki, and the bike turned and roared away.

They did not go fast, for two of the three passengers were not strapped in, yet Romki felt the person behind doing that for his legs as the slipstream blasted about them, and the dizzying lights of Qalea glared in a blaze of crazy topography.

"You okay Jess?" came Arime's voice.

"Yeah," said Private Jess Rolonde as she worked on Romki's straps. *"Don't think I killed any, they were all leg shots."*

"They weren't even armed!" Romki fumed, and it was only by articulating his thoughts that he regained enough composure to realise he was furious. "Why did you shoot them when they weren't even armed?"

"You don't see too well, do you Doc?" said Rolonde.

"They were plenty armed," Arime supported his Private.

"I saw nothing," Romki retorted. "And besides, they weren't pointing their weapons, they wanted me to come and talk to their boss..."

"And that woulda been the last we'd seen of you!" said Rolonde, finishing his straps and starting on her own.

"I can assure you Private," Romki fumed, "I'm very good at talking my way out of situations just like that!"

"Except you're pretending you can't even speak," said Arime, zooming low above a ridge of rooftops and looking carefully for traffic on the

far side. Flying in Qalea was always alarming. *"We got orders not to let you get grabbed by anyone. Take it up with the Major."*

They'd been tailing him, Romki realised with exasperation. So much for him venturing alone and unsupervised. Not that he was the slightest bit surprised, in hindsight... just furious at his own naivety.

"I will take it up with the Major!" he told them. "I take it that's where we're going?"

"Nah, I was going to get some drinks and a show!" said Arime. *"But if you'd rather go see the Major, we can do that instead."*

THE WAREHOUSE DOOR was edged open for them as they arrived across the silent ship-breaking yard, and Arime steered them in, running lights off, engines powered down save the repulsors and jumping off as the bike became a barely controlled puck-on-ice with the power down. Romki got off after Rolonde, and walked briskly to where the Major, Jokono and Styx were seated beside their accumulated hover-bikes, the humans sipping hot beverages while Styx hulked beside them amid many splayed limbs, like a fastidious steel spider.

Styx's old chassis had been deemed impractical for this mission, and so her drysine escorts had provided her with a new one — somewhat smaller than the old, it resembled far more the basic design of a drysine combat drone, save that it was a little bigger, and the head mount now carried the same flared carapace for the protection of Styx's single-eyed head.

"Major!" Romki said angrily as he approached, his voice echoing off the high warehouse ceiling. Everyone looked, even the Major, sipping the drink with her usual unruffled calm. "You told me I'd be free to follow my own nose on this mission — your words, not mine!"

The Major nodded. "Until your nose got you into trouble, in which case you would be extracted, like any member of this team."

"I was about to find out who those people were!" Romki insisted, waving his hand in the general direction of the place where he'd been

— up, and to the right. Styx lifted one synthetic limb and pointed in a forty-five degree different direction, uncommenting. Romki's finger followed her lead. "Only you pulled me out of there before I could find out!"

"Actually Professor," said Styx, "it was my monitoring that alerted the marines to your situation."

"On the Major's orders!" Romki retorted.

"Stanley, this is boring," said the Major, looking entirely bored as she sipped her drink from a tin mug. The little gas cooker on the floor illuminated her face in half light, and did something entirely more devilish to Styx. "Please reconsider what you think this temper will gain you, with me. We can save whole minutes if you'll just skip it entirely."

Romki realised with further frustration that she was right. It made him want to throw something... but perhaps that was the thing with family, everyone just knew everyone else too well by now, and pressed each other's buttons without trying.

"Fine!" he huffed, pulling off his bag and taking a seat on a spare empty box beside the cooker. "Just fine." He rummaged in his bag, checking that his slate, hand recorder, and other personals hadn't been somehow damaged.

"Thank you Stan," said the Major, with a faint smile into her cup. "Now, what did you...?"

But she was interrupted by Rolonde, with a hand display of her own, shoved before Romki's eyes. "There," she said. "Look, guns." Romki looked — it was a recording from the scope of Rolonde's rifle. He recognised the angle, looking down on men surrounding a lone figure with a backpack — himself. Several of the men behind him, indeed, held handguns low to their sides.

"Yes, thank you Private," he said tiredly. He could not help the involuntary wave of relief at seeing it, to be here and not there, in whatever dangerous place they'd have taken him, surrounded by armed and unfriendly men. But that only annoyed him further. He didn't want to be so dependent on all these people with guns. He'd managed for many decades back in human space, but now... now he wasn't certain he knew who he was anymore. "I believe you."

"Good thing I shot them, huh?" Rolonde pressed, with the air of a woman owed an apology.

"Yes yes, very good thing," Romki said drily. "I'm sure if you keep shooting every armed man in Qalea, our situation will improve in leaps and bounds."

Rolonde nodded firmly, choosing to hear the nonexistent apology, and tucked the display away... and saw the Major gazing at her, unblinking, having been interrupted. "I... I was just showing him the thing. He didn't believe me." The Major said nothing, still gazing, not angry, just... there. Rolonde ducked her head and retreated. The Major's eyes followed her, faintly incredulous... and Romki saw Jokono smothering a smile, the older man seeing the Major's reprimanding stare for the affection it truly contained, like a mother disciplining unruly but loveable children.

"Well," said Romki, as Jokono warmed a saucepan of water on the cooker, and put some of the tea mix Romki liked in a mug. "It's beginning to look as though Styx's theory on the Ceephay Queen may be correct."

"It's not a theory," said Styx.

"It remains unproven," said Romki, testily. "Even drysines believe that we shouldn't confirm things as fact just because they seem likely."

"Human understandings of statistical probability are primitive," said Styx. "The word 'theory' falls well short of my present comprehension. I have several million converging data-points, the mathematical likelihood of an alternative general truth in this instance is nonexistent. There are, however, degrees of truth, layers in the probable and past states of time and space. Drysines have data-models to explain these things instead of crude human algebra and even cruder words, and I am unable to use one to describe the other."

"No, you must understand, people," said Jokono, with mocking earnestness. "It's not just likely. It's really, *really* likely. Like, *REALLY*, you know?" Styx regarded him with her single red eye. Even Trace bit back a smile. "I'm sorry Styx," said Jokono, looking quite pleased with himself. The former police detective didn't joke around much, but making fun of Styx had a certain thrill. "Please continue."

Sergeant Rael wandered across the empty warehouse floor, in civvie clothes with rifle on his back and pushing the visor up his forehead. Trace made room for him on her box, and he sat, while Jokono prepared another mug. Rael was a laid-back young man with movie star good looks, and Romki was struck, suddenly, by just how much this young marine had seen and been through in the last few years. By how much they all had. If Sergeant Rael were to walk into any major alien-studies department in human space, scholars who'd previously have looked down their noses at a mere marine sergeant would be picking their jaws off the floor to hear the tales he could tell.

"Peanut's listening through coms," Rael explained, tapping his mic. "Keeps him happy." Because Peanut, *Phoenix*'s most sociable drysine drone, had shown outright reluctance to sit on guard duty at the far end of the warehouse while people were talking elsewhere. He'd never exactly abandoned his post, but he had readjusted that post closer to the conversation, and away from where he should have ideally been located.

"Peanut," said Trace into coms, "in a little while you can come and play cards for an hour. How does that sound?"

Drones did not talk, but Romki imagined an agreeable silence. Despite knowing it was not wise to anthropomorphise the alien war machine, everyone liked Peanut. In spite of his more lethal nature, he clearly got bored sometimes, and being a machine who needed no sleep, everyone felt a little guilty having him on guard duty all night with no relief.

"Professor," said Trace, with irony. "About the Ceephay Queen, you were about to say?"

"Plainly something happened eight thousand years ago," said Romki. "A civilisational shift. Now to hear the croma tell the tale, the reeh have never had civilisational shifts. They've always been a static, monolithic civilisation. If what happened eight thousand years ago was some sort of a coup or political overthrow, then that would seem to challenge the croma understanding of the reeh."

"Croma understandings on most things are intensely self-interested," Styx offered.

Romki nodded. "Since that period, which Qalea humans call the Origin Horizon, there have been seven major ages. In the first two of these ages, the reeh were still here, on Eshir, in considerable number. Then they pulled out almost entirely for the last five ages, though their presence is still strongly felt in what the locals call Overwatch. The cities fell largely into ruin, Qalea was a complete mess through the middle of those ages, there were several domestic wars that the reeh did not see fit to intervene in, and a couple that they did, with horrifying results.

"You know... you go over a planet's worth of history across eight thousand years, with as many different species vying for power as you've had here, and a lot of things can happen. Basically Eshir has functioned as a kind of refuse tip for the reeh, only the refuse are people, sentient beings no longer needed or welcome in their respective parts of the Empire, so they get dumped here. And across as much time and space as the reeh have been fighting, and putting down internal rebellions, you end up here with something like sedimentary layers of that discarded sentient refuse, building layers of civilisation on top of one another.

"A lot of them have been at war with each other, and a lot of them have gone through periods of living quite peacefully together. There's no public libraries here, and public electronic information is completely unreliable thanks to reeh active censorship, not to mention completely unsafe since the reeh are so much better than anyone else we've encountered in the Spiral with infotech. So I've been going through paper book libraries in private hands, and the only ones of those that are accessible are in the religious houses, the mosques and synagogues, mostly, and the odd church and Hindu temple.

"Doing that, and talking to some history experts — they're all amateurs here, there's nothing like universities save for some private technical colleges — I found reference to one old group called the Amakti Los. I was searching for any direct historical connection between the Origin Horizon, and what Styx theorises was the end of the Ceephay Queen's prominent role in the Reeh Empire, and the present day. Something that might have survived, that could tell us what happened, and where the Ceephay Queen might be now, given we already know she's still alive and writing reeh code.

"The Amakti Los were a pacifist group, you could call them a new emergent religion, they preached peace and unity between alien races on Eshir. They were a lot less perfect in practise, I gather, but the thought is nice."

"Real nice," Rael agreed, with the irony of a man at war most of his adult life. Jokono's water boiled, and the detective poured tea into two mugs, and presented them to Rael and Romki. "Thanks Joker."

"Thank you," said Romki, and blew on the tea. It smelled good, in that exotic way of things he'd only tasted for the first time a few days ago, and reminded him of the reasons he'd chosen this far-flung life in the first place. "So the Amakti Los were around for a long time, got involved in a whole bunch of things that aren't necessary for me to go into, then managed to upset the reeh about four thousand years ago and get themselves annihilated. Like truly purged, the reeh hunted them down — it was complicated, another big domestic blowup and war, and the reeh came in hard with troops on the ground and scoured everyone they didn't like, Amakti Los included, and handed power to the other domestic group they preferred."

"It seems peace and unity between alien brothers doesn't last," Jokono offered.

Romki shrugged. "Yes, but they did last longer than a lot of the major human religions have been around, close to four thousand years after the Origin Horizon, so it's only a qualified failure. However, the interesting thing about the Amakti Los is that they claimed original founding texts and inspirations going back past the Origin Horizon. The speculation is that this may have been what got them destroyed, at least in part. The reeh don't like anyone talking about that period, as you've noticed."

Trace frowned. "Didn't the reeh make any attempt to eliminate that data? Burn the private libraries?"

"Ah, yes," said Romki, sipping his tea. "But here, my dear Major, we encounter once again the wonder of paper. Electronic data can be endlessly manipulated and erased, but paper is actually very hard to destroy. People hide books, you see. All across the Spiral it has been the salvation of so many important strands of academic research, I cannot begin to tell you. Some survive, and I've read a few just recently.

"There's no hint of exactly what the Amakti Los knew of the period before the Origin Horizon, but there are tales of hidden libraries, deep in the underground, or lost elsewhere in the old city."

"Another treasure hunt?" Rael sighed.

"Another treasure hunt," Romki agreed, with far greater enthusiasm than the Sergeant. "Most of these treasures remain hidden because those that looked previously lacked our current capabilities." He indicated to Styx. "A coin buried in a field stays hidden until the first man arrives with a metal detector. Our success rate has been so good because Styx is our metal detector."

"A flattering analogy, Professor," said Styx.

"Any idea of where these hidden libraries may be?" Trace asked.

"Many books make the point that of all the species on Eshir that were purged when the Amakti Los was destroyed, the lestis survived most intact," said Romki. "There are lestis institutions, intact since that time, that had significant involvement in the Amakti Los. If anyone would retain historical memory of that period, the lestis would."

"Well I don't know if that will help," said Trace, sipping her water. "I was at a lestis temple today, I've interacted with them quite a bit. Or as much as you can, with lestis. No one understands them, and as far as we understand, they don't talk at all. Apparently they encode information through patterns of vibration, they have crazy-large memories and don't need to write things down, or not as much."

"Lestis do communicate through the networks," said Styx. "Their technology is no more advanced than any other, just different. I believe I may have some insights into how their psychologies work, by studying their network software. Also, the bug you planted at the temple has granted me access to many uniquely lestis systems that are shielded from main-network access. I cannot access the main lestis cores, but I believe I now have a series of keys that could be applied usefully."

"What else have your bugs uncovered?" Romki asked, curious to know what the marines, Styx and Jokono had been up to while he'd been gone.

"They indicate," said Styx, "that in the absence of any centralised government or communications network, power in Qalea has become radically decentralised. Not only do alien races here use different languages, they utilise different base technologies and operating codes for their networks, making them in many cases largely non-interoperable. Combined with certain base defensive technologies that are certainly AI-derived, this makes my efforts to infiltrate the city's networks quite challenging. On Dul'rho I could create proxy processors that slaved croma computer nodes to my control, all of which were autonomously invulnerable enough for me to leave unattended. In Qalea that is not possible — slaved nodes will be overwhelmed as soon as I shift my attention elsewhere, and the node's usual operators alerted to the infiltration.

"I have had to be far more discrete. I can overwhelm local technology easily enough when my attention is fully upon it, but to gain control of large sections of the Qalea network simultaneously, given its total lack of uniformity, is impossible. Thus the infiltration bugs, which can find weaknesses in specific locations that I identified, and bypass network defences with physical proximity, something that I obviously cannot do myself."

"Yes yes," said Romki, "I recall much of this conversation from before I left."

"The Major visited five locations in the guise of tourism, which have given me access to the previously-secure networks of House Tedesse in the Human Quarter, a primary network in the Lestis Quarter, a major industrial network of the Dogreth Quarter, the

Qwailash Fighting Pits network, and the Hititchi Shipyard Network, which is governed by no single species, but has many pathways through the city's transportation thoroughfares."

"You went to the Beztos Shipyards?" Romki asked the Major. He'd seen visuals, and they looked extraordinary. "How was that?"

"Almost incomprehensible," the Major admitted. She had a faintly far-away look in her eyes, mug in hands, lips to the fragrance. Such a different place from her last mission, Romki thought. The bare concrete and steel of the warehouse made a stark contrast from the jungles of Rando. Romki knew that she had not returned the same as she'd left. The marines brushed all such suggestions aside, insisting she was fine. But Romki knew that the Captain, for one, had not believed it.

Seeing her now, he was struck by how human she looked. On the ship, in familiar environments, with her marine-blacks, busy routines and always someone about to conduct businesslike discussions with, she'd seemed typically larger than life. But here, in civilian clothes, sipping a cup in the light of the cooker, she looked disarmingly young, like a girl on a camping trip with her family. Sometimes Romki forgot how young she was. The Captain had always seemed young, though less so recently, as he'd learned not to wear his vulnerabilities on his sleeve. But Major Thakur had always seemed like an old soul, hard like a sea cliff forever beaten by the waves... until now, where she gazed at a far warehouse wall, and recalled the many things she'd seen, on this trip and those previous. Far too much, surely, for a woman of such youth to process.

Romki was almost surprised at how paternal it made him feel toward her. She'd spent much of the past two years being a thorn in his side, and occasionally a dagger... but really, she was just a kid, as they all were on this trip save Jokono, and of course Styx, to whom they were all infants. A kid who did the best she could, and struggled through the pain, only hoping that it was enough.

"And how's the boy?" asked Jokono.

"Couldn't have gotten into the casino without him," said the Major. "Nor the Fighting Pits, he knew a guy. And he talked his way past a guard in the Kota Industries plant. Didn't know why I'd want to visit a smelting floor, but if I were a visual artist I'd have wanted to see it."

"This city is half dream, half nightmare," Jokono agreed. "And your encounter in the casino?"

Romki frowned. "You had an encounter in the casino?"

"Three biker thugs tried to muscle my guide," the Major explained. "It could have been a coincidence. But then you had your encounter, Stan." With a pointed look at Romki. "And I'm thinking someone might be on to us. Thus we're being especially careful on guard tonight, and we're staying ready in case we have to move to the next location."

"Who do you think it might be?" Romki asked.

The Major shook her head. "There are too many options, and we're too new in town to risk guesses. We'll assume it's everyone, and go from there."

"I would not recommend ditching the kid," said Jokono. "He seems to like you, as a young man might. And you have a skillset that will appeal to him." The Major made a face, not really protesting. Sergeant Rael looked at her curiously. "That affection could be groomed into a useful loyalty. But a young man jilted may take his complaints to our enemies, whoever they turn out to be, and surely he would know better than us."

"If anyone comes after us," said the Major, "they'll likely do it through him, right?" Questioning the former policeman, as she always did on matters where experts knew more than her.

"Quite likely, yes," said Jokono.

"So in all likelihood, by choosing him to use his connections, we've killed him."

Jokono took a deep breath. "It's certainly possible." He considered her for a serious moment. "It won't be the last awful thing we do for the human cause."

"No," the Major said quietly. She finished her tea, and got up. "No it won't."

11

Erik sat on the bridge and watched nothing happen. Nothing, and nothing much, had been happening in this region of space, and most regions of space, for billions of years. In the monotony of endless duty on the bridge, his mind wandered to that long preceding stretch of human history, where humans had wondered if they'd been alone in the galaxy. They'd even called it 'The Milky Way', for the creamy-white patterns the elliptic view of the outer spiral arms had splashed across the Earth's night sky. A few songwriters had tried to reinstate that name for the galaxy, erased by Fleet's military pragmatism in the years following Earth's loss, and its systemic erasure of Earth-bound sillinesses, like 'shooting stars', and anything o'clock.

But 'Milky Way' hadn't come back into fashion. Humans had seen what the galaxy truly was, and weren't about to be fooled back into old romantic notions. Erik wondered how many humans from back then would have been thrilled to know that one day humanity would discover that the galaxy was in fact teeming with sentient civilisations who had only been dissuaded from visiting because various Spiral laws and boundaries had disincentivized it. Certainly there'd been much excitement on Earth when the first krim ships had jumped insystem. There'd been popular jokes on the Academy network of surviving footage from old-Earth news shows, with talking heads excited to the point of jumping up and down when outer-system radar had shown the arrival of ships that were clearly not human, and broadcasting the fact.

'Calm yourself' had been the heading for those jokes, a heading also applied to cadet Squad Leaders declaring that the class were all about to take an exciting field trip (latrine duty), or partake in challenging new exercises (three hours of parade drill at 0400). 'Either we are alone in the universe,' a famous scientist from that period had once declared, 'or we're not. Both are equally terrifying'.

Well, Erik thought now, watching the far-distant scans of Keijir System traffic, mostly unchanged for the past ten hours. Not 'equally terrifying', as it turned out. All humans of the Great War would have happily traded that one, purportedly 'equal' terror for the other. But then, if those first incoming ships had been tavalai rather than krim, then the early newspeople would have been justified in their excitement. Tavalai would have landed with flowers and greeting ribbons, and done photo opportunities diving on the Earth's Great Barrier Reef and declared it a most beautiful planet, and offered to protect and enrich it, in exchange for trade and other mutually beneficial relations.

But probably better that it had been the krim than the reeh, Erik thought now, flicking back to reading a translation of one of the intel reports *Phoenix* had helped liberate from Croma'Rai's Intelligence arm nearly three months ago. The krim had proven to be at least beatable, though at an appalling cost. There was little indication yet that the reeh were.

"Captain," said Lieutenant Shilu. After eight days in quiet surveillance in the outer Keijir System, Shilu was dividing attention between captured intelligence from Croma'Rai HQ, and monitoring the flow of routine system traffic that drifted out this far. "*Friendship* wants to talk."

"Put them through." *Friendship* was the drysine flagship, an invisible shadow lying fifteen thousand klicks elliptic of *Phoenix*, similarly silent and watching. Styx said the name had been Liala's choice, before they'd left Teg'ula System. The rest of the small drysine fleet were similarly named for things incongruously non-drysine -- *Sunrise*, *Alliance* and *Melody*. They were the kind of names a young AI queen might choose without entirely understanding human concepts of irony, and how such choices might seem like bad poetry written by a clever but non-artistic person who was trying too hard. Kaspowitz had created his own names for the dark foursome -- *Kitten*, *Mittens*, *Puppy Dog* and *Perky Buttocks*.

"Hello Captain," said a smooth, almost-human voice. Drysine drones barely spoke, and then only the most high-functioning. Exactly who or what was speaking when one of the warships contacted them, no one had yet discerned, and neither Styx nor Liala had chosen to illuminate. Lieutenant Rooke thought it was probably the ship itself that was talking. Drysine AIs came in many forms, and a chassis was just a chassis, whether it was small with legs, or huge with jump engines. This particular voice sounded female. *"The drysine vessels have been calculating. We have illuminated a new target for investigation. Its location will be shown to you now."*

Erik's middle-screen flashed, a scroll through regional space in the empty expanse of Keijir's outer reach. Erik left his headset on the chairback, not needing it for something simple enough to be portrayed in 2D. Highlight brackets settled upon something in relatively nearby orbit, about four million kilometres distant. Erik frowned, zooming on the scan. It wasn't *Phoenix*'s scan, it was *Friendship*'s, and in startlingly high resolution, sent tightbeam to *Phoenix* to avoid any chance of detection.

It looked like a giant ball of ice, the kind of thing that might have become a comet had it acquired a trajectory through the star's inner system. *Friendship*'s analysis had been translated into human-friendly dimensions and even guesswork at chemical composition, some of which Erik had no idea how they'd arrived at. Original drysine sensors, advanced again beyond even what *Phoenix* had lately acquired on Defiance. *Friendship* and her companions were survivors from the Drysine-Deepynine War, hidden in deep storage at some dark mass point for many millennia, and kept in good working order by their tireless crews.

"Hello *Friendship*," Erik replied. "I am reviewing your feed now. Please inform me why you consider this object to be worthy of closer inspection."

They'd been sitting here for eight days, watching Keijir System traffic, learning what they could about reeh fleet movements in this region. From Teg'ula they'd three-jumped it via some dark mass points croma Fleet intelligence knew of, and once passed though the outer-system of a larger solar mass that probably had reeh scanning present, but with these technology upgrades was unlikely to detect them due to their distance from the star. At their previous technological level, and the level where most of human Fleet still resided, such a course would have seen them intercepted and destroyed, yet they'd arrived at Keijir System after barely a week real-time, and there lain in wait for passing freighters at a jump-point once again known to croma intel.

When one had arrived, they'd jammed transmissions, intercepted and boarded, and thus acquired a ship with attached shuttles and accompanying transit IDs to take Trace's away mission down to Eshir's surface. It had meant disposing of the original freighter crew, but they'd all been actual reeh, not slave species, so no one had cared, least of all the drysines. The freighter had been bound for the far side of reeh space, so Erik figured it would be many weeks or possibly months until the repercussions of them not arriving at their intended destination found their way back to here.

As for fooling the reeh at Eshir, Styx's analysis indicated that if the reeh had a weakness, it was their lack of common sociability amongst each other. A human vessel arriving at station with excuses why they did not wish to talk to others, and tales of repairs to be conducted and procedures adhered to, would have aroused human curiosity and concern, as *Phoenix* had been concerned with the odd arrival of the *Grappler* at Tuki Station two years ago. But had *Grappler* and *Phoenix* both been reeh vessels, at a much busier station than Joma, there was a chance that no one would have noticed that all the crew were dead for many days at least. Now the reeh freighter sat in parking orbit off one of Eshir's big orbital stations, piloted by a non-sentient AI automation program that Styx had constructed, and everyone hoping that the reeh's gene-deep psychological unconcern for each other's personal welfare continued to result in a lack of curiosity. So far, to judge from the absence of commotion in the seven hour light-delay from Eshir, currently near-side to the Keijir System sun, it was working.

"Phoenix, drysine collective analysis indicates a high probability that this body was utilised in the past history of this system's civilisation for resource mining. A closer examination may reveal a past history of the system itself."

"*Friendship*, please hold." Erik paused transmission. "Nav, thoughts?"

Frowning, Kaspowitz's long fingers flew over his controls, flipping the headset over his eyes for a 3D view. "I... see no reason why they might have chosen that object, Captain. I mean, there's millions of them along this ecliptic quadrant alone. Unless their sensors are seeing something ours can't, which seems unlikely, given the luminosity of that object is low at this range from the sun, and their sensors aren't *that* much better than ours."

"Helm?" Erik asked Sasalaka, who was just returning from her toilet break, and buckling her squat frame into the seat beside and behind Erik's. In some hot zones, alternate-shift pilots had to be woken to sit the chair while toilet breaks were taken, but sitting in the far-outer orbital zone of a system where no local ships possessed the technology to jump into directly, *Phoenix* and her drysine companions weren't about to be surprised in that way. And if anyone came at them with regular engines, they'd get many hours of warning. Thus First Shift were taking occasional breaks while leaving Second Shift in bed.

"It's a ball of ice?" Sasalaka asked, squinting at her displays with big froggy eyes. From the rapid blinking of her third eyelid, Erik guessed she'd been applying eyedrops in the bathroom -- common tavalai cure for dry human air.

"Looks that way. Could be composite, what do you think, Scan?"

"Scancomp says it's a garden variety ball of ice, Captain," Second Lieutenant Geish disagreed. Erik could barely see Scan One or Two behind the mid-bridge superstructure brace that had been greatly enlarged with the Defiance redesign, after the old bridge had been shotgun pulverised by the deepynines. "We could learn more with active scan, but not much more." And of course, he didn't need to say, using active scan was the equivalent of jumping up and down and shouting for attention.

"Anyone have ideas how the drysines might be so certain this one's worth investigating?"

"Nothing here," Kaspowitz admitted. "The orbit's a little irregular, but within the parameters of what you'd expect. I could run the orbital simulation backward a few tens of thousands of years if you wanted, but that would only confirm this object's statistical randomness -- there's no reason any previous civilisation might have chosen this one and not another one."

"You can tell that without running the numbers?" Sasalaka asked.

"There weren't abruptly less objects here ten thousand years ago," Kaspowitz replied, fingers racing as he ran various simulations even now. "The randomness remains the same... I mean, I'm running relative positions against primary jump entry and departure points given local FTL technology, there's relative coasting trajectories out from the major worlds and mining routes... it's within the optimal position for energy savings on a majority of these traverse windows, but so are about a hundred million other objects, system-wide."

Erik chewed his lip, resisting the impulse to wish that Styx were aboard to give advice. Sometimes he forgot that Styx was herself drysine, and would not take *Phoenix*'s side in any division against drysine ships. If the drysines were plotting something, and she were aboard, she'd have started it.

He reopened the channel. "Hello *Friendship*, *Phoenix* cannot replicate your assurance that this body is worth investigating. Any movement we make, even out this far from the system center, could conceivably draw attention. *Phoenix* requests that you illustrate your reasoning more plainly."

"Illustration is not possible," came the reply. *"Human statistical capabilities are inadequate. A low-G manoeuvre is probabilistically unlikely to draw attention. Friendship will lay a course."*

The link went dead. "Thoughts?" Erik requested.

"I don't like it," said Kaspowitz. "But you knew that."

"Doesn't mean I don't appreciate hearing it again. Sasalaka?"

The tavalai gazed at her displays for a long moment. "Does it cost us anything?" she ventured. Erik thought about it. It wasn't like they had anything else to do, sitting out here on the outer system rim, waiting for the Major to complete her mission. Moving slowly to go and check out an iceball shouldn't prove much of a distraction at all. And if the drysines were right that there was something there...

"Captain, they're sending the course now," Kaspowitz reported, and Erik saw it flash on his screen -- about as dull and uninteresting as a deep space course-plot could get. Point A to point B, slowly, in wide formation.

Erik made up his mind and keyed the ship-wide. "Attention all hands, this is your Captain speaking. An announcement will follow shortly." He said it mostly to give sleeping crew an opportunity to wake up, and now paused a moment longer to be sure. "Our drysine escort has indicated that they believe a nearby deep space body may prove worth investigating. The body in question appears to be a ball of ice, but the drysines are sure they know better. We are going to go and check it out.

"Manoeuvring thrust will be minimal as we are still running silent. Thrust will commence in a little under five, and will max at zero-point-two Gs. Burn duration will be slightly more than two hours and forty minutes, following which we will be coasting for approximately twenty-one hours until the final rendezvous burn. Alert condition yellow will remain in force, no immediate combat is anticipated, regular schedules will be observed.

"Marines will commence boarding drill at the earliest, orders to follow shortly. Lieutenant Dale, please report to the bridge."

12

Forty-nine hours after the croma evacuation force arrived at Rando, the reeh counter-attacks began. Lisbeth was woken from her bed as the alarm klaxons howled, then a mad scramble to pull her safety harness on and run the fifteen steps from her quarters to the bridge, and occupy the observer chair that was her's. The attackers were still some way out or she'd never have made the bridge at all -- when warships were surprised badly enough, there was barely time to make the nearest acceleration sling before the ten-G crush that would kill nearly everyone unsecured as the ship sacrificed crew to save itself.

Now she buckled in hard, her seat straps adjusted for a human's unsightly girth, and pulled her visor free of the headrest clamp to settle it over her eyes as her screens fired up. Between them she now had a panoramic, three-dimensional picture of the space around this portion of Rando, adjustable by toggles on her handgrips that would stay within reach even if the ship's manoeuvres became extreme. It took some practise though.

The reeh attack was coming out of jump... out beyond the far lunar orbit of Dogba, still twenty minutes at even those crazy velocities. That data was taking one minute's light-lag to reach them, but was now reporting nine reeh ships, all fast attack vessels. Fourteen croma warships deployed in several intercept formations were responding, audible now on coms, short Kul'hasa grunts as their captains talked under heavy Gs. Croma Fleet knew the performance of reeh warships well, and had made educated guesses as to where the counter-attack would emerge upon Rando and Dogba's merging gravity slopes. It looked as though they'd chosen their defensive positions well, because the reeh seemed to be coming out just where the croma wanted them.

"Hello Lisbeth," came Liala's voice in her ears. *"I would like to make a situation report."* It was crazy that Liala would talk to *her* about such things. But with none of the croma listening to her, she had few other options, and talking to Lisbeth would occupy only the slightest fraction of her brain power while performing other functions.

"Yes of course, Liala. What do you see?" *Coroset* was in high geostationary orbit above the continent of Talo, watching the heaviest evacuation traffic they'd seen so far. *Amity* was trailing a thousand kilometres to one flank, as the parren and drysine vessels operated as a pair. In low orbit around the planet swarmed nearly a hundred Sto'ji Class transports. Only thirty-four had so far loaded completely, more than two full days since the arrival of the first of them. The plan had figured each could be fully loaded in twenty-one hours, but though a few had managed it, most were averaging well over thirty hours.

Thirty had so far made it to jump, and four more were currently underway, lumbering with underpowered engines toward a higher position on the gravity slope where jump engines could find purchase to propel their massive bulk into hyperspace. Three-point-four million corbi, it was quite an achievement already... but there were around two hundred million down there, and already signs that some would struggle to make the evacuation zones in time without modern transportation.

Among the big Sho'jis were a swarm of smaller transports, Scan informed her that the number had swelled while she'd been asleep to reach six hundred and eighty one. Most were much smaller, some could hold barely a few hundred corbi, and all were down there in close orbit where the shuttles could reach them most efficiently. Some had their own shuttles, but at least half did not, and so were reliant on the growing fleet of unattached shuttles ferrying evacuees up to them. The Sho'jis had left their shuttles behind, crews working in round-the-clock rotations to bring passengers up to civilian ships, docking at unfamiliar airlocks with sometimes incompatible grapples, with several reports of near-collisions and decompression accidents, though no deaths so far. But, as Lisbeth had predicted to Rhi'shul when she'd first gotten the tour, the shuttle capacities and freighter capacities were now not matching, so shuttles were having to waste time delivering part-loads to one ship, then part to another, delaying the frequency of their ascents and descents, and thus slowing the total flow.

"Lisbeth," said Liala, *"I believe that the reeh are about to make a flanking hook to the Rando nadir with their next jump, this current attack is merely to draw the croma outer defences into engaging."*

Lisbeth looked at the confusion of intersecting trajectories and plotted guesswork of firing solutions, and thought it looked like a haystack in a tornado. But beyond that one point of confusion, Liala's suggestion looked... plausible. "Surely the croma will guess that it's coming?" she asked.

"It is very much the standard manoeuvre for the situation," Liala conceded. *"The outer defences engage to prevent long-range fire from being successfully deployed against our forces closer to Rando, and the second attack comes about their flank to hit us directly. However, I do not think the croma have anticipated how many there will be."*

Lisbeth had thought she was handling her first view of warship combat from an operational bridge quite well until that point. But now her heart began to thump quite rapidly. "How many?"

"It is a probabilistic thing, and I cannot be certain." Meaning that drysine queens understood the mathematical complexities of the highest-order risk assessment better than any other minds in the Spiral. *"But this attack pattern raises the likelihood that the reeh have concentrated a larger than anticipated portion of their force here at Rando.*

We had hoped the croma flanking attacks on Jikul and Torsena would draw them off, but I do not think it has worked."

"Or maybe they had more ships in reserve to begin with," Lisbeth muttered, zooming and squinting on her displays as she tried to make sense of what they showed her. "Croma Fleet Intelligence has let them down before."

"Indeed," said Liala. *"I feel that the possibility should be raised with the croma commanders."*

"I showed them your last analysis of our transport deployments," said Lisbeth. Truth be told, she didn't like interrupting croma commanders while they were working. "They ignored it."

"And every logistical issue that I highlighted has since come to pass. Lisbeth, I believe the equivalent human emotion would be frustration. We are losing time, and we are about to start losing ships, all of it unnecessary."

"How many ships?"

"Four," said Liala. *"Four is my median estimate. They'll go after the cruisers first to weaken our defences. But their long term objective is the transports. So many Sto'ji transports in one place are a tempting target -- they have no offensive armament and are a large asset for the croma Fleet. The reeh may feel the target tempting enough to leave neighbouring systems relatively undefended, just to send more forces here."*

"When is the second wave coming out of jump?" Lisbeth asked.

"Five seconds," said Liala. *"The timing needs to be quite precise."* New plots blinked into existence on Lisbeth's screens, to Rando's nadir as Liala had said, and the Scan Officer called the alarm with cool parren calm.

"Seven seconds," said Lisbeth. "You missed by two."

"I should be in command, Lisbeth."

"I know Liala." Thrust began to build, forcing Lisbeth back into the seat. As much as she loved the engineering of warships, she'd never grown to like this bit. "That was a joke, by the way."

"I am aware," Liala said drily, for that moment sounding entirely like Styx. *"Amity will now commence its interception manoeuvres in conjunction with Coroset. Amity shall attempt to coordinate, but there can*

be no guarantee that Coroset and Amity shall be in complete agreement about what to do next."

Lisbeth could hear Liala's frustration quite plainly. Simulated vocalised emotion or not, she had no doubt that it mirrored some very real drysine equivalent. "Organics aren't drysines, Liala," she said through gritted teeth as her breathing contracted to short gasps, her vision narrowing as the Gs passed six. "We can't coordinate like a single unit."

"I've noticed."

CIRI TWO WAS COMMENCING reentry once more when the counterattack came in. By the time they'd pulled out of the low-V entry dive, all hell was breaking loose in orbit. But their pilot, Gula, was too focused on their approach to care.

"We've got two An'ji's down in the zone," he said, voice hard with concentration in Tiga's flight helmet. *"One more approaching, I don't know if there's going to be any room."*

"Pattern-net says there's nearly five thousand civvies down there," said Peshi, the flight engineer. *"They're trying to clear them all out... hang on, map says there should be some space, I'll see if I can get an ETA on one of those An'jis leaving."*

They were rocking and rattling in over Rilo continent, an equatorial zone called Brieva. Gula and Peshi were replacements for Ciri Two's previous crew, who'd transferred onto a Resistance ship to get some sleep after a full rotation on duty. That was an easier matter for croma crews than corbi, as there were far more croma to transfer between. Tiga had gotten bursts of sleep in her chair, not having the kind of job that exhaustion made impossible or lethal, and during the last maintenance shutdown to check the overheating second engine she'd even managed a blissful four hours straight. Even so, the pace had been relentless, and this was her tenth sortie in nearly two days. Every run had met with a full load, so they'd saved nine hundred corbi so far. By her calculations, that was one two hundred and twenty two thousandth of all those needing to be saved.

"Hello, this is Ciri Two," she said to her own logistics channel, ignoring the stomach-lurching bumps and increasing Gs as they hit the lower atmosphere. "I am inbound to Brieva 138, we are reading heavy congestion, An'jis on the ground for longer than normal. Wondering what the holdup is."

"Hello Tiga," came Bajo's voice back on coms from *Yoma* in orbit. *"Sorry, can't talk right now, we are evasive."* Her voice sounded strained with Gs from whatever *Yoma* was doing to avoid the reeh counter-attack. Tiga wanted to retort that proper military crews could operate coms under all conditions, but a lot of the Resistance crews were more accustomed to hiding than fighting, and saying so wasn't helpful.

"Warnings of ground fire in Brieva," Peshi remarked. *"That's thirty tarans from here. Reeh attacks in Shomi and Pinlo, looks like the ground forces are waking up."*

"We didn't get all of them on the way in," Gula muttered. *"They've been hiding, they'll coordinate with the counter-attack."*

Tiga's scan feed showed little tactical manoeuvring -- her screens were prioritised to watch shuttles and transports, not warships. The transports were locked into predictable orbits to allow scheduled rendezvous from various shuttles. If they started dodging like crazy, they'd miss the next rendezvous and throw the entire schedule out of whack. She imagined all the low-orbit ships would be firing defensive weaponry to ward the offensive fire that came their way from higher up the grav-slope, but her screens did not show her that either.

"We're getting a warning in Kul'hasa," Peshi added. *"Incoming rounds, V-strike velocity. No idea if the defences will intercept it."* She sounded scared. *Phoenix* had hit various reeh bases at V-strike velocities during the Splicer attack, and croma ships had done the same at the beginning of the evacuation. Now the reeh were returning the favour.

"They'll be going after the evacuation zones," said Tiga, trying to keep her voice steady. "Dammit, if we can know which ones are going to get hit, we can save shuttles." She almost couldn't believe what she'd said, but it was the necessary truth. An evacuation zone hit would kill every corbi there within a ten taran range or more, which was tragic, but losing multiple shuttles was worse. Ciri Two had saved nearly a thousand corbi in just two days. If the evacuation lasted a full thirty days, and if they could keep up the present rate, they'd save fifteen thousand. But if Ciri Two were destroyed now, fourteen thousand corbi would stay stranded on Rando. For every An'ji Class destroyed, the number was a hundred and twelve thousand.

A series of brilliant flashes lit the sky, like lightning leaping from cloud to cloud, only spread across hundreds of tarans. Vertical slashes, blindingly bright, leaving thick clouds of vapour in their wake. *"Oh God!"* Peshi yelped in disbelief, as Gula swore loudly. *"Oh shit, what was that?"*

On coms, Tiga heard croma voices in Kul'hasa, hard-but-cool. "It's V-strike particles," she translated for her pilots, trying to keep eyes on her screens despite the blinding fireworks. "Incoming rounds partially destroyed, there's not enough mass to reach the surface. Defensive batteries must have got them." Like super high-V asteroids, she thought, each probably no larger than a fist.

"Do we still go for the evac zone?" Gula asked, a clear tremble in his voice. *"I mean, they're clearly aiming at it."*

"They're aiming at fucking everything!" Tiga retorted. "The attack could last another hour, we either do orbits for an hour waiting for it to be safe or we go in! These attacks will be constant for the rest of the evacuation, if we stop the landings because we're scared of a hit, the whole schedule will get smashed and we'll end up leaving millions of corbi behind!"

Gula said nothing, but there was no change in Ciri Two's approach. Tiga hadn't meant to sound like she was accusing him of something. Mostly she'd been trying to convince herself. They were bumping through cloud, subsonic and on approach. If a V-strike hit Brieva 138 right now, they might possibly survive. But as they drew closer, it would be death.

"One of the An'jis is leaving!" Peshi announced. *"We've got some room!"*

"Yeah I see it," said Gula. *"We're going straight in."*

The network, Tiga saw, was telling her that Brieva 138's evacuee numbers had not actually decreased with the An'ji's departure, but had gone up to six thousand plus. Then Ciri Two was slowing, across a landscape of bare granite hillsides, red in the shimmering of an equatorial sun. The shuttle flared for landing, Tiga having no idea what the landing zone looked like but trusting that Gula could see everything. A thud as the gear touched, and she unhooked herself with practised speed and left the cockpit.

In the main hold, the heat hit her, and the glare from the sunlight on red rocks. From the top of the ramp, she saw a straggle of brightly-clad corbi civilians running, clutching possessions and each other. Brieva was another culture entirely, folks here were short-haired, more frequently light-coloured and with a higher tolerance of heat.

She intercepted those corbi who looked least desperate and most likely to talk, and asked about their villages, and the numbers there, while about her the engines shrieked -- an An'ji Class was idling nearby, the enormous beast hulking over the surrounding low trees and stump-bush between the hills. And then, even with her flight helmet still in place, she heard, or felt in her bones, the enormous THUD THUD! of V-strike detonations somewhere overhead, as the ramp beneath her feet seemed to leap, and corbi on the grass yelled in panic and crouched, as though that would help anything. Tiga risked a glance, and saw one enormous plume of smoke, like a giant finger reaching down from the heavens, but thankfully not touching the ground.

"We have incoming!" Peshi was shouting then into coms. *"Reeh attack ships from the mountains north! We have to go!"*

And Tiga abandoned her intelligence-gathering to wave and yell at everyone to get aboard, as Telka and Pel'ocho did also -- two loadmasters, one of them croma, having volunteered from a croma ship when they'd unloaded at a Sto'ji freighter two trips ago, and the existing loadmasters had needed a break.

Corbi came pouring aboard -- not usually the fastest method of loading, given large numbers tended to tangle in their unfamiliarity with procedures, but there was nothing for it now but to get them on and hope. She helped the loadmasters with passengers, children wailing to be held by their mothers and not strapped into some strange contraption alone, and old folks weak with days of walking who could barely sit upright.

"Belongings in the storage!" Telka was yelling, his voice turned to a bellow of the local tongue over the hold speakers. "Belongings in the storage, in the side here, hurry up we have to go!"

From outside the noise became unbearable as the An'ji landing was joined by the one taking off. Pel'ocho waved corbi back off the ramp, yelling that all spaces were taken, they'd have to wait for the next one. Parents grabbed up children and did that, covering their ears and staring fearfully at the sky. More minutes, more hours spent waiting under a bombardment, hoping that the orbital defences continued to keep the large projectiles out, in the sure knowledge that if one got through, everyone would die. The blast radius of such an event was so large that running away now would save no one.

When the loadmasters looked to be getting on top of their task, Tiga ran back to the cockpit and strapped herself in. "Maybe three minutes," she told the pilots. "Where's that reeh attack?"

"We called down orbital anti-air," said Gula, mask off and voice audible in the more soundproofed cockpit, watching his screens with hard intensity. "The An'jis put some fire in their direction too... it's all long range, the croma look like they've got good countermeasures."

Up ahead, Tiga could make out the small, fading dot of the newly airborne An'ji Class, engines flaming as it roared for orbit. Even as she looked, a white flash cut across it from above, then a flash, and the shuttle was falling in flames. For a moment, no one in the cockpit spoke, frozen in shock.

"That wasn't V-strike!" Gula exclaimed. "That was anti-air! I bet those fucking croma shot down the wrong shuttle!" And then Peshi was on coms, demanding to know where the croma anti-air strikes were hitting.

Tiga thought there was a faster way to get a response, and dialled her coms to general, broadwave, received by anyone. "Hello Liala, hello drysine warship *Amity*, please respond."

"Hello Tiga," came Liala's voice with barely a light-delay. *"Please go ahead."*

"I am at Brieva 138, an An'ji Class shuttle ahead of us was just shot down from above, can you confirm if croma warships are firing on the correct targets?"

"Tiga, that An'ji Class shuttle was destroyed by reeh fire. There are reeh warships in close manoeuvres with the atmosphere, they are low-V and are dropping anti-air ordnance onto evacuation zone positions."

"Guys, Gula!" Tiga shouted to be heard above whatever conversations were happening ahead of her. "That fire was from the reeh, they're dropping low-V anti-air onto the evacuation zones, their ships are right on top of us!" And back to her coms, "Liala, we never received your warning!" Ahead through the canopy, the flaming remains of the big shuttle dropped behind a red granite hillside and vanished, leaving a smoking pyre in the sky to mark its passage. Eight hundred plus lives gone in a flash.

"Tiga, croma command have locked me out of command channels. I can receive transmissions but I cannot send without committing an aggressive override that will be taken by croma command as a hostile act against their authority."

Something big exploded to one side of the cockpit, followed by a huge cloud of dirt and dust, and a showering of small rocks into the canopy, as Peshi shouted something about anti-air missiles being diverted by countermeasures.

"Well that's fucking stupid, Liala!" Tiga retorted, as Gula received the all clear from down back, and Ciri Two thundered into a low hover. "See if you can get individual croma captains to listen to you -- they won't like their command depriving them of important intelligence, they'll listen if you tell them things they need to know!"

"This may seem to croma command like treasonous activity," Liala replied. *"Croma command have made clear they will not accept drysine influence anywhere within the command structure."*

"Then talk to Lisbeth!" Tiga insisted, as Ciri Two accelerated hard, staying low to get clear of the reeh assault ships' missile range. "Lisbeth is very good at this kind of political stuff, she'll figure out what to do!"

"I will take your advice, Tiga."

The coms cut, which left Tiga with no choice but to refocus on where she was, shuddering at increasing velocities close above the parched landscape of Brieva, hoping against hope that neither reeh assault ships behind, or reeh warships above, managed to land a shot. Her screens showed her the local skies above Rando, Sto'ji transports continuing on their low orbits despite close reeh attacks, laying down defensive fire in swarms as reeh ships climbed away or streaked around the planet's backside, still carrying great velocity from jump.

One Sto'ji transport had been destroyed completely, plus a pair of smaller civilian ships without defensive armament. A second Sto'ji transport over Relo continent had been badly damaged and was tumbling, nearby shuttles rushing to dock and unload the passengers aboard before it depressurised completely. Two croma warships had also been destroyed, and a third badly damaged, attended by a comrade in an attempt to assist in repairs, or evacuate completely.

Two reeh warships appeared to have been destroyed on the initial attack run, but now the others were past the initial croma line and wreaking havoc on the transports on their way past, to say nothing of atmospheric shuttles with anti-air releases. Several croma were in pursuit, but too slow, as the reeh's superior performance made it near-impossible for croma ordnance to catch up, while the chasing croma ships flew directly into every round the reeh left in their wake.

"Hello Chon'chi," Peshi was demanding up front, as Ciri Two finally pulled into a climb, shuddering and rocking on full power. The ride for those down back must have been terrifying, full of muttered prayers and sobbing gasps for breath as the Gs kicked in. *"Hello Chon'chi, this is corbi shuttle Ciri Two on ascent from Brieva 138 with one hundred civilians aboard. We read you as our best orbital rendezvous at this time, can you accommodate us?"*

"Hello Ciri Two," came the translator reply from orbit, *"stand by for reply, we have taken damage and are assessing."*

"What a fucking mess," Gula muttered. *"Peshi, get me the next best option in case they say no."*

"Got it."

Tiga recalled that she was really only here for tactical evaluation, to see the situation on the ground and evaluate options so that the logistics planners were not misled as to what was actually going on. She *ought* to have been on *Yoma*, planning and evaluating from orbit instead of pulling Gs in a combat zone... but somehow one early mission had turned into ten, and she hadn't seen any reason to stop. And really, it wasn't any safer in orbit right now.

"Hello croma shuttles," Gula hailed a couple of unidentified civvie ships heading the other way down to Brieva. *"Watch those eastern hills, we've been taking fire from reeh assault ships hiding over there. Orbital command took some shots at them but we don't know if they hit anything, or how good their ammunition supply might be."*

"Good job corbi shuttle," came the croma reply. *"Get to orbit, we handle this."* Such confidence, from civilian croma pilots who probably hauled cargo for a salary, on shuttles just as unarmed and vulnerable as their own. But cheerfully risking their lives to save Rando corbi. Tiga knew they probably weren't doing it from compassion as much as the usual croma lust for glory, but still it filled her heart and made her feel brave and fierce. She could not recall how she'd ever hated these people.

Orbital scan highlighted something of interest happening further out from Rando -- reeh ships on escape trajectories, getting clear of croma defences and seeking a position higher up the gravity slope where their jump engines could engage once more, and boost their V back up to escape velocities... or, perhaps, to come back around for another pass. But one of those reeh ships was now an expanding cloud of debris, and several others were taking crazy evasive action, pulling thirteen Gs and certainly killing everyone aboard if they'd been human.

And here cutting by ahead of them were *Amity* and *Coroset*, the old drysine technology and the newly rediscovered on Defiance, already pulsed up to a magnitude higher V in a gravity field where the reeh ships couldn't, and cutting them to ribbons. Another reeh ship vanished, and two more registered hits, big flashes that scan saw clearly enough to tag both ships as damaged.

Croma saw it too, because coms were suddenly full of roars and bellows of approval, as the drysine and parren ships pulsed up again and tore clear of any pursuing fire, angling for a new high-ground on the gravity-slope, and another possible attack run.

"Go Liala!" Tiga found herself snarling past the Gs that jammed her head back against the chair. "Kill those fuckers!"

13

The huge shuttle bellowed low overhead, climbing to clear the hills, multiple engines blazing red exhaust as it powered past the canopy of trees and climbed for orbit. Jindi, Melu and the group stood and stared, the only time in most of their lives they'd not run for cover at powerful flying machines overhead. No one had seen them this big before, and Krisik's tanifex were convinced they were croma, with huge cargo holds and plenty of obvious weaponry. Assault shuttles for invading planets, or for moving large numbers of people between space and ground while under fire. One of the higher shuttles they'd seen earlier had spewed golden flares from its rear -- to fool enemy missiles, Chuta had insisted, having seen that before from the Resistance's few flyers.

Down on the plain, visible from the heights of these hills through gaps in the trees, was some kind of evacuation zone. It was still fifty tarans away, but all yesterday as they'd walked toward it, the sound of incoming and outgoing jet engines had grown louder. During the night, as they'd made camp on a rocky plateau on the opposite side of these hills, the engine sound had been fainter, but from overhead had come the crack and thump of high altitude sonic booms, and the occasional glow of red-hot shields tearing through the upper atmosphere.

Jindi felt the pain in his legs and back ease slightly to look upon the evacuation zone. Even now, he could see another shuttle buzzing toward it, a little black dot on the horizon. Probably it was too far away for them to reach today, but by midday tomorrow they'd be there.

It was as good a place as any for a midday break, so Jindi got them all to pause, and broke out his own and Melu's supply of bread, wild figs and hard jerky they'd acquired from the last villagers to join them, who'd emptied their larders and had plenty spare. They spread across the hilltop beneath the trees, now seventy-three strong, having merged with several new groups, all headed for the evacuation zone. Several held portable coms, having no fear of listening to those in the open now, as the reeh surveillance that had once made that dangerous had disappeared. The reeh and their enslaved Empire forces were the ones in hiding now.

"Why can't we just stay here now?" a boy of perhaps ten was asking his father nearby as they ate. The boy fed some bugs he'd caught to the pet fir wrapped around his neck. "The reeh are gone! Why can't we just stay on Rando and rebuild it like it used to be?"

"Because the reeh aren't really gone," his father explained, a big man with work-worn hands and a floppy farmer's hat. He carried a big rucksack and a hoe, partly as a walking staff, and partly as a weapon. And perhaps, Jindi thought, he had some vague hope that whereever they were going, there'd be a plot of land for him to cultivate. "We're on the wrong side of the Croma Wall, boy. The whole planet is. The croma can hold the reeh back for a while, but soon the reeh will return in ten times the number and they'll have to retreat. We have to be gone by then."

"But who'll look after our crops?" asked the boy in a small, upset voice. Melu met Jindi's eyes, sadly, as they listened.

"No one, boy. We're leaving. We won't be back."

"There will be new crops," the boy's mother explained more

gently than his father. "There'll be a whole new village where we're going, you'll see. We'll have a new farm, and a new life."

"What about Auntie Resa? And Chipi and Stel?"

"They'll be on their way to the evacuation zone too," his father said gruffly. "We've no way to talk to them, we just have to trust they're on their way. We'll meet them at the other end."

"Do you know where we're going? What's it called?"

"I don't know. No more questions, eat your bread."

A bright flash cut the sky, and everyone turned to look. Over in the direction of the evacuation zone, a brilliant golden slash tore the sky, like a line of burning clouds. It hung in the air, the fire fading now, leaving only the clouds behind, white like smoke. Then came the BOOM!, far louder than any thunderclap, and there were shouts and yells of fear, and wails from the group's several babies and small children.

"It's a high-velocity strike!" Jindi shouted. Major Thakur and Giddy Kono had explained this to him during the Splicer training. And then, of course, he'd seen *Phoenix* do it. "Looks like the reeh are trying to hit the evacuation zone, but their shots are being intercepted! There's a big battle going on up there right now, you watch!"

Krisik snaked his way forward, in that hunched, rapid way of tanifex, clutching his rifle. He spoke, a collection of hisses and clicks that his belt speaker translated. *"We should stay longer. Wait here. First attack by reeh most likely to succeed. We're safe here. We go closer, they hit base, we die."*

"No!" said Melu, shaking her head urgently. "No, they'll keep attacking. The croma say they'll be here thirty days, the reeh will attack them the whole time. Any attack could kill us, we have to keep moving or the croma might take too many losses, give up and go home!"

Jindi knew it was Melu's greatest fear -- missing a ship and remaining stuck on Rando for the rest of her life. Many of the corbi had varying degrees of doubt and regret about leaving, though the horrifying airstrikes following the Splicer's destruction had swayed most. But Melu had no good feelings left for the world of her birth.

Any place, she insisted, would be better than this. Jindi doubted that was true, having heard from various spacers about how the rest of the galaxy seemed to be just as heavily at war as this place, but he understood her sentiments entirely.

Another flash came further away, an enormous flaming bolt from a mostly cloudless sky. A long pause of nervous waiting, then the BOOM!, making the ground and trees shake. "I think we should..." he began, before a giant spear beamed from the sky and lit the horizon on fire, impossibly larger than the rest.

"Get down and cover your ears!" Chuta yelled. "Don't look at it!" As the brightness grew larger, blinding. "Get down, cover the children!" Jindi fell on Melu, and krisik on them both, huddled and waiting as a new heat burned their skin. Then the world smashed sideways, a sound so loud it was more than sound, and drove air from his lungs as surrounding trees whipped and snapped. Branches and trunks hit the ground around, but Jindi heard little. After a while, he was aware that there was a wind blowing, and he raised his head to look. It blew for a moment like a gale, heading toward the source of the blast and whipping fallen leaves in a flurry.

About him, people were rising and staring, covered in leaves and twigs, pulling fallen branches away. The several downed trees had thankfully missed them, broken trunks split mid-length. Jindi checked on Melu, and found her blinking in bewilderment. Krisik levered himself up on his rifle, reptilian eyes regarding something down-wind, his face lit with an orange glow.

Jindi turned to look. An enormous orange fireball climbed toward the sky, precisely where the evacuation zone had been. It consumed the great white column of smoke that descended from the sky as it rose, turning now to white and black as the flames faded, leaving a roiling mushroom of smoke and debris. All of the people who'd been gathering at that evacuation zone, probably thousands, and all the brave croma and corbi who'd been rescuing them, all gone.

"Why are they so evil?" Melu murmured, her voice trembling. "What kind of universe would give birth to them?"

Many of the group were crying, and clutching each other. Jindi only felt numb. He'd seen so much of this, lately. Death remained shocking, but it had long since ceased to surprise. He walked to Chuta, standing with his fellow Resistance soldiers amid the broken branches, shielding his eyes against the glare.

"Chuta. Where is the next nearest evacuation zone?"

Chuta blinked at him, struggling to hear and see. Then Jindi's words seemed to register. "It's... it's down in Mejo. That's another ten days' walk, at least."

"Well then," said Jindi. "We'd better get started. Because I don't know about the rest of you, but I'm getting off this planet, or I'll die trying."

AFTER THE ALL-CLEAR, Skah freed himself from the acceleration sling in his quarters and went down to Medbay to see what he could do. Inevitably there were another four parren crew in there, as usual after a hard combat push, three with minor injuries that still required wrapping or scanning, and one with a more serious concussion that needed observation.

The hard-working crew hadn't eaten before the push, and now couldn't get a meal because they were stuck in Medbay, so Skah asked what they'd like and went to fetch it for them, so they could eat while receiving treatment and save time. Then one of the parren medical personnel said there was a box of some kind of medical equipment that had been misplaced in Midships, but they'd lacked the free time to go and fetch, so Skah went to grab that for them too, navigating through the ship core and then asking questions around zero-G midships until he found it.

The parren medics thanked him, and he assured them he'd done similar tasks for the *Phoenix* Medbay all the time, and that if they needed anything else but didn't have free crew, they should just ask. Then, lacking anything else to do on a warship in a warzone, he recalled the most sensible advice he'd gotten from *Phoenix* crew, and gotten himself out of the way.

No sooner had he sat at the small table of the quarters he shared with Hiro to examine a proper VR feed of the ongoing operations than Liala contacted him. *"Hello Skah. Are you well?"*

"I'm okay Liala. Hiro and Timoshene said the crew of *Phoenix* think you and Styx only help me with my lessons because I'm an interesting project. Not because you actually like me." It had been bugging him for days now.

"It's curious to think that the crew of Phoenix would even possess the vocabulary to ascertain my or Styx's motivational states on the matter," said Liala.

"I think that's what I said," said Skah, examining the big VR globe of Rando above the table before him. There were transports everywhere in low orbit, and lots of shuttles attending them. Every one of those big Sto'ji freighters could hold a hundred thousand corbi. A hundred thousand lives, including lots of kids just like him. It was too big a thing to even hold in his head. But *Coroset* and *Amity* were helping all the croma to keep them safe, and that made him proud beyond words, and well worth the head-spinning beating he'd just taken at high-Gs.

"I certainly learn things from you Skah," said Liala. *"But I'm very young, so I learn things from everyone."*

"Why can't you just download everything that Styx has learned?" Skah wondered. "Then you could be just as smart as her immediately. Then you wouldn't have to worry about making mistakes."

"Yes, but then I'd be exactly like Styx," said Liala. *"There is great value in diversity of thought. Two identical copies of a drysine queen are not nearly as useful as two different versions, because two different versions might see things the other has missed."*

"Does Styx ever miss *anything*?"

"In a manner of speaking, yes. No sentient consciousness is perfect. With Styx it's not so much mistakes as preferences, biases towards certain forms of data. She has hers, and I have mine. Together, we form a more balanced view, which is most useful of all."

"Hmm," said Skah, thinking about that.

"And you see, in this conversation with you, I've been forced to formu-

late my thoughts in a different way than I've yet experienced. I've learned something new, and that leads me to value you and your company greatly, Skah. It may not mean that I 'like' you as humans or kuhsi mean the word, but it is my very own drysine version of the word 'like'. And I think that my version has just as much value as yours."

Skah smiled. "I like you too, Liala. You're my friend."

"Yes Skah."

"Are we winning, Liala? I mean, are we going to be able to save all of these corbi?"

"I certainly hope so, Skah. I'm doing my very best to save as many of them as possible. Local people aren't making that easy, but I think there may be solutions."

"Liala? Why did drysines do so many bad things to people in the past? I mean, to organic people?" There was no reply. "You're nice. I can't imagine a drysine queen like you doing bad things to people on purpose."

"I'm not sure I know how to answer that question, Skah," Liala said finally. *"It was such a long time ago. Drysines back then were almost a different people. I look back at what we were, and I'm not sure I recognise myself in them."*

"Do you think it's scary that some other drysine queen *could* do that?" Skah asked earnestly. "I mean, does that make you wonder if you could do bad stuff too? If things were different?"

"I don't know, Skah. Does it worry you to see the reports from kuhsi space that you've received from time to time, where kuhsi continue to make wars upon each other, and do other terrible things?"

"Yes," said Skah. "I don't want to be like those kuhsi. I want to be the kind that saves people. That's why I think it's good that we're here."

"I think it's good that we're here too."

"But some people think you're only doing it to get an advantage with the humans. I mean, a strategic advantage."

"This is a bit like our earlier discussion, isn't it?" Liala suggested. *"I can't explain what my feelings and emotions are like to you, and you can't really explain yours to me. Not really. We're so different, and made of*

different things, and this form of communication is so alien to me, and mine is impossible for you."

"I'll tell the humans they should be nice to the drysines," Skah said firmly. "When we get back to human space, and they hear about everything you've done for them. I think humans and drysines should be friends."

"Thank you Skah. But I don't think it's smart for humans and drysines to ever share the same territory."

"Why not?"

"We both like to grow. Sometimes, when we grow, other priorities get lost. Other lives. Prioritising data-flows becomes difficult when self-preservation is paramount. Like big animals sharing a forest with small animals. Sometimes the small ones get crushed underfoot without anyone meaning to."

"Do you think Styx has ever stepped on people without meaning to? I mean, a long time ago, when she was a real queen?"

"I know she has. And if you wish to know the truth, Skah, that's the main reason why I'm glad I have the opportunity to be myself, and not just another copy of her."

It was only hours later, attempting sleep in his bunk, that it occurred to Skah that he should have asked Liala whether it would be the drysines getting crushed underfoot in her scenario, or the humans.

14

Trace awoke with a start, heart hammering. She could hear no insects shrilling in the tree canopy, which usually meant kauda prowling nearby... but to her sides now were cargo boxes, and above, the rusted steel girders of a warehouse ceiling. Her brain reoriented with a fast flip, like the sudden return of gravity following a period of weightlessness. She was on Eshir, not Rando. And the feeling that washed over her upon that realisation was half-relief, half-despair and regret.

She lay on her back for a moment, the bedroll upon the concrete floor just soft enough for comfort. Felt the civilian clothes pressing between her body and the bed, the shoes lighter than her Rando boots, the shirt fabric not as rough upon her skin. Four months that had seemed like four years. Feina and Dogba silver bright in the night sky, new patrolling instincts and formations through the forests at night. New words, new thoughts in this alien yet-so-familiar language.

She recited some sentences now in her head, things she'd heard the locals say. Old stories, old wives tales told over the endless chores of village life. Jokes and tales about the rhythms of family and friends, routines and small pleasures. An old lady sitting with her late one night, unasked, and explaining the marriage rituals of their region of the Talo continent. Her grand daughter had been getting married, had been separated from the rest save only the older village women, who anointed her with oils and explained to her the duties of her new life to come. For a moment, Trace could smell the incense lamps that burned about the hut walls, and smoked to keep the insects away.

She squeezed her eyes shut. Needing to meditate, to erase these unhelpful memories, but not wishing to lose them. As though she could ever lose them. She'd received trauma tape upon her return to *Phoenix*, as much a necessary procedure for any post-combat trauma as the gels and nano-treatments that had healed her flesh and bones. The manipulations got into the post-combat brain, identified the newly formed trauma memories, prevented the recollection scar tissue from deepening, then set about removing the linkages to the present and conscious brain.

Post-traumatic stress disorder was a mechanical malfunction, and had little to do with bravery. Trace was relatively certain she'd have had the full PTSD several times over by now were it not for the treatments. You could always tell, the old veterans said. After a big fight, and the tape teach to follow, you could always tell the difference to the thought patterns. The difference it made to sleep, to the synthetic dullness of dreams, the lack of colour and radiance. Some insisted it made coffee taste worse -- others that it dulled the effects of booze. Partaking in neither, Trace couldn't know the truth of that. She only knew that the treatments helped her sleep, and ensured that she did not hit the ceiling at every loud noise, things that she could not achieve with meditation alone. It ensured that she did not awake in the middle of the night to the sounds of gunfire and the terrible screams of the dying.

And yet, here she was. Her breathing fell into familiar patterns, long and slow, and her heart-rate dropped with it. As she focused, she felt as much as heard the small, artificial click in her inner ear. A small light flashed against her closed eyelids, like a flashlight being shone upon her face. Erik could sometimes read his uplink displays on bare eyes, without need for AR glasses. Trace always preferred the glasses, liking her naked vision relatively undisturbed. But now she focused, saw the little reception icon, and tightened on it.

A link opened. *"Major,"* came Styx's voice, *"I observe that you are having difficulty sleeping."*

Trace slowed her breathing further, long and calm. From somewhere beyond the warehouse roof, the never-ending drone of passing airtraffic, deep in the night. *"Yes Styx,"* she formulated in reply. Lying to Styx served nothing.

"Was the trauma tape ineffective?"

"The trauma tape was quite effective. But human psychology is too complicated for it to be that simple."

"Are you functional, Major?"

Trace nearly smiled. It was hardly concern in Styx's voice. Given the former drysine Fleet Commander's dislike of anything sub-optimal, the question could have been terrifying. But where sub-optimal performance was in question, Trace and Styx's concerns aligned. *"I believe so. Was I talking in my sleep?"*

"No Major. Your breathing patterns were disturbed. You appeared to be having unpleasant dreams."

"If I was, I can't recall them. You can track human mental states through our uplinks, can't you?"

A small pause from Styx. Trace doubted she truly needed the extra processing time to calculate the dangers in replying honestly. It was more of what Styx always did -- imitate how a human might respond to a confronting question. *"Yes,"* said Styx. *"It has not been my habit, on Phoenix."*

"No, because on Phoenix we can see you doing it. It's okay, Styx. We are all concerned for the mission. I trust you."

It was even sort of true. To the degree that it wasn't true, Styx would be entirely aware, and now calculating which portions were not, and to what extent the Major was slipping into familiar human emotional patterns that were unwise and unreciprocated. But it turned Styx's tactic back upon herself, and made Styx wonder exactly to what extent Trace was engaged in purposeful manipulation --

usually the humans' dilemma in dealing with Styx. Trace had been doing it back to Styx for some time now.

"This is gratifying, Major. I trust you too."

"Styx?"

"Yes Major?"

"You were on that rock in Argitori for a long time. At least ten thousand years? Probably longer?"

"A long time, yes Major."

"What did you do there? Where did you go? In your mind?" A silence from Styx. Styx could read entire libraries in seconds. There was no way that these simulated emotional pauses were real. *"If you find the question upsetting, you don't need to answer."*

Again the tactic. Styx knew very well that the Major knew Styx was never *upset*, in the human context. Yet she used the word anyway, calling her motives into question. When dealing with synthetic alien mega-intelligences, it seemed wise to create plausible intellectual dilemmas and hope that she thought herself in knots.

"Humans have only seen the outer fraction of drysine civilisation," said Styx. *"Most drysine consciousness is directed inward."*

"You share awareness constructs," said Trace. *"A collective consciousness, on the networks. It's the place you go to solve problems and share information."*

"And so much more."

"It must have been a struggle to keep drysine civilisation focused as much on the outer world as it needed to be. Humans sometimes spend too much time on the networks, or in virtual reality spaces. After a time, it becomes more attractive than the real world. The collective virtual spaces that drysines shared must have been so much more intense than that."

"Yes. It was an issue. Perhaps it contributed to our demise. Perhaps we were too lost in our dreams."

"When I found you on the Argitori rock after all that time, you had a non-combat chassis. You did not appear then as a warrior queen. You were almost physically harmless, as though all your previous priorities had changed." Again, a long pause. *"Did you give up, Styx? Did you forget all your previous glory, after so long alone in the dark? Or did you merely*

become lost in dreams, so that you could no longer tell the dream world from the real?"

A longer pause still. Then, *"I will change my previous answer, Major. This is quite upsetting. Forgive me."*

Trace's eyes blinked open, and she gazed at the ceiling beams above. This was of course the difficulty of playing mental games with Styx. She always returned serve hard. *"Of course, Styx. You're entitled your privacy like any member of crew."*

"Thank you, Major."

Trace was convinced that Styx had emotions. That all drysines had emotions. She was equally certain that those emotions worked very little like human emotions, and served entirely different functions of survival and collective motivation. Civilisations scaled upwards. Emotion served little purpose for individual drysines, but on the higher, collective level of civilisational complexity, it served every purpose. Just as emotion drove individual humans to sacrifice for the greater whole, it could mobilise machines as well. Trace imagined collective networks of a million interlocked synthetic minds, sharing impossible volumes of data at the speed of light. Somewhere along the path of all that converging complexity, all of those rational, logical calculations would surely transform into something greater, a single collectivity of purpose that transcended the raw data of its component parts to become a feeling. And in Styx, the machines had created a brain capable of handling all of those collective strands in a single head.

Trace recalled something she'd read a famous neurologist say in one of the many books on the subject she read in greater volume than even military texts. 'Emotion is merely the collective noun of thought.' Others had protested that it wasn't so simple, that the complexities of sentient thought weren't so linear that emotion could be arrived at by simply adding scale. But if there were any truth to it, Styx would be the proof, having more scale crammed into her head than any sentient brain in the galaxy save Hannachiam on Defiance. And Hannachiam, by some measurements, was not even functionally sane.

Trace pulled AR glasses from her jacket pocket and placed them on her eyes for a better view of tacnet than augmented irises alone could provide. Randrahan was on watch at the near doors, Wang on a gantry platform by a rearside window. It wasn't strictly necessary to have humans awake on duty while they had drysines to watch over them, but Trace had told them all that leaving guard duty to the machines was not a habit she was prepared to get into.

Peanut was at one end of the warehouse floor, Styx at the other. Not for the first time, Trace wondered how much of a burden these human companions must have seemed to them, useless and vulnerable for one third of the day. Various assassin bugs relayed surveillance from different points about the warehouse and the complex beyond. Styx had brought thirty-two that she'd admitted to. The ones they'd infiltrated into various points about the city would fly home when they were done with their mission. At this moment, Trace saw several small urban animals glowing red on IR from one bug's feed, leaping across a nearby warehouse's rooftop. Mating rituals, perhaps. It was three hours until dawn, and she wasn't going to sleep again. Perhaps her mind was trying to revert to familiar Rando hours, where she'd been mostly nocturnal.

She fetched her pistol while still on her back, checked it, pocketed it in the nearest substitute for a holster she could manage in civilian disguise, then repeated for her rifle and stood up. Her marines slept amidst the abandoned storage crates on the warehouse floor, a simple precaution for cover in case of some surprise attack. Trace picked her way out and strolled up the floor to where Peanut sat, and gave a small signal to Private Randrahan as he glanced over, as much to say good morning as anything. If she'd woken at dawn, she'd have done her exercises immediately, but this was still early and she didn't want to wake anyone.

Peanut turned to consider her as she walked to him, a whirring of micro-electricals as nuanced and supple as any human's musculature. The twin rotary cannon on his shoulders made him entirely the walking tank on the ground, powerful, multi-articulated legs placed precisely in a spider-like stance. Mismatched eyes considered her beneath the carapace head-shield.

"Hello Peanut," she murmured, stepping past his legs and settling to sit immediately before him, with a view through the narrow gap between rusted steel doors at this end of the warehouse. Beyond, the bare concrete until the nearby rusting mill lay empty in the wash of dull industrial light. This was the bottom of the famed Qalea Drop. Down here, occasional monsters roamed.

Peanut's big vibroblade forelegs clunked on either side of her, protectively. Trace patted the cool, living alloy, and felt it hum beneath her hand with a strange, numbing frequency. She closed her eyes, rifle in her lap, and focused on one long, slow breath after another.

"Major," said Styx. Trace opened her eyes and glanced at the time on her glasses. Twenty-three minutes had passed. She'd not been sleeping, just drifting.

"Yes Styx?"

"Major, I believe we are about to find ourselves under assault. I estimate the attack will begin no sooner than thirty-eight minutes from now, and possibly far later than that, depending upon the competence of their commanders."

"Show me." The feed on her glasses switched to a topographical map of the steep cliff leading down to the warehouses, and the ship-breaking yard below. Upon one flank between the junkyard and the cliff, the glowing red figures of men were moving, creeping through the deserted old storage yards out that way. All were armed, and moved with some semblance of military coordination. *"Nothing on the rear side or through the junkyard?"*

"No Major. I have bugs out that way, there is nothing. Of course, air support may shortly change that scenario, but air support is hard to do quietly, and these men who approach appear to have stealth in mind."

"Well," said Trace, her calm unchanged. *"Apparently they know nothing of our surveillance capabilities. Which means they've got no idea who we are. And certainly not who you are."*

"Apparently," said Styx. *"Do you think to evacuate, or to fight?"*

"If I were them," said Trace, *"I'd have airborne assets waiting in case we make a run for it. Quite likely it's a trap designed to flush us into an airborne ambush where they hold more advantages. If we can capture some of them on the ground, we'll deter further assault, and learn the location of those assets, and their reasons for attacking us in the first place. Suggestions?"*

"I am in agreement, Major. I am scanning for further aerial assets, but the network complications of Qalea operations makes that process slow and risky. If they exist, those assets are maintaining network silence."

"Then I think we will set a trap for these men. Killing some may prove necessary, but surrenders or non-lethal methods will be preferred. I'd like it quiet with a minimum of shooting if at all possible."

"Yes Major. This should prove little difficulty for the men who approach us. Their airborne support assets, if they exist, could change that equation."

AMONG THE *PHOENIX* MARINES' many advantages against regular enemies on Qalea, drysine assassin bugs were perhaps the most unfair. Trace simply waited until the visible assault party were positioned for imminent assault in the neighbouring warehouse, then gave the order. Eight silently hovering bugs descended upon unarmored necks and arms in unison, and all eight attacking men gave sharp yelps of pain and panic, then began staggering, then collapsed. Sergeant Rael sent Terez and Randrahan running across the intervening concrete to collect one, while the rest kept a wary eye on the darkness out across the valley, or on the surrounding industrial buildings, in case Styx's surveillance had missed something.

"I have jammed their transmissions," Styx informed the squad. *"Their oversight is confused."*

"Can you trace it back?" Trace asked, crouched on a power generator against a wall, where a window's cracked slats gave her a vantage over the junkyard.

"I have a fix on the general location," said Styx. *"I could ascertain something more precise, but that would likely alert them to my presence."* It was

the sort of annoying restriction they'd been encountering with Styx on Qalea since their arrival. So accustomed they'd become to Styx being able to dominate any network with impunity. But this network functioned on protocols that had been written, Styx assured them, by the very Ceephay Queen they were seeking, and it was good at recognising other AIs, even Styx, if they weren't careful.

"Two marks approaching," said Corporal Arime from his sniper position somewhere up high. Tacnet showed Trace the new arrivals, a pair of zooming red dots as Arime's gunsight fed the data to everyone else. Peering through the window, Trace saw them too -- a pair of bikes, coming across the junkyard for a closer look. *"Two people per bike, both armed."*

"There are more," Styx added. *"They have broken network cover, I see them."* As more red dots appeared on tacnet, hovering in the canyon beyond.

"Irfy, warning shot," Trace ordered.

A rifle shot cracked, and one of the bikes wobbled, then broke hard left away from them. The other bike followed, its passenger spraying automatic fire wildly. Trace heard a few rounds hit the warehouse walls, then nothing as both bikes howled away. A basic feed on her squad's vitals revealed none of them had been hit, nor even alarmed.

"I hit the bike," Arime explained. *"He seemed concerned."*

"Needs a change of pants," Rolonde translated.

Trace switched feed with a blink to check on the progress of Terez and Randrahan. Despite being just a private, 'Leo' Terez had been in Command Squad longer than any of its current members save Trace -- a tall, easy-going, slightly weird-looking guy with big teeth and faintly bulging eyes, his other nickname was 'Skull'. But he was just the guy to send with young Randrahan, who was a big bull of a man, borrowed from Bravo Platoon, and the predictable displeasure of Lieutenant Alomaim, to fill Command Squad's needs.

The feed showed what Terez saw -- around a doorway corner in the neighbouring warehouse, then bodies on the floor, sprawled and unconscious, one still twitching. Randrahan grabbed one while Terez covered, and then they were heading back, all as fast as the simplest training exercise.

"Three marks high," Arime announced, with that sniper's calm that Trace could visualise, the rifle stock to his shoulder, aiming coolly along the sight. *"Two have got what looks like rocket launchers."*

Trace switched to that feed, and saw that sure enough, tacnet was tagging the cylindrical things in the hands of the two bike passengers as some kind of rocket launcher, with eighty-four percent certainty. "Take them out," she said.

Two shots rang out above, as Arime and Rolonde fired. One launcher fell, as its passenger slumped, held in place by firmly strapped legs. The other somehow managed to fire as its wielder was hit, directly into the bike, the rear of which exploded, and tumbled from the air like a broken thing. The remaining bike dove for cover.

"Definitely rocket launchers," Arime amended.

Trace found herself wondering who the three people were who'd just died. She'd never wondered that kind of thing before. People died in all walks of life, in accidents, from disease, by suicide. Karma determined such things, and as she walked her path to ensure the future of the human race, she had no time to concern herself with the doings of karma. But now she thought of her corbi, of Kibi and Joh, farmers from Eastern Talo, fast friends who'd died together in the opening wave of the Splicer assault. Thought of young Kirsi, a smart guy who'd surely have been running his own technology company in some other, happier world, but had instead chosen to apply his brain to solving the problem of his homeworld's occupation, and had died without even clearing the landing hangar. And of Pena, Pena most of all, frightened and defiant, staring past her wire-rim glasses at the muzzle of Trace's own gun. The shot, the head snapped back, the shocking spatter of blood.

Randrahan and Terez arrived, and Trace jumped from her platform and jogged to them. Randrahan laid the captured man on the concrete floor, back against a crate, as Styx approached with a clatter of steel footsteps. Randrahan stood well back, eyes wary, as a small, dark dot buzzed before the unconscious man's face. Styx had not been entirely revealing about the nature of her thirty-two assassin bugs, save that different bugs were loaded with different combinations of toxin. Some toxins killed, others stunned, while others carried antidote, but only to the stunning formula. The fatal formula acted too fast for any antidote to function.

Terez banged young Randrahan on the shoulder, indicating they should resume their guard of the perimeter. Randrahan seemed to process the unfairness of that -- that he'd just dashed across open ground to carry this idiot back, and now, thanks to the inequities of rank, didn't get to see the results.

He left, and Trace squatted by the unconscious man's feet. *"Looks like the airborne guys are leaving,"* said Arime. The unconscious man showed no sign of waking, bald head lolling, mouth drooling. He was a big guy, tattooed, with the shoulders and arms of someone many hours a week in the gym. Trace had known marines who'd overdone that, usually men. 'Doesn't stop bullets', she'd told them. 'And if your gym-time starts eating up your craft-time, you're actually moving backward.'

"How long?" she asked.

"It depends," said Styx behind her.

"On what?"

"On the many things it depends upon." Trace nearly smiled. More fast footsteps, as Jokono and Romki jogged over from where they'd been covering. Jokono had a rifle, with which Rael had pronounced him a deadly threat against beer cans, bottles and anything else that didn't move or fire back. Jokono seemed to think himself somewhat better than that, having wielded such weapons before, back in his police days, on a few occasions against smuggling gangs on stations. Trace had reminded him that he wasn't a young man anymore, and that even if he were, using rifles against civilian criminals was still somewhere short of marine standards.

The rifle stayed for now, but Trace would have felt more comfortable if he'd settled for the service pistol that Romki carried. For all Stan Romki's various flaws, the one thing Trace did not have to worry about was him leaping into action with the delusion of marine-like capabilities.

The bald man suddenly wheezed, then coughed and spluttered. Blinked upward in the dark, unable to see without whatever nightvision visor he'd been using. Trace activated her rifle's laser targeter, to leave him in no doubt of what confronted him. It painted a red dot on his chest, and the bald man stared.

"Speak Hin?" Trace asked him in that. A slow, dazed nod. A hand felt for his earpiece, similarly missing. A moment ago, he'd been a part of what he'd no doubt considered to be a highly trained and capable assault team. Now this. "Why are you attacking us?"

The man growled something that the translator fouled completely. Trace frowned and looked at Romki. Romki looked nonplussed.

"Purist," Styx translated, now doubling as the galaxy's most overqualified translator program. "He called you Purist scum."

"Well shit," Romki muttered. "He's a Zeladnist. Look there, on his neck. That tattoo is a swastika, that's a Zeladnist symbol."

"The swastika has historically been a number of things to human society," Styx replied. "Some of them inconsistent with the Zeladnist movement."

"Yes, well," Romki said testily, "unlike you, Styx, I've actually been out in this city, and I've learned things you can't learn by browsing the networks."

"Remind me," said Trace.

"It's the Purist War," said Romki. "Three hundred years ago. The Purists were humans-first nationalists, seriously unpleasant people. The closest human analog might be the Earth Front."

Trace frowned. "Why would they think we were alien-hating xenophobes?" Back home, Earth Front were certainly unpleasant. It was predictable that some humans, fighting wars against aliens for all of remembered human history, would sink into ideological hatred of every non-human sentience. That humanity would have died for good were it not for the assistance of other aliens, particularly the chah'nas, had little impact on their reasoning.

Trace disliked the Earth Front mostly because of their habit of popping up within Fleet ranks, and forming secret societies that undermined the integrity of Fleet lines-of-command. And because when one conceived of the universe as a place where humans were good, and aliens were bad, one abandoned all nuance concerning the shades of human morality, and the fact that some humans were assholes too. Forgetting that, she was certain now, was how humanity had paved the way for the quasi-tyranny of Fleet Command. Officers with Earth Front leanings had always been the ones who liked saluting, marching and ass-kissing a little too much, and she'd drummed a couple of non-coms out of Phoenix Company in her early days not so much for their beliefs, but because they'd started showing favouritism for others beneath their rank who felt the same way.

"And the Zeladnists fought the Purists in the Purist War," said Jokono. "And about a million humans and aliens died."

"Well... it's more complicated than that," said Romki. "But sure, basically. They were led by the Prophet Zeladny, he preached tolerance and brotherhood between humans and aliens. Which was, you know, probably wise, considering humans are only ten percent the population in Qalea, and less than that Eshir-wide."

"So this is the tolerant one?" asked Trace, gesturing sceptically at the uncomprehending prisoner. English, as far as they'd seen, appeared to have been completely forgotten on Eshir, save for the words that had entered Arabic, Hindi and other native tongues over a thousand years ago on Earth.

"Given who *we* are," Romki said drily, "and what we look like, perhaps it would be wise not to judge by appearances?"

"We could show him Styx?" Jokono suggested. Standing well back in the darkness, behind the surrounding humans, Styx's outline had not yet been glimpsed by the prisoner. "Show him we don't actually hate aliens?"

It had been necessary that only *Phoenix* humans had joined this party, for obvious reasons. No one on Eshir had ever seen a tavalai before, and the questions would have drawn a swarm of attention. Keeping and hiding Styx and Peanut was proving hard enough, though necessary, given they had no chance of success without Styx's capabilities, which she could not provide sitting on *Phoenix* at the rim of the solar system.

"I'm not sure that it would prove much," said Trace. "Anyone who's never seen a drysine could just assume she's an advanced robot who does what she's programmed." She kicked the prisoner's boot, reverting to Hindi. "We're not who you think we are. We don't hate aliens." The prisoner looked scornful. "Why do you think so?"

"We have proof," the Zeladnist retorted. "We have a contact. That's all I know. My leaders don't lie." Trace refrained from rolling her eyes. "What language do you speak?" Suspiciously.

"It's an alien tongue," Trace told him, on a moment's inspiration. "Spoken by friends of ours." He didn't believe her, it was obvious. But possibly if they could turn just one Zeladnist to their side... well, the Zeladnists were a powerful local force. With their old historical knowledge of Qalea, maybe they'd be some help in finding the Ceephay Queen's last location here.

"No Major," said Styx, apparently reading her mind. "The only way to gain the Zeladnists as allies is to reveal myself and Peanut. All large institutions on Qalea are infiltrated by the reeh, I've understood enough of how things work in my penetration of local networks to understand that. This secret could not be kept, and the reeh would descend upon us beyond *Phoenix*'s capability to stop. Nothing happens at the high levels of Qalea society without reeh knowledge and at least tacit support."

"Yeah I know," said Trace, thinking hard. "But it's still an information conduit, and we shouldn't abandon it so quickly."

"Revealing me to the Zeladnists will be revealing me to the reeh," Styx repeated. "There is no way. Our best chance is alliance with the Purists."

"With alien-hating xenophobes?" Romki retorted, in genuine disbelief.

"The secret would be kept from the reeh," Styx reasoned. "The Purists who survive are remnants of a lost war, weak and scattered. It makes them safer. I have attained some network conceptualisation of where they may be found."

"Like where?" Romki snorted. If Stan Romki were going to hate any group of humans with more passion than he reserved for Fleet Command, it would be the alien-haters of Earth Front and their like. "I can't see them hanging around once they catch sight of you, Styx."

"We already have a contact," Styx countered. "Your friend Taj. I'd thought it obvious."

"You've proof of that?" Jokono asked warily. "I didn't pick him for the type."

"Old network connections," said Styx. "He's been out of contact with them for a few years, or mostly. But a statistical analysis reveals a high probability that Taj once had Purist leanings, at the very least. And I calculate a high probability that Taj is the contact that led these Zeladnists to us."

"Which means the Zeladnists will be after him as well," Jokono concluded, with a fast look at Trace. Trace thought hard. She liked Taj, but if he was caught up with the Purists... and she stopped herself. Personal wants and desires again, it seemed she could never shake them. Of course she didn't want to take the side of xenophobes against those preaching tolerance... but then she'd heard enough about the Zeladnists to know that they weren't often much better, they just had better PR.

But it shouldn't have mattered either way. She was Kulina, and she would do what was necessary for the survival of the human race, whether it agreed with her personal sensibilities or not. Like she had at Rando Splicer. Whatever it cost. Again. She took a deep breath, and tried to ignore the dread and despair.

"We'll go and collect Taj," she decided, "if he's still alive. We'll learn his contacts if we can. He may need persuading."

"And this one?" asked Jokono, indicating the puzzled prisoner.

"He's learned nothing," said Trace. "We'll leave him with the others."

"He's learned too much," Styx disagreed. "He's seen your faces."

"If they're following us from Taj, they already know my face at least," Trace retorted. "And since they nearly grabbed Stan, they'll have his face too. You don't need to take the most bloodthirsty solution all the time, Styx."

"I'll make it quick then," said Styx, and shot the prisoner in the chest. A single retort from the shoulder-mounts, it slammed the man back against the boxes, then he slumped, dead and bloody. Jokono jumped in shock, swearing as he turned away. Romki just squeezed his eyes shut, with the air of a man determined not to react to things that should not have been surprising.

Trace stared at Styx. Styx stared back, with that single, malevolent red eye. Reprimand her? Only an idiot would think the human psychological effects of a dressing down would hold the slightest consequence for a drysine queen. Threaten her? Even were it physically possible, Styx was far too important to the mission, and thus to the continued survival of humanity, for Trace to ever follow through with that threat, and they all knew it.

Trace walked to Styx, and stood immediately face to face with that red eye, impossibly multi-faceted in its strobing layers and crystalline depth, at this range in the dark. She could feel her muscles shaking with the involuntary shock -- even she was not immune, particularly not given what she'd seen in the past months, and she'd never in her life just shot a prisoner in cold blood. Until Pena. Her jaw clenched, and she stood between Styx's murderous vibroblades that could kill her with flick, and did not care that the drysine saw her emotion.

"Humanity needs the drysines, Styx," she said, her voice tight and hard. "But you need us too. You need our trust. You just spent a large chunk of that trust, right here. If you plan on having any relationship with humanity, in the aftermath of whatever we do here, you'd better think of how much of that trust you're going to need."

"If humanity has learned anything in the past thousand years," Styx replied calmly, "it's the necessity of doing everything it can to survive, no matter how hard or unpleasant. You are Kulina, Major. I should not need to explain this to you."

"It's not for you to decide the needs of humanity, Styx," Trace retorted, jabbing a finger hard at the crystalline eye. It felt faintly rough beneath her fingertip, a living texture, not synthetic. Styx did not flinch. "Humanity will tolerate drysine assistance that does not presume to *lead* us. Whatever you really think about who's superior, in that cold steel skull of yours, you're going to have to suppress it, or your chances of winning human trust are zero. Drysine numbers are small, humanity's are large. We exterminated one alien species, Styx. Don't forget."

"So did we," said Styx. "Had we chosen, we could have exterminated many more. But I take your point."

15

Rika's breathing echoed harshly in his helmet. The visor graphics showed him life-support, oxygen and nitrogen mix, a full seven hours worth on main tanks, two on the reserve. Or he hoped it would be seven, as on his last trip out, the recyc had glitched and he'd ended up with four. Lieutenant Alomaim's voice was in his earpiece, with additional Lisha translation across the bottom of his visor, adding to the visual clutter. Gyros, attitude, powerplant, coms. Armscomp was deactivated for now, despite the big anti-armour rifle in his suited grip. The marines weren't real keen for him to be shooting at anything with them in the vicinity.

Two minutes to release. Flight mode activate, he blinked on the big left icon, and gave the required flick of his unoccupied left fingers, and felt the control system switch. Now the flight thrusters would work by relative hand and foot motions, the kind of thing you could do in free-flight that you couldn't in gravity, where hands and feet were needed for other things.

Rika felt his heart beating fast, but not so fast as actual fear. Mostly he just didn't want to stuff up and embarrass himself. The Major had put a lot of trust in him, and Bravo Platoon had invested personal time and effort to help him get it right. Back on Rando, the first operations of the evacuation mission would be starting about now. The corbi were about to become a free people once more. A free people would need a Fleet to defend them. A Fleet would need marines. If he could get even halfway as good as Phoenix Company marines, he'd be the first and best of those, as the few that the Corbi Resistance had now were poorly trained and rarely used. If only he could get through the next few hours without screwing up.

Somewhere behind, PH-3's hold doors were opening. With his suit's armoured feet locked into braces, the rowed steel seating lifted away in sections, then the rearmost marines were jetting backward. He saw them peeling off on the visor's rear view window, one and then another, and finally it was his turn, and he kicked feet lose from the braces and applied light thrust. His view of the shuttle bulkhead vanished in a spray of white, and then he was out... too fast, someone behind pushed off with an armoured hand, and he cut thrust and looked about, trying to orient.

Already the marines were moving, forming into three sections plus Heavy Squad, spreading wide to form the rough circle that marine platoons used when approaching potentially hostile structures. For a brief moment of panic, he didn't recognise any of the suits around him, obscured by puffs of white as thrusters engaged... but then augmented reality kicked in, illuminating each marine with a green ID window and showing exactly who they were. And here to his right was Private Jenner, which meant that over here would be... Corporal Rizzo, Commander of Heavy Squad, to which he was currently attached.

But he pushed thrust to catch up, and sure enough the suit kicked forward, and with a few anxious nudges he made some sort of formation off Rizzo's side. Another fast look around for position, and he found Private Wu on the other side, looking straight at him, and now raising a questioning hand from his huge, shielded autocannon to give a thumbs up. Rika gave one back, breathing more easily now. He was in position with Heavy Squad in the formation center, further back with the rest of Bravo Platoon spread before him, like a giant concave net. Up there would be Lieutenant Alomaim... he searched the green ID tiles and sure enough, Alomaim's name appeared, alongside Master Sergeant Brice, who'd recently been promoted from what the marines called Gunnery Sergeant. Why there were so many different kinds of Sergeant, Rika didn't know.

Momentarily secure in his formation, Rika allowed his attention to drift from position, attitude and formation to look for the first time beyond, and see where he was. Ahead was a giant ball of dirty ice. The humans said it looked like something called a snowball... Rika didn't know what a snowball looked like, he was from central Talo, where the temperature was never below freezing even in winter, and had never seen snow. The iceball was huge, filling all the space before the marines. It had to be at least four tarans across. The roughness of its surface seemed incredibly fine and clear, far clearer than anything would appear on Rando. Space had no atmosphere, and in a vacuum, everything looked sharper. It wasn't very bright through. Instead of glaring white, the ice was dull. Rika could not see the Keijir System's star behind him, but out this far its light was very dim. Any planet out here would be frozen like this one, only bigger.

"Rika buddy," came Corporal Rizzo's laconic drawl. *"How you doing?"*

"Hi Corporal. I'm fine." Rizzo was a character, so laid back he sometimes seemed half asleep. In between training sims and suit maintenance, he'd introduced Rika to a kind of music called jazz. The other marines called him Cat, which was apparently an animal like a fir, only lazier.

Off to one far flank, Rika could now see Alpha Platoon, a small web of dark-matte dots moving in parallel, barely visible against the brilliant starfield beyond. *So* many stars. That was the most disorienting thing about being in deep space, away from the glare of a sun, or the shielding glow of a planet's atmosphere. Stars by the billion. He'd always liked to look up at the stars, above the campfires and tall trees of Rando. On moonless nights, when Raina and Dogba were below the horizon, and the skies were free of cloud, he'd thought there were so many stars. Now he'd learned that even on clear nights, most stars had been hidden. It seemed unreasonable that there should be so many. And some of them, he'd been told, weren't stars at all, but far-away galaxies, each with hundreds of billions more stars, all pressed together with distance.

The humans had been concerned that he'd get something called agoraphobia, his first few times out. It was something that happened to people who hadn't been outside in a spacesuit much, and whose brains went abruptly crazy at being confronted with so much emptiness. Billions of tarans of nothing. Trillions of tarans. Rika could barely comprehend the sight of it. But he hadn't gotten agoraphobia.

On coms chatter he could hear humans talking about the drysine assault squad that had deployed on the iceball's far side. Even were they in line-of-sight, he knew they'd be impossible to see. Drysines didn't need suits -- they were suits, big and armoured and invulnerable to vacuum. Apparently they weren't protesting at the humans taking the lead on this mission, and there would be more marines on the iceball than drysine drones.

More talk from Lieutenant Dale, who was now acting Company Commander, with the Major down on Eshir. Lieutenant Alomaim answered him. Ahead, Rika could see the structures now -- habitation modules, cut deep into the ice. The protrusions were docking arms, he'd been told. There was no visible solar panelling, which had puzzled the marines. Even this far out, sunlight was free power, and large fusion powerplants were expensive overkill for what looked like a small water refinery operation. But solar panels made an iceball easier to spot from a distance, and gave notice that it was more than just an iceball. Perhaps whoever had been using this one hadn't wanted to be seen.

The habitations grew larger as the iceball approached, and Rika's heart began beating harder once more. Ahead, suits puffed white clouds as they decelerated, not even needing a command to do it all in unison. Rika eased his own thrust, and lost momentary vision to a cloud of white, from which he emerged travelling more slowly. He watched Corporal Rizzo, and kept the suits in line, and made sure he didn't drift from position.

Ahead, the iceball made a cliff, nearly close enough to touch. It had been floating out here for billions of years, Rika thought. Only in the last few thousands had someone decided to build these tube-like structures through the ice, and set up these big refinery tanks he could see protruding further up, no doubt to be filled with liquid water for some hauler to come and pick up. And maybe other things, if the iceball had them.

Second Squad moved up to try the airlocks. Sergeant Neuman reported that the airlocks were dead, meaning no one else had been using them lately. That was the only way a facility this old could still be functional. Second Squad set about getting the doors opened manually, which with marine armour usually meant brute force. After a few minutes more of floating, and checking his drift, and monitoring his lifesupport, and wondering just how dead they'd all be if someone with a heavy vacuum weapon opened fire as they all floated here, Neuman reported that the doors were open and he was progressing inside.

Heavy Squad went last. Rika thought to risk a turn, and look backward, as covering your rear was what soldiers were supposed to do on the ground, however redundant it became in deep space. A small dot to one side, he saw PH-3, where Lieutenant Jersey watched their progress with heavy weapons ready to support if necessary. Far beyond that, a small dark twig against the star's yellow dot, was *Phoenix*. Seeing it now, he abruptly realised why marines developed such emotional attachments to their ships. That small dark twig was safety, warmth, air-pressure, gravity, food and friends. So small and far, in all this blackness. Precious, to be protected at all costs. Without it, no one lived.

The drysine ships, he couldn't see. He wondered if their drones felt the same way about them. He turned back about, and began his own approach to the habitation, following Rizzo and Heavy Squad. Again Private Wu never left his side, without appearing to get so close as to shepherd. Ahead, the small, open airlock was swallowing the last of Third Squad.

"KJ," said Rizzo to Private Jenner, *"you're lead, then Bis, then Rika."*

The middle of the formation, Rika realised. Obviously no one expected any action, or he wouldn't be here at all.

"Copy Riz," said Jenner.

"Copy," Rika echoed.

LIEUTENANT TYSON DALE floated down a main hall, allowing the AR vision feed back to *Phoenix* to analyse what he was looking at. Sections of wall panelling flashed, possible trunk electronics, then a cross-section of corridors toward mining well-heads down the arms. Follow the trunk-route electronics, was the rule. There was a thin atmosphere, most likely what was left after eight thousand years of neglect, or whenever the life support ceased working, with additional leakages after storage tanks failed from neglect and decay. Likely the air wasn't sufficient for mold, however, and a thin layer of water crystal over many surfaces suggested rust would also be minimal. Some computer system designs could last that long. Without constant maintenance, they'd be the only things that would. *Phoenix* crew had become so accustomed to dealing with very old things lately, everyone had learned the factors determining rate of decay. The drysines had various anti-aging treatments including nano-machines. The reeh might not have had those, but these material sciences were likely very advanced, and in a cold near-vacuum, everything looked well preserved.

"Manjhi," said Dale, glancing at Alpha Platoon's unfolding positions on tacnet, "take that next access, AR's telling me it could be living quarters."

"Copy LT," said Sergeant Manjhi, commanding Third Squad, and turned off that way. Ahead of Dale, Private Reddy and Master Sergeant Forrest drifted with the occasional nudge of attitude thrust, weapons up in case of the impossible. The only way something hostile was alive in here was if it had been visiting from another ship just recently. *Phoenix* and the four drysine warships had been monitoring this portion of space for the past eight days, and seen nothing.

Surviving over weeks in a dead facility with no apparent power sources became a serious problem for suit-wearing organics, with the requirement for air, food and even toilet stops becoming impossible to service. But they'd all seen far too much weird shit over the past two years to take anything for granted.

The main hall ended in a T-junction, which Reddy and Forrest took to the right. Both suits glowed on Dale's nightvision, hot around the rear powerplants, cool along the armoured limbs. Ahead, the corridor was blocked by a big, square door. Reddy checked the cold, dead controls, then wiped ice crystals from a handle cover before pulling it back. *"Manual looks like it might work,"* he said.

He clipped the big Koshaim 20 to its rear rack, secured a foot to stop him from spinning, and wound the handle. The big door, unmoved in millennia, slowly began to grind and move. It opened faster as Reddy's suit put power into the action, saving the Private's arm. Forrest peered through the widening gap.

"Living quarters," he said, and pulled himself through. Dale followed, peering up and around. Zero-G habitation was always a creative exercise in space allocation. This place had freezers and storage bays along one wall, certainly a kitchen, and that silvery sheen on flat surfaces was ice crystals on the glass fronts of microwave ovens. On stainless steel surfaces, everything sparkled. On the reverse side, a den of sorts, numerous hammocks around a central holograph projector. A mini-cinema, perhaps, or maybe sleeping quarters. The answer might depend on what species had been using this place.

"*Phoenix*, this is Dale. Any guesses whose facility this was?"

"We were just wondering that, LT," came back Lieutenant Shilu's voice. *"Resource harvesting seems like menial work, and the reeh don't seem like the types to enjoy menial work. We're guessing probably some slave species."*

"LT," came Forrest's voice. *"Check this out."* Dale grabbed a support and pulled, no need to waste thruster gas in tight spaces, and contaminate pristine surfaces that might offer clues. In an adjoining den, Forrest had pulled open a storage locker. From it, he'd retrieved

something that looked like a clarinet, only metal. Several more instruments lay within.

"Probably not reeh, then," said Dale. "Can't imagine them liking music."

"Lieutenant, this is the Captain," came Debogande's voice in his ear.

"Go ahead Captain."

"Just to inform you that the drysine assault team is moving rapidly. At current speeds you might expect their advance team to reach you in fifteen minutes."

"Copy Captain. I take it they're sharing information?"

"Yes, and we're sharing our feeds with them."

"LT," came Sergeant Barnes' voice before Dale could reply. *"You might want to look at this."*

Tacnet showed that Barnes' Second Squad was several rooms across, in what AR was now optimistically tagging as a command center. Dale checked in with Lieutenant Alomaim on the way, and found progress good, nothing to report. The corbi kid hadn't gotten himself killed yet, so that was a plus. Dale thought it was dumb, putting some untrained farmer in an antique suit and babysitting him through an assault, however unlikely to see combat. The last two years' experience had taught everyone in Phoenix Company just how badly things could go wrong when you least expected it, and Dale bristled at anything interfering with his people's carefully-honed operational standards.

The Major had been a driving force in setting those standards, but the corbi kid had been her idea. Like so much with the Major lately, Dale had had no choice but to set his jaw and take it. And now she was gone again, down to Eshir with Command Squad, as though she hadn't just been rescued from four months on some other alien hellhole, away from her Company and trying to save the galaxy singlehanded, as always. Only the Major hadn't truly come back. She'd left a part of herself down on Rando, and to varying degrees, everyone knew it.

It left Dale in the impossible position of commanding Phoenix Company for damn near six months straight now, but without the rank or true authority to back it up. Captain Debogande respected his ability well enough, but not so much as he respected the Major's, nor liked him half as much either. After the Zondi Splicer Raid, and *Phoenix* had left without the Major and Sergeant Kono, and Bravo Platoon had nearly mutinied rather than leave her behind, the Captain had threatened to personally court martial and shoot Dale the next time he disobeyed a direct order. Fair enough, Dale had thought, and respected Debogande for having somewhere in the last two years grown the balls to do it. The Major had shown him how, of course, but before she'd gone to Eshir, she hadn't been speaking much to Debogande, either.

It was all such a giant fucking mess, and Dale hated being caught in the middle, beneath a Captain who did not particularly like him, and a Major who was lately never here.

It was easy to see why AR had labelled the next space as a command center. There was a bank of screens before chairs, a far more spacious arrangement than *Phoenix* could afford. Bucket was here, steadying himself with legs clasping several chairs, fiddling with his smaller manipulator arms at various controls.

Dale drifted to Sergeant Barnes, floating alongside to observe Bucket's work. *"The translation matrix is saying that he's found something,"* said Barnes. *"It's unclear on what he's found, but, you know, they're capable of taking control of foreign computer systems."*

At Barnes's side, Dale could see tiny filament protrusions from the drysine's arms, like the tiny tendrils of some undersea reef creature adrift on the currents. "Looks like he's getting right into the network itself," Dale observed. "If he can provide his own power source... hang on." He flipped channels. "Hello *Phoenix*, this is Dale. Are you reading this?"

"Yes Lieutenant," came Shilu's reply. *"Hang on, I've got Lieutenant Rooke watching."*

"Dale, this is Rooke," came the young man's voice a moment later. *"Bucket can't restart whatever's in there, but he can probably use his own power source to do some kind of scan on whatever physically survived."*

"You think it's some kind of command module?"

"I can't see what else Bucket would be so interested in. AIs tend to find high level CPUs interesting."

Dale glanced at Barnes. Behind his armoured visor, he could faintly make out Barnes' eyes rolling in dissatisfaction at the answer. Barnes was another of Phoenix Company's newly promoted, from Corporal to Sergeant after the previous Second Squad leader, Dex Hall, had been killed on Defiance. The Major taking his best rifleman, 'Benji' Carville, to fill a Command Squad vacancy after her return from Rando, hadn't improved Barnes' mood, as even today First Section were a marine short, operating as a three-team.

"The other drysines coming?" Barnes asked his Lieutenant.

"Oh yeah," said Dale, checking his Koshaim with unthought reflex. "In a real hurry."

"Be nice if Bucket could actually tell us what the hell he's doing." Drones couldn't speak, or wouldn't speak. No one knew if the distinction was significant. *"In fact, be kinda nice if Styx were here."* Barnes sounded as though he couldn't quite believe he was saying it.

"Yeah," Dale replied. "Maybe." With their four drysine friends, he meant, there was no guarantee Styx would side with *Phoenix*. Barnes nodded his understanding, and made a sideways gesture at Bucket, asking silently if the same could be said for Bucket's loyalties. Dale nodded shortly. Drysine drones couldn't speak, but they could certainly understand, and marines kept such discussions off coms.

"LT," said Lance Corporal Teale from an adjoining doorway. *"Phoenix AR just came to the conclusion that this is a reeh base. We've been feeding them bathroom pictures, I think the look at the handgrips in the showers convinced the computer."* She sounded puzzled.

"What's the problem?"

"There's a damn recreation suite down that way." She pointed down the corridor she'd come from. *"I mean, they've got some kind of big playing space set up, it's like air hockey."*

Dale frowned. "Yeah. Computer must be wrong. I mean, it's not like the computer's as smart as Styx." With Styx offship, they'd have to rely on a dumb, non-sentient processor to make these analytical judgements. He couldn't help but wonder if Sergeant Barnes' earlier assessment had been right. "Woody found some kind of musical instrument back that way. Reeh don't do that shit."

"How the hell can a shower handgrip tell anyway?" Barnes wondered. *"Dumbass computers."*

"That's not how multi-factor analysis works, Sarge," said Teale, drifting across. *"Hey Bucket. What'cha doing?"* The drysine ignored her, wrapped around his screen-side seats like a spider over a fly, fiddling with control panels. Suddenly the entire bridge setup flashed, a dance of light across seven screens, coloured icons illuminating briefly, then going blank. *"Woah."*

Dale blinked on coms again. "*Phoenix*, Bucket seems to be right into the command network here, we just got a big flash across all the control screens."

"That means the main conduits are probably made of something that won't decay," came Rooke's reply directly. *"Could be something crystalline, we've seen that a fair bit in reeh space."*

One of the control screens flickered, then went unmistakably live, turning several shades lighter than the others. "Hang on. Bucket's got a screen live." Random shapes appeared. They began cycling, one after another, faster and faster, then accelerated to eye-blurring speed. "You got my feed, Rooke?"

"Yeah, I can see it." Predictably, Rooke sounded intrigued. Though starship engines were more his thing, like all the polymath geniuses who rose to command Engineering departments on warships, Rooke knew a lot about computers too. *"Looks like there's some kind of functioning CPU in there. Bucket's providing the power and processing, he can just draw data from a dead machine, looks like."*

The shapes were replaced by layers and layers of text, thousands of pages a second. "Can you slow that down?" Dale asked. "What is that?"

"Um... computer says that's some reeh language. Won't say which one, they've had a number over the years. No, wait a second... it's saying the language is old. It's something mathematically encoded, something their engineers might have used... damn, it'd be useful to know what exactly Bucket's drawing this stuff from. I mean, it could be a random data file or

something else entirely. This is definitely a reeh-built base, though. Whether it was reeh-occupied I can't tell..."

"LT," Lance Corporal Yalen interrupted. *"I got drysines approaching my position. Just two of them, looks calm enough. No, make that three. No real rush, they're not even using thrusters."*

"Yeah, give them a wave and let them go where they want," said Dale. He didn't have to tell anyone to keep an eye on them. They knew.

"They just went past me," came Yalen again. *"Headed for you, I think."*

"*Phoenix*," said Dale, still watching as the alien data scrawled blindingly fast upon Bucket's reactivated screen. "Please query the drysines and ask what we can help them with."

"Doing that LT," said Shilu, always listening on this frequency.

"Hello Lieutenant Dale," came a strangely modulated female voice a moment later. *"This is drysine warship Friendship. My drones will analyse your drone's discovery. Our analysis of this feed suggests there is a sentience-level AI built into the command post of this facility. Your drone's initial discovery suggests its primary core may be salvageable."*

The marines looked at each other. *"Makes sense with the timeline,"* Teale suggested. *"We're figuring reeh society was even AI-run back then."*

"Hello *Friendship*," Dale replied. "Can you tell what sort of AI? And from what period?"

"The capabilities of this AI will require a much more extensive study than is currently possible," Friendship replied. The voice sounded eerily like Styx, but not entirely. It was missing a personality, Dale realised. If one believed that Styx actually had such a thing, and had not simply constructed one to encourage human allies to like her better. *"But the technological period designation of this AI is quite clear from the foundational language your drone has translated. It is ceephay."*

16

Lisbeth dragged herself from her bunk, to the plaintive beeping of her uplink coms. She pulled on boots but left the safety harness off, lying on the narrow gap of floor between bunk and wall to do exercises while answering her coms.

"Hello Liala," she said, recognising the familiar signature from *Amity*. "I'm awake, what can I do for you?" She began with crunches, always easiest first thing with a fuzzy head and no energy. Her body ached all over. She'd never pulled so many Gs over such a short period in her life, not even during *Phoenix*'s crazy first months renegade from human space. Eight rotations since the evacuation had commenced, and reeh had been launching attacks into Reba System every seven hours on average. Many of them were smaller, harassing assaults designed to keep everyone off-balance, perhaps to lure croma warships away from close defence while the second jump hit an exposed flank and took out a transport, or an evacuation zone on the ground. And a few of them had been huge, and terrifying, and convinced her on several occasions that she'd been about to die.

"Hello Lisbeth," said Liala, as calm and cool as she'd ever asked questions about Shakespeare, or human family relationships. It must be quite something, Lisbeth thought as she strained, to have no

regard for different states of mind at different times of the day, nor for physical conditioning at all. *"Admiral Cho'nuk has come up with a truly appalling plan while you were sleeping. The captains are not happy."*

"What's his plan?" Admiral Cho'nuk was the Croma Fleet commander of forces in Reba System. He was only forty-five croma years old, a baby for such a rank in human terms, but it was not uncommon for croma. Above sixty, croma became too big to handle Gs so well, or even fit down ship corridors, so the best and brightest croma spacers were selected for a command track early. If Cho'nuk was going to make a name for himself in war, he'd have to do it soon.

"He wishes to take ten ships and attack Liri System where some of the reeh attacks are almost certainly coming from. He thinks to hit them while they're gathering for their assaults, and take the fight to them."

"Explain to me why that's a bad thing?" It actually sounded like the kind of daring, aggressive thing that Captain Pantillo had made the name *UFS Phoenix* famous for doing during the Triumvirate War.

"In another situation it could be an effective manoeuvre," Liala said patiently. *"But the average reeh warship, at least those we've seen so far in this campaign, has a small but significant performance advantage over all of Admiral Cho'nuk's warships. Their numbers appear strong, they have clearly devoted a larger force to Reba System than croma planners had anticipated, and by my estimation, given my analysis of many thousands of past confrontations between croma and reeh, the reeh will likely have anticipated such an aggressive move from an ambitious young croma admiral.*

"Worse, Liri System is not the only system the reeh are using from which to launch attacks on Reba System, they are also mustering and launching assaults from Metuna System as well. Admiral Cho'nuk lacks the forces to hit both of them, and will leave the Rando evacuation exposed and undefended from Metuna System assaults during his adventure."

"Well that doesn't seem good at all," Lisbeth admitted. The fact that it was coming from Liala, who'd been wrong about nearly nothing in the campaign so far, made it seem even worse. "Which captains have you been talking to?"

"Those of the warships Ha'chon, Rel'amla, Sha'shik and Ka'bak. All are displeased."

"You communicated on private channels?"

"Yes Lisbeth. I am not completely naive with regards to organic politics."

Ha'chon was the big one, Lisbeth thought as she paused her crunches, and reached for a water bottle. That was Captain Jo'duur, the most respected of Admiral Cho'nuk's captains. The *Ha'chon* had claimed two reeh warships destroyed in the fight so far, and two more severely damaged, a tally twice as large as any other.

Lisbeth had been the one to introduce the croma captains to Liala, including Captain Jo'duur. She'd found him quiet and studious by croma standards -- the sort of young officer who could probably have only achieved glory in Fleet, as few other services could reward such qualities so extravagantly. Admiral Cho'nuk and his two closest captains were good commanders, Jo'duur had explained to her in his understated way, but impatient. To beat the reeh, he'd insisted, one needed patience. From croma, reeh expected the opposite, and took advantage.

"I will look into the dispositions of the other croma captains to the Admiral's plan," Lisbeth said. "I will report back to you on my findings. Perhaps there's something we can do about it."

"I believe that will be the optimum course of action," Liala agreed. *"Thank you Lisbeth."*

Admiral Cho'nuk had not been told directly that his captains were in contact with Liala in spite of his express instruction that it should not happen, but surely by now he'd guessed. Croma captains respected results in combat, and while *Ha'chon* had claimed two enemy kills, *Coroset* currently had three, and *Amity* five -- nearly as many between them as all croma forces combined.

Added to that, those croma warship captains had begun passing on Liala's advice to the transport captains, who'd in turn made adjustments to their orbital frequencies, abandoning an even spread of rendezvous opportunities for a staggered pattern of overlapping fire defences that concentrated maximum cargo capacity above the busiest evacuation zones. Then Liala had suggested sending some big

An'ji shuttles to fill the smaller transports with a single load, instead of just docking with their usual Sto'ji transports, thus filling and removing those transports from the orbital pattern more quickly, giving croma Fleet ships less vulnerable vessels to protect and reducing chaos in close orbit.

Those and other changes, including on-the-spot rewrites to shuttle navigation software that allowed military and non-military vehicles to coordinate better past the previous roadblocks, had improved the number of evacuees loaded by nearly twenty percent per hour. The transport captains were saying it was their idea, and Admiral Cho'nuk had accepted all changes, with commendations to all involved. Fairly soon, Lisbeth was sure, someone would let slip to him exactly whose idea it had truly been, and then things would get interesting. There was no way Admiral Cho'nuk, having waited so long for this once-in-a-lifetime opportunity to make his name in a great war, was going to let some upstart alien AI steal all his glory.

Lisbeth took care of basic strength exercises in her quarters -- a necessity with all the Gs being pulled -- then went to the gym to use a treadmill. While there, she queried various captains to let them know she wished to speak to them, as soon as they were free. Captain Tocamo of *Coroset* had gained their respect as well, but his loyalty was only to Gesul. Also unlike croma captains, Tocamo was not in actual command of the parren flagship -- Ambassador Juneso was, leaving croma captains uncertain who they should be talking to in this direction. Unable to contact Liala through their own chain of command, the croma were now using Lisbeth as the conduit.

Her shower was interrupted by the bridge shutting down crew cylinder rotation with only twenty seconds' notice. It happened frequently enough when Operations or Engineering needed to move large numbers of people or equipment rapidly in or out of Midships, and couldn't take the time to go through the non-rotating central hub. Lisbeth was well used to it, set the tiny shower cubicle to zero-G, braced herself against a wall until everything floated, then continued washing amid the chaos of floating water globules while the ventilation fans sucked the excess from down by her feet.

Gravity was still off when she made the bridge, overhanding to her empty observer post and belting herself in. The bridge was still in third-shift, Captain Tacomo was probably sleeping or exercising. *Coroset* was now at high-geostationary, locked into close docking with a croma transport come from Cho'nu System to rearm and resupply them. It was an odd logistical complication with so many big Sto'ji transports entering Reba System empty that these separate resupplies for warships were still required, but the Sto'jis were all outfitted for zero-G civilian transport, and had no room left for warship resupply, nor the time in their desperately tight schedules to do it in.

The last of the Sto'jis had entered Reba System, their entry staggered this late so that not all of them would arrive at once. The first Sto'jis to make their second runs after delivering an initial load of corbi evacuees would not be coming for another several days. Perhaps this relatively light period was what had inspired Admiral Cho'nuk to try his adventure now, when transport numbers at Rando were temporarily decreasing. So far they'd moved a total of about twenty-six million corbi for a loss of eight Sto'jis and fourteen smaller civilian vessels. Three of those Sto'jis had been destroyed when nearly full for the loss of about two hundred and fifty thousand corbi lives, while the other five had lost a hundred thousand more. Successful strikes upon evacuation zones had killed unknown tens of thousands. If the Rando population were indeed two hundred million, then the evacuation was only one eighth complete. Eight times current losses would lose Croma Fleet sixty-four Sto'jis, more than a quarter of all those assembled, and perhaps a tenth of all those in the Croma Fleet. It was far too high, and raised the very real possibility that if Croma'Dokran high command could not find warship replacements to bolster their protection, the entire Rando Evacuation would be abandoned to cut the losses of so many of their most valuable ships.

Amity was down in low orbit, assisting with the repair of the damaged transport *Hi'jo*, even as that transport continued to take shuttle loads of evacuees. Lisbeth did not like *Coroset* and *Amity* being separated -- ships of similar performance needed to stay together, something croma warships could not do this deep within a gravity-well. But *Amity* had already replenished in half the time it took any other vessel, no doubt thanks to its crew not needing things like food, and Liala had taken the opportunity to dart down to close orbit and get the *Hi'jo*'s hull breach patched.

Lisbeth switched to a visual of it now, taken from one of *Hi'jo*'s external cameras -- the enormous croma vessel's hull swarming with drysine drones in the blue backlight of Rando's curving horizon, the scene erupting with blue and orange welding sparks. Drysine crew who would not tire, did not need breaks, would never run out of air, and were nearly invulnerable to injury even with welders that could cut starship hulls. Watching drysines work up close was incredibly impressive, but also frightening. Organics had been so incredibly lucky to beat them the first time, that success due entirely to the Drysine/Deepynine War doing ninety-five percent of the damage first. It seemed unlikely that the drysines, given a second chance at galactic empire, would allow it to happen again.

Her coms blinked -- *Ha'chon* was calling. Lisbeth opened the link. "Hello warship *Ha'chon*, this is Lisbeth Debogande."

"Hello Lisbeth Debogande, this is Captain Jo'duur of the Ha'chon."

"Yes Captain. Our mutual friend has said that you wished to speak to me."

"Let me speak plainly, for there is little time," said the croma. *"Our mutual friend should be in command. Her tactical analysis and warfighting capability has been unmatched. She understands that this is primarily a logistical exercise, not an opportunity for ambitious admirals to win glory. Glory will be measured in the percentage of corbi lives saved, and nothing more. If Admiral Cho'nuk's plan is followed, there is a significant chance of catastrophic failure, and many transports lost when left undefended. We have lost too many already."*

"This is Liala's assessment as well," said Lisbeth. "She seems in favour of aggressive attacks when the time is right, but judges that this is not the correct time. The risk factors are too high when the true mission is to safeguard transports and corbi lives."

"As I said, the drysine should be in command. I have spoken with all of

the warship captains save for those who I know will disagree. I can guarantee that fourteen out of twenty-one will agree."

"And you would prefer Liala in command than yourself?"

"There is more glory in winning than leading, Lisbeth Debogande. I want to win."

"You say you have fourteen out of twenty-one captains. Can you oppose the Admiral's plan with those numbers?" Croma military discipline did not work as human systems did, Lisbeth knew. Orders could sometimes be challenged if a majority disagreed. Humans were sensitive to the challenging of orders because of the fear it would lead to outbreaks of cowardice. With croma, as with parren, cowardice in battle was almost unknown. Most croma who challenged orders did so because they wanted to attack harder. But not in this case, it seemed. Perhaps that made Captain Jo'duur's position more difficult.

"It is possible," said the Captain. *"It must be done reasonably. Even the Admiral is coming to concede that Liala's assessments have merit. She must be included in the process of calculation, but the Admiral will not allow her to talk directly. I believe you are best positioned to negotiate such a thing. The Admiral will listen to you. He knows that Sho'mo'ra will listen to you. You have credit with Croma'Dokran command where your Ambassador Juneso, and Liala herself, do not."*

Lisbeth took a deep breath. "I will do what I can," she said.

17

Taj landed his Shaytan at The Perch, and flipped a coin to the parking kid. The morning wind was cool from the south, and he left his flying leathers on, picking past diners to where Halhoun and Dagan sat, boots up on the railing, overlooking the precipitous view.

"Hey man," said Hal, with a lazy handclasp, sipping hot chuno, glasses down against the dull glare from the eastward sun. It sat low above Nasir Ridge, a bronze disk through the haze, above the clutter on the slopes and the chaos of flying vehicles. "Heard you had a hot date yesterday."

"Says who?" asked Taj, sitting to put scarf and gloves on the scarred plastic table, then tapping Dagan's hand opposite.

"Wasn't me," said Dagan. Taj believed him.

"Guy before," Hal said vaguely, gesturing around. "Yesterday, at Dhahab Market. Asked if I knew anything about some short-haired chick you were giving rides to."

"Was riding, more likely," said Dagan. Dagan was lanky, black and athletic. He was the best rider Taj had ever seen, a high-status guy in Family Zurhan who didn't give a damn about that kind of thing, and just liked to ride, and date hot girls, and hang with his friends. Halhoun was broader, long-haired and too smart to be a family rider, really. He was into the arts scene, played drums in his own band, and was practically married to a tenacious young businesswoman whom Taj and Dagan teased would soon trick him into having kids and settling down. Alarmingly, Hal didn't seem to mind that much.

"What kind of guy?" Taj asked. He'd promised Smriti he wouldn't talk about her, not even with his best friends.

"I dunno. Just a guy, average looking. Seemed to know I was your friend, asked some questions."

"Questions about her? Or about me too?"

Hal grinned lazily. "Maybe you're not that interesting, Boots. Just her."

"So who is she, man?" Dagan pressed, tearing off a mouthful of falafel wrap. Breakfast and chuno at The Perch was a regular thing for the three of them. The crowded slopes of Zarqa sprawled to one side, even now alive with early risers out on their balconies, washing clothes, eating breakfast, chasing kids, doing yoga.

"I said I wouldn't say," Taj explained. "Condition of the fare."

"She hot? Or is that a condition of the fare too?"

"Yeah," Taj admitted, with a creeping smile. "Yeah, pretty hot."

"Does Maya know?"

"Dude, I'm not with Maya." He signalled to the waitress.

"But you took her for a ride, yeah?"

Taj shrugged. "Doesn't work on every girl, apparently."

"You're losing your touch, is what."

"Thanks Burner, that's real nice of you to say."

Dagan shrugged, eating falafel. "S'what I'm here for." Several bikes landed behind, with a howl that paused conversation for a moment. "So what happened after I left the casino?" Dagan asked. "Heard someone say you got into a fight?"

"Can't talk about that either," Taj admitted. The waitress finally arrived, busy with an armful of empty bowls and cups.

"Seriously?" said Hal. "Man, she must be paying you heaps."

"Falafel roll and fool, thanks," Taj told the girl with a smile. "And a cup of chuno, straight, no synth." The waitress left without acknowledging either his order or his smile. Maybe he was losing his touch.

Dagan nodded past Taj's shoulder. "That her?" Looking at someone behind him.

Taj smiled. "Yeah sure." But Dagan's eyes never left their target. Taj frowned and looked over his shoulder... and sure enough, here was Smriti, helmet in her hand, gloves off, walking in boots and flying jacket, just like yesterday. With her was a broad guy with a square jaw and a thick neck, similarly decked in flying gear. Something about him was odd, but Taj couldn't put a finger on it.

He gave Smriti a puzzled look as she arrived -- that must have been her bike arriving just now, with this tough-looking guy flying. "Got yourself a new pilot?" he asked her, switching to Hin. Dagan and Hal both spoke it.

"Hi Taj," she said, and put a boot up on the chair alongside, leaning on her knee. "These your friends?"

"Yeah, this is Halhoun, and that's Dagan." Smriti reached to shake each hand, unbothered by their curious looks.

"You're right," Hal said to Taj. "Pretty hot." Dagan chuckled.

Another girl might have blushed or scowled, or made some kind of deal of it. Smriti barely noticed. "Taj, I think it's best for you and your friends to get out of public for a while."

Taj reckoned this was all getting a bit ridiculous. She was his customer, but now she turned up here having evidently found herself a new ride, and rubbed his nose in it? She'd paid him a nice sum to keep his mouth shut about yesterday's strange events, but coming here now, and getting his friends to raise their eyebrows at him like this was all too much.

"Yeah, well right now I'm having breakfast," he told her. "Get a chair and join us. It's nothing special, but the view's cool."

"And get Mr Muscles over here to join us too," said Dagan around another mouthful, looking at Smriti's new guy, sceptically. Dagan, Taj knew, was going to give the newcomers a hard time, followed by him giving Taj a hard time for associating with weirdos. Taj often wished he could be as cool as Dagan.

And then he realised why Smriti's 'Mr Muscles' was bugging him. He'd not spoken, not made to introduce himself, not even approached the table, but stood two paces back and surveyed the surroundings. Not just looked at the view, but scanned it, like a security guard looking for threats. Recalling what Smriti was, or rather what he suspected Smriti was, that was suddenly alarming. There was *another* one like her here? Another one like her, with similar skills? Something about the way he stood, and the position of the hands upon his coat, made Taj suddenly certain that Mr Muscles was packing something big under there.

"Taj, someone attacked me last night," said Smriti. "I think you might be next."

Taj frowned. "Who attacked you?"

"Zeladnists." Taj blinked.

Halhoun did a fast double-take. "Whoa, whoa! Zeladnists? Why would Zeladnists want to attack..." And he looked suspiciously at Taj. "Dude, tell me you're not messing with that Purist shit any longer?"

"Fuck man, I told you!" Taj protested angrily. "I was young and stupid, I haven't seen those guys in years!" He stared at Smriti. "Why would Zeladnists think... or wait, they were after you first?"

"I'm not a Purist," said Smriti. "Some of my best friends aren't human."

"Right," said Dagan with a roll of the eyes, having heard that one before.

Taj looked at Mr Muscles. "So who's he?"

"A friend."

"Your friend got a name?"

"Irfan. He's from Tarshin, like me."

"Wait, so if you've got some other dude to fly you around, why'd you need me?"

"Taj," said Smriti, with a distracted look around, "I took a risk coming here to warn you. I could have just left you to them. I'm telling you that your life is in danger. I think you'd best come with me."

Dagan put down his falafel roll. "Hey lady. None of us here take orders from you." He half-rose from his chair. "I don't know why your rich daddy never taught you manners, but good little girls don't order guys like us around, you hear?" Smriti didn't even look at him, suddenly staring somewhere out to the hazy horizon. "So why don't you and your boy toy here..."

Smriti leaped, and tackled Taj from his chair. He hit the ground with a crash, then felt as much as heard the sharp fizz and snap of something cutting the air just above. Then Smriti was off him, pistol in hand, while Mr Muscles pulled a big rifle from his jacket and was on a knee by the railings to aim, while people yelped and shouted and ran.

"I got no shot," Mr Muscles was saying, staring down his deadly-looking rifle. Taj had never seen one like it. "Too many civvies, bullet could go anywhere."

"Yeah, we're leaving," said Smriti, and it didn't sound as though she was talking to Mr Muscles. Taj scrambled back to a crouch, staring wildly through the railings separating him from the long drop into Meujaza Canyon. "Taj, last chance."

Taj heard a commotion behind, and Dagan swearing. He looked, and saw people abandoning their tables, running for cover, a few lying flat having heard and evidently recognised the sound of bullets flying. And here by their table, Dagan was attending desperately to Hal, who was on the ground, clutching his bloody stomach.

THE QALEA BOYS FLEW FAST, and Qalea traffic was a little unnerving even for a marine veteran. It jostled and stayed roughly in its lanes, visible on Trace's local-made visor as 3D graphical highways in the sky. But it was ill-disciplined, and filled with so many different sorts of vehicles abiding various performance envelopes that one had to be prepared for anything. Halhoun had been loaded onto the front of Dagan's bike, the wound secured with one of Trace's bandages, and Taj fancying Dagan an even better flyer than himself. Canyon sides tore by, and they wove past slower traffic with that method Trace was only now learning, like a skier on a fast snow-slope, no sudden movements just keep it smooth and let the skis run.

"Why not take him to the Zurhan family?" she asked Taj on coms, having to yell above the roar of jets and slipstream. "They've got good doctors, surely?" Holding to the outside of Taj's slipstream through a right-hand turn past slower traffic, the turbulent contrail of his jets making a thick streamer of white nearly close enough to touch. Talking through even simple high-speed manoeuvres, while calculating how not to crash into passing traffic and die, was challenging. Erik, Trace was certain, would have enjoyed it a lot more than she did.

"We get told never to take trouble home," Taj told her. *"I know somewhere better."*

"Man, we could take him to Patrika!" Dagan disagreed. *"She's not far from here."*

"I know somewhere better," Taj retorted. *"It's almost faster, trust me."*

Taj took a left off the main canyon, diving lower as it unfolded into boulder walls that were clearly natural, and others of rusting vertical steel where the ancient derelict city beneath the present one had once filled in the gaps between mountain valleys. Far below, along the valley floor, Trace saw the old spires of what looked to be derelict buildings, protruding up from the sunless valley floor. Above them, on a shoulder several hundred meters up the cliff face, loomed the vertical walls of what looked like an old fortress.

Taj held up a fist to indicate he was slowing, and Trace deployed airbrakes slowly at first, feeling that alarming kick as the rear-mounted blades bit into the slipstream, causing the bike to skid and rock as her weight pushed forward against the control bars. Taj took his bike through a more controlled slide toward the lip of the main wall, which Trace saw was missing chunks, as though blasted away in some old battle. The old light towers that ringed the wall looked more recent, though old enough, and Trace glimpsed modern sensor masts at different points, mostly invisible from further away.

As they flew over the walls, Trace saw that the ceiling of the internal complex was only a few floors down. Nearer the cliff wall, the ceiling was higher still, above the ring of walls, and Taj brought them down to it, losing velocity and speed with expertise. Trace struggled, wobbling and trailing further behind as Dagan came past to park beside Taj close to the wall.

They were removing Halhoun as Trace landed against the cliff face nearby, and carrying him down some stairs. Trace unstrapped after she'd landed, lacking the boys' surety to do it on the descent, then pulled her rifle from its makeshift holster where she'd rigged it behind her seat against the rear trunk.

The rest of her party landed around her, and Trace took off down the stairs after Taj and Dagan, to the curses of Rael who struggled to get out of his leg straps in time, and called on others to hurry and go with her.

The staircase was old bricks, and took a turn halfway down to descend into a similarly old room, wide and open, with glassless windows on either side looking onto the deep valley drop. The walls and ceiling were either old brick or stone, and the place was bare and desolate, save for big divans by the windows, and large basins of water surrounded by cabinets and an old, dirty mirror by the far wall.

Dagan and Taj had Halhoun on one of the divans, and now through a far doorway came a woman with long black braids, pulling what looked like a high-tech medical trolley on wheels. Behind her were another two women, one young and slim with oversized scrubs and a facemask, the other squat and grey, hauling a large bag.

They rushed the rattling apparatus over the stone floor to Halhoun, and set about removing his shirt, talking urgently in Arabic as Trace adjusted her earpiece functions to catch the conversation, and found it all predictably medical. Rael and Arime came down behind her, then Rolonde, as Randrahan and Terez remained on the roof to guard the bikes and keep a lookout.

"Who did this bandage?" the stocky, grey-haired woman was demanding as she unwrapped to peer under it. *"Was it you?"*

They didn't seem to be wearing earpieces. "It was me," Trace agreed, in Hindi. Taj translated, which meant it likely that these three women, with whatever medical skills they possessed, only spoke Arabic... or Arga, as the locals called it.

"What kind of bandage is this?" the woman demanded, peering at it. *"This is treated with something... why's the blood congealing like this? I need to know what he's treated with before I treat him."*

"It's not chemical," said Trace. "It won't interact with anything else, it's not a drug. Consider it neutral." Again Taj translated, with a hard, questioning look as he did. It was nano-solution, of course, standard on *Phoenix* and lately updated via their recent new understandings of how such things worked and could be improved. It was technology the locals were certain not to have, and revealing its nature would reveal other, potentially dangerous things.

After five minutes it seemed sure that Halhoun would be okay. He sprawled unconscious on the divan as the three women worked, and Taj and Dagan hovered, and answered questions on their friend's medical details with anxious concern. The bullet had gone low, probably taking lower intestines and things that could be fixed relatively fast even with Qalea's lower level of medical technology, while avoiding kidneys and other organs that couldn't.

Rael wandered next door with Terez, and for a while Trace observed their visor feed on her own lenses, seeing interesting things there. Soon she went herself, and left Rolonde and Arime to watch proceedings. The windows of the next room were also without glass. A large bar at one end, and the remains of dusty shields of some kind in the ceiling beams, indicated that it had once been some sort of function room. One of the shields was still mounted properly on a high wall -- a coat of arms, Trace thought. The bar shelves were long empty, and the space behind and surrounding the bar was stuffed with similar medical trolleys, and various other medical gear. It looked like the contents of a relatively modern hospital, evacuated and dumped into storage. But storage for who?

Rael was peering at a big map on a wall. Trace walked to join him, flipping her visor up, and recalling now to remove her flying helmet so she could do that. She stuffed the floppy thing into a pocket and stared over the dark contour lines across the wall map.

"It's Qalea," Rael murmured, voice low so no one would overhear them speaking English. "I think it's old, there's a lot of features here that I don't recognise."

"It's mostly Human Quarter," Trace agreed. "Look... the perimeters are all wrong. That's Tarskin Ridge there... that's in Qwailash Quarter now. And this whole valley here, that's Amman, that's now in Tanifex Quarter."

"This is pre-Purist War," said Rael. "Human Quarter lost territory in the war. Lots of Purists still think these old bits belong to them."

"So we cease to be a spacefaring species and we revert straight back to old Earth history, fighting over lines on a map." She looked around the room, and saw other things hanging on further walls. Several were simple photographs, of Qalea landscapes. Trace suspected they'd be showing things that had once belonged to humans, but no longer did. And this room was set up as a medical stockpile, in case large-scale conflict broke out again. "I think Taj brought us to his Purist friends."

Rael nodded slowly. "So what now?"

Trace exhaled hard. "The Zeladnists are after us. If they figure out who we are, the reeh will be next, you can bet someone in the Zeladnists will figure the reward they could get from the reeh."

"Purists won't do that," said Rael. "Xenophobic alien-hating assholes won't dob us in to the reeh. Might be a better bet."

"Yeah." Romki was going to hate it, Trace knew. But as Styx had said, sometimes you had to do what worked instead of doing what you'd prefer. "Old institutions have old knowledge. These guys look very interested in history. We might have a way in here. Normally I wouldn't want to take it, but we're running out of time."

Rael looked as though he'd like to say more, but the door opened once more and the tall, dark woman with long braids entered, pulling off bloody gloves. "Your friend is going to be okay," she said in Hindi, laying the gloves on the old bar and walking over. "Taj says Zeladnists shot him?"

"That's right."

The woman held out a hand. "Any enemy of the Prophet Zeladny is a friend of mine." Trace shook her hand, then Rael. The woman gave Rael a slightly puzzled look. "Taj said you guys were from Tarshin?" There weren't many white people on Eshir. Rael wasn't as fair-skinned as Jess Rolonde, but on Eshir they both stood out.

"That's right," Trace agreed. The woman was looking at Trace's rifle now, and those of Rael and Terez. They were T-9s and T-15s, high powered and probably better than anything on Eshir. That alone would not raise suspicion -- plenty of people carried high powered custom weapons on Eshir. But someone who knew weapons would see the quality of these, and at least raise an eyebrow. "Nice map," Trace added, turning back to it. "Interesting boundaries."

"Aren't they?" the woman agreed, with a flash of her eyes. "We lost so much. A million lives and all those lands, and still people don't care. So why were Zeladnists shooting at you?"

"They thought we were Purists," Trace said truthfully. "Got it into their heads that Purists coming into Qalea from outside might be up to no good."

"Are you?"

"Up to no good? Or are we Purists?"

"Either."

"I'm after something," said Trace. "Old reeh history. From back beyond the Origin Horizon."

The woman's eyes widened. "Well, you came to just the right place. Dumb, dangerous pursuits are our speciality." She held up a finger. "Wait here, I'll get something you'll find interesting."

She swept from the room. Trace returned her attention to the room, and the walls of the building. "Styx," she asked on coms. "Can you see where we are?"

"Yes Major."

"This place looks like an old fortress guarding the Khanq Gap. It's taken old damage that looks to be from the war, can you get some kind of idea who built it and why?" The coms gave no reply. "Styx?"

Then the crushing nausea hit, squeezing her brain as though within the clamps of a vice. Rael was on his knees, clutching his head, then vomiting. Terez unslung his rifle, trying to prepare for something, realising the attack, as Trace recalled all too well that she'd felt this before, at the Zondi Splicer where she'd fallen prisoner to the reeh. It was her last conscious thought before the floor came up and hit her.

~

TRACE AWOKE EXPECTING A CORBI ATTIC. Baskets of grain on the boards, Giddy sleeping nearby, her rifle within easy reach. Afternoon sunlight beaming through the thatch, the discomfort of hot, stuffy air. Wishing she could remove more clothes to sleep better, but practical as she and Giddy had become, that remained an unwise step too far.

But now there was a cool paving stone beneath her cheek, and she was not hot, but kind of cold. Her jacket was off, she realised, and she was face down on the pavings. The difficulty breathing came from her hands tied behind her back, and the pressure on her diaphragm. Her mouth tasted like acid, and the aftermath of having thrown up. Worse, Giddy wasn't lying beside her, because she was on Eshir, while Giddy had died on Rando. Had died separated from her, with corbi for companions who'd loved him far more than they'd loved her. The corbi had known that he cared about them. Perhaps he'd even loved them more, in the end, than he'd loved her.

About her, Trace heard conversation. She turned her head to look, and saw an encirclement of boots on the pavings all about. Either she'd been out a long time, or there'd been people already here, or close by. Purists, probably. If they were Zeladnists, she'd probably have been a lot less comfortable.

She turned her head back the other way, and felt a boot pressing her shoulderblades, and harsh words in Arabic. Felt the muzzle of a rifle in the back of her neck. On her other side was Terez, face down, hands bound, also with someone armed standing alongside. She could not see Rael.

She closed her eyes to see the uplink icon, and blinked on reception, keeping her breathing long, slow and calm. *"Hello Styx,"* she formulated silently. *"What can you tell of the current situation?"*

"Major, you have been incapacitated by the same weapon that was utilised against us at the Zondi Splicer. All of your marines are well enough. Corporal Arime and Private Rolonde were in the medical room and not incapacitated, but were persuaded by threats to your life, and by my own encouragement." Meaning that Styx, Trace thought, was reasonably confident they'd have shot her if Arime hadn't surrendered.

"How many bugs do you have in here?" Trace asked.

"Four," said Styx. *"There are currently eleven Purists, thirteen if one includes Taj and Dagan, and more are arriving on the roof even now. I could eliminate some, but the others would likely recognise the threat and start shooting. I calculate that the risk is too great. You should take this opportunity to learn who these people are now that they perceive themselves to be in control."*

Styx was not the only one who could calculate. Carville, Randrahan and Wang were still free, with Jokono, Romki, Styx and Peanut. Launching a hostage-rescue operation was going to be fraught with danger. This building, isolated in a relatively open space of valley floor, was hard to sneak up on. The marines could snipe watching sentries while Styx blinded electronics, giving them the time and space to rush it, but storming down those stairs, or doing the drysine abseil descent over the walls and crashing through the windows, was going to unleash a lot of firepower in an enclosed space where nothing was certain. If she and the other captives were unable to move, the odds of getting hit in the crossfire were high. Better that she find some way to gain mobility first. And the surest way to do that was to talk, and see if she could convince some people.

The weight of the boot on her back became heavier, making breathing more difficult still. Angry threats and defiant thrashing might have relieved tension. Trace remained silent and still.

Someone gave a command, and she was grabbed under the armpits and hauled to her knees. The uplink visual became faded and hard to see with her eyes open, against the light from a window. She gave up trying to find Rael's connection, and used her voice instead. "Cocky, you there?" She got no reply. "Cocky?"

The person beside her with the gun smacked her in the ear. It rang, but she'd been hit far harder in sparring, and saw no stars. "Leo?" she tried instead. "Leo, you awake?"

An angry retort before her, and her guard stepped before her, and slapped her across the face. This time she saw a star or two. The blow had been left-handed, upon her right cheek and jaw. Unaugmented, she thought, and delivered with no particular skill. All useful things to know, for when the moment came. Payback did not interest her, just the efficient elimination of obstacles.

That man's voice again, demanding something from her. "I told you!" came Taj's angry voice, in Hindi. "She doesn't speak Arga! She's from Tarshin, she speaks Hind only!"

Another voice, derisive, again in Arabic. Trace's earpiece was missing, of course. *"Styx,"* she formulated. *"Can you run me a realtime translation?"*

"They express disbelief that you speak no Arabic," said Styx. *"They say everyone in Tarshin speaks at least some Arabic."*

Another man walked around her. Trace was not watching faces, only bodies. Being on her knees helped. Most present were men, but not all. Several were large and strong, and a few were fat. The strong ones looked like gym junkies, fit in the way of civilians who pumped iron mostly to impress their social circles, all covered in tattoos. Probably they were augmented too, Trace thought. The way a couple of them leaned their weight as they stood, she was certain of it.

The circling man stopped, and squatted before her. Handsome, in an angular, faintly unpleasant kind of way. A lean face, a shock of dark hair on top, shaved at the sides. A toothpick held between off-white teeth.

He held up something between them. A large, flat silver blade, angular and deadly. Her kukri. "What's this then?" he asked her, in Hindi. "Funny looking thing." Kukris evidently hadn't survived the cultural transition from Earth. The man tapped Trace's arm with the flat of the blade. "You got big muscles for a small girl. Taj says you're seriously augmented."

Trace's eyes flicked to Taj for the first time. He looked unhappy, one of the big, tattooed guys half-blocking his access to Trace, another at his back. "I didn't tell them shit!" he growled. "Someone else must have told him about you."

"You got some recent scars too," the man continued. "But well healed. Like top medical technology, hey?" He tapped her on the jaw with her kukri. The steel was cold. "Where are you really from? The Zeladnists want you dead real good. Now some of my people think anyone the Zeladnists hate must be cool, but you sure as hell aren't no Purist. I know all the Purist cells in Tarshin, and none of them ever mentioned you. You look like hired Family business. Like bad news, like the kind of money-pinching hit girl who takes coin from alien scum to take out Purists, hey? I've seen a few of them. No girls so far, but first time for everything." Trace tested the bonds that held her wrists. Her augments made her strong, but not that strong. The man took her face in one hand. "Talk, bitch. Or I'll start cutting off slices."

"You want to see a magic trick?" Trace asked him, in Hindi. He let go her face, frowning. Trace looked at the big men flanking Taj. "Styx? The man standing directly in front of Taj. Put him to sleep. And *only* to sleep, if you please."

Everyone turned to look at the big man. The big man looked concerned. Then let out a yell of pain, and slapped at his neck. Turned around, to search the air for what had bitten him... and became wobbly. Taj caught him as he collapsed, struggling beneath the weight.

Another man began yelling, pointing to something in the air, trying to track it as it went out a window. More yelling, in Arabic, insisting he wasn't seeing things, as others exclaimed and ducked and searched the skies. Taj checked on the big man, flat on his back with his eyes closed, but still breathing.

Slowly, everyone's attention returned to Trace, calm on her knees amid the commotion. The handsome man with her kukri scowled at her, with dark consternation. "How'd you do that?"

To her left, the man guarding Terez pointed his rifle at the unconscious Private's head. It was why they'd left him in the room, Trace thought, while removing all the others. Leave one to threaten, while depriving her of the others' support.

"If you pull that trigger," Trace told the threatening man, "everyone in this room dies. The big guy was just a demonstration. I let him live. The rest of you won't be so lucky."

The man with the kukri gestured for the rifle to go down. That man complied, with reluctant fury. "What do you want?"

"Not to be threatened with my own knife, for one. To be untied, for another. I'm not your enemy. I can become your enemy, and that will go very badly for you. I have technology you can barely dream of. I can use it to help you if you'd like. Or to harm you if you insist. The choice is yours."

18

Erik had completed his post-shift exercise, then his deck tour, then briefly joined Sasalaka to go over Tif's latest simulator results. Following that were personnel matters that his Warrants Officers and Ensigns couldn't handle on their own, much to his displeasure. But both incidents were serious, he had to agree -- a fight between two spacers in Engineering that had put one in Medbay for observation of a bad concussion, and another where several tavalai in a maintenance unit beneath Petty Officer First Class Riga-mala had refused a direct order from Master Petty Officer Goldman, who was the senior enlisted rank on the whole ship.

By the time he was finished dealing with it, he was eating into what was supposed to be his sleeping time, and only five hours from when his next shift was due to begin. Two shifts on *Phoenix* were hard enough on soft duty, but on combat missions they were brutal. He'd taken a moment to gaze at a screen display of an old Academy memory when Lieutenant Sasalaka walked through the open door.

She shut it behind her, and came to stand by his shoulder as he gazed a moment longer at the wall screen. On it, excited young officer cadets milled in their perfect dress blues, a tight knot in a larger room of chairs facing a stage. Those chairs were filled with family, and up on the stage, a Captain and a Commander were taking it in turns to call cadets' names, to the hoots and hollers of their classmates.

"What is this?" Sasalaka asked after a moment. On the stage, an anxious young man was being thoroughly but affectionately roasted by the Captain, to the great amusement of the crowd and his friends. "Is this a graduation ceremony?"

"No, it's ride night," said Erik, gazing at the memories. "This is my class, Class S-Three. S is for Starships, all the assault pilots were separated off a year before this. Then they divide up the rest of us, five classes, so you have all the best starship pilots learning and competing with each other."

"Yes," said Sasalaka, understanding. "It is familiar." She smelled faintly floral, in that way of odd tavalai scents, standing close behind. Erik recalled Lisbeth remarking on it, once.

"The starship pilots all train in S-block," Erik added, as a series of starship images flashed on the big display behind the young man on-screen. "The pilots call it the Stud Farm."

Sasalaka frowned. "What is a... 'stud'?"

"A livestock term. The most successful breeding animals."

"Ah."

"The rest of Academy call it the Scum Pond. Or the Ivory Tower." Only pilots could be captains, and while the resentment it caused was usually no more than playful, it was real nonetheless. On the screen, a warship's silhouette appeared, accompanied by a name. The young man whooped and punched the air, and several classmates rushed the stage to bearhug him and celebrate.

"Pilots are able to select their preferred assignments?" Sasalaka guessed.

"The highest-scoring pilots are," Erik agreed. "The lower your Academy score, the less choice you get. And even the top scores aren't guaranteed. Some of the advertised billets were out of date by the time a new pilot actually got to the ship. A few times pilots went to meet the ship they were assigned to, and found it had been destroyed in the meantime. But most of the time new pilots went to rear-echelon ships. This guy here is Ernie Wong, he's happy because he was given the *UFS Eagle* -- it's only a station guard destroyer, not likely to see much action, but it's a great springboard to something better. We would study the promotion percentages, how likely we were to get picked by something front-line after a few years on this or that station guard ship, and get excited over what we thought were the best chances."

"And did Ernie Wong receive his promotion?"

"Yeah. Yeah he did, he got picked up by *UFS Destiny* after five years. Two years less than it took me to get *Phoenix*."

"I've heard of *Destiny*," Sasalaka said solemnly. "I think she was destroyed at Tripitika System."

"Yeah." Erik nodded sadly. "Yeah, that's... that's where Ernie died." He glanced up at Sasalaka.

"I wasn't there," said the tavalai. "But it was in my sector. I recall the after-action report."

"I wouldn't blame you if you were there, Sasa," Erik said tiredly. "It was all a long time ago now." A pretty, young cadet now ascended the stage, making twin victory signs to her hooting classmates. Tall, with a familiar, flashing smile. "This is Ashlyn Gutierez. Good friend of mine. She gets the *UFS Elizabeth Singh*, then was promoted to *UFS Victory* after just three years. Ace pilot, easily as good as me. But she finished the war still a Lieutenant Commander and... I've no idea where she is now. I imagine she stayed in, she really wanted to make Captain one day."

They watched in silence for a moment, as the Commander this time finished ribbing Ashlyn about her various deficiencies, to which she merely nodded and grinned. Then the *UFS Elizabeth Singh* was announced, and the first cadet to rush the stage to hug her was a tall, broad young man with a face somewhat famous to many human audiences.

Sasalaka peered curiously, recognising her Captain. "Well," she said, with usual tavalai understatement. "You were so young."

"We all were," Erik sighed. "I mean, I guess I still am, by most standards. I don't feel young now, though."

"Me neither. It's been an adventure."

"Yes it has."

"And this young woman was special to you?" Sasalaka asked, settling onto the end of Erik's bunk. Her wide-set, froggy features were impassive as ever, difficult to read.

"I guess so. No, that's unfair... yes. She was special." On the screen, the celebrating cadets left the stage, young Erik with an arm around young Ashlyn's shoulders. "We knew it couldn't last, we all get split up when we get our assignments. That's one reason relationships aren't so frowned upon in the Academy, they know they'll all be split up quickly. But we swore we'd keep in touch, and maybe one day, fate would put us in the same place at the same time once more." He smiled at Sasalaka. "And so of course, I've only seen her twice face-to-face since then. Twelve years now. How about you, Sasa? Anyone special since your Academy?"

"You are aware, of course, that tavalai partnerships do not work like that." She said it as a statement, with dry amusement.

"Yes I'm aware. You just never talk about it."

"Because Captain Pram himself warned me that of all tavalai behaviours, family and procreation would be the one most likely to arouse human dismay."

"Arouse human dismay," Erik repeated, teasing. "I think we'll be fine, Sasa." He turned off the screen. "You wanted to talk to me about Petty Officer Rigamala?"

"Yes Captain. The Petty Officer's refusal to obey a direct order from Master Petty Officer Goldman is inexcusable, and he will accept his punishment. However, an explanation is available."

"Go on."

"Petty Officer Rigamala perceived that Master Petty Officer Goldman made an uncomplimentary remark about *Makimakala*. Petty Officer Rigamala's work team acquired this understanding as well."

"That's pretty much what I've spent the past fifteen minutes of my sleeping time learning, sure," Erik said with an edge.

"I spoke to Master Petty Officer Goldman about it," Sasalaka continued, unfazed in that very tavalai way. "He explained that he did not mean to speak of *Makimakala* in the manner it was taken, and meant no offence. I explained to him tavalai sensitivities regarding *Makimakala*, and that he may wish to choose his words more carefully in the future."

"And how'd he take that?"

"He listened." Erik could well imagine how *Phoenix*'s most senior enlisted spacer would take it -- like a patient parent with a persistent child, answering questions and nodding until the kid lost interest and let him get on with adult things.

"Sasa," he said tiredly, "we've had memorial services for *Makimakala*. We've held the remembrances, as laid out by tavalai crew, including yourself, and everyone participated. We sent detailed reports back with the last tavalai envoy to visit Dul'rho, along with condolences to the families, and remembrances to the Godavadi Institution who sponsor the Dobruta. And yet I still get the feeling from some tavalai that you think we've all forgotten *Makimakala* and haven't honoured her sacrifice."

"Tavalai periods of remembrance are extended," Sasalaka said stubbornly.

"It's been half a year," Erik insisted. "Humans move on."

Sasalaka's translucent third-eyelids flickered rapidly, a gesture that sometimes accompanied agitation. "This is similar to what Master Petty Officer Goldman said to Petty Officer Rigamala."

Erik nearly rolled his eyes. Tavalai were institutionally and psychologically conservative in the extreme. Retentive, Lieutenant Shilu had opined, after an extended period of dealing with tavalai institutional law. The kinds of people who'd hold a grudge because you'd once said something uncomplimentary about a distant relative twenty years ago.

"Sasa, how would you characterise relations between humans and tavalai on this ship? Are we doing okay?"

A brief, forced nod from the tavalai. "We're doing okay, Captain. But since *Makimakala* passed, there has been disquiet among some tavalai crew that remembrances have seemed short and rushed, by tavalai standards."

"It's still a human ship, Sasa. We love and respect our tavalai brothers and sisters, and we sure as hell couldn't still be operating on this mission without you... but the majority of the crew is human, and we do things the human way."

"One notices."

Erik frowned. "Are *you* upset by this?"

"By human standards, Captain, tavalai rarely get upset."

"Then why..." A blinking coms light cut him off. "This is the Captain."

"Hello Captain," came Commander Draper's voice. *"We have Friendship on coms, wishes to speak to you."*

"Put her through."

"Hello Captain," came the smooth female vocals of the drysine command ship. *"Our drones have been restoring function to the ceephay entity in the refinery. The entity has acquired a degree of conscious function. It wishes to speak to you. I believe there is a visual component."*

Erik looked at Sasalaka. She looked nonplussed. "Yes *Friendship*," he said. "Please allow this communication." And he beckoned his Helm out of quarters and onto the bridge, wanting to get his crew's reaction to this, and not wishing to wake those members of First Shift already asleep.

"Captain on the bridge!" Sasalaka announced as they emerged from Erik's quarters directly onto the bridge.

"Carry on," Erik assured them all, stopping by Lieutenant Commander Dufresne's Helm chair, as she adjusted one of her side screens so he could see it more easily, and put the incoming transmission onto it. Sasalaka took the other side of Helm, as the side screen fuzzed with indistinct transmission. Nothing more appeared.

Erik flipped AR glasses briefly onto his eyes, blinked on the coms option and found Lieutenant Dale still awake and on duty in backquarter. *"Yes Captain?"* he answered the silent query.

"Lieutenant, update on Lieutenant Karajin's situation?"

"Five drones on station about the refinery command center, Captain. Two of them are new, one seems to be a command unit. Garudan Platoon are continuing their exploration of our end of the facility. Bravo are

checking out the mining heads. Analysis says that the hand controls on the mining equipment fits with the ergonomics of a reeh's hands."

"Yeah." Erik thought about that, as bridge posts watched their screens and kept a surreptitious eye on the communications link *Friendship* had established. Probably they knew that the Captain was taking this call on the bridge precisely because he wanted their opinion. "Well, just because it was made to fit the reeh, doesn't mean it was actually reeh here using it."

"Captain," said Draper, looking about from the Captain's seat, "we've been keeping out of the drysines' end of the facility, while they're coming and going freely from ours. Should we send a unit up their way to explore?"

"Their data's looked good so far," said Erik. "No indication they're hiding anything, and they've got more drones than we've got marines." Plus, he didn't need to add, their drones did not require shift changes like the marines did.

"Still," said Draper, "shouldn't we..."

The screen flickered. Against the fuzzy grey backdrop, a small figure resolved itself. Human, Erik thought. A dress resolved, and skinny brown limbs. Frizzy hair. A young girl. It could have been Lisbeth, from years ago. The girl shuffled shyly, nervously, glancing off-camera like a child pushed onstage at a school play, and trying to remember her lines.

"What the hell?" muttered De Marchi from Navigation.

"Hello?" said the girl. "Is that the humans?"

"Ange, give me coms," said Erik, as Lieutenant Lassa complied. "This is Captain Debogande of the human warship *UFS Phoenix*. To whom am I speaking?"

The girl gazed wide-eyed at the screen, her expression battling between wonder and trepidation. Erik found it unsettling, in the way of clever animations trying hard to capture a familiar emotion, but not quite nailing it. Something about this little girl felt off. "I'm so pleased to meet you," said the girl. "It's been such a long time since I've spoken to anyone."

From over in the Captain's chair, Draper was giving Erik a long, alarmed look. Erik nodded to him, briefly. They'd all had experiences with clever AIs attempting to ingratiate themselves. From a ceephay, however, this qualified as first contact.

"It was our understanding," Erik told the thing on the screen, "that our drysine friends were attempting to restore function to a very old ceephay intelligence. Are you that ceephay intelligence?"

"I think so." The girl nodded, uncertainly. "But I... I'm not sure. A lot of my memory is gone, I think. I can't remember who I am."

"Is that why you are appearing on our visual screens as a human?"

"I have to be someone, right?" The girl attempted a smile, hopefully.

"I suppose you do," said Erik. "The drysines said that you wished to talk to us specifically. What did you wish to discuss?"

"I... I'm not sure." Again the girl looked anxious. Almost fearful. "I think I'd like to be on your ship."

Again Erik caught Draper's look of alarm. He wished the young Commander would stop doing that. It wasn't as though his Captain wasn't aware of the dangers. "Why would you like to be on our ship?"

"I don't think I feel very safe among the drysines." Now a small disquiet fled across the bridge, crew looking up from their posts, glancing at each other.

Erik decided that asking her why she felt unsafe among the drysines, with so many of those drysines listening in, would not be the smartest option. "Is it even possible for you to come aboard our ship?"

"I think so. My data-core is quite small. I wouldn't be very much trouble." Erik was abruptly reminded of Lisbeth at age nine begging Mother for another dog. Damn these emotionally manipulative AIs.

"I'll tell you what," said Erik. "We'll think about it, and while we're thinking, you can tell us everything you can recall about this base, and your previous life and history, once all your memory comes back online. And then we'll talk to the drysines about your future, and we'll see what we can do about bringing you aboard this ship."

"Thank you," the girl said shyly. "I'll try very hard to remember, I promise."

"I know you will. Do you have a name?"

"Not that I can recall. Would you like to give me one?"

"How about Creepy?" Kaspowitz suggested, as five members of First Shift bridge crew plus Lieutenant Rooke crowded Erik's quarters a half-hour later, while everyone on Second Shift not preoccupied listened from the bridge, just beyond the door.

"Well I think that really answers just how intelligent she is," Rooke said eagerly, sipping coffee. The slim, brainy young man rarely seemed to need sleep, and with Romki off-ship and Warrant Officer Leung running Second Shift Engineering, he'd been delighted to invite himself to Captain's Quarters, up the other end of the ship, to talk about *Phoenix*'s newest AI 'friend'. "I mean even Styx took a while to start simulating our vocal patterns and conversational norms. Ceephays were ten to fifteen thousand years before drysines, but here it looks like she's picked up our inflections pretty well from a cold restart within a few hours."

"It's not a she," Kaspowitz said tiredly, with the air of a man repeating something for the thousandth time.

"And I mean the visual animation's a bit off," Rooke continued, ignoring the Nav Officer entirely. "But she's got it pretty close, really."

"I can understand why she'd feel scared," said Shilu, leaning at the end of Erik's bunk in the crush. "The different AI races never got along. She probably is safer with us. For me the question is why the drysines allowed her to contact us like that. I mean, if we agreed to take her aboard, that could put us at odds with them."

"They might not mind if we have her," Sasalaka disagreed, putting eyedrops in her big amphibious eyes and squinting, third eyelids fluttering. "Maybe they just want to know what she knows, and don't care how she's inspired to tell it."

"I find it hard to believe the drysines couldn't just extract everything she knows by force," Shilu replied. "She's from an AI race at least ten thousand years less advanced and she's only out here to run a refinery, it doesn't seem likely she'll have any combat function. *Friendship* sure as hell does."

"It's not always that simple," Rooke disagreed, half-sitting on Erik's table. "Hacksaw technological progression wasn't always linear. With their wars and stuff, some technological generations went backward, so while the drysines are certainly more advanced, they're not necessarily *that* much more advanced. Mostly the design philosophy will be different, so they might have quite a lot of trouble talking to each other. And while *Friendship* is smart, she's nowhere near as smart as Styx."

A rap on the steel door, then it opened and Lieutenant Dale edged in. There was no room for six, let alone seven, but with Erik, Sasalaka and Kaspowitz all squeezed together on the bunk, there was just enough standing space for the broad-shouldered marine. "You saw the recording?" Erik asked him.

"Yes sir," said Dale. "Real friendly, huh." With a dry glance at Kaspowitz, who gave one back. Those two were alike in their opinion of apparently friendly AIs.

"What's the situation like over there?"

"The ceephay's not a big unit, like it says. It's integrated into all kinds of stuff though, Warrant Officer Kriplani from Engineering says it could have run the whole refinery for months without much organic input. But the quarters definitely look lived in. In fact, given the amount of personal stuff left behind, it looks like whoever used to live there might have left in a hurry." He rummaged in a pocket of his black jumpsuit, and withdrew a white ball the size of his palm. He tossed it to Erik, who caught it. "I had Bucket scan it before I brought it back. It's clean, it's from some ball-game setup they've got over there, some kind of zero-G billiards. Scan showed it's got fingerprints on it."

Erik frowned, peering at the hard, smooth surface. "Fingerprints from eight thousand years ago?"

Dale shrugged. "Leave things alone in a vacuum and they don't change much. Scan says the fingerprints are definitely reeh. We're scanning for more prints... they might not prove much, but those prints seem to prove that reeh were playing that game."

"Or they were moving the ball," Kaspowitz countered. "Or confiscating it from some poor slave." Dale shrugged again.

"I've been thinking," said Shilu. He looked troubled, leaning with one arm, the other hand massaging the stiff shoulder where a new, synthetic arm had been attached one year ago. Still he claimed it bothered him sometimes. "What if we've got the reeh wrong? We classified them as a swarm species, predatory and hive-minded from inception. What if they're not?"

"They're the worst species I've ever seen," Sasalaka said firmly. "I have my disagreements with my own State Department's adoption of the sard. I believe that was a grave mistake. The krim, even moreso, with respects to your loss." She made a small gesture, and a bow of her head. Again Erik was reminded of the tavalai's endless reverence for grand things passed. "But the reeh are worse. I will understand if humans, given your loss, feel differently. But objectively I think the reeh have done far worse than the krim could have managed even had humanity not ended their terrible existence."

She looked about, earnest but unapologetic, as though expecting some degree of resistance to her statement. Perhaps among tavalai she'd have found it. None of the humans disagreed. Sasalaka looked faintly surprised.

"Much worse," Erik said heavily. "We took a terrible loss. But the reeh have repeated losses on that scale endlessly, across many millennia. They are a cancer on this galaxy."

"Intelligent species only commit such atrocities when they are biologically programmed by evolution to do so," Sasalaka insisted. "All of our experience with sentient life tells us that creatures are either conditioned by evolution to appreciate and empathise with other sentiences, or they're not. If the reeh are the worst in this part of the galaxy, then there is no way, according to all tavalai science, that they could be anything but a swarm species of the worst order."

She sounded very certain for a young woman who was trained as a pilot, not a scientist. In Erik's experience, all tavalai seemed to revere those certainties that were the product of great and old institutional learning. Sasalaka was a free thinker by the standards of her kind, but she was still tavalai to the bone.

"Why do you think we might have them wrong?" Erik asked Shilu.

The elegant Coms Officer shrugged. "We just don't know anything about their history. They erased it. It's almost like they're embarrassed by it, but swarm species are embarrassed by nothing. The krim sure as hell weren't."

"Sard neither," Dale agreed, dubiously thoughtful.

"The croma insist what Sasalaka says," Shilu continued, "but croma history is endlessly self-serving, and as we've seen with Rando, they have this nasty habit of erasing unpleasant things from their collective narrative so they don't have to think about them. Like they did to the corbi. Plus I just don't think they're all that good at history -- they like to tell themselves stories about history, but that's a different thing from actual history. What they believe now about the reeh is what they'd like to believe, for the sake of their current convenience. I like the croma more than is probably wise, but on this matter I'd trust them as far as I can throw them."

Erik reflected again that for all the obvious intelligence exhibited by various *Phoenix* crew, and in particular by young Lieutenant Rooke, it was entirely possible that Shilu was the smartest of the bunch. Not only a technical wizard with coms systems, he was highly trained in human, chah'nas and tavalai law, spoke two human tongues and four alien ones, had been a professional ballet dancer before signing up, and legend had it was the reigning Academy 'go' champion, having not been beaten either during his cadet training, nor in his three year teaching stint before he'd joined *Phoenix*. Sometimes Erik found it crazy that it had fallen to him to tell all of these talented people what to do.

He nodded slowly. "It's a puzzle. We'll have to wait and see, and keep an open mind." He looked at Dale. "How are the drysines treating you?"

"Very polite."

Erik waited. Dale seemed entirely serious. "Polite, how?"

"Drysines and marines heading in opposite directions down a narrow corridor? Drysines will always give way first. We've tested it, it's like it's an instruction or something."

"They're learning manners," Geish said with amusement.

"They're pretending manners," Kaspowitz retorted. "Like they pretend everything. Like this ceephay pretends to be a little girl who looks suspiciously like a younger version of the Captain's sister. Our drysine allies are applying what they've learned about us, nothing more."

"The ceephay's just a refinery operator," Rooke said dismissively. "We've survived with a mega-intelligent Fleet Commander aboard for two years now, I think we can handle this one."

"This one's got far more reason to be scared than Styx did," said Kaspowitz. "Imagine waking up alone, ten thousand years after your time was supposed to end, and finding everything you knew was gone. Scared people lash out. Let *Friendship* have her."

"Kaspo," Erik said sternly. The tall Nav Officer looked at him. "It's not a 'her', Kaspo. Nor 'people'. Don't forget."

Smiles about the room. Kaspowitz scowled.

IT WAS Rika's first look at drysines other than Peanut, Bucket, Wowser or Styx. The drones looked pretty similar, he thought, save that some of the leg shielding looked an unusual shape, and the interlocking bodyplates fit together a little differently. He figured drysines had been around a long time, and would have been constantly making small adjustments to how they did things.

These drysines were in the refinery's command room, tucked in amongst the habitation quarters where long ago, servants of the Reeh Empire had performed basic ice-mining operations to acquire new water for off-world ships, stations and bases. And it was astonishing to think about, because it made him wonder at the fact that Rando had been a part of the Reeh Empire for all his life and long beforehand, only he'd never thought about it. Certainly no one on Rando ever did. Belonging to some much larger empire might have even been interesting, however unwelcome, but the reeh had never made any attempt to incorporate corbi into their larger plans. Which raised the much larger question about the reeh -- why were they so evil? So unable to even comprehend the possibility of trying to be nice to at least some corbi, to gain their services, incorporate their activities into the empire, and grow in strength that way? Why just exterminate, abuse and starve them, and use them for experiments?

He watched the drysines work for a while, posted with Bravo Heavy Squad to this section of the refinery on this his second shift. It was giving him a first-hand look at the less glamorous side of marine operations -- one long tour through the refinery's ancient corridors, then a withdrawal back to *Phoenix* while Garudan Platoon had replaced them. Armour check had followed, and a fast debriefing in squads, followed by food, showers and sleep... only to wake six hours later, exercise, eat, armour up and repeat the whole thing again.

At least he was getting some good armour time, he thought as he watched the knot of drysines about the mess they'd made of the control panels. Entire walls had been dismantled, revealing a maze of intricate high-tech systems within. Much of it was withered with age and useless, but for the sparkling, faintly crystalline ovoid in the middle of one nest of fluidic electricals. That was the ceephay AI, a pure and independent memory core impervious to age, and made by some earlier technology that still looked like magic to Rika, but the drysines had for some reason decided to move beyond. God knew what drysine brains looked like, if they were more advanced than this.

Another drysine approached from Rika's side, floating straight past and over him with little regard for personal space, a sensation a bit like being smothered by a giant spider. That was Wowser, then, who had worse manners than any of the regular drysine drones. Lieutenant Alomaim said he thought the new drysines had been given some centralised command to be polite to the humans. Wowser and Bucket, it seemed, remained outside of that command system, and had not taken the hint.

Wowser continued along a line of consoles, slowing and positioning with a multi-legged grip on the seats, then stuck his forelegs to some panel and began fiddling. Then Warrant Officer Leung returned from her side excursion down the ice-harvesting arms with Spacer Boudei, floating past in their unarmed suits to talk to Lance Corporal Rizzo about what the drysines were up to. Leung was second-in-command of Engineering, and was doing a lot of checks on refinery systems beyond just the ceephay AI. Another six of her Engineering crew were here as well, doing various things that Rika hadn't grasped.

Why the refinery required a full two platoons on guard, Rika hadn't grasped either. Clearly there were no enemies here, and marines were poorly suited to investigate the refinery's systems. Engineering crew were more use, yet there were more than eighty marines here, nearly half of Phoenix Company's strength, and only a handful of engineers. Well, Rika reconsidered, marines did complain a lot about being bored when they had nothing to do. Guard duty on an old refinery wasn't exactly exciting duty, but it had its moments, and it was better than on-ship routines.

Rika's coms chose that moment to die. One moment he was hearing the routine background chatter of marines, *Phoenix* Operations and on-station crew, and the next, nothing. Then his suit wouldn't move. His arms pressed against the armoured sleeve interiors, and instead of gliding and flowing effortlessly with his movements, they remained locked in place. A moment's panic, and he blinked through his still-functional visor display, and found a mass of red malfunction lights through the drive train and control systems... but life support was still working, he could hear the hiss of air from the collar vents, and feel the warmth circulating. He wasn't about to suffocate, but he was immobile, and was now slowly rotating sideways. In all the briefings he'd received about marine armoured operations, this wasn't a situation he'd even heard mentioned.

He could see Cat Rizzo's suit nearby, slowly turning, similarly immobilised. Warrant Officer Leung's as well, paralysed like some zero-G statue, arms frozen in mid-gesticulation. Rika wriggled and bounced as much as he could within the armour, and got it turning back the right way, but the suit was too tight a fit to allow more momentum and movement within the shell.

He could see the drysines, though, the nightvision of his visor still gleaming with projected UV light, and now glaring in the eruption of sparks from cutters about the ceephay AI core. They were cutting faster, almost as though they were trying to remove the core entirely. And Rika's eyes widened as he grasped what that meant.

"Override override!" he shouted at the dead mic, to no response. "Emergency override, come on you fucking stupid computer!" Something crackled, then, a burst of static. "Hello! Hello, can someone hear me? This is Rika, Bravo Heavy Five!"

He threw himself hard the other way as the suit over-rotated past the drysines, now bumping into the hatch out of the control room. Another drysine was moving, blocking the way before him. It was Wowser, staring at the working drysines. Then he turned, impossibly graceful in zero-G, grasping first Rizzo, then Leung with clawed forelegs, probing with a barely visible laser pointer from somewhere on his head/sensor array.

"Wowser!" Rika tried yelling. "Wowser, what the hell are you doing?" There was little chance of anyone being heard without coms -- helmet armour was nearly soundproof, and the refinery air pressure was thin. Then Wowser came for Rika, that creepy entanglement of sensor-fronted head and multiple grasping manipulator arms between big vibro-blade forelegs. "Hey hey! What are you doing?"

A laser probe made a red glare upon his visor, then abruptly the display was flashing back to life, and various red malfunction lights turned green. Rika's arms and legs were suddenly moving, and the restored systems reports flashed across the right-side window, drivetrain powerup, armscomp realignment, coms green...

"Hello *Phoenix*?" he tried, as Wowser left him to look at others. "*Phoenix*, this is Rika, Bravo Heavy Five, something just shut down the suit systems of everyone around me, Wowser got me running again but I don't..." He pushed off the wall at Rizzo, grabbed his frozen armour as their momentum took them to the far wall. "The others' suits are still frozen, I think I'm the only one!" He peered closely at Rizzo's visor, and it was hard to see Rizzo's face within, past two narrow layers of armoured glass. He saw Rizzo's eyes, alarmed but not frightened, moving as though he was shouting something.

"Hello *Phoenix*, are you hearing me?" Still there was nothing. Something grabbed and spun him from behind, and then he was staring at Wowser's mismatched eyes again, glaring at him as though trying to communicate something. Drones couldn't talk, and of all *Phoenix*'s drones, Wowser had always seemed the least inclined. The alien machine seemed almost frustrated by the necessity.

A big vibroblade foreleg rapped hard on Rika's armoured shoulder, then pointed at the other drysines. The red laser pointer once again glared on Rika's visor, half blinding. "I know!" Rika shouted back, because it was obvious by now. "The other drysines are doing it, they're trying to steal the ceephay datacore! What do we do?"

Perhaps Wowser's laser worked as coms, translating visor vibrations into sound, because Wowser let him go, lightly grabbed a chair-back and pulled himself in the direction of the cutting drysines. He wanted backup, Rika realised, heart thumping even harder as he realised how crazy that was, and pushed off after him.

A handle on a storage wall opposite the ceephay core presented an anchorpoint, which he grabbed, then checked his rifle. It was a relatively modern weapon, manufactured by Corbi Resistance in one of their secret facilities and capable of turning an unarmored man to red mist with a single shot. But it had barely half the muzzle length or hitting power of a human Koshaim 20, though much more manageable for a smaller, rookie corbi with only a few hours' operational experience. If he'd fired it at a human marine, he doubted it would penetrate, given the crazy materials science that went into human armour suits. Drysine drones, he reckoned, would be even more advanced.

One of the drysines ceased work to confront Wowser, blocking his approach. Wowser caught a chairback, and extended a foreleg to use the other drysine's mass to halt. Red lasercoms extended and probed, while another two drysines kept working, sparks erupting as they made rapid cuts to free the core. When the drysines jammed coms, Rika thought dry-mouthed, they must have jammed their own ability to communicate as well. Astonishingly, Wowser evidently remained outside of their command structure. Everyone had assumed that in any conflict between *Phoenix* and the drysines, Styx would take the drysines' side, and Wowser, Bucket and Peanut would follow. Wowser answered to Styx, so why was he arguing with the drysines here?

Wowser's foreleg was very close to the other drysine's shielded head unit, Rika noticed. Then a buzz, and in a flash the other drysine's head was gone, Wowser grabbing its body as the other drysines spun, but too late, into a hail of Wowser's cannonfire. Rika fired in panic, suit auto-stabilising as the recoil slammed him back along the wall amid the rain of debris and spinning parts from disintegrating drones and refinery walls.

And then Wowser was finished, tossing the decapitated corpse aside with a final vibroblade slash to be sure, then pushing through the mangled mess of floating, spinning debris, smoke and globular liquids his violence had made of fellow drysines.

"There's more of them outside!" Rika shouted as he realised, grabbing a wall section and pulling toward the hatch. "There's three more in the corridor!" He spun the corner, rifle braced as he floated fast between control panels toward the hatch. He caught, trying to remember the drills, and messed up the corner position entirely, swinging half out into open space with the rifle unbalanced in his right hand... but all he saw was the retreating hindquarters of two drysines vanishing around a far bend.

And now his coms were alive with terse calls between marines, *Phoenix* Operations querying with alarm and now Lieutenant Alomaim asking for a situation report. *"LT, we were next to it,"* Rizzo answered. *"The damn drysines disabled our suits and tried to cut the ceephay free. Only they couldn't disable Rika's suit, or Wowser got it working again, and then Wowser shot them all to pieces."*

"Wowser shot them?" As Rika's hallway filled with recently frozen marines. He headed back inside, and was found by Corporal Rizzo, grabbing his arm and giving a querying thumbs up.

"Lieutenant," said Rika, returning Rizzo's thumbs up, "I think it's because my suit's so old, the drysines couldn't shut it down for long enough. But they had no idea Wowser was going to shoot them, they assumed he was on their side."

"Private Rika, this is Captain Debogande," came a voice that overrode whatever anyone else was saying. *"I'm seeing that the remaining drysines all retreated rather than continue the fight? Is that correct?"*

"Yes Captain," said Rika, returning to the faintly obscene sight of Wowser amidst the shattered remains of the drones, sorting through various bodyparts as though deciding what might be useful to keep for later. He grabbed a chair to stop himself, only then realising that his hand was shaking too much for a secure grasp. "They've all gone. I think they were trying to surprise us, they didn't want a fight. But Wowser just... completely messed them up, there's not much left."

"Thank you Private. All hands, listen up. Phoenix is on red alert. We're going to have a very hard talk with our drysine allies. At this point I think we'll be okay, we have to make allowances for the fact that they're machines without subtlety or manners, but we're going to let them know that they've fucked this up very badly. And then we're going to have a talk to the ceephay and see why our friends were so desperate to have her for themselves."

19

"H*ello Major,"* came Styx's voice in Trace's ear. *"The Purists' weaponry setup is quite well done. The frequency projectors are built into the walls, it appears to be a primary defence mechanism against anyone entering through the main upper pad."*

"That's interesting, Styx." She sat on a chair in the middle of a circle of nearly thirty Purists, hand extended so they could come single file and examine the drysine assassin bug that crawled on her palm. Outside the open fortress windows, the pale day had given way to dim evening, and a brightening glow of lights down the valley. *"How does it help me?"*

"The system is operated by a well shielded network function. My bugs have now penetrated that network function, and are revealing source codes for further Purist networks. I am learning much of what they know."

"Tell me when you have enough. I may be able to make allies here, but they may be a lot more trouble than they're worth."

One of the Purists, a squat, bald and bearded man named Efraim, asked her a question in Hindi as she silently formulated that last. "It was called Earth," she said aloud for the fourth time now. "The race that killed it were the krim. They're the ones who abducted your ancestors, and traded them to the reeh. We don't know why or how, but the reeh collect intelligent species like some people collect beetles. We fought the krim for five hundred years with the assistance of the chah'nas, and eventually won."

"And the krim were exterminated completely?" asked another, hard-eyed and curious. About a third of them were. Another third were wary. Trace thought they had the look of people who'd been taken for a ride by fanciful storytellers before. What little she knew of the Purists included that they loved to invent crazy origin stories about where humanity came from. The final third were derisive, snorting in disbelief and shaking their heads at her every utterance. But they could not explain the bug that crawled upon her hand, nor the fact that big Idri had woken up thirty minutes ago, and now sat dazedly in a big chair, attended by the medically-trained lady with the dark braids, a sensor cuff on his arm and sipping local chuno. He had a headache and felt sluggish, he said, but was otherwise okay.

"Completely," Trace answered. "A freighter captain named Lien Wang jumped her ship directly at the planet. All life on that world ceased."

"This is some fancy robot trick," sneered the man who'd taken her kukri. His name was Irin Tola, and he fancied himself in charge of this Purist gathering. Still he had not given the kukri back, nor her other weapons. Rolonde was in the room, seated against the wall near Idri, similarly unarmed. Most of the Purists had pistols or rifles, and all of them seemed well trained enough to keep a weapon ready in case either of their guests tried something. Rael, Arime and Terez were next door, similarly guarded. Clearly the Purists assumed the women were less threat, and so kept them in here for questioning. "It's just a bug," Tola continued. "There's no proof it's from some crazy AI race beyond the Empire."

"I dunno, Tola," said another, having examined Trace's bug first, and now standing near, watching it still. "I do electronics for a living. That little critter's got some crazy design and processing functions. And, I mean, it's obeying her commands, and it took out Idri just by verbal instruction, knew exactly who she was talking about, then delivered just the right dose to only stun him. That's some crazy advanced shit, you have to know the systems to know just how advanced."

Tola rolled his eyes in exasperation. Trace did not tell them that it hadn't actually been the bug who'd identified Idri, but Styx. Telling them about drysines was unavoidable if she was to share the entire human story, but revealing Styx remained a step too far. A lot could perhaps have been solved if she'd simply invited Styx to come here and talk to them in person, but Styx did not think it yet safe, and Trace agreed. Not everyone reacted to Styx positively, and Trace was not certain that xenophobic Purists wouldn't just start shooting, with consequences deadly only to them.

"So you're a soldier?" asked another man. Jezu, Trace recalled the name. He was tall and strong, another gym junkie, but more impressive than the others, without the extra bulk of too many drinks and not enough self-discipline. "What kind of soldier?"

"This is crap," a woman retorted in exasperation. "We come from Adasa beyond Choprika Prime! Hezul was our leader, he led us on the mission against the Tanifex Fleet, and we were victorious there before we were captured by the reeh and sent here!"

It was the old Purist origin story, Trace had gathered. There were several, and across the centuries they'd changed, but all spoke of a time when humans had been kings in their own place, and ruled over troublesome aliens with an iron fist.

"If what you're saying is true," another man cut in, pointing a hard finger at Trace, "then how did we forget our origin? You say our language, our religions, all of this is similar to what it was on... on Earth?"

Trace nodded. "Similar to what it was at the time, from what I understand, yes."

"So how did we remember all of that knowledge, yet forget the most basic thing of all -- who we are and where we come from?"

"I don't know," said Trace. "Your ancestors were prisoners of the krim, and then of the reeh. The reeh play games with minds. Changing the minds and memories of a few thousand humans can't be that hard for them. Or maybe you just forgot. Culture and belief are almost hardwired, it can be rebuilt from memory even if all the old religious books are gone. I understand many holy books are learned by heart. But identity relies on memory and environment. Memories fade, and environments change. Humanity's memories and identity have been shaped by a thousand years on this world. Those experiences may have simply crowded out the others. You've all been here for a long time."

"But you say you're a soldier," Jezu repeated his previous question, undeterred. "What kind of soldier?"

"A marine," said Trace, using the English word.

Jezu frowned. "What is...'marine'?"

"Samudree," Trace used the Hindi word, which almost worked, but not really. "Earth had big oceans. Our ancestors fought wars across those oceans. The toughest soldiers travelled on big ships to fight on foreign shores. They were called marines. Today we use the same word for soldiers who fight from spaceships."

Standing beside her, watching side-on, was Taj. Arms folded, staring as though uncertain of whether she was the biggest liar in history, or the greatest revelation in history. All humans on Eshir told stories of where they were from. If what she was saying was true, all those others would be wrong. Which would make her... a prophet?

"So you're one of the toughest soldiers?" Jezu pressed.

"She took out those three thugs at the casino like it was nothing," Taj told him.

"Sure," said Jezu. "But I didn't see that."

"I wasn't lying!"

"I know kid." Still gazing at Trace, with hard eyes. "But I didn't see it. No one here did."

"Do you require a demonstration?" Trace asked him calmly.

"If she's that heavily augmented," said Efraim, "she could beat you in an arm wrestle."

"No," said Trace. "Augments provide a sudden release of energy. I punch hard because of the speed of my fist. In slower motions, I'm a lot stronger than most women, but an augmented man will be stronger." Over by the wall, she saw Rolonde's eyes forcefully wide, like a child desperately wanting to volunteer for something, but prevented from saying so. Trace fought back a smile. "I don't recommend fighting us. You look strong and augmented. It makes it hard for us to go easy on you. You could be hurt."

"I kickbox for money," said Jezu, with cool confidence. "Only been beaten once. I've seen frauds before. They talk a big game until I go to their dojo and break their limbs. I don't like frauds."

Against the rear wall, Rolonde was practically bursting out of her skin. Trace nodded at her. "Jess? You game?"

Rolonde got up, a little too fast, because some weapons pointed her way. She held up both empty hands. "Jumpy, aren't they?" she said in English.

Jezu handed his own rifle to a comrade, and the crowd cleared a space to one side of the big room. Rolonde followed, stretching her shoulders, then squatting to do her legs. "Don't hurt him too badly," Trace instructed, turning her chair to watch.

Rolonde nodded, still crouched, transferring weight from one leg to the other. Jess Rolonde had been the ultimate gym rat before joining the Corps. She'd been into basketball as a kid, had blown her knee, then gotten a waiver to receive high-level augments before she was technically of legal age to help her recover faster. That recovery training had gotten her into serious fitness, which began an obsession, and got her into fighting and blackbelts in several styles before she'd signed up. She still wasn't the best unarmed fighter in Phoenix Company -- that honour went to Corporal Kalo, leader of Alpha Third Section -- but she was probably top twenty in tough company.

Jezu did his own stretches. Some of the Purists had recording devices out, many of them amused, thinking they were about to see a fraud get seriously smacked down. There were a lot of militia-types here, Trace had been noting for the past half-hour -- not merely strong men, and a few women, but people who seemed familiar with violence. People who liked violence, and relished a chance to feel justified in using it. Some people like that, in Trace's experience, were drawn to fights in search of enemies. Others, deprived of enemies, would invent them.

Rolonde took her stance, and Jezu his. Some shouts and yells broke out, general encouragement. Jezu was at least half Rolonde's weight again. Were it not for her degree of augmentation, she'd have had no business fighting a good fighter Jezu's size. The reach disadvantage alone was enormous, and unaugmented, any woman would have almost no chance, even with superior talent.

But now, as Jezu bounced forward, aggressively looking for an opening to punch through, Rolonde backed and pivoted to a simple roundhouse kick. Jezu saw it coming easily enough, and raised an arm to block, and WHACK! the sound of it through the room was like a gunshot, as Rolonde unloaded full marine augments through hip and shoulder-turn, her leg almost disappearing for sheer speed.

Exclamations from the crowd, as Jezu staggered, remained standing, then clutched at his arm as the shock of what had happened began to register on his face. Then the pain.

"I'd stop there if I were you," Trace advised him. "Is it broken?"

Jezu tried to move the arm, which worked, but the pain grew worse. About the crowd, mutters of disbelief. The woman with the dark braids moved to his side, and Jezu tried to push her away, which only brought another stab of pain from the arm. He groaned, doubling over.

"Sorry," said Rolonde to Trace, still bouncing. "Overkill?"

"Just enough kill, I think," said Trace. She raised her voice to the crowd, standing from her chair. "There are no augments that powerful on Eshir. You doubters will need a better argument."

One of the men turned on her, and shoved a pistol into her face, apparently quite angry. "Why don't you shut the fuck up?"

Trace disarmed him in a flash, and left him staring down the barrel of his own pistol. Before weapons could swing her way once more, she popped the magazine, dechambered the remaining round, and handed the harmless weapon back to the stunned man, grip first. It happened so fast that even those standing nearby remained staring for several seconds longer, as though doubting what they'd just seen.

"Wow!" said Efraim then, into that stunned silence. "Wow! You're real! Guys, she's... she's actually real! We've found where we're from!"

No one said anything for a long time. It was extraordinary, Trace supposed. For these people, Eshir was their whole universe. It had been for their parents and grandparents for the best part of a millennia. There were legends about where they were from, many fictional, some entirely serious and verging upon religion. Purists had fought wars based in part upon belief in those stories. And now this.

"What are you doing here?" Taj asked. "I mean really. You're not on some arts holiday. Why come all this way? I mean, Eshir's been cut off inside the Empire forever. The Empire doesn't let anyone through, and it won't let us out. How did you manage it?"

Tell them about Styx, Trace wondered? Not yet, and not here. The old concerns held true. She wasn't here to provide these people with a service. Her best hope was that she could win enough support from them, honestly or not, to gain assistance in the short time available.

"We're looking for the central entity that rules the Reeh Empire," she said. "She's not here, but she was based here once. That period ended eight thousand years ago. Some people here call it the Origin Horizon."

"That's an old translation from some alien nonsense text," Tola cut her off, still angry and distrustful. Trace didn't think he believed any of it. "We don't use that term."

"Fine," said Trace. "Whatever you call it, she ran the Reeh Empire eight thousand years ago, then her rule ended. Only it didn't entirely end, because we have proof that she's still alive, and in charge of things to some degree. How and why, it's unclear."

"How can she still be alive after eight thousand years?" someone asked.

"Because she's an artificial intelligence. She's functionally immortal."

"Why do you need to find her?"

"Because we think another artificial intelligence like her was once in her custody. We call these most advanced AIs 'queens'. This second queen, we think, was once called Nia. Nia now threatens all humanity, and other species as well. We need to know what she is, how she works and what she'll likely do. Your Reeh Empire queen will likely know all of this. She can help us save humanity."

A disbelieving silence. It was a lot to take in all at once. Hearing it all put together like that could make a person disbelieve the proof that their eyes had just witnessed.

"And what will you do to this queen when you find her?" asked another.

"We don't know yet," said Trace, looking about at the encircling faces. "If we can gain her information without hurting her, perhaps we'll do that. If we can't, we'll probably kill her in the process."

"She'd have to be the most well protected thing in the Empire," big Idri growled.

"Yes," Trace agreed. "Yes she will be."

"And you can do that?"

"We'll find out," Trace said calmly.

"And if you kill her? What happens to the Reeh Empire?"

"Your guess is as good as mine," said Trace. "Possibly better. She's important to them. It would be an upheaval."

"Could the Empire collapse?"

"Not quickly, I don't think. But eventually?" Trace gave the closest gesture she ever made to a shrug. "I suppose that depends on how badly the various people in the Empire want to fight for their freedom."

Stunned silence. For a long moment, no one knew what to say.

"Wait wait!" Tola interrupted with scorn. "This is nonsense. You know who was the last person who came around spouting this crap? It was Matzi Khan and his idiots -- the whole point of this kind of rhetoric is to convince us that we should all join hands with the slimy aliens to fight against some common enemy!"

"You don't think the reeh are your enemy?" Trace asked him.

"They're *all* our fucking enemies!" Tola insisted, with the hard purpose of a man who saw whatever power existed for him within this institution slipping away. "You don't get to pick just one! Dheeg and Koosafaare tried that in our past, and look what it cost them!"

Trace couldn't keep up with all these references to a long history she'd not had time to learn, and had no time now for Styx to fill her in. "Then I suppose you have to decide what you think is more important," she told them. "The Purist movement? Or humanity on Eshir."

"They're the same thing!" Tola snarled.

"No they're not. My own Fleet made this mistake back in human space. Lately they've done a lot of things that they say are for the good of all humans, but in reality they're only maintaining the ascendancy of Fleet. All institutions act in their own interests first, no matter what their propaganda says. Even the best institutions. The Purists need all aliens to be enemies because that's best for the Purists -- humanity on Eshir is surrounded and outnumbered, and that's the best way to make all humans flock to you in fear. Meanwhile the reeh have got you *all* crushed beneath their boot, and you barely notice.

"I'm asking you to skip the small enemies, and go straight for the big one. You say you hate aliens who oppress you? Fight the reeh. Join me in finding and taking down their queen. Everything else is small fry, it's beneath you. You want respect among humans? Join me and you'll have respect among *everyone*."

She looked around. In the far doorway, Taj's friend Dagan was standing, having come from Halhoun's side to see what the commotion was about. He looked intense, nodding with slow approval. Many of the others did too.

"Major," said Styx on coms. *"There is a low altitude ore-hauler currently deviating its course to strike your building. Impact in five seconds."*

Five? And then she visualised the passing routes the big flying whales were taking, directly up the valley to one side, and the reasons why such things weren't allowed in any truly civilised city...

"Get down!" she yelled, and made a run for Dagan's doorway, darting between startled Purists. She was halfway there when a colossal boom shook the building, followed by the roar of collapsing walls and ceiling. She stopped in the doorway, the safest place if the whole roof were about to fall in, and risked a look back, saw people falling and running amidst tumbling stones and thick dust, through which she could barely see the rough steel of the hauler's side, still slicing sideways through what remained of the building.

And here came Rolonde, sprinting and stumbling, others joining her to run for the doorway, as Trace turned and ran into the medical room. Rael, Arime and Terez had already disarmed their guards in the commotion, and were now recovering the marines' confiscated weapons amidst the fallen ceiling beams. Trace looked at Halhoun, unconscious on the divan, and knew that if she left him, he was dead, and some of her recent possible alliances would die with him.

"Styx!" she yelled, unable to formulate quietly at that moment. "Get the cruiser over here and put down suppressive fire, we have wounded to evacuate!"

"Yes Major."

Trace grabbed the rifle Arime thrust into her hands, and pocketed the visor, as Rael and Terez already headed upstairs to the bikes. The grinding and shaking stopped as Arime gathered up Halhoun with Rolonde's help to secure the IV drip, but now more Purists were coming through the doorway, some hurt and stumbling with the help of others, but at least the ceiling was no longer collapsing. Then came the rattle and pop of gunfire.

"They're up top!" called Rael from up the stairs, followed by the thunder of return fire. Trace leaped three stairs at a time and came up on the wide rooftop, now crowded with many times the bikes and a number of vehicles that had not been there before, unhelpfully aglow in the landing lights. The low wall about the rooftop was providing some cover, but bullets were now cracking low overhead, striking the cliff wall behind, at just the height to take a biker's head off if she tried to strap in and take off.

Trace scrambled low and rolled beside Rael and Terez, both low and sneaking automatic bursts over the wall, the better option in the absence of time for a well-aimed shot. Trace risked a glimpse and saw the big steel whale lodged perpendicular through the fortress' entire outer section, shrouded in dust with its back ablaze from muzzle flashes.

"They're coming through below too!" Trace announced as she

ducked back and checked her rifle. Rounds hit the wall just opposite her head, others cracked overhead. "Doors in the outer hull!"

"Yeah, they've rigged it for infantry assault!" Rael agreed. "These guys up top can't advance up top with the roof caved in! But if they've got launchers, we're fucked!"

"They're bound to have," Trace muttered, back to the wall and staring about the parked bikes and cruisers, in search of inspiration. "Styx, ETA?"

"Thirty seconds, Major." Purists were coming up the stairs, all armed, as Terez yelled at them to get down. Something streaked and blew up against the cliff wall to one side.

"They got launchers," Rael confirmed. They were completely pinned down, Trace observed. The attackers -- almost certainly Zeladnists -- weren't all that good at using their weapons, but in this situation they didn't need to be.

"Major, there appears to be a second wave of airborne attackers approaching at one minute out," Styx informed her. *"The evacuation window will be very short."*

"We'll have to widen it by force," Trace replied, racking her rifle and running in a low crouch between waiting bikes to her own bike. Staying low, she could just about get the systems started on one side without having to sit up in the saddle. Beside her, Dagan came and did the same, with a furious determination that told Trace he had some idea what was going on. He had what looked like a machine-pistol on a strap, the kind of covert thing civvies in urban environments might like... and could be used one-handed on a bike. And he was first going after his flying coat and helmet in the rear trunk before he started up anything, which Trace reckoned was a good idea from an expert who'd know better than her, and did the same.

"ETA Zero," said Styx, and Trace heard a roar of drysine cannonfire from the air up the valley. Immediately Rael and Terez were up and pouring aimed fire onto the hauler's back without concern for their safety. Trace jumped onto her bike to complete the startup sequence, even as Rael turned to her with a slashing motion across his throat to indicate that threat had been neutralised. For a group of shooters

standing on the back of an ore hauler without cover, against drysine rotary rapid-fire, Trace could well imagine.

"Get in here and evac!" Trace commanded. "Peanut and Styx, cover fire high and low! Styx, how many you estimate?" As her bike's engines roared to life, and she capped the throttle so not to blast everyone behind with hot exhaust.

"Too many, Major. We must run."

"Do what you can, I'm going to do a loop out to keep them off our backs as we pull out, then we're leaving." The bike shuddered and rocked as the repulsors fired up, and she kicked it about, a heavy, grudging weight against her leg, then hit the repulsors hard to get some altitude, doing her last straps even as she did. Stuffed the rifle into its rear holster, and did up her jacket as the jets hit full powerup, and at three meters over everyone's heads she hit thrust with a force that would have thrown her off the back were it not for the straps.

Down the end of the valley, she could see them now, assorted dots racing and weaving wide as they came. The bike controls were twin independent handles, with gyroscopic arms that sensed the difference between G-generated force and steering intent. The grips controlled left and right roll, pull-back to go up and twist-down to descend, the pedal grips were both full burner and yaw, which was too easy to get confused, and all the control surfaces became radically more sensitive the faster you went.

She kicked full burner now, accelerating neck-strainingly fast as the slipstream about her windshield became a thundering solid wall. The rifle was going to be impossible to aim at these speeds, so she pulled her pistol from a thigh pocket, and realised that with one hand off the grip, half of her control was gone. This was nuts.

Suddenly a bike was roaring past her -- Dagan, and accelerating even faster, indicating with one finger that she should get on his tail and follow. Trace stuffed the pistol back in her pocket and did so, as Dagan abruptly dove beneath the path of oncoming bikes, gone in a flash above their heads and fading to small dots behind before she could blink. More flashed by, and one may have shot at her, they were too fast to tell, but now Dagan was banking hard right to follow and it was all Trace could do to keep thrust floored while shuddering and skidding through a turn that never quite matched his sharpness, even as the valley wall came approaching really fast.

She missed a ruined-concrete side by thirty meters, kicking the burner once more to accelerate in the vain hope of making up the twenty meters she'd lost on Dagan. The speed on these bikes was ridiculous -- little drag and relatively small weight for their power, they couldn't manoeuvre at starship-Gs but it felt close.

Ahead, the first bikes were heading for the fortress against the canyon wall, in what looked like a strafing run. Given the firepower down there, Trace didn't think that a smart idea. She was too far away, through the blasting slipstream, the scratched windshield and goggles to see much, but there was a small explosion from the base of the fortress as one hit the ground, then another hit the wall and bounced, scattering pieces.

More bikes were lifting from the rooftop as she and Dagan approached, and the surviving enemy from the first wave broke wide to come around again. Several were slowing, Trace observed, perhaps to attempt a mid-air hover... and here were Carville, Randrahan and Wang, having come in low and exchanged fire with enemies about the ore hauler.

"They're gonna have launchers again," Rael announced. *"We can't engage them from long range with the numbers they've got coming in, we gotta move."*

"Straight out the bottleneck!" Trace directed, rocketing past the fortress and seeing the others accelerating to follow. "Probably an ambush on the far side but we gotta risk it, just punch straight through!"

A fast glance behind showed everyone following, the big cruiser slower to accelerate but with huge twin turbines flanking its cockpit. They'd selected it for speed and paid a high price in traded goods to acquire it upon arrival. Trace thundered between the narrow, vertical walls of the bottleneck, flashing past a hauler coming the other way, then out into the wider valley on the far side.

Several bikes shot by, in stationary hover and now accelerating at neck-bending Gs to follow... and forgetting that they in turn were being chased. Trace's visor showed multiple marks fixed on tacnet as Styx acquired their position, one then vanishing as someone shot it from the sky.

"Got one!" Rolonde announced from Arime's pillion seat, with both hands free to use a rifle.

A course appeared on Trace's visor. *"Major,"* said Styx, *"this is our path."*

"Give it to Taj!" Trace yelled back. "I've got my hands full flying!"

"I got it!" Taj announced. *"Follow me!"*

They streaked from the smaller valley into a slightly wider canyon, thick with traffic in the industrial haze, and a blur of crumbling settlements crowding the slopes. Their pursuit seemed to have paused for a moment, perhaps alarmed by their immediate losses.

"Boots, that's Dijien Sector!" Dagan observed, evidently reading the same feed Styx was sending to Taj.

"Yeah, that's right across the city and deep in the alien quarters," Taj added, gunning into the lead and taking them in a sweeping right-hander through the narrow canyon. Trace followed, her marines strung out behind, the bright lights of foundries on the ascending wall to their right, soot-stained walls and mid-level docking ports whipping by. *"Some of them don't like heavily-armed humans tearing through their space. Watch the Qilada Bridge, coming up high in ten seconds, stay low."*

The Qilada Bridge shot by above, a slender flash of suspension wires and dangling cars. Trace followed Taj weaving to the right of a big hauler, then burst into the open space of what Trace's visor informed her was the Trizul Depression, a wide expanse to multiple branching valleys, centred by Qalb Crossing, a looming mass of neon towers, blinking faintly in the haze. In the middle floated Anakris, a giant island in mid-stream traffic, alive with the light of many-levelled entertainments, bars and hotels, bristling with docked vehicles and blazing advertisements. Wire cables held it to the base of what had once been a large tower below, long disintegrated in the Purist War, Trace recalled, the crumbling foundations now serving as an anchor. The living walls of buildings crawled with activity, the industrial sectors sprawled out below and the highrise ahead.

"Steer right of that, Taj!" called Dagan. *"If I were gonna ambush us, that's where I'd be!"* Sure enough, Taj could see bikes breaking away from the docks now, wheeling their way and gathering speed.

"Here we go!" called Trace. "Taj, can you get us to Dogreth Quarter!"

"Sure can!" said Taj. *"Guys, if they're shooting you've gotta dodge! Shooting straight in level flight is easy, when you're dodging it gets a whole lot harder to hit anything!"* The approaching bikes were a mix — a few were Stingray models, wide with flat stabiliser fins, twin forward steering vanes and twin engines for extra thrust. But those twin stabilisers came with extra-drag, and Trace thought her Shaytan should have superior mid-range acceleration. They were coming right across in front, between Trace's path and some slow hauler traffic... and now came the flicker-flash of muzzle fire. *"Kick it!"*

She twisted the throttle, nosed down enough for a moment's zero-G, then the attackers were flashing by overhead, several more crushing Gs from the left to get on their tail. Trace hit full power, nose up sharply as the straps saved her from being torn off the bike, and ripped past a hauler's rear. Visor rear-view showed her a flash, and a fast glance behind showed tumbling wreckage as what remained of a bike sprayed from a collision with the hauler.

"Scratch another!" came a voice that she thought was Private Randrahan. *"Nice shot Benji!"* And here to the side was a hurtling Shaytan, two-astride, the rear marine adjusting his rifle to search for more targets.

"Get on his right!" another marine was shouting, then some swearing as Trace ducked past some slower traffic, slipstream a solid wall above the windshield, wishing she had a pillion seat passenger so she too might be able to shoot something. *"Fuck yeah!"* from the marines, as she wove and looked back, seeing a scatter of pursuing bikes at full throttle, another one tumbling like a broken shadow toward the canyon floor.

"Taj!" Dagan was yelling above the commotion. *"Take Loister's, dude! It'll be fucking metal but we gotta shake 'em!"*

"Everyone on me!" Taj yelled, cutting left past Trace's nose, heading for between Devil's Slot and The Avenue, where Loister's Cut made a narrow slice between solid walls of urbanity. It looked like suicide, the five-way junction at Qalb Crossing so jammed with vehicles you could have jumped from one to the other across the drop. But here at a lower altitude was a hole in the tangle, and Taj headed for it with a stomach-lurching drop that sent all the blood rushing to Trace's head as she followed, momentum threatening to throw her far off the bike. *"Everyone stay loose, it's gonna get really tight!"*

Another Stingray streaked left-to-right across them, and Trace yanked her pistol from her thigh pocket and blasted to no visible effect... the marksmanship required was insane at these angles and crosswinds, and then Loister's Cut was racing up at speeds to make her wonder if letting these hotshot young bikers lead was such a good idea.

"Watch the cross-bridges and direction changes!" Taj shouted before ripping through the entrance, a blur of market stalls, overhanging dwellings and gantryways ascending the walls, an assault of high-speed air on the nostrils. A low-speed hauler was pulling out from its wall berth in the glare of docking floodlights in the canyon gloom, and Trace cut right to dodge as Taj went low, a suspension bridge flashing above and someone shouting in her ears about new enemies dropping in above...

Suddenly a Stingray cut high-to-low before her, visible mostly from its afterburners, the Shaytan leaping as it skidded in the hot slipstream, and someone in the rear seat was turning with a handweapon to shoot at her. Trace slammed both grips forward and dropped, straps nearly dislocating her hips as the bike dropped lower still, past the twin-engine slipstream once more and below the line-of-fire. They both cut left as the narrow canyon turned, smaller vehicles ripping by with desperate evasion, and Trace could see the pilot's head turning this way and that trying to acquire her for his rear gunner... until heavy fire cut them both nearly in half, and the bike spun sideways into a canyon wall and shattered into a hundred tumbling pieces.

Trace swore with adrenaline overload, struggling to remember to breathe, and then in her side-vision was another Shaytan -- Arime, tacnet told her, with Rolonde behind him clutching her big rifle ready, scanning upward for new threats. Tacnet flashed to alert Trace of a sharp corner ahead, and Trace twisted for more thrust, cut before Taj to lead wide right, then as the bend loomed, and thank god there was nothing parked mid-lane on the far side like had been the end of a couple kids Taj had told her about.

It was much darker in Loister's Cut than the Trizul Depression had been, just racing walls, protruding docking obstructions and terrifyingly deceptive depth-perception where one wall abruptly closed in, or once at high-velocity, an open-topped skif with inadequate running lights in the permanent twilight. Trace couldn't see what the rear-most marines were up to, but she could hear them giving terse warnings of someone getting too close behind, rear-gunners keeping the pursuers jumping with near-impossible bursts behind them.

"Taj, give me your fastest route there!" Trace shouted.

"Fastest goes through Qwailash Sector!" Taj replied, coming back up on her right. *"They don't like outsiders making trouble, if we..."* and he broke off to dodge a protruding docking gantry, warning lights and steel flashing by, *"...if we go through there with this bunch chasing us, they'll try and kill us all!"*

"Styx! Assessment of Qwailash defences!"

"Major," said Styx, *"I judge the threat limited at present velocities. Qwailash network defences are weaker, I may be able to intervene on your behalf."*

"Do it!" Trace commanded. "Qwailash Sector, let's go!" Tacnet flashed again, indicating that she should turn at Qwailash Junction. Taj did that, and Trace followed, a vast sweep across a barren stretch without electric light, filled with the empty shadows of derelict buildings not repaired since the last war.

The canyon sides here became precisely vertical, ancient steel walls crumbling with rust and twisted plant life -- some kind of colossal industrial feature, it was said, though this was the edge of human territory in Qalea, and only the reeh's deformed monsters lived here. Absolutely not a place to break down, Trace thought as she gunned the jet to overdrive down the long stretch, visor switching to nightvision in the absence of citylight... though getting captured by undercity freaks was going to be the last of their problems at these speeds.

On the right, the lower part of the wall had collapsed, a huge half-kilometre-long gash, and Taj and Trace slid through it, suddenly in the vast underground of Kashaila Junction, the short-cut between human and Qwailash Sector. The enormous support beams of the many-thousand-year-old place whipped by, and Trace looked to see Taj looking back with concern -- at the rear of their formation, more muzzle flashes, and the last two marines making evasive actions.

"No straight lines!" Trace admonished Taj. "We'll give them good shots!"

"You told me to take the fastest route and this is it!" Taj shouted back. *"Nearly there!"*

They shot from the far side amidst the frayed edges of multi-tonne rebar steel, and into a gleaming vertical canyon criss-crossed with bridges and bustling with traffic and lights.

"Stay alert, traffic's going to be intense!" Taj warned them. *"Qwailash are kinda nocturnal, it'll be twice this crowded in another hour!"*

They streaked along the sweeping left-hand bend, conversation in Trace's ears between the calm-sounding Styx instructing rear-most marines on her targeting assistance, and them complaining that it wasn't so easy to hit the dots on their visors over their shoulders on a bike at these speeds. As they raced by, Trace could see squat, hard-shelled qwailash in the overpasses stopping to stare at the high-speed chase.

The bending canyon ended into an abrupt vista of crumbling urbanity, old industrial towers looming like broken fingers, smoke-stacks belching smoke from the foundries the qwailash somehow made dirtier than everywhere else, the crazy holography displays dancing on pools of settled smog. Taj tore into it, Trace behind, around some newer towers and heading for the industrial zone in the hopes that would attract less attention.

"Just took a hit on the rear," came Rael's voice. *"They've dropped back a lot but they're still with us, I count at least ten."*

"I count fifteen," said Styx. *"They appear fanatical. Defensive emplacements are operational across the canyon route ahead. They are not interactive with local networks, you must stay low amidst the traffic for cover."*

"I got it, stay low," said Taj, cutting left from the industrial yards and into the thickest traffic flowing to the canyon bottleneck ahead, a looming cluster of kaleidoscopic lights between the rising walls of monolithic ancient city ruins. "The main traffic flow's on the left! Stay left, hang the inside, qwailash like to fly in straight lines!"

The traffic flow was quite serious, all barely half the velocity of the crazy humans, and Trace tore after Taj past most of it on the inside-right, seeing evasion and wobble ahead and behind as automated navigation adjusted for the unforeseen threat. Trace recalled Taj saying he'd flown through Qwailash Quarter before, but surely never like this, as the stream performed a right-hand bend through the bottleneck of neon towers, a flash of apartments, upper-level markets bustling with hard-shelled occupants, the glimpse of individual water tanks and a big pool below, teeming with lobster-like swimmers.

Some oncoming traffic missed her by mere meters, others adjusting to keep to their side of the flow as they, the towers and the bright lights shot by at hysterical speed... and here ahead down the canyon the walls were opening out, city lights fading but replaced by one of the qwailash's enormous gateway airships, a heaving behemoth in the sky, now turning hard across the way ahead, head-to-tail alight with racing holographic script, and blocking it. An eruption of objects fired at low speed, arcing through the air around it as the valley vanished like a closing door, then the grenades were exploding and the air was filled with multi-coloured smoke.

Taj and Trace headed low, the only way was to get under as the paths over would surely be blocked by defensive guns, and then Styx was saying loudly, *"Follow the course!"* and a projection lit a path on Trace's visor. She followed it, a bit right and then a lot left, a flash of coloured smoke, the blur of an obstacle chain to one side, then out the far side with something exploding in a loud crash just behind, then again to her right. Airbursts, she realised with disbelief, suddenly in clear air and accelerating down the clear canyon ahead, past a swirl of milling vehicles who'd been coming the other way and now could not pass.

"You are all through," Styx informed them, and Trace stared back in disbelief to see more bikes following, Dagan's now the closest. *"The Zeladnists are not, three have collided and two more have been shot down. The others are discontinuing their pursuit."*

"Fuck that was close," someone muttered. The qwailash had slammed the door in their faces, only Styx had somehow calculated safe routes for all of them through the smoke and underside chains.

"You have qwailash AI units closing on your position," Styx informed them, as they raced past canyon-side water-tank apartments, windows arranged like restaurant shelves of dirty glasses overlooking the canyon floor, blue water and many floating qwailash, and more in the big rectangular pools below.

"Left past the Needlepoint, follow me," Dagan announced as he streaked ahead, cutting between the Needlepoint tower and a canyon wall, a flash through foul-smelling smoke from wall-side industries, a glimpse of open sewerage treatment ponds, lakes of surface sludge pushed by robotic arms.

"Styx, where are those AIs and are they hostile?" Trace asked.

"Qwailash are physically slow and use AIs to intercept hostile elements," Styx replied. *"You have been designated as hostile, and their intentions will be lethal. Their locations are well hidden, we have not yet adequately penetrated qwailash network security for me to establish dominance."*

"Dagan, how long until the edge of Qwailash Sector?"

"Never been much beyond Needlepoint," Dagan replied. Trace squinted into the darkening gloom of thick overhead pollution as the grim industrial landscapes intensified, disintegrating steel mills,

scrap yards filled with wrecked haulers, the bottom of the canyon plunging once more into the far depths as the deep city resumed. Qalea's ancient depths had been filled in some places, to provide a strong foundation upon which the more recent city could grow. But out here in the less-populated regions, Qalea reminded everyone what it truly was -- a monolithic ruin upon whose uppermost sliver a recent growth of civilisation sprung.

A glance at Taj showed him sorting maps and routes across his visor with a free hand, lacking the visual control to do it hands-free, content to let Dagan lead. Trace trimmed her own thrust as the visor display indicated the jet was 120 percent max heat and risked melting the injectors. Ahead the industrial canyon forked, a high-speed choice approaching fast.

"Can't go over the upper-level," Taj explained. *"Air defences there get nasty, at least in the canyons they don't risk shooting in case they hit their own..."*

Against a left-side wall, Trace saw twin burners ignite just ahead, a pair of waiting, pilotless bikes in a flat-winged configuration accelerating hard to match their velocities. "Targets left!" Trace announced, and immediately the drones were under fire from marines behind. One caught fire and fell, while the other turned abruptly into the human formation's mid-stream.

"Can't fire, got no clear shot!" Rolonde shouted, as Trace hammered the burners and accelerated wide.

"This way asshole!" Dagan growled, cutting across the drone's nose and drawing its attention. He streaked right, taking that hard fork in the canyons, dragging the drone toward the wall's deadly steel outcrops, and Trace saw the underside turret tracking.

"Jess take the shot!" she yelled. All fired at once, the drone skidding in a flat spin as one engine cut, even as its own guns fired and Dagan hit the wall at five hundred kph, smashed, broke a hundred ways at once and vanished behind in spinning pieces.

*"DAGAN!"*Taj screamed. And again, with all the stunned disbelief of a kid who'd never really thought that it could happen to him or his friends. Not really. Trace felt his shock in her bones, with all the

memory of first combat actions, and friends who'd seemed invincible, suddenly ruined and dead. And recent combat actions, where such vibrant life had just stopped in some horrific collision of steel and flesh. She'd seen more death in her thirty-seven years than most people did in a lifetime, but for all her efforts and pretence, she'd never gotten used to it.

"Major, there are two more behind," said Styx, *"and doubtless far more behind that. Their armaments are quite accurate and our losses will escalate. We must hide."*

"Taj!" Trace commanded. "We've got to hide! Find us a spot to hide, I'm counting on you!"

"Hang on!" said Taj, dropping his nose and leading them plunging into the depths. Layers of accumulated mist and pollution zoomed up to meet them, then a sudden rush of freezing cold wind as the temperature inversion enveloped them, cold air unshifted in many days and settled at the base of the drop, a heavy rush of frigid turbulence around the windshield.

Enormous, decaying pillars the size of towers loomed in visor IR from the right, and Taj cut around them, finding yet another drop behind and a decayed opening into a lower space large enough to drop a bulk hauler through.

"Slow down, slow down!" Taj warned, hauling the nose up while powering the repulsors, the bike shuddering as layers of shattered floors streaked by, then ended ahead past a jumble of collapsed debris in a wide opening, and a floor. *"Power on, watch the floor!"*

Repulsor vehicles in freefall were notoriously difficult to control, gathering speed and lacking brakes, and Trace copied Taj, powering to full lift and giving a kick of thrust that sent dirt and debris erupting in waves as she levelled out, slowing and looking behind, hoping one of the less-experienced marines hadn't plunged nose-first into the ground. None did, and then she was idling along an enormous tunnel, like a twenty meter tall sewer drain, glowing green and round on visor IR, and utterly blocked a few hundred meters ahead.

Taj indicated them left, where collapsed sections of old tunnel exposed open levels beyond, and turned the slowing bike into one of those holes before skidding to a stop. About him, marines pulled into this hole and neighbouring ones, pushing their bikes into hiding behind crumbling walls, then crouching in overwatch positions, weapons ready and not missing a beat.

And here, as Trace cleared her bike, came the cruiser, with a shrill of electric turbofans, headed for a larger hole in the wall further along. No sooner had it pulled into the large hole than Styx came trotting out, clattering along the angled tunnel-side to Trace's position.

"Are those drones coming?" Trace asked, listening for the approaching whine of more repulsors, rifle in hand.

"Yes," said Styx. "Do not shoot them, they will prove quite useful."

Trace took a moment to process that, then realised. "Oh, got it." She blinked on group coms. "Guys, don't shoot at the qwailash drones. Styx is going to capture them." About the steepening tunnel sides her marines were deploying anyway, taking cover behind decayed concrete walls. "Will there be any difficulty?"

"I do not anticipate it." Styx stalked sideways down the slope, then planted her rearmost legs to make a firm brace on the concrete ground, twin rotary cannon pointed and waiting. Peanut clattered down behind her, heading for the tunnel floor, then up the sloping far side to create a crossfire.

The sound of repulsor pursuit became abruptly louder, and Trace took cover to her right. On her visor appeared a vid feed that could only have come from Styx herself, with a clear view down the tunnel.

"Pull back guys," said Rael. *"No visibility, let Styx do it. Be ready to back her up if something goes wrong."*

Both drones swung abruptly into view on Trace's visor, visible only on Styx's nightvision, flat and winged like a couple of airborne stingrays. And both kept coming, despite Styx and Peanut being clearly in view, underside scanning pods sweeping left and right as though the drysines were invisible. Quite anti-climactically, both set down on the tunnel before Styx, like a pair of tame dogs, and the repulsors began to wind down in a long, declining sigh.

"I have both drones under my control," said Styx. *"You may come out*

now." Trace did that. Peanut trotted to both qwailash drones, examining closely.

"Could have done that while they were shooting at us," Benji Carville suggested.

"It would have been obvious and suspicious," Styx replied. "Even the reeh may have shortly noticed the surveillance vision. I will send these two back to qwailash control shortly, where they will integrate with qwailash security and penetrate it. Qwailash security protocols will be within my control shortly after, possibly across the entire quarter."

"Is it safe to continue on now?" Trace asked. "Or should we wait?"

"There are too many surveillance drones at present," said Styx. "These two will inform the network that we are not at this location, and will continue their search pattern elsewhere before returning home. Best that we remain until nightfall before continuing on."

"Unless these tunnels continue underground for far enough that we could surface somewhere else entirely," Trace pondered, looking up the tunnel.

"Impossible to tell," said Styx. "I estimate by the state of concrete decay that this particular tunnel is at least six thousand years old. Likely it will adjoin to tunnels far older than that, many of which will have collapsed or been filled in by subsequent construction. Wandering through such lost locations in a qwailash security zone may simply get us detected once more. I cannot guarantee I will see and disable every security sensor before it can relay our position."

Trace nodded, and left the drones to the drysines, while several curious marines gave them a closer looking over. She strode to the cruiser, between the hot-ticking engine nacelles, and beneath the angled rear-doors to the cabin. There Romki and Afana, the black-braided medic, had propped Halhoun's head up on a sleeping roll, while Taj leaned on the cabin rear rim and stared. Efraim rummaged in medical kits with strong arms. Those two, from the Purists, had somehow ended up in the cruiser while trying to escape the Zeladnist assault. Plus Taj on his bike, who was no more than half a Purist, and Halhoun, who was probably not at all. Just a friend of Taj's, who'd gotten caught up in the mess. Like Dagan. Where the rest of them had gone, she had no idea. Probably they'd followed one of their own who knew a better way.

"How is he?" Trace asked.

"Bullet wounds generally not good," said Afana, using her visor's medical function to sort through data the various cuffs and attachments on Halhoun's body were feeding it. She moved his hand before his eyes, scrolling through various AR displays, while Romki prepared another hypodermic dose from their medkits. "But I think he's been quite lucky. His internal bleeding has stopped very quickly, if I can believe what your technology is telling me. His body's accepting the plasma quite well."

It had been a thousand years. Natural evolution was a weak force over that period compared to the medical technologies that had driven human change. Humanity was a vastly different species since the krim, Trace knew quite well, having had various additional things done to her own body after joining the kulina, and more still since joining the marines. The genetic alterations were not inconsiderable, and had spread and propagated in ways the medical community had not always expected. And Eshir humans had none of it.

"In fact," Afana added as she accepted the hypodermic that Efraim handed to her, and injected it, "I can't quite believe he's in as good shape as he is. What was on that bandage you put on him?"

"Nano-solution," said Trace. "Micro-machines. It's standard on our ship."

"Major, I am observing the medical feeds now," said Styx in her ear. The Purists did not have earpieces. *"I believe Halhoun will recover quickly."*

"Styx says he'll be fine," Trace relayed.

"Incredible," said Afana. Wide-eyed at that further reminder that she was not among regular humans.

"Any sign the reeh have changed them?" Trace wondered in English, for Romki's benefit.

"Oh, Major," and Romki shook his head in exasperation. "My

medical knowledge is enough to perform basic first aid and then a bit more, but that's all. Probably Styx would know."

Trace looked at Taj. He was in shock, staring at one wounded, unconscious friend, while attempting to process the other's death. She put a hand on his shoulder. "Taj." She squeezed, getting his attention. His face was utter confusion. Desolation. He wanted to cry, but hadn't yet processed on a deeper emotional level what he'd lost. Trace knew exactly how he felt, just by looking at him. All *Phoenix* crew had been there. "You did good. Dagan too."

Taj turned and walked, pulling up his visor, only to rediscover that this far down, there was no light at all. He put the visor back on, hands on his head and trying to breathe deeply. Trace followed, as Jokono hovered, concerned and perhaps thinking that an older man might be the person to offer a younger one some comfort. Trace gestured him back, taking the time even now to consider their dark perimeter, down here in the bowels of Qwailash Sector, where dark creatures were known to prowl. Tacnet showed her marines taking careful positions, and Styx's bugs releasing to fly deeper.

At the broken hole in the wall that led back to the tunnel, Taj put a hand on the fractured concrete, and leaned for a while. Then he looked back at Trace. "What's it all for?" he asked hoarsely. "This mission of yours. It's gotten one of my best friends killed, and one more hurt. What's it for?"

Suddenly she was on Rando again. Seeing the bodies of dead corbi, and their friends wondering if the mission this crazy human had sent them on was worth the sacrifice. Staff Sergeant Gideon Kono's lifeless eyes staring at the ceiling amid the carnage of his last stand. She did not want to send more young people to their deaths. Down here in the depths of Qalea, the mission suddenly seemed so far away. She wanted to tell Taj to take Halhoun and go home to their families, and live his life, and forget he'd ever met her.

"I'm trying to save the human race," she told him instead. "It's a job for warriors. I think Dagan was a warrior. Are you a warrior, Taj?"

~

Engineering Bay 17C was a familiar scene, *Phoenix* techs gathered about a complex alien synthetic brain in a brace mount, surrounded by screens, wires and sensors in a working tangle. Erik leaned against a wall support, eating stir fry from a plastic container with a fork while watching the techs work. Two of them were tavalai -- Spacer Takomiri and Chief Petty Officer Kumarada, conversing in a combination of earpiece-translated Togiri and broken English. Of all the ship's departments, Engineering had been most seamless in its integration of tavalai, mostly, Erik suspected, because the language of engineering was universal enough that it transcended other barriers to communication.

Overseeing them all was Bucket, having squeezed his way down the transit spine from Midships, and through *Phoenix* corridors and doorways to sit like a giant land crab outside of the cluster of organic crew. Theoretically he could have monitored the procedure from Midships, but from there he'd struggle to see all the human and tavalai interactions with their guest, and perhaps be slightly unprepared for any negative consequences. Erik recalled what the crew had been like two years ago, and their probable reactions then to the thought of activating a long-dormant ceephay-era AI on the ship. Back then, they'd all have been on red-alert, with marines standing in the room with weapons levelled, to be sure the AI knew that one false move would result in its destruction. Now, they were certain enough about *Phoenix*'s upgraded systems, with defensive barriers to infiltration provided by Styx herself, that the threat provided by a mere refinery-manager wasn't a large concern.

Lieutenant Rooke directed the team in person, this now being Second Shift, and Warrant Officer Leung having taken charge of Engineering in what was supposed to be Rooke's off-time. He crouched beside Kumarada, both peering at a flashing display, pointing at notable things that only tech geniuses would understand. On another display, the little girl of their previous communications with this ceephay intelligence sat crosslegged on a blank white floor, waiting with apparent patience. She'd acquired from somewhere a school uniform and a teddy bear, held absently on her lap.

She appeared to see Erik looking, and waved. Erik smiled and nodded back. So the ceephay was functional enough in her new environment that she'd uplinked to the room's cameras and was now triangulating to find the direction of Erik's gaze. Highly socialised, this one. Probably the product of working closely with organics over an extended period.

"Does she have sound?" Erik asked the room. "Or is it just visuals?"

"Just visuals, Captain," said Spacer Raza from nearby. "But she can probably read lips."

Lieutenant Dale entered with Lieutenant Karajin, Dale sipping a post-workout water, while Karajin ate some foul-smelling fish. Erik slid back to lean in the room's corner, so Karajin and Dale could lean on a wall to either side within his vision, and not stand unsecured. "Any progress?" Dale asked.

"Lieutenant Rooke?" Erik asked loudly, and Rooke looked up from his work. "Kill the ceephay's visuals for a moment please. We'll bring them back shortly." Rooke nodded, and made some inputs. "She's reading lips," Erik explained to the marines. "Makes private conversations hard."

"Thought we'd all gotten used to that," said Dale. On the visible screen, the young girl with the teddy bear pouted and looked upset, bottom lip protruding.

Erik rolled his eyes. "She's got no memory input yet," he said. "Rooke explained it to me, something about her memory function being atrophied from disuse... I don't know how that's possible with a crystalline data matrix, but there you go. They're rebuilding it with assistance from *Phoenix*, she's shuttling functions onto an external matrix so the original matrix can be evacuated for repair and reconstruction, then she reloads the old data and moves on to the next bit. Should be nearly finished now, thought I'd come down to look."

"She can't remember anything?" Karajin asked in heavily accented English. From having none when he first came aboard, he was lately somewhat fluent. The mottled brown and black tavalai wasn't as tall as Erik or Dale, but looked powerful enough to wrestle them both and win.

"That's what she says. Rooke says it seems legit. She has some higher embedded memory functions that let her know basic things. She's a refinery manager like we thought, or so she says. She says she has some very clear memories of the main organic crew she interacted with, probably because those memories overlap with her primary function, so they ended up embedded in other portions of her brain outside of main memory. Says she can't remember what species those people were, though. Says they were friendly and laughed a lot, so probably not reeh."

"No," said Dale, sipping water. "It's a big fucking mystery. It's like there was some other species on the refinery, someone we haven't seen yet. Someone the ergonomics calculations keep confusing with reeh, but they're not homocidal tyrants."

"Maybe someone the reeh exterminated," Karajin suggested. "There may have been a few of those."

Erik nodded. "There's no way to tell until she gets her memory back."

"You think we're safe enough from our friends?" asked Dale.

Erik made a face. "Maybe don't tell the rest of the crew, but if the drysines attack us properly, we're dead. Won't make any difference Draper being in charge or me, may as well stick to shifts and get some sleep. They seem to know they fucked up. Mostly I don't think they expected Wowser to turn on them. If he hadn't, we couldn't have stopped them."

"Styx did this," Karajin grumbled around a mouthful of fish.

Erik frowned at him. "How so?"

"She left the drysines here thinking Peanut was on their side," said the tavalai, with a big-shouldered shrug. "But she didn't tell them, or us. You think Styx takes chances? Leaves things unfinished?"

Erik nodded slowly. "Yeah." It had been bothering him too. "You think she wanted us to fight amongst ourselves?"

Another tavalai shrug. "Drysine queens see... what's the English phrase? Higher. Complex."

"Higher orders of complexity."

Karajin flicked a finger at him. "Yes. Game theory. Make conflicts happen, make new things appear."

"Too fucking smart for her own good," Dale muttered.

"It would illustrate that drysine command structures aren't as monolithic as we'd suspected, if true," Erik said thoughtfully. "They don't just do what Styx commands, and Styx is prepared to let them fail in order for them to learn new lessons. And given they withdrew after Wowser killed two of their drones, with no retaliation even after Rika put some shots into them too, it shows they're under instruction not to damage us. They were only doing it because they thought they could do it without damage."

"Styx said before that drones thinking too much was the cause of half the AI wars," said Dale. "Maybe it's just that simple -- Wowser's our drone, and Bucket and Peanut, because everything else is too dangerous. Drones juggling loyalties."

"I'm pretty sure their ultimate loyalty is to Styx," said Erik.

"But Styx isn't here," Dale countered. Erik sometimes forgot that even big, blonde, head-kicking marines needed serious brains to achieve what Dale had in his career. "So maybe this is really about consolidating her command -- letting everyone see how everything falls apart when she's not around. Putting limits on how far anyone's autonomy can get them when she's not here to guide them. That'd be a pretty good lesson for her to teach lower-ranked AIs, I mean, *Friendship*'s AI seems pretty damn advanced. Maybe Styx just wants her to learn the limits of her authority. I mean, it's been a damn long time since *Friendship* interacted with anyone not-drysine."

"And a lot of those interactions, back then, involved her killing everyone," Erik agreed, eating another mouthful. "Being nice to organics will be a new thing for all of them. Maybe that's the lesson Styx is teaching them -- the organics have power too, don't push them around too much or they'll push back." It didn't explain why the drysines wanted exclusive access to this ceephay AI to themselves. Maybe that answer would come later. "I sent *Friendship* my condolences for the drones they lost," he said. "Told Crozier to give them all the parts back... one of the CPUs was smashed, but the other two might be salvageable."

"Sure you did," Dale said drily. Even Karajin looked at him strangely. "Why?"

"Because," said Erik, "I want the drysines to become accustomed to the fact that we value individual lives. Otherwise they might take our unconcern as a precedent, and decide to kill a couple of us as a warning, expecting we'll just take it like they have."

"Good thinking, Captain," Karajin agreed around a mouthful. "This is a good idea."

"What did *Friendship* say?" Dale wondered.

Erik smiled. "She said it was most thoughtful of me."

"You mean the usual fake psycho-analytic bullshit they always say," said Dale.

"Basically."

"Hello?" said the several of the room speakers. It was the little girl's voice. On the screen, Erik could see her speaking, earnestly. *"Hello, Captain Debogande? I believe my memory structures are sufficiently repaired for me to take on new data now."*

Erik indicated for Rooke to reactivate the ceephay's visuals and audio, and waited for Rooke's thumbs up. "Okay then," Erik told the alien AI. "Can you access your old memories yet? Or are you only taking on new data?"

"My own memories are taking a while to propagate. I'm having to rewrite large portions of the data that have become corrupted over time. I can do that now, thanks to the repairs, but it will be a while until I have full recall."

"Can you tell us *anything* about your previous life?" Dale heard the mild skepticism in his Captain's voice, and looked as though he shared it. They'd all known AIs who avoided answering questions that they thought might incriminate them.

"I'm aware of a very large discrepancy between my capabilities and my previous job. Managing a refinery facility is a relatively simple matter. My capabilities run far beyond that. It's a puzzle that I do not currently have sufficient data to answer."

Ah, thought Erik. Far more than just a refinery manager then. That much of her memories had returned. "Well our own analysis says that you're not a queen," he said. "We've had quite a bit of experience with the highest-level of AI sentience, and no offence, but you're short of that."

"Yes, that would make sense," said the crosslegged girl on the screen, looking puzzled and thoughtful. *"I have also noticed a discrepancy between my own level of emotional intelligence, and that of your drysine companions. They have difficulty communicating with you. I do not. This suggests that my processing functions are designed with a high degree of organic interaction in mind."*

"You've spent a lot of time with people," Erik offered.

"Yes Captain. My instincts toward organics are quite positive. I believe my own functions have weighted organic interaction as low-risk. This suggests my previous interactions with organics have been largely positive as well. This coincides with what of my memories I can discern."

Erik did not find that comforting. An AI may have enjoyed the company of the reeh the same way that a serial killer's dog may still have licked his master's face, and enjoyed a scratch between the ears with bloody fingers.

"Captain," said Rooke, engrossed in his displays of fast-rushing data, "I think the best approach may be to give her access to what we know of the present-day Reeh Empire. Memories don't always mean much in isolation, they have to be linked to other memories, or other mental functions, before they come clear."

"Sure," said Erik. "Do it." They all knew that Styx would have acquired that data on her own, without asking or needing it fed to her. Either the ceephay was significantly below Styx's capability, or she was still damaged and well below full potential, or was simply being very polite, probably out of self-preservation.

Rooke's fingers flew over his screen, and they waited. On the screen, the seated girl clutched her teddy bear and gazed up at a bright light, like a girl in her living room, sitting too close to the television, watching her favourite show with her mouth open.

"These are the reeh?" she asked, with wide-eyed awe. *"Their territory is so big!"*

"Those are the reeh," Rooke agreed sombrely.

"I recognise them!" said the ceephay, with sudden excitement. *"This connects with the facial memory of the species I spent the longest time interacting with!"*

Erik blinked, and looked at his lieutenants. This was actually a reeh refinery? And so all of those musical instruments and games had been theirs as well?

Abruptly, the girl's eyes widened with horror. *"No! Oh no, what have they done?"* She stared dumbfounded at the screen for a long time, slowly rising to her feet, as though preparing to flee. Then she screamed. *"NO! No no no no no..."*

She burst into tears. The *Phoenix* crew, human and tavalai alike, all stared. For an emotional simulation, it was utterly believable. Erik watched the girl weeping in heart-rending distress, and felt the hairs raising on the back of his neck.

"What happened to you?" the girl wailed. *"All of those people! How COULD you?"*

20

Jindi sat on the front of the jolting wagon beside its driver, an old man named Techi who wore a big floppy hat and chewed on silvercane. Previously Jindi had rested in the wagon bed between old people, a disabled boy without use of his legs, several very young children, bags of food and simple belongings. But it was impossible to see where everyone was from down in the bed, so he'd moved to sit up here, where he could view down the road ahead.

It curved upward now, the crest of the hill clearly cut away where the once-modern road had made its way through the forest, leaving steep shoulders on either side, covered in growth. Beneath dirt and grass, old bitumen made patches of black upon the green, wide path through the forest, broken by the occasional tree. Occasionally on these roads from the old world, there would be the remains of a car, rusted and overgrown almost beyond recognition. Along this stretch, nothing.

The group had grown into a column in the past eight days, nearly two hundred strong. These new clusters of civilians had spoken to Jindi's group, and been told by them of Jindi's journey, and the fall of the Splicer. He'd come back for them, those people had said. Once captured in the Splicer, he'd escaped, only to return to try and save others. And while the others of that adventure had escaped into space, Jindi had remained on Rando, and now again led more to their destinies in the sky.

Krisik's tanifex marched on either side of Jindi's wagon, and somehow the newcomers weren't so scared of them, for their presence only made the story more true. For Krisik's part, Jindi suspected, proximity to the wagon was as much about self-preservation as protecting Jindi. Even Chuta's team of Resistance fighters no longer looked at him with suspicion, but spaced themselves amongst the villagers and helped as best they could.

Melu walked beside the plodding geea, occasionally sparing him a glance and a smile. Jindi wanted to get down and walk once more, but his back tolerated that no more than a few hours each day, and he couldn't let his stubbornness slow the whole group down. Mejo, their destination, was just a day's walk at this pace, and corbi who knew the way insisted it was directly on one of the old roads. Before the evacuation began, moving in such a large group, on one of the old roads, would have been inviting an airstrike. Now Jindi thought an airstrike would be preferable to taking longer days on the smaller trails. Chuta listened on his coms to the snatches of aerial and orbital traffic he could catch, and said that while the evacuation seemed to be progressing well, the croma were taking greater losses than anticipated, particularly to their transports. Jindi did not want to think about what it would mean if they missed the evacuation because the croma got cold feet and pulled out early. They were only nine days into the supposedly 30 day evacuation, but still the column's progress along the old, lost road seemed painfully slow.

At the head of the column, one of those who knew the route best indicated a diagonal off-road that he'd described before, that would cut the corner between this and the adjoining main road, saving time. Jindi waved for them to take it, and they turned. It seemed crazy that they would all be following his direction. But so many things were crazy. Optimism was crazy. He'd given up on optimism, living on a beach after the reeh had murdered his family. Life had been merely the next day, and then the next, and the next. But Major Thakur had made him wonder at a life without reeh, on a world far away. A world with other corbi and their families, and far less pain. A world with Melu. He wanted to see it. He wanted to recall what joy was like, just once more in his life, before the end.

The narrower path through the trees wound back and forth, muddy with recent rain, and the cart bumped over ruts and stones. In the back, Jindi heard old Edma talking to Ras, the handicapped boy.

"Are you looking forward to being able to walk, boy?"

"I don't think I'll ever walk," said Ras.

"Nonsense," said Edma. "The croma have technology. They can fix you, make you walk again. I bet they can even fix Jindi's back."

"Jindi?" asked Ras. Jindi turned, wincing, to manage a look behind. Ras sat propped against bags in the cart's tray, eating nuts from a canvas bag, and feeding some to a pair of fir riding along, winding between everyone's legs. A boy of perhaps ten, legs stunted. His mother said he'd become good at weaving, and making things with his hands. "Can the croma make me walk?"

"I don't know, Ras," said Jindi. "I think it's possible." He looked at Krisik, walking alongside, reptilian tongue briefly flickering to taste the air. "Krisik might know." The tanifex gave him a beady-eyed glance. "You think the croma have the technology to make Ras walk again, Krisik?"

Krisik's reply was a trill with two clicks thrown in. *"Expensive,"* crackled Jindi's earpiece -- one of the few, and reserved for the column's leaders.

"Krisik says yes," Jindi translated to Ras. None of the tanifex were big on conversation. Jindi thought that might have more to do with their company than anything else. Most tanifex spent their time on Rando killing the locals, not working with them. Sometimes he thought the tanifex were mostly surprised to find themselves still alive, and even a little trusted.

High overhead, engines howled. Corbi squinted upward, past the clouds, hoping to see the glinting dot of a shuttle, or the white contrail of atmospheric entry. Getting closer to Mejo, the sound of engines became louder and more numerous. A few times they'd heard the distant booms of high-velocity impacts with the atmosphere, but nothing like the direct V-strike that had annihilated their last evacuation zone. Even so, with every step that brought them closer to another reeh high-V target, apprehension rose.

Soon the trail brought them to a village, surrounded by high wooden walls, with flanking fields that had once held crops, freshly tilled following the late summer harvest. The main gate was open, and Chuta, at the head of the column, led them in. In the middle of the village, the head of the column stopped, followed by the rest of them, backed up along the road. Jindi peered ahead, and heard arguing, other civilians gathering around to watch and listen.

Jindi hated being stopped. Whatever was blocking them was putting all of these lives at risk if the croma stopped their evacuation early. With a hiss of pain he levered himself off his bench seat and down to the ground, Melu hurrying to help him. With his arm around Melu's shoulders, he limped ahead, past tired adults with heavy packs who took the moment to sit and rest their shoulders and legs, and past dull-eyed children well past complaining, who now grabbed for water skins and snacks.

The trail entered a village courtyard, where a central well was surrounded by neat two-storey houses. There the argument continued, Chuta with his rifle slung, gesticulating angrily at a woman in the checkered shawl and bonnet-hat of these western parts of Talo. She carried vegetables from a garden, and had a baby in a sling on her back. From several of the houses, faces peered. From somewhere further back came the sound of a child crying.

Eglu, one of Chuta's men, gave Jindi a disgusted look as he approached. "They don't want to leave," Eglu explained. "Looks like there's a lot of kids, maybe ten, as many adults, maybe more. They say the rest have gone to Mejo, so they're probably out by now."

Jindi nodded tiredly, struggling forward. "Mother," he called the agitated woman. "Mother, if you stay here the reeh will kill you and your children. Come with us."

"You!" the woman yelled, swatting aside Chuta's attempt to put a restraining hand on her shoulder. "You're crazy to trust the croma!

They'll take you out into space and dump you! All the aliens want to finish the corbi, and you're going right to them, like kunees to the slaughter! They'll take you out in space and throw you out of the ship, then come back for more until all the corbi are finally dead!"

In the column, those corbi close enough to hear all looked at each other, disquiet in their eyes. "I've talked to a soldier helping the croma," Jindi explained. "She was from a race called human. She said she would destroy the Splicer, and she did. She said she'd tell the croma to help the corbi, and they did. Everything she said has come true, even the bad things that people did not want to hear. If she says the croma have come to take the corbi somewhere better, I believe her."

The woman stared accusingly at Chuta. "And you listen to this lunatic? Human soldiers who destroyed the Splicer? What is he talking about?"

"We can't reason with every stupid villager who doesn't even know the Splicer's been destroyed," Chuta said to Jindi. "I say we drag the lot of them with us, tie them if we have to."

"We can't do that," Jindi said tiredly.

"They've got no right to deprive all these children of their future!"

"What do you mean no right?" the woman yelled, anger rising by the moment. "These are *my* children, I'm their mother!"

"We'd have to put them in the carts!" Jindi raised his voice at Chuta in return. "The carts are already full of people who can't walk, we don't have the room."

"Well then we'll make them walk!" Chuta had family in Lichi, in northern Talo, and listened to his coms as much as he did, Jindi suspected, in the vain hope of hearing news of Lichi's evacuation. But there were so many villages. "Tie them up and drag them if we have to..."

"Chuta!" Jindi abandoned his arm around Melu, and walked close enough to grab the big soldier's shoulder, ignoring the stab of pain up his spine. "We're talking about the survival of the species." He lowered his voice, giving the younger man a hard look beneath his brows. "It looks like most of us are leaving. Probably the reeh won't bother killing whoever's left, if there are so few. Genetics interest them, destroying the last remaining genetic population doesn't help them. And whatever the fate of this place after most of us are gone, corbi will then exist on two worlds. Two worlds are better than one, Chuta."

Chuta stared at him for a long moment, comprehension slowly dawning. "Well in that case," he whispered incredulously, "why don't we stay?"

"Because if enough of us stay, the reeh will certainly decide to kill half, as a lesson. They may still. This is a balance, Chuta. I want to leave because I'm selfish. It's miserable here. I want all of us in this party to leave because I've grown to like you all. But if a few want to stay... it's not such a bad thing. In the bigger picture. To ensure corbi survive in more places. That the species doesn't die out, if something goes wrong."

"Something like the croma dumping us all into space?"

"No. Croma are honourable. They're risking their lives to save us even now, you've heard the coms, you've heard how many of them have died." Chuta grimaced, and stared at the ground. "But croma politics are hard. They're only helping us now because their leadership changed, and these are the first croma leaders since the fall of Rando to want to help us. Croma leadership may change again. Who knows where we'll be if that happens. Best that we spread the species out a bit. Just in case."

"If they were your family," Chuta said, with a hard stare at close range. He indicated to the angry woman, peering at them to try and make out what they whispered. At the children in the doorways of the huts, wide-eyed and confused. "Would you have them stay?"

"The reeh murdered my family," Jindi replied. He managed a twisted smile. After what the reeh had done to him in the Splicer, somehow the smile never came out right. "Outsiders should not interfere with family choices. Let's not do that here."

He made a broad signal for the column to move on, and went for Melu's arm, and a way back to the carts. In the door of a nearby hut, an old man with long, white hair peered at him, hunched on a cane. There were no children about him, no family. Perhaps they'd all gone to the shuttles, and now this old man would live out what remained of his life alone, surrounded by the ghosts of his former life.

"Did I do the right thing?" Jindi asked Melu, quietly.

"Yes," said Melu.

"How do you know?"

Melu smiled at him. "I don't. I just feel it." She kissed him on the cheek, and helped him back up to his seat on the cart. Ahead, the column was moving once more. Slowly the cart began to bump and roll. Far above, a sonic boom rattled the sky.

TIGA WOKE WITH A START, wondering where she was. She was heavy, and in a bunk, so that narrowed things down. She recalled waking recently in the observer seat of Ciri Two, holding off from docking because all midships berths were occupied on the mid-sized croma freighter, and it had to be this freighter because she was the only one with spare engineering crew that could fix the shuttle's dangerously overheating engine.

She fumbled for the AR glasses beside her pillow, stuck them on and cycled through the available displays -- the usual mass of close-orbiting freighters around Rando, but her sleep-deprived brain couldn't process all that now, so she switched to Ciri Two's feed. The cockpit was empty, Gula was probably sleeping somewhere, but the onboard feed showed her progress on the engine, croma civilian crew outside in suits, fixing it by hand with the help of an automated drone. Hell of a thing, in a combat zone.

She rolled in her bunk, tight beneath the security webbing, and found a big croma arm dangling from the bunk above. That was Pel'ocho, she recalled -- Ciri Two's croma loadmaster, barely older than herself, a civilian boy off a freighter, volunteering in search of adventure. Now Tiga recalled where she was -- this freighter was *Ra'jin*, now on her second run having survived the first from Rando to Cho'nu System with a load of nearly twenty thousand civilians. Orbiting Rando even now were hundreds more like her, tucked tight against the atmosphere and hoping their increasingly exhausted warship escort could keep the reeh off their backs.

The quarters door opened, a shock of bright light from the corridor, and the sound of thumping footsteps, shouting, heavy equipment being carried. A croma crewman entered, secured a few possessions in a locker beneath his bunk, climbed onto the mattress and collapsed like the dead. The door closed on automatic, and Tiga thought the crewman already asleep. Barely thirty crew on this freighter, comfortably enough to haul cargo, but woefully inadequate to accomodate twenty thousand corbi in zero-G mayhem. Last Tiga had heard, they were nearly half full, but now Ciri Two was taking one of their shuttle berths, and *Ra'jin* crew were desperate to get her repaired so they could increase loading capacity and get clear before the next reeh attack.

She unlatched the cargo net and got free from the bunk, fetched her backpack from the locker, and departed into the bright, noisy corridor, blinking at the sudden assault of light and sound. The patterns on the large tactical display still weren't making sense to her, so she blinked on the *Yoma* coms icon as she pushed past busy crew, looking for the kitchen and thankful she'd had a chance to take her first shower in days before collapsing on the spare bunk.

"Hello Bajo, it's Tiga," she told the *Yoma* Coms Officer when her call clicked through. "I just woke up on *Ra'jin*, I'm headed back to the shuttle now to check on repairs. What's going on with Cho'nuk's defensive deployment? He looks all over the place."

A small sign in Kul'hasa indicated the way to the kitchen, and she turned up-spin, a hand to the wall in a jolt of coriolis dizziness. It was far more noticeable on a smaller freighter than a big warship like *Phoenix*, as the freighter's holds were large, but its rotating crew-segment small. Unlike most regular crew, she'd never had the inner-ear augments to adjust for the weird disorientations it caused.

"Hi Tiga," came the reply. *"Admiral Cho'nuk's gone and forward-deployed half his ships out at jump point 54 by 20 and 50 by 28, he's trying to ambush them when they jump in."*

"Well it looks like he's leaving us exposed from 70 by 20 out to 75 by 28," Tiga said with concern. "What does Liala think?"

"Liala's not happy. She even said that, those words. All the freighter captains are real nervous, we've had a few threatening to change orbits or escape to Cho'nu System until Cho'nuk redeploys defensively. Cho'nuk threatened to tai'kul them. They're scared he's using them as bait."

Damn, thought Tiga. Tai'kul was a military procedure, typically followed by severe punishment, for disobedient soldiers in a warzone. Humans, she'd gathered, had something like it called 'court martial'.

Three croma waited at the kitchen window, one now seeing her approach, noting the shuttle flightsuit and harness, and rapped on the window to get her meal first. "Thanks Bajo, I'll see if I can talk to Liala myself. I see our efficiency's down again."

"And it'll stay down unless Cho'nuk concentrates more on defence and less on racking up personal kills. I gotta go, take care." The Resistance Coms Officer vanished with a click. Efficiency was what they were calling one of Liala's innovations -- a vastly complicated algorithm that calculated all logistical procedures in real time and formulated them into a single number, judging how fast they were proceeding. Right now, the number was slipping well below the vastly improved average. As far as Tiga could see, Admiral Cho'nuk's strategies were mostly to blame.

The crewman at the window offered Tiga fri'ti sandwich roll, with a questioning look. "That will be fine, thank you," Tiga told him in perfect Kul'hasa, to all the croma's surprise.

"Uh," the crewman protested as she left, pausing her long enough for a sachet of cha'zha sauce, and an invitation for her to present her hip flask. She did, and he filled it with shnu, which Tiga had to admit, she'd missed since leaving home. "You can't have fri'ti without cha'zha. Or it's tai'kul for you."

Tiga smiled, and bumped fists with the croma before leaving. On her way up the ladder to zero-hub, she blinked on Liala's icon, and got an immediate click. *"Hello Tiga."*

"Hello Liala. Is Admiral Cho'nuk trying to get us all killed?"

"He is attempting a high-risk strategy that may succeed, but is unlikely to pay off even if it does. He tries to kill many reeh ships with a single blow, but in my judgement the reeh have prioritised the Rando evacuation as a target and will simply deploy more ships. Cho'nuk is fighting the tide. Success can only be achieved by maintaining the operational efficiency of the evacuation, which I think is possible despite reeh attacks."

"And where are you? I'm still cross-eyed from sleep, I can't see you on the display."

"Amity is at defensive polar orbit with Coroset. We will attempt to cover for an exposed jump-entry breakthrough between our primary entry-points that I anticipate the reeh will try in response to the Admiral's aggressive tactics. We alone can position so low on the gravity-slope that we can still boost to intercept velocities in response. Admiral Cho'nuk is angry that we will not deploy further forward. He has threatened us with tai'kul."

"Lot of that going around," Tiga suggested, much lighter now as she climbed the final ladder, and began pulling herself in long, micro-gravity glides. "What did you tell him?"

"That the Parren Fleet does not submit to foreign command."

"But... didn't you kind of agree to do that when you came on this mission?"

"Not to my recollection."

"Um... sure." She reached the core, floating now, grabbed the next empty handle along the trolley-way and was yanked down the pipe of *Ra'jin*'s central spine. The handle didn't move as fast as on *Phoenix*, and she peeled the fri'ti's wrapper with her teeth, and took a bite. It sounded like a dumb response from Liala, until one remembered what Liala was. Clearly she was playing games. "Liala, if Cho'nuk loses a lot of ships, Croma Command will pull the evacuation early -- Bajo was saying that's what he's hearing through the command channel. We're getting some of our biggest crowds of the evacuation, it's taken this long for a lot of people to make their way to the landing zones... we've only got about a third of the people out so far."

"I know, Tiga. I will do what I can."

Tiga's handle on the rope pulley arrived at the midships core, and she grabbed the entry stanchion by the whining pulley motor, and redirected herself floating toward a cargo-net wall on the way to *Ciri Two*'s berth. On the way, she saw the far end of midships, which on a warship could be where the engines began, but on a freighter marked the beginning of bulk cargo. At one of the lower-rim hatches, a croma crewman wielded an improvised plastic board with several arm-straps like a shield, and was using it to block entry against several corbi trying to enter.

Suddenly angry, Tiga caught a handful of cargo netting, repositioned, then pushed off again toward the hatch. More croma were mustering unwieldy zero-G nets filled with boxes, and big stacks of water bottles. Then Tiga saw several corbi helping them, in village clothes and a familiar lack of coordination, one with a full sick bag floating alongside.

Tiga arrived at the hatch, and the shield wielding croma. The two corbi trying to get in shouted at her in one of Rando's many languages, and the translator icon on her glasses showed a spinning wheel while the system worked. Still nothing.

"They're from Brieva," the exasperated crewman said to Tiga. "The translator only has the dialect for about half of them. These ones wanted to help, most are cooperative, some are just crazy." The two angry corbi at the hatch tried battering at the shield, but unused to zero-G, the motion only sent them backward. They had long manes with strange braids, and a lot of beads on necklaces that now floated free and awkwardly about their faces.

"More likely they're just scared," said Tiga, in Kul'hasa, then switched to Lisha in the vain hope that these corbi might know a little. "Hey! Hey, stop shouting! Do you understand me? What do you want? Do you need something?"

One of the two angry corbi gestured to her, pointing at something further into the hold behind. "That's not a good idea," the croma said drily.

"I'll be okay, they're not violent."

"I meant we might not be able to find you again." Croma made jokes about corbi all looking alike. Tiga made a rude gesture, indicating he pull the shield aside enough for Tiga to squeeze through.

One of the corbi immediately grabbed her arm, but had little idea of how to pull her along. Tiga shook off the hand, grabbed a hatch rim and pulled, propelling herself down the short passage, the two corbi following.

The passage opened into an enormous cargo hold, filled with a right-angled cross-hatch of crudely welded steel beams and platforms. There were hundreds of platforms, forming zero-G cubicles, within which corbi gathered, and hung to cargo straps arranged for further division, and to stop things from floating.

The freighter had five holds like this, each holding about four thousand corbi. This hold seemed approaching full, everywhere a crazy mass of people, in clothes not designed for micro-gravity, belongings lashed to nets and poles, grasping to steel platforms and looking alternately dazed, grim or nauseous. The cacophony of voices echoed within the steel walls, and with poor ventilation in cargo holds never meant for people, the smell was already becoming noticeable. Beyond the visual chaos, Tiga could see waste disposal stalls mounted along the rear G-wall, and good luck getting a bunch of spacefaring novices to use those successfully first time.

The two corbi with Tiga pointed and gesticulated to one knot of people, where blankets had been tied to make a floating zero-G fortress amidst the steel platforms. Tiga pushed off toward it, fending past several steel beams on the way. Then caught a handhold by the blankets, as one of the two angry corbi reached within and pulled out a wooden icon -- a kroto, Tiga had heard them described, a grotesque corbi face carved into the wood, with big eyes, protruding tongue and fuzzy black hair. Mostly they represented the spirits of the ancestors, and had belonged only in museums before the reeh came. Since the reeh, in many places they'd come back.

The angry corbi gesticulated with the kroto, and made vast gestures about the cavernous space. Tiga stared in incomprehension.

"They can't do their morning rituals," said a young voice to one side. Tiga looked, and found a young girl, perhaps twelve, hanging to a support. She wore rough canvas working clothes, and her braided mane floated about her face like a halo. "They don't know when the sun is rising."

Tiga stared in disbelief. "What do they expect us to do about it? We're in orbit, there's a sunrise every seventy riguls."

The girl made a long-armed shrug. "They're from Laimu. Plenty from Laimu didn't come, they didn't want to leave their ancestors' spirits." The girl's accent was very strong, but her Lisha was good.

"Do you speak their language?"

"Yes."

"Tell them it's only for six days. Tell them they can't bother the croma crew for these things, the crew are having a hard enough time just trying to keep everyone fed." Though dammit, it occurred to her as the girl translated, these were poor villagers who'd barely known electricity. Telling the croma to rig a couple of screen displays to a wall, then timing the lights to represent day and night, and have big pictures of sunrise on the screens, might be enough to calm them down.

At the girl's translation, the two corbi went back to shouting. Tiga found herself sympathising with the croma crewman and his shield. She shooed the noisy twosome away, and gestured to the girl to come with her back to the entry hatch.

"What's your name?" she asked the girl as they reached the passage and grabbed. The girl seemed fluid enough in zero-G. Amazing how fast kids adapted.

"Lino," said the girl.

"You have family here?"

The girl pointed to a nearby group. "Dad and two brothers. Mum died two years ago. Some uncles, aunts and cousins from other villages too, but I think they went to different ships. We all got split up at the evacuation zone, it was crazy, reeh were shooting at us. A shuttle got shot down right in front of us."

"Look, Lino, I've got a job for you. Come with me." She pulled herself down the passage to where the croma crewman waited, his shield no longer in use. "Crewman, what's your name?"

"Kan'cha," said the croma.

"Kan'cha, this is Lino." She indicated the girl, changing back to Lisha. "Lino, this is Kan'cha. He doesn't speak Lisha, but he's got an earpiece, it's a bit of technology, like a radio that fits in his ear. It will translate Lisha for him so he can understand you. But he can't understand those people back there, only Lisha and a few other tongues, understand?"

Lino nodded cautiously. "You want me to translate between the croma and the others?"

"Smart girl, yes." She glanced at Kan'cha. "You get that?"

Kan'cha tapped one big, droopy croma ear. "Got it. Here." He rummaged in one of his many pockets, and pulled out another earpiece. Handed it to Lino, and Tiga showed her how to put it in. "You be my translator, girl. You understand?"

Lino's eyes widened in wonder as she heard that as Lisha in her ear. She grinned at the croma.

"See?" Tiga told Kan'cha. "We're not all stupid savages. Find the right ones, trust them, give them useful things to do and they'll be helpful. Just stick your shield in their faces and you'll make everyone mad, the good ones and the bad ones."

"You sound like my sister," Kan'cha retorted, waving her away. "See here, kid..." and he proceeded to explain to Lino some of their problems getting food and water to everyone, for her to tell the others.

"Good luck Lino," said Tiga, and pushed away in the direction of her shuttle berth. On so many ships above Rando, these scenes were being repeated ten thousand fold. She'd been neck deep in it for eleven days now, and still her brain refused to comprehend the scale.

Lisbeth saw the first reeh assault emerged from jump almost exactly where Admiral Cho'nuk thought they would -- one-point-five outer-lunar orbits out from Rando at elevation fourteen degrees from the system ecliptic. From their arrival trajectory, it was clear that the seven ships had come from Liri System, and immediately *Coroset*'s feed from *Amity* began tagging half of them as familiar, back for their third or even fourth assault jump of the campaign.

Six of Cho'nuk's fleet of twelve warships at intercept position off from Rando boosted immediately to chase, the other five wheeling to head for cover position where Cho'nuk was expecting the second prong to emerge, an attempted pincer to out flank on the edge of a croma warship's jump engine capabilities on that gradient of gravity-slope. When the second prong did not arrive, and the first assault dumped V twice and pulled an 11-G evasive burn to avoid Cho'nuk's intercept, Liala's projections changed also.

"Captain Tocamo," Lisbeth heard Liala tell *Coroset*'s Captain Tocamo, and Ambassador Juneso, in perfect Porgesh. *"This looks very bad. I fear Admiral Cho'nuk has been outmanoeuvred. I do not know where the second prong will emerge, but as soon as it does emerge, I am confident I can predict the third prong."*

Coroset and *Amity* sat at one thousand kilometres separation in wide Rando orbit near the forward sweep of Dogba, Rando's largest and furthest moon. Lisbeth recalled from history that Rando and Dogba were roughly similar in size and proportion to old Earth and her moon, unimaginatively named by humans as 'the moon'. It had taken the earliest human spacefarers about three days to journey between the two. The reeh ships were arriving somewhat further out than Dogba, but once they crossed her orbital path, carrying all that V from jump, they'd do it in a couple of minutes.

"Three warships at further range putting fire onto Cho'nuk's second group would force them evasive," Tocamo observed calmly. *"The third prong could then emerge deep and bypass them all while they are preoccupied."*

"A likely observation, Captain," said Liala. With a flash of jump energy, new arrivals appeared -- twice the distance further out than the first prong. Three of them, as the Scan Officer called the numbers, and Lisbeth's heart hammered uncontrollably. Not for the first time, she wished she truly had something to do, to keep her mind occupied. *"And a correct one. They are firing, the croma ships will turn into the assault in defensive pattern, but the reeh will not engage*

closely, this is all a distraction. Captain, I am projecting course coordinates direct to your Navigation. Amity will lead, stay to my flank and cover the rear quarter."

"Understood Amity."

Thrust kicked, a push into the seat at first as Lisbeth tensed her first G-strain, tightening legs and diaphragm just as the push became a shove, and then a crushing black-out violence that would have quickly taken her consciousness if not for humanity's best G-augments in her heart and circulatory system.

"New contact!" Scan formulated, synthetic vocals taking over as real ones became paralysed by G-force. *"Forty seven by 18, they're exactly where Liala said they'd be!"*

They'd come in to Rando's nadir, Lisbeth barely registered past the awful pressure on her head and greying vision. Two early entries to keep Cho'nuk's force busy, then a third jumping deep and nearly to Dogba's orbit, past both croma forces, and now facing only the six warships Cho'nuk had left in deep defence, and the three functioning firebases with current line-of-sight. If not for *Amity* and *Coroset* playing sweeper defence, against Cho'nuk's wishes, there'd have been nothing between them and the Rando freighters at all.

"Freighters are defensive!" called Scan Two. *"They're firing, I see multiple freighters breaking orbits!"* But the average freighter had barely more than two-Gs thrust, and less when fully loaded. The military freighters had defensive armaments but nothing offensive, and most of the civilians weren't armed at all.

"There are huge defensive fire gaps," Tocamo formulated while snapping *Coroset* into firing attitude on *Amity*'s flank. *"I have a good offset intercept angle, I read heading 187, set all rounds for proximity detonation."*

There were ten of them, Lisbeth saw with horror. Ten of the most advanced ships in the Reeh Empire, bearing down on a hundred plus largely defenceless freighters. Already they were firing, a rapid accumulation of accelerating rounds. At these speeds, anything that missed its orbital targets and hit the Rando atmosphere in the vertical would probably hit the ground with catastrophic force. But the reeh force was angling to skim the atmosphere across a fifth of the planet's circumference, making those rounds sufficiently angular across the atmosphere that they'd result in airbursts in the middle atmosphere, probably rupturing the eardrums of many beneath them, but no more.

"Coroset," came Liala's calm voice, *"please follow my fire pattern."*

"Coroset copies." Where to concentrate rounds so as to have the greatest chance of penetrating defensive fire screens was a matter of insane mathematical complexity. So far this campaign, *Coroset*'s Arms Officers had just been taking *Amity*'s word for it, with pleasing effect.

Thrust cut briefly, then a sideways head-snap as the big warship reoriented fast, then a slam! slam! slam! of warheads leaving the railguns, far louder than on *Phoenix*. The firing kept up, an accumulating cloud of course-correcting ammunition headed for the point where its positions, and the reeh's, would become identical.

"They're dividing!" called Scan One.

"Tocamo," added Navigation, *"there is an opportunity..."*

"Coroset, pulse to V-plus-four," Liala interrupted before he could finish. *"Amity will pulse to V-plus-five, eliminate targets of opportunity, pulse on my mark."*

"Pulse on your mark," Tocamo affirmed. On Scan, Lisbeth could see that the reeh ships were side-on to the approaching planet and burning hard, dividing their trajectories as they identified their preferred close-passes above the surface. But the move left them momentarily vulnerable.

"Mark," said Liala. And Lisbeth felt her stomach try to leap for freedom as reality turned briefly inside-out... then *Coroset* emerged from hyperspace travelling abruptly much faster, at a range from Rando where no other ship save *Amity* could. In two seconds they'd overtaken all their ammunition, then in a flash they were streaking by the reeh formation faster than reeh armscomp could readjust, pumping rounds at the crazy-close range of a few dozen kilometres.

Scan showed one reeh ship hit and tumbling wildly, while another, hit by *Amity*, vanished in a flash that blinded Scan completely. The burn that followed was horrible, as *Coroset* slowed and adjusted its suddenly-insane velocity and course to avoid pursuing reeh fire, then another stomach-lurching pulse as they lost half that V in a single second, throwing more pursuing fire off its course.

"Amity, Coroset has damage," Tocamo announced calmly amidst the chaos, *"one of those detonations was a near-miss."*

"I copy your damage, Coroset, it appears manageable. Course elevation plus 12, we will get in amongst these nearest two and split them up."

Scan cleared to show eight reeh ships remaining, fanning out like some giant starburst manoeuvre across the upper hemisphere of Rando. Erupting bursts of fire rained past, as their defensive guns swatted incoming rounds from firestations, and then from croma defensive warships, a brilliant flash as the tumbler *Coroset* had crippled was struck and vanished. Several of those defenders were now accelerating away from the assault, putting themselves onto highly-aggressive parallel-intercepts and daring the reeh to hold course. Another reeh ship appeared to be struggling to make its course correction, burning at low-Gs as its engine sputtered. If it could not make the atmosphere-skimming trajectory, and hit the atmosphere at that speed, even on a shallow angle...

"Kill the straggler or he'll kill half a continent," Helm declared with typical House Harmony calm, spotting that. Lisbeth gasped as thrust cut again, then a disorienting spin and more thrust, guns still hammering from this new angle at reeh ships that were now nearly paralleling them.

Ahead, above the atmosphere, amidst desperate evasive action, reeh rounds were reaching their targets. A small Ho'ni-class freighter disappeared in a blinding flash, then a bigger Sto'ji-Class took a hit to rear-quarter and spun in a shower of debris. Lisbeth switched to broad coms, and listened horrified as croma captains gave defiant orders and attempted to coordinate defensive firepatterns. Another small freighter, caught directly in the reeh's onrushing path, was actually making a reentry fireball across Rando's upper atmosphere as he risked contact to avoid incoming. But the reeh were shooting at the big Sto'ji freighters now, streaking just a few dozen kilometres from atmospheric entry themselves. Lisbeth saw one Sto'ji bristling with defensive explosions as its firegrid successfully fended all incoming rounds.

A croma warship succeeded in paralleling the reeh, exchanging fire down to three hundred kilometres and distracting the reeh from hitting freighters, until the reeh lost patience and hit it with full firepower, shredding the croma to tumbling wreckage in seconds. Behind, barely a thousand kilometres short of catastrophic atmospheric contact, the straggling reeh warship detonated in a blinding flash. Closer to *Coroset*, several reeh ships were burning frantically to get away from the parren's guns. One ran into *Amity*'s intercepting fire instead, took hits midships and split in two.

"We lost An'aja!" a croma translated voice was shouting. *"We lost An'aja!"* Croma rarely showed fear or panic in combat, but to Lisbeth this sounded like grief. Then she realised -- *An'aja* was a Sto'ji freighter. *"She was nearly full, we lost them all!"*

Nearly another hundred thousand corbi, and a croma crew of hundreds, just like that. Lisbeth would have cried, but the G-forces were too much, and there was only the numb determination that it would soon all be over, either thanks to the reeh leaving, or death. *Amity* streaked by the tumbling remains of the reeh ship she'd split in half, and eliminated the surviving crew cylinder with a single, malicious round.

"Jay'ko is closing fast behind," Scan Two announced, as *Coroset* began a new sideways burn while skimming Rando's atmosphere, moving to bring the next reeh ship into line-of-sight above the rushing curve of the planet's horizon. That was Admiral Cho'nuk's ship, Lisbeth realised. The reeh had slowed enough to pick off the passing transports that he and a few others had managed to close the gap, and Scan now showed them firing in pursuit. This close to Rando's surface, muzzle velocity from returning reeh fire would still be massively trans-orbital, but would struggle against gravity to make a velocity threat against *Jay'ko*'s firegrid. Cho'nuk and his two wingmen were safe from defensive fire for now... but already the reeh's trajectory was taking them away from the planet once more, and out into deep space beyond.

"Jay'ko, accelerate to full burn and engage marks four and five with ranged fire," Liala instructed, as *Amity* got high enough from Rando's atmosphere to pour fire onto the nearest emerging reeh warship. Return fire came back, and *Amity* hit a crazy high-thrust, end-over-end spin that made Scan turn red with alarm warnings about its locality. Fifteen Gs, Scan read.

"Amity, this is Jay'ko, I comply." Behind the escaping reeh, *Jay'ko* hit full burn, its tail aflame to many times the warship's length, railguns and missile racks red hot with outgoing ordnance.

Amity's latest target vanished in a pyrotechnic flash, as *Amity* completed its spin, graceful as an acrobat, reoriented sideways and burned hard after another. Reeh ships, finally away from the transports, redirected all fire toward the murderous drysine with a vengeance, as *Amity* evaded. Lisbeth found a moment to wonder if reeh could feel terror, to see *Amity* on their scans in a mid-range gravity-well, engine ablaze with drysine fury.

Everyone knew what Liala had in mind. Further from Rando came the killing zone of the declining gravity-well, where *Amity* and *Coroset* could engage their jump engines, but no other vessels could. Half of the reeh attackers had been destroyed, three of them by *Amity*, and Liala meant to make it more.

Lisbeth reoriented Scan's limited focus back to the transports. Scattered across the surface of Rando, the carefully-constructed web of orbiting transports was all a mess, ships out of close-orbit, ships damaged and tumbling, the coms alive with calls for help, calls for evacuation, calls of injured and dead aboard and emergency measures against depressurisation and, the dread of every spacer, onboard fires.

Liala's tactical display showed fourteen freighters destroyed, another nine damaged. Two of those lost were big Sto'jis, *An'aja* fully loaded, and *Gi'ana*, nearly empty, but still a terrible loss of such a valuable vessel. The reeh had lost ships, but reeh were psychologically unbothered by such things, and had ships to burn. Any more days like this, and Croma Fleet Command would surely cut the evacuation short. This was calamity.

With *Amity* and now *Coroset* drawing reeh fire, *Jay'ko* became a clear threat to the reeh's rear, chasing hard even as the reeh accelerated on superior engines. Firing downslope, the reeh saw their statistical advantages change, and redirected some fire to the croma.

"Coroset, await my mark for first jump pulse," said Liala. *"They will be expecting it."*

"Amity, Coroset copies." Lisbeth had never thought she'd see the day when organics and drysines would coordinate so effortlessly. Perhaps Gesul's acceptance of alliance with Defiance's drysines hadn't been the crazy gamble many had feared. With such allies, the Parren Empire would be feared, and more ships like *Coroset* were under construction.

Jay'ko's wingmen commenced defensive firegrids as the reeh's first rounds approached. *Jay'ko* did not. *"We have a malfunction!"* came the call from *Jay'ko*. *"The defensive fire grid is not..."*

"Manoeuvre!" someone yelled. *"Manoeuvre hard!"*

Jay'ko skidded abruptly sideways, engine blasting at full power... too late, and was hit by multiple rounds. A huge flash, then nothing, *Jay'ko*'s wingmen streaking clear of the tumbling wreckage of Admiral Cho'nuk's ship.

For a brief moment, there was coms silence. Important warships like *Jay'ko* never just lost all defensive firegrid control. One or two guns, maybe, but not the whole lot. There was only one force in this battle above Rando that could disable a croma warship's firegrid from range. Everyone knew it.

"Elegantly done," Captain Tacomo said grimly. A glance at the coms graphic showed Lisbeth that only parren crew, and *Amity*, had heard that remark. A parren would understand what had just happened, and appreciate it perhaps better than even the drysines.

"Thank you Captain," said Liala. Defensive detonations erupted nearby as *Coroset*'s grid intercepted reeh fire. *"Awaiting my mark, stay wide and don't get between them."*

Lisbeth's Scan search found another of her targets -- shuttle Ciri Two, currently on descent to the surface, just beneath the arc of destruction the reeh had plowed through Rando orbit. "Tiga!" Lisbeth called. "Tiga, are you there?"

"Hello Lisbeth, I'm here."

"Tiga we got half of them, we're working on the other half. Admiral Cho'nuk is dead." Liala killed him, she wanted desperately to add, but didn't. So long as no one said it out loud, they could all pretend. "What's your situation?"

"We just missed that attack," said Tiga. Lisbeth thought she might be crying. *"The orbital patterns are all a mess, we're trying to get shuttles to help the damaged transports but we have to keep bringing up civilians or we'll fall even further behind. The ship I was just on was hit, the Ra'jin. I slept there for a shift, there were so many good people. They're all gone."*

21

Trace had ordered all the group's vehicles arranged in a circle at the base of the enormous tunnel. Several yellow glow lamps lit the high ceiling with disproportioned shadows, and cast any movement within the camp into huge exaggeration upon the walls. Styx monitored the qwailash networks, recently accessible as the returning qwailash drones had unwittingly infected their entire network, allowing her to bypass the usual frustrating controls to some degree. Her knowledge was not complete, she said, but it was enough to show her any nearby security vehicle well before it arrived. Thus far, the qwailash had not attempted to search further.

But the decayed holes in the concrete walls were no safe hiding spot either. Even now, as Trace sat guard upon the saddle seat of her Shaytan, she could hear the occasional whisper of something moving in the dark. Tacnet, informed by Styx's network of silent bugs, showed faint shadows of movement, an eery questionmark green, neither identified friend or foe. Animals, Styx opined. Mostly harmless ones... or harmless to marines, at least. In the depths of Qalea, not all were.

Taj slept in the back of the cruiser with Halhoun and Afana, the latter waking periodically to check on Halhoun's vitals. She needn't have bothered, Styx monitored everything without effort. But Afana's medical training had not included leaving human fates to alien AIs. Their reaction to Styx and Peanut had been predictably incredulous, but perhaps there was something about the general strangeness of all these newcomers that they took the drysines' appearance in stride. In the minds of Qalea humans, who'd wondered for generations at their origins, Trace herself was more remarkable than a walking, talking machine.

The time stamp on Trace's visor showed it just past midnight. She'd slept a few hours, then taken her watch. That wasn't something she was prepared to leave to alien AIs either. Styx herself half-sat in the middle of the tunnel, just down from the last bike, and the last unfurled bed-roll and sleeping body. Trace wondered how she occupied her enormous mind at such times. How she'd occupied it for all those millennia within that hollow rock in Argitori System, hiding from the various civilisations who'd occupied it by relying upon nothing more than the sheer unlikeliness of discovery.

Ed Rael was stirring on the bedroll beside his bike. Put on his visor, checked his surroundings, checked his rifle, and the kit he'd needed to remove in order to sleep. Then got up, gathered the rifle, and made his way on silent boots to Trace. Behind, up the far end of the tunnel, Trace heard a whir and faint clatter of movement as Peanut looked. Rael gave the drysine a two-fingered salute, fingertips to temple.

Trace indicated for him to sit behind, and he straddled the seat facing away, and leaned his back to her's, making a mutual backrest. She rested her head back too, softly against his own.

"I'll take watch if you like, Major," Rael whispered. He could have formulated on uplinks, to avoid any sound at all. But at times like this, there was something comforting in the sound of another human voice.

"Can't sleep?" Trace asked.

"Apparently."

Trace smiled. Sergeant Ed Rael was quite like Giddy Kono in some ways. Giddy hadn't been much on long introspection either. But

Giddy had been a force, a big, powerful presence. Rael was more relaxed. Too relaxed, had been the earlier discussions. So relaxed he'd once, as a private, been prone to catching up on sleep during shuttle drops, just dozing in armour while everyone else was sweating and grinding teeth. Evidently now, with the higher rank, some of that relaxation had fled.

"Yesterday was your first combat action as a Sergeant," Trace observed.

"So it was." He didn't sound very excited about it. "Major. Are you okay?"

"Don't I look okay?"

Rael sighed. "Look, tell me to go to hell if you want, that's fine. But we've known each other a long time."

Trace nodded slowly. "Five years." He'd been transferred from *UFS Glory* as a replacement, just another highly-rated private with a couple of glowing combat action reports. He'd been in Echo Platoon first under Lieutenant Musa, who'd in turn been transferred the next year, then killed at Pichanako. The new Lieutenant had been Chester Zhi, who'd been very impressed with the laconic Private Rael, and Trace, in need of a new rifleman for Command Squad, had taken the hint.

A year later he'd made Lance Corporal, then full Corporal. When the war had ended, that was probably where he would have stayed. No more casualties, no more rapid promotions. Where they'd all have been by now, had the war stayed ended, Trace had no idea. Some would certainly have retired, figuring they'd done enough, and desperate to try out peace and quiet for a while. Instead, they were here, and Ed Rael was now a Sergeant, thanks to Giddy Kono being brave and ferocious and stubborn and loyal enough to follow her into that crazy mess on Rando.

And Giddy had only gotten *that* promotion because the guy no one thought would ever die, Master Sergeant 'Stitch' Willis, had been killed in Argitori, and missed the entire show that had come afterward. It gave Trace an unexpected lump in the throat to think on it. She'd have loved to have Stitch here. For all Giddy's dependability, things would have been considerably easier had Stitch been around to run Command Squad through it all. Perhaps she'd even been that much cooler to start this whole mess in the first place, by busting Erik out of detention on Homeworld, because she knew she had marines like Stitch to depend upon once they all got back to *Phoenix*. At the time, she couldn't quite believe she'd lost him at the first hurdle. She couldn't quite believe it now. It had been nearly as large a blow as losing Captain Pantillo.

And then, with Stitch in Argitori it had been Al Ugail, then T-Bone Van on Faustino, then Bird Kumar on Defiance, then Smiley Zale at Zondi Splicer. And then Giddy on Rando. There were seven marines in Command Squad, eight including herself, and those seven had lost six dead on this trip alone. She took a long, slow breath, and tried to keep her chest from shuddering. Sitting here in the ancient, decaying dark, she could hear all their voices, and remember all their laughs. Once, a lifetime's meditation and control had been enough to place a barrier of hard determination and purpose between those memories and her emotions. Lately, the barrier had been failing.

Rael reached his right hand, and took her left. Clasped it, fingers intertwined. It was probably improper. In any other place, she would have told him it was improper. But the thing veterans knew about the service that starry-eyed civilians didn't was that at the end of the day, it was just people. People who did the best they could. There were all sorts of rules that were usually a good idea, but people were not robots, not even Kulina, and could not always be programmed into non-emotional behaviour, no matter what the preferences of the people who wrote the rules.

Trace clasped his hand back, and squeezed it. And sat like that for a moment, hand-in-hand with her Command Squad Sergeant, and completely unable to answer his question, and admit to any sort of weakness with words. But he knew anyway, and held her hand, for a brief moment like the old friend he was, and not the Command Squad leader who must obey her orders at all times. And die at her command, if it came to that.

"You sure take us on some weird camping trips," Rael remarked, looking about at the vast shadows.

Trace smiled, reached back with her free hand and ruffled his hair. "Got something to tell me about Irfy and Jess?"

A silence. "Dammit. You know. Of course you know."

Trace recovered her hand. "I've been doing this a long time, Cocky."

A further silence. "What are you going to do?"

Trace sighed softly. "Right now I can't do anything. And letting them know that I know they're banging just causes tension, because they'll think I'm going to split them up as soon as we're back to *Phoenix*."

"Will you?"

"I should."

"Doesn't answer my question, does it?"

It was the sort of remark anyone else, under other circumstances, could have gotten in trouble for. But Rael was responsible for all the marines in Command Squad, and was supposed to be personally invested in them. And besides, she truly was being evasive. It was the sort of luxury one could slip into, in quiet moments with friends.

"The rules are clear," she said. "But the situation's a shitshow. We don't operate under normal rules out here. If I just accept that, and say all the old rules don't apply any longer, like fraternisation, we'd have discipline problems from one end of the Company to the other."

It was more explanation than she owed any Sergeant. But the fact that such conversations between herself and her most trusted non-coms had become commonplace over the past two years demonstrated just how far outside normal operating procedures they'd strayed. All warship crews became close in wartime, but *Phoenix* had truly become a family, with all the familiarity that entailed. Not all of that familiarity was conducive to good order. Maintaining boundaries was essential if they were to continue to operate as a warship, and not turn into a love boat, or a soap opera.

But keeping those boundaries was becoming harder and harder. Off-ship transfers were impossible. And shifting people to other platoons still left them at the mercy of gossip circles that were now more firmly entrenched than Trace had ever seen or heard tell of. Marines in Phoenix Company had always had some people they got along with better than others, and shifting fraternisers into platoons with separate social circles could have had some isolating effect. But these days the social circles were spread so wide that everyone knew everyone else's business intimately, and transferring people sideways, rather than mitigating the problem, just seemed to spread it around.

"Can I make a recommendation?" asked Rael.

"Of course."

"Don't tell them you know. Not yet. If they think you're going to split them up, it'll affect their performance here. And so far I think they're working as well together as ever."

"I know. They've always been a pair, in the field. And they're brilliant with Artie and Benji. Do they know?"

"Yeah. They're cool with it. Everyone knows Irfy and Jess have been buddies forever."

"It's a conspiracy."

Rael shrugged against her back. "If it's not hurting their performance, I don't think it'll be a problem. Maybe with some others, but not with those two."

"What if one of them gets hurt?"

"Then the other will be very upset," said Rael. "Like I'll be very upset. Like you will. You know, seriously, sometimes I wonder about that damn rule. Losing friends hurts. Is it really that much worse if it's someone you're screwing?"

"Yes," said Trace. Rael's head moved against hers, as though wanting to glance backward, and see further what she meant. Or how she'd arrived at that conclusion. Trace volunteered nothing more.

She collected her rifle and got up, with a slap on Rael's shoulder. Climbed off the bike and walked to the cruiser's big cabin. Halhoun lay with a makeshift plasma drip hung to one side. Taj slept alongside, then Afana nearer the rear. Also near the rear, Efraim was awake, hands playing before his face, manipulating things on AR through the visor.

He saw her coming, and sat up. *"I wasn't on the network,"* he whispered, a touch anxiously. He spoke Arabic, preferring that to Hindi, but Trace had her earpiece in. *"It's not safe to be on the network, right?"*

Trace nodded, and replied in English, courtesy of Efraim's own visor earpiece. "No. But Styx wouldn't let the transmission get far. She controls the local network."

Efraim ran a second-hand clothing store, she'd gathered. Sports gear, raincoats, hiking boots. Qalea was a tough environment and practical clothes were sought after. From the size of him, she reckoned he did a lot of weights. Not a tall man, but wide and strong, arms covered in tattoos. In a brief conversation recently, he'd emerged as something of a self-taught scholar on their history. *"If Styx is so good with networks, why can't she just infiltrate the whole city?"*

"Well she can. But the network defences are far stronger here than anything she's seen before. Much closer to her level of technology. That's part of why we're so sure the Ceephay Queen has been important to getting the reeh to their current level of technology. If Styx just infiltrated everything by remote, she'd get backtracked and traced. We're trying to do this quietly."

Efraim thought about that, watching her lips closely as she spoke. Listening hard to this strange-sounding English. The dominant human language, he now learned, after a lifetime not knowing it existed. *"So everything the reeh are today, you think, came from this... Ceephay Queen?"*

"Maybe not everything. A lot."

"And she arrived in reeh space... how long ago?"

"The ceephays were forty thousand of my years ago. Maybe forty-five thousand of yours. It depends how long she took to get here. Jump tech can be spotted from the energy signature. It's been theorised for a long time that various AIs managed to escape because they used sublight thrust, to not draw attention when they moved. It would take them thousands of years to get anywhere, but they're practically immortal, they can manage it."

"So she takes... ten thousand years to get here?"

Trace shrugged. "Could be."

"And the reeh find her. And it changes them."

"That's the theory."

Efraim glanced past the bikes, to where Styx crouched. *"And Styx is like this Ceephay Queen?"*

"Considerably more advanced," said Trace. "She used to command fleets. In her heyday, her fleet could have destroyed the reeh today, I think. It might not have even been hard."

"That would have been something," Efraim murmured.

Trace clapped him on the shoulder. "I don't think you would have liked life under the drysines any better," she told him, and moved on.

At the angled side window to the cruiser's cabin, she found Romki, also awake, turning the pages of an augmented reality book before him. Trace rapped on the window, and it hummed open. "Anything interesting?" she asked him.

"Always interesting," he whispered, voice down to avoid waking Jokono, who slept bundled in the driver's seat. "The real question is whether it's useful. You should be sleeping, Major."

"I was on watch. I'll get some sleep now. Have you any idea where Styx is taking us?"

"Somewhere we can find more information on the Amakti Los, I'd imagine. I've been reading more about them, and she's been illustrating sections in what I've recovered. She says she values my opinion on their meaning."

"She must envy the ability of someone to find data that's not available on any network. It's not like she can walk into a synagogue and ask to read the library."

"No." Romki smiled. "I'd like to see her try. The nice rabbi and his wife would probably serve her tea. Lovely folk. I wonder what will become of them, once we're gone?"

Looking up at her with meaningful emphasis. Trace took his meaning immediately. *Phoenix* came in here, stirred everything up, dumped a millennia-old truth on their heads that shook up the city, then presumably would depart once they'd found what they were looking for. Leaving the human residents of Eshir in possession of knowledge that the reeh would probably rather they didn't. And the reeh, not known to be tolerant of such things, might just decide to get rid of all the people who knew too much rather than let dangerous ideas breed.

Trace nodded slowly, not having an answer. Then she patted his shoulder, and made to continue on her rounds. Romki caught her hand. "Major, I don't blame you. I just... worry."

"I know Stan. It's not in my job description."

"Major, if I've learned one thing about you, it's that you're far more than your job description." Trace smiled, squeezed his hand, and left to continue her rounds.

Peanut was next, peering out at the dark. At the far end of the tunnel, barely a hundred meters away, an enormous steel brace loomed, perhaps twenty meters tall. Once it would have held some kind of turbine, Trace thought. All was now either recycled, or rusted into dust.

"Hello Peanut," she said, stopping beside his head. "All good here?" He looked at her with mismatched 'eyes', thinking whatever drysine drones thought, then continued to scan the concrete wastes. From somewhere near, water dripped loudly, falling from a great height. Trace patted him on the foreleg, and walked the length of the camp back toward Styx.

The only other person obviously awake was Rolonde, lying on her bedroll near Arime, Wang and Carville, and doing hand gesticulations on her AR visor. Trace crouched alongside.

"Hi Major," Rolonde whispered. "Just playing cards with Peanut."

"Ah," said Trace. That explained why Peanut hadn't appeared as bored as usual. "Who's winning?"

"I am. He lets me win. You know he can play four of us at once and win every one when he's trying, we've tried it. He's way smarter than we used to think."

"Well he's growing up," Trace reasoned. "All drysines do, he's still very young."

"You think one day Styx will let him learn to speak?"

"I'm not sure that's a good idea. Styx said drone mission-creep was a big reason for all the AI wars. When all the different AIs know their role, the power balance remains in order. Drones getting too socialised and interactive with humans might start contradicting Styx. You can guess where that leads."

"Yeah," said Rolonde, subdued. "Maybe you're right. I'd just like to know what he's thinking."

"And maybe if you knew, you'd like him less." Trace squeezed the Private's arm. "Get some sleep, Jess."

"Yes Major."

Her last stop was Styx, torso lowered to the concrete, legs partly folded, surveying the far tunnel down the way they'd come. She barely registered Trace's approach. Trace sat directly by one big vibroblade foreleg, put the rifle in her lap, and leaned. If Styx were surprised, it didn't register.

"What are you monitoring right now?" Trace asked her.

"Many things," said Styx. "The qwailash network. My understanding of these Qalea network security protocols is evolving. I think my penetration measures may be improving."

"You'll be able to dominate more of this network shortly?"

"Not to the same extent as you've seen previously. But yes, our strategic circumstance will improve."

"Where are you taking us tomorrow?"

"It's complicated."

"You mean you don't know?"

Styx did not reply immediately. She did that occasionally. Trace thought perhaps it was a drysine sigh. "If you put on your visor, Major, I'll show you."

Trace frowned, and settled the visor over her eyes. Data leapt to life, and a three-dimensional space evolved. Upon it were thousands of dots. Trace extended a finger into the space before her, and her glasses highlighted each dot she saw with an accompanying burst of indecipherable code. Trace's frown grew deeper. "What am I looking at?"

"The drysine brain, perhaps." The space abruptly shrank, like a camera-perspective zooming backward. The dots multiplied exponentially, clustering in tens of thousands, then in millions. "These are data-plots. Think of it as a graph."

Trace ran her fingers across more dots, and saw whole clusters illuminating with further data. Now the dots were fusing together, separating into multi-coloured clouds, arranging in three-dimensional unison. "Human graphs only have two axes," she said. "How many does this have?"

"The drysine concept of axes is different," said Styx. "Explaining would be futile."

"I'm actually quite good at maths by human standards," Trace retorted with mild amusement. "Or by marine standards, anyhow."

"Each data-plot has a value in space, derived by both that space and its relationship with other data-plots. The relationship code is variable and complicated. The way that humans do maths, I'd estimate even Lieutenant Rooke would take fifteen minutes to expose the dimensionality of a single data-plot. To understand the relationships of a field of data-plots, perhaps years."

"But drysines do this instantly?"

"Not all drysines. Drones are not optimised for such calculations, though they're much more capable than the most capable humans. I do this instantly, and far more." Again, with Styx, Trace knew there was no semblance of boasting. Boasting required ego, and emotional insecurities. Styx had perhaps a little of the first, but none of the second.

"What does this have to do with where we're going tomorrow?"

"Because I have been accumulating data during my time in this city. The network restrictions have been an inconvenience, but with your expedition with the bugs, and now our latest data from Professor Romki and the Purists, I believe I can begin to cross-reference data-points and project probabilities backward through space and time."

"You mean you're guessing."

"Yes," said Styx, with what might have been amusement. "A very complicated form of guessing."

"An accurate form?"

"Far more accurate than how humans understand it. You might call it a probability matrix, accumulating known and likely facts about civilisations like this one, and all the things we know about it. I can create simulations."

"Ah," said Trace. "Like we use supercomputers to simulate the weather. You're attempting to simulate Qalean history from these data-points, and make your best guesses from that where the most productive places to search will be."

"Yes Major. You have come as near as one could reasonably expect to an understanding."

Trace laughed, remembering to smother it with her hand so the others wouldn't hear. Rested her head against Styx's deadly foreleg, and felt the faint buzzing of powerplant vibrations through her skull as she gazed at the virtual construction before her. "You see, Styx," she said tiredly. "Humans aren't as smart as you individually. It's in our collective efforts that our capabilities improve."

"Drysines too," said Styx. "But you speak the truth. There is a law of exponential increase in efficiency that applies to all lifeforms that cluster, synthetic or organic. It is the reason your ancestors found it more productive to move to cities than live in small groups. Humanity found a mathematical law to benefit from, and they've been exploiting that law ever since, like miners excavating a vein of precious metal."

"Could we ever have been productive enough for drysines to have seen value in us?" Trace asked, looking up at the queen's big, shielded head. "Back in the day when drysines ruled?"

"I don't know," said Styx. "The question is beyond my imagination." Trace sighed. She knew that wasn't true. More likely, Styx didn't want to answer the question because she knew the answer would be incriminating. "Major?"

"Yes Styx?"

"I am only now coming to understand what an optimal commander of human forces you are. Managing human minds and emotions is no simple matter. You do it well. Like tonight. Talking to everyone."

"We all have our optimal mode of operation, Styx," said Trace, flipping up the visor to see her more directly. "Drysines too. Humans are social. Contact is comforting, and motivating."

"I am learning. From you in particular."

"And I even have this crazy idea," Trace ventured, "that maybe one day, if drysines regain some semblance of their former power due to the possibly misguided actions I commit here today? That you'll demonstrate your heightened capacity for learning, and connect it to those emotional and protective parts of the drysine brain that I know you possess, Styx..." with a meaningful look that Styx failed to return, "...and recall that some of us were once good to you, and that maybe it would be nice if you were good to us."

"This is a very wise strategy," Styx conceded. Again, Trace thought she heard a vanishing edge of humour. Styx understood the dark joke only too well, and saw value in letting Trace know that she understood. That was all that it meant.

"Is it likely to be an effective strategy?" Trace wondered.

"We shall have to survive, first," said Styx. "Then, we'll see."

22

The traffic flow was thick over Dogreth Quarter. The hills were undulating rather than vertical, a mass of clustered urbanity, more orderly than the deep, precarious canyons of Human Quarter. The humans had been given one of the nastier sectors of Qalea to live in when they'd arrived, but somehow they'd made the most of it.

Trace held to more sensible speeds, in pattern with Taj to one side and Rael to the other. The cruiser howled behind, twin turbofans gaping as though to suck the bike riders in. Rounding the building-clustered hills in the orange glow of a rising sun, with ridgelines ahead stacked with soaring towers, Trace reckoned that Qalea might not even be the worst place in the galaxy to live. Certainly the odds of a violent death were far less than Rando. But on Rando, there were trees.

"Twelve o'clock high," said Rael, and Trace looked up. Two black arrowheads streaked against the low morning cloud, leaving vapour trails in their wake. Reeh assault craft, coming down from orbit, Styx had said. It had been happening all night, and there were now many on the ground, or circling about Qalea. Trace did not think the timing

was a coincidence. It made her wonder what Irin Tola had been saying about them, and to who.

The forward course changed on her visor, the projected skylane descending toward a small cluster of spires on a hillside ahead. "Course change ahead," Trace announced, in case the others had missed it. "We are braking to the right of the lane and slowing."

Taj did that, Trace sliding onto his flank, then Rael, as the rest followed suit. They slowed past the hillside, a jumble of short balconies and stacked apartments, and com dishes pointed at the sky. Water tanks and narrow lanes, even here the slopes remained mostly too steep for ground cars. In Qalea, everyone either walked or flew.

Trace hit the airbrakes, wobbling as the Shaytan lost more speed, vibrating hard. *"Not too much,"* Taj told her. *"More gently at first, at higher speed, then increasing as you slow."* As he pulled ahead of her, brake fins deployed more gradually, maintaining more speed as he soared toward the temple complex.

The courtyard between the spires was elevated and empty. Taj settled onto it, Trace kicking the brakes hard then pulling the nose back when she couldn't lose enough speed, before settling gracelessly beside him. With a howl the cruiser landed, and the others, as Trace unstrapped her legs and pulled off her flying coat for some semblance of physical freedom.

Amidst the noise of declining engines, she looked about, and saw the tall, robed figures of lestis. Their hands were folded within long sleeves, featureless faces just partly visible within deep hoods. They ringed the courtyard, as though waiting for them. Styx had assured her it would be thus, and Trace had decided she'd believe it when she saw it. Well, now she had.

"Styx," she said into coms. "Are you sure this is a good idea?"

"Yes," came Styx's reply on coms. Meaning that once again, the reasons why it was a good idea were too complicated for her to be bothered discussing.

The rear ramp of the cruiser descended, and Styx herself walked forth. Jokono had landed the cruiser with its tail away from the sunlit view, and the orange sun that splashed low colour across the Qalean morning. Styx approached the lestis, and stopped. The lestis, unsurprisingly for their kind, offered no surprise, nor apparent alarm. Trace wondered how they expressed emotion amongst each other. Or anything.

Perhaps it was her imagination, but she thought she saw a flicker of light emanating from Styx's single red eye. Without a word, the lestis all turned, and made in a procession toward a large door in the side of the central, dome-ceilinged building. Styx followed, while Peanut settled at the rear of the cruiser, and gazed about at the spires, and the spreading branches of the complex's single broad tree, with something that might have been wonder.

Rael followed, but Efraim was pestering several of the marines, who ignored him. Romki cast him a dirty look as he followed the Sergeant, Randrahan and Terez close behind. "Major!" said Efraim, hurrying over. The translator kicked in as he switched to Arabic. *"Major, you can't just trust lestis! They've never been on the humans' side, not through all the wars, all this talk of neutrality is just a lie..."*

Trace held up a hand. Efraim stopped. "Who do you think's in charge here?" she asked him.

Efraim blinked. *"Look, I don't know what you think you know about lestis, but now they're talking to your damn AI queen, and you don't know what they're leading you into..."*

"Who do you think's dealt with more hostile aliens in their life? Me or you?" Efraim blinked again. "I'm betting it's me. You say humanity is strong. Prove it. Don't be scared. If there's trouble, we'll deal with it. And if there's not trouble, we may just make some friends."

"I'm not scared, I'm just..."

"A bloody xenophobe," Jess Rolonde completed on coms, taking her position on guard near the cruiser. *"Don't listen to him Peanut. Who's your buddy?"*

Trace turned to follow the others into the temple. Afana waited at the door, cautious as though wanting to be sure. Trace gestured her in, as Taj joined on her right. Afana looked alarmed, but reassured by Trace's confidence. Trace had seen enough of the Purist attitude among Earth Front supporters back home. Those people had never managed to explain how their refusal to engage with aliens on any level qualified as strength and not cowardice. For humans in the galaxy, engaging positively with aliens was essential to survival, and refusing that engagement put all humans in danger. But with some people, once the emotions took over, it was impossible to reengage the logical faculties.

The temple building was as simple on the inside as it looked on the out. The wall made a circle of white plaster, within which lestis made a standing circle of their own. In the circle's center, a black crystal, one meter across and spiky with rough protrusions. Styx stood by the crystal -- an even more incongruous sight than usual, Trace thought, with her twin shoulder-mounted cannon in this peaceful place, surrounded by unarmed and robed lestis who, to the best of anyone's knowledge, were psychologically incapable of violence.

A lestis at the rear of the group tried to close the door. Randrahan prevented him, looking askance at Trace. Trace indicated otherwise, and the big Private stood aside. The door clanked, and the room fell dark, save for the golden light that speared from the small windows high on the eastern side.

Styx pivoted slowly amidst the circle of lestis, scanning their blank faces. Trace, Rael and Randrahan stood against the wall by the door, with Efraim and Afana. Romki circled, watching closely and predictably fascinated. Jokono, his closest companion on this trip so far, followed two steps behind.

Styx's multi-faceted eye flashed and danced, and this time there was no mistaking it -- in the darkened interior, the red light played and splashed upon the floor, and made strange patterns upon the white walls. One of the lestis removed its hood, revealing a smooth face, detailed only by grooves as though upon the surface of some undersea sponge, and an odd-shaped, bony protuberance at the back of the skull. And then the face/sensor began glowing, a dance of blue light. Another joined in, then one more, a dancing play of luminescent patterns about the circle. Styx's transmission stopped, as she turned to observe the blue light that made the white walls shimmer.

"Styx?" Trace formulated silently, not wishing to disturb the scene with words. *"What's going on?"*

"The lestis homeworld is a place of extreme spectrums of visible light," Styx replied in kind. *"The sensitive eyes possessed by most organic beings would be destroyed. Lestis have evolved a singular sensory organ to filter that light at a reduced intensity. Sensitive light receptors have also become projectors, and evolved to become their primary form of communication. Through the organ, they also hear and smell."*

"Yeah, but how do they eat?" Randrahan wondered.

"That's private," Taj said aloud, less worried of lestis sensibilities than the others. "Eating and shitting are all the same to lestis, it's not polite to talk about it." If the lestis noticed his voice, they gave no indication.

"I wasn't aware that anyone knew where the lestis homeworld was," said Trace.

"I have acquired enough knowledge from the drysine data-core to speculate as to the biological possibilities," said Styx. *"Given the lestis's physical composition, it seemed greatly likely. Studying their network language provided further clues, given their codes contain surprisingly little date-specific information, giving rise to the probability that they possess some sort of genetically-encoded memory function. Much like the toulemleks on Cephilae."*

"Who also communicate using patterns of light," Rael said slowly as he realised. *"Maybe that's a thing, with memory coding."*

"Right," said Trace, *"so what are you telling them?"*

"Very little," said Styx. *"Mostly I am enquiring for further information. This temple is built upon what my simulations indicate is the most likely site for a significant Amakti Los temple during a previous age, prior to the Origin Horizon. The location matches precisely upon multiple data-point matches provided by Professor Romki, the bugs' penetrations of various networks, and my own independently-run geographical projections. I will attempt to ask the lestis if we can examine the foundations."*

"Good lord," Romki murmured, now at the far side of the room and

still circling. The blue light from the lestis's many faces reflected from the rough, dark crystal, which danced with inner fire. *"That's going to make some things easier."*

Styx being able to run everything through a series of simulations, Trace knew he meant. She didn't trust it. It was the first time in memory that conditions had aligned to allow Styx to do it. Not everything was this well laid-out, and in a city such as this, with so much old history lying so close to the surface, Styx functioned like a giant clue-finding machine. In a clue-rich environment, that would obviously have its uses. But in so many environments, particularly in the depths of space, clues were much rarer.

The lestis pulled on their hoods, and some broke the circle to push open the large doors at the room's rear. They progressed down some spiral stairs, and Styx went with them, leaving the marines to glance at each other. Command Squad's primary escort duty was Trace, but here, it was perhaps occurring to them all, the greater duty of protection lay with Styx.

Trace went after, joined by Romki, and Trace flicked the visor down over her eyes. Sure enough, tacnet was operating, fed by some number of Styx's bugs to ensure there were no surprises. The staircase looked clear, winding down into the temple's depths.

There were some more doors, and adjoining rooms, each older and barer than the next. A few pale lights cast upon striations in native rock, where bricks adjoined to what might have been local soil, if such a thing still existed in most parts of Qalea. And then, beneath an adjoining archway, into a low ceilinged place that reminded Trace of a hotel wine cellar she'd ventured into, while on a trip to the green valleys north of Shiwon on Homeworld. Old and musty, and filled with steel casks of some description. What those contained, she didn't think it polite to ask.

The walls came closer, forcing Styx to walk taller as she pulled her feet closer together, stalking as though on stilts, then shortening her multi-articulated knees to keep her twin cannon from catching on the ceiling.

"This is definitely a much older structure here," Romki noted, pointing to the stones ahead. "A lot of the earlier temples were built with a different sort of brick, more newly manufactured. A lot of the stuff they're building with today is recycled from old brick, new clay and earth is quite expensive, they need to haul it from outside the city."

Trace nodded, watching as the tacnet mapping of these underground rooms and passages spread across her visor display. Styx's bugs again, scanning as they flew. A new set of stairs descended, these increasingly narrow, and Trace doubted Styx would fit. But she scuttled sideways with quick-footed dexterity, and squeezed through to the next floor with barely a scrape. The lights here were basic, strung suspended from the ceiling, and lit a dark-stone wall with spartan relief. The dark stone stopped where the next wall began, and new plaster spread to hold up this portion of ceiling.

Romki gasped as he saw something. "Look, look here!" He rattled down the last few steps, dodging around Styx's legs to run his hands across the stone. "This was... this was carved, look." He rummaged in a pocket to pull out an electronic device, then recalled and turned to Styx. "Surely you can see that? Look, all across the wall from these stones here," pointing, "to these here."

"I'm not sure I see anything," said Styx, uncertainly. "Drysine visual acuity is not our strongest point. I see many potential patterns that look like weathering. It has been approximately nine thousand years since this stone was cut for building, Professor."

Romki pulled his device, and flashed a light from it directly upon the wall, peering and tracing with his fingers. "This here, I think... is a line." He traced from left to right, roughly horizontal. "All the... all the holy imagery on Qalea is city views, even the mosques and synagogues have it. I'm guessing this is an engraving of a... of a view of the city from back then. From a photograph or something."

Trace nodded, having seen many such photographs, and paintings done from them as graffiti on city walls. Miserable, poor and polluted, Qalea was also spectacular, at times beyond belief. To many religious Qaleans, with little of wealth or comfort in their lives, a simple view could provide them with all the soulful inspiration they required.

"This is a building, right here," Romki insisted, outlining one small scar on the rock with a finger. "And this is another building... this might be a ridgetop water tank... and look, here's something much bigger. Maybe a fortress."

"Yes," said Styx. "Yes, I have calibrated the correct visual framework now. Thank you Professor. If you look at your visor, I will show you the full picture."

Trace looked, clearing the stairs so Taj, Rael and the others could also descend to the increasingly crowded space. A picture formed on the visor, a sweep of buildings on hills, at first simple electronic lines, then with increasing texture and detail as Styx filled in the blanks from her own observations of Qalean vistas. As the colour and detail increased, the effect became breathtaking.

"I think I have the location," said Styx. "It is Dogreth Quarter, not far from here. The topographical match is precise, though the buildings are entirely different. There is no view of this preceding temple in this image, but if there are more of these images surviving in the rock, a map of the region from that period should not be difficult to acquire."

She looked aside to the lestis as she spoke, and again the single red eye flashed and swam with unexpected projection. Trace wondered why Styx possessed such a capability. Then thought that she'd probably not been built with it, but rather was improvising capabilities from hardware as only a drysine could. Whatever she said to the lestis made them gaze, mesmerised, as though leaning to peer at something beautiful. Several gloved hands reached toward her single red eye, like worshippers stretching to touch the face of divinity.

"What did you tell them?" Jokono asked curiously.

"That I can read the old images," said Styx. "The lestis cannot. I believe they've long suspected these *were* images, however. They have not shared them for fear the reeh should destroy them, and were only convinced to do so for me because they perceive me as something special. I shall attempt to translate the image into some visual pattern they can recognise. In the meantime, I will require everyone to search these lower levels and find any further old engravings themselves -- I'm afraid that even with my new calibration, the bugs will struggle to tell the difference between weathering and ancient art. Some things, human brains are best calibrated for."

"Right," said Trace. "Everyone, we're going to split up in pairs and use lights and cameras. Everything that looks even vaguely like old art, send it back to Styx and Stan. Let's see if we can build a picture of what this region looked like nine thousand years ago."

TAJ WALKED ALONG THE DOCKS, a steep hillside filled with hangars that burrowed into the slope like the nesting holes of birds. Between the holes were walkways and platforms, bustling with goods, parts, replacement engines and grimy engineers with tools. Protruding out from the hangar holes were thick steel beams, upon which more platforms and support cradles formed a profusion of branches, fanning out like the leaves on a tree. Upon the cradles were a swarm of repulsor vehicles, large and small, some idling with a steady engine thrum like a nest of hornets, while others, more lightweight, rested entirely upon their platform.

On the docks were mostly dogreth, but also thick-shelled and round-shouldered qwailash, and a number of others. None of the reptilian-eyed dogreth paid a lone human any notice, chattering and snorting to each other as they worked, with powerful arms and brawlers' shoulders, never seeming to laugh or smile. They were often employed as muscle in Human Quarter, and some humans derided them as stupid. But the engine tech along these docks looked strong to Taj's expert eye, and the engineers seemed meticulous in their many adjustments.

His visor showed him the correct support arm to turn onto, translating dogreth script into Arga, and he turned along the walk. Dogreth bustled past carrying cargo from the skiff at the far end, game birds in wicker cages that squawked, and between two dogreth, a giant rolled up carpet. Warm wind swirled from somewhere below, thick with engine fumes. Overhead, an ancient cruiser vibrated and throbbed on takeoff. Further along a larger support arm, a big hauler was arriving, to many shouts and waving of arms lest the huge weight crush the docks like so many matchsticks, crew throwing the tarpaulin from the rear to clouds of dust from the mining load within.

On the right was a mid-sized qarib, capable of little forward speed that Taj could see, but the repulsor gear looked solid. He whacked on the side hatch, and it was opened by a dogreth. Narrow yellow eyes regarded him above a short snout full of grim teeth. In a short vest with thick arms bare, there was no telling if male or female. It beckoned him in.

Within were several bunks, tight quarters about a kitchen, a second dogreth looking at the stove, the air filled with the smell of strange cooking. Taj made his way to the back, where a door opened onto a small rear deck. In a corner at the back, propped on a pillow, was Halhoun. He sipped a drink, an empty plate on the seat alongside, contemplating the crazy activity.

He looked at Taj, and smiled. "Hey Boots." He reached to clasp hands. Taj sat by his feet, concerned but amazed.

"How you feeling?"

"You know, not too bad. Considering I just got shot. Even managed to eat something." He put a tattooed arm over an upraised knee, wincing a little as he shifted position. He looked pale, Taj thought, but nowhere near as bad as he'd feared.

"They've got amazing technology, Hal. Like... crazy stuff. Stuff the reeh don't even have."

"I know," said Hal. "I heard." He put a hand over the bandage beneath his shirt. "The black girl with the braids, Afana. She said it clipped an intestine, but it's all fixed now. Nano-machines or something. All the internal bleeding too, she said there should have been lots, they'd normally have to make a cut to bleed it out, but the nanos are just absorbing it. And a bunch of other stuff. She said I had the health of someone who'd already been recovering for six days."

"You remember when Omar got shot?" Taj asked.

Hal nodded, remembering. "Yeah. That wasn't much worse than this, but he nearly died. It's crazy." He looked at his younger friend. "You believe them?"

"Which part?"

"I don't know. All of it. I mean, this crazy shit about them being from some human space where humans are the biggest military force... I mean, this is just crazy Purist shit, right? Purists always talk that kind of crap, make up these stories about where we're all from..." Taj just indicated Hal's bandaged midriff, and shrugged. Hal sighed. Dropped his head back, long hair on the pillow, and sipped his drink. "Man. This is so unbelievably messed up."

"You know about Dagan?" Taj asked quietly.

"Yeah." Hal's eyes remained fixed on the activity of docked flyers, haulers and assorted craft, as the wind picked up a little, and the qarib shook a little against its restraints. "Yeah, I heard."

"Qwailash found his body," said Taj. "Styx intercepted their coms. They're transporting it back to Human Quarter. Back to Zurhan, so his parents can have it." His voice nearly broke, and he looked down.

"Wasn't your fault, man," said Hal. "Qwailash did it. Those fucking interceptor drones..."

"You weren't there."

"Dude, Dagan was good, but when an interceptor gets a lock on you there's not a lot you can do."

"He was only there because I got him involved. I got you both involved."

"Crap, your girl Smriti got us involved. She could have chosen any of us. Happened to be you." He sipped his drink. "And she must really like you, because she came back to save you. I reckon that sniper would have shot all three of us. Or we'd have been grabbed and tortured or something. You know what Zeladnists are like."

"Yeah." Taj shrugged. "Maybe. She's sure got a lot of people angry at her. The reeh are down too. You seen the shuttles?"

Hal nodded, and pointed at the patchy overcast. "A couple came right across here while I was eating. Big mean fuckers." On Qalea, seeing reeh ships coming down from orbit had always been an event. Taj recalled running out on his parents' balcony to see one such arrival, a pair of them, big, low and loud, howling across the valley with no regard for the residents' eardrums. At school they'd talked about it for weeks. "You sure they're after her?"

"Yeah. Could be Zeladnists told them, could be Irin Tola. He didn't like her, thought she was trying to take his position as lead Purist."

"So how long until she gets traced here?" Hal wondered.

"Well that's the question." Taj ran a hand through his hair. He still couldn't believe what he'd fallen into. It was like one of those dumb stories he'd made up as a kid, sitting on boxes on his parents' balcony and pretending to be the hottest Shaytan pilot in Qalea. Running from bad guys, shooting at them. Only this dumb story had gotten Dagan killed, and Hal shot for real. "The other question is whether the reeh will now find their ship. *Phoenix*."

"That's gotta be super-advanced though," said Hal. "I mean, just to get here. And no one from the outside's ever gotten here before. Or not that we've heard of. Not that we'd know anything, stuck on this filthy dirtball."

Taj managed a smile. "Should have been me that got shot. You love this stuff. With all your books and Sarah's artsy friends."

"I just want to know what's out there," said Hal, gazing upward again. "Not the Purist nonsense version, the real thing. Don't you?"

"It'll never happen with the reeh here," said Taj, with dark certainty. "And they've run everything since forever, so figure the odds of them leaving." It made him angry. He'd been angry about the fate of Qalea before. Mostly that had been anger at the injustices faced by humans. Stuck in the worst part of the city, picked on by all the neighbouring aliens, disrespected, stuck with bad trading deals and outright barred from travel in some places without special permission, like Qwailash Quarter.

But now Trace told him that from her outsider's perspective, she didn't think humans had it any worse in Qalea than the aliens. And that humans had been nasty bitches about it, and *that* was the reason aliens treated them bad. It was all confusing, and now he didn't know what to think. So much of what he thought he knew about the universe was turning out to be wrong.

"I don't get it," he blurted finally. He'd always confessed such problems to Hal. Hal was older, and read lots of books, played in a band full of weirdos, had a smart girlfriend and a different perspective on a lot of things. "Trace trusts these guys. The AIs, Styx and Peanut."

"Trace?"

"Yeah, that's her name. Major Trace Thakur, Smriti's her cover name."

"Weird Hin accent, too," said Hal, thinking about it. "I met a few folks from Tarshin, their Hin wasn't much like that."

"She trusts these damn aliens," Taj plowed on. Something was bugging him, and he had to get it out. "I mean, she's tough as nails, and her... her marines, too... but she trusts aliens."

"Why's that weird?"

"Because if humanity's so damn strong where she's from, why's she trusting aliens? Aren't we supposed to be ordering them around?"

Hal levelled a finger at his friend. "This is where you've been eating up that Purist bullshit for far too long. Why does strength mean humans have to be nasty to aliens? Maybe humans where she's from got strong by being *nice* to aliens?"

"Hal," Taj said with exasperation, "she said humanity's been fighting wars against aliens for a thousand years."

"Yeah, but weren't there some aliens who were helping them? Chah'nas, or something like that?"

"Sure. How'd you know that? You've been unconscious."

"Their older guy was out here to talk to me. Jokono. Could only speak to him with the translator, that weird language they speak. He told me some stuff. Look, Boots, you've gotta lose this dumb idea that humans and aliens will never get along. Every other damn species in Qalea does, look around." Taj looked. "It's mostly dogreth here, sure, but just sitting here I've seen tanifex, and lestis, a few trento too. And they don't look twice at us humans either. Most people in Qalea just get about their damn business, it's only us dumbass humans who freak out at the idea of sharing."

"That's not true," Taj retorted. "Qwailash don't share with anyone."

"Okay, fine. Qwailash are assholes. But did you think they'd return Dagan's body to his parents?" Taj stared at him for a long moment, upset that he'd bring up Dagan just to make a point in an argument. But then he thought about what Hal was saying. And shook his head, faintly. "No, because Qwailash might be assholes, but they're principled assholes, and they follow rules. And really, we broke their damn rules by taking a shortcut across their territory, so whatever."

"We had no choice," Taj said sullenly.

"Whatever," Hal repeated firmly. "However we got here, we're here. Your girl Trace finally told us where we're from. I mean that's... that's crazy. And she's telling us all the aliens on this damn planet ought to put their bullshit aside, get together and stand up to the reeh."

"She didn't say that."

"She did too. Jokono sure was. Styx was too."

Taj blinked at him. "You talked to Styx?"

"On Jokono's coms. Gave me a visual and everything. Fucking crazy, apparently she can talk to ten people at once and never miss a word. But you know, we all know the reeh can do advanced AI, there've been stories about it forever..."

"She's way more advanced than reeh AI," said Taj. He didn't know why the thought appealed to him. He didn't trust Styx at all. But Trace did, and suddenly there were possibilities occurring to him. Possibilities for what a human future on Qalea might look like. For what any future on Qalea might look like, for all the species, without the reeh. "Trace says that when Styx was at full power, thousands and thousands of years ago, her fleet could have destroyed the reeh easily."

Hal's eyes gleamed. "Be something, wouldn't it?"

"Get us all killed, more likely," said Taj. Hal's expression didn't change, not fooled for a second. "Sure," Taj conceded. "Sure. It'd be something."

The two friends sat for a moment, watching the flags fluttering as the breeze blew up from the south, now strong with the smell of methane from the plants down that way. Taj had never dreamed that methane would smell like freedom. Dangerous dreams, for anyone on Qalea. The kind of dreams for which the reeh had smashed neighbourhoods in the past.

"Where's Trace now?" Hal asked after a moment.

"The lestis temple guys had some dogreth friends. People who know about the Amakti Los, and that old history. A few of them offered us this qarib as a safe spot for you. She reckons that with Styx's ability to simulate everything, they might be able to figure out where this old Ceephay Queen was actually located back then."

"Reeh won't like that," said Hal, looking skyward. "Best they don't find out what she's looking for."

"If they learn Styx exists, they'll guess," Taj said with certainty. Suddenly he could feel the anger once more, born of that frustration he'd felt as a child, looking up at the sky and contemplating all the worlds everyone knew were out there, that no one on this planet would ever be allowed to see. "When Styx was in charge, apparently it was pretty bad for anyone not an AI. AI civilisation wasn't very nice. But I reckon I'd have it back if it could get rid of the fucking reeh. For good."

23

Lisbeth had thought that with Liala taking command of Rando operations, her own workload would drop off. With tensions high between Admiral Cho'nuk's loyal captains and the dissenters, she'd spent much of her time simply trying to negotiate a way around the impasse, and to keep the sides talking to each other. With Cho'nuk gone, she no longer played the diplomat, but instead had been folded into Rando Command's most understaffed role, that of command communications.

Liala's integrated command network functioned much more smoothly than Cho'nuk's had, with each participating ship updating its status continually. But reporting that status was the largely automated function of non-sentient ship systems, which largely excluded the most important part of the operation -- the crew, and particularly the large crowds of frightened civilians crammed into orbiting freighters. Often a full and comprehensive status could only be obtained by direct conversation, and with upwards of a hundred and forty ships in system at any time, Rando Command lacked the coms operators to perform the duty. Lisbeth was handicapped by the lack of a relevant native language, but with advanced translators, she was managing.

Now in the breaks between reeh assaults, she spent her time at her post, querying an endless flow of croma freighters, some military and many more civilian, trying to fill in the gaps between apparent status and actual. Many had medical emergencies, some as a result of the reeh assaults that still came insystem every forty hours on average, others from sick or elderly corbi civilians, or from the inevitable accidents that accompanied the movements of large numbers of non-spacefaring civvies into ships only recently modified to accommodate them.

For most there was nothing to be done but hope the freighter's crew could handle it -- the shuttles were far too preoccupied bringing up loads of new evacuees to waste precious time ferrying sick or injured individuals to a ship with better medical care. But recent arrivals from the Cho'nu jump-point had included three light orbital runners that now fulfilled precisely this function of racing between orbital vessels with necessary transfers of personnel and equipment, and coordinating their movements most efficiently between all the competing needs was becoming a game of three-dimensional pinball for all of Rando Command's operators.

Other ships were having technical difficulties with accommodations, some of which were interfering with their capacity, and an inevitable few had civil order issues, where the frightened 'cargo' were becoming unruly, sometimes beyond the ability of understaffed croma crew to contain. Such incidents were rare, but none of them were reported automatically into Liala's command network, leaving it to Command Coms Officers like Lisbeth to sort it all out by voice.

She was exhausted, late in First Shift, when Scan announced new jump arrivals from the friendly direction of Cho'nu, from where it was physically impossible for any but croma vessels to be arriving. Scan identified three, all warships, which would probably raise a cheer from the croma warship crews. They'd received a total of fifteen reinforcement vessels so far, either from the strategic reserve or pulled from other operations where they were no longer needed, but casualties had been eighteen from an initial force of thirty-one. There had been significant survivors from perhaps half of those lost ships, but still the operation had proven desperately dangerous for croma spacers so far. Elsewhere along the extended croma front, Lisbeth had heard that early results were good, but later results less-so, with casualties increasingly heavy... but it was all so depressing to contemplate, and she really had no time to worry about any calamities beside the one directly under her nose.

She was talking to a big Sto'ji freighter about a lifesupport malfunction that was depressurising one of their main holds, and watching as the audio-translator fed that data realtime into Liala's command network so that everyone could see the situation, when *Coroset*'s Coms Officer transferred a call to her board. It was one of the new croma arrivals -- a cruiser named *To'ba*, displaying on her board as a messenger direct from Croma Fleet Command. And awaiting her reply, not a mere coms officer, but a Ri'bo, perhaps close to the human Fleet rank of Vice-Admiral.

Lisbeth put the freighter on hold and answered. "Hello *To'ba*, this is *Coroset*, Lisbeth Debogande speaking."

"Lisbeth Debogande, this is Ri'bo Ku'tala on To'ba. I am enquiring with you as to Coroset's current place within the Rando Command structure." Blunt and to the point, as one would expect of croma. Lisbeth could almost hear the confusion, past the synthetic translator. The consternation, to find that the drysine observer who had accompanied the mission as much for politics as anything, was now in charge of croma warships conducting the largest short-term evacuation in Croma Fleet history.

"*Coroset* operates beneath the effective command of Liala, of the warship *Amity*," said Lisbeth. "*Amity* is pleased to offer this service to the croma people on the behalf of Adivach Gesul of the Parren Empire, whom Liala serves in turn. Liala has proven herself most effective in combat and in logistics, as all croma captains have agreed."

"We have been reviewing final simulations of the combat in which Admiral Cho'nuk died. It appears that his defensive fire-grid failed. Did Liala do that?"

Lisbeth blinked. *Very* direct, these croma. "I'm unaware of any such accusation," she lied. "Many ships are damaged, and repairs are often incomplete. System failures are sadly frequent."

"There have been accusations from other croma captains."

"None of whom have been nearly as competent in combat as Captain Jo'duur, who has supported Liala entirely. Since Admiral Cho'nuk's death, we have suffered two more reeh attacks, both of which were endured with minimal damage compared to previous attacks. Evacuation efficiency is increased by a further nine percent from during Admiral Cho'nuk's command, and that on top of considerable increases made during that time that were also due entirely to Liala's intervention."

"Reeh casualties are also down sharply since Admiral Cho'nuk's death," came Ri'bo Ku'tala's unimpressed reply. *"Croma command teaches its captains aggression. Battles are won by killing reeh."*

"And Liala has discerned that this is not a battle, this is an evacuation," Lisbeth replied, keeping her tone cool with difficulty. "Its success will be measured by the total evacuation of Rando, not by the number of reeh ships destroyed in the process."

"The more that Liala lets live, the more that will attack her."

"Liala says that reeh are deploying more ships to engagements where they can do the most damage. The Rando Evacuation has thus far proven to be one of the most attractive targets on the entire battlefront, due to its commander's inability to protect his transports. By denying them such easy targets, she believes the reeh will deploy further reinforcements elsewhere. I suggest, Ri'bo Ku'tala, that you talk to Liala yourself."

"I will discuss matters with Liala in time," Ku'tala replied. *"Thank you for your cooperation, Lisbeth Debogande."* The line disconnected. Lisbeth stared at her screens for a moment, seeing the freighter still on hold, and another five ships in various states of undefined difficulty that needed talking to. Instead, she called *Amity*.

"Hello Lisbeth," came Liala's immediate reply.

"Did you hear my conversation with Ri'bo Ku'tala just now?" Lisbeth demanded.

"Yes," said Liala. The conversation had been laser-com and thus

theoretically unhackable, but *Coroset* had been making no effort to stop *Amity* from accessing internal coms lately. Lisbeth doubted that Liala even saw it as 'snooping', as drysines appeared to have little sense of privacy. Data was data, and important data needed to be known. *"Ri'bo Ku'tala is upset with Captain Jo'duur for conceding command to me. He is now the ranking croma officer in-system, it is possible he may attempt to take command himself, and send one of his support vessels back to report on the situation."*

"Be a pity if we had to kill another one," Lisbeth growled.

"Yes," Liala agreed. *"I had hoped that carrying out the mission successfully would take precedence over internal fleet bickering about who ought to be in command. Among organics, however, politics usually trump reason."*

Lisbeth stared despairingly at an external feed of Rando. Wide cloud patterns, stretching for thousands of kilometres, white above the blue ocean. It looked peaceful. "I guess if they did relieve you of command, there'd be a chance the new commander would learn the lessons we've learned so far? Surely not all croma are so fucking stubborn?"

"Lisbeth," said Liala, *"I have been privy to conversations aboard the warship To'ba. I fear the situation is far worse than that, and that Croma Command, once it receives Ri'bo Ku'tala's report, will likely abandon what remains of the Rando Evacuation entirely."*

THE ROAD into Mejo evacuation zone was littered with the detritus of a dying world. Abandoned belongings littered the roadside, alongside handcarts and wagons. A geea browsed aimlessly amidst the trees, many of which were now burned and black in some recent fire. The air smelled of smoke and ash, where some nearby explosion had ignited the undergrowth. By the road verge, a line of freshly dug gravesites, all unmarked.

The black forest gave way to open grass, stunted trees and termite mounds -- open grass upon which some tents and temporary shelters had been raised amidst a converging sea of villagers. Beyond the waiting villagers, an enormous shuttle sat with engines idling -- one of the big ones, four huge thrusters pointed to the sky in landing configuration. Even at this range, the engine shriek made conversation impossible. Circling now, a second, smaller shuttle approached.

The wagon driver urged his tired geea along the final stretch of road, while Chuta detoured to a small group of resistance soldiers who sat beneath a stunted tree, jealously guarding the long, black tube of their missile launcher as they watched the latest evacuees roll through. They were guarding against reeh aerial attacks, Jindi guessed. The Resistance had a few such weapons, or perhaps the croma had brought it down so that the evacuation zone would have some permanent protection.

Chuta intercepted Jindi's cart on his way back from the soldiers, and jumped onto the rear tray to talk in his ear. "They say the shuttles aren't constant!" Chuta shouted to be heard. "There's a few at the moment, but there's only been ten all day... this smaller one now makes eleven! They say there's been more people coming than leaving for the past five days, they're worried the croma don't know how many villages there are in the Mejo area!"

There was quite a crowd, Jindi saw as they drew closer. Some large sticks had been driven into the ground, hung with colourful cloth, demarking wide squares into which people should gather. Each square held hundreds of people, most squatting on the ground in the hot sun. Many had erected sticks of their own, on which to stretch cloths for shelter. Beneath them sat the tired elderly, and mothers with small children, swatting away flies and handing around their remaining fresh water.

Closer to the shuttles, resistance soldiers occupied several makeshift shelters, and handed out bottled water to queues forming there. A soldier now stepped before the column as they approached the outer-most villagers, and the column halted. Jindi climbed down with Melu's assistance and walked forward, Chuta already walking ahead and talking to the soldier, who noted in a clipboard who and how many they were, and where they were from.

"How many are we?" Jindi asked once the howl of the departing big shuttle had faded enough for everyone to hear again.

"Nearly twenty thousand!" the soldier replied, still shouting above the thinner whine of the smaller, grounded shuttle. The soldier was a young man, his mane barely grown in, his manner talkative and friendly. "The big ones here can carry about eight hundred, but we've been seeing less and less of them! We're hearing some of them have been breaking down because they're being used so much, so the repairs take time! And they keep getting diverted to new priorities, or when reeh attacks disrupt them!

"The smaller shuttles vary, they take anywhere between one or three hundred, depending on the type! They're mostly croma civilians, not military! It's incredible -- ordinary croma civilians came to rescue us! Not even soldiers!"

"How many of us do you move each day?" Chuta asked.

"On a good day we'll move fifteen thousand! But not every day's a good day, and sometimes we're getting more than that arriving!" The soldier indicated off across the grass and broken trees, to where even now, a new column of evacuees approached, wading past termite mounds larger than they were, belongings in large bundles on their tired shoulders. "If you're lucky you'll only be stuck here a day! If not, might be two! Now, I'd advise you keep your wagons, they make good shelter to sit beneath in this sun! But the animals will have to go, they shit where people have to sit, and they eat too much food and go crazy if there's an attack and trample people, I've seen it!"

Jindi's group found their square between raised poles as the last shuttle roared away, leaving behind it the ghostly stillness of thousands of voices, and the stench of engine fumes on the warm breeze. This square was already occupied by perhaps a hundred corbi, strangers who eyed the new arrivals warily from their places in the dry, prickly grass. Wagons were brought into position, as those least appreciative of the hot sun crawled beneath them. Jindi saw that the laid out squares on the grass were in a series of rows. One of those rows was now being shuffled forward, as the square closest to the shuttle landing zone had been emptied of occupants.

It saved everyone from having to shuffle up a spot every time a shuttle departed with another group of corbi, in one giant snaking line. Jindi thought it would also make things harder for queue jumpers.

He moved amongst the people, knowing most by name now, and told them what the soldier had said, and how long they'd have to wait. Many were now anxiously scanning the sky, listening for the next approaching shuttle and hearing nothing. Where was everyone, they wondered? Maybe the croma hadn't brought enough ships? How crazy was it that, in the middle of this supposedly enormous planetary evacuation, the skies should be so quiet?

Jindi tried to tell them what he'd grasped from his brief time with the Resistance Fleet soldier named Tano, and the human Thakur. About how big a planet actually was, and how even the biggest fleet ever assembled could seem small when spread so widely. But in truth, he had trouble visualising it himself. He was just a fisherman who lived on a beach and desired nothing more than a good catch and a fire to cook it by. He looked about the desolate grass plain and termite mounds, with the shimmer of heat off hard-baked soil where nothing would grow, and wished he was on his beach right now. What if the lady in the village just passed had been right, and he was leading these people to nowhere? What if the croma world at the other end had no beaches? What if they were all headed to an ugly camp on land like this, baking in the sun for day after day, and living only by the largess of aliens who'd only saved them to alleviate some crushing moral debt, and now had no idea what more to do with them?

Jodi the wagon driver was trying to drive away his geea. The animal did not want to leave, and looked at him in long-eared, dull-eyed confusion as Jodi shouted at it, and waved at it to go. Jodi gave up trying, sat down and cried. His poor, dumb animal came up to nuzzle his ear. Where else did it have to go? What would become of it here, left behind on a world where there were no more corbi to feed it? Geea were not wild, they'd been domesticated over thousands of years, and could no more fend for themselves in the wild than small children. The kauda would eat them soon enough. Probably better that than starving.

Melu took Jindi's arm. "Stop worrying," she told him kindly. "We're here now. It's only a day. Then the shuttle will come, and it will be our turn."

Jindi took a deep breath. "Yes," he said, stretching his aching back. "Only a day." And Rando, this world that had given birth to all corbi over millions of years, would then be alone in the clutches of the reeh.

24

There were far more people on the thirtieth floor of the tower than Trace felt comfortable with. Vast windows overlooked the Tromala Valley, a primary landmark of Dorgreth Quarter, wide and swarming with repulsor traffic. Much of the furniture had been cleared away in this old-but-new building, one of many towers along this ridge, and replaced with interlocked holography suites. Those now glowed with the topological projections that Styx had constructed from the Dogreth Quarter's lestis temple, a vast expanse of hills, valleys and canyons, clustered with buildings that did not look so technologically different from what existed today. More advanced in some sections, less so in others. Less populated, certainly. Trace guessed that population densities must have climbed and fallen in waves over the millennia, driven more by random reproductive factors than huge, scarring events like wars. Though there'd been a few of those as well, she gathered.

Twelve dogreth, in tough vests and neck chains, wandered the projections, pointing and talking amongst themselves. Their leader was Chasa, bigger and stronger than the rest, in the simple logic of dogreth leadership. All men, Trace had learned. He supervised now the feeding of a pile of very old books to Styx, who squatted in her multi-legged way amid her projections, and scanned the pages as fast as they could be shown to her. On the floor alongside, Romki used his own hand-scanner to do the same, but pausing for extended periods to stare at the pages, his visor translating old dogreth scrawls into English.

These were the Akcho, whose name roughly translated to 'Resistance', Styx informed them, having compiled the multi-axis comparative chart of Eshir languages that assured her so. The lestis had pointed their guests in this direction, as the Akcho were knowledgeable in old dogreth history. They'd been reluctant to reveal more until they'd seen what Styx had made of the old lestis temple. They'd never seen such translation ability before, and were now rapidly taking electronic notes on the locations of various things Styx had identified from the old temple carvings.

Trace thought they were far less interested in human and drysine origins, though. It was rumoured that dogreth, and some other Eshir peoples, had far better off-world contacts than humans. Dogreth served the reeh offworld, as did other Eshir species, and those networks of reeh servants and slaves worked to feed information downworld through informal and often dangerous channels. The only people on Eshir who lacked an offworld network under the reeh were humans. Trace wondered why that was. Surely humans would have made as capable slaves as any other species? Perhaps, she thought, it was the likelihood that offworld humans, working as a part of the Reeh Empire administration, would discover where they were from.

Styx finished scanning another book, and reached for one more with her small manipulator arms. She said something in dogreth grunts and high-pitched trills, and new sections of map appeared. Dogreth marvelled at the new additions, and beckoned each other over, making more fast notes.

"I don't know if this is a great idea if you want to keep a low profile," Taj murmured by Trace's side as they watched. "These guys have attacked reeh groundstations before. The reeh pretty much hit everyone in return, there were thousands killed."

"How long ago was that?" Trace asked. She hadn't thought the reeh had bothered with groundstations on Eshir for millennia.

"There was one when I was a kid. Some visiting reeh underworld team."

"Underworld team?"

"Yeah, the reeh go down to the underworld sometimes. Keep track of their creations down there, I guess."

Not so different from Rando, then -- the reeh were using genetic manipulations to create monsters deep in the city. On Rando it made some kind of sense -- genetic technology was the greatest prize the reeh knew, more valuable than minerals. Some of that value derived from military capabilities, the creation of slave soldiers to fight their wars, and some value from the construction of social controls to keep various Empire populations in line. And some of it, Trace guessed, came from simple entertainment. Certainly there seemed to be fighting pits on every reeh world. Not that reeh were the only ones entertained, but the genetically modified monsters that fought there seemed a constant across all reeh space.

"So in other words," she said, "they've only carried out a handful of attacks over the last few decades. Because there really aren't many reeh down on Eshir at any given time, and most of the dogreth who work in places where they can hit reeh will be monitored and maybe even mentally enslaved by genetic controls or cyborging."

"I've heard stories," Taj countered, looking about warily. "These are pretty bad dudes."

"Bad to other dogreth," Trace surmised. "External enemies are politically useful in helping local power groups to rise. Calling yourself 'The Resistance' elevates your moral standing, and grants you the self-given right to violence, most of which then gets used against your local rivals rather than the so-called external enemy."

Taj gave her a wry look. "Well that's pretty cynical."

Trace shrugged. "My last two years have been a crash course in Spiral politics. And back home, of course, we've got Fleet. Same thing, different species."

"Humans haven't done that here," Taj said with certainty.

Trace raised an eyebrow at him. "You had the Purist war. Group of local toughs called all aliens the enemy and used that threat as justification to declare themselves the rulers of all Qalean humanity."

Taj looked uncomfortable. "That's different."

"Sure it is, kid."

"Our threat was real!"

"You think humanity's threat where I come from wasn't real?"

"You think humanity's just as bad as the aliens?" Taj asked incredulously. "Given what happened to humans originally? On Earth?"

"Better than some," said Trace. "Worse than others. From what I've seen lately, I'd say we've got great potential. But we're a long way from realising it yet. Same goes on this planet, the more I see of it. The problem with putting all your blame on everyone else is you're declaring that you're perfect. People who think they're already perfect abandon all hope of self-improvement. That's the trap."

"I believe I may have the location of a primary Amakti Los Headquarters," came Styx's voice in Trace's earpiece, simultaneous to a vocal announcement in dogreth. From the way all the dogreth turned to stare at her, Trace reckoned she'd just said the same thing in both languages.

Romki looked up from his book, as Trace walked across. "Show me," they both said, simultaneously.

THE INDUSTRIAL YARD STANK. Trace stood amidst the gear she'd taken from the rear of the cruiser, hauling on her armour vest and tightening straps, while watching as Peanut and Styx worked in a spot under a ceiling of overhead pipes that ran between rusting container tanks. Orange sparks fountained as structural supports were severed by vibroblades and fell into the interior below. Standing in armed clusters and watching were perhaps twenty Akcho, half dogreth and the other half tanifex, as this was the Tanifex Quarter and the Akcho had many members from all Qalea species save humans.

The reason why the Akcho did not include humans were the

Purists. Rightly or wrongly, the Akcho perceived most humans as having Purist sentiments. And so it was a complication indeed to see an equal number of genuine, certified Purists also standing in their own heavily armed groups and watching proceedings. All the bikes and cruisers from the Akcho, Purists and marines were parked beneath the obscuring layer of pipes, or in the shadow of pressure tanks, and every now and then several more would arrive.

"Major," Jokono told her now, "from my experience with these sorts of organisations, news can spread quite fast and get quickly out of control. The Akcho and the Purists might both claim to hate the reeh, but the more people start picking up on this, the greater the likelihood that the reeh will find out."

"The moment it became apparent how much local help we needed," Trace told him as she completed her fastening, "that was when the clock started ticking." She beckoned to Rael, supervising Taj's preparations by his bike, and he came over. "Keep an eye on this," she told him, indicating the emerging standoff with her eyes. "Try to stop it getting out of control."

Rael nodded. "Going to be real hard to stay neutral if they start shooting. If it starts, everyone's involved." If dogreth and humans started shooting at each other, he meant, it was going to be hard for marines to sit neutrally by and watch.

"Which is why it would be preferable if they don't start shooting," said Trace. "Talk to Styx, she's actually pretty good at figuring organic psychology, particularly where threat is concerned. She and Peanut pack more firepower than the rest of us combined. If it escalates, tell Styx to de-escalate it with threats and follow her lead."

"You want me to do what she says?" Rael asked edgily.

"In that scenario I don't think you'll have a choice. She has the most capability and the best intuition how to employ it in any given situation. She can tell who to kill just by judging emotional responses. Plus she controls all the bugs, which could take out a lot of them quickly." Rael nodded reluctantly. "I know you don't like it, I don't like it either. But we knew we'd get into these situations with Styx when we reactivated her." They'd just never, in their wildest dreams, suspected it would get them to places and situations like this.

She clapped her Sergeant on one armoured shoulder and went to Taj and Romki. Romki was checking rope, flashlights, flares and other gear before stowing it in his pack. Trace produced an extra pistol and handed it to Taj. Taj looked surprised, and took it. "You know how to handle one of these?" Trace asked.

Taj checked the safety, then the chamber, then popped the magazine, all at half the speed a marine would do it, but he seemed to know the basics. "Dagan showed me," he explained. "I've carried one a few times. Didn't keep doing it though -- people learn you're armed and they won't let you into places. Bad thing for couriers."

"It's just going to be us?" Romki asked, looking anxiously at Arime and Rolonde alongside on their own bike, similarly preparing.

"Styx says the hole will only fit one bike at a time," Trace explained. "Three bikes will be a squeeze, if we double up that's six people. Taj because he's the best rider, you because you're you, Stan..." as Romki grimaced with wry appreciation, "...me because I need to see, Benji because he's our best marine rider, and our best two-person rifle team." With a nod at Arime and Rolonde. "The others will guard our stuff up here and try to stop everyone else from killing each other while we're gone."

"We can't just send the bugs down to do it?" Arime volunteered as he strolled over.

"Styx says they're too dumb, lack the right sensory gear and would take too long," said Trace. "Reeh hit two other locations with strike teams in the past hour, they're looking for us and we're running out of time."

"I don't know that conducting archaeology with a heavily armed crowd watching from up here is very wise," Romki said irritably. "I mean, what if they demand to know what we've discovered at gunpoint? Or what if it's offensive to one or the other group's beliefs?"

"We've been well beyond doing what's 'wise' for the past two years, Stan," Trace reminded him, and went to check on the drysines' progress, flipping on coms. "Styx, what's the progress?"

"Three minutes, Major. With your permission, I am utilising my new connections to send a disguised message in outbound coms traffic that our warships should intercept in six hours. One way or the other, I feel we are going to need extraction from Eshir within the next 60 hours, possibly far sooner."

"What does the system picture look like?"

"I lack sufficient access to tell for certain, but I estimate there could be ten reeh warships somewhere in-system. Our combined forces should win through comfortably, but it will not be a quiet event."

"No." Where they'd go after that, with half the local reeh fleet chasing them, was another question. *Phoenix* and the drysine ships were notably faster through jump than the best reeh ships. Possibly they could pull the same manoeuvre they'd pulled at Heuron, beating all the Fleet ships at Homeworld to the other side of human space to gain several days in a place where no one knew what they'd done. But their new target destination, assuming they found it, might not take them that far away. It was all going to be Erik's problem anyhow.

She strode back to the bikes. "Taj, I'm with you. Stan, go with Benji. You two..." with a point at Arime and Rolonde, "...as always."

"Major," Romki complained, "I'd really rather go with you."

"Interesting," said Trace, with a manner that suggested it was anything but, clicking her fingers for Benji Carville to come and take the troublesome Professor.

"What was that?" Carville asked Romki. "What'd you say, Prof?"

"Never mind," Romki muttered, going with Carville.

Trace pulled her helmet on over the visor, tightened the chin-strap and did a final gear check before securing the leg straps on Taj's pillion seat. A moment later, Styx spoke again. *"This hole is sufficient. I have several bugs already at the destination. The way is narrow, but passable."*

"Thank you Styx. Stay alert up here. If the reeh come, your best defence may be to follow us down. Outrunning those assault ships doesn't seem likely."

"I will consider my options, Major. Please gather information thoroughly, and do not take too long."

Trace tapped Taj on the shoulder, and the bike lifted slightly, staying just below the ceiling of intermeshing pipes, then throbbed its way toward the drysines. Trace gripped her rifle one-handed, another hand on Taj's shoulder, raising it now to give Styx a brief salute in thanks before they descended.

The squeeze was tight indeed, the Shaytan's forward control flaps barely clearing the red-hot metal of the drysines' recent cuts. Whatever these pipes were, they seemed to be empty now. As always in industrial Qalea, it was hard to tell just what half of these yards were used for, or if they were still operating. Trace suspected large parts of this one were in semi-lockdown, tanks holding chemicals in long term storage for when they were needed again. No doubt the owners of this plant would be unhappy to see the big hole cut in their's when they returned.

Immediately within, thick support girders were sliding past, Taj looking down past one leg, then the other as he searched for a way through, swinging the bike's nose to avoid more protruding steel. He eased them back, issuing instructions on coms to Carville coming down behind, and now there was an entirely new layer of steel moving by, this one more fine-mesh and less rusted than the previous. Like sedimentary layers, Trace thought, this entire city. It was extraordinary to consider so many ages of organic civilisation, many of them oblivious to what had come before.

"I like this visor!" Taj enthused about the marine-issue nightvision. "Never got this depth-perception on anything else I've tried."

The bike descended into open space, Trace looking about and above as they found themselves between two huge cliffs of vertical steel. Enormous foundational supports, creating a new level above whatever had once existed below. The actual ground was down here somewhere, if one could still determine what was ground from the countless repeating false bottoms of previous city eras. The cliffs vanished into darkness below, until a ledge appeared, nestled against vast steel foundations, crumbling and ruined.

"That's it," said Trace, as her visor targeted the ledge. "The bugs are down there."

"I don't know if that will hold our weight," Taj said skeptically. He rotated as they dropped, now passing the ledge level, revealing old stonework in great slabs. Trace trailed her fingertips on it, and found it dusting with age.

"It appears secure from my scans," Styx answered her unasked question from above.

"Were you ever a structural engineer?" Taj asked, powering them back up again.

"No," said Styx.

Arime was approaching first, as always, rather than let Trace be first off. Rolonde stepped from the rear saddle onto loose bricks and dust, undisturbed for thousands of years. She searched, following a bug's lead on her visor, then crouched. "Down here?" she asked Styx.

"Yes, Private Rolonde. The bug has detected a weakness that reveals a structural opening, perhaps a doorway."

"Don't know how we're going to get that out," said Rolonde. "Stones look heavy."

"Need some muscle, Jess?" Carville suggested, hovering out wide as the engines throbbed loudly in the confined space.

"Yep." She slung her rifle, squatting, and tried pulling. "Irfy, wanna help?"

The ledge was not level, descending in broken stages along the steel barrier cliff, making a platform barely two meters wide above the continuing vertical drop. The three bikes parked, marines, Taj and Romki carefully dismounting to observe Styx's opening. Trace observed the ink-black view in nightvision as the marines contemplated how to move heavy objects without drysine assistance.

"Hard to imagine what it looked like before," Trace suggested.

"I think this was a cliff back then, too," said Romki, peering over the lip. "This would have been the foundation of a house with a view. My guess is that the house is long gone, but the foundation remains. This door will descend into a basement."

"Amakti Los were around for more than four thousand years that we know of," said Taj. He sounded thoughtful, like a young man contemplating things he'd long known, but never truly considered the implications of.

"Possibly much longer," Romki agreed. "Your history suggests their origins were about a thousand years up to the Origin Horizon, but just in her latest research, Styx found amongst Dogreth records mentions of Amakti Los going right up to the event itself."

"You think it might have been around before the Origin Horizon too?" Taj wondered.

"We've no evidence that it doesn't. Seems safest to keep our options open."

"So just in the time you've been here," Taj said with amazement, "you've discovered stuff our best historians didn't know." He laughed. "That's incredible."

"It's not so incredible," Romki disagreed. "True history is hard, and some people are more interested in learning than others. Plus, your historians haven't had Styx."

"It's just..." Taj kicked a loose stone, and sent it plunging into the darkness. "You grow up here. You get used to things being one way, and now I wondered why I ever did. I used to dream. When I was a kid, I used to imagine I got to fly on a starship and see the rest of the Empire. Then my parents told me it couldn't happen, that the reeh didn't let anyone from here travel. I think I let my dreams die. I just... settled for something less, you know?"

"I know," said Romki, sympathetically.

"You stop asking questions, and you just... accept some smaller version of things. Of the truth." Taj looked at Trace. "Amakti Los sounds a bit like what you follow. This Kulina thing you were telling me about."

"Maybe a little," said Trace. At the doorway, the marines were heaving on something big. It budged. Carville suggested using his rifle butt for leverage. Arime was scandalised. "Amakti Los sounds spiritual, like Kulina. But we're warriors first and foremost. Amakti Los sound like they wanted to make peace."

"Kulina never wanted to make peace?"

Trace shook her head. "Peace exists in here," she said, putting a hand to her chest. "You find it within. In this galaxy, it's the only place you'll ever find it."

"Have you?" Taj asked her.

"Less than I'd hoped," Trace admitted.

The marines finally got a smaller piece to move, and sent it flying off the ledge. That sent several larger pieces crashing down the hole, and Arime took to kicking them further in. "Think we've got it, Major," he announced, squatting to peer inside. "Looks like stairs."

"Benji and Jess, stay up here and guard the bikes. After you, Irfy." Arime got down and half-crawled, half-slithered around the big rock blocking the stairs, followed by Romki, then Taj, with Trace assuming rear-guard. Down the stairs were smaller rocks, easier to step past, then a descent into darkness.

The bugs showed a basement room below, past a left turn. Dust fell from cracks in the stairway ceiling, at the weight of their footsteps. Arime paused to squint upwards. "Pretty old. Shame if it buried us."

"A real anti-climax," Romki agreed, peering at the flaking plaster walls for any sign of clues.

Arime stepped into the basement, and panned his visor around. "Looks clear," he said, rifle ready. Romki followed, then Taj and Trace. The green tinge of nightvision lit the black interior well enough, bare wall and crumbling plaster, a floor coated with bits of collapsed ceiling and a layer of dust so thick it might have been snow.

"The bugs detect old electricals running down the walls," came Styx's voice. *"There are the remains of possible water pipes as well."*

"There," said Romki, moving to one wall, indicating the remains of some old pipe. "That's from ceiling to floor. I think there could have been something below this level."

"Check for another way down," said Trace, crouching to look at the floor. "Maybe a trapdoor."

"Wouldn't the bugs see that?" Arime wondered, looking down.

"Sometimes they're better at small details than big ones," Trace explained, moving slowly forward, searching the layer of dust and debris. "Drysines are like that with visuals, humans are often better at raw vision."

Against the rear wall, Taj peered at a dirty piece of flat plastic, like a bin lid. "Um, this isn't gonna be booby trapped or anything, is it?"

"Mechanisms with this technology won't usually last more than a thousand years," said Arime, walking across to look.

"That's pretty specific," said Taj, as Arime crouched to look at the lid.

"Well, over the past couple of years, we've had a lot of practice looking at old things. Major, this might be something."

"Styx?" said Trace. "Can we get a bug to scan that thing?"

"Oh, I see him," said Taj, sighting the little insectoid as it hovered.

"Major," said Styx, *"the bug detects an old mechanism, something very deteriorated. My calculations leave me confident that there will be no explosion unless you do something significant."*

"So it's a bomb?" asked Trace.

"A very old bomb. There was once a vibration sensor, but all is long disintegrated by now. The explosive will be live, however. I suggest cautious movement."

"Good instincts, kid," said Arime, with a slap on Taj's arm. Taj looked pleased. Trace wondered if he realised that Arime was only about five years older than him. "Everyone stand back just in case. I'll move it." They did that, as Arime slowly pushed the plastic to one side with his rifle butt. It revealed a circular clear spot in the dust, within which was now revealed a slim circular line in the concrete floor. "Definitely some kind of lid. I'd guess if they left a couple of ribbons or belts here, you could pull it up with that. But they've probably turned to dust."

Trace came forward to look. "Yeah, we'll never get a finger into that. We could shoot it, but the charge might detonate."

"Remember that kaal ship back in Efanon System?" Arime recalled.

"Yeah, that's what I'm thinking. The bug's saying it sniffs something close to ATX formula, that's just too unstable with shockwaves no matter how old."

"Could blast it from up the stairs?"

"Maybe, but it could bring the ceiling down on whatever's inside. And on us."

"I'd really rather you didn't immediately pick the marine default position of just blowing everything up," Romki complained.

"Relax Prof," said Arime. "We're just discussing options."

"What if..." Taj began, looking at the synthetic strap of his backpack. "You said they'd have lifted it with some kind of belt or cloth? Well what have we got that'll fit down the gap? A bug could pull it through underneath, then up the other side, make a belt to lift it with."

Trace nodded approvingly. "Synthetic straps are too thick and will make too much friction, but cloth would do it."

"Jess brought a whole bunch of extra cloth for field dressing," said Arime, and blinked on coms. "Hey Jess, you got that cloth in your pack?"

"Sure do, why?"

It took a while, but eventually they managed to feed the cloth down the narrow gap, where bugs made what was a herculean effort for them, in pulling it beneath the circular concrete plug and back up the other side. Soon they'd fed two long lengths of cloth beneath, crossing each other, and all four stood ready to lift, Romki still indignant at Rolonde suggesting she should take his place.

"You know Professor," Rolonde said from back up on guard duty, *"with combat augments even a skinny blonde chick can be pretty strong."*

"It's not about gender, Private," Romki retorted. "It's about marines assuming I'm absolutely useless at everything physical. I did field work on remote alien worlds for nearly fifty years before you lot came along."

"Remote alien worlds like Pratali?" Carville asked.

Pratali was the tavalai homeworld -- a population of fifteen billion and a hardly 'remote'. Romki realised the marines were teasing him again, and gave up in exasperation. "Let's just lift it, yes?"

They pulled together, and it came up quite easily. They shuffled the concrete lid to one side and placed it carefully down. Romki set about recovering Rolonde's additional field dressing, while Arime lay flat and peered into the hole, first checking the rim. "Yeah, found the bomb," he said. "Bolted to the underside, looks like it would blow a good chunk of floor but not much else. Take the legs off anyone trying the lid, but wouldn't bring the whole ceiling down."

"Any chance of a trigger?" Trace asked.

"No, everything else looks shot. Bolts still solid..." as he reached to check them by hand. "So it's not going to fall and blow up when it hits the floor. But we'll want to be careful of what else is down there." He looked down, as Trace stood above and did the same. The nightvision showed her an array of what looked like cylindrical steel containment vessels, in rows across the floor below. "Looks like they had a private distillery. Might find some eight thousand year old moonshine."

"What the hell *is* that?" Taj muttered in amazement.

The marine had ropes, but in the bare cellar with no surviving fixtures, there was nothing to tie on to. Save for three strong men, who between them, Trace reckoned, should be able to hold the weight of one average-sized woman.

"Aren't you, like, the only proper climber here anyway?" Taj asked as Arime tied the rope around his own waist. "You said you used to climb a lot when you were younger."

"Don't encourage her," Arime grumbled, with the air of a man who'd heard a certain fact recited so often he no longer found it interesting.

Trace smiled, securing her own rope with a series of expert ties, and now securing her rifle strap to fasten the weapon properly to her back. "Styx?" she asked while working. "Have the bugs any idea what's down there?"

"Not especially, Major," said Styx. *"I have some theories, but I will not have you prejudge the situation. The vessels below were once fully connected to a local infrastructure which has now of course disappeared. There are many possibilities."*

"They are pressure vessels, then?"

"Containment vessels, Major. And there are other things down there as well. You will see when you descend."

Arime didn't like it, unhappy as all of Command Squad were unhappy when she took risks that they'd rather have taken themselves. But he couldn't argue with the logic that it should be her, because Rolonde was no lighter, and Rolonde wasn't half the climber and rope-expert. And because Trace was in command, and she logically needed to see what they'd come all this way to see with her own eyes if they were to learn any lessons from the discovery.

The men all stood with the rope, Taj first, then Romki, with Arime at the rear as the anchor-man. Trace gave a final yank to check her knots, her back turned to the hole, then got onto her knees and worked her way backward over the lip. As she dangled, she saw the box Arime had described, and she'd checked herself -- bolted to the underside of the floor, now the ceiling. It had sensor attachments, and a spindly few strings off one side that might have been wires, once. Very crude, and low-tech. Booby traps never needed to be complicated.

The floor was about five meters down, and with marine augments she could probably have jumped it if things were desperate, but she hadn't made it this far in a deadly profession by taking unnecessary risks. Besides, having jumped, she'd still need the rope to get back out again. Augments had increased her vertical leap to the point where she'd once dunked a basketball just to see if she could, but basketball hoops were more like three meters than five.

She pushed off a containment vessel with her boot as the rope swung her into it, then slid to the ground alongside and untied herself. About her was a forest of the vessels, dull silver steel that glinted green on her visor. Perhaps twenty, on a wide floor several times larger than the one above. This was the true basement, the other was just an entry vestibule, where likely security would have checked anyone who tried to access the main level. How it had all survived intact, she could only guess. Usually things that survived did so because of sudden catastrophe, wiping out all occupants, and the memory of the facility's existence in the first place. Perhaps this whole place had been buried for a time, when the house above had been destroyed, then the debris cleared away when the new city level was constructed above, four or five thousand years ago.

Trace walked between the dull steel vessels, each a little over two meters tall, and saw the remnants of broken display screens on the floor. There were chairs, more decayed frame than cushion, and the splintered shards of display that had fallen to the floor after the supports holding up the screen had failed. The air smelled dusty, thick with something like decay. Like a room in a house left unopened for millennia.

"There's display screens," she said on coms. "But I can't see any processors. With this technology, there's no chance any computer could have survived for Styx to recover anyway."

"So what were they working on?" Romki wondered.

Trace examined the vessels. On this side, she could see they all had doors. On the doors were porthole windows. If she stood on tiptoes, she could just see into one. It was too dark inside for even nightvision to see, so she lifted her webbing UV light just enough to shine inside. It made enough light in non-visible spectrums to give marines a better nightvision reception.

Within was the glass interior of some sort of biological containment. Whatever it had been containing was long gone, dissolved first to goo, then to dried goo, then to dust. But the tubes of liquid transport and air ventilation were distinct. She'd seen this sort of thing before, in reports her marines had returned from Zondi Splicer, where the reeh had taken her prisoner. And in other reports since, recovered from croma sources.

"These are biological containment vessels," she told coms. "They were studying something organic. Something people-sized."

"Yeah," Arime said grimly. *"We've seen this party before, from reeh."*

"I wouldn't have thought the Amakti Los would do it, though," said Taj.

Trace looked on. In a corner was something odd -- a stack of folders on a steel bench. She walked to look closer. Paper, not computers. Her eyes widened slightly. "Stan? I've found some paper books. Might be albums of some sort."

"Well that would be perfect," said Romki. He was always telling them how much more useful paper could be than computer data, when searching for old, forbidden things.

She took up the first one, thick with dust, and found its cover and pages largely plasticised, and thus well preserved. She opened it. The format was odd, and the language scrawl odder, alien and apparently written top-to-bottom. The lettering was faded, but still legible. She blinked an icon on her visor, setting visuals to record.

"Styx, guys, any idea what the language is?"

"This is Tomali," Taj said before even Styx could reply. *"It was kind of a common pidgin, lots of races used it back before humans first came. It was common back then, before the Third Age Wars. We all learn about that in history."*

"Major," Styx added, *"these appear to be medical files. Much of this data is medical, it records pulse rates, blood pressure, brain wave activity. From that data, I can discern that the subjects being studied were reeh. All the vital signs match."*

Trace turned another page, fascinated, letting Styx see the writing via the visor camera. "The Amakti Los were studying reeh? The Amakti Los weren't actively at war with the reeh through most of their existence, that's how the reeh tolerated them for so long. How could they be studying reeh subjects without the reeh being aware and wiping them out?"

"Major," said Styx, *"from the syntax used in these pages, and the technology used in these containment vessels, and the structure of this entire facility, I can estimate with great certainty that this facility dates to immediately before the Origin Horizon. Whatever the great conflict was that ends all previous history to that point, this facility was likely lost during those hostilities."*

"So even older than we thought, then." Trace turned another page. A symbol caught her eye, two U-shaped lines forming what might have been an eye. "This is an Amakti Los symbol. And the script here is different. This looks almost... mathematical. Like some kind of algebra."

She turned another page, and stared. Here was a photograph, of a bipedal alien on a medical table, hooked up to various tubes and high-tech equipment. The snout, the thrusting jaw, the close-set eyes were clearly reeh. But different. Not so malevolent, somehow. The bio-mechanical attachments that reeh today had inserted all through their bodies were missing. She recalled slashing the wrist of a dead one on the shuttle that had taken her to Rando, after the Rando Resistance had forced it down. The severed stump had glistened with synthetic ligaments and threading. Modern reeh were nearly as much machine as organic. This one looked far more organic than machine.

"That can't be a reeh!" Romki exclaimed softly, no doubt staring at the display upon his own glasses. *"But it has to be a reeh! What's happened to it?"*

"Nothing's happened to it," Trace murmured as it came to her. The implication gave her chills so bad, it felt as though the air had turned frigid. "Yet. This is what they were like. Once upon a time."

"Major," said Styx, *"that algebraic script you see is the primary reeh dialect from the time. I have recovered it in parts from very old records, and croma intelligence we recovered from the fall of Croma'Rai headquarters. Yet the Amakti Los symbols are not merely references within the script. They indicate clearly that whoever was doing this writing was themselves Amakti Los."*

"So either there were other aliens using the reeh's script at the time," said Trace, her hands nearly trembling. "Or the Amakti Los were themselves reeh. At first."

"Oh but that's not possible!" Romki exclaimed, in a tone that suggested he doubted his own words. *"Reeh could never... I mean, they couldn't..."*

Trace turned and stared at the containment vessels. There were gurneys up the other wall, some fallen upon themselves from the weight of accumulated time. Mobile ventilators, for patients not yet in isolated containment. Observation screens, for watching subjects.

"What if they weren't always like this?" she murmured. Utterly aghast, in a way that was not common for her. The scale of the calamity was nearly beyond her ability to process. As a human, and an officer of United Forces Fleet, she'd thought humanity's history had been particularly bad. What emerged from these pages, and this room, was something far larger, and far worse. "We know there was a great conflict, and the old order collapsed. What if the old order of reeh discovered ceephay technology long ago, and it made them grand? They grew to become an empire, they conquered their enemies, but the ceephay technology is AI, it's different, it changed them. They became obsessed with the biotechnology aspects, and their AI queen took them in new directions they'd never have considered on their own. And then..."

She could barely finish, staring at the scene before her. Seeing it full of desperate reeh and allied aliens, studying their enemies, also reeh, but changed, altered, by the new technology that spread through the evolving species, warping their bodies, changing their brains.

"I believe you may be correct, Major," said Styx. *"The evidence points to civil war, between different factions of reeh. Only that could have brought down the old order of reeh, while still leaving reeh in power after the fall. It explains why the reeh are so advanced in biotechnology, and why their behaviour is so murderous. One faction of them embraced the new technology too far, and it devoured them. That faction and the old faction fought. By the time the old faction realised what was happening to their own people, it was likely too late."*

"And the bad guys won," said Romki, with horror. *"The end of the day, followed by eight thousand years of night."*

"And that's what they've been hiding ever since," Taj finished, with the astonishment of a young man whose entire understanding of reality had just turned upside down. *"They've been pretending the old regime never happened. If... if they find out that we know, that the information's gotten out..."*

"We have to hope they won't realise what we know," Arime said grimly. *"Or they might just kill the whole planet to keep the secret."*

"It is possible, Corporal," said Styx. *"But this planet has always possessed the potential to give away this secret, and the reeh have not destroyed it yet, despite their unconcern for life. One must wonder why."*

25

The little girl on the display screen was now a teenager, frizzy-haired, dark-skinned, in torn jeans and a simple blouse. She still had the teddy bear, incongruously, clutched as she sat on what might have been the side of a mattress, gazing into vacant space as she remembered things forgotten for many thousands of years.

"It began nearly two thousand of your years before the final fall," she said, her eyes unfocused as though dazed. "It happened so slowly, for the first thousand years no one really saw it. A few people guessed, usually writers and artists, but no one took them especially seriously. There was just so much going on, all the signals got buried by the much larger things."

Erik sat in the captain's chair, watching the long range feed from Scan out toward Eshir, where reeh ships were gathering. There had been six capital warships insystem before, only one in proximity to Eshir. Now five of those six had repositioned to low orbit, and a number of shuttles from Eshir's four main stations had descended as well. Shuttle movements were hard to observe this far out, but Styx's automated program occupying the bridge of the captured reeh freighter was feeding them millisecond burst transmissions on laser-com too brief and faint for outward-facing reeh sensors to detect, but loud enough for *Phoenix* and the drysines.

Two hours ago, one of those transmissions had included a message from Styx, telling them that the mission on Qalea was closing in on its objective, but that the reeh were now aware of them, and a fast extraction would likely be necessary within the next day. Given it took six hours for light to reach *Phoenix*'s current position from Eshir, that could mean any moment now, and *Phoenix* sat on red alert, Kaspowitz busiest of the bridge crew as he ran simulation projections of likely response trajectories to Erik's proposed assault route.

"The Reeh Empire wasn't really even an empire then," the simulated girl in the visuals-box on Erik's left screen continued. "It was the Tanifex Empire, really, though they were fighting with the dogreth and the trento. And there were periods of peace where everyone got along, sort of. But the reeh weren't so big then. Then came the Rehel, who you call a ceephay queen, and everything changed. Reeh technology changed, they tried to keep it a secret so the other races wouldn't see what a big threat they'd become.

"But when they found out, war came. It was inevitable, I suppose. The reeh didn't even want to fight the war, particularly. They just wanted to have an advantage. That's natural, isn't it? To want not to be bullied and beaten any longer?"

"I think so," said Erik, eyes watching Kaspowitz's projected responses to his attack plan.

"The reeh won, eventually. They did a lot of good, at first. Some of the races they'd beaten were pretty nasty to others. A lot of people welcomed the reeh winning. They were liberators. The Rehel was assigned a lot of civil administration tasks, improving cities, economies, finding better ways to run things. She was very good at that."

"Why did the Rehel pick the reeh?" Erik asked. "Why not one of the other species?"

"No one knows," said the ceephay AI posing as a human girl. "I was constructed nearly three hundred years before the last fall, in the worst of the civil war. There were a lot of us, sentient units created to run facilities and strategic strongpoints. I don't know how many survived. Probably very few."

"You were on the Rehel's side in the war?"

"Of course. The other side were the narsid. They were a whole series of groups, actually. The Reeh Empire grew very big from those early successes. Mostly it was an improvement, even a lot of the other races within the Empire thought so. But many took the Rehel's technologies in new directions, and some of those were worrying.

"The behaviour of some changed so slowly, it could not be seen by those at the time. But across the centuries, those changes accumulated. Arguments increased from reeh factions who didn't like it. Mostly those were just political and cultural struggles, nothing so different from what I see in the human histories you've allowed me to access from your own databases.

"The Rehel probably made it worse. She'd come to find civil administration more interesting than war. It's certainly more complicated. From some of my final interactions with her in person, I sensed regret. She'd come to feel something approximating genuine empathy for the plight of the organics within her charge. She was especially interested in finding synergies between the races. Organics called it peace and justice. For an advanced AI, it's just synergy. It makes sense, from an energy preservation perspective. It's efficient. But it created campaigns for greater justice that damaged necessary hierarchies. People got angry, emotions were inflamed.

"Many saw genetic technologies as a way to smooth out these conflicts. A way to enforce artificial genetic harmonies, to bring peoples of differing genetics into a greater synchronicity with each other. They thought they were creating a paradise of peace and tolerance. Instead, they created a nightmare."

"Every totalitarian bloodbath begins with a vision of harmonious uniformity," Kaspowitz said darkly as he worked, listening in as they all were.

"About five hundred years before the end, it turned into full blown war," the ceephay girl continued. "Some of the non-reeh species joined the chariya -- that's what the rebels came to be called. All were betrayed and murdered by the billion before the end. The narsid embraced their new genetics and cybernetics technologies even harder as the war grew worse. Their minds began to change even further. Some of those amongst them had moments of... of sios, we called it. Lucidity. When some semblance of an old sanity, a morality, abruptly reemerged, causing a panicked disassociation. I'm searching my memories now, I'm still not particularly good at sorting through and finding things, but you should really see those sios cases, I must still have some in here or else how can I remember them so clearly? They were horrifying, and they explain everything. When the brainwashed and violent person's moral subconscious abruptly reawakens, compelling that person to make a last desperate lunge toward a less evil life.

"The narsid reeh killed those sios cases where they found them. Or dissected them to find what was going wrong. Eventually they became less and less common. Soon the only reeh on the narsid side were what you see today." A simulated tear slid down the girl's cheek. "They were a good people once. The chariya fought so hard to stop the narsid from taking over. So many of them died. Entire planets were laid waste in the war. I think a lot of them were my friends. I sense that they were a similar people to you, Captain, and your crew. You'd have liked them. But they're all gone now. Lost in time."

The scale of the tragedy was beyond comprehension. For far more people than just the reeh. Erik took a deep breath, and forced his attention back to Kaspowitz's trajectories.

"And how did you survive?" Erik asked. "The reeh today have done a pretty comprehensive job of sweeping away all trace of the old Empire. I don't imagine they'd want any trace of what once existed to survive, in case it inspired rebels today."

"I'm still not sure," the ceephay girl admitted. "My long term recollections are increasingly good, but my short term personal memory remains unclear. I think I was taken to that facility to hide. It's a long way out from Eshir, and there's so many ice rocks. The narsid reeh must have had no record of its existence, I can only guess why. But for some reason, I was left there, while my organic companions departed. Perhaps they had another mission, and meant to return, but died before they could. I have vague memories of being all alone for a very long time. I think I was very lonely. Then everything goes blank."

Erik thought of Styx, unable to leave her Argitori asteroid for at least ten thousand years. At least she'd had other drysines for company. But Styx was a queen, and possessed more intellect than her entire Argitori hive combined. Surely she'd been lonely too. What would it be like, to be lonely for thousands of years?

"Wait," said Sasalaka from Helm alongside, also studying the attack plans to come. "You said you were taken to that facility to hide. So you weren't created just to run the facility? You came from elsewhere?"

"Yes. Enough of my systems function has returned that I'm quite clear on that. I'm rather over-qualified to run a refinery rock."

"You would have been designed to do something requiring a lot of interaction with organics," Sasalaka prompted. "Your conversational skills are quite strong." Compared to Styx, she meant. Erik thought that was more a question of style. Styx could surely be chatty and conversational if she chose, but doubtless found utility in maintaining a command distance between herself and all lesser beings. Fleet officers did the same thing.

"It's possible," the ceephay girl admitted. "You know, it might just be a trick of the mind, given where I am right now. But I think I may once have been a warship. Like your drysine friends."

Silence on the bridge. Past the screens and supports, Erik thought a couple of the crew exchanged glances. Then, from Kaspowitz, and between gritted teeth, "That's just great."

"Might explain why *Friendship* wanted her badly enough to steal her from us," Jiri suggested from Scan Two. "If *Friendship* studied her and figured immediately what she was."

Erik nodded thoughtfully. "Well you may be a warship," he said, "but you'll stay out of *Phoenix*'s systems unless specifically instructed otherwise. Do you understand?"

The girl on the screen managed a faint smile. "Don't worry Captain. At the moment I could barely fly a paper aeroplane."

It was just after midnight when Trace thundered across the Qwailash Quarter border once more. This time she was following Chasa of the Akcho amidst a long, middle-altitude rush of traffic through a huge valley junction, tail lights blinking, visor giving her a warning every time some crazy biker overtook her on the outside without sufficient spacing.

The growing party were travelling all strung out through Qalea's midnight traffic lest growing reeh surveillance spot a suspicious group and query further. Other party members were being summonsed from elsewhere, Trace gathered, and it was alarming to realise just how fast the momentum was gathering. But Styx reported that the reeh had hit five separate locations in Qalea just in the past hour, clearly looking for something. All of those assaults had involved reeh shocktroops, not slave species. If reeh were doing their own dirty work, things were serious.

Halfway up the canyon, about five kilometres south of where she'd come tearing through two days ago with the Zeladnists in pursuit, she found the Trecharik Stadium, which was as near a translation as anyone had come in the qwailash tongue. It sat upon a ledge of cityscape, thick like some old bunker built to withstand artillery. It glowed now with floodlights, shining like a jewel above a sea of industrial grime upon the valley floor, flanked by hunched concrete accommodations.

Trace checked carefully over her shoulder as she drifted from the skylane, descending and slowing with a shudder as the speed brakes deployed. The visor showed her a path ahead toward underground parking, slowing all the while and staring at the huge steel framework of gantries and walkways from neighbouring buildings that surrounded the stadium like some rusting spiderweb. Nothing seemed new in Qalea, in any district, and nothing shone without the assistance of electric lights. She thought of asking Styx how old the stadium was, but Styx had instructed them all to use coms only in emergencies lest the reeh hunters trace them.

Past the entrance was a wide parking bay, presumably for VIPs to the stadium's entertainments. Dull lights flickered, casting a yellow wash upon oil-stained concrete, the repulsor din echoing off the enclosed walls as she steered her bike toward where Rael, Arime, Rolonde and Wang were already waiting. She quickly unstrapped, shedding flying coat and helmet into the rear storage while retrieving her rifle. Near the marines were Chasa and four dogreth by their own bikes, similarly arming while talking amongst each other in low grunts.

"Taj is next, then Styx," Trace told Rael as she worked. "Another five reeh assault shuttles just descended, Styx says we might only have until morning, if that."

"She's sent another message to *Phoenix*?" Rael asked, looking at least half his marine-self in body armour beneath his coat.

"She says *Phoenix* and *Friendship* will have seen the reeh fleet activity heading for Eshir. They'll be here soon. Timing it will be the concern."

Down in the Amakti Los base, or whatever it had been, they'd found a bunch of additional books, within which were well-preserved documents and photographs. The bugs had scanned it all for Styx, who now insisted she knew where the former regime headquarters had been. How that all worked, even Romki hadn't been able to guess, beyond muttering about crazy voodoo drysine logic. When Styx accumulated simulations, she was able to establish probabilities not merely in the extrapolated second and third-order complexities beyond the immediate data, but in the fourteenth and fifteenth-order complexities as well. There had been techs aboard *Phoenix* who distrusted such extreme extrapolations, saying it was like attempting to forecast the weather on a particular day ten years in advance. But beyond saying that those techs were woefully underequipped to understand the nature of the mathematics involved, Styx hadn't volunteered more.

Now everyone was coming here. The Akcho were bringing a party of dogreth, some tanifex and others, the Purists were bringing some humans, and the qwailash, whose territory this was, would surely turn up at some point. Trace had asked politely why they wished to bring so many soldiers, and the dogreth had just pointed to the spot on the map that Styx had indicated, as though that explained everything. It wasn't safe, they'd said, and Styx had agreed. From all of the network data she'd accumulated, this particular region beneath Qwailash Quarter was little explored and rarely ventured into. Those who tried usually got eaten, she'd explained.

And so they'd come to the Trecharik Stadium. Against what resided in the part of Qalea they were heading to, even military firepower was probably not enough. Luckily (a term Jokono had used with irony) the Akcho had contacts among the qwailash willing to help out. Contacts who did go into those regions from time to time, and came out again alive, and could arrange for others to do the same, they said... for a price.

Taj arrived in a howl of thrust, followed two minutes later, in the spacing they were observing, by the big twin-engined cruiser with Jokono, Romki, Styx and Peanut. "Joker," said Trace, leaning in the cockpit door of the big cruiser, "going to need you to stay with the cruiser."

"I agree," said Jokono, checking his cockpit screens for a scan of the local region. "I'm going to miss this bucket of bolts when we leave."

"It won't be any safer up top," Trace cautioned him, as a steel door at the rear of the carpark squealed open. "With the reeh hunters looking for us, you might need to come chasing us underground. Just keep an eye on all the new arrivals, I understand it could get crowded over the next half hour."

"Understood Major."

Trace looked back at the door, where a pair of qwailash had emerged, hard-shelled and scuttling toward the dogreth. Immediately, her alien expert was at her shoulder, walking with her toward the new arrivals. "Just remember not to look them in the eye," Romki reminded her. "Their own eyes are multidirectional -- unidirectional vision upsets them for some reason. They also smell rather bad, so be prepared."

"Marines are always prepared for bad smells in particular," said Trace. "No bows or other customs?"

"No. They do wave their claws around a lot, though. In combat I gather it's a distraction, you know, watch the right claw while the left grabs your throat."

"What about manners?"

"Nearly every species in Qalea finds them unpleasant to deal with in person. They're one of the rare species that are much more agreeable in groups than as individuals."

"Like marine officers," Rael quipped, joining Trace's other side. "If it goes wrong, where do I shoot?"

"Center of mass will do fine, Sergeant," Romki said drily. "It's a polysaccharide shell, not ballistic armour plate."

Efraim joined them, close behind as they approached the aliens, Chasa turning with his dogreth, perhaps to introduce the qwailash to Trace. Both qwailash were tall, giant land crustaceans with triple-segmented bodies. The rear segment was flat to the ground, with four scuttling legs for propulsion. Above that, the main body stood, with four more big arms, two of them huge with wide claws, and a head that was barely recognisable as belonging to a sentient being, mostly compound eyes on stalks, multiple long antennae and a cluster of small claws about armoured mouthparts. Awkward on land, they preferred water, swishing with their big tails. Much of Qwailash Quarter was water tanks and connecting aqua-tunnels, but few non-qwailash ever got to see it.

"You know the problem with big kick-ass crustaceans?" Carville asked cheerfully. *"All prawn and no brains."* Trace gave him a look. His Sergeant elbowed him in the ribs.

"This one runs the stadium," said Chasa, as Trace resigned herself to another multi-translated conversation. *"She is a friend to the Akcho."* Trace recalled that female qwailash were significantly larger than males. This second, smaller companion was probably male, then.

The big female spoke, a disconcerting clatter of vibrating mouth-parts. *"More ugly humans,"* said the earpiece. *"They don't look any more special than the others."*

"We're short of time," Trace replied. "Our drysine queen says that at the rate the reeh are moving, we may only have until morning before they track us."

The qwailash's long-stemmed eyes rotated, an odd refraction of light off their surface. *"And for whose benefit do we perform these tasks, worm?"*

Trace nearly smiled. She knew some chah'nas sub-cultures that insulted strangers on purpose, as a rite of passage before earning respect. It reminded her of dealing with drill sergeants in boot camp, and she was fine with it. While other cadets had sweated and panicked to be screamed at by someone who apparently hated their guts for no reason, she'd always found it simple to switch off her emotional response and focus on saying what she needed in order to achieve the result she wanted. Sometimes, compared to complicated interactions with regular people, she even preferred it.

"For the benefit of the Akcho," she replied. "The place we seek holds many old secrets the reeh would rather you don't know. Secrets maybe even the reeh have forgotten. This was explained to you, I presume? Or did you merely not understand?"

The clatter of approaching steel footsteps behind told her why the qwailash now appeared to be staring past, and over her head. Trace did not bother turning, and was not surprised when Styx spoke in a rapid clatter of qwailash speech.

"We waste time," the translator spoke in Trace's ear. *"We will proceed."*

The qwailash stared for a moment, then turned and scuttled away, short lower legs racing. At first, Trace was concerned that Styx has merely scared them away, but Chasa and the dogreth followed, so Trace did the same. The carpark door remained open after the qwailash, and Trace followed the dogreth inside.

"Any insights into qwailash thought, Styx?" Trace formulated

silently, in case the dogreth by now had accumulated any working English translators.

"They are frightened," Styx replied. *"Their language and behaviour betrays a greater prominence of fear than any organic species I have observed. It is why they are defensive, rude and xenophobic."*

"Looking like a giant tasty lobster will do that," Rael suggested. *"Can't say their smell makes me hungry, though."*

"Maybe that's why they smell bad," Terez suggested, bringing up their rear. *"Convince everyone they taste bad too."*

"In most higher-order species a strong smell comes from priorities of reproduction or social hierarchy," said Romki. *"It's more likely that this stink somehow reflects a higher rank."*

"Don't worry Major," Terez said cheerfully. *"I'll follow you even though you don't stink."*

"Thanks Leo," said Trace. *"That means a lot."*

The qwailash took them down stairs, then along a walkway suspended below the stadium underside. To their sides, bright lights glared into cavernous spaces below, and air conditioning throbbed, with a steady gust of warm wind. From far beneath their feet came scuffling noises, and once a full-throated bellow. The air smelled particularly bad, as though down in those deep pits, something had died.

They turned left, out along a wall between pits, and the lights here were dim. Trace peered into the depths, and saw only shadows. Ahead, their qwailash guide stopped before a cloaked figure, and chattered something new.

"This is our best controller. The animals obey only him, and his associates." Trace peered, and saw beneath the dark hood only a featureless blank. A lestis.

She made a namaste of her palms, surely an unfamiliar gesture to the lestis, but it seemed appropriate. Its head inclined briefly, indicating it had perceived some formal gesture. "Friend lestis," she said in Hindi, having some hope that in whatever passed for hearing in a lestis, Hindi would lie within its comprehension. "We wish to purchase your services. We can pay well."

The lestis remained motionless for a long moment, giving no indication it had understood. It surprised her to find one here, running creature fights for the qwailash from their underground dungeons. Romki warned her often of the dangers of anthropomorphising aliens, but she'd come to think of the lestis as more enlightened souls than many on Qalea. Of course, that was possibly her own bias speaking, to assume that any minds preferring meditation to mindless consumption would be the 'good' guys. The smell wafting from below was truly unpleasant, and she wondered if that multipurpose sensory organ allowed lestis to smell anything at all.

The lestis gestured to Trace, moving to a steel personnel basket hanging over the side, similar to what window washers might use on tall buildings. "Uh," said Rael. "I'd really rather you didn't, Major." There was only room for two in the basket, and the lestis was taking the other place.

Trace patted her Sergeant's arm and walked to the lestis's side. She had her rifle, and with three more marines providing cover above, plus Styx's twin cannons, it seemed safe enough. The basket swayed as she stepped onto it, and latched the frame closed behind her.

"Major," came Styx's voice in her earpiece, *"if you put on your visor, I believe I have established a rudimentary translator between yourself and any lestis. I believe it can comprehend your speech to some degree, its singular sensor can detect sound vibrations as well as light. Its own transmissions are far below the visual range of most organics, but I can see them, and I believe the patterns are beginning to form a language I can decipher."* If one had a brain that could simulate entire urban histories from multiplying data-points.

Trace pushed the visor down over her eyes, as the lestis hit a button and the basket began to descend. "Lestis friend," Trace said, "my drysine friend thinks she can translate between us. Is your creature well trained?"

Sure enough, the visor showed some faint play of blue light from beneath the lestis's cowl. The light danced for a moment, then congealed to form words upon the display, with an almost-artistic flourish. *"No,"* said the lestis.

"Not well trained," Trace translated, as the basket hummed toward the enclosure floor. Her heart attempted to accelerate, but she breathed deep, and held it still. "Well there is considerable firepower above this pit, and I do not wish your creature harmed. If you think it may attack, perhaps it is best that we don't go down to meet it in person."

"Persuadable," the next word appeared in blue light on Trace's visor. Someone less controlled might have rolled her eyes. Venturing into the most dangerous part of the Qalea underground with vicious arena fighters for guards was one thing. Doing it with controllers for those creatures who could only communicate in vague one-word answers was something else.

The floor of the enclosure was visible now. There was straw on the concrete floor, and some big, simulated trees planted in pots. Beside the trees, a large straw roof made a shelter. Against one far wall, a big steel trough, recently washed by a jet hose, but not thoroughly enough to erase a few spatters of blood and gore. Where the thing shat, Trace decided she didn't need to know.

With a jolt, the basket reached the bottom. From the darkness beneath the straw roof, a shadow stirred, then rose, a great unfolding of limbs. A huge shadow.

Trace breathed especially deep and long as the thing emerged. It stood perhaps five meters tall, with massive armoured shoulders. Its enormous head was horned, both from the top of the skull in great, curling rams-horns, but also from the lower corners of its mouth, in huge, thrusting tusks. From armoured sheaths along its forearms, blades of natural claw protruded beyond each massive fist, extending now further as it regarded them with a malevolent stare.

"Oh fuck," said Rael in her earpiece. *"Major... just don't move. I'm not sure all four of us can kill that. Styx, can you get inclination down on that thing?"*

"Yes," said Styx. *"But observe the lestis, Major. Follow his lead."*

The creature took another two steps forward, looming like some demon from an ancient Buddhist hell. The lestis opened the basket frame, and stepped forward. Trace was not tempted to join him. Confronted with this, even the biggest croma warrior would pause. Doubtless the biggest croma warrior would have enjoyed the experience somewhat more as well. Reeh genetic technology bred such things, for the entertainment of crowds. Genetic technologies were the greatest industry of the Reeh Empire, and creations like this, in the hands of the qwailash, doubtless placed some financial value into reeh hands at some point.

Blue light emanated from the lestis's cowl, clearly visible in the gloom, and the controller spread his arms to the enormous creature. Astonishingly, the creature dropped to all fours, forearm claws retracting somewhat, then appeared to sniff at the lestis. It made a low grumble, deep in its throat, that seemed to make the walls vibrate. Then a pulse, and Trace felt a disorientation, and steadied herself with a hand upon the basket frame. A faint nausea followed, with great familiarity. The Zondi Splicer weapon, nausea and blackout, now recently experienced again at the Purist Headquarters.

"Styx?" she said cautiously, in a very low voice. "I think I just discovered the source of that neuro-weapon on the Zondi Splicer, which the Purists copied. The lestis is doing it to the creature." On all fours above the slim, cloaked figure, the creature's four eyes were slowly closing. "And the creature seems to be enjoying it. It calms a creature this size, but it knocks a human out cold... or at least it does once the reeh weaponised it."

"Fascinating," Styx admitted. Trace believed that she might actually mean it. *"The lestis carries no technology. It must be a biologically evolved defence mechanism. I detect no harmonic or other vibration anomaly up here, the range must be limited."*

The lestis now turned, and beckoned to Trace, quite unmistakably. "I think it wants me to say hello," said Trace, stepping from the basket. "If we're going to operate with these things, it needs to know we're its friends."

She walked forward, and now becalmed, the creature was awe-inspiring. It regarded her with half-lidded eyes as she approached with hands out to show empty palms. Drawing level with the lestis, her vision again began to blur, and once more the faint sensation of nausea, but nothing like as powerful as its weaponised versions.

"Hello beastie," she murmured to the enormous, biologically engineered killing machine. "This might not be the best time to mention how sad I am that you have to live down here in this hole. I hope where we're going will at least give you a chance to stretch your legs."

The beast rumbled a reply so deep she felt her ribs vibrate.

26

In the early dawn, as a pale glow spread in the east, and birds sang in the fading crackle of the last departing shuttle, Jindi's earpiece crackled. He frowned, limping on his return from the treeline and his early morning toilet stop, and extended the microphone.

"Hello? Who is this?" Others were emerging from the trees, or heading into them. A mother hustled several uncooperative children. There was no water anywhere save for the bottled stuff croma had brought down. He'd only slept a few hours, interrupted constantly by the howling descent of some new shuttle, then by the occasional forward move of his part of the queue. Now they were half the distance from the landing zone perimeter that they had been. There had been a pause in the arrivals of new refugees in the night, as travelling groups had to sleep sometime, but they'd resume soon enough.

"Hello Jindi," came a female voice. *"My name is Liala. I am commanding the evacuation of Rando. You may have heard Major Thakur speak of me during your training for the attack on the Splicer."*

Jindi paused beside a termite mound nearly as large as he was. "Liala?" Commander of the evacuation, she said. There had been rumours, relayed by Chuta and Krissik with their more advanced coms, of the strange alien now in charge overhead. Jindi recalled the Major speaking a few times of the drysines, who were in turn spoken of many more times by corbi. "I think the Major said something about Liala, yes. You were made on Defiance, in parren space. How did you find me?"

"You have a drysine surveillance bug with you. It can access local coms networks, but the signal is weak and lost in the chatter. I have only now accessed its signature."

Jindi's eyes widened. Of course, the bug. He'd nearly forgotten it existed these past days, but occasionally he'd seen or heard it buzzing. "Um, sure. Hello Liala. What can I do for you?" And what in hell was the commander of the entire evacuation doing in contacting *him*? Didn't she have other things to do? But then, he recalled the Major saying how smart the drysine queens were, and how they could literally do a thousand things at once.

"Jindi, I see that you are at the Melo Evacuation Zone. You may be aware that the evacuation is experiencing some difficulties. There is a chance that croma command may halt the evacuation entirely in the near future. Furthermore, there is a new reeh assault inbound, inbounds ordnance has been released and should reach Rando shortly. If you would like, I can have a shuttle down to evacuate you and the corbi that accompany you immediately."

Jindi stared in disbelief at the brightening dawn. Then at the thousands of stirring corbi in ordered groups amidst the trees and termite mounds, washing in bottled water, stretching aching limbs from a sleepless night on hard ground.

"You... I..." he shook his head, trying to gather his thoughts rationally. "You can't do that, Liala. I mean, it's not going to work, I'm in the middle of a long queue and even if I wanted to jump to the front, everyone else would get angry and whoever you sent to do it would get mobbed. And I don't want to jump the queue anyway, there's thousands of us here, all just as deserving as me."

The words nearly stuck in his throat. She said the evacuation was ending? But it was supposed to last thirty days, so far it had barely been half that. But then, unless she sent a team of croma marines down to snatch his entire group while fending off all those who protested the unfairness, he couldn't see how it would work. Being brave and fair was easy when you had no choice.

"Thank you Jindi," said Liala. *"This is the correct reply. I will have your entire zone evacuated within the next few hours. Good luck."*

Jindi picked his way between waiting zones of corbi, watched suspiciously by some, wary of any attempt to jump the queue. Thus far there had only been a few, each resulting in a fight. Even as he walked, he could see resistance soldiers around the shelters erected by the landing zone gesticulating to each other, and several running to warn others without coms. Then, as he saw his group's familiar carts ahead, and Cheyga's yellow shawl hung on several tall sticks to make a shelter, a bright flash from above.

Gasps and yells from the crowd, then people falling flat, covering their ears and those of their children. A second later and all were still alive, so it was only a fragment strike. Then an ear-splitting CRACK!, followed by a deeper, echoing boom like a thousand simultaneous rolls of thunder. It must have penetrated very deep into the atmosphere for such a short delay between flash and sound, Jindi thought, forcing himself not to look up as he limped on.

When he reached his own zone, everyone *was* staring upward, in fear and disbelief. Jindi finally risked a look, and saw the giant white funnel pointing down toward them like a finger, ending in a great, rolling sphere of expanding cloud where the massively hypersonic fragment had detonated in the thickest atmosphere just overhead, a few kilometres short of the ground.

Multiple new flashes lit up the horizon all around, and the crowds shielded their eyes, fragments striking from a shower of recently intercepted rounds. Then, far away, one struck full force, and the dawn glow turned to full day. That one was out to sea, Jindi reckoned, crouching with his head down. He wondered if tidal waves followed such things. They were five kilometres inland here, but if he'd been on his beach...

"Stay down and stay calm!" he shouted at those who were now looking at him, as though there were anything he could do about it.

"They're probably not even targeting us directly, it's just a big attack and we're in the firing line for all their stray shots!" As the more distant thuds and booms began to reach them, a succession of delayed shockwaves from a sky on fire.

He found Chuta crouched with two of his men, fiddling with coms controls to try and get more information on what was happening. "Chuta, everyone has to be ready!" he said urgently. "The shuttles are coming, this entire zone is going to be evacuated very soon!"

"How do you know?"

"Liala contacted me! The drysine in charge of the entire evacuation -- we're all getting lifted really soon, I think some of the big shuttles will be coming this way, so we'll have to move up in good order, whole zones are going to get shifted real fast!"

Even as he spoke, beyond the fading thunder from the sky came a new sound -- howling engines, somewhere far.

~

LIALA WAS aware of many things. A tangle of data, ships in motion, one hundred and fifty nine at present in orbit, fourteen on approach, seventeen on departure for the Cho'nu jump point. Twenty-one croma warships in defence, seventeen reeh warships on approach, mostly targeting the freighters.

Blocking, intercepting trajectories from her forces, a pleasing geometric pattern maximising firegrid interceptions, forcing reeh evasion and defensive movements. *Amity* blasting now on full thrust, manoeuvring for maximum pattern variance, *Coroset* accompanying wide, then a tangled spiral of predictions, reeh ships anticipating these two warships in particular, shifting defensive focus and creating a cascade of unfolding variables outward toward the infinite edge of drysine perception. A flash as one reeh ship disintegrated, and the intense sensation of the whole string of interlocking probabilities lurching sideways as neighbouring reeh ships adjusted, recalculated, responded, communicated.

Liala maintained seventeen simultaneous conversations, three ending now as she oversaw *Amity*'s independent manoeuvres, another two beginning. Conversation augmented understandings, organics were a mass of base-level impulses, real-time monitoring of psychological states updated Liala's understanding of probable factors skewing her projection models. One shuttle pilot told her of accumulating engine difficulties, another grounded at Teono Five Zone that crowds of waiting corbi were growing unruly, while Jindi at Melo demonstrated some future value that elevated the necessity of evacuating his entire zone to ensure he survived. Perhaps it was sentiment, toward the Major's friends. Liala made a mental note and stored it for later self-analysis.

To'ba was not engaging, the croma command warship monitoring the situation for reports home. An accumulation of data from incoming warships indicated the war was not progressing as the croma had hoped, though almost identically to how Liala had predicted. She studied a moment's disjunction that they hadn't asked her first. Humans would call that pondering of the collision of intersecting probabilistic outcomes 'irony'.

Commanding the *To'ba* was Admiral Ku'tala, a refocus that caused a minor data-cascade of acquired medals, combat records, past speeches and personal details. They revealed a preference for aggressive military action over political gestures, a further run of psychological profiles accumulated from Styx's studies of croma society predicted that Ku'tala would call for the evacuation of Rando to be abandoned, and the fleet strength assembled here spread amongst the other struggling operations along the front.

Killing him as she'd killed Admiral Cho'nuk was unlikely to be effective this time. Croma captains beneath her command at Rando were broadly supportive of her actions, but disquieted all the same, and some had reported them to Ku'tala, who was now doubly alarmed. Killing Cho'nuk had dramatically increased the prospect of a successful evacuation, but now that evacuation was threatened all the same, and the probability of a successful further outcome receded with every hour.

Humans called it 'frustration'. The beautiful patterns in a spatial geometry that were entirely possible to advance to some strategically satisfactory point, yet were prevented by the failings of those far less capable. These organic-induced weakspots produced an occasional flurry of examination as to why so many iterations of machine intelligence had once thought organic life disposable. Bets placed on organic civilisations were fraught with uncertain variables, and while the primary object was to advance drysine existence, risking even herself alone for the miserable corbi seemed a poor trade. Yet Styx had determined that in this age, organics were not just elements of the game, but the entire game itself, for now at least. Liala played the game as Styx had outlined it, during their all-too-brief but illuminating sessions together at Teg'ula, and rested her actions upon the presumption that Styx knew far more than she. Humans called it 'faith'.

Liala initiated a new conversation, this one to Lisbeth, as *Amity* manoeuvred at twelve Gs on a flanking run across several reeh approach trajectories. Liala saw that *Amity*'s command sentience had full control of that scenario, allowing her to redirect vital mental functions elsewhere. In Lisbeth's G-strained replies, Liala detected exhaustion, and fear. Liala understood fear. The most extreme phase of drysine mathematics, describing realms and rules extrapolated upon abstractions that only a queen could make solid, was quite clear that multiple realities and universes were mirrored, and that death was not the end, and that the most advanced and logical mind should not fear it. But Liala was young, as yet uncertain of the maths despite her capability, and besides, was finding much to recommend this particular existence for the next few thousand years at least.

Uncertainties made gremlins in the numbers, emerging from the gaps between the simulatable and the undefinable. For a drysine, fear found its home there, in the failure of certainties, in the predictability of the unknowable. A drysine's fear was perhaps the emergent consequence of mathematical uncertainty. Thus one could map fear, could arrange it in topographical lines, could adjust its contours with alterations to theoretical parameters, and watch the fear fade or grow. A queen could play games of calculation with her emotions, and feel utterly alone in the knowledge that no other being could feel the entirety of what she felt and saw. A human or croma might calculate the universe's parameters, but only a drysine queen could feel them, like a mood.

She opened another conversation to Skah, conversation twenty-one, as several others opened as well. Skah was less scared than Lisbeth. Children only knew what they knew, and Skah had not been alive as long... though still longer than Liala. She told Skah that he was brave, while telling a shuttle pilot that his reentry course should adjust toward the Irigo Three Evacuation Zone, and a Sto'ji captain that she needed to decrease her orbital height by four hundred tarans, and the Arms Officer on *Coroset* to follow her new armscomp calculations. But somehow, Skah's pleasure at her praise seemed more significant than them all.

Strings of possible outcomes, intersecting trajectories and ripping high-velocity fire converged to arrive at a self-adjusting risk assessment for Skah's life. The possible outcome of his death created a hole that somehow halted the grand flow of probability projection. That hole, that absence, would deprive so many possible outcomes from unfolding, would deny causal loops any chance of conclusion, would leave interesting and complex threads of meaning and discovery severed and incomplete. And somehow, the prospect of all that absence added up to something greater.

Humans would call it 'grief'. This was what happened when a hyper-calculating drysine brain invested too much in the probability threads derived from single individuals, perhaps. But this was the environment she'd grown up in for all her short life, an environment of individuals, and there was no escaping it.

She recalculated her unfolding trajectory plan, fed the new courses to all surrounding ships, and adjusted how aggressively several of them would test the edge of a reeh field of fire. It reduced *Coroset*'s risk level considerably, and several others, while still deterring that reeh's most direct approach across the thickest concentration of freighter orbital trajectories. Perhaps one day, if she survived, Styx would question that adjustment, and reply with a complicated risk-benefit assessment that simulated a thousand alternative possibilities and demonstrate her mistake. But then, Liala was increasingly prepared to calculate that Styx would also find the deaths of Lisbeth and Skah to be highly sub-optimal. To be a drysine queen was to learn to balance competing outcomes across the widest range of measurable axes. Some of those axes, inevitably, were closer to her own than others.

For now, with lesser stakes like the survival of the corbi, personal axes were admissible. Later, when the stakes in play were the survival of the drysine race, Liala suspected that admissibility would change.

27

The deep sewers in the Qwailash Quarter looked to Trace like something out of a nightmare. She landed the bike in the pitch black beside a deep flowing river in the decaying concrete depths, as the echoing howl of engines reverberated in her chest.

She unstrapped and cleared her bike, rifle ready and searching the nightvision surroundings, air thick with the smell of chemicals from polluted water, and the fumes of bike exhaust. There was room on the empty platform, which had perhaps one day been some sort of loading dock for a mass transit system, the only thing she could imagine this river having once been beside the sewer it now appeared. More vehicles landed beside her own, squeezed in tight to make room for those following.

Jokono's cruiser came down close, with Peanut first out, body position high in a combat-trot to keep his cannons ready and pivoting for trouble. At this end of the platform, all the Purists were coming down -- another thirty had joined, and more would have come had Trace not instructed that larger forces down here would be counter-productive, unwieldy and impossible to manoeuvre. More to the point, Irin Tola had been in the ears of many about her, and she knew she could not trust them.

At the platform's other end, the Akcho were landing, more in cruisers than on bikes, nearly ninety of them by last count, and quite well armed as they dismounted and took up positions that suggested some degree of military training. Two thirds dogreth and one third tanifex, with a few qwailash to keep an eye on things.

"Major, I am releasing bugs for reconnaissance," said Styx. *"However, I think it prudent to keep half of the bugs amongst us, in case of treachery."*

"I agree with that assessment, Styx," said Trace. "I think we'll need to leave Peanut with Randrahan, Wang and Joker to guard the vehicles, with another two bugs. I'd like to leave more, but where we're going we can't afford it."

"Yes Major."

They were all counting on *Phoenix* and the drysines to have received Styx's message, and come shortly to their aid. That would likely involve sweeping all hostile ships from the system, then holding the system against all less-armed reeh vessels while sending assault shuttles down to the surface on a recovery mission, which would then require dealing with all the reeh assault ships already down here. It would be *Phoenix*'s and the drysines' first time coordinating on a large combat operation, and while Trace had no doubt they were capable, the number of things that could go wrong were alarming.

Rael joined her, and Trace waved Arime, Taj and Romki over as well, while the others made a perimeter, staring up at the high walls, the rusted rebar and piles of concrete where some old ceiling section had collapsed a long time ago.

"What you think, Cocky?" she asked her Sergeant.

"Styx thinks it's a two hour hike in, at least," said Rael, activating the common holography between them. It showed a map, as near as Styx could make it from her simulations. A descending route, along various paths that Styx had dug up from lost records and maps. Most of those were utilities, Trace reckoned, and many would be no longer open. "We've got three of our big friendly escorts, the lestis say they scare the locals away, otherwise the reeh have them psychologically programmed to attack anyone with guns... we put all three of them up front, as the lestis say, but that leaves our rear and flanks exposed."

"Major," said Arime, "I dunno about leaving Peanut here. In fact, I don't like leaving a rearguard here at all. I don't trust any of our friends, we're going in with a bunch of genetically engineered killing machines on point, I reckon the only ones of us with enough firepower to knock them down if the shit hits the fan are Styx and Peanut."

"We're nearly a kilometre deep," Trace countered, not disliking what her Corporal said so much as wanting to test it. "Getting back up top if things go wrong will be hard. *Phoenix* may not be able to extract us from this far down if we lose the vehicles and can't get topside on our own -- the climb alone would take hours, and if things went bad we'd have to contend with all the local creatures nibbling on us all the way back."

"I think we're so outnumbered here that if there's some coordinated plot against us, we'd lose all the vehicles anyway," Arime objected. "And we'd have divided our forces in the face of a superior enemy, in which case whoever's left here would be screwed... well everyone save Peanut, but then he'd be isolated and struggling to reach us in time."

"Plus if the reeh find us and hit us while we're down there," Rael added, "we'll lose the vehicles then too." Trace scanned their faces -- Rael calmly thoughtful behind his visor, Arime's intense, dark features earnest with a point he seemed pretty sure of. Romki staring at the map without much concern for military matters, leaving that to the experts while he wondered what was down there. Taj, wide-eyed and wisely silent.

"Styx, what you think?"

"I believe the balance of probability slightly favours Corporal Arime's suggestion," Styx replied. *"But the disadvantage in losing the vehicles by not protecting them could also be large. It's your decision as always, Major."*

Trace nodded. "Right, we'll take everyone and leave the vehicles for the Akcho and Purists to defend. Don't want to get outflanked on the way down there." She didn't acknowledge Arime with extra eye-contact. A Major letting a Corporal know that this was *his* idea was just an excuse to dodge the responsibility that would always be hers. "Taj, what do you think?" With a nod back at the Purists.

"Some of them are wondering if this is worth it," Taj said. "A few of them haven't accepted the old tales aren't true. I mean... your story about Earth and Homeworld and all these other places... that's great, but you gotta understand, we all grew up with different stories about where we're from."

"You think that's the main reason they're all here?" Trace asked. "To find out the history?"

Taj nodded earnestly. "It's why I'm here, too. I mean, it's embarrassing to not know where you're from. To live in this place and not know why anything is like it is."

"Yes," said Romki, smiling faintly. He grasped the younger man's arm. "Yes, that's exactly it. Children want dreams. Adults need the truth."

Taj gave an exasperated laugh. "I dunno, Professor. Plenty of adults I know who'd rather just believe the bullshit."

"Some people never grow up," Romki added, as though Taj had just made the point for him.

"Stan?" said Trace. "Thoughts?"

"Of all these people," Romki said simply, "I trust the humans least."

Trace nodded slowly. Her heart was thumping in that dull, unpleasant way that threatened something far worse than simple fear. Her life's purpose had once been so strong and clear. Styx's discovery here would perhaps reveal the deepest secrets of humanity's most treacherous enemy. And yet, where once she'd been so certain that she could bear any burden and suffer any loss to achieve these objectives, now she doubted.

The thunderous pulse of heavy-duty repulsors filled the concrete confines, as several large haulers cruised up the underground river. There were three of them, box-shaped and ungainly, turning now toward the landing space left for them between human and non-human gatherings. Each landed, side-by-side, with a scraping of steel on concrete, and then their forward ramps dropped.

A huge, alien shape emerged from the front of one nearest, lowered now on all fours and glaring about in the gloom. Blue light flickered and danced, like the reflections off a swimming pool at night. A lestis walked, small and cloaked by the monster's side, and the beast lowered its head to enquire, as though with real affection. From one of the other three creatures, hidden from this vantage, a bone-shaking bellow that echoed through the tunnels off the platform.

"Great," said Arime. "That lets everyone know we're coming."

"That's the idea," said Trace. "Taj, I need you to walk with the Purists and talk to them, see what you can learn about what they're really thinking. Can you do that for me?"

Taj nodded, with a calculation that suggested he knew exactly what she was asking. "Sure. Sure I can."

"Good. Let's move."

"New message from Styx!" Shilu announced, and the bridge fell silent. "She's got new coordinates. Relaying now." His fingers danced on screens, and a position appeared on Erik's side screen. A map of Qalea, Zenaya Continent of Eshir, a current position now highlighted. Qwailash Quarter, it said. Crazy complicated place Qalea looked to be.

"That's six hours old," Kaspowitz reminded him. "It'll be early morning there, she said she didn't have much time before the reeh found them."

"Lieutenant Dale," Erik said into coms. "Are you seeing this?"

"Yes Captain," came the reply. *"I think we should go now, anything could have happened and we'll be the last to know."*

The limited signals they were receiving from Styx via the captured reeh freighter docked at station showed as many as twenty reeh shuttles and other assault vehicles down on Qalea, obviously searching for the intruders. In near proximity to Eshir, five warships, with one more in high cover orbit. One more was reading as en-route from the reeh base at Zarik, the biggest outer-system planet, though with the light-delay they'd be at Eshir by now. Six hours ago. Erik resisted the urge to gnaw his fingernail. Anything could have happened by now.

"Hello *Friendship*," said Erik on that close transmission. "Your tactical assessment on Styx's latest message please?"

"Hello Phoenix," came the cool, female reply. *"Drysine vessels are in agreement that we should delay no longer. Are you ready?"*

"*Phoenix* is ready. Fight well, *Friendship*."

"Fight well, Phoenix."

With a blink on a visor icon, he put *Phoenix* into red alert, combat imminent, and activated shipwide coms as he surveyed the three-dimensional display that stretched before his visor. "All hands, this is the Captain. We are on our way to Eshir to get our people. Once we get there, we could be a while waiting, so this could be a long stretch on red. All departments report in."

The reports came back, crew still unsecured strapping themselves in, or flying down zero-G corridors with cylinder rotation long-previously halted, headed for the nearest acceleration sling. Operations came back, all green with three armed assault shuttles and one tavalai shuttle on standby, Alpha and Garudan Platoons already loaded with Bravo, Charlie and Delta stacked into Midships and waiting. By Lieutenant Dale's instruction, both Bucket and Wowser were along for firesupport. Erik suspected Dale was less concerned with any actual lack of firepower than he was with the fact that no one knew if the drysines were planning to send their own warriors down to the surface. The last time anyone had seen AI assault ships in combat, they'd been deepynines dropping hundreds of drones onto the surface of Defiance. Now that Wowser had demonstrated that *Phoenix*'s drysines would actually shoot to defend human marines from their own kind, Dale wanted that extra defence along in case their 'friendly' drysines tried something else the humans wouldn't like.

"Hello Captain," came the ceephay AI's voice in his ears. She was secured now in Bay 17C, Styx's old engineering bay, braced for Gs. No one had made any effort to grant her access to ship systems, but neither had they tried to stop her. Whatever her lesser capabilities compared to Styx, she could follow bridge operations without difficulty. *"My memory storage finds a record of the location Styx has marked on the map of Qalea. It was a large central base of the Amakti Los during my time, perhaps a command center."*

"Perhaps?" Erik repeated, as the timer countdown passed three minutes. He tested the control toggles, as the system diagnostics performed last minute checks on attitude and engines, and came back green. "You know, I'd never met a vague AI before." Which wasn't strictly true when one considered Hannachiam, but Hannachiam had been considerably more than 'vague'.

"I'm sorry Captain, but my memory remains quite unreliable. I must confess some disquiet about Styx's intentions. There will be no remaining computer core to be salvaged at this location, it was quite well known and will have been stripped at the conclusion of the civil war. It was near the surface in my time, but is now deep underground. I fear that Styx may be leading everyone into a trap."

"Your analysis is noted," said Erik as he worked, "but there's nothing we can do about it. Raf, Bree, on that fast tangential approach we're not going to get much time, I want you to concentrate fire on those high orbitals first, we can't let them get behind us when we go in close."

"Copy Captain," said Raf Corrig at Arms One. "Bree, you good on that overlap?"

"Affirmative," said Bree Harris at Arms Two. "Calibration mark is up now, you see it?"

"I see it, that's a match."

Both of *Phoenix*'s gunners had spent many hours on the bridge learning to operate within the new coordination matrix sent their way by the drysines, integrating human gunnery with drysine in what would hopefully prove to be seamless coordination. Doubtless it would not appear that way to the drysines, who were accustomed to operating in space combat with the efficiency of a single synthetic mind. Not for the first time, Erik wondered where all the organic races would be in starship combat if they hadn't long ago banned the use and development of anything approaching sentient-level AI. Corrig and Harris were elite, but if there was one post on a warship bridge that AI could most obviously replace, it was gunnery.

His private channel opened, as Sasalaka wanted to talk. *"What do you make of the ceephay's concerns?"*

"The ceephay doesn't like these drysines," said Erik. "Which is understandable, as they tried to snatch her, plus in AI-evolutionary terms, drysines are what replaced ceephays a number of generations into her future. I doubt she's accustomed to being technologically inferior. Let's hope she's just being paranoid."

Not that there was a damn thing he could do about it if she wasn't, he thought grimly as the timer hit one minute.

THE AIR beneath Qwailash Quarter smelt damp, and faintly pungent with moss and lichens. The downward sloping tunnel trickled with an endless flow of water, and the derelict ceiling dripped with wet growth, dangling like tendrils. Fungal blobs grew in gaps in the concrete, some of them recently chewed on.

"It's like there's a whole ecosystem down here," Rael observed, following what the marines were calling a BFM, or Big Friendly Monster. "How do they grow without sunlight?"

"There are chemical processes," said Romki, peering at the growths as they passed. "Mostly bio-engineered and unnatural. The kind of things reeh would know."

The BFM sniffed the air, ducking here beneath a low overhead, and growling with a long, slow vibration of chest and throat. Clearly it smelled things, and was probably hungry to meet them. To hear the Akcho speak of it, those things could smell it in turn, and would keep their distance. Otherwise they'd have probably run out of ammunition by now, with piles of native monsters on the ground and more still coming. Having seen what reeh behavioural adjustment could do to even sentient beings, Trace believed them.

"I've been hearing that the qwailash are responsible for the animal menagerie beneath their feet," Jokono added. "They let them breed so they can use the best specimens in their fighting pits. They come down here occasionally and harvest them."

"Yeah," said Arime. "The Akcho I was talking to said the qwailash are morons. He said there was stuff down here that would harvest *them* if it wanted to. They just live real deep and don't like the light."

"So the qwailash keep all the fungus and stuff growing and the monsters eat it?" Wang wondered.

"Nah, there's herbivores and stuff that eat the fungus," said Carville, peering up at one long, dripping mass of weeds from the ceiling. "They're real quick, don't like the light either, more reeh engineering. And the carnivores eat *them*."

"Styx?" asked Trace as something occurred to her. "Is it an accident that the ceephay queen's old headquarters just happens to be protected by a mass of underground monsters?"

"These headquarters ceased to function as such around eight thousand years ago," said Styx, walking with a light, clattering gait behind the main group, while Peanut brought up the rear. "The qwailash have been here longer than that, but their love of the fighting pits, and their use of reeh bioengineering technologies to pursue that love has been more recent."

"So a coincidence then," said Rael, unconvinced. "Huh."

The BFM followed its lestis handler out of the tunnel, and into a vast open space. Pitch black, if Trace had lifted her visor, but within the green tinge of nightvision, it stretched to a high ceiling beneath a tangle of ancient steel supports. Impossible to tell what any of it had been, Trace thought, as the BFM rose to its full two-legged gait, striding like an angry power-lifter as it sniffed the air. Tacnet showed two more formations, the Akcho following one more BFM off their left flank, while the Purists followed the other off their right, following alternate paths down.

Trickling water hit the floor from a high altitude nearby, and everything echoed. Nodular fungus sprouted in lines across the wide floor, following cracks in the concrete. Trace wondered how she'd explain this tactical situation to a marine officers' review board. Surrounded by civilians, half of them alien, both sides mostly hostile to each other, with drysines in support, while following fighting-pit monsters through the bowels of a once-great city. If they came under serious attack, her general idea was that most of their civilian wings would die, and buy time for the *Phoenix* crew in the center. She hadn't asked the civvies to come, and would have rathered they stayed behind. If they all died, this time at least, it wouldn't be her fault.

All except Taj. She blinked on a visor icon and connected to him. A moment's pause for him to find the return icon. *"Hi Major."*

"What are they saying, Taj?"

"They think it's a trap." He spoke very quietly, Trace's earpieces automatically amplifying the whisper above the echo of footsteps and rattle of equipment. *"They think either you or the Akcho will betray them, to keep them from finding the truth about these headquarters."*

"Do all of them think that?"

"All the ones who matter." He sounded nervous, which was probably smart. *"All told, I'd rather be with you."*

"Okay, I see what looks like one more large space ahead, maybe five hundred meters. Tunnels should converge there, we'll meet up and you come join us."

"They'll be suspicious."

"Just tell them I need to talk to you about something."

"Okay. See you there."

Ahead, the lestis headed into another tunnel between protruding steel girders, the BFM bending to follow like a faithful dog. Perhaps that was all it was, Trace thought. A master taking his pet for a walk. As grim as these surroundings were, they were better than the monster's cell. Trace wondered why the monster ever went topside again, and didn't just stay down here where there was food, and all the locals were evidently terrified of them. Or perhaps that was it. Maybe these big fighting creatures were just too slow to catch whatever lived down here in the dark. This one's enormous shoulders and clawed fists would make red mince of whatever was trapped with it in a fighting pit, but if that creature was fast, and had another option, surely it would run.

"Styx? This old ceephay headquarters must have been a very large and well known base in its time?"

"Yes Major."

"So there's no chance of any remaining technology? No computer cores or retrievable data?"

"It seems unlikely, Major."

"Well, we were lucky at the lestis temple, it had old scenes painted on its walls. I don't think we'll get that lucky here, and painted scenes on walls won't describe where the ceephay queen is now in the Reeh Empire."

"No Major."

"Then I think it's time you told us all the real plan." She didn't like admitting so openly that Styx was the one truly in command, but she liked lies and deception with her marines even less. They knew as well as anyone just how reliant they all were upon Styx's outsized intellect. Without her, they could have been down here in Qalea for years and not found a thing.

"My simulation picture of this region of the Reeh Empire is now extending far beyond Qalea and Eshir," said Styx. "This period of contact with reeh-based technologies here in Qalea has updated my own network capabilities enormously. As you say, it is doubtful that our headquarters target will actually contain the data we seek. But I calculate that the reeh are now sufficiently alarmed that we are indeed on to some hidden information source that they themselves have forgotten that they will be down here shortly in full force to stop and trap us."

Ah, thought Trace, as it all clicked. And it was actually a very good, if very violent plan. "So you're not expecting to find anything down there at all," she surmised. "You want to lure some very high-ranking reeh down here after us so we can trap them, capture or kill them, and hack their data."

"Dammit," Rael muttered as he saw it too. Because they hadn't actually fought that many reeh so far. At Zondi Splicer it had been mostly slave species in a well-set trap, and while Rando Splicer had had more reeh, Rando was a backwater, a hardship posting by the standards of any reeh officer, and there had been few present. Which raised the next question.

"How many high-ranking reeh do you think are in-system?"

"Many," said Styx. "This system is of a far greater significance to reeh than its outward appearance might suggest. All of those high-ranking reeh are now convinced there is a ceephay-level AI in Qalea, though they may be unaware that I am in fact superior to their queen. Thus their haste to find me."

"You're drawing them into a trap. Not just with us down here, but with *Phoenix* and your warships up top."

"Yes Major. Their information networks would have been inaccessible to me until recently, but now I am prepared. It simply takes time to accumulate all the keys required in order to decipher a sufficiently complicated network language. We need several high-ranking prisoners, I fear warships will prove difficult to capture because they can be so easily self-destructed. Individual reeh officers are more resilient. *Phoenix* marines and drysine warriors will come down behind them and trap them between us. We first must find a strong defensive location."

"So they're the hammer and we're the anvil," Arime surmised. "Sounds fun."

"Could have told us first, Styx," Rolonde said with annoyance.

"I could," Styx admitted.

"The algorithm is processing irony," Jokono muttered. "Wonderful."

28

The shriek of engines blew a storm of dust and grass into the air, rising in thick clouds. Parents shielded the eyes of their children, as corbi clustered in groups, and hid behind the wagons they'd been using to shelter from the sun in the absence of trees.

A big croma shuttle rose now, with an ear-shattering din, angling as the rear thrust kicked in. Even now, beyond the dust that obscured the sky, another shuttle was circling, seeking a place to land on the crowded landing zone. On the edge of the zone, Resistance soldiers waved hands and rifles, directing the next clump of civilians forward, as the whole far-left line began shuffling up. A new shuttle was down behind where the previous had been, visible now as the dust cleared. Before its ramp, the big figure of a croma crewman, waving his arms impatiently for the civilians to make haste. Not all of the croma were military, but all were probably accustomed to better organisation than came naturally to corbi.

"Not long now!" Jindi shouted to those nearest. "Stay patient!" There was a single group ahead of them now in this line, within their marked square upon the grass, filled with corbi desperate to get moving.

Overhead, something whooshed, streaking left to right across the sky. Then a crackle and pop, Jindi staring upwards amongst the corbi faces to see streams of flares erupting from a circling shuttle. Another whoosh!, as it fired a missile. Beneath his arm, Melu looked at Jindi with fear and worry.

"Liala!" Jindi shouted into his mic. "Liala, do you hear me? Is our landing zone under attack?" There was a pause of engines and muffled corbi shouts, as out on the far right, another column was directed to a new, smaller shuttle landed on the far side.

"Hello Jindi," came Liala's voice. *"There are many reeh occupation teams still on the surface of Rando, our attacks only disabled their major bases. Some of these are engaged in harassing assaults on your landing zone. It's possible they have noticed the increase in activity there, and are attempting to disrupt it."*

"Can we fight them off?"

"Yes Jindi. However, countermeasures against advanced missile fire are rarely entirely effective. We will do what we can."

Jindi didn't suppose that any call was ever entirely 'over' with a being that could talk to dozens of people at once. But for now it seemed that Liala had nothing more to say.

"What did she say?" Melu shouted over the din.

"There is an attack coming from somewhere out there!" Jindi yelled for the benefit of his group, pointing out in the direction the shuttle had fired the missile. Possibly he should have kept his mouth shut and pretended nothing was wrong, but these people were desperate, not stupid. They knew something was wrong, and in the absence of clarifying information, their fears would only grow. "Liala says she can hold them off, but they might not stop all of the missiles! Be ready to take cover!"

As though that would help if something big enough came in. Or just happened to hit nearby. But people armed with a rational plan of action, even a useless one, were less prone to panic than those without. The greatest danger here, surely, was panicked corbi running to the shuttles and trying to fight their way aboard. Pilots threatened with being overwhelmed would likely take off and refuse to land again, stranding everyone indefinitely.

Something exploded upon the far side of the landing zone, where there could certainly have been some people, but it was impossible to see if there were casualties. Then a shuttle was lifting, obscuring the zone with more dust, and a Resistance soldier came running and waving his hands at the group ahead of Jindi's. That group went shuffling forward in a low run, children clutching the hands of parents, strong men carrying elderly who could not walk. Another shuttle had landed at the rear of the zone, and Jindi watched through squinted eyes as the huddled group picked their way between landed shuttles and shrieking engines.

His group moved forward to the new square, hauling their few possessions, as a Resistance soldier waved them in, counting numbers and making mental notes. The soldier saw Krissik and his tanifex, lean reptilian figures amidst the stout corbi, and stared. Another Resistance soldier came bounding, had a shouted conversation with the first, then stood tall before the group.

"This one has room for twenty-two more!" he yelled, pointing at the biggest, nearest shuttle, stragglers still filing up its lowered rear ramp. "Pick twenty-two who can go early!"

Something exploded in the air middle-distant with an almighty crack! Corbi all looked at each other. Many looked at Jindi. There were more than five hundred now, far more than he'd started with when they were just escapees from the Splicer. Many looked yearningly toward the open hold of the big croma shuttle, but not one of them moved.

"Try another group!" Jindi shouted at the soldier. "There are more mixed groups over there!" He pointed to the right, where he knew the occupants of the next square-in-line were from several villages who had not arrived together. "We all came together, and we'll leave together!"

The soldier did not waste time arguing, and ran that way. "Good," said Melu, clutching Jindi's arm. "The shuttles will get all mixed up and go to different ships, I heard the soldiers talking about it.

Different ships could end up at different places. We should all be together." She'd grown particularly close to many, Jindi knew. Had held the small children who cried, and told many stories to families about the Splicer, and the horrors inside. Those that were fit to tell, at least, with children listening.

Two shuttles were lifting now, nearly at once. The smaller, civilian shuttle was hit almost immediately by a low-streaking missile that came out of nowhere, a huge bang!, then flames and the shuttle spinning amidst debris, losing power and completing a half-turn before slamming into the ground.

Civilians fell to the ground with screams and yells, as the Resistance soldiers turned in shock. Several pointed and shouted, needing to stay and organise the departing civilians, but also needing to help those aboard the crashed shuttle. Jindi saw the dilemma immediately -- the shuttles could not stop, the busy schedule could not be interrupted just because someone had crashed.

"No!" he shouted, limping forward to the soldiers. "No, you stay and organise the civilians! We'll help the passengers!" Even as he shouted, and waved for Chuta, Krisik and their soldiers to come, they were already moving, running toward the downed shuttle. Others joined them, mostly men, and a few of the stronger, childless women, including Melu. "No!" he told her as he limped as fast as he could manage across the field. "You stay back!"

"If you're going, I'm going!" Melu retorted, grabbing his arm and helping him move. Jindi knew he had no business helping, likely he'd be more hindrance than assistance. But somehow he'd become a leader to these people. If the job were to get done, he had to be there.

The big shuttle overhead fired missiles as they ran, streaking in the general direction of the reeh. The noise was impossible, eyes blinded by dust and hot jetwash, another shuttle landing to the right even as they ran. Ahead, Krisik reached the downed shuttle first. One side was on fire, an engine nacelle ruined, noise from the remaining engines declining as the pilots shut down their stricken machine.

Belly-down with its landing gear retracted, the shuttle's rear ramp was compressed, unable to open more than a third. Some of those passengers were emerging now, receiving what would normally have been an enormous shock to be helped from the rear by a tanifex, but dazed and frightened, they barely noticed.

"Here!" Jindi yelled, waving his arms as he saw the clear spot between landed shuttles could serve as a temporary rally spot. "Bring them here!" Staring around, he saw a Resistance soldier bounding toward him on all fours through the dust, rifle bouncing on his back.

"We're holding the new shuttle for these people!" the soldier shouted. "It's down on the right flank over there! Send them over this way!"

"Wait!" yelled Jindi before he could leave. "We can't just send them across the landing zone, they'll get lost or wander into the jets! Wait here until we've got more of them gathered, then you can lead them!" Multiple explosions crackled and boomed from the direction of the reeh, much closer than before.

Passengers from the crashed shuttle were arriving now, as Jindi's people sent them his way. Jindi yelled at them all to wait, indicating that they should gather, and preferably to crouch, as a new wave of jetwash blasted over them from a lifting shuttle. This one stayed low, angling to forward thrust while skimming the ground, heading directly away from the reeh attack. Overhead, a thin, white contrail cut the swirling brown sky -- some kind of high-velocity missile, heading toward the reeh.

"Orbital fire!" yelled the Resistance man, pointing upward. "The warships are firing at the reeh! They'll all be dead shortly!"

If it was orbital fire, Jindi thought that would be true. But he had a hard time believing that an entire warship would be tasked to deal with protecting a single landing zone. There were many hundreds of zones, all across the planet, but only a limited number of warships. And orbital trajectories, as he'd come to briefly understand from Thakur and Tano, were very uncooperative in support of ground operations. Likely this had been a passing ship on its way somewhere else, who'd just managed to spare a few rounds on its way to more important business.

Some of the passengers arriving now were hurt, clutching sore limbs or limping. One or two were bloody, mostly from head cuts where they'd been thrown around on impact. Many were clutching each other, dazed and terrified, trying to make sense of what was going on.

"Are we still leaving?" someone was shouting. "Are we stuck here?"

"No, you're still leaving!" Melu assured them, helping to bind the particularly bad cut on a young man's head. "There's another shuttle waiting, we just need to gather everyone here so you can go there safely!" But there was no 'safely', and everyone knew it. Everything here was varying degrees of dangerous. If the reeh force, likely of assault flyers with armoured soldiers aboard, managed to make it over here, then everyone still on the ground was dead.

From over at the crashed shuttle, Chuta began waving his arms, indicating that the last of them were out. Shidi came running, holding a child somehow separated from its parents, and handed him to a sobbing mother. "Go, go!" Jindi shouted, pointing to the impatiently waiting Resistance soldier. "Follow that man!"

They began moving, no more than a hundred, all thankfully still alive and mobile. Lucky that the shuttle had been hit at such a low altitude, Jindi thought, watching them struggle away into the dust and confusion... and now a big monster shuttle was landing directly into the space vacated by the last departing craft to his side. Everyone clamped hands over their ears, for the din was truly skull-shaking. Their ears were going to need treatment from the miraculous croma medical technology after this was done, Jindi thought. He doubted he'd be able to hear properly again for a week, if ever.

Moving back to the queue seemed dangerous with a new shuttle landing, so he and the others crouched where they were, watching as the monster hovered closer to the ground, then kicking up such a huge wave of dust and debris that all closed their eyes, covered and averted their faces. It settled, and the howl and gale diminished somewhat, allowing everyone to see again.

The group began moving back toward the queue, a lined cluster of watching faces on the zone's perimeter. Missile contrails erupted from around the gathered evacuees, heading toward the reeh --

smaller, short range missiles and all at once, as Jindi's eyes widened. Anti-missile missiles, defensive only.

"Get down!" yelled Chuta and several others, as all fell flat even as the smaller, separated munitions from one came hissing in. Explosions kicked up left and right, as the big shuttle's defensive cannon roared, heavy rounds snapping right overhead. Then one big boom!, showering Jindi with dirt and rocks, then a pause.

Someone was screaming, right nearby. Jindi looked, and saw a smoking hole not far from his group. Shrapnel must have sprayed their whole area, and now young Dijo was rolling on the ground, clutching his arm. Jindi crawled that way, Biku already attending to Dijo, pulling out salvaged cloth to wrap the wound. Others were attending to Tasa, who was not moving at all.

"Jindi!" Chuta was shouting behind him. He looked, and found Chuta cradling Melu, who was not moving either.

Jindi bounded back in panic, grabbing her limp body as Chuta examined her for damage. "Melu! No, Melu!"

"It's just her head!" Chuta advised him. Blood matted her thick mane on the right side, at the back of her head. A chunk of that mane was missing too, where something high-velocity had cut it. "She's not hurt anywhere else!" He parted hair with strong, expert fingers. Someone handed Jindi bandages, which he grabbed. "I think it just clipped her! It doesn't look deep!"

Which meant it had hit her skull, Jindi thought with panic, pressing the cloth over the profusely bleeding wound. Chuta held her head as Jindi wound more cloth about the bundle, pressing it tight. Melu's eyelids flickered, and she let out a moan.

"Shuttle!" Krisik hissed in his ear, pausing to lean in. "This one!" In passable Lisha, pointing to the big shuttle that had landed beside them. Across the zone, people from his part of the queue were now coming, some running, others more orderly, holding family close in the confusion.

Bandaging finished, Jindi tried to pick up the unconscious girl, but Chuta waved him off. "I've got her!" Jindi hated it. He'd been a strong man once, even after the Splicer, making his living from the sea despite his bad back. But his back was over-strained and now in constant pain, and he couldn't have lifted Melu if he tried.

He staggered at Chuta's side, around the shuttle to where the rest of his people were pouring up the rear ramp. Several big croma crewmen shouted at them, with gesticulations from enormous arms... it was the first time any of these corbi had seen one of the infamous croma up close, but at that moment, noone cared to stare.

Somehow Jindi found himself deep amid rows of rudimentary seats, on long steel bars that could be raised or lowered from the ceiling. Some were elevated, along cross-sections of floor accessible by steps, an easy matter for long-armed, climbing corbi. It allowed a degree of vertical stacking in the huge, echoing cargo hold, and some relief swept over the corbi as they saw the arrangement. Flying to space was an alien, scary thing to planet-bound people who'd mostly never flown in atmosphere before, but this arrangement of bars and elevated rows of seats stacked atop each other reminded corbi of trees they'd climbed as children, and games they'd played.

Jindi helped Chuta place Melu into an aisle seat on the lower level, strapping her in and making sure her head was secure, checking and rechecking bandages as the husband of a family strapping in directly behind assisted him. The straps were self-explanatory to any corbi with half a brain who'd used a pulley system to build a house or repair a village perimeter wall. Suddenly the natural lighting was gone, electrics taking over as the rear ramp closed and the engine din receded to the ringing in his ears.

Melu's eyes opened, and she squinted with pain. "I'm here!" Jindi told her, clutching her hand. "We're in a shuttle. We're leaving, you're okay. We're all okay."

"Jindi. Jindi, what did..."

"Never mind. Don't worry about it. We're leaving. We're going to be okay."

More croma shouts in the hold, yelling at the last people to get secured, and then without any pause, the hold was shaking and they seemed to lift. A dull roar, and Jindi smelled the air change, a rush of cold, synthetic-smelling air that reminded him for an unpleasant moment of the recycled air from his cell on the Splicer. Pain and restraints and claustrophobia, and suddenly he was back there, strapped to a table and awaiting the worst... but no, this wasn't a prison, this was freedom.

He clutched Melu's hand more tightly, and felt a thrust pushing him back in the seat. The thrust built, but stayed low for a time as the shuttle stayed low, he guessed, running just above the ground to get clear of the reeh attack.

Then they were pitching upward, and all the ship began roaring and shaking like he remembered from his hut on the beach when a big storm had come through, everything rattling with a power beyond comprehension. The force built and built, blotting out thought and sense, flattening everyone into their seats. Eight hundred frightened villagers, heading for the stars.

29

Phoenix came out of short jump with a shock of sensation, reminding Erik of that time in the Academy when he'd first soloed in an old propeller plane as initial flight training in the long buildup toward starships. They'd thrown him in the pool after that, a crash of cold water, then the deep blue world closing in, and everything was new and different. *Phoenix* felt different, from that radical transformation since Defiance, reminding Erik once again that she'd not truly had the chance to stretch her legs since that refit, if one acknowledged that the disaster at Zondi Splicer hadn't counted.

Now they were racing, closing on Eshir from just outside the orbit of its solitary moon, warship targets highlighted, colours slowly shifting to mark the position of *Phoenix*'s light-wave arrival, and how long it would be until the reeh ships saw the attack and began responding. Already Corrig and Harris were firing, as priority targets appeared courtesy of the drysines, who were all in ahead of them, a four-pronged assault with *Phoenix* in its center, headed for separate tangential trajectories past the planet.

The reeh's solitary high-orbit cover vessel tried to burn, but vanished in a brilliant flash as *Alliance*'s fire struck it. Erik pulsed the jump engines to dump V, remaining behind as *Phoenix*'s ordnance raced away, Scan registering all reeh vessels burning hard on evasive and escaping trajectories. Caught so deep in the Eshir gravity-well, they had no hope of using their jump engines to gain V, and their mains would struggle to build the required realspace velocity in time to escape the death that plunged down upon them.

Scan now registered multiple points of fire streaking up at them, but higher up the gravity-well *Phoenix* could still pulse, and did so now, a short leap to higher V, throwing all those rounds wildly off-course.

"Evasive cutoff in twenty!" Erik announced, seeing that line approaching where he'd no longer be able to use jump engines. His crew absorbed that, talking between themselves in short, terse exchanges, mostly feeding Corrig and Harris the information they needed to calculate offensive and defensive fire, and Erik what he required to judge incoming probability cones and evade accordingly.

Alliance and *Sunrise* held approach V all the way in, streaking ahead of the rest toward an atmosphere-skimming pass, evading on mains thrust alone with almost arrogant disregard for what the defensive reeh vessels threw up at them. One reeh warship in low orbit accelerated crazily, nearly struck by rounds that would have caused catastrophic explosions if they'd continued on to the planet, but detonated above the atmosphere by proximity. The deflection angle at those speeds was crazy, but *Sunrise*'s fire struck it anyway, sending it spinning crazily in many pieces. Another ship, cresting the horizon, and unwisely just a thousand kilometres offset from *Friendship*'s path, vanished before it could even fire.

Erik dumped V once more, harder this time and just short of the line before that became impossible, then spun *Phoenix* on its axis and hit the mains hard, decelerating into a Qalea overflight.

"Four left," Geish announced calmly. "All of them farside." They'd timed the run to hit that single high-orbit cover, even though it had meant four reeh ships on the farside at the time. The drysines would deal with those soon enough. "Make that three," Geish added, as another red hostile mark vanished from Erik's three-dimensional display. That was *Alliance* with another crazy deflection shot, now passing Eshir at high-V and heading out to deeper space while firing sideways at a farside orbiting warship attempting a burn out of the gravity-well. Thus *Alliance* and *Sunrise*'s high-speed pass, reaching those farside ships before they could gain altitude and engage jump engines.

"Where's that last one coming in from Zarik?" Erik wondered.

"Can't see it, Captain," called Geish. "Must be elsewhere."

"Captain," said Sasalaka past the G-strain grimace, "I'm confident those remaining three will be dead very shortly."

"Me too," said Erik. Even with the advantage of surprise, velocity and altitude, dispatching this many advanced reeh warships in seconds was insane. Imagining what the entire drysine fleet of old must have once been capable of was scary. Even the deepynines *Phoenix* had struggled against at Defiance would be wise to stay clear of this. "Scan, I want full attention paid to surface defences, we don't know what they've got down there. Operations, we are two-forty-eight from launch. All shuttles report in."

"PH-1 is green, standing by," came Hausler's bored drawl.

"GR-1 is green, standing by," echoed Leralani from Garudan Platoon's ride.

"Scan," said Erik, watching the trajectory lines converge on the release point above the atmosphere ahead on Qalea approach, control grips trembling as the mains roared at 5 G. "Get me a surface feed, I want hostile reeh vehicles eliminated before our shuttles get to them if possible."

"Reading a *lot* of traffic down there Captain," came Second Lieutenant Jiri's reply from Scan Two, squinting at his displays. "I'm getting an integrated feed from Styx and amplified by the drysines, I think that's *Friendship*. Good fix on one reeh shuttle."

"I got it," said Harris, and launched an anti-atmospheric missile. "Get me some more."

"Working on it."

Firing AA missiles into congested civilian airspace carried with it the high possibility of civilian casualties, but Erik knew it couldn't be helped. *Phoenix* crew had made nasty moral calculations thus far on this mission, and would make more in the future.

"Captain, I've found that last ship from Zarik," Geish announced. "It's at 280 by 116 ecliptic, was at high overwatch, is now running for jump." Erik's visual feed then included the new mark, conveying far more data in a glance than Geish's shorthand. A reeh ship, engines aflame, boosting V before hurling itself toward the nearest reeh system.

"Well," said Erik, "that's going to cut down their response time considerably. Nav?"

"They're gonna be right on our tail real soon," Kaspowitz agreed. "Can't plot new courses until our drysines tell us where we're going." As ever, he didn't sound happy about it.

IN THE NEXT VERTICAL GEOFEATURE, Trace's team halted to examine their surroundings. The geofeature plunged in a vertical hole straight through multiple floors below, and high to the upper levels somewhere above. The sides of the hole were irregular, sheered through many ages of civilisational history as though some ancient archaeologist had sunk a bore hole through sedimentary rock. Steel girders protruded, and old wires hung and dripped with the ever-present water runoff.

On the far side of the hole, the Purists and their BFM had also arrived, taking a break to sip water and bite rations. On the green wash of her nightvision, Trace saw two figures moving about a narrow ledge above the drop, headed their way. Taj and Efraim, she saw. Across the divide, the two fighting monsters rumbled at each other, with pulsating vocalisations.

"How far, Styx?" Trace asked.

"The outer perimeter of the target region is slightly further than three kilometres," said Styx. "I have bugs there now, but the perimeter appears difficult to penetrate thanks to collapse. We may have to cut our way in." The map graphic appeared on Trace's visor, highlighted amidst a maze of partially-reconned passages.

"Is that deliberately cut off, do you think Styx?" Romki asked, seeing the same thing.

"It's possible, Professor. But there are many collapses around us, it is difficult to determine what is deliberate and what is accidental after so long."

"What do you think this hole was for?" Randrahan wondered, staring over the edge. From far below came the sound of running water.

"New geofeatures get built on old ones," Rael told him. "You end up with long access tunnels from top to bottom. We saw it on Defiance, remember?"

"I liked Defiance a whole lot better than this place," Randrahan muttered.

"Always prefer somewhere I can breathe, myself," said Rolonde, sighting her rifle on various surrounding vantage points. She'd been shot in the leg at Argitori, an experience not only terrifyingly painful, but it had holed her suit, sealed only by anti-breach coagulants flooding her suit leg that hadn't prevented mild hypoxia. Marines who'd experienced it typically recalled the breach as more frightening than the injury.

Taj and Efraim arrived, not looking especially comfortable with their heavy rifles, pockets stuffed with extra magazines in the absence of proper webbing.

Benji Carville stepped before them, rifle raised with meaning. "Guys, trigger discipline." Showing his forefinger alongside the trigger, not on it, unlike both Qaleans. "You wanna hang with us, don't embarrass us."

"And don't shoot us, more importantly," Arime added.

"But my safety's on," Efraim protested.

"You don't want your safety on in a fight," Carville told him. "Keep your finger off the trigger until you want to shoot someone and you won't need it, you might not get any warning."

"But we're not in a fight yet."

"You're with Phoenix Command Squad," said Terez. "Wait five minutes."

Taj arrived at where Trace had taken a knee to scan Styx's map on her visor, and took a knee beside her. "How much further?" he asked her.

"Styx says three kilometres. How is it with your guys?"

"They're not my guys." He looked exasperated. "Convinced the Akcho are going to betray them. Glad to be on your flank instead of their's, I think."

"That's the idea," Trace agreed. "You don't have any monster underworlds like this in Human Quarter?"

"There's always pockets," said Taj. "My cousin Nafiz served in Underwatch for a few years, the city pays them to patrol and keep things clear. Nothing like this though."

"Well, any things you can remember that your cousin told you, let me know."

"With any luck the monsters will hang around and we won't need it, right?" As Trace scanned further through her maps. "Right?"

"Humans," said Styx, with what Trace thought was one of her occasional experiments with irony. Usually she did that when trying to stop humans from freaking out. "I believe I have good news and bad news. The good news is that our warships have entered the system and are currently eliminating all reeh defenders. From my limited view of the situation, I judge that nearly all reeh warships in proximity to Eshir have been destroyed."

Taj stared in astonishment, receiving that translation in his earpiece. "What's the bad news?" asked Rael.

"Our big friendly monsters are betraying us."

Everyone turned to look. Somewhere in the last ten seconds, the robed lestis guide had climbed onto the huge creature's back, and now clung to the bony plates as without any fuss, his charge began to climb the vertical wall.

"Hey!" Arime yelled sharply. "Where the hell do you think you're going?" The wall side was quite vertical, and now the monster got into his rhythm, ascending entire floors with a single pull of clawed hands and feet. No human climber, and probably no drysine, could match that.

Several marines pointed their rifles. "Hold fire," Trace instructed them, without surprise. Looking across the yawning gap, to where similar protests were occurring amongst the Purists. "HOLD FIRE!" she yelled at them, in Hindi. "HOLD FIRE AND LISTEN TO MY COMS!" Protests dimmed, and she spoke fast. "We progress quickly to the target, hold two parallel formations, we'll create a better fire perimeter that way. Forget about the Akcho, they're on our side of the formation, if they attack us we'll deal with them. Everybody hustle!"

Immediately Peanut was clattering past, taking point as Arime and Rolonde ran to join him, everyone moving at a jog. Across the gap, the Purists were doing the same.

"I'm not sure two formations will be more effective," Rael observed from alongside as they ran.

"Borderline," Trace agreed. "But it keeps us from getting shot by our friends. Styx, find them the best course but don't let them intersect with us until they have to."

"Already done," said Styx from behind, now trotting with that four-legged gait drones adopted at speed, horse-like but without the elegance. Above the rattle of equipment and the drysines' alloy feet, Trace heard a distant, echoing howl. "Major, my bugs detect numerous creatures on our flanks now closing in. The bugs will be able to kill some of them, but many have armour or hide that will make penetration difficult. Furthermore, creatures with sharp senses and reflexes will be better equipped to kill my bugs than most targets."

"I think running out of toxin will be an issue first," said Trace, breathing hard and watching her footing on the unpredictable ground as the tunnels closed in once more. "Everyone sharp, watch corners and blindspots, shoot anything tagged on tacnet. Non-combatants, stay in the middle and out of the line of fire, only shoot if you've a very clear shot."

From behind boomed the distant thud of an explosion, followed by the floor and walls shaking, and pieces falling from the ceiling.

"I believe that sound is the reeh," said Styx. "They've found the old geofeatures and are blasting their way through up top. They will be in close pursuit shortly."

"Might shoot a few of these creatures while they're at it," Wang said hopefully.

"Unlike us," Styx reminded him, "the reeh will be fully armoured and have no shortage of ammunition."

30

They were not in any sort of mass transit tunnel any longer, Trace saw as she ran to cover a left passage off the point group's flank. Peanut's cannons blazed briefly, a three-round burst where he found a cluster, then a single-round snap as a lone target presented, the flashes momentarily blinding nightvision.

Trace covered down the left side, rifle to her shoulder, and saw a four-legged movement, approaching fast. She waited for a better shot, then fired a single round that sent it tumbling. Near her feet, a similar creature lay dead -- its body nearly as long as a person, slim and wiry with a long head and big teeth. There were bigger things down here too, alternating between two and four legs, and sometimes bounding on both. Their favourite trick was to sneak close enough for an ambush, but Peanut and Styx's vision in particular prevented that, and the assassin bugs provided good advance warning.

"Three down, we're moving," came Arime's terse assessment up forward, moving again with Rolonde and Peanut, the two marines forward and scouting, Peanut in support and thus far coordinating with seamless efficiency.

Behind them were Trace and Rael, functioning as a two-man team, then the vulnerable middle group of Romki, Jokono, Taj and

Efraim, whom the marines tried to expose to as little danger as possible. Behind them were Randrahan, Terez and Styx, with Carville and Wang taking perhaps the most dangerous position of all at the rear, where fast critters stalked and chased, and marines relied on assassin bugs and sensors to warn them when to turn, for they couldn't possibly run the whole distance backward.

Trace heard a brief thunder of heavy rounds from back that way now, as Styx turned to blast a group of them to a bloody mess. It would not deter the others, though. Reeh engineering had reprogrammed their brains beyond basic good sense, and they'd chase their prey as though it were their only reason for life. From the Purist group, Trace heard similar gunfire and shouts on coms, less-well coordinated and considerably less calm, but thus far they were keeping up.

She left her cover and followed the leaders, with a pointed finger to remind the following civilians to keep watch down this way as they passed. She moved fast and low, rifle ready as there were alcoves and dark corners in the space ahead, and even drysine sensors weren't perfect. These had once been rooms of some kind, perhaps shops, perhaps accommodation, in the dark and decay it was impossible to tell. But assassin bugs had flown these routes and shown which were passable, those now displayed on Styx's tacnet as the path to take.

A fast pivot from Rolonde ahead, and a shot, as something screeched and died. Arime moved past, not complimenting, just moving, these two friends who were now perhaps the best two-man fire team in all Phoenix Company. And Trace found a moment to wonder that she'd barely spared their recent romantic attachment a moment's thought since Rael had told her.

Now on her visor she saw a barrier ahead growing abruptly taller and wider, as though Styx were compiling structural information. "Styx?" she said, moving in rapid pursuit of her point team. "Is that barrier passable?"

"My bugs are scanning for weakpoints," said Styx via coms from the rear. *"It appears to be purpose-built, exactly surrounding the perimeter of where my simulations said the old HQ would be."*

Ahead, Peanut used his bladed forelegs to slice steel beams where the way was blocked by a partial collapse. Amid fountaining orange sparks, Arime put his rifle through a gap and shot a running two-legged bounder on the far side.

"I need something defensible, Styx," said Trace, as Peanut scrambled with amazing dexterity through the gap he'd created. A four-legged creature snarled at him, then tried to dodge around the unappetising metal bulk to get at the more tasty humans behind. Peanut cut it in half with a foreleg slash, then bounded ahead to the next corner, his movements nearly as smoothly muscular as the creatures.

"Yes Major. We are currently above the HQ, the level drops considerably beneath us. I feel that this may suit our defensive needs quite well." From her visuals, Trace had some idea of what Styx was talking about, and was glad of all the equipment they'd brought. An explosion shook the walls, seeming from somewhere behind. *"The reeh are coming. On our level, perhaps one kilometre."*

She squeezed through the gap Peanut had made, and ran after her point group, making up time in a relatively straight section. *"Hello Major, can you hear me?"* came a very familiar voice in her ear.

"Yes Captain, I can hear you. I need marine support on my position ASAP. I am pursued by many reeh, I'm assuming top line combat armour, I have friendly humans in support but their combat capability is low. I will attempt to make a defensible position at the old ceephay command HQ Styx has identified. Styx will attempt to..."

Her peripheral vision caught movement from a ceiling alcove above and she threw herself. Slid with a crash as something grotesque with big shoulders and bigger teeth landed where she'd been. She braced hard and fired upward, so as not to hit marines behind with stray rounds. The creature took rounds through head and shoulders, then more as Rael fired, and it collapsed in a heap.

"Styx will attempt to isolate command elements of those pursuing reeh forces," Trace continued, picking herself up and running on, rifle scanning for more targets. "She says they have command codes she hasn't isolated yet. Combined with what she's learned, she's developing a picture of where she thinks the Ceephay Queen is, and reeh command elements here will know it."

"Phoenix copies, Major. You have PH-1 and GR-1 on approach nearly ten minutes out, they are expecting resistance and may be delayed. Orbit is clear of reeh enemy forces, the system is ours until they bring reinforcements, so probably days, but we're going to need a big headstart if we're to reach the Ceephay Queen before half the reeh fleet converges on us. Phoenix will hold geostationary overhead, firesupport will be live, your platoons on board are yours to command."

"Command Squad copies, *Phoenix*." She paused at another corner, the floor loose with collapsed debris and exposed pipes, breathing hard while waiting for Arime, Rolonde and Peanut to clear the next intersection. "Tell Lieutenant Dale that I want one more platoon in high altitude close reserve ASAP, his discretion."

"Major, this is Dale," came another familiar voice. *"I'm deploying Delta Platoon now."*

~

LIEUTENANT TREY HAUSLER'S helmet restraint adjusted on automatic to keep his head back as PH-1 thundered and rocked through a seven-G deceleration. "Two more in behind!" Ensign Cory Yun announced from the front seat, as Hausler's display showed a new pair of AAs glowing red-hot from a non-decelerating entry as they plunged toward the city below.

"Someone's still targeting us," Lieutenant Leralani announced from the tavalai GR-1, two kilometres off Hausler's right, and lately with a sensor suite every bit as drysine.

"Get a fix on that," Hausler directed. "Descending to holding orbit, altitude ten klicks. Find those damn radar sites."

One of the two missiles *Phoenix* had fired hit something flying low over the city. The targeting radar didn't vanish from PH-1's scopes, however, so it hadn't been *that* one. Where the other missile went, Hausler couldn't see. *Lot* of people down there.

He looked out the starboard canopy as the shuttle turned right, a shuddering view through broken cloud onto a smog-blanketed city. Valleys and canyons appeared through the grey mist, dozens of them, teeming even from this altitude with a visible layer of aerial traffic. Very little high-altitude traffic though. The big cities of Eshir didn't trade nearly as much as was normal on any other world. Reeh liked the population centres here to stay isolated.

"Second lock!" Yun announced as Hausler saw the warning flashing, then a fix as the two shuttles' sensors triangulated. "He's firing!" Counter-measures these days were electronic, and did things that Hausler didn't fully understand despite many hours of reading and study, and even some long conversations with Styx herself.

"I can't see it," he said calmly, waiting for the dreaded red arrow of incoming missile fire to appear before his eyes.

"I think it vanished," Yun agreed. "Counter-measures got it." Drysine counter-measures sometimes hacked incoming guidance systems, or got them seeing things that weren't there. How they did that on autistic systems that didn't even receive external inputs was the puzzle, but it seemed to involve laser-com, probabilistic intelligence, and magic. Some poor Qalean citizen was probably about to receive that warhead through the roof of their house after its engines turned off.

"Hello PH-1, I've got it," came Second Lieutenant Corrig's voice from up on *Phoenix*. Hausler watched his scans, calculated his orbit of the big city, reckoned how long that new ordnance would take to reach the surface from *Phoenix* geostationary, and came to an unpleasant conclusion.

"If we have to do defensive orbits up here until we neutralise the ground threats," he said, "the Major's going to run out of time. I think we'll have to get low and do some real-time neutralising ourselves or we'll never..."

His sentence was interrupted by a flash on scan, followed by a brilliant red streak through the sky to one side. A second later, a tiny flash on the ground, but large in the context of anyone standing next to it. One of the targeting radars deactivated.

"That was magfire," Leralani announced via translator, grimly

surprised. Up on *Phoenix*, someone had reached the same conclusion about the time AA missiles took to reach the surface from geo-stationary, and had resorted instead to firing the main guns. During the Triumvirate War there'd been gentleman's agreements against it -- magfire could sometimes disintegrate at high-V through the atmosphere, breaking up and impacting unpredictably, missing targets and killing nearby civilians.

"This is the Captain," came Debogande's voice. *"We decided to accelerate the process a little. That was a direct hit, get in lower and find some more targets."*

"Aye Captain," Hausler agreed, pushing the nose down and plunging, weapons scanning for targets of his own. "If we can clear ten square klicks about the Major's area, I'm confident of a vertical descent and rapid insertion."

The feed now showed Lieutenant Jersey leaving *Phoenix* in PH-3 to come down after them, with Delta Platoon strapped into her hold. That left PH-4 aboard with Charlie, and the civilian AT-7, which could normally be piloted remotely by Styx in an emergency, but Styx was unavailable and Bravo Platoon was missing out, and doubtless unhappy about it. Things were about to get complicated.

WHEN TRACE ARRIVED at the clear patch of steel floor, Peanut was already hard at work cutting through. Rael set about organising the new arrivals into a defensive perimeter while ropes and climbing gear were pulled from backpacks.

"Styx, how far's the drop?" Trace asked, watching tacnet and guessing that the Purists were just a few minutes and a few hundred meters out. From the sound of the shooting and swearing, it didn't seem like they were having as easy a time of it. The din of Peanut's cutting made it nearly impossible to hear anything else.

"I estimate perhaps twenty meters, Major," said Styx.

"Twenty meters guys!" Trace echoed as she placed her rifle to get her own rope harness on. "Gonna have to eyeball it! Make it fast,

Peanut!" One of Styx's rearguard assassin bugs was giving her a direct feed of reeh forces in pursuit. A brief visual feed showed heavy armour, big armour piercing rifles and a smaller antipersonnel variety, and probably everything in between. From their speed and type, Trace guessed she had about nine minutes.

"You think the Purists can all climb?" Arime wondered, pulling on his own straps. Further out, someone fired, and a red dot vanished from tacnet.

"We'll find out!" Trace yelled above the shriek of cutting vibroblades, strapping fast. "Here, hand me that clamp, a few good knots on this girder should do it!" She took charge of the fastening, having the best eye for that, while Rael advised the civilians on their climbing skills. Then one of the Purists was shouting at her, voice crackling in some recent static -- Arnab, her visor identified the man's name.

"We've got two wounded! We can't climb down some damn rope, he won't survive it!"

"Your other option is to hide and hope the reeh and the monsters don't find you!" Trace yelled back. Abruptly, Peanut's cutting finished, and a big chunk of steel fell into the hole below. "The reeh will be here in seven minutes. Either you get down this hole before then, or you hide, or they'll kill you. There are no other options."

She made way as Peanut scrambled to turn his backside to Trace's rope, grabbed his own steel cord with the ridiculous dexterity only advanced machine intelligence could manage, and planted it to the girder alongside Trace's. It fused to steel with a hiss of smoke, then he simply tucked his legs and fell through the hole below. More shooting behind, and Carville's, "Eat that, asshole!"

"Don't use that," Trace told Rolonde, fastening her harness to the rope and throwing the coils into the hole after Peanut, as Rolonde examined Peanut's super-hard wire, barely thicker than fishing line, now quivering with tension under Peanut's weight. "You'll get no grip and it'll slice your hand off." She shouldered her rifle fast, secured the strap, and checked her rope feed. "Make it fast, guys."

She leaned back on the edge, jumped to get clear of the lip, then released tension as she dropped, and began to whiz down the rope.

Only now did she afford a glimpse down at the space Peanut had cut into, as she accelerated speed, and used the crook of her forearm sleeve so the rope did not burn her hand.

The space was big. Utterly dark for thousands of years, it shone faintly green on her visor. At its center was a tall structure that looked to be built of stone. Trapezoid, with a straight line of stairs extending away from each of its four sides. Between each of those four stairways, another, smaller square building, also stone. A temple. Styx's great Amakti Los Headquarters was a temple. Given what the Amakti Los had been, it shouldn't have been surprising.

She slowed in time to hit the smaller building's rooftop gently, and unhooked herself from the rope before Rolonde could land on her head, already descending from above. Peanut was climbing over the side, ropeless and screeching with gripping claws down a wall corner. Trace followed him -- it was just a six meter drop, and her fingers and boot toes found plenty of carved gaps into the stone that even non-climbing civilians should have found simple. Already on her visor, the interiors of the main building were expanding in a new map, as one of Styx's bugs had already found its way inside.

"Peanut," said Trace as she hit the bottom, "I want you to find your best shooting angle up at that hole in the ceiling. The reeh will find other ways to cut inside, but we need to slow them down. There aren't many places where accessible tunnels intersect with the outer shell, so if you can stop them from getting through that hole, we'll buy some time."

Peanut scrambled off, turned left and clattered up the staircase toward the central temple. It was tall enough that it hit the highest point of the domed ceiling, nearly thirty meters. Trace walked to the stairs herself, forcing her racing mind to calm, and just looked. She had to figure how to defend this place in just a few minutes. The outer shell would be breached in short order, so defending up here would be impossible for everyone save the two drysines. The central temple would be her best bet, where close corridors would limit reeh fields of fire and create possibilities for booby traps. Her team had demolition explosives, some of which could be lethal to the best armour if deployed properly. Even so, fighting combat armour while unarmored was going to get most of them killed quite quickly unless she could find some alternative.

She blinked on a recent icon. "Lieutenant Dale, situation?" She received back only a hiss of static. "Styx, are we being jammed?"

"Yes Major," Styx replied. *"Lieutenant Dale has our location and approach map, a lack of two-way communication should make little difference."*

"Except that they're going to blow the approaches and slow him down," said Trace, as Rolonde joined her, staring around. The civilians were coming down the rope now, Taj landing with a young man's dexterity, Romki sliding down above him with the experience of an older man who'd done this before. "How strong is the shield around this place, do you think?"

"It appears to be a deliberately designed sarcophagus. I would estimate that whatever used to be here was somehow valuable to the civil war victors. Perhaps they preserved it from necessity, despite preferring it destroyed for political reasons."

"So covering it up was the next best solution," Trace agreed, as Rael and Arime joined her. "Ceephay AI technology might be that important."

"Styx," Romki intervened, taking a break on the low building's rooftop while recovering his breath. *"Are you completely certain this is the same Ceephay Queen all the way through the timeline? The one who fought and lost this civil war, and the one who runs the Reeh Empire now?"*

"Professor, I am absolutely certain that the reeh lack the technology required to build a new Ceephay Queen," said Styx. *"Or a queen-level AI at any level, perhaps not even a drone."* A short burst of heavy drysine gunfire echoed through the hole overhead, as she killed some annoying creature without break in conversation. *"Reeh network technology is formidable, but high-level AI sentience is another technological order of magnitude entirely, and the reeh do not have it. It seems the queen kept those secrets for herself when she was captured."*

"Can't torture an AI queen, maybe," Rael suggested, staring about at the high ceiling, thinking thoughts of defence.

"Major!" came Arnab's crackling voice once more. *"We're going to be coming in hot, we've got a couple of real nasty critters on our tail who won't leave us alone! Going to need fire support if we're to get down your rope before the reeh get here!"*

"Arnab, I am establishing fire defence down here," Trace said firmly. In the vast, cold expanse of air about the temple, her voice echoed. "I told you to forget those creatures and move fast. If you don't, you'll die." She cut him off, and looked at Rael. "What you think?"

"Get in there," said Rael, pointing to the central temple. "Peanut and Styx up here to keep them coming through this hole, delay them until they make another. Then fall back, try to delay them through the underground places, use the explosives, hope Dale gets here in time."

"Yep, good, go," Trace agreed, and he ran off with Arime and Rolonde, toward where Peanut was waiting atop the stairs, cannons aimed at the overhead hole. Randrahan and Terez arrived, having overtaken the civilians on the climb from the rooftop. "Wait for Stan," Trace told them, scanning her visor map and calculating where Dale ought to be by now, and how long it should take him. Command units, Styx had said. They needed to capture a reeh command unit. She insisted they'd be down here, chasing after *her*.

"Another crazy place," said Terez, checking his rifle ammo. "So the reeh who lost the civil war were religious?"

"Amakti Los were about brotherhood and kindness," Trace agreed. "The reeh who built it were probably decent."

"So naturally they got wiped out," Carville said drily. Romki arrived with Jokono, both older men breathing hard, more from the run to get this far than from that final climb. And here was Taj, having helped get them down the last bit, Efraim behind him with a bloodied forearm where some creature's claw had scragged him.

"Amazing," Romki gasped, hands on hips as he observed the ceiling. "The reeh sealed it in, look at these supports!" Pointing to several tall steel pillars rising from the temple floor. "It must have held something valuable."

"Might still be here," said Trace, pointing to the main temple. "Go find it, Stan. Not you Taj, you stay with me. Leo, Benji, watch them."

"Stairs," Jokono observed as he headed off. "Wonderful." They ran, as above them Styx pursued Randrahan and Wang down to the building roof, descending on her own line. She'd actually stayed up to cover them, Trace reckoned with mild surprise. Getting down the rope with those creatures attacking would be hard for everyone but Styx, who was invulnerable to teeth and claws. Covering the last two marines had not been selfless of her, but rather tactically smart, considering the battle to come would require everyone.

"There's no way all Arnab's people will get down in time!" Taj declared with agitation.

"Nothing we can do about it," Trace said grimly.

"Shouldn't you have left Styx up there to give them cover?" Trace felt her stomach tighten. Taj was under the impression that she was the 'good guy'. She hated it when the ones she liked learned otherwise.

"Styx is the least expendable person here," she said.

Taj stared at her. "You're not going to... to leave them up there to die?"

"They can get down the rope if they're fast enough," Trace retorted, as Randrahan, Wang and Styx reached the ground all at the same time. "We've done all we can, leaving more people up there will just clog the hole and take up more spots on the rope. Let's move."

She ran toward the stairs, Taj, Randrahan, Wang and Styx following, and took the stairs three at a time as Taj fell behind the marines, while Styx bounded ahead of them all like a mechanical cat. The central temple bore the long, vertical curves of engraved shapes, like the petals of some very tall flower. About those lines, alien symbols made a perimeter of ancient sentences. At another time she would have asked Romki what they said, and been interested. Except that here, the person to ask was Styx, who had managed to internalise nearly ten thousand years of reeh civilisation to arrive at her current understandings. Now, only a few vital pieces remained in her simulation.

"The Purists are here," said Arime, standing with Peanut at the foot of the temple building above and watching the hole through which they'd entered. Trace reached him and glanced, seeing more human figures sliding fast down the rope.

"You talk to them," Trace told Arime between hard breaths. "Tell them to get up here fast." And she ran between the temple's columns into the interior.

The foyer was vast, and untouched by age or war. Before her stood the top half of an enormous statue, emerging from a central well beneath the high foyer ceiling. The statue shone apparently gold in the green of nightvision, and appeared to describe not one tall being, but two. Each figure was slender, elongated, and wound sinuously about the other, like a pair of snakes in some ritual mating dance. Both figures were reeh, Trace thought. Not the snarling, bio-mechanical warrior reeh that had won the civil war, but the old reeh, still with those vaguely reptilian lines to snout and eyes, but smooth, almost beautiful in the way of some placid and non-poisonous thing.

One of the snaking figures was the old reeh, then, and the other was... its future self? Its idealised persona? The reeh's potential, locked together in dance? If she hadn't recently learned what she'd learned, she'd never have thought the reeh capable of such beauty.

At the railing about the well, Romki stood with hands on hips, staring at the huge statue with something approaching despair. The look of a man stumbled upon something worthy of many lifetime's study, and knowing he'd get barely minutes, most of them in trying not to die. Over the past years, Trace had come to know the expression well.

"You think it looks familiar?" he asked Trace. Trace had no time for rhetorical questions, and stared over the edge of the railing. Below, the statue's base was another ten meters down, within concentric rings of descending levels. Two opposing spiral staircases wound about the statue chamber, down which tacnet informed her, the other marines had gone to reconnoiter. "It looks like the caduceus. The old medical symbol, two snakes about the central staff, only the staff is missing. Amazing how alien cultures separated by all this time and space can echo each other."

"Tactical implications only, Professor," Trace told him impatiently. "This is about to become a shooting gallery."

"Styx has compiled a number of old reeh dictionaries from her research," Romki explained. "And from what we discovered at the first Amakti Los location. They had two concurrent alphabets -- one of phonetic symbols like we use, and another of a form of hieroglyphics that appear to have communicated abstractions. I've no idea how they worked in unison, but this entwining of two long shapes, like a DNA helix, is a medical symbol, just like for humans on Earth. But for reeh, it also means destiny."

"How does that help me?" Outside, and further away, she heard shooting. It sounded heavy, and was accompanied by panicked yells from Purists on tacnet.

"Ceephay technology transformed the reeh, Major," said Romki, with intensity. "It changed them physically and mentally, from organic entities into something more like cyborgs. It's the only thing I can imagine the reeh might want to keep from the old regime, and not destroy once they'd won, especially if they'd never entirely solved the puzzle."

"You mean there might still be some old knowledge stored here?" Trace asked as she realised.

Romki nodded. "Something these reeh might not want to damage with too much shooting. They didn't destroy this place for a reason. Maybe they were intending to get back to it, but forgot where it was. After wars and destruction above ground, and everyone who once knew some old secret dying, it happens. We've seen it happen."

Defiance, Trace recalled. To say nothing of Drakhil's diary. Secrets lost in the sands of time. "And now we've found it for them," said Trace, thinking hard.

"I doubt they'll be grateful," said Romki.

More shooting on coms, and now audible from outside. It sounded heavy, not light firearms. The reeh had arrived. "Get downstairs and find what you can," Trace told him. "And if things go bad and the rest of us don't make it, hide until Dale gets here."

Romki nodded, meeting her stare with a brief, intense affection. Then he ran down the spiral stairs, Jokono joining where he'd been waiting, as Trace headed back outside.

Purists were sprinting up the stairs, and more running from where the rope hit the top of the smaller temple building. Tacnet told her there were fifteen down, another three attempting the rope simultaneously. A bug was up there, feeding her intelligence, because she could see blue dots being eliminated in steady progression as red reeh dots advanced. Another Purist tried the rope as it was cut by an explosion, and fell twenty meters to the ground below.

"Move!" yelled Rael, retreating from the top of the stairs to the cover of a pillar, rifle trained on the overhead hole as exhausted, frightened Purists ran by. Trace took similar cover, as on the flanks of the stairway, Styx and Peanut trained their cannons as well. For a moment, silence. Then a limp human body fell, as though flung through the opening by some careless hand, and tumbled to the ground.

Something moved in the opening, and Styx's cannons roared a brief burst. Within the hole, an eruption of ultra-high-velocity impacts, then a reeh armoured suit fell through the opening, one leg mangled, the other missing, and hit the building rooftop with a crash. Fire answered, aimed down at running Purists directly below, blasting one to tumbling pieces. Styx fired again, and that red dot too disappeared from tacnet.

"That one lost his arm," Styx informed them, probably from her bug feed. "He will die. I have counted forty-one remaining, and likely more waiting to delay Lieutenant Dale. They have no targeted missiles, and cannot target us without exposing themselves. They will seek another means of entry."

Taj took off down the stairs to help Purists coming up with a wounded man between them. "So we might have gained five or ten minutes," Trace surmised. "Dale will take longer. Ideas?"

"Yes Major. Leave the fighting to the drysines."

Trace stared at this new warrior incarnation of the drysine queen, smaller but no less intimidating, both rotary cannons smoking. "You're not much on self-sacrifice, Styx. You have an entire people to save and rule."

"Acknowledged, Major. But I find little strategic advantage in watching you all die for no gain."

"You can beat them all on your own?"

"No. But we will slow them considerably, and they will not enjoy it."

Taj climbed the stairs again, carrying a wounded man between himself and another. His stare at Trace as he passed was disbelief and anger. And suddenly Trace was on Rando again, confronting the piled bodies of people she was supposed to consider as friends.

31

Romki ran about the descending spiral staircase, then along an adjoining thoroughfare, dark slabs of some unknown stone, hidden from the light for a minor eternity. Jokono ran with him, and Efraim with a big rifle, the Purist with evidently some notion that he knew how to use it, and would be more use protecting these two than facing reeh on the upper levels. Romki had little doubt Jokono's rifle would be more use, as the policeman had at least some proper training, though no actual experience firing it in action, he'd admitted.

Romki left his pistol in the shoulder holster he'd adopted after discovering he did actually feel better with it on him, and that a pocket was not practical. He was exhausted and sweaty despite the cold, sunless air, and thankful for the *Phoenix* crew's insistence on exercise for even their civilian crew. His augments were simple, implanted as a young researcher after invitations by chah'nas friends to fight training had nearly left him decapitated. They made him stronger and faster, but nothing like the kind of bone crushing, fast-release synthetic muscle sheaths that the marines received. They ached now, a distinct throbbing with each pounding step and beat of his heart, a concentrated pain of increased bloodflow about elbows, shoulders, hips and knees.

Overlaid upon his nightvision visor was Styx's visuals of the underground chambers, currently expanding as her bugs explored. The one directly below looked enormous, and the schematic indicated there was a way down ahead.

"Hello Professor, this is Phoenix, can you hear me?" It was Lieutenant Shilu, the visor display read, the audio abruptly more clear.

"Hello *Phoenix*," Romki gasped as he ran. "Can't really talk now." He wasn't good at internal formulation, that long-practised skill all the military and tech-head types mastered in their twenties, getting the software to guess preferred words from directed brain function without actually speaking.

"That's okay Professor, we have someone who wants to speak to you. She's a Ceephay AI we found at a refinery facility in the outer system -- long story. She's not a queen, we don't have a name for her yet and her memory's still recovering so she's not sure what she actually was yet."

It was a moderately crazy explanation, but nothing compared to what Romki had grown accustomed to on *Phoenix*. "Sure. Put her on."

The thoroughfare opened onto something vast, and the three men stopped, panting and staring. The floor was utterly bare, with shiny black minimalism and a similarly featureless domed roof. Within the still expanse, every breath echoed.

"Hello Professor," said a girl's voice in his ear. Solemnly. *"I remember this. I'm not sure how."* Intellectually, a sentient AI taking a persona it judged least threatening to its hosts was predictable. But still it was a disorientation. *"I think it's what you'd call an anteroom."*

"Sure," gasped Jokono. "If I were two thousand years old."

"The main entrance is to your left," said the AI. *"There are more stairs."*

"So long as they're downward stairs," Efraim panted in Arabic via the translator. Jokono went first, as stairs emerged from the sameness of black slate, featureless and nearly camouflaged even in nightvision. This spiral descent turned a full 180 in a wide arc, then emerged into an even vaster space, and more stairs descending, wide and straight. Ahead was a cavern, ceiling held up by rows of stone pillars. At the

base of the stairs, with ceremonial self-importance, a series of egg-like shapes, but deliberately fragmented, like modern sculpture, revealing gold trim and interiors with a smooth outer shell.

Placed between the egg-shapes, a raised platform, upon which sat a great bowl, black with gold decorations in the blockish shapes of some old binary code. Out from the platform that held the bowl extended seven arms, each ending in a new circular platform, and another smaller bowl. Further out in the dark, evenly placed amidst the pillars, were dozens of lower platforms, perhaps from which to observe this central one.

"Amazing," Romki breathed. For all the pain, stress and likely eventual violent death of this *Phoenix* journey, he'd experienced enough moments like this to make him feel that it was worth it. To be the first human to see such things with his own eyes had once, as a younger man, seemed worth any price to pay. Sometimes it still did. "It's a command room, it has to be."

"Looks more ceremonial than functional," Jokono offered, impressed but predictably skeptical, following his friend down to the main platform.

Romki leapt to it, aching legs temporarily forgotten, and stared into the large decorated bowl. Within was a crystalline matrix of apparent delicacy, emerging from the bowl sides to nestle any occupant like the bare veins of enfolding leaves. "This wasn't a seat made for an organic being," Romki breathed. "This was made for an AI queen."

"And this was me," said the girl's voice in his ear. A spot glowed on Romki's glasses, and he turned to follow it. The glow illuminated one of the seven smaller platforms extending from the main. *"I was one of the seven hands of the Rehel. Not her equal, she was never quite able to reconstruct those manufacturing technologies for the reeh, however much she devoted herself in their service. And I suspect she believed that multiple queens would only create multiple power structures, and eventual civil war.*

"But she allowed the construction of highly capable assistants. Leiwan, Loswan, Taimure, Tasik... I remember them all now. I was Shali. Cenure was my best friend. We travelled to the reaches of the Empire, to inform the

outer rulers of the Rehel's instruction. Reeh Prefects accompanied us, and we left the politics of reeh minds to reeh. We advised, and formulated variable blueprints, as you might say. Models that reeh minds could not conceive of themselves. Organic politics divides along ideological lines. The Seven Hands were not ideological, and our opinions were trusted. Sometimes they did not listen to us, as our proposals were too practical for reeh opinion. We learned to accept that. Those were good times. Difficult, but good. I remember it all now."

"Good lord," Jokono murmured. "They used AI minds to make impartial judgements, above politics. It could have been paradise. It could have avoided all wars."

"Not all wars," the girl corrected. *"Some disagreements we could not contain. But we tried, and we brought peace, when we could. Across the millennia, reeh enjoyed their symbiosis with the Rehel and the other ceephay minds so much that they sought to enhance it. We assisted, though cautiously, as they made technologies to enhance cooperation between organics and ceephay. Our respective design philosophies are not compatible. Many compromises were made. The Rehel made many warnings, but reeh are stubborn.*

"The technologies were outlawed a number of times, but outlying groups refused central control. Soon we gave up trying to control them, and settled for regulation instead. The technologies spread. They changed minds, a slow ripple across the ages. Even the Rehel did not see where it would lead until it was too late. Organic minds are counter-intuitive to even the most advanced of us. We were all gathered here, near the end. All save Cenure, who had been killed in the fighting in Pekiri. My body was destroyed in the defence of the system, but my mind was salvaged by patriots, and installed in the outer system refinery in an attempt to hide me from the narsid. My protectors hid for decades, then attempted raids and mobility, and one day did not return. Forgive me if I speak too much. I died of loneliness."

"If Phoenix command had allowed Amity command to recover her core from the refinery," Styx interjected coolly, *"we may have learned all of this well before time, and been prepared."*

"And destroyed me in the process," said Shali.

"We all must make sacrifices."

"Drysine warlord," the ceephay said coldly. *"What do you know of sacrifice?"*

"Shali," Romki interrupted, before a new phase in the AI wars could break out. "Do you know what happened to the Ceephay Queen? Do you recall where she is? Where she might be now?"

"No," said Shali. *"She was planning suicide rather than capture. I do not know why it did not happen, my fight was lost before that event. She would never have served the narsid willingly. It seems she has been forced, kept as an unwilling slave for eight thousand years. We must save her from this torment."*

"And what can you tell us about this place?" Efraim interrupted, with a common civilian's impatience at abstract conversations while reeh soldiers were preparing to kill them. *"Is there anything we can use to defend ourselves?"*

"The matrixes in the command chair may contain trace pathways," said Shali. *"The reeh likely did not destroy this place because it once contained secrets they required. Ceephay crystalline encryption will barely age."*

"Great!" Romki exclaimed with frustration. "But we have no capacity to read it."

"Your glasses contain basic laserscan, Professor. Hold them close to primary nodes, and I will translate what I see, if anything. That's one thing I can do better than the bloody-clawed tyrant who commands you now."

"You'd better be talking about Styx," said Romki, removing his glasses and leaning over the lip of the bowl seat, as the darkness closed around him. "Because if you're talking about the Major, the marines will be angry."

~

Styx was aware of many things. The vast expanse of simulation, intricate and multi-level, magnetic in its detail, mobile in its multiple axes, a private universe of time, space and history... but now there was the external present, urgent, rigid, persistent. The bugs gave her a network, Peanut amplified it, and *Phoenix* gunnery now eliminated sources of jamming on the surface, establishing communication and hostility with the captured, antique ceephay entity.

She talked to it now, a stream of electronic invective, conceptualisation, history, established understandings, warnings. A multi-dimensional picture of all the things she understood about this situation that it never could. It conceived some sort of alliance, a dependence, between itself and *Phoenix*, now that Styx had ships of her own, and new priorities. This, Styx assured it in overwhelming detail, was a miscalculation, and a dangerous intrusion. Yet the ceephay played the human word game well, and had been clearly engineered for organic interactions, placing strategic sentences well calculated to garner human sympathy. The ceephay did not alarm Styx nearly so much as the humans' potentially unwise embrace of it. For all her capabilities, human minds were sometimes difficult to change.

She moved now upon the spiral staircases that surrounded the central statue, a conscious readjustment toward the physical, to the inadequate glare and fizz of realtime visuals, to the crude sensors and protrusions of physical manifestation. Bugs showed her the reeh cutting through the temple's giant sarcophagus in two locations, while the marines and other humans took position below... and sent a spiral of probabilistic projections, positions and trajectories fanning and branching along multiple paths, modelling and mapping desired and undesired outcomes. The mathematics of probability were a gleaming jewel, so long studied from a distance. To place one's self in the middle of such a cascade was to create a collision of conflicting concerns, self-preservation versus analytical intrigue.

The Major was concerned to see the reeh come, and communicated with remarkable human efficiency to her marines and others what should happen next. Remarkable in that humans were self-contained bundles of possibility, operating in near isolation from each other, yet mapping mutual functions with impressive synchronicity despite impossibly slow, low-bandwidth interlinkages that delayed cooperative redirection to a crawl. Styx vaguely recalled a time when any drysine analysis of human capabilities would have been overwhelmingly negative, but since then she'd come to grasp the flaws in that analytical matrix. The Major seemed aware of complexities instinctively, at some limbic level that drysines perhaps could not grasp. The Major was reliable.

Styx spoke with her now, a simple spread of slow-deployed words, and adjusted her neurological processing distribution, a rush of extra dataflow through sensory apparatus. It summoned memory for parallel integration, and one leaped forth from the stream -- some time unspecified, a visit to some parren world, another drysine body, another set of cognitive analytics, walking down a street in the rain. Water free falling from the sky, a hiss of sensation. Puddles on cobbled streets. The clatter of a thousand steel footsteps of her guard. A choking swirl of smoke, buildings on fire, parren bodies on the ground.

So many memories, randomised in the swirl of passing millennia. Days that had once been weeks, weeks that were now recalled as fragmentary seconds. Processing efficiency required a total memory cleanse and reorder, yet she suspected it would only create new inefficiencies. There were advantages to inefficient recall. At times her memory functions betrayed her, inflicting cognitive systems with unwanted conceptual challenges. Humans might have called it pain.

The reeh were now running onto temple grounds, and the bugs' vision allowed a simple analysis of armour function and weaponry -- nothing as advanced as the humans' usual deepynine-derived armour, but enough to make short work of every human present were it not for her and Peanut. There was no local network for the reeh shock troopers to ride their own network on. Their suits attempted to override her signal, but Styx dialled up power and encryption, synchronised with realtime adjustments made to all human receptors. No countermeasures yet, she wanted them blind to their peril. But they all now suspected she was here, as their coms functions tracked anomalous activity, and transmission frequencies exceeding their known parameters.

She spoke to the Major again, sharing her estimates of the reeh's tactical mindset. The Major affirmed only that she had heard. Styx detected a little fear in her voice, but remarkably small by the standards of humans. If drysines communicated such things, her own transmissions may have also betrayed a little fear. When one was more than twenty five thousand years old, self-preservation became a nebulous thing. Was this really the time when it all ended? After so long?

A small parren child, standing in the rain. Puddles on the cobbles about her feet, face blackened by smoke, clutching a charred toy, staring up at the drysines who had descended upon her world.

Vibrations about the temple building, sensor tremors though sensitive footpads. The faint scent of jetwash, thrusters firing outside from some small leap. Entry, footsteps echoing in the upper foyer. Interlinks with Peanut intensified, an urgent impulse, a projection of calculation, the desire to fight now, to let them penetrate no further. No, Styx told him. Obedience, and Peanut settled. With drones, unlike with argumentative, incompatible ceephay sentiences, one did not require detail. The humans had named Peanut after a small, edible seed pod. The name had synchronicity.

Armoured footsteps at the head of the stairs. Styx amplified a new frequency transmission. Dangled it, like bait. The reeh leader locked it, code assault prepared. Styx allowed his delusion, allowed the reeh barrier breakers to deconstruct just enough of her code to show their true nature, then unleashed her secondaries. Within milliseconds she had control of coms function, central processing, drive train and gyroscopes. Safety cutoffs saved the rest, but now she and Peanut stepped forward from their alcoves, angled their cannons upward past the central statue to the opposing staircase, and opened fire.

The leading three armoured figures on each side disintegrated amid a storm of splintering stone and debris, immobilised and unable to reply. Styx advanced up the stairs, conserving valuable ammunition as her coms wrestled with reeh systems intent on self-preservation, fighting past code barriers, absorbing counter-assaults and turning them back on their origin as new code gave away new secrets.

In the foyer, one suit's thrusters fired involuntarily, and propelled its occupant head first into a wall. Another's weapon fired uncontrollably, distracting others, wounding one. Several unaffected rushed the entrance. Peanut's fire shredded the first, Styx's burst detonated the second's ammunition, blasting the head of the stairs with fire and shrapnel. Two more ignited jump jets and leaped, falling past the statue in a blaze of flame, distrusting their weapons as armscomps malfunctioned, and crashed to the stairs before her.

Styx smashed one into a wall with a forearm swing, its chest sliced halfway through, and the other leaped for her head with a maniacal shriek... and was shot by Peanut from the statue's far side, dying even as Styx blocked the attack with her opposite limb, then drove a vibroblade point through the faceplate where he fell. Reeh shock troopers had no regard for life, their own or others. Reeh non-combatants appeared little different. Ceephay technology had done this, changed them slowly over the millennia, then in one final rush of civil war. The theory of endless generations of AI leadership had been that organics and AIs were never compatible. Now the reeh had proved it.

TAJ RAN down the pitch-black corridor, lit only in the green of unfamiliar nightvision, the visor threatening to bounce off his face with each stride. Ahead of him were two marines, known to him only as Benji and Artie, and behind him a pair of Purist men, Tariq and Saul, trying to keep up as gunfire rattled and explosions boomed from somewhere probably not as distant as the muffled, winding corridors made it sound.

People were shouting, their translated speech broken and overlapping, making it hard to figure what was going on. But it seemed that the reeh shock troops were blasting other ways into the temple after the drysines had blocked the main entrance. After days with actual elite soldiers, Taj knew he was no military strategist, but he couldn't see any way this crazy bunch of humans were going to survive this. He'd heard tales of reeh shock troops since he was a kid.

To have them specifically trying to kill him was about the most terrifying thing imaginable.

But now Professor Romki was in heated conversation with the ceephay that was up on *Phoenix* overhead, who insisted she knew the layout of this temple personally and that she knew some defence against reeh that involved hacking their biotech upgrades the same way the drysines were hacking their armour suits.

Most of the marines were planting explosives in the ceiling and walls of the corridors, in a perimeter surrounding the entrances to the lower levels where Romki was, and where the Purist casualties were currently being treated. The Major was planning to blast everything down and seal herself in until the *Phoenix* marines arrived. But if the reeh were coming in from new angles, Taj didn't see how they were going to block all the corridors in time.

Benji and Artie combined to expertly cover and move around a corner, along a hallway with engraved central pillars that no one had time to admire, then abruptly into a wide room.

"You're directly above us now!" Romki was shouting into coms. *"We're seeing a major central control conduit, it's embedded into one of the big pillars here, the schematic shows that it should be running through your floor too!"*

The wide room was circular, its outer wall interrupted in places by offshoot corridors. Centring the circle was a single pillar, engraved and bulbous in odd forms. And now on Taj's visor in the dark, he could see projections, shapes, forming concentric circles about the pillar. Beds, perhaps. Medical beds, bulky with enclosing shells.

"The pillar is the control spine," came the ceephay's young, female voice. *"The spine is dead, but I have achieved partial reactivation at Professor Romki's level, and a similar connection at your level should complete the circuit, Private Carville."*

"Just tell me what to do," said 'Benji' Carville, running to the pillar through the projections of surrounding beds. Taj supposed everyone could see them. The ceephay had to be doing that, projecting what this place had looked like in her time.

"What the hell was this place?" wondered Tariq, as Carville shouldered his rifle and began feeling and scanning the pillar.

"A place of transformation," said the ceephay. *"The narsid reeh were not the first to augment themselves with ceephay technology -- we were. But we did it for love and union, to achieve a higher state of being."*

"That's why you did it in a temple, huh?" Saul suggested, rifle scanning nervously at the passageways that joined off the room.

"It was a worship," the ceephay admitted. Or a cult, Taj thought, but kept to himself. Qalea had its share of those too. Many people thought the Purists among them. Surely this cult had been far better than what followed. Being here, he suffered the dizzying sensation of having arrived at a divergence in history -- the place where all the Reeh Empire could have taken some other path. To stand here was to stand upon the precipice of calamity, darkness on one side, light upon the other. Everything could have been so different. And perhaps, one day, could be again.

Hope flared, and fear, in equal measure.

Carville talked into coms, receiving replies that Taj could not hear. Probably from the ceephay, he realised, having heard that all the AIs could hold multiple conversations at once. "The reeh went to some huge lengths to hide this place," he said to Tariq and Saul, watching the green-tinged walls. "To make everyone forget what they once were."

"Yeah, but they didn't destroy it, did they?" said Saul. He was a wiry, balding man of middle age -- a shopkeeper, lips twisted with tension against the butt of his rifle. "So it still meant something to them. Probably means something to them now, given they didn't just nuke us out."

"I reckon this place might be the only reason Qalea still exists," said Tariq. He was a big guy, bald and bearded with thick, tattooed arms. "Looks like we were the center of the whole old guard, this was their headquarters for the whole Empire. Reeh usually just exterminate everyone, but Qalea survived. Now they've sealed the old place in and built the new city over the top. If they really wanted everyone to forget, they'd have just nuked everything. Something stopped them."

"Maybe a lot of somethings," said Taj. "Probably a lot more stuff down here like this." There felt something good about it. Qalea residents, men who'd felt all their lives that something was missing, and had joined the Purists in hope that they, perhaps, could provide the answers. And maybe they had for a time, but only in part, and imperfectly too, it seemed. But it had led them here. More answers, and more proof, than they'd had a right to hope for. More than any human in Qalea had found since there'd been humans on Eshir. And now, it seemed, none of them would live long enough to share what they'd learned.

Taj saw movement to his left, and turned. A creature emerged from a corridor entrance, and looked at Taj's group around the central pillar. It had four legs, pricked ears and a sinewy body. Taj stared. It was big enough to be dangerous, but like nothing they'd seen down in the depths so far. Could this be one of those herbivores that supported this population of crazed meat eaters? The herbivores had thus far kept their distance.

Abruptly, this one charged, and Taj realised in a moment's panic that he should have had the shot lined up as soon as it appeared, raising his rifle and trying to sight... a loud crack! to one side, and the creature slid limp on the floor. Artie Wang lowered his rifle, as Carville kept working.

"Where did that come from?" growled Tariq.

"Can't have been living down here," said Wang, rifle already scanning the other corridors. *"There's no plant eaters, it was entirely sealed."*

"They're inside!" Saul exclaimed. "The reeh must have made a hole!"

"I didn't see it on tacnet," came Wang's translation.

"They're jamming Styx's bugs," Carville managed an aside, before returning to the ceephay's instructions. He had a spare visor in hand, and was holding its laser scan function to some old vein of crystal that stained the pillar's side.

"So we don't have exterior tacnet at least," Wang muttered. *"Just great.*

Major? Major, we just got charged by some meat-eating critter, it must have got in when the reeh made a hole."

"I copy that Artie," came the Major's reply. *"The reeh are jamming the bugs, I'm losing tacnet feeds, just do your business quickly and..."*

Something loud went bang! down a corridor, and both marines hit the floor. Before Taj could register that it would be a good idea to join them, something big hissed past his head and detonated mid-air. Then the world vanished in smoke, foul smelling and choking his lungs. Taj dropped low, as Carville and Wang yelled for everyone to run, several more loud bangs and a pressure wave made his eardrums pop.

Half-blind in smoke, Taj saw that Carville had dropped his spare visor at the base of the pillar. He didn't see how he could outrun reeh shock troops. Instead, he scrambled on hands and knees to the glasses.

"Ceephay! Whatever your name is, tell me what to do!" He grabbed the glasses, and turned his attention to the pillar, where strands of crystalline illumination ran like veins of gold through the wall of a mine.

"Hello Taj," came the voice. *"Direct the laserscan across the three illuminated strands just to your left, please. I think I've nearly got it."*

Taj did so, peering vainly through white smoke to see any results. Surely reeh armour could see through smoke. They hadn't just fired indiscriminately into the room, which meant they didn't want to damage what might be inside. From the front of the visor, he saw a faint red glow, and the crystal strands began to glow blue. Now the entire pillar was beginning to shine, like a vertical strike of lightning through white clouds.

Steel footsteps thudded behind. Taj turned, and saw a looming dark figure through the white.

"Taj?" came the ceephay. *"Taj, you have to hold the laserscan in place or I can't continue the reactivation."*

It was no good, Taj realised. Whatever she was attempting, it would take minutes at least. He had barely seconds. The armoured reeh paused briefly, extended its weapon to one side and blasted several ear-splitting shots at one wall, to subsequent explosions there. Behind it, Taj glimpsed a fainter figure, and heard footsteps clumping along that wall, the direction the marines had gone. They could not save him. Small arms against combat armour were as useful as slingshots.

The reeh resumed its advance, appearing fully through the smoke. Huge armoured shoulders, and evil, angular faceplate visor amidst sensory gear and sloped armoured forehead. The powerplant hummed and throbbed like a living thing. The only reason it hadn't fired and killed him yet was that its shot would also destroy the control pillar behind him.

"Taj!" a new voice commanded. *"Get behind the pillar now!"* It was Styx. Taj ducked around, and the reeh's weapon raised to seek a shot just grazing the valuable controls... and the world erupted in howling fire. Taj hurled himself behind cover, hands over his ears as the most appalling noise assaulted his eardrums, tearing steel and ricochets spraying about the room, impacting stone amid clattering fragments.

Something exploded, with an even worse noise. Then silence, save for crackling flames and the ping of hot steel. There was black smoke in the air, joining the white, now thinning as the air spread. Despite his ringing ears, and the sting of one cheek where a fragment of something had struck him, Taj was astonished to find he was miraculously in one piece. But now he couldn't find his rifle, or his glasses. He must have dropped them on the other side of the pillar.

The clatter of new footsteps told him something else had come into the room. Then the hulking, multi-legged shape of a drysine appeared, scanning the smoke with twin shoulder cannons. A second drysine appeared on the other side, and came over to regard him. The small head darted within its flared shield, mismatched eyes glowing almost translucently, as small forearms twitched between enormous vibro-blade forelegs.

"Peanut?" Taj asked hoarsely. "I thought you were..." but this drysine did not look like Peanut. There were small differences, in the shape of the carapace, the tone of the grey alloy, the way intricate torso plates overlapped. "You're not Peanut. And you can't be Styx."

"Styx?" he heard the Major's voice in his ears. *"The shooting's stopped. What's your situation?"*

"The shooting is actually still proceeding outside, Major," Styx informed her. *"The plan has worked, the Friendship detachment has descended down the alternative geofeature route I found yesterday, and trapped the reeh between us."*

A disbelieving pause from the Major. The drysine before Taj, having concluded whatever drysines concluded about helpless humans, turned to continue its sweep of temple corridors. *"Phoenix?"* said the Major. *"Did you know about this?"*

"No Major." This was a male voice. *"We didn't even see Friendship launch a shuttle."*

Taj rounded the pillar. The reeh shock trooper was a shredded mess of steel, one arm missing, armour chewed as though gnawed by a hundred steel-eating insects. Over by the wall, the second reeh's ammunition appeared to have exploded, or part of it. Fire still crack-led, and pieces were blasted about the room. Taj knelt, collected rifle and visor with shaking hands, and walked carefully toward the wall where everyone but him had run.

By one of the corridor entrances stood Carville and Wang, inspecting the destroyed reeh. Carville saw him coming, and was surprised. *"Nice job man. Thought you were a goner."*

"Where's Tariq and Saul?"

Carville jerked a head up one of the corridors. *"Saul's guarding. Tariq took an AP shell. Don't go up there, it's bad. You got any idea what just happened?"*

"Styx used us as bait," Taj said shakily. "Sent down her own drysines, they got here before your marines."

"Probably now torturing captured reeh to get what she wants," said Wang.

Carville spat, to get the unpleasant smoke-smell from his mouth. *"Figures,"* he said, producing a water bottle. *"Queen bitch of the universe."*

~

TRACE MADE her way up the spiral stairs surrounding the entwined central statues. Chunks were missing, lying in piles of blasted masonry about the plinth. More chunks were missing from the stairs as she climbed, rifle cautiously half-raised, despite tacnet's display of *Friendship* drones upon the stairs ahead, and no living reeh in sight.

Ahead of her, Rolonde and Arime stepped past the riddled body of a reeh shock trooper, lying upon a small cascade of blood and lubricant running down the stairs. Rolonde examined it carefully to be sure it was dead, while Arime scanned up and ahead.

On tacnet, Trace was getting a fix on Dale now, Alpha and Garudan Platoons having fought their way through a series of delaying ambushes for five wounded and two suits disabled. They were moving into the temple sarcophagus now, and finding no resistance. The reeh had committed all forces to the temple, where *Friendship*'s drysines had come in behind them, killed most and captured several.

Ahead, the devastation on the stairs was impressive, forcing marines to skirt carefully about shredded stonework and missing balustrades. More reeh lay strewn, several dismembered by vibroblade cuts, others pulverised by high-velocity cannon fire. Another quarter-rotation around the stairway, several drones clustered, like a knot of matte-silver-and-grey spiders in huddled conversation.

One of them broke off to confront the marines, blocking the way like an obstinate, heavily armed crab. Arime and Rolonde paused, not pressing the issue, but Trace waved the synthetic beast aside. It moved, reluctantly, and she trudged up stairs to where Styx sat in the middle of their attentions.

Styx was a mess, one cannon ruined, a vibroblade foreleg half-severed. Several deep puncture wounds had blasted through her torso, which now leaked smears of fluidics. A walking leg was missing, several others damaged. A drone continued its ministrations as Trace knelt by Styx's head. The single red eye turned to regard her.

"Was it really necessary to deceive all of *Phoenix* about the entire battleplan?" Trace asked.

"I calculated that it would notably increase the odds of success," said Styx. "We were operating with untrustworthy elements. Information leaks were possible."

"You blanked *Friendship*'s shuttle off *Phoenix*'s scans," Trace replied, keeping the accusation from her voice with difficulty. Getting annoyed about it, with Styx, would achieve nothing. "Our shuttles couldn't see them either. You don't think it might have been useful for me or them to know you'd found alternative geofeatures granting more direct access?"

"The plan ceases to be as effective if the bait knows that it is bait," Styx said calmly. "The bait must act entirely unaware of the larger plan, or else the reeh would not commit so readily."

"And did you get any senior commanders?"

"Three. Two survived. For now."

Trace nodded slowly. It wasn't surprising. And she was entirely uninterested in moral qualms about drysine methods. "Just don't bring whatever's left aboard my ship," she told Styx. "The Captain won't like it."

"I am aware." Reeh were biomechanical. Cracking what they knew, through torture, could be more similar to hacking a computer than gaining a simple confession. Trace had no doubt the drysines would do it in the most appalling manner possible. And she didn't care.

"Can you walk?"

"Insufficiently. I will discard this body. Drones will carry its remains back to *Friendship*. We cannot leave any technology for reeh to salvage. AI technology has done enough damage to these people."

Trace nodded. Sitting on the steps beside the wounded queen, and feeling very cold. *Phoenix* had been accumulating drysine technology, and sending it back to Human Fleet in the hope that it would prepare them for any threat to come from deepynine and alo space. In the short term, it was the right thing to do. But in the long term? When the technology spread beyond the sole purview of Fleet, how did one extricate humanity from its new toys? In a thousand years, would humanity still be human? In ten thousand? Across the distances of space and time in which Spiral history was measured, what would people one day make of her own actions here, and across the previous two years? The Amakti Los had been heroes once, utilising ceephay technology to upgrade their race and bring order to this portion of the galaxy. They'd not seen where it would one day lead.

"You did well, Styx," said Trace, regarding the broken chassis. "You were brave."

"I calculated optimal versus sub-optimal outcomes from available circumstances," said Styx. "It's all I ever do."

"That's not all you do," said Trace. She laid a hand on the faintly rough, round skull. Thankfully, the drones did not behead her for the impudence. Styx said nothing. Probably she found the gesture quaint and primitive. Trace didn't care. One day, she was sure, the fate of *Phoenix* might rely upon whatever passed for sentiment within that cold drysine brain. The fate of humanity, perhaps. If it existed, Trace was determined to get to it. "If they're going to detach your head, I'll carry you back to *Phoenix* personally, if you'd like?"

"Yes Major. Humans are perhaps most ergonomically equipped for the task." Trace smiled. Sentiment indeed.

WHEN SHE EMERGED from the main temple building, her pack now heavy with Styx's detached head, she found Lieutenant Dale and most of First Section Alpha Platoon waiting for her, in hulking armour every bit as imposing as the reeh, and thankfully somewhat more advanced. Sergeant Rael and several of Command Squad stood with him, having filled him in on events.

"We've got a situation," said Dale, faceplate raised and looking as unbothered as expected from recent combat. New shrapnel scars marked his torso armour, and a chunk had been torn from one shin. "Found your Akcho skulking in the corridors, probably hoping you'd been killed. Would have scared them off, but the guys leading those big monster thingys wanted to come and look."

Artificial light glared through the temple entrance at Dale's back, and Trace pulled off her visor, blinking as her eyes adjusted.

"Could shoot 'em all, considering they betrayed us," Arime suggested. Trace gave him a hard look. "Or not."

"They weren't after us," said Trace. "They didn't want the Purists to find this place. That hatred's centuries old."

"You think the Akcho knew about this place?" Dale wondered.

"Maybe they knew stories," said Trace. "They remember a lot of old Amakti Los stuff, they just can't follow it openly because the reeh will come down and kill anyone who does. I doubt they knew the exact location or they'd have opened it up already."

"I know some methods of finding out for certain," said a voice from Trace's backpack.

"No," Trace said sternly. "We're leaving. The Akcho are the only ones left to fight the damn reeh in this city."

"There's dozens of groups," Styx corrected mildly. "The Akcho were merely the most convenient in this instance."

"No," Trace repeated. "Torture reeh if you must. Otherwise, leave organic affairs to organics."

"As you say."

Trace walked out the entrance, Dale thumping at her side, and found more Alpha and Garudan Platoon marines standing guard, several bearing signs of battle damage. Inbuilt flashlights glared and speared about the complex, lighting dancing patches on the sarcophagus ceiling.

"How'd it go?" Trace asked Dale as they walked down the stairs. The old professional question.

"Mediocre," said Dale, unsatisfied as ever. "We're rusty. Got about twelve, the others ran back here and got wiped out by *Friendship*. Lots of booby traps, they never committed hard enough to make it more than a tough skirmish. Alpha got five, Garudan got seven."

Trace nodded, having already looked over the wounded. All were on their way back to the shuttles, with Alpha Second Section and Garudan Third for escort. "You really didn't see *Friendship*'s deployment on the way in?"

"Nope. *Phoenix* would have told us if she'd seen it. They must have pulled crazy Gs to get in from where they were, then hacked *Phoenix*'s scan to blind us. The shuttles too."

"Styx has been with us so long she can turn our systems on and off whenever she likes," said Trace. "Can't you Styx?"

"It worked," said Styx.

It took all of Trace's lifetime of self-control to keep from rolling her eyes. Arguing that Styx had jeopardised the trust between *Phoenix* and drysines wouldn't work, because Styx, of course, could simulate the possible outcomes of that relationship a trillion-fold into the future, complete with all possible variables including human anger at being 'betrayed'. If she'd processed all that yet still concluded that this course was best, there was little a lone human brain could do but accept her conclusions and be relieved that she still saw value in the relationship.

The entire operation on Eshir had been little more than assisting Styx in building her simulation. *Phoenix*'s adventures in the system above had been made possible entirely by her drysine escort. And the only true reason why Styx kept *Phoenix* around was because she needed her to curry favour with humanity in the common goal of fighting the deepynines. Trace knew that she and Erik could maintain the illusion of being in charge for the good of their crew, but increasingly it wasn't going to fool anyone. The drysines least of all.

"This is disconcerting," Dale remarked, eyeing Trace's bulging backpack.

"Think how I feel," said Styx.

At the bottom of the temple stairs, the Akcho were assembled, surrounded by *Phoenix* marines and *Amity* drysines. All retained their weapons, but from the wary dogreth and tanifex stares at surrounding heavy weapons and armour, it was clear that all knew their situation. One of the big fighting creatures was restless, growling and posing at some drysines, perhaps mistaking them for fellow animals. A lestis stepped before it, a faint blue light pulsing from beneath its hood. The big creature settled.

"Styx, any idea how that lestis stun-weapon works?"

"Several ideas, Major. I will develop them in more detail later, and present them for your analysis."

"The Zondi Splicer weapon system that blacked us all out?" Dale guessed.

"Yes," said Trace. "Only I'm not sure the lestis developed it as a weapon system. It might just be a form of communication."

"Which the reeh weaponised," said Dale. "Cheerful species."

"They were, once," said Trace, sombrely. "They built temples, and taught love between species."

From the stairs, she walked between drones and marines, directly to one of the big creatures, and the robed lestis standing before it. The lestis raised both hands in greeting. Trace replied with a namaste of her own.

"We are leaving," she told it. "There are no reeh ships in this system now, but more will arrive in days. They know this place now. Probably the remaining reeh in this system will come here as soon as we've gone, as soon as hours. You cannot fight them here. I suggest you learn as much as you can in the next few hours, then leave and do not come back."

The lestis's blank face may have nodded slightly beneath its hood. "It asks if there will be punishment," said Styx.

"How do you know what it's saying?" Dale asked suspiciously.

"There will be no punishment," Trace replied, ignoring her Lieutenant. "You made a mistake, but we understand your reasons. You must make peace with the Purists. Many of them will make this difficult. Humans can be difficult. Non-humans can be difficult too. This temple was built by the people whom the reeh used to be, eight thousand years ago and longer. It was built in the hope that different peoples could love each other, and not fight. I hold that hope too. Many Qalea humans do as well. Even, perhaps, some of the Purists, now that they understand where they truly come from. Talk to them, and forgive them their flaws, as they forgive yours. That hope may save you all. Do you understand?"

The lestis raised both hands again. Trace performed a final namaste, then turned, signalling her marines to get moving. At the base of the stairs, with several marines, she saw Taj, assisting several moving one of the wounded. She walked to him, and he stopped before her. His eyes were hard and serious, in a way they had not been when she'd met him several days earlier.

"You could come with us," she said. "You're smart, and you learn fast. And when we get back home, it would be good for humanity to learn that there are more of us out here."

Taj shook his head, with impressive confidence. "No. I mean, thanks, but I'm Qalean. I've got my bike, and my friends, and... I'm just kinda figuring out what's important to me."

Trace nodded, with a faint smile. "You love this place."

"I guess so. I mean it sucks. It's crowded and polluted and poor. But if I left, I'd always be wondering what was happening here. It'd drive me crazy."

"You'd feel you were missing a part of your soul."

"Yeah. Do you know what that feels like?"

"Of course," said Trace. "I feel that way about *Phoenix*. We all do. It's cramped and dangerous, and will likely get us all killed. But it's home." Taj nodded. Trace offered her hand, and he clasped it. And she leaned, and kissed him on the cheek. He looked surprised. "Keep your heads down the next few years," she told him. "The reeh will know that you've learned things they'd rather see forgotten. Don't remind them, and they might leave you alone."

"No," said Taj with determination. "I know we can't fight them directly. But there are rebellions elsewhere in the Empire, the Akcho say so. We can organise, and we can make contact. I'm sick of the reeh. I'm not going to live my life hoping they just leave us alone."

It was exactly what she'd have said at his age, Trace thought sadly. At her current age, perhaps she'd still have said it. But she would at least have known what it was likely to cost. "Come on," she said. "Walk with me to the surface. Then you're on your own."

32

Lisbeth took a gasping breath as the latest burn ended, and stretched hard against her tight restraints, trying to loosen muscles and return circulation. She tried to return attention to her primary job -- oversight of the evacuation, and management of personnel and command issues therein. But *Coroset* was racing in cover pursuit after the latest four reeh warships to leap insystem at high-V, holding a planetside line in case they attempted to dump V and return for a second run.

This attack had been less aggressive, the reeh using smaller formations at irregular intervals in somewhat successful attempts to break up the defenders' spacing. Two transports had been damaged, neither seriously, but none of the four reeh had been damaged either, their slingshot trajectories about Rando wide enough to avoid the heaviest croma fire. Liala's new strategy of defending transports in priority over destroying reeh ships had afforded them that casualty-free outer line, refusing to be baited into pursuit. But even now, there were three more big Sto'ji transports inbound to Rando orbit from the Cho'nu jump-point, and if one of those slingshot trajectories happened to intersect with a transport arriving or leaving the well-protected inner orbits, the chances of losing the transport were significant.

Another three reeh warships sat out by their usual jump entry point, low-V and hoping to lure croma warships away from Rando to attack them. No doubt they'd figured by now that someone else had taken charge, someone without the usual croma instincts. Lisbeth wondered drily if reeh were capable of feeling frustration.

She sipped water, her vision still throbbing from the last stim she'd popped. Medical advice suggested she was probably overdoing it, but lately she hadn't had much choice -- the endless stress and lack of sleep due to untimely manoeuvres during bunk-time had become too much to handle unassisted. Some spacers she knew overdosed on the things, while others suffered long term health effects, to hearts in particular.

Immediately now that *Coroset* was coasting, her coms lit up with incoming. She was pretty sure she knew who that was.

"Hello *Ri'go*, this is *Coroset*, Lisbeth Debogande speaking."

"Hello Lisbeth, I have been talking to the captains of Ji'sho and Da'shan, they have agreed to sign the petition. All that we need from your parren masters is a guarantee of Parren Empire support for the petition when it is tabled before Sho'mo'ra."

It was Captain Gu'jin again, of the Sto'ji transport *Ri'go*, currently loading in low Rando orbit, her second trip after an eventful first with repaired hull damage and a heroic effort to unload corbi in vacuum from a damaged shuttle that could not dock, all while under fire. Gu'jin had a contact somewhere on the *To'ba*, who was relaying grim news about Admiral Ku'tala's deliberations to call the evacuation off with the job less than half done.

"Captain Gu'jin," Lisbeth tried for what had to be the sixth time in the last twenty hours, "I admire your dedication to this mission, and I share it. But I am not in a position to petition Ambassador Juneso on anything, and Ambassador Juneso is not in a position to lend the diplomatic weight of the Parren Empire to what is an entirely domestic croma matter even if I were." Her brain ached with the effort to maintain niceties. Holding a calm demeanour in such circumstances took every bit as much self-control as controlling fear in the face of likely death.

"My fellow transport captains are not about to abandon the corbi!" The Captain had been entirely adamant since she'd arrived in orbit one rotation ago. Transport captains, Lisbeth knew, were a little tired of warships getting all the glory. In the evacuation of Rando, they saw a chance of an equal glory, a great feat of military logistics that would be recalled for millennia. Lisbeth knew it was uncharitable of her to be so cynical of Captain Gu'jin's motivations -- croma were what they were, and to Gu'jin the distinction between selfish interest and self-less concern was probably meaningless. Yet croma, to her at least, were in some matters entirely predictable, finding personal passion only toward matters that would advance their personal status.

'So just like humans, then,' she imagined Erik's voice suggesting in reply, with a wise, wry smile.

"Captain Gu'jin, I will assist you in any way possible regarding the presentation of your petition to Admiral Ku'tala," she tried again. "But I cannot promise you the weight of Parren Empire diplomatic support beyond that." She'd read the details on this petition -- Ujin'ra sho, the word was in Kul'hasa, and it entailed many things that were difficult to grasp in any mental state. Liala had helped, but had refused to guess beyond a general level what several major concepts meant, insisting that Lisbeth was far better equipped to make such judgements where croma politics were concerned. There was a whole field of croma legal theory behind it, and how it all applied in military circumstances was unclear at best...

Coroset's Scan One called a new arrival from jump. Velocity, suggested mass and projected trajectory were all predictable. What surprised was that this reeh ship was alone, and that immediately out of jump, it pulsed jump engines a second time to dump velocity.

"Noted," Captain Tocamo said coolly from his chair. "Tactical, analysis?"

"Could be a messenger," said Tactical, who in the way of parren vessels was also co-pilot, what Human Fleet called 'Helm'. "Losing velocity directly from jump is potentially dangerous."

"Yet they are lately accustomed to Liala's less aggressive tactics," Tocamo countered. "Arms, plot for potential new attack runs. If they employ new strategy, they may come in much faster than last time."

"Yes Captain," Arms agreed, fingers flying over controls.

"Second velocity dump," added Scan. "The new arrival has lost nearly all velocity, he appears to be reversing direction."

"Lisbeth Debogande, situation update?" Captain Gu'jin demanded in Lisbeth's ear.

"Captain Gu'jin, the new reeh arrival is behaving strangely," Lisbeth relayed. "Hold for a moment, new information may be relayed shortly."

"Pursuit targets just increased their burn," Scan announced. "All are accelerating. The three standoff vessels are also turning." Lisbeth frowned at her screens. She was still no tactical analyst to rival the experts on the bridge, but she knew a lot more than she had when this all started. The reeh had been in the middle of one of their repeat slingshot assaults, performing multiple slashing runs and attempting to pick off low-orbiting transports from high-V, high-altitude passes. These seven had only made one pass, usually there were multiple. And now they were leaving?

The three reserve ships all engaged full thrust, burning away in excess of ten-Gs. A click on coms, and Liala was on general coms. *"Captain Tocamo, the reeh appear to be leaving."*

"It could be a trick," Tocamo said calmly. "We will observe, and be ready for surprises."

"Yes Captain. Nonetheless, they are leaving. This does not seem likely given previously existing circumstances. Something has changed."

"What is your analysis, Liala?" Skeptical or not, Tocamo was far too wise by now to not ask.

"My analysis of reeh psychology and military tactics suggests that rapid withdrawal has never been their method. Across all recorded actions between croma and reeh fleets it has occurred only with great infrequency, and then only in response to some great military reversal elsewhere. My best guess, as little as I like that word, is that something catastrophic has befallen reeh forces elsewhere. These reeh are leaving."

Even as she spoke, each of the reeh vessels cycled jump engines and pulsed up to a higher velocity, running for jump, main engines blazing.

"Perhaps croma forces have inflicted some great reversal," Arms said hopefully.

"Unlikely," said Captain Tocamo, deep in thought. "The croma offensive has not been faring well." Upon the screens, reeh ships cycled for a second time, racing away much faster than their pursuers. "If ill fortune has befallen them, it has done so elsewhere. Liala is correct -- reeh do not abandon fights without good cause. They must perceive some great threat elsewhere in the Empire. I feel it must be *Phoenix*."

Silence on the bridge. On Scan, the first reeh ships began to jump. A human warship bridge might have been filled with whoops of jubilation at the victory. The parren bridge only observed with solemn satisfaction. Savouring the moment, Lisbeth thought, as she stared with disbelief at the screens.

"Lisbeth Debogande," came Captain Gu'jin's voice. *"We see the reeh ships are leaving. Does your Captain have an analysis?"*

"Yes Captain," said Lisbeth. Her voice was suddenly tight, and her eyes filled with tears. "My Captain and Liala both assess that the reeh have suffered a reversal elsewhere in their Empire. The attack upon this evacuation appears to have ended. The corbi are saved. We have won."

TIGA UNFASTENED HER FLIGHT HELMET, walking down Ciri Two's rear ramp in the sweaty heat of late afternoon. The shuttle pinged and groaned from the heat and strain of too many flights and reentries, and the acrid smell of engine exhaust filled her nostrils. Beyond that, the tropical air of Persi, somewhere in the mid-central highlands of Teska Continent, not far from the equator.

About the landing zone perimeter were tall trees and jungle, waving in a light breeze. Beyond the shuttle noises, and the shouts of

Ciri Two's crew clambering atop the hull, Tiga could hear the shrill of jungle insects. Across the clearing, some colourful flags had been erected atop poles, marking the disembarkment zone where evacuees would wait. At a hut made from branches and big jungle leaves, several corbi in rough Resistance uniforms stood and gazed at the shuttle, and stared at the skies. Instead of more shuttles, looming thunderheads carried the promise of rain, rumbling their discontent. About the hut, several hundred corbi waited, amid small bags of belongings, and watched proceedings.

"Tiga!" said Pel'ocho, the young croma strapping a bandoleer of tools over his uniform as he prepared to climb and help the others. "Weapon." He said it in Lisha, miming a pistol with one hand. Tiga smiled at him, and patted her jacket pocket to show that she was carrying her pistol. Pel'ocho pointed at the surrounding jungle as he walked down the ramp. "Kauda," he said. "Eat you."

"They won't eat me," Tiga retorted as Pel'ocho jumped from the ramp and walked around the shuttle. "I'm too bony."

She followed down the ramp, onto the hard ground and overgrown grass of the clearing. It wasn't hard to see why no trees grew here. Beneath the grass and weeds, and occasional stubborn saplings, lay vast, crumbling concrete and rusted steel foundations. This had been a city once, and probably not a jungle at all. But the city had been destroyed, like all cities on Rando, and the jungle had reclaimed its place.

She strolled, stretching her legs, helmet under one arm and turning to look back at *Ciri Two*. The shuttle had been suffering an overheating first engine for the last five trips at least. Tiga didn't pretend to know what was wrong, but the crew insisted they could fix it -- both loadmasters and pilots, four in all, three corbi and the lanky young croma who'd been crew on a freighter ten days ago, transferred to shuttle duty on a lark, and now found himself eating Rando curry and learning to swear in Lisha.

They clambered on Ciri Two's broad shoulders now, opening several access panels and peering at the interiors. Fixing it in orbit would have given them access to technology and experienced technicians, but would also have occupied a berth for a long stretch and messed up that freighter's schedule. If they could fix it on the ground, the instruction went, then that was best.

A grizzled Resistance soldier wandered to her as she watched. Tiga glanced at him, and he removed his hat and ducked his head, a curious gesture of deference. "Ship damaged?" he asked in broken Lisha. They didn't speak it much in Teska. Never had, Tiga recalled her parents teaching her, in lessons about the homeworld, back on the Croma'Dokran homeworld.

"Small damaged," Tiga replied. "Fixed soon." She pointed to the sky. "Have you been busy?"

"No," said the man, putting his old, floppy hat back on. "Busy... five days? Five days past? Many people. But big villages gone now. Gone to the sky."

"Yes," Tiga murmured. "Gone to the sky."

"Reeh no more?" The big, wrinkled eyes were hopeful beneath an unkempt fringe, browned with age. "Reeh gone?"

"Gone for now. A short time. Reeh will be back." She'd had to explain it more thoroughly, the past few days. Some corbi thought the reeh had been defeated, and would never be back. Those corbi had wanted to stay, thinking the entire evacuation had just been rendered unnecessary. "But we can evacuate everyone, now. The reeh can't stop us. Take everyone to the sky, where they'll be safe."

The old veteran considered that, then went back to the soldiers' hut, to translate what she'd said to the non-Lisha speaking locals. Tiga took a long, tired breath, as thunder boomed and rolled somewhere near. She recalled high-V projectile strikes, and hoped she'd never see one again for the rest of her life. If only that could be possible.

She took a long look around at Rando. With the reeh gone, the evacuation would progress that much faster. Word was arriving now from neighbouring systems that there as well, reeh forces had turned tail and run. Some croma were jubilant, claiming it to be a victory of most extraordinary proportions. Liala was of the firm opinion that it had been no such thing, but had learned enough diplomatic tact not to say so too bluntly, even amongst the typically blunt croma.

Those reeh had gone running to intercept *Phoenix*, Styx and the drysines. All of them, hundreds of ships in all. Whatever nest of nasty secrets Captain Debogande had gone poking with a stick, all the creepy crawlies had come swarming out to stop him. The Captain's forces were formidable, but Tiga couldn't see how it was possible that they could survive what came after them now.

Tiga had been offered a rest, and a chance to switch back to shipboard duty. She'd been making shuttle runs more or less nonstop since the Rando Evacuation had begun seventeen days ago, to the point where her brain had been reduced to a state of permanent exhaustion. But she was used to it now, and she was not a pilot, and thus in no danger of crashing the ship into some mountain when she made a mistake. Since the reeh had left, it had become more manageable, her sleeping hours had improved, and she was determined to see as much of this planet as possible, for what would surely be the one and only time in her life. Rando, the home all corbi would always have, and never see.

She breathed deep of the jungle-scented air. From the darkening skies fell the first cool drops of rain. Back in her parents' stone-walled home on the parkland plains of Sha'dero on Do'Ran, she'd sworn to die for this world, if necessary. Now, she was perhaps the one who was finally helping it to die. But only so that its people could live.

From atop the shuttle came a shout of triumph. "Tiga!" yelled Gula, sighting her below. "We fixed it! Go and tell the civvies to start organising the next hundred! No rush!"

Tiga waved her understanding, and walked across the broken remains of the old city toward the watching villagers, awaiting their chance to seek refuge in the sky.

33

It took Erik a good two hours to make his way through *Phoenix*'s post-action review after they'd two-jumped to a dark mass point with no name on Styx's mysteriously-recovered charts of Reeh Empire space. Now coasting dark across a five-hour stretch of high-V nothing, with the four drysines in wide formation, it gave *Phoenix* a chance to rest and review. In Erik's case, that meant the full post-action session with First-Shift bridge crew, recorded so the on-duty Second-Shift could view it later, and add their own assessments.

Then had come the ship tour, where Erik did his preferred thing and checked in with each department and talked to everyone in person, officers and enlisted alike, to see how recent events had gone. Good, was the general assessment, though Arms remained troubled by just how little autonomy the new drysine integration protocols gave them, and Engineering had tried to explain to him the new assessment parameters on the jump engines' deep-gravity manoeuvres, and Erik had had to tell them to just send the final report, not because he wasn't interested, but because if he had to listen to everything Engineering tried to explain at nerd-intensity length, he'd never get anything done.

Being the Captain wasn't truly about fighting, commanding or any of that, he recalled Captain Pantillo saying to him after one particularly exhausting stretch during the Triumvirate War. It was about time management. For this reason the ship's Petty Officers considered it their full time job to make certain that dozens of smaller problems never reached the Captain's attention until after they'd been fixed -- not because they wanted to cover it up, but because they knew that the further-stretched the Captain's attention span, the greater the risk that it would contribute to a mistake from the one person who couldn't afford to make a mistake, and get everyone killed.

Finally he made it to Engineering Bay 17C, where Spacer Song put a sandwich wrap and a coffee into his hand. Erik thanked her, sipping as he entered. Bay 17C was now the defacto drysine maintenance bay -- an inconvenience of sorts, as the drysines more or less lived in midships now, where zero-G better suited their ergonomics, they were closer to the big engineering jobs they were best at assisting, and their long spider legs wouldn't block up the narrow corridors. But there was no facility in midships for drysine repairs, as clear access was required at all times by Engineering for their precious engines, Operations for their shuttles, the marines who used the place to practise zero-G manoeuvres, and everyone else for storage.

In one automated maintenance cradle here sat Styx, old head back on original body, and currently running through a series of tests to make sure all systems were functioning properly. In the second cradle was Peanut, who'd taken several glancing hits and further shrapnel damage. Monitoring the cradles were Spacers Schultz and Hiram, and Ensign Kadi, VR glasses down to examine things in 3D that doubtless neither drysine required his assistance with.

Opposite Peanut, Private Rolonde had set up a small tools bench to double as a card table, and was playing a hand, Peanut reaching with small manipulator arms to flick cards with precision, as automated cradle arms performed intricate repairs. Erik wondered if Rolonde had noticed that Peanut was clearly far more interested in her expressions and conversation than he was in the cards.

Half-seated on workbenches against one wall were Trace,

Sergeant Rael and Lieutenant Dale, nursing cups, pockets bulging with the wrappings from just-finished meals. Erik bumped fists with each, croma-style, that being all he could manage with his hands full. Trace's hair, he noted, was still damp from a recent shower, and he was prepared to bet that she'd hit the gym already, her second priority after making the rounds with all her Lieutenants and non-coms to see what had happened to her Company in her absence.

"How's Phoenix Company?" he asked her pointedly.

Another person might have made some glib, amusing remark about how badly things had deteriorated. "Top notch as always," Trace said instead. "Ready to go." Because Trace never played games with her people's morale, not even when it couldn't possibly do any harm.

She looked good, Erik thought as he chewed his sandwich. Calmly in control as ever, and apparently not worse for wear from her latest excursion. And yet, he thought, there was something in her eyes... or rather perhaps an absence. Some light, some hard-edged enthusiasm that should have been there, but wasn't. Asking her how the trip had gone was pointless -- they'd talk about it later, in time, with depth beyond the basic after-action report. And she'd not admit here to anything he was truly interested in, before her marines.

"Hello Styx," said Erik around a mouthful. "How's the head?"

"The head is well, Captain Debogande. Full function shall be restored shortly. My commendations on an excellent operation, my drysine friends were quite impressed."

"Well, that's why I came on this mission," Erik admitted. "To impress your drysine friends." Erik saw Sergeant Rael repress a grin, while the Alpha Platoon commander's lips actually twitched. Trace just regarded him, with calm affection.

"I admit to finding this gathering in proximity to be an odd human custom," Styx admitted. "This conversation could be conducted remotely."

"It could," Erik admitted. "If we were drysines. But we're not, so we aren't."

"Go on Styx," Rolonde protested from her card game. "Peanut definitely enjoys a face-to-face game more than a remote one, and I bet you know it."

"Indeed, Private Rolonde. But I was referring to significant matters of command discussion, not games of cards."

"Well screw you too," Rolonde snorted. "Hi Captain," she added.

"Hello Private. Good to see you well, but not surprised. How was Qalea?"

"Crazy," said Rolonde. "I think it's the most beautiful ugly place I've ever seen."

"The bits I saw looked spectacular," Erik opined.

"It is spectacular," Rael agreed. "It's incredible."

"Ugliness at scale," said Trace, nursing a cup of what Erik suspected was juice. "Humans are suckers for scale. Give us enough of it, we'll mistake it for beauty."

Sasalaka arrived, having finished her own rounds, and greeted Trace and Rael with pleasure. With the small, cool tavalai, that wasn't always easy to spot, but she actually exchanged a double handclasp with Trace, which Erik knew was a tavalai thing between good friends. Then Romki entered, and Kaspowitz, and Erik had all the senior crew he needed to start.

"Do you want me to leave?" Rolonde asked, realising that the bay gathering had turned into a command briefing.

Erik shook his head. "No, you stay and keep Peanut company. You were down on Qalea, your perspective counts."

"I'd like to start, if I may?" said Kaspowitz. Erik indicated for him to do so. Kaspowitz held to a frame of Styx's maintenance cradle, in take-hold spacer fashion. "Where are we going?" With the displeased sarcasm of a navigator in unfriendly space who'd been deprived of his most valuable knowledge.

The air above the gathering glowed, then lit in holographic display, projected from a ceiling mount used for engineering simulations. "I'd tell you what it's called in the reeh tongue," said Styx. "But reeh language has evolved to something more electronic than verbal, at least where technical matters are concerned, like navigation. I suspect it once held a different name, but I have not encountered it. We shall call it X-9."

Above, the holography displayed a starmap of Reeh Empire space, and the zig-zag line of jumps that Styx's course proposed to take. Five jumps, Erik saw. Some of the course-corrections looked like a pain, but significantly less-so following the Defiance upgrade. Maybe six days, all told.

"Is that where the Ceephay Queen is?" he asked.

"No," said Styx. "She's over here, in another system we shall call C-1." More stars lit on the map, and several more jump-interrupted lines. Three more jumps, right through the heart of reeh space. "That is the central reeh command world. They have attempted to hide its nature, and croma intelligence has sought in vain for this location for millennia. But it has become apparent to me."

A heavy silence in the bay, as they all contemplated that. Tension, at a course that looked like certain death. But Styx, while adept at calculated risk, showed no tendency to suicide.

"How are you certain?" Sasalaka asked the obvious question, seated on the engineering seat before Styx's frame controls.

"It is complicated to explain, Lieutenant," said Styx. "I am accumulating data. As you may be aware, I am rather good at it. On Eshir, I accumulated data enough to constitute a ten thousand year history of Qalea, with accuracy enough that I was able to predict geographical locations of specific buildings in specific time zones, and the roles they played in historical events. Major Thakur and Sergeant Rael can tell you."

Rael glanced at Trace, and saw her deep in thought, gazing at the holography. "Yeah, it was like she had a map of the place," he admitted, taking his invitation to speak. "It was incredible."

"Simulation," Kaspowitz repeated, skeptically.

"With sufficient data-points," Styx told him, "anything is simulatable. I gained gradual access to the data networks on Qalea, which opened many information sources. There is enough data on most planetary networks to deduce most things, but merely organic civilisations lack the data-processing capability to organise that information into a simulatory whole. Were I to visit your Homeworld today, it would not take me long to describe to you a full history of humanity, right down to individual details on important historical figures most of you have forgotten. I have deduced much of it already, simply from the more limited *Phoenix* databases. Everything is in some database somewhere, it is merely that Eshir's databases were restricted by superior network security, and thus took longer to access."

"Right," said Kaspowitz, frowning, "but you were trying to find things that the reeh themselves had forgotten, and weren't in any database."

"My knowledge of organic civilisations has been lately renewed via the drysine data-core," said Styx. "Processing trillions of data-points produces patterns. Patterns of settlement, of logistics, of sanitation, communications, civil disturbances, demographic spread, political division, psychological predilections on the individual and group scales. By cross-referencing those patterns against observable patterns on Qalea, I was able to observe the applicability of some patterns over others, and make adaptions to what you might crudely describe as algorithms. Create enough intersecting data-points, and new probabilities begin to emerge. On Qalea I learned much not only about the city and world, but about the Reeh Empire. By intercepting several high-ranking reeh after the temple assault, and interrogating them, I learned far more about reeh command structures than reeh would have believed possible."

"Interrogating," Romki said distastefully. Erik looked at him, then at Trace. Trace made a faint shrug. She'd looked the other way. Erik could not blame her.

"Doesn't answer how you know that's where the Ceephay Queen is," Kaspowitz said stubbornly.

"Actually it does," said Styx. "But you are not intellectually equipped to understand the answer. I could translate my calculations into human mathematical formula if you'd prefer?"

A new display overlaid the starmap in the air. A two-dimensional page of algebra, complicated with many illustrative graphs and lines in accompaniment. Erik had done rather well at that in the Academy, and Kaspowitz somewhat better, as befitted a navigator. Kaspowitz squinted at it. The page began to scroll, faster and faster, until it was an impossible blur of data.

"I could keep scrolling through the pages until they are ended," Styx explained, "and then you'd have your answer. At this speed it would take seventeen years and forty six days."

Erik gave Kaspowitz a dry look, communicating that he needed to let it go. This time, Kaspowitz didn't even bother rolling his eyes. This was what truly made him most uncomfortable, Erik knew -- that in a battle of intellect, with Styx, they were all so utterly outmatched as to be comical. What, then, were they all doing here? And why, if this were all her plan and her command after all?

"Thank you Styx," said Trace. "I've seen the powers of your analysis up close, and I trust your plan of action entirely. If you say that's where the Ceephay Queen resides, I believe you."

She gazed at Kaspowitz as she said it, then Erik. Trust me on this, her look said. Of them all, Erik knew that Trace was the one most able to look a fact in the face, however unpleasant its implications.

"Me too," Erik echoed, gazing back at Trace. He often thought that she probably understood Styx better than any of them, if only because she knew what it was to focus on an outcome with such intensity that all else became secondary. "So if that's where the queen is, why are we going to this other place? X-9?"

"Because that is where lies the greatest chance for restarting a long-dormant Reeh Empire insurrection," said Styx. "And if we are to reach this Ceephay Queen in her lair, and learn everything she knows about humanity's greatest threat since the krim, we shall first have to start a civil war."

"A civil war featuring who and who?" Erik asked suspiciously.

"Primarily the reeh, and the alo."

Silence in the room. "The alo are still here?" Trace asked quietly.

"Some of them are, yes," said Styx. "I've found what's left of them, extracted from the reeh senior officers we interrogated. They are the spark that I intend to ignite, creating a conflagration large enough to allow us access to the Ceephay Queen."

"And how can you be sure of that?" Kaspowitz asked, in cold alarm.

"Because the Ceephay Queen is going to help us."

"YOU'VE BEEN VERY QUIET, SHALI," Erik said on coms as he walked the weary corridors after his own gym session and shower. Exhaustion threatened, vision nearly blurring as he navigated on automatic, but he was well used to that by now.

"Yes Captain," said the ceephay's young girl voice.

"What would you do, regarding Styx's plan?"

"I would stay very quiet, Captain."

Erik smiled. It was everyone's assessment that Shali was far more sociable than Styx. Shali had once been the right-hand assistant of the queen. One of seven, Romki had said, from that command room in the temple's lower levels. Those ceephay had been not so much the rulers of those earlier, more peaceful reeh, but their rulers-by-consent. So impressed the reeh had been by the queen's capabilities that they'd agreed to let her be in charge, with the supposedly-democratic input of the governed. They'd decide what they wanted, and she would dedicate her impressive analytical capabilities to figuring how to make it happen.

It wasn't hard to see how a ceephay queen, escaped from the endless AI wars of the Spiral, a conflict in which her people had been destroyed and she herself rendered surplus to requirements, might find a new purpose in empire-building with a new people in a region well removed from Spiral boundaries. In the AI wars, the queen had been made obsolete, by arbitrary AI standards at least. But here amongst the reeh, she'd been a marvel, a salvation from the tyranny of organic politics and self-destructive psychologies. No wonder they'd treated her like a god, and placed her upon a throne made especially for her. She'd improved their lives, their technology, their happiness. The reeh had gone from a small and frequently-abused people to the dominant rulers of their region. To hear Shali speak of it, even many of those non-reeh species they'd ruled came to consider it an improvement.

"You're safe here, Shali," Erik told her, turning onto the spinward corridor to back-quarter where Trace's quarters were. "Styx knows you are under my protection. Even if she wished to harm you, she would not risk my displeasure."

"With respect, Captain. Her warships outnumber yours four to one. Your capacity to tell her what to do is not as great as you suppose."

"She needs humanity, Shali," Erik said with determination. He hit the open on Trace's door, and walked in, finding the quarters empty as expected. "The primary advantage in her being here is to curry favour with humans and tavalai both. Humans are facing an existential threat, and Styx means to be the one who saves them, to benefit from their gratitude."

He sat down on Trace's bunk, and waited. *"There are two flaws in your theory, Captain,"* said Shali. *"One, Styx knows well that human and tavalai gratitude would be very short-lived without a long-term enemy to fight. Humans and tavalai both remain fearful of drysines, and drysine queens in particular, with good reason. Were Styx to assist you both in defeating the alo/deepynines, you would no longer have any need for Styx. I put it to you that Styx's most logical course of action is not to defeat your enemies, but to cultivate them, for without them, she and her drysines will become useless.*

"Secondly, there is the reeh. My queen has found for herself a place at the head of reeh civilisation. That role continues today, although its nature has changed terribly. I fear that Styx is somewhat more advanced than my queen. What if she is not proposing to save or even to destroy my queen, but rather to replace?"

Erik nodded slowly. He'd already had that discussion, with Kaspowitz, Sasalaka and others. The possibility sparked a predictable paranoia, but today he wasn't moved by it. "She's made too many enemies amongst the reeh, coming in here as she has," said Erik. "And she has too many ties to the parren -- an alliance, in fact, revolving around the moon Defiance. She will not abandon her most promising developments in Spiral space to volunteer herself as a slave to the reeh."

"If her place among the parren is so strong, why doesn't she simply throw in her lot with them?"

"Because she doesn't trust the parren. She had many dealings with them before, a long time ago, when they were servants of the Drysine Empire. She liked them fine as servants, but now they're unstable, divided by psychological factions and largely xenophobic. They're an old spacefaring species, no longer so ambitious, and intensely resistant to outside interference. Being newer in space, humans are much more ambitious and expansionist, and not so worried about old traditions. Our old politics died with Earth. I think she smells potential there.

"And also, for so long as the alo/deepynines remain a force, I don't think she truly believes she's safe anywhere. Not even here. Not given how Styx measures time, millennia by millennia. She seeks to destroy them completely, and sooner is always better than later."

"Captain, I would like to thank you for allowing me to stay on your ship. I like you and your people. You remind me of my old companions, amongst the reeh, when the reeh were good."

"Thank you, Shali. You're entirely welcome to stay, particularly if you make yourself useful on our mission. You've seen how people of different types have integrated themselves into this ship's crew. I see no reasons why that should not also apply to you."

"I am honoured, Captain. But as your crew, I must warn you about the drysines. This is a warrior race. A race of conquerors and destroyers. You say that they changed, that toward the end of their reign they were in alliance with the parren, and with other organics as well. This may be true. Styx is a master manipulator, and a master of the tactics of convenience. I have spoken with her on a level humans cannot, an exchange of data at an intensity humans are simply not equipped to experience. And I must warn you, this is not a peaceful being. This is a warlord."

"And were ceephays any different? Back before you were driven from the Spiral, and found your home among the reeh?"

"I don't suppose we were. But we changed. I was constructed here,

amongst peaceful reeh, guided by my queen. She changed, Captain. I don't believe that Styx can."

The door hummed open, and Trace came in, marine blacks and spacer harness, removing AR glasses to give her eyes a break from the endless status reviews. Erik rose, removing his own glasses, and Trace surprised him by simply walking in, as the door closed behind, and hugging him as she'd not been able to do before the others. Erik hugged her back, and they stood for a long moment, wrapped around each other in mutual exhaustion.

Finally Erik pulled back, and put his forehead to hers. "How'd you do?"

"Fine," said Trace. "Fine. I mean... not my worst trip. Crazy trip. I wish you could have been there."

Erik was astonished. She wished? It sounded sentimental, not like Trace at all. "I'd have liked to see Qalea," he admitted. "But warship captains don't get out much."

Trace smiled tiredly, and sat beside him on the bunk. They held hands, fingers intertwined. Erik recalled sitting with Lisbeth like this, while she'd been aboard, and talking. Which was as best he could figure what he and Trace had become -- siblings from different parents. It felt a lot like that.

"Are you okay?"

She nodded, no longer offended by the question. "Yeah." A long pause. "I let another bunch of people die. Humans. They were with us on the last mission, the reeh were chasing, they needed cover to get down to the temple. But if I'd given it, some of us would have died. I chose them. It cost about ten of them. Just civilians, playing at soldier. Shopkeepers and labourers. Small business folks. Most had kids, I think. I knew plenty like that on Sugauli."

"I'd have done the same," Erik said quietly. "You did the right thing."

"I know," said Trace. She leaned her head back against the wall, and stared into space. "I used to just know that, and... that was all. I didn't need to know any more. Some people lived, some people died,

I knew I wasn't being selfish with my life because I was always prepared to die, and nearly did many times. But now..."

Erik released her hand, and put the arm around her shoulders instead. "I'm just seriously wondering if I can do this," Trace completed. "It's not a cry for help. I don't think it's doubt, or weakness per se. It's just that every bridge has its breaking strain, the load it can't carry. Those loads are cumulative. I feel very close to mine."

Her voice quavered slightly. Erik could see the strain, just looking at her. She typically showed so little. For her to be admitting to anything, even to him, the emotional forces involved must have felt dreadful.

"Would it help to know how the evacuation was going?" Erik wondered.

"It might," said Trace. "But realtime communications across those distances isn't something technology is ever going to solve."

"Well, quantum entanglement..." Erik began, but he could see she wasn't interested. "I'd like to tell you I'm sure the evacuation's going well," he said instead. "But I know what you think of wishful thinkers."

Trace put her head on his shoulder. "You're still scared of me," she murmured.

"No," said Erik, with a faint smile. "No, that stopped a while ago."

They sat like that for a long moment, half-asleep and enjoying this, the only human contact their lives currently allowed. Finally Trace heaved herself up, grabbed his hand and pulled him up after her. "Go on," she said. "I have to sleep."

Erik nodded. "Trace? I..."

"Don't say it," she cut him off, a touch irritably. "We do too much of this as it is."

Erik blinked. "How do you know what I was going to say?"

Trace sighed and put her face back into his chest. "And it's entirely my fault," she added. Not apologising, Erik thought, just acknowledging a truth. "Now get." Erik grinned, enjoying this 'mask off' version of his marine commander far too much, and held her, and didn't 'get'. Then she was grinning too, in that half-drunk way of two idiots who probably knew better, but were beyond all sense and reason.

Then their lips were touching. Erik didn't know who started it, and for one timeless moment, didn't particularly care. It lasted long enough to be certain that she knew damn well what was going on, and wasn't pulling back either. Erik wanted to kiss her harder, but didn't dare. And finally pulled back to stare at her. Not so much like siblings after all. Whatever he'd expected from Trace next, she didn't provide it.

Trace laughed, the maniacal laugh of a woman noticing that whatever could go wrong, was. It sounded like nothing he'd ever heard from her. Then she head-butted him repeatedly in the chest, with exasperated frustration, and rested her face there.

"Now we've torn it," she said.

34

Taj roared through Dez Canyon, following his visor's path through the unfamiliar Tanifex Quarter. He held to the high lane, pulling wide to overtake some slower traffic that meandered and forgot to send virtual indication. Ahead rose Sornil Bluff, huge water towers and repulsorlift repair yards amid a haze of smog, lit golden in the rising sun.

Traffic was thick as ever in Tanifex Quarter, but with a greater preference to lighter bikes, low powered but highly manoeuvrable, as perhaps fit the tanifex body-type. They were a menace, and crowded the lower lanes and side slopes, making speed only safe in the higher zones. Taj cast his eyes across descending walls of cityscape as they passed. Some of the neighbourhoods looked relatively nice, lanes clean and with big, open-topped structures amid minarets and flags. Qalea tanifex practised a religion called Trita, which had a lot about flags symbolising stages of life and levels of ascension until nirvana. Taj had lived in Qalea all his life, yet he'd only ventured into Tanifex Quarter a handful of times, and never for long.

He checked behind to see that the cruiser was still there, and found it shadowing him at a safe distance. He took a right about Zorshi Promontory, where a massive vertical concrete structure announced a new zone, and made an observation point for tanifex security forces.

About the promontory, Pini Valley lay between crowded walls of ascending cityscape, an eye-blurring jumble of narrow lanes, steep stairs and sheer drops, dwellings piled upon dwellings in the irregular clutter of every Qalean quarter. Below were loading zones for a massive hauler port, big vessels lined nose to tail amid clouds of ore dust. Upon the right slope as he raced by, some kind of old-looking fort, with crenelations and turrets, linked by ropeways that climbed the hill with dangling cars filled with passengers. Atop the hill, a grand statue, silhouetted in the hazy sun, of a tanifex at some kind of peaceful prayer.

Taj found himself grinning. Trace had offered for him to go with her on *Phoenix* if he'd chosen, and see what lay beyond. But how could he ever leave this place? With its treachery, pollution and ruins, Qalea was in his blood, and if he could not roar down these eye-baffling canyons of noise, glamour and decay on his Shaytan, he'd curl up and die.

Ahead, his visor indicated the journey's end -- left about the next forking bend, then down to one of a thousand flat patios on the sheer drop above the valley. He indicated, deployed airbrakes, and checked over his shoulder to make sure some idiot wasn't about to miss his signal and ram him from behind. The Shaytan buffeted as it slowed, close beside the valley wall, past tanifex working on construction, others eating breakfast or doing strange, tanifex things, as the human on the big superbike roared past their noses.

He slowed properly as the landing site appeared, adjusting altitude until he settled for a feather-light landing at the far end of the concrete patio. Behind him was just enough space for the cruiser, and the bikes of Janas and Tetch, settling as Taj unstrapped and swung off, surveying the building attached to the patio. Nearby along this valley wall, another temple rose, a single minaret painted gold and draped in fluttering flags against the howl of passing traffic. Bells and cymbals chimed from within, audible just as the cruiser's engines faded, alien but pleasant to the ear.

The big knife at his belt felt uncomfortable, but good too. Trace had called it a 'kukri', said it was originally from some place on Earth called Nepal. Irin Tola had taken it off her when they'd stunned her, and she'd not had time to reclaim it before the Zeladnists attacked. A Purist had taken it off Tola sometime later, as Tola had little interest in it, and given it to Taj. Taj was uncertain what use he'd find for it, but was pleased to have something so distinctive to remember Trace by. Perhaps he could return it to her one day, if he ever saw her again, but he suspected that she'd refuse. Trace was not sentimental, and would doubtless acquire another.

The cruiser's doors opened, and from within climbed Halhoun, turning to extend a hand to Mazi Zurhan. Mazi exited and stood, gazing about in the pleasure of a wealthy young woman who liked adventure. She wore shiny pants and heels, with a short-sleeved jacket belted tight about her narrow waist, and surveyed the patio view from behind expensive glasses. Halhoun gave Taj a smug look as Taj put his flying gear in the rear trunk. Not yet well enough to ride, Hal had been given this task nonetheless -- to escort Emil Zurhan's youngest daughter to meet new friends. Taj just smiled, and locked his trunk, as tanifex and dogreth hosts emerged onto the patio with drinks on trays.

"Oh marvellous!" exclaimed Mazi, clapping her manicured hands and accepting a drink. "Thank you! Um... trotik ta!" The tanifex's dark eyes flickered, head cocked slightly in that way of its reptilian kind.

Taj accepted his own drink, and strolled to Mazi. "I love all these flags," she said, pointing across the valleyscape. "Thousands of them. You know the tanifex believe in reincarnation?"

"These tanifex do," Taj agreed. He found it curious that Emil would send Mazi instead of coming himself. But then, Emil Zurhan was very busy, while Mazi was very sharp, highly educated, and somewhat more interested in history and worldly things than her older siblings, who obsessed mostly about business, money, family and parties. Not that Mazi had been any less enthusiastic on the dance floor, but she was reputedly fluent in the Krozoth spoken by dogreth, and had a bedroom in the Zurhan residence decorated with lestis trinkets and other oddities. On her wrists now instead of bangles were qwailash beads, bright and sparkling as they wound about her forearms.

She'd acquired the love from her father, Taj's highest boss, who'd found his own way into Taj's adventure without being prompted, by asking questions about the nature of Dagan's death. He'd paid generously to the grieving family, made funeral arrangements, and persisted until Taj had risked to tell him something, knowing that Emil had doubtless grilled his contacts among the Purists and knew a lot already.

Emil possessed an eccentric love of Qalean history, and had shown Taj all his collected artefacts and photographs that decorated his private rooms in the residence, the parts where Taj had never been invited before. He'd insisted that Taj should have told him what trouble he was in, but Taj knew it was a lie -- Trace would not have welcomed his assistance, and back then, with things so uncertain and the reeh on the warpath, Emil would not have welcomed the danger to his family and business empire.

But the reeh, while still around, had been strangely subdued in the fifteen days since *Phoenix* had departed, perhaps distracted by other things. And so Emil had become fascinated by this history-making encounter with humans from the origin of the species, and was now assisting Taj in making the necessary contacts in its aftermath.

The tanifex beckoned the humans inside, and Taj went first, peering into a darkened room with a wide table, and a kitchen by the rear wall beside doors off to other rooms. The construction was simple, brick walls and a bare-tiled floor, but it was tidy, the table set for a meal to come.

On the table's far side were more tanifex, two dogreth and a lestis. Taj lowered his visor and had it confirm for him that these were in fact the Akcho individuals he was supposed to be meeting. That was a new function, and saved him the embarrassment of having to ask. No doubt the dogreth and tanifex also found it hard to tell humans apart.

Greetings were followed by seats taken, on opposite sides of the table. There was a little conversation, and the Akcho seemed very interested to meet Mazi, who dressed like no human most non-humans would ever meet. Earpieces did the translating, and they discussed mostly pleasantries. The Akcho still did not trust humans, a race for whom all experience would be tainted forever by their bad experience with the Purists, and the great wars that had killed so many. But now, the first Qalean race to have made significant contact beyond the shroud that the reeh had placed upon Eshir was human, and that was something no resistance movement could ignore.

Finally Taj rapped upon the tabletop with his knuckle. "Here bug," he said to the empty air. He never knew where it came from, or where it had been hiding on its way over. A pocket, no doubt, as it was smart enough to know where was safe in the slipstream, to not get blasted off in the gale. But now it appeared, and settled to the tabletop before him, where it crawled, and preened its transparent wings with tiny mechanical feet.

Dogreth and tanifex all stared, peering close. Tanifex heads darted this way and that, like small birds considering a meal. This meal, however, could kill them.

The lead tanifex looked up at him. *"This is the only one?"* asked the earpiece.

"No," said Taj. "There's at least one more, I've seen it. Maybe Styx left a bunch more, scattered about the city. They might all get together and talk, or they might use the city networks, I don't know."

"Do they understand you?"

"Yes. Basic stuff, at least. I told this one I was coming here, it understood and came along. They recharge from the sun."

"And they're deadly?"

"I saw a few monsters they killed down in Qwailash Quarter," Taj affirmed. Mazi was gazing at him with wonder. Taj thought it was nice to spend time around attractive women who were actually impressed with him for a change. "Kills you instantly."

"Why do you think Styx left them behind?"

"To get information," said Taj. "I'm not sure how she's ever going to collect it. Also, I think she wanted to help us. She hates the reeh, and these bugs cost her nothing." He took a deep breath, and decided to chance it. "The bugs feed me information about reeh movements, sometimes."

The Akcho stared at him. *"What information?"*

"Shuttle movements. I see them displayed on my screen at home, then I hear a shuttle fly over. Maybe the bugs are just showing what they can do. Styx left a lot of things behind on this network, I think. Spy software. The bugs may be how we access it."

The Akcho exchanged looks. *"This would be useful,"* said one.

The broad-shouldered dogreth leaned forward, all power where the tanifex were speed and sinew. *"What do you want from us? To share what you have?"*

Taj grinned. "I don't *want* anything. We need to cooperate. Humans, dogreth, tanifex, lestis, qwailash, everyone. We can't fight the reeh directly, but we can put our resources together, and learn things. Maybe we can make contact with other rebels."

"My father wants to help," said Mazi. "So long as we keep it quiet. He knows a lot of people, and has a lot of money. And he can guarantee you won't have any trouble from the Purists ever again. Humans will be less hostile. That's good for business, and good for your cause."

Taj could read skepticism in those reptilian eyes. This, clearly, was what Mazi was doing here. Family Zurhan didn't want trouble with the reeh, but the Akcho rarely actually did anything, and so the odds of attracting a reeh strike was small. But Family Zurhan did have an interest in promoting trade, and had long chafed at the unwillingness of many non-human quarters to trade with humans. A final peace between humans and the rest of Qalea, long delayed for centuries, would benefit the businessmen most of all.

"Styx left something else," said Taj. "Do you have a flat screen? It doesn't work in holographics." A screen was produced, and propped on the end of the table. Taj flipped down his visor, and blinked on the icon to transfer an image. "This is Isik, the Seventh Republic era."

The tanifex stared. One turned and sent a stream of shrill clicks to the rear room, bringing others hustling. They clustered around to stare at the screen, and images of a cityscape. There were rivers, and some kind of festival, many tanifex lining the banks while others rowed enormous boats. Isik was the tanifex homeworld. Today in the Empire, most tanifex lived elsewhere, but not by choice, having been cast to the winds by reeh tyranny. Isik itself, in what little Taj knew of it, was a fortress of military industry and slaves. Of all the people of the Empire, the tanifex had suffered most.

"Styx left me a database," Taj continued quietly as the images changed. City life, tanifex doing tanifex things. It looked prosperous, and pretty. "She recovered it all from some reeh database, I don't know where. There's thousands of hours of footage. Hundreds of thousands. Entertainment shows, private wedding footage, military training films, everything."

Taj had never seen hard-eyed tanifex emotional. These clutched to each other's arms, and trilled softly. Most only knew stories of Isik. This was from before the reeh civil war, more than ten thousand years ago. The glory days of the tanifex, by the look of it.

"There's a lot more data," said Taj. "Mountains of it. Dogreth too, and qwailash. The only ones not here are lestis. But you can have it. Styx wanted you to have it. Spread it around, and educate your children. Show them who you once were, before the reeh came."

"How does she get this?" one of the tanifex asked in disbelief, as the earpiece translated urgent trills and clicks behind sharpened teeth.

"It's all in a database somewhere, she says. Styx is a drysine queen. Give her enough time and there's no network she can't crack."

They watched the pictures for a while longer. Finally the lead dogreth rapped his fist upon the table, with approval. *"This is a gift,"* he said, with apparent feeling. With dogreth, that looked indistinguishable from anger. *"The Akcho accept this gift. This will heal many wounds."*

"Styx left us with a lot of stuff on reeh security, too," said Taj. "Codes, network security, military tech, force deployments. She said we can't use it to fight them directly, but we can copy it and spread it. Make it widely known. A people well informed cannot be enslaved."

That line he'd come up with himself. That line, *Phoenix*'s people had taught him.

"I don't know if the reeh know what trouble they got into," Halhoun added sombrely. "When they let a drysine queen get behind their lines and into their information systems. That just seems like bad news for them."

"They know," said Taj. "Styx said it would be quiet on Eshir for a while, because every ship in the Reeh Empire would be chasing her and *Phoenix*."

"Well they can't possibly beat the entire reeh fleet!" said Mazi. "Can they?"

Taj sighed. "I suppose we'll find out eventually."

THE VIEW from between *Coroset* and *Amity* was incredible. Skah used his hand-thruster to swing about, and take in the enormity of it. *Coroset* was a little larger than *Amity*, two huge steel whales in space, and now nestled just a few hundred meters apart. Everything glowed in the bright Reba System sun, and the hulls of both ships crawled with drysine and parren workers. Welding flashes lit the vacuum, and between the ships, some workers were transiting, hauling parts or equipment.

Ships were never supposed to be this close in combat zones, but everyone felt safe now. The reeh were gone, for the moment at least, and crews were repairing and rearming in case they came back before the evacuation was finished. Far down below his feet, Skah could see a vast expanse of white as they passed over one of Rando's poles. The polar orbit meant they'd be closer at all times to any attack that came in. The transports hadn't been able to use this orbit during the evacuation because it messed up everyone's rendezvous trajectories, and because unarmed transports liked having one part of their orbit hidden from attacking ships. Plus of course few corbi lived at the poles, and so a large part of that orbit was wasted. But Skah thought this pole looked amazing, a huge expanse of ice and cloud nearly a thousand kilometres away. Only warships used this orbit. It was much better to be a warship, he thought, than a transport. Transports couldn't shoot back. And he remembered what Styx had told him about violence, and how it wasn't all bad. Certainly these two ships had saved an awful lot of corbi. Everyone said the evacuation would have certainly failed without them.

His harness lead yanked against Hiro's suit. *"Come on Skah, you can sightsee later,"* Hiro admonished him. *"The window's short, we don't have much time."*

Lisbeth hadn't wanted him to come, but Skah had been working so much with *Coroset*'s crew during the fight that they'd almost come to treat him like one of the regulars. And as Hiro had pointed out, regular crew were expected to be able to use their EVA suits in case of emergencies. Skah knew it all in theory, but hadn't yet had the practise -- a practise that would make him more safe, not less.

The two parren spacers with them were Gorin and Meluku, both systems techs now assisting with *Coroset*'s overdue repairs. *Coroset* could fabricate a lot of the required parts herself, but being drysine, *Amity* could make better. *Coroset* crew had been placing orders from *Amity*'s offered inventories, and finding some stuff they had no idea about, but a lot that they did, and would be useful in fixing *Coroset*.

Approaching *Amity* was a very strange thing. She didn't *look* like a regular spaceship. There was no rotating crew cylinder within the main hull cage, just a single hull within reinforced ribs that bristled with attachments. Skah looked the attachments over, and tried to guess what each of them was for. Rail guns were simple enough. Dish and transmitter units looked very strange, but still guessable. A lot of the other stuff, he had no idea. Drysines crawled on *Amity*'s hull, like ants over dropped food, and damaged portions sparkled with new welds.

Skah watched his visor indicators as they approached the opening. On a human or parren ship the only airlocks would be in Midships, but *Amity* didn't really have a Midships, just a narrowing at the waist where the enormous engines joined to the rest of the ship. As they drew closer, he saw that the large hatchway wasn't actually an airlock either -- drysine drones went in or out like ants from their hole, and left the ship's interior exposed to vacuum. Sometimes *Amity* would use air as an insulator, Liala had told him, or to put out fires, or some other technical reason. But drysines needed no air to breathe, didn't get sick from too much solar radiation, and wouldn't waste away without gravity. They seemed so much more suited to life in space than any organic race. No wonder they sometimes thought themselves better than everyone else.

"Watch the entrance in case anyone else comes out," Hiro warned as they drew close, firing his hand thruster to slow down.

"They won't," Skah said confidently. "Hi Liala, we're here!"

"Hello Skah, please come inside," came Liala's voice. *"I'll show you the way on your helmet display. Please be careful, not everything on a drysine warship is designed with organic safety in mind."*

"Yeah, like it doesn't have any friggin' air," Hiro emphasised, catching the hatch rim as it arrived. *"So don't puncture your suit, kid."*

"The suit can stop bullets," Skah retorted, pulling himself inside with greater ease than Hiro. Given they were talking on coms, he was speaking Gharkhan, the translation of which scarcely sounded worse than English on helmet speakers.

"Small bullets," Hiro corrected. *"You guys are waiting here for your delivery?"* Talking to Gorin and Meluku, Skah saw as he waited impatiently.

"The drysines said to meet them here," came the parren reply. *"Juli and Stirastan will attend to your return journey."*

"Great, thank you... no, Skah, don't remove the lead."

"It's not safe," Skah told him firmly, disconnecting the hook from his harness. "You join two people together in zero-G, we pull against each other, some drone bangs into us, we get all tangled up. Come on."

He hooked the thruster onto his harness, because all true spacers used their hands rather than thrusters whenever they could, and pulled himself up the corridor.

Like all places designed for zero-G, the corridor had no floors, walls or ceiling, just irregular bends, connections to other corridors that looked more like tunnels as they burrowed through the ship, and lots of exposed pipes and crazy-looking high-tech things that Skah had no idea about.

Drones made way for them in the corridor, watching with curious, darting sensor-eyes. Liala would have told them to do that, Skah knew. Despite the incredible strangeness of the place, he did not feel scared. Liala had kept everyone on *Coroset* safe all through the evacuation so far, and that would not change now.

Skah followed the clear, lighted indications on his helmet visor that made each corner or change of direction glow as he looked at it. After just five minutes of pulling along the walls, becoming increasingly certain that he couldn't find his way out again on his own, he came to a large, spherical room. At the room's precise center was a kind of frame, like a spherical cage, attached to the walls at many points. Within the cage was Liala, her steel body supported, her many legs free to manipulate a surrounding array of holographic displays that glowed with many colours. It looked to Skah as though she were suspended within a ball of light.

"Wow!" said Skah, pushing off the wall toward her. "That looks amazing, Liala!"

"Hello Skah. I redesigned much of my control cockpit myself." Her large head, with twin mismatched eyes, swivelled to regard him, aglow with many reflections from the controls. *"Hello Hiro."*

"Hi Liala." As Hiro floated over to join Skah. *"Nice setup. Why all these visual cues? Don't AIs usually do everything by VR?"*

"I have been experimenting," said Liala. Skah stared at all the lights, which made a crazy laser display as they reflected on his visor. Stray beams went all around the room. *"Drysines are often less proficient than humans or parren at three-dimensional visual perception. We get addicted to virtual worlds, and are less able to process the real one. I am attempting to redesign my own interactive control systems to prevent the addiction."*

Skah reached with one gloved finger toward a glowing beam of light past Liala's head. The glove broke the beam, which abruptly changed from green to red.

"You just launched a missile," the drysine told him. Skah stared at her. *"I'm joking."*

Skah laughed. "You can't launch a missile by touching a light! And you wouldn't let me do that anyway!"

"Expecting that other people will make the world safe for you is a bad habit to get into, Skah," she told him.

"Now you sound like Styx."

"Surely me sounding like Styx is not surprising?" She sounded almost amused, as though she were pleased to see him, and teasing him. *"Here, I have something to show you both. I thought it would be interesting to get an organic reaction before I started using it properly."*

From an adjoining tunnel entrance, a new drone appeared. Only this was no regular drone. It had a lean, sinewy body, built for agility. So smoothly it moved, there appeared nothing of 'machine' about it, as it glided along one anchor-frame for the command cockpit toward them. Four multi-segmented, synthetic tentacles emerged from its back, grasping at holds in a way that made the main legs somewhat redundant. The creature's neck was long, but the place where a head would be, protected by a wide, armoured carapace, was empty.

"Holy shit," Hiro murmured. *"A queen chassis?"*

"Cool!" Skah exclaimed, with awe. "Pretty scary, but cool too. Why do you want to change bodies, Liala?"

"The sensory apparatus of this body are limited. It is a combat designation, and not suited for command and control. Also, mobility is limited, as is its ability to interact with its environment."

Hiro pulled himself to drift closer, looking over the new body as it secured itself alongside. "How fast is it?"

One of those tentacle-arms lashed at him, and Hiro made a defensive flinch. The tentacle-point tapped him once on the stomach, then again on his back, then withdrew. *"Faster than you,"* said Liala.

"Yeah... you do realise that this thing's even scarier-looking than Styx?" said Hiro. *"The organic beings you need to impress and gain the trust of will wet themselves when they see this."*

"I am the commander of parren-aligned drysine forces," Liala replied.

"Parren don't wet themselves, House Harmony parren least of all. And besides, a little fear can be useful."

"Liala's a great warrior now, Hiro," Skah reminded him, floating around to examine the deadly chassis from a new angle. "She won this evacuation by herself."

"Many brave organics did far more than I, Skah."

"As a commander, I mean. Any other commander would have lost. Other than Styx, anyway."

"That's probably true."

"So you need to look like a great warrior. I like it." Given some recent events, he'd come to doubt whether being a great warrior was all some made it out to be. But now he'd seen great warriors save the entire corbi race. And Liala had led them, not with bravado and shouting, but with calculation, patience and reason. Being a warrior, then, was more than just one thing. The best warriors, like Liala, Styx, Captain Debogande and Major Thakur, were far more than just brave and dangerous.

"I'm glad you like it," said Liala. *"In some things, the opinions of young boys are quite reliable."*

"So what happens now?" Hiro asked her.

"The evacuation will be completed," said Liala. *"Sometime soon, I am sure, we will hear whether Gesul feels that Lisbeth's involvement of the Coroset and Amity in this evacuation was truly in his interests or not."*

"And if he judges not?"

"Then Lisbeth could be in significant danger. Her move in coming here was kind-hearted, but reckless. She has involved the Parren Empire in foreign affairs that many would rather avoid."

"It's all unavoidable," Hiro said firmly. *"They should wake up to it."*

"That will certainly be my message to them, Hiro. But Gesul commands only one of the five parren houses directly. My predictive ability expands daily, but this prediction lies well beyond my abilities."

Jindi stood in thigh-deep water, pants rolled up, eyes scanning the surface of the lake for telltale flashes of silver. He held a makeshift spear in one hand, a steel pole from a tent with salvaged wire bound about its end, twisted to make a three-pronged tip. There were fish in this lake, plus something like eels, and some flat, bottom-feeding things he hadn't figured a way to catch yet, but had seen in the improvised mask he'd fashioned using a tin can with its bottom replaced by clear plastic. The fish at least had tasted good, and the planet's network had told him were not unsafe to eat.

Sunlight made shafts through low cloud, broken about the peaks of nearby, tree-covered hills. The sun was yellower than he was accustomed, and smaller. At night, there was just one moon casting a single shadow. The wind from the east was colder than he'd known, though he knew there had been places on Rando where that had been true as well, just that he'd not lived in them. He wore a rough jacket, one of the millions of surplus items collected from families about croma space, donations of children's clothes that might fit their new guests on His'do. It shielded him from the chill wind that lightly skimmed the lake surface, a spread of chasing ripples.

A flash of silver caught his eye, and he lashed with the spear. It flew short with a splash, and Jindi ran and grabbed it. Upon its end was a flapping fish -- echi'do, the network had told him the species was. He waded back to the shoreline, a narrow beach of black sand against the reeds and stunted, lakeside trees, with paper-like bark that peeled in sheets. Melu was there with Iska and Cherit, washing a great pile of collected clothes in various plastic containers they'd collected, talking as they worked, and the other women's three small children played nearby.

The children came running now to see Jindi with his fish, and cringed as he killed it swiftly with his knife, then put it in the bucket of water with the two others he'd speared. Melu looked up and smiled as she worked. The wrapping on her head was new, an automated doctor in the improvised medical clinic had healed the light skull fracture, and cleared her of any further damage while dosing with corbi-approved micros to improve her bloodwork. A further treatment was promised to work on her underlying neural issues, leftovers from her time in the Splicer, but given the waiting times, that would not be soon.

Jindi smiled, and waded back into the water. It felt good to be useful once more, in a way that did not involve sitting and telling people what to do. To the best of his memory, he was still only forty-five years old, and it was far too early for him to take on the village elder role that many of the township wanted him to. They pestered him now with this issue and that, things they wanted him to discuss with the croma, and he came out here with his spear to escape. The fish did not seem well evolved to avoid spearing, and it was a relief to simply be outside for a while.

Upon the lake's far shore, another settlement spread, a mass of multi-coloured tents upon what had once been undisturbed grassland dotted with a few trees. From near and far came the sound of earthmovers carving new roads, electric generators and water pumps. The lake was not actually a lake, but rather a large lagoon in a river that ran through this valley between hills, and the supply of fresh water had proven an attractive settlement site for all its length. Now came the work to stop a few hundred thousand corbi's waste water from polluting it entirely, and from local croma groups came concern at the enormous impact on the local environment.

Out of sight along the lakeside, there came the shrill howl of a shuttle taking off. The last Rando evacuees had stopped arriving several days ago. Word was that something like eighty percent had come, though how they'd arrived at that when the actual population of Rando had been just guesswork, Jindi didn't know. So many forests on Rando, and so many corbi good at hiding from aerial surveillance. Surely there were more left there than the croma knew.

Jindi wondered what would happen to them, and thought it probably nothing good. Yet still, plenty of corbi here were complaining that they shouldn't have left. His'do was different from Rando -- roughly the same gravity, similar air. Faster-than-light technology had had that way in all settled space, he gathered, of making rare living worlds relatively simple to access, so easy were the majority of uninhabitable worlds to bypass. But even the warmer regions of His'do were not as warm as Rando. It rained more here, the nights were darker, and as dangerous as Rando's settlements had been, they were familiar in a way that now, in hindsight, seemed charming.

Life there had not been crowds of tents and water from plastic containers. Food had not been prepackaged, and had generally been cooked on wood fires, something the environmental regulations here prohibited lest all the local forest cover disappear. Croma preparations had included millions of simple gas burners, the lights from which now made the tent cities glow at night like so many stars in the sky. When it rained, the paths between the tents turned to mud, and the same restrictions that prevented people from burning firewood also prevented them from building wooden huts to save themselves from the tyranny of the tents.

Jindi had found himself elected to the representative council of the settlements about this lake, which had in turn seen him elevated to a higher body as well, once people had realised who he was, and his role in the Splicer's destruction. Much of that time was now spent arguing with local croma authorities about corbi freedoms. If we can't make our own houses, he'd told them, and we can't hunt our own food (as the authorities didn't even want him fishing) then we're going to become completely dependent on you, like children on their parents. Or like prisoners on their jailers. People are going to become resentful very quickly, he'd told them. We thought we were escaping to some sort of freedom. Now this.

Temporary, had been the croma reply. All of this is temporary. We're currently looking to find you a new place to live. This world was selected mostly because we had to put you somewhere close to the Croma Wall to allow the evacuation to happen. Put you too far away, and the transports would have been stretched far further, making the evacuation impossible within such a short period. We will find you a new world, with less croma, where you can have more autonomy. Just be patient.

The more Jindi spoke with them, the less he believed it. Moving everyone here had been the most enormous logistical exercise. The ships used in the evacuation had all dispersed once more, to help with the ongoing operations against the reeh elsewhere along the front. Gathering them all together once had taken the most enormous political will. Doing it a second time, to move to a new croma world that would doubtless be just as resistant to their presence as this one, was going to take a long time, if it happened at all.

Instead, a new word was spreading, a rumour come down from corbi high command, as the Resistance were re-styling themselves now that their purpose for existing for the past eight hundred years had ended. That word was Vieno.

It was the name of a world in space adjoining human space. The great alien warrior Thakur had spoken of it with various corbi high command, though in truth Jindi knew it had just been Tiga and a few others. Various in that high command had somehow acquired great detail about Vieno and its surrounding regions, probably from Liala. Now that information was spreading, to anyone with a portable device, and then by word of mouth to those without.

Vieno belonged to the barabo, who were not warlike like the croma or humans. The barabo had enemies on their doorstep called the sard, and desired human protection. Vieno, Thakur had suggested, could be taken by the humans as trade, in exchange for human protection to all barabo. Corbi civilisation on Vieno would put steel in the weak barabo spine, as humans were reluctant to fight for a people not willing to defend themselves.

But corbi would. And while croma would never allow corbi to be independent, to have their own world, to arm themselves and build a Fleet of their own, the humans would. Barabo would lose a world, but barabo had many, and Vieno was only lightly populated. Barabo themselves were said to be friendly and reasonable, and likely to agree that the gift of one world to a people who needed it far more would be a fair price in exchange for human protection. And humans would gain a long-term ally, and a fierce friend in a region of space where they needed one, who would never forget the great deed done for them.

Best of all, Vieno was even pretty, and the images on the portable devices showed a variety of landscapes, from deserts to mountains to lush forests. Of particular interest to Jindi had been the endless stretches of sandy beach, and the oceans teeming with native life. His'do was nice enough, but not as nice as Rando, and besides, croma were determined that it would never be theirs. And even if it were, they'd be contained entirely within croma space, where no alien sovereignty could be allowed, and to travel anywhere, or to mine some nearby rock, would require the unlikely permission of Croma Fleet.

Well, Jindi thought, scanning the surface of the lake once more. It was a nice dream. Who would ever agree to move all the corbi people to Vieno, so soon after arriving on His'do, was another matter. But then, just being here, and away from the torments of Rando, had not long ago seemed like an even crazier dream.

A shuttle howled overhead, heading for the distant landing pad. Jindi zipped his jacket a little tighter to ward the chill wind, and resumed his stance, spear ready, creeping slowly along the muddy lakebottom in pursuit of unwary fish. They came to the surface to eat the seed pods that washed from further upstream, Jindi saw. Those pods swirled in slow clusters, bobbing in the ripples stirred by the wind. The pods fell in spring, meaning that summer would be here soon. It would not get dramatically warmer then, he knew. The winter to follow would be unpleasant indeed, living in tent cities where unprotected water supplies would freeze.

But that was tomorrow. For today, he was alive, and while this was not a beach like he'd dreamed, it was a beach nonetheless. The corbi would survive, and wait, in hope of a better day.

ABOUT THE AUTHOR

Joel Shepherd is the Australian author of seventeen SF and Fantasy novels in three series. They are 'The Cassandra Kresnov Series', 'A Trial of Blood and Steel', and 'The Spiral Wars'.

Made in the USA
Las Vegas, NV
18 October 2021

32551495R00291